D1012610

HERE

&

THERE

JOSHUA V. SCHER

HERE
&
THERE

47N⬤RTH

This is a work of fiction. Names, characters, organizations, places, events, and incidents are either products of the author's imagination or are used fictitiously.

Text copyright © 2015 Joshua V. Scher
All rights reserved.

No part of this book may be reproduced, or stored in a retrieval system, or transmitted in any form or by any means, electronic, mechanical, photocopying, recording, or otherwise, without express written permission of the publisher.

Published by 47North, Seattle

www.apub.com

Amazon, the Amazon logo, and 47North are trademarks of Amazon.com, Inc., or its affiliates.

ISBN-13: 9781503946842
ISBN-10: 1503946843

Cover design by M.S. Corley

Printed in the United States of America

May 16, 2011

Dear Josh,

I hope my "care package" finds you well. Wish I could say it left me that way. Who knew FedEx delivered Pandora's boxes, right? I'm sure you must be looking over the edge of my letter, staring down at the unstable innards bound in an oversized leather briefcase, sealed with duct tape, and cradled by packing peanuts, wondering, "What the fuck did Dan send me?" It's a beast. Trust me, I know. Probably dislocated your FedEx guy's lower lumbar-region. Lift with your legs.

 When I first found all this, my mother had already been missing for close to a year. I'm not sure if I took possession of her report or it me.

 Things were always that way with Hilary.

 "Why in hell did Dan send me . . . ?" I know. I *know*. I didn't really have many options. And honestly, you're the only guy I know who might actually be able to help. Who am I to ask a favor, right? We bump into each other up at Brown last spring; before then we only hung out after a handful of run-ins around the city in the years since college. I don't know, man, I hope your heart is still big and your tolerance for bullshit still miniscule.

 All I'm asking is that you take a look, and if you believe me—no—if you just think there's something here, help me drag this behemoth out into the light. Just look inside, please. No promises necessary. Take a glance and see if it grabs you. It got me with the first line I happened upon:

"It was the second time he had broken the basement."

Who the hell breaks a basement? Twice? I stumbled upon the thing while cleaning up my mother's past and sifting through the jigsaw of skeletons in the back of a closet, ten fathoms deep. When I read that line, I knew. This was it, my cipher. This would help put the pieces together and give me more closure than a closet could ever contain. I was sure that somehow this aberrant phrase about a broken basement was the tip of the iceberg, just sharp enough to crack open the case and let me peer inside—and find my mother.

I didn't tell you any of this that afternoon we ran into each other up at Brown, 'cause, well, how do you just unload something like this on someone? Plus, back then I was channeling through my own river of shit, locked in with my tunneling tunnel vision. And honestly, the last thing I wanted to do was explain to anyone how my mother had vanished. I didn't want to explain anything about her at all. It never went well. The last time I tried, I was fourteen and got sent to boarding school as a result. I mean sure, it stopped me from crawling into bed with my mother every night, but it didn't bring my dad back from the dead. That looks weird as I write it. It wasn't at the time. It was the only way I could cope. What do I know? I nursed till I was three. Psychologists' kids are always fucked up.

Did I mention yet that I miss her?

I'd always been scared about losing my parents. What kid isn't? I just went a little above and beyond. I had nightmares. Not your run-of-the-mill, wake-up-a-little-scared, turn-on-a-night-light, and go-back-to-sleep nightmares. No. I had slam-awake, screaming, drenched-in-a-cold-sweat, shiver-in-fear-for-the-next-three-hours nightmares. And they started galloping through my head at a very young age.

Maybe I was having premonitions about my dad's death. He was an artist, or wished he were: an artist dressed in lawyer's clothing. My earliest memories are of him wearing stained painter pants and a T-shirt blotched with color. Whenever inspired, he would sneak off to his art studio on O Street to "keep the paint from drying out." Maybe he should have let it go. Maybe it was the paint that killed him. All the carcinogens and lead and mercury and sarin gas and who the hell knows what else. Maybe that's what gave him nonsmoking lung cancer. Twin tumors blossomed in each lung, replicating to their hearts' content and my father's demise. The doctors told him to stop eating artificial sweetener and instead to spike his coffee with massive doses of chemo cocktails, but those cells wouldn't stop splitting. It took only four months from diagnosis to demise. That's the velocity of death.

I was thirteen.

But you know all this. And I know all about your year of death and the whole high-school-classmate-killed-by-lightning thing. I've learned something new though since our tête-à-têtes from sophomore year. I've learned about the abeyant hell that is the lack of death.

Legally speaking, the courts don't consider someone dead until seven years after filing a missing person's report. Dead in absentia. My mom's only two years in. Well, two years plus however long it took me to realize she was gone in the first place.

It had been at least a month since the last time we had talked. (According to the police investigation, my phone records stipulate it had actually been thirty-eight days since my mom and I had talked.) Some small talk, some work talk (me, not her, she rarely talked about her work), a little dancing around romantic relationships talk (again, me not her), and lastly a fight. As always, it escalated to a game of emotional chicken that ended with one of us hanging up on the other. I called her a few weeks after that. Left a voice mail. It's hard to say if she had disappeared by that point, because my mom could hold a grudge. So fuck her for being so stubborn. She didn't want to talk, fine by me.

At the time I was at a company called Anomaly, which was defiantly "not an ad agency." No, no. We were executionally agnostic market innovators who utilized a multidisciplinary approach to unravel the advertising enigmas of the modern media arena. We eschewed the old and embraced the numinous. We thought we were hotter than a lava monster shitting in a deep fryer turned up to high. I myself was the head of Innovation and Intellectual Initiatives, III, the Trinity of Me, or Tri-Me for short.

Being the steward of strategy was no easy task at a place like that. To make it work, I not only had to con an entire bullpen of bullshitters, I had to make it stick to the fan like it was covered in airplane glue. Looks like a Brown semiotics degree had some use in the real world. Who would've thought that my fabricated thesis about the utilization of reflections in Pierre Menard's remake of Baudrillard's *House of Mirrors* (a film, mind you, that itself was a complete fabrication of my imagination) would give me a corporate

4

edge? I mean, how many different ways can someone describe how when a driver sees a red octagon atop a pole on the side of the road, he knows to stop, even if he doesn't see the letters S-T-O-P? He "reads" the sign. That's it. That's semiotics: brand recognition, for academics.

With my days flooded by the deluge of Anomaly, my nights were inundated by the tide of Toby. Do you remember him? I think you met the night we ran into each other at the club, K-OS. You were there with that insecure producer named Doubtie, I think. Toby's the guy I grew up with in the "alleys" of Foggy Bottom, while you were living large up above Woodley Park. Toby had become my very own Manhattan Virgil, ferrying me along a river of spirits around the nine circles of the Lower East Side. We'd start out downing ambrosia at Milk and Honey, sipping over-priced mojitos through stainless steel straws, sweetened by the nectar of exclusivity. I always thought it was a cloying attempt at a speakeasy in a city where Prohibition was a bar on the Upper West Side. Still, the mojitos were delicious, and the dark, retronouvelle twenties décor reflected in the copper-tiled ceiling had a certain charm. Even if we all knew that, behind that thick velvet curtain of exclusivity, there was a garbage-choked Delancey Street. From there, we would stumble to any one of a bevy of hip scenes, so cool they needed only a monosyllabic name: Branch, Tree, Land, Sea, Salt, Bread, Rain, Spice, and the coup de grâce of creativity—Bar.

Well, late one night, Toby and I found ourselves in a renowned lesbian bar in the West Village. I was swinging for the fences and doing about as well as a one-legged kid at kickball. Toby, on the other hand, couldn't even raise his drink to his lips as it was weighed down by the diesel dyke hanging on his arm. Jesus, that body-building gay girl had more muscle than a Blue Bell cow and less body fat than a Eurasian model. There I was commiserating with a suicide grrrl about how we always end up with loonies with extra crazy sprinkled on top, and there he was, murmuring into a sinewy ear, talking Hippolyta right out of her magical girdle. My only conciliation was stealing sips of Toby's bourbon. And damnitall if while leaning in to purloin another slug, I didn't overhear his athletic ornament whisper an inquiry as to Toby's preference for anal. I couldn't believe it, not only was Toby picking up a lovely lady in a lesbian bar, he had found one that could make a porn star blush. Having long since hit my limit, I took that as my cue to head out.

I wandered homeward, clip-clopping along the side-walk, watching my shadow circle round me to avoid the street lamps. I must have had a lot more of Toby's bour-bons than I'd realized, because the next thing I knew I woke up sitting on a bench in Union Square. A patch of drool had blossomed on the collar of my peacoat. My breath condensed into plumes of sighs. Fall was coming. My phone BEEPED/VIBRATED in my pocket. That must have been what woke me.

It was a text from Toby. *If a diesel dyke ever asks if ur into backdoor action, the answer is always NO.*

BEEP/VIBRATE: *I think she jammed a coatrack up my arse.*

I grinned so big it hurt my ears, watched the clouds of my breath evaporate, stood up, and glanced at the frenetic digital clock that glowed eight stories above the southeast corner of the park.

It was 4:52.

It was the 30th.

It was my mother's birthday.

Like I said, it took a while for it all to coalesce in my head. I left long messages for her while riding the Acela down to DC. Called her again from the cab. And shouted her name as I unlocked the front door to my childhood home. I spent the entire weekend in the empty house. I waited, I watched TV, I snooped through my mother's bedroom, closets, drawers. Everything was there. No missing underwear or suspiciously absent luggage. However, it also wasn't like there was a cigarette in the ashtray still quietly trailing a ribbon of smoke into the air over a glass of milk, still wet with condensation. Just a rotten, desiccated orange on her desk and a busted water pipe in the basement weeping from an early frost. Like she just went out one day and never came home. That's how I explained it to the police. Except her car was still in the garage.

The folks at Anomaly were nice enough about the whole thing when I told them I wouldn't be in for a few days. I called Toby. He offered to come down, but I didn't see the point. The FBI and I were already going through the house and her office looking for clues. The Bureau got involved due to my mom's position with the government—with DARPA—the Defense Advance Research Projects Agency.

It had been a while since I'd stepped foot in her office. It looked the same, pretty much, just felt like everything had been shifted three inches to the left. At the time I wrote it off to memory echo. Mom's term. She came up with it to explain how memories tended to persist, but distort a little. Fade, but not uniformly, in patches. Like how in an echo certain syllables still get punched clearly, while the other parts muddle into gibberish due to the destructive interference.

That's what I thought it was. Back then.

Before all this.

Still, it was all there. Her desk in the corner, her book-shelves filled with *The Drama of the Gifted Child, I & Thou, In Contradiction: A Study of the Transconsistent;* the DSM-IV-TR—her ergonomic lounge chair in which she did the majority of her work: listening to patients, tak-ing notes, and of course her trademark Psynar®-ing; the abstract wooden sculptures that looked like 3-D Rorschach tests (even though she always denied it); and the oriental rug, bordered by not one, but two leather couches. These weren't the prototypical Freud-mind-fuck leather couches. You know the kind, the armless, dimpled-cushioned, psy-choanalytic sofas with the raised back. She had way too strong a sense of irony for that. No, these were just your typical Design Within Reach leather couches. Still, these artifacts were exactly the type of thing semioticians get off on. What better symbol to signify therapy than a leather couch? I guess a Polaroid of Freud sucking on a thick, long phallus of a cigar would trump it, but in a pinch: leather couch.

She wasn't just any run-of-the-mill, tell-me-about-your-childhood kind of therapist. My mother was a Pneumagrapher . . . or more colloquially put, a mind-mapper. The authorities would bring her in, after some aberrant occurrence, to reverse engineer the psychological state of the perpetrator. This was less criminal profiling and more demonic possession. She wasn't just called in for any old crime, though. They only used her when it was open-ended, when something needed to be shaken loose.

Once she was summoned after Alan Teleos, the serial kidnapper, was killed during his attempted arrest.

She found the secret lair where two of his intended victims were slowly starving to death. Another time she was brought in after that student went on a shooting spree at Virginia Tech University. The ATF asked her to ascertain if he was an individual who had a psychological break or rather was the by-product of a confluence of insidious memes that could be diverted and dispersed through government regulation. And on three separate occasions, I can attest to my mother taking sudden vacations to undisclosed destinations within twenty-four hours of three different terrorist attacks. I can only posit that she was needed to determine whether these were multitiered attacks with still-pending targets or something along those lines.

My mother would inhabit the scene of the crime; she would delve into the landscape of her subject's life. She'd read his books, taste his food, study his life, take volumes of notes, and then sit in her ergonomic chair, collating iterations of what was and what ifs and Psynar® her way into his skin. Psy(chological) na(vigation) r(anging). In navigating her subjects, my mother tracked the footprints of their animas, listening for memory echoes and following them right inside the hollow. You see, objects, things . . . they muffle acoustic reflections. Only empty places can house echoes of lasting clarity. So she went spelunking around the caverns of their minds, sat inside their empty dwellings, and sent out waves of empathy that bounced back. She let iteration after iteration wash over her until she could "see" it. See how they felt.

Once her talent was recognized, she was ushered into the upper levels of anonymity through a variety of "classified" government agencies. While her Psynar® was what originally attracted the attention of these shadow walkers, her success was due to another trademarked innovation, her PsychoNarrative®.

With Psynar® she could map out the subconscious of her subjects and sound the depths of their psyches. However, it was only useful to her. But the PsychoNarrative®: that puppy took her data and interpolated the shit out of it, transforming it from a visceral, singular immersion into a transportive, engrossing, almost seductive window of access to others. It provided the higher-ups with insights they could assimilate, integrate, and implement. Simply put, she used the good old-fashioned time-travel and mind-reading technology of a good book and wrote a story (cleverly disguised as a report) they couldn't put down.

Based on my mother's doctoral work, PsychoNarration taps into ancient neurological roots tied to crucial parts of our social cognition dealing with both the telling of tales and the enjoyment of them. She discovered all this by studying the have-nots, by poking and prodding those with dysnarrativia, which is basically a state of narrative impairment due to brain damage. These poor souls can't separate between narrativity and personhood. Essentially, in losing the ability to construct narrative, they lose themselves. Am I me or the character of me? I can relate.

Anyway, the habit of engaging the world around us through narrative is hardwired into our central nervous system. It's why storytelling is one of the few human traits universal across cultures and throughout history. Folktales even predate the written word. What do you think those Neanderthals were doing painting bison and deer on their cave walls in Lascaux? They were telling one of the three basic stories and tapping into our common, underlying biology. As Jeremy Tsu summarizes the theory of Patrick

Colm Hogan, professor of English and comparative literature at the University of Connecticut, "As many as two
thirds of the most respected stories in narrative traditions
seem to be variations on three narrative patterns, or prototypes . . . The two more common prototypes are romantic
and heroic scenarios—the former focuses on the trials and
travails of love, whereas the latter deals with power struggles. The third prototype, dubbed 'sacrificial' by Hogan,
focuses on agrarian plenty versus famine as well as on
societal redemption. These themes appear over and over
again as humans create narrative records of their most basic
needs: food, reproduction and social status." We're pro-
grammed to respond to them as our very survival depends
on it. Hence, the power of PsychoNarratives®.

Psychologists like Mom call this immersion in stories
"narrative transport." It's crucial for social interaction and
communal living. It's how we learn empathy. It's why lines
like *my bedroom ceiling fan is spreading rumors about me*
strike a chord in us. We make stories out of everything.

My mother hammered her quill into a psychic scalpel and lobotomized the shit out of an inner monologue.
What propaganda was to cinema, PsychoNarrative® is to
storytelling. Her reports were beyond influential, they were
the tablets from on high. Which is why they were locked
away, thrown into the oubliette of CLASSIFIED. And
most likely why she hid this last report.

When I uncovered the documents you now have, there
was no DCPD, no FBI, no NSA, no acronyms of any sort.
I didn't find it for some time, not until I stared at the key
she left for me. And when I say key, I don't mean figuratively, but an actual, physical key. Like I said, she had a
healthy respect for irony.

It had been over nine months since her birthday weekend. Toby and I were sucking down martinis at Olive (we had progressed to two-syllable joints). I was bitching about my recent rent hike, when Toby just sort of blurted out, "What about your mom's house?"

I didn't get it at first. Telling him that while a town house in northwest DC was styling, it would make the commute to SoHo a tad long.

"No, I mean like you could subsidize yourself by renting out your mom's house. Not like there's a mortgage on it or anything. With the money you get you could probably even move out and get yourself a sweet loft."

I blinked at my glass of gin.

I wasn't upset, just more shocked. Stunned that I hadn't thought about it. It had been nine months, and somehow I had carried my mother's disappearance to term. Her, the house, hope—I had kept it all in some sort of abeyance. It's not like I was in denial or anything, I was on the phone with the FBI every other week. But it was her house. I mean, yeah it was our house, but it was my mom's house. I guess it was denial. But I deserved a little denial in my life. I didn't have her anymore, no Mom to cuddle and comfort me. But I had the house that still reeked of the scent of childhood. The house that she might open the front door to any day now.

Toby ordered another round for us, and offered to drive me down.

So there I was, sitting on the edge of my bed, in my old room that hadn't changed since I left for college. On my walls hung prints of paintings by Magritte, Escher, Dalí, Kandinsky; a poster of Einstein; and a Norwegian Moose Crossing sign. (I was nerd-chic before it was hip.)

Bookshelves were stocked with everything from *The Yearling* to Tolkien to *Hamlet* to Kesey. Soccer trophies and annual sports-team photos stood guard over my bureau, and stacks of comic books cluttered my closet.

Toby was downstairs, mothballing my mom's study. I was in my room, staring at a poster of *Dalí from the Back Painting a Person at the Window from the Back Eternalized by Six Virtual Panes Provisionally*. In the left foreground is the back of Dalí. He sits at his easel, paintbrush in hand, and leans to the right of it to look at his subject, the back side of a woman in a blue-striped house dress and a ribbon necklace, leaning on a windowsill. She stares out at a seascape. Opened inward, a six-paned window stands guard behind her. Reflected in the glass, divided up by the coordinate plane of windowpanes, is the woman and the face of Dalí leaning to the right of his easel. In the window's reflection you can see the ribbon draped around the woman's neck twists like a Möbius strip, and a key-shaped pendant dangles from it.

This painting had always been a favorite of mine. The stillness of the craft, the facing one's self, and the secrets within the reflection. More than just themes, in this portrait Dalí simultaneously creates and compresses depth. It seemed both intimate and infinite. A little unnerving unless you just went with it, otherwise it'd just do-si-do with your middle ear. Even the key, which seemed locked in the distant reflection, at the same time bulged with proximity. The effect was hypnotic.

Something was off, though. I stumbled out of a middle-distance stare, wobbled back into two-dimensional analysis, and forced myself to focus. The key still really came out at me.

I stood up and approached the print. The image of the key was not an image at all; it was an actual key. *Ceci n'est pas une pipe*, my ass. It had been glued onto the painting. I tried to delicately pry it off, but after a few tentative snaps with my fingernail, I just ripped it off with a piece of the woman in tow.

So there I was, staring down at this key that, to my discombobulated mind, had somehow been magically transported from one world to another. It looked like an old key, worn, stained with some old paint, a piece of poster stuck to it. What the hell had it been doing there, like the Purloined Letter? More importantly, what did it open? I know you've already jumped ahead of me at this point, but you have to remember, at the time I wasn't in the most incisive of mental states. And then I turned it over, and it all snapped into focus.

On the back of the key, underneath the piece of poster, were more blotches of paint. I knew those blotches, like a suicide girl knows her tats. It was the key to my father's old art studio.

It was exactly like he left it. Preserved like a shrine. Canvases leaned against the walls, tubes of paint scattered asunder on his drafting table, easel, and an almost finished painting. It was a portrait of my mother when she was younger. The brushstrokes seemed blatantly impressionistic as if each blot was made up of a tiny picture. And in fact, they were. As I moved close to the canvas, the portrait of my mother dissolved into a collage of a thousand little portraits of me.

I took it all in: the clutter, the silence, the thick air that smelled like my father. She had kept my dad's studio all these years. Her little secret. Her little piece of him.

That's when the tsunami of guilt hit me. Knocked me right off my feet and left me dazed, in the middle of the floor, on my ass. Here I was sitting in the middle of this shrine that my mother had preserved all these years, while back at the house, Toby mummified my mother's china in Bubble Wrap.

What was I doing? Putting the final nail in my mother's coffin? No, not even. Worse. I was burying her alive.

I needed to stand up, get my sea legs, march myself back to the house, and put an end to this lunacy. Rent hike be damned, I wasn't going to close the door just yet.

If I weren't looking at things from my particular lowly vantage point, I would have done exactly that. But instead I noticed something of an anomaly. A briefcase. A black leather, oversized, catalog briefcase. Which was somewhat of a bibelot of conformity ensconced beneath a drafting table cluttered with tubes of paint, brushes, and sketches.

I crawled over and dragged it out from the shadows. It felt like it was filled with mercury. With a few determined tugs, I overpowered its static friction and hauled that disobedient puppy into the light.

It didn't look like one of my dad's old cases. Nor did it make any sense that he would have brought it here, to his sanctuary.

The combo locks were securely fastened. I tried the obvious combinations: 123, 321, 789, 987, and all the triple repeats like 000, 111, 222—so much for my inner hacker.

I sifted through the disheveled studio looking for a knife, scissors, a can top, anything sharp. He had to have cut the canvases with something. Once again, the portrait caught my attention. I stood and stared, played back and forth with my focus: my mom, to a million me's, back to my mom, back to me . . .

That's what gave me the idea. I dashed back to the briefcase and scrolled through the numbers until both combo locks read 315. My birthday. They popped right open.

The case was stuffed full of folders, papers, reports, transcripts, and notes in her handwriting. It was one of her PsychoNarratives®.

I had rarely caught glimpses of her filing them away in her office. From what I could tell, they were always neat, well organized, streamlined. Nothing ever this prolific. Maybe it's because it was unfinished. Maybe they all started this way, and then she would whittle them down over time. And for some reason, she hid it here and left me a personalized trail of breadcrumbs and a scavenger hunt of memory echoes.

I had every intention of going through the whole thing right then, like some sort of masochistic Sisyphus. I pulled out a hunk of manila folders, set them on the floor next to me, and picked up the top one. She had written diagonally down the front, like an e. e. cummings poem, the title:

here

&

there

And for some reason, in the moment, staring at her handwriting, I felt overwhelmingly vulnerable. I was not safe. I had to get it away. Hide it. Cloister it in some hermetic safe harbor. Up until that moment, my father's studio had been an asylum, but once I had found it, opened it up, and let the air in, its cloak of secrecy started to disintegrate. Soon the hungry, watchful moths would flutter in and devour it.

I would hide it in habit. Continue on with my life as if nothing had happened. Put her stuff in storage, rent out her house, and go back to New York. Only instead of using the extra money to move into a loft, I decided to hand over the cash to an ex-girlfriend of Toby's. For a little cheese, she rented me a carriage house tucked away behind apartment buildings, in the middle of a block, at the bottom of Hell's Kitchen.

I know, it sounds nuts, but I needed a hideaway and had to make sure I wasn't being followed. So like always, I'd periodically hit some bars on Ninth Avenue, ending up at a nondescript door on 40th Street, with a single red light over it. It was the entrance to Siberia, a low-frills bar that was large, unadorned, and had a voluminous lower level. But that's not why I'd go there. I'd go there to use the door in back that opened up into the rear of Bellevue, another bar, which had its own entrance on Ninth. Once discharged, I'd swing down the avenue, and make my way to 357 West 39th. I'd open the two security doors, walk past the stairwell leading up to several floors of apartments, beyond the row of garbage and recycling cans, and out yet another back door. I'd cross the wrought iron bridge spanning a cement "courtyard" and unlock the door to the carriage house. On the entrance level there would be a kitchenette and an empty living room; on the top level, a bathroom and a bedroom with a mattress resting on the floor; and on the courtyard level, another bathroom and bedroom with a fold-up card table, a chair, and my mother's leather, catalog-sized briefcase.

The place needed to be all but empty. For the echoes. So I'd go and immerse myself in her report and try and track the echoes of her words. If I could just follow them to the source, I'd find out what happened. I'd find her.

If only it had happened that way.

How could I have known then that by the time I was far enough in to begin to put the pieces together, the picture would have already changed? At that time, I didn't know if I was going mental or if my mother had gone round the bend while Psynar®-ing. The only thing that was clear was our shared sense of paranoia. But at least we were determined.

Unfortunately, so was the other side.

I've been running for a long time now. So long it's hard to differentiate between pounding heartbeats and pursuing footsteps. All I know, with any real clarity, is that my only chance of getting through all this is to publish it.

I need you to get my mom's story out there.

The more I thought about it, the more it made sense, for a variety of reasons:

1. To protect myself. Once this is published, the powers that be will have to either acknowledge or deny the existence of this report, my mother, and the accident. No matter what track they take, I'll be safe from any government retribution. It would be too obvious, not to mention suspicious, were I to meet some tragic end.

2. To possibly find her. If my mother has not disappeared completely into the void, if she is still alive, then with this, I can send her a message. I can let her know I found the inheritance she left me.

3. To save her. This was her last narrative. Her last words. I'm trying to keep her alive.

I can't publish it myself because it's too dangerous to slow down. I'm hot on her trail, and the last thing I want to do is give them the time to catch up and catch me. By the time you read this, if you've gotten this far, I've already left the country. If I find what I'm looking for, somehow I'll get in touch.

If you think it's got any legs, help me take it for a run. Market it as my memoir or Hilary's. And if publishers are too skittish to bite—sell it as goddamn fiction. Make yourself the author and change the names if necessary. Do whatever it takes.

I realize that it won't be easy. Very few people have ever heard of my mother or PsychoNarrative®. Her entire report focuses on an unverified, paradigm-shifting discovery and a military project that doesn't officially exist.

Even Reidier—the star, as you'll see, of this massive clusterfuck—is a ghost, a phantom pariah. Brown University removed him from their public records. Informally, they justify this as necessary in order to expunge any of the bad PR concerning his "lab accident." All they'll acknowledge is that Reidier and his family were killed while he was performing an unauthorized experiment, layering Bose-Einstein condensates with deuterium while using a pulsed beam of photons from an ALS to ionize the electrons, which caused it to fragment into a severe "Coulomb explosion."

If you believe my mother's records, though, this had absolutely nothing to do with Reidier's work and is not even close to what went down.

Read this and ask yourself, what would you do in my shoes? Either my mother was an imaginative storyteller with an immense and serious case of OCD, who one day just upped and left her life behind—left me; or she was a soul mapper and scribe of the State, whose testimony had to be annulled.

From what I can tell, she started not too long after the incident. DARPA hired her to decipher if it all was an accident or sabotage. And in either case, they needed her to find out what led up to it.

I think she did just that.

Your friend,
Daniel Brand

PS *In the beginning is the deed.* ~Goethe

I

Every man takes the limits of his own field of vision for the limits of the world.

~Arthur Schopenhauer

Knowledge, its pursuit, its mastery, is merely an illusion of comprehension that conveniently distracts us from our limits.

~E. Tassat, "Fencing in the Liminal State"

"My life is a lovely story, happy and full of incident."

~Hans Christian Andersen

Name the greatest of all inventors. Accident.

~Mark Twain

All those ~~involved in~~* privy to *The Reidier Test* found themselves (and continue to find themselves) in complete and utter agreement as to "what happened." DARPA had gathered its top brass, a handful of military personnel, and physicist Kerek Reidier, along with his family, for a test on September 14, 2008, of a top-secret Department developmental program requiring so much energy that it necessitated the USS ███████████ aircraft** carrier to act, essentially, as a battery. Shortly after sunset, with the Navy's help, DARPA ferried everyone over from the Newport Naval Station to the Navy's decommissioned bunker—which had been recommissioned by DARPA for Reidier's lab—on Gould Island, a small isle at the bottom of the Narragansett Bay tucked between Jamestown and Newport. At 8:58 p.m. a switch was thrown, and a brilliant white light, similar to a magnesium ignition, engulfed the northeastern end of Gould Island, immediately accompanied by what's best described as a thunderclap. The bunker and the USS ███████ were no longer there, and all those present at the test are presumed dead.

---

* This is a handwritten edit by Dr. Hilary Kahn of her report.

** The name of the specific aircraft carrier utilized was redacted by DARPA.

While the classified footage of the fallout is both awing and unnerving, it merely encapsulates the spectacle of it all, not the essence. The significance lies in the before. Not the what, but the how. The moments before the test initiation, as captured in the lab video records,[1] reveal a striking contrast to the catastrophic aftermath.

Donald Pierce, the Director of the Strategic Technology Office within DARPA, struts around the Plexiglased observation area, shaking hands with fellow brass. The heads of the four other technical offices of the Department are present: Director of the Tactical Technology Office, Dr. David Walker; Acting Deputy Director of the Defense Sciences Office, Dr. Carol Eberhart; Director of the Information Processing Techniques Office, Dr. Wendy Morefield;

---

[1] Throughout the lab, a host of video cameras documented any and all activity within. The system was originally implemented at the insistence of Reidier, who viewed it as a resource for reviewing and replicating any "unplanned or unaccounted for factors." The video was recorded onto lab hard drives and backed up through a secure network on storage towers in Brown University's CCV (Center for Computation and Visualization), as well as on computers in Reidier's home.

and Deputy Director of the Microsystems Technology Office, Gregory Pica. Rear Admiral Russell Wisecup, Naval Station Newport's Commanding Officer, is in attendance as well, along with various other military and Department personnel.

Director Pierce makes it a point to personally interact with every member of the gathered audience. With some, like David Walker, Director Pierce shakes hands without letting go. Instead, he maintains his grasp, and pulls them in, leans toward their ear, and offers a conspiratorial whisper. With others, Pierce similarly transforms the handshake into a bear hug, only to lean back and announce his pleasure that so-and-so could make it to their little show. These are his respective supporters and skeptics. After several minutes of this, everybody finds their seats, and Pierce says a few words.

"All of us here understand the excitement and the hardship in preparing for our nation's future. Some of us, through our ambitious and varied enterprises, have set out to develop, master, and harness all that which is possible. Others here have sought to bring about and tame the impossible. Tonight, I hope we accomplish a little of both. This achievement would provide us the ultimate tool. We cannot imagine how a successful test will completely change the world as we know it, nor comprehend the importance of this newly discovered phenomenon. At the very least, for our nation, it will forever alter international relations, rendering war practically obsolete, saving not only American lives, but the citizens of any would-be aggressor. This technology will liberate humankind. Thank you all for your support, your criticisms, your contributions, and your participation here in this incredible event."

Event . . . Pierce's use of the term is telling. "Event" demarcates the sense of hope and optimism present in driving toward *The Reidier Test*. The assumption of a positive happening. The presumed knowledge of what will happen at a certain place at a certain time. It's a managed and celebrated occurrence.

Terminology has played a crucial role in the fallout after *The Reidier Test*. While those in the know found themselves (and continue to find themselves) in complete and utter agreement as to "what happened," many have also unwittingly engaged in a subconscious battle of semantics on how to label what in fact occurred. In our day-to-day lives, we often shrug off this type of disagreement with a dismissive, "We're just arguing semantics." More often than not, this is seen as the moment of agreement. The dispute has been resolved; until this point the two parties thought they were arguing toward different ends, and now it's apparent that they were saying the same thing, just in different ways. Semantics.

The type of terminology utilized in discussing *The Reidier Test*, however, lies at the very center of the conflict. How it's described cannot be shrugged off with the assumption of moot inconsequentiality. Rather, its label utterly affects what it is. The exponential effects of this cannot be overestimated as we hold the potential to either defuse or detonate the volatile situation in the naming of it.

In the various postdisaster interdepartment memos I have been copied on, *The Reidier Test* has been referred to with a variety of nomenclature including: the happening, the occurrence, the phenomenon, the episode, the enterprise, the feat, the attempt, the hazard, the Super SNAFU, the Major FUBAR, and the Atomic Clusterfuck. The two most consistent monikers have been "the incident" and "the accident." It is these last two terms that successfully encapsulate the rest. And it is the distinction between the two that necessitated my services.

In order to learn from the mistakes, and capitalize on further iterations, the Department must first accurately classify what *The Reidier Test* was.

Was the experiment a failure and why? Clearly the experiment did not work, but it might not be an experimental failure. Instead it may have been an attempt at the impossible.

Was it human error or the very unwieldy nature of the act itself? Was it sabotage?

An *incident* is inherently singular in its occurrence. A one-time thing. It's a distinct piece of action, one that is demarcated with boundaries. Still, incidents are not separate from a continuum. They can be connected to something else, without being a part of it. An incident carries with it the connotation of diminished importance: an act that didn't warrant a full-blown name. We most often find this in military jargon, such as an international incident or a border incident. By using this terminology, the hope is to minimize or at least contain the matter.[2] Perhaps in referring to *The Reidier Test* as an incident, Department members are hoping to do just this. Contain what happened. Minimize its importance. Separate it. Insulate it so, like a tumor, it can be excised, and in doing so the Department could move on as if it never happened. Or perhaps by circumscribing it, it can be safely quarantined and thereby allow the Department to proceed further down the Reidier road, comfortable that what happened was an isolated incident.

Accidents, on the other hand, are an altogether different type of beast. Bear in mind the root of the word: *ad-* "to" plus *cadere* "fall." Every accident is an act of falling—an act devoid of control, an act impossible to govern. There is no inherent singularity within. An accident could happen again and again. By definition, its occurrence is always undesirable, unintentional, and unfortunate. But accidents also are so very valuable because they are devoid of fault and blame. Of course, this cuts both ways. While accidents often lead to damage, sometimes they are merely unexpected events that can occasionally yield wondrous results. Still, chance and fortune do not make

---

[2] Paradoxically, doing so emphasizes what it is not, rather than what it is. Inherent to an incident is ignorance, a lack of articulation, and an inability to describe. It induces aphasia, which ratchets up fear, and thereby heightens the impulse to contain.

dependable partners. It is not too difficult to understand why some at the Department would be eager to avoid blame, while others would be frustrated by the inability to replicate results.

Long before the jargon balkanization within the Department, competing terminologies were finding footholds in Providence's various network affiliates. NBC's WJAR provided all-day coverage of the "catastrophic accident," while ABC's WLNE provided minute-to-minute updates on the "Gould Island Incident." Oddly, while Fox's WPRI based in East Providence had a running banner on Ocean State of Fear, its Providence counterpart bounced all around from "tragedy" to "marine mishap" to "waterloo" to "cataclysm" to "debacle" to "disaster."[3] Despite the frenzy of captions, the majority of the news coverage focused primarily on the fish kill: the swaths of dead marine life that washed up on the shores of both Jamestown and Newport, and the Naval Station (NAVSTA) on Newport. Suppositions were made about oil spills, chemical pollution, secret Naval weapons testing,[4] and algae blooms brought on by global warming. The algae bloom was supported by the discovery of a film/residue that coated some coastal rocks. (It was later determined that this was very fine iron/manganese/cobalt-based dust, not algae.) There was almost no mention of an intense, incinerating flash of light. WJAR's meteorology report referred to an aberrant lightning discharge, but that was about it. As the news is essentially a visual medium, the imagery of fish kill occupied significantly more airtime than nomenclature or reporting.

---

[3] It's more than likely that the mass media's contradictory coverage contributed to the Department's own epidemic of misnomers.

[4] The Pentagon promptly issued a press release, which stated unequivocally that there had been no weapons testing at Newport NAVSTA, secret or otherwise. Its remote test facilities are located at Seneca Lake and Fisher's Island in New York, and Dodge Pond, Connecticut. Neither of these had run any weapons test in the past three weeks. One month later, the Navy's website issued a small announcement about a retired aircraft carrier having been sunk off the coast of Puerto Rico for a coral reef rehabilitation project.

None of the stations ever mentioned *The Reidier Test*, or Reidier himself. A few weeks after, the Providence *Journal* ran an obituary on Reidier referring to his untimely death in a freak lab accident. No connection to Gould Island was ever made or has yet to be made publicly.

Having considered the various factions within the Department, as well as the sensationalist impulses of the twenty-four-hour news cycle, we can see that the classification of *The Reidier Test* has as much, if not more, to do with the observer as with the observed. Nevertheless, it is also important to consider Reidier's own worldview. He vehemently denied the idea of accidents. As he himself said while discussing serendipity at a colloquium, ". . . It echoes tones of divining and fortune smiling down on you, but really it's just a highfalutin way of saying you pulled something completely out of your rear end . . . The thing is, though, you would have never discovered your answer to begin with if you weren't already looking for it. Archimedes didn't take a bath and accidentally discover that the volume of displaced water equals the volume of the displacing object. He was already trying to figure out how to calculate the density of King Hiero's golden crown. It just happens that he found the answer in the tub. 'Chance favors the prepared mind,' as Pasteur said. Without intent, accidents go unnoticed or are misunderstood; with intent, they cannot, by definition, occur. There are no such things as accidents."

Reidier's passionate insight is both compelling and revealing. And if we take a page from a book of one of his favorite authors, we find yet another perspective. According to Isaac Asimov, "The most exciting phrase to hear in science, the one that heralds new discoveries, is not 'Eureka!' but 'That's funny . . .'"

It would be wrong to dismiss this etymological unpacking as merely an intellectual exercise of wordplay. In analyzing the connotations and denotations of the terminology, what we are attempting to uncover are underlying motivations for using this word or that one.

What is gained or sacrificed in choosing one noun over another? Who profits or loses from it? To grasp the significance of this, one need merely read any of the various periodicals covering the Israeli-Palestinian conflict. Do they refer to the Palestinians as defenders or aggressors, victims or perpetrators, liberators or jihadists, freedom fighters or terrorists? Even our own history changes with this same duplicity of language. In the 1770s, the British were outraged by the terrorist campaigns waged against their honorable Red Coats. Ben Franklin noted the malleability and power of language: "A rebellion is always legal in the first person, such as 'our rebellion.' It is only in the third person—'their rebellion'—that it becomes illegal."

Words build ideas. Ideas build ideologies. Ideologies build nations. *The Reidier Test*, however, could render all of this meaningless.

It is important to not be distracted by all the magnitude and grandeur of the ideological and literal creative destruction. At its heart, the narrative of *The Reidier Test* is a human story about a man, his wife, and their children. On another video feed, following the commencement speech to his colleagues, Director Pierce enters the control room where Dr. Kerek Reidier prepares and his family sits. His young twin boys sit at opposite ends of the console: Otto on the left side, Ecco on the right. Eve Tassat, his wife, stands behind in a corner, dressed in a hunter-green blouse and a faded red sweater with waist tie. Her arms wrap around herself, one over the other, in a *V.* Her hands just poke out of the stretched sleeves of the sweater and hook over her shoulders.

Reidier adjusts a few knobs, calibrating off of a monitor.

"You boys going to do the honor for us?" Pierce asks the twins.

Otto looks up, smiles, and nods vigorously. Ecco looks over at his brother and nods too.

"How's that, Eve, not only does your family get to watch your husband make a miracle, your boys get to be a part of it and start it all off?" Pierce says.

She looks up at him for a moment. "It *ease* quite compelling, Pierce," she replies with only a trace of her French accent.

"I had to pull a few strings to get all of you in here." Pierce gives Eve an expectant look, perhaps in anticipation of a thank-you. When it doesn't come, he continues unfazed. "A momentous day indeed!" he says, no longer looking at her. His eyes follow Reidier on his adjustments. "Not just the final frontier, beyond the frontier. Not even. No. It's the destruction of frontiers altogether."

Eve doesn't respond. Her face is devoid of expression. Her hands, however, keep flexing and relaxing and grasping her shoulders, while she stares at Otto. It's difficult to tell, with the complete lack of cinematography, but there might be tears in her eyes.

"The finale of frontiers," Pierce quips to himself.

Reidier, still focused on the console, absentmindedly paraphrases the first law of thermodynamics. "Nothing is ever created or destroyed." Before Pierce can counter, Reidier stands up and announces, "We're ready."

Pierce straightens himself. "It will work?"

Reidier faces Pierce. "Is your floating battery out there going to give me the ▮▮▮▮▮▮▮▮▮▮[5] of power I need?"

"Absolutely."

"Then my physics will work."

Pierce puts his hand on Reidier's shoulder. "You've definitely earned yourself a vacation. But first, let's change the world. Wait till I'm back in the observation deck."

He exits.

From off of the back of a chair, Reidier picks up, of all things, a tattered tweed sport coat, adorned with worn elbow patches and a lapel

---

[5] The specific amount of energy required was bleeped out by DARPA.

pin made from an old computer transistor. He puts on the jacket and straightens his brown velvet tie.

Reidier looks at Eve. She gives the slightest of nods. The corners of his lips flutter up briefly. He walks over to Otto and opens up the Plexiglas cover over the button in front of the boy.

"Wait until I tell you," Reidier says.

Otto nods.

Eve moves to stand behind Otto and places her hands on his shoulders.

Reidier walks over to Ecco. In similar fashion, he opens the button cover in front of Ecco.[6]

Once again, Reidier admonishes, "Wait until I tell you."

Ecco smiles up at his father.

Reidier stands behind him and glances over at a monitor. It shows Pierce taking his seat in the observation area. Reidier places his hands on Ecco's shoulders.

For a moment, the four of them stay perfectly still, a tableau of the nuclear family: mother, father, and twin boys, mirror images of each other.

"On 'go,' boys. Three, two, one, go."

The boys press their respective buttons as Reidier says something to himself, but the audio garbles it into guttural gibberish as the video interference begins. The image freezes. Some areas transform into static, lines pixilate, artifacts randomly pop up. Still you can decipher the four of them, until the next iteration of interference. The images of all four of them stretch sideways in a wavelike pattern and split, so now there are eight of them, and then the video goes black. It all happens in a matter of seconds.

The hard drives at Brown and at the Reidier home cannot back

---

[6] As far as my research shows, there was no scientific purpose for having a separated two-button "ignition" system. Rather, like with a nuclear missile launch, it serves merely as a safety measure.

up instantaneously. Depending on the cycle, there can be anywhere from an eight to a sixteen second delay. This is why we never actually see the boys press the buttons.

None of those present survived. No remains were ever recovered. Officially, the immense power the test was pulling from Pierce's floating battery or some unforeseen, exothermic factor vaporized all living matter within a hundred meter radius.

Still, there's something perplexing about that final image of the four of them.

There's a similarly intimate moment in the last recordings of the Reidier home footage.[7] It's in Eve and Reidier's bedroom. It's the night before, according to the video counter, 12:21 a.m. Eve sits on the bottom edge of their queen bed. She's wearing old gray sweatpants and a white ribbed tank top. She's staring down.

Reidier shuffles down the hallway and into view. He leans against the doorway, dressed in flannel pajama bottoms, slippers, a V-neck undershirt, and fittingly, his tweed sport coat. He watches his wife, his head tilting to the right like a confused beagle. Reidier bites his lower lip and sighs.

It's the sigh that gets Eve's attention. She shrugs, her eyes finally pulling up to find him. "I know. I know."

---

[7] Reidier had installed a similar set of cameras in the home office/lab in his basement to record all of his lab activity. These cameras only saved footage to his personal computers in his home office. The above-referenced footage, however, is from Reidier and Eve's bedroom. Without the family's approval or knowledge, a nanosurveillance system was integrated into their entire home by the Department. The Microsystems Technology Office stated this was a precautionary measure to protect the Department's intellectual property along with the human assets (aka the Reidier family) from competitive interests, i.e. foreign governments and multinational corporations. See Chapter XI.

Reidier smiles and shuffles across the room to the edge of the bed. The two of them sit there, side by side, staring down.

From one of the high-angle camera feeds,[8] we can follow their gaze. In front of them, on the middle of the carpet, is a zipped-up suitcase. Folded on top of it lies the faded red sweater.

They were planning a family vacation regardless of the outcome of Reidier's test the following day. As Eve put it, the trip would be either a "much needed celebration or refuge."

They lean against each other at the edge of the bed. "Wear it tomorrow," Reidier says.

"It doesn't go with my favorite blouse. I'll look like a color-blind leprechaun at a Christmas party."

The two sit on the bed for a moment and then burst out laughing. He wraps an arm around her back. Eve curls into Reidier, snorting laughter into his armpit, their bodies shaking with amusement. Reidier kisses the top of her head.

It's a rare moment of relief for them. Somehow, in this mundane suggestion, Reidier and Eve found a way to cut through the months of tension and alienation they had endured.

Eve slept that night.
Reidier did not.

Instead, a few hours later he's sitting on the floor of his sons' room. He rests with his back against the nightstand between their two beds. Reidier barely moves. He just rubs his thumb against his forefinger

---

[8] Thank you to Deputy ▮▮▮▮▮▮, for facilitating the release of the hours of videos from these multiple feeds.

absentmindedly. The only sound is the synchronized breathing of the twins.

Less than a half hour later, Reidier is downstairs in his home office/lab in the basement. The footage is discontinuous, jarring. It is not from the Department feeds, but recorded with his computer's webcam. Reidier obviously made this recording himself, but without any decipherable purpose or method. Instead, it's a disconnected montage of half thoughts and disjointed moments. The overall effect suggests that he randomly, and sometimes accidentally, hit the record and pause buttons. There's no indication of any review or editing. More of a stream of consciousness, or unconsciousness as the case may be.

The first shot is of Reidier at his desk, still in his pajama bottoms and sport coat. He faces the camera in a whispered testimonial. Reidier's manner and tone are conspiratorial, bordering on paranoid. "It's all about tomorrow. If I'm right, then . . ."

A quick smile curls at the corners of his lips and flattens back out. He nods to himself, then finally stops. "It solves everything. You'll see, Kai. Then we'll—"

He abruptly turns around and stares up the stairs. He appears to be searching for the source of a noise that either didn't occur or didn't get picked up by the computer's microphone.[9]

After almost half a minute, Reidier turns back to the camera. He leans in close to the camera and confides, "The ceiling fan is still trying to eavesdrop." He shakes his head. "Don't think it can hear down here. But it doesn't matter. It still can't read Leo's Notebooks."

Jump-cut to his empty chair. In the background, Reidier, wearing an eye-patch on his right eye, paces back and forth, holding, of

---

[9] There is no corroborating Department nanofootage of the basement.

all things, a wok. He makes small circular motions with it as he walks. From inside the wok swishes out the tinny sound of metal on metal.

Jump-cut to a God shot (presumably Reidier holds the webcam above, pointed down) of the wok. At the center of it sits a metal marble. Reidier's hand comes into view and spins a second metal marble around the wok's lateral surface like a roulette ball. As it spirals down, the other marble jumps away from the first, as if pushed by an invisible force. It's disorienting at first until you realize the two marbles are similarly charged magnets. They move in tandem together, circling the center. Every now and then Reidier reaches his hand in and nudges one. Instantly, the other moves in response.

Jump-cut to Reidier sitting with his back to the camera at a three-quarter angle. He seems completely motionless, possibly asleep. At the bottom left corner of the screen, a fluttering movement catches the eye. He holds an unframed photograph. He tilts the photo ever so slightly back and forth. Due to the angle, the dim lighting, and the general low quality of webcams, we cannot see what's in the photograph.

After this, there's one more jump cut to a final testimonial, although its intent is debatable, as it might have simply been an accidental recording. Reidier faces the camera, but his eyes are focused below it, on the computer screen. He shifts from right to left. His eyes similarly shift in the opposite direction. It is unclear as to what he is looking at, but his behavior suggests that he's staring at his own live video image in a webcam window. This interpretation is further bolstered by Reidier's parting whisper, "We are never who we were."

That's the last shot of the discombobulated montage. The only other recorded activity that night is Reidier walking up the stairs, shuffling down the quiet hallways between the upstairs bedrooms, and climbing into bed with Eve.

During one of my visits to the Reidier house, after the Test day, I think I found the photo Reidier was looking at that night. It was face down in the wok. The magnetic marbles were still holding each other up against the conical sides, about an inch above the center.

The photograph was taken a few years ago when they were living in Chicago. Reidier and Eve are standing in Navy Pier Park with the Great Lake behind them. It's a sunny day. Reidier and Eve hold hands. Reidier smiles at the camera, his head tilted toward his wife. Eve is looking down at one of the boys, dangling in front of Reidier, fast asleep in a Baby Björn.

In interpreting the webcam footage, especially compared to the previous mundane Eve packing moment, one wonders about Reidier's psychological state. Indeed this suspicion has already been explored in numerous intra-Departmental e-mails under the guise (and sometimes outright accusation) of inquiring about the connections between genius and madness.[10]

The hypothesis that these two are related has existed for centuries. Historical and psychiatric research shows higher rates and intensities of psychopathological symptoms in creative individuals. Or more properly put, that individuals with creative, "outside of the box" thinking exhibit a higher incidence of symptoms associated with mental illness. Still, a trend does not signify correlation or causation with any statistical significance.

Dean Keith Simonton, PhD addresses and classifies these trends

---

[10] Extrapolating the inquiry, if Reidier the genius also ended up being Reidier the madman, then human error if not sabotage becomes a much more likely, and more easily digestible, explanation for what went wrong.

in his May 31, 2005 article for the *Psychiatric Times*, "Are Genius and Madness Related? Contemporary Answers to an Ancient Question" (http://www.psychiatrictimes.com/cultural-psychiatry/are-genius-and-madness-related-contemporary-answers-ancient-question). Simonton summarizes the three basic conclusions in this matter:

1. "The rate and intensity of psychopathological symptoms appear to be higher among eminent creators than in the general population . . . On average, the more eminent the creator, the higher is the expected rate and intensity of the psychopathological symptoms . . . Depression seems to be the most common symptom, along with the correlates of alcoholism and suicide."

2. "The rate and intensity of symptoms varies according to the specific domain of creativity. For example, psychopathology is higher among artistic creators than among scientific creators."[11]

3. "Family lines that produce the most eminent creators also tend to be characterized by a higher rate and intensity of psychopathological symptoms."[12]

---

[11] According to one study, 87 percent of famous poets experienced psychopathology whereas only 28 percent of the eminent scientists did so, a figure close to the population baseline (Ludwig, 1995 - *Ibid*).

[12] The majority of this evidence comes from the results of the Minnesota Multiphasic Personality Inventory (MMPI) and the Eysenck Personality Questionnaire (EPQ) (Gough, 1953). Still, it is nowhere near as conclusive as it seems. While creative individuals score higher on psychopathological symptoms, they rarely score high enough to indicate a psychopathology. Rather, their scores fall somewhere between normal and abnormal. Furthermore, as Simonton notes, elevated scores on psychoticism are associated with independence and nonconformity, features that lend support to innovative activities. In addition, these score levels are associated with the capacity for defocused attention, which enables ideas to enter the mind that would normally be filtered. One must also consider that these creative individuals also score higher on other characteristics, such as ego strength and self-sufficiency, which dampen the effects of psychopathological symptoms.

Psychologist Mihaly Csikszentmihalyi, known for his work on flow, has spent over forty years studying creatives and their processes. What he has found common to all "geniuses" is not madness, but rather discipline. Perseverance through bout after bout of trial and error—this is what's required of the mind of a genius. "Discipline is not a hallmark of minds in the throes of emotional distress. 'Despite the carefree air that many creative people affect,' writes Csikszentmihalyi, 'most of them work late into the night and persist when less driven individuals would not.'"[13]

All of this is a grant-fueled, academic way of saying that at best the link between genius and madness is inconclusive. Nevertheless, Reidier does not seem to be exhibiting any symptoms of a psychotic episode or suicidal depression. This is supported by the previously described lab footage the day of the Test. Reidier seems focused, in control, and disciplined. In spite of the "absurdity" of his behavior in his home office, he seems to behave in as normal a manner as anyone would alone, in the middle of the night, before a possibly monumental, career-making day.

These moments are not the meaningless testimonials of a lunatic. They are the private utterances of a focused, albeit anxious, man.

This is bound to unsettle some within the Department as it leaves several crucial questions unanswered.

Who is Kai?

What and where are Leo's Notebooks?

What's the significance of the wok and the magnets?

And why is there only one boy in the photograph?

---

[13] Hara Estroff Marano, "Genius and Madness, Creativity and Mood: The myth that madness heightens creative genius," *Psychology Today* May 07, 2007.

Public interest in the Gould Island incident/accident barely took hold in the public consciousness and waned in the weeks following *The Reidier Test*. Gould Island was uninhabited and sold to the State of Rhode Island and the Providence Plantation. Cleanup of the marine-animal carcasses was completed within ten days. Human casualties were never reported by the Department. The structural survey of the nearby Newport Bridge revealed no damage. And the busy season of summer had been over for weeks.

Probably the most significant reason for *The Reidier Test*'s lack of prominence on the nation's radar was the date: September 14, 2008. Lehman Brothers filed for bankruptcy only a few hours later at 1:45 a.m. on September 15. The national news networks ran the story all day, cutting back from images of Lehman employees removing files and belongings from 745 Seventh Avenue to shots of the Stock Exchange as its shares tumbled over 90 percent. The country was overwrought about economic implosion and unconcerned about an actual explosion (incidental or accidental) a couple hundred miles up the Eastern seaboard.

There was a follow-up piece to Reidier's obituary, noting the contributions he had made in the world of quantum cryptography while working for Centre Spatial Guyanis (CSG),[14] the French spaceport near Kourou in French Guiana. It mentioned how Reidier created the R00 protocol,[15] which improved the information reconciliation and privacy amplification of the previous BB84 and E91 protocols. There were no letters to the editors in response to this piece or any printings of eulogies from colleagues.

This last point brings up a unique aspect to Reidier's work. Even with all of the corporate investment, intellectual property stakes, and

---

[14] Guiana Space Center.

[15] Named after its inventor and the year he published it.

consequent gag orders within the scientific community, it has continued to maintain open communication and a collaborative spirit.
Reidier's work, however, was and remains a completely isolated and
insulated pursuit. As of yet, no one in the Department has clarified
whether this was solely at DARPA's insistence or due to Reidier's own
preference. It's difficult to assign the proper term without understanding his motivation, which could range from paranoia to com-
petitiveness to insecurity to pathological self-reliance. Interviews
with friends and colleagues suggest that Reidier was eager to discuss
colleagues' work but consistently dismissive or cryptic about his own.
He did, however, have a tendency to "drop in" on friends and coworkers with seemingly random but incisive questions about their
respective specialties.

Regardless of the motivation, it is clear that advanced measures
and protocols were instituted in order to maintain the highest level
of secrecy. All outside intellectual input and mechanical production
was compartmentalized into fractured and redundant tasks, and
then outsourced to a wide array of independent contractors with no
classification access. I suspect that the five Deputies of the
Department insisted on exceptional, top-secret status for two reasons. One, obviously, to protect the Department's investment and
maximize its strategic utility if successfully developed. And, two,
there was no foreseeable benefit to sharing information: Reidier was
ahead of all of his colleagues working in the field of teleportation.

While other scientists, mathematicians, and engineers were still
trying to understand, create, and harness teleportation of information, Reidier was already fine tuning what we can approximate as
matter transmission.

Curiously, among teleportation researchers, Reidier was solely
known for his cryptographic contributions and his entertaining philosophical lectures. He published no papers or articles in the field and
is rarely referenced by colleagues in their publications. Still, although

less than a few dozen people with the highest clearance may know it, Reidier was *the* teleportation expert. In 1967, *Star Trek* introduced the idea of teleportation to the masses, but, until Reidier, no one had come anywhere close to making this a reality.

Of course others were making significant contributions in the field. In 1997, while Reidier was working on his PhD, Anton Zeilinger, at the University of Innsbruck in Austria, performed the first practical demonstration of teleportation using entangled photons to "transmit" Bell polarization states.[16] In that experiment, 75 percent of the teleporting events still couldn't be measured. To this day, no one has managed to devise a complete Bell-state analyzer. Independently, at the University of Rome, Francesco DeMartini had developed a way around this 75 percent problem by riding information shotgun on an auxiliary photon.

In 1998, Jeff Kimble managed to teleport complete light particles (not just their quantum states) at CalTech's Norman Bridge Laboratory across a lab bench of about a meter. The year 1999 witnessed the development of the 3-qubit quantum computer[17]; 2000 saw the creation of the 7-qubit quantum computer. In 2002, a quantum key was transported across twenty-three kilometers of open air by the UK Defense Research Agency. In that same year, Indian physicists Sougato Sharma and Dipankar Home at the Bose Institute in Calcutta showed how it might be possible to entangle any kind of particle, not just photons, electrons, and atoms.

While all of this was both impressive and slightly impenetrable, it all seemed amateurish compared to what Reidier was allegedly working on. And what exactly was that? It's been more than a little challenging to put the pieces together and arrive at a clear picture in light of the paucity of public records, the overzealous Department censorship of Reidier's documents (even though I'm expected to

---

[16] See Appendix.

[17] See Appendix.

learn Reidier's mind, I'm not privileged enough to be able to read his thoughts), and the tragic reality that everyone who had enough clearance to understand or at least see Reidier's work was killed while attending *The Reidier Test*.

I'm alone in this without a map.

Obviously, the Department has not brought me in to interpolate and analyze Reidier's physics. I'm sure that's been fractured apart and dispersed to thousands of scientists for segmented analysis, none of them remotely aware of how the whole is truly greater than the sum of its parts.

In any case, it's not the physics that's important here. If it were, I wouldn't know any of this. No, it's Reidier. He's the key. Something he did or didn't do. Something hidden except to him.

The Reidier Test wasn't about physics. It was about Reidier. And Eve and Otto and Ecco. Only through them will we ever know what happened. Accident or incident. Tragedy or miracle.

TITLE CARD: **GALILEE 6:21**

TITLE CARD: **EXPERIMENT 7**

CONTROL ROOM, GOULD ISLAND FACILITY - 2007-07-17
09:44

Dr. Reidier at console. Wears tweed sport coat -
brown, elbow patches, lapel pin, size 42 regular

Addresses camera . . .

                    DR. REIDIER
                     (sighs)
        Experiment seven, Inanimate
        Transfer. While attempts four
        through six did successfully
        teleport whole atoms and molecules,
        the macro, cubic structure was not
        preserved. Instead of reconstituting
        a cube, a pile of remarkably fine
        graphite dust was received.

INT. MIRROR LAB - SAME TIME

As Dr. Reidier continues, the Mirror Lab comes
to life. Fiber-optic cables, circumscribing
the Entanglement Channel, flare red for several
seconds, then morph into an orbiting white light
as the Entanglement Channel opens.

                    DR. REIDIER (OS)
        In an effort to counteract the
        dissociation, the catalyzing quark
        burst has been raised to ███████
        ██████████

The Boson Cannons and Pion Beams twitch to
life. SOUNDS of the rapid ACCELERATION and
DECELERATION of GEARS as they take a series

of readings. Once complete, they settle into optimized focal positions.

> DR. REIDIER (OS) (CONT'D)
> Furthermore, the quark color wavelength has been altered ████████ ████

The Quark Resonator emits a SOFT, HIGH-PITCHED DRONE as it powers up.

> DR. REIDIER (OS) (CONT'D)
> As with previous attempts, Inanimate is uniform carbon, graphite-layered, planar structure in a cube with sides measuring 81 mm.

INT. CONTROL ROOM - SAME TIME

Dr. Reidier tilts open the Plexiglas cover of Contact Button Alpha. While at far end of console, IS1 O'Brien does the same with Contact Button Bravo. Dr. Reidier absentmindedly taps his lapel pin twice, in a ritualized manner.

Dr. Reidier and IS1 O'Brien simultaneously engage Contacts.

CUT TO:

MIRROR LAB - SAME TIME

SPLIT SCREEN, on right side CLOSE-UP of an empty reinforced-acrylic sphere over target pad.

LEFT SIDE, CLOSE-UP: graphite cube sits inside reinforced-acrylic sphere over the transmission pad.

Cube remains perfectly still.

At 2007-07-17 09:47:11.5709411 a quiet THRUM
coincides with the inside of the transmission
acrylic sphere being suddenly coated with
residue [subsequently determined to be a
heterogeneous mixture of atoms and molecules
ranging from P to Rb (including a variety
of compounds within this range); the lowest
concentration of elements consisting of Al
and Y, whereas the concentrations increased
from both extremes toward Fe, which had the
highest].

NOTE: While undetectable to the naked eye, when
high-speed footage was slowed down, a phenomenon
was detected for the last 800 picoseconds on
the left side. During this increment, a seeming
digital artifact appears on screen as the cube
seems to tessellate then (slightly) shudder.

RIGHT SIDE, at 2007-07-17 09:47:11.5709411, the
graphite cube appears. On the outside of the
acrylic sphere, frost immediately accumulates.

CONTROL ROOM - 09:47:17

IS1 O'Brien reads information off a screen.

                    IS1 O'BRIEN
          Initial scan, structural integrity
          intact.

Dr. Reidier nods, sighs, collapses back into his
chair.

INT. MIRROR LAB -

The HIGH PITCH of the Quark Resonator fades out
as the machine powers down.

GEARS SPINNING NOISE ramps up and down as the
Boson Cannons and Pion Beams retract.

The circling indicator lights surrounding the
Entanglement Channel orbit to a standstill, flash
green, and then switch off.

II

A house is not a home unless it contains food and fire for the mind as well as the body.

~Benjamin Franklin

Where thou art—that—is Home.

~Emily Dickinson

Excerpts of Interview Transcript and Author's Psynar® Notes with Clyde Palmore, Professor of Materials Engineering, Brown University

April 3, 2009

"It was the second time he had broken the basement. Eve was gone for the weekend. She had taken the kids to New York, I believe. See some family, catch a show, you know the drill. Anyhow, she was gone, and Reidier was working down in the basement. He had set up a makeshift lab down there—well, a pretty high-end makeshift lab actually. I imagine Eve had been getting on him about late hours and staying in the office too much. The basement workshop was sort of a compromise. At least it was Reidier's attempt at a compromise."

Clyde lets out a curt snort and shakes his head. More a befuddled amusement than a gesture of judgment. He's a cherubic, middle-aged man with a shock of wavy gray hair. He carries his weight mostly in his gut but wears it well. It sort of lends an outward physical softness to his easy, welcoming demeanor. This is further emphasized by his rumpled casual attire: dark blue Polo shirt, wrinkled khakis, and a limp sport coat that dangles off the back of his chair.

Clyde rubs the back of his right thumb along the crease in his Polo shirt where his belly dives into his chest. A dark patch of sweat bleeds out, demarcating the change in topography. "I sort of got the feeling that it was more of a jury-rigged gesture than an actual solution."

"How's that?" I ask.

"Well," he leans back in his chair, securing his sport coat's precarious position, "I guess it was his tone. Very curt. Tense. Urgent, bordering on panic. Clearly, there was a lot of tension down in that basement."

"That's pretty specific of you."

"Somebody calls you in the middle of a Sox game on Saturday afternoon about how he broke the house and how quickly could you get there, it tends to stay with you."

"I'd imagine so. So you went over?"

"Right over. Anybody else calls you, saying something like that, you laugh and hang up. But Reidier, well he just wasn't a prankster. Yeah, let's leave it at that. Plus, you always knew that with Reidier it was going to make a great story."

"Broken homes often do. At least according to Tolstoy."

Clyde laughs. "*Anna Karenina*, right?"

"I'm impressed."

"What, you think just 'cause I'm an expert at load engineering stress I don't dabble in literature?"

"Not at all, Professor Palmore."

He chuckles some more and winks at me. "I had a fifty-fifty shot, it was either that or *War and Peace*. Anyhow, this was a more literal predicament, not literary, otherwise that would have been right up Eve's alley."[18] He winks again. "There was a crack with an amplitude of up to nine centimeters at points that ran about three and a half meters laterally through the concrete foundation of Reidier's basement."

"How did he do that?"

"That's exactly what I asked . . . But Reidier, he had this frantic look in his eye. He just stared at the wall and asked 'Can you fix it by six p.m., Sunday?'"

"That's when Eve would be home?"

"Exactly. He told me it had to be just us, and I couldn't tell anybody. Eve couldn't know. She'd leave him, he said. She almost had the last time, apparently. I told him it's just concrete, but he kept shaking his head saying she'd leave him, she'd leave him."

Clyde stops short. He rubs his thumb along the crease in his shirt again. His mouth turns inward, as he sucks in his lips.

He looks up at me, across the desk. "I guess it's all right me talking about it now. Since uh . . . I guess it's ok. If you think it'd help your report."

"I'm not even sure this story has to go in. It just gives me a better understanding of what led up to—how everything unfolded," I assure Clyde.

He nods. "Anyhow, we did it. I had to come down here and pilfer my shotcrete gun."

"Shotcrete?"

"Sprayable concrete. The wet process is best for high-strength applications. It's good for reinforcing and averages about 5,500 psi. I

---

[18] Presumably, Clyde is referring to Eve being a Visiting Assistant Professor in Brown's Comparative Literature Department.

added some accelerators to the mixture to get it dry as fast as possible. Then all we had to do was smooth it down with an air sander. We were done by lunchtime on Sunday. The only problem was the discoloration."

"The patch was a different tone?"

"Yeah. I said Eve probably wouldn't notice, but Reidier was not about to risk it."

"So how'd you guys match the color?"

Clyde grins. "We didn't. Reidier had a computer projector down there. He pointed it at the patch, found an image of Picasso's Bullfighter on the web, threw it up on the wall, traced it, painted it in with black paint, and voilà, our very own Purloined Letter. See, you're not the only one who can make literary allusions."

Through Clyde's bizarre anecdote, we find a window into the Reidier household. It's a home held together by tension, very much in danger of snapping apart both figuratively and literally.

Tension is a unique type of interpersonal stress. It must, by its very nature, build. It is not something that can spring out of a single incident or misunderstanding. It's an artifact of a couple's history requiring investment and stakes. Likewise, it cannot be unbound with a single gesture—at least not safely or constructively. Pressure can be relieved with a variety of situation-specific tactics. An explosive confrontation can be diffused, but not dismantled. Without a systematic teardown and rebuild, however, it's only a matter of time before the tension coils around and pulls everything taut.

Unfortunately, too often in relationships many of us don't have the foresight, the tools, or the wherewithal to disentangle ourselves from the roots of the tension. We tell ourselves it's not the right time to do a proper unraveling. We just need to wait until things relax, we convince ourselves. And then we inevitably wait too long, we wait until we're bound up in an agglomeration of knots and gnarls, too entangled and too turned around to even be looking the right way when something snaps. Our lifeline begins to fray with all the weight pulling on it, and we're beyond unprepared. We're so wound up, we can't even think straight, and all we can focus on is how to cut out a little slack.

That's what happened with Reidier and the basement. Disoriented by stress, hampered by fear—fear of professional failure, fear of losing Eve and the boys—he had a knee-jerk reaction, and he ran with it. Fix the basement. Fix the basement and everything will be ok. Eve will be ok. His work will be ok. And the house will be fine.

Phillip Moffitt, founder of the Life Balance Institute,[19] explores this myopic mind-set in much of his writing. He observes how the rationalization is always "the same—'Once this situation is remedied, then I will be happy.' But it never works that way in reality: The goal is achieved, but the person who reaches it is not the same person who dreamed it. The goal was static, but the person's identity was dynamic." In Reidier's case, the goal was clear and achievable.

The basement foundation is cracked.

He had done something like this before. It had been a problem.

Eve can't handle another incident. She won't handle it.

Fix the foundation. Fix Eve.

What he didn't realize is that he was addressing the wrong problem. Reidier was trying to fix their house—a static goal. Eve wanted him to fix their home—a dynamic desire.

Belongings are never just objects. They're metaphors. Something happens, an emotional alchemy of sorts transforms a thing into a possession. It happens every day, all the time. A young child plays

---

[19] Note: Phillip can also boast an impressive, more "conventional" CV. He was the editor-in-chief and chief executive officer of *Esquire* magazine for most of the '80s. He has coauthored numerous books, holds a black belt in Aikido, and has served on the boards of the C. G. Jung Foundation in New York and the C. G. Jung Institute in San Francisco.

with a bunch of beads and string for an arts and crafts project. A parent thinks nothing of it, until a bead goes up the nose, a scream pierces the air, a family drives to the hospital, and a green bead is removed from deep within the nasal passage, washed, and strung on a blue string to dangle from a father's neck, metamorphosed into his most valuable piece of jewelry.*

---

* I haven't thought about this for years. I was playing with Remi Allens. We went to Hoey Camp together Mondays through Fridays from 9:00-11:30. In the fields out back, the big kids would play baseball with Mr. Hoey as the automatic pitcher. Inside, Mrs. Hoey would monitor the Ping-Pong and bumper pool tournaments and run the Arts 'n Crafts activities. I don't think there was a family within a ten-mile radius of that place that wasn't rife with woven pot holders, gimp bracelets, and bead necklaces.

Most days I played baseball. Even though I was technically a little kid, I knew how to hit Mr. Hoey's underhand knuckleball. It was raining that day, though, and the game was called. While some undaunted souls still braved the elements, climbing the slippery jungle gym or playing chicken with centripetal force on the playground merry-go-round, I felt the call of the indoors.

As typically happens on rainy days, the Ping-Pong tables were mobbed, and the bumper pool had a queue ten kids deep. Arts 'n Crafts it was. Mom had made me swear off potholders after I finished filling the second drawer with my handwoven masterpieces. So beads it was.

Remi sat next to me. She had already finished weaving some purple and pink gimp into a tight box-stitch key chain and was currently working on the ever-elusive spiral stitch to make, of all things, a pulley system. A gimp show-off if you asked me. Still, it was impressive, and I found myself paying less and less attention to the bead necklace I was making.

By eleven thirty we had Remi's pulley system anchored with a bag of marbles applying enough tension to the system to hoist a Ping-Pong paddle into the air. Meanwhile, my bead project was in a sad state that more closely resembled a three-day-old candy necklace ravaged by seagulls than a strand of colorful pearls. Mrs. Hoey, the altruistic liar that she was, suggested I take it home to finish up my beautiful start there. Clearly, she did not want this piece of junk cluttering up her craft table scaring away other would-be boy and girl artisans.

"I'll help you finish it this afternoon," Remi whispered. "Your mom will love it."

I just raised the left side of my mouth in a half smile and kind of nodded.

"She doesn't even need to know I helped," Remi added.

The other side of my mouth turned up, completing the smile. We gathered up supplies and headed out the door.

Remi lived four doors down from us. I didn't know it at the time, but her parents were getting divorced. So three afternoons a week, Remi came home with us. Which is how she and I ended up in my playroom working on bead necklaces.

There we were, sitting on the floor, me handing Remi beads, her shaking them down the string to join their counterparts. And somewhere along that assembly line of two, I noticed that the beads were just about nostril size.

My mother heard the scream in her office.

"Lean back and let me see," she ordered after running down two flights of stairs. "It's really up there. I don't think I can get it."

I was nothing if not diligent.

Dad, who happened to be home early that day, was no help either.

Remi just sat quietly and watched. She didn't say anything until the four of us were halfway to the hospital.

"Which bead did you stick up there?" she asked.

"The green one."

"Oh," she sighed. "That was my favorite one."

My father lost it. He couldn't stop laughing. I didn't get it. Remi didn't get it. Mom smiled at him, though.

The doctor got it out. Remi joined us for pizza. And the necklace remained unfinished.

A few weeks later, I was helping my father rake cut grass in the yard. He leaned over to hold open a garbage bag, and his shirt collar fell open. Circled around his neck was a blue string. And dangling from the string was my green bead.

Mom gave it to me after he died. I keep it in a jewelry box in my underwear drawer. I just went to look for it the other day, after reading this section. It wasn't there. Not in the box, not in the drawer, not on my bookshelves, or in any of my files. I tore up the entire place. No necklace. It must have gotten misplaced in one of my numerous moves. I dumped every drawer, swiped all the books off my shelves, overturned every plastic storage bin.

Gone.

On the way here, though—I'm taking a two hour lunch, and I needed to get away from the weightless phrases of advertising and sink into my mother's words—I walked by a bead store. This part of Hell's Kitchen masquerades as the Garment District by day. I bought a green bead and a blue string. And I made a replica.

It's now hanging off of a single nail in the center of the otherwise barren beige wall in the bottom floor of the carriage house. So when I lean back from the table, to take a break from Mom's report, I see it there. Hanging.

It's not the original. Never been in any kid's orifice, that I know of.

Not exact. Not the same. Close enough, though, I guess. A doppelgänger of sentiment. It's not the object anyway. It's the memory. Still, I like to see it, look at it, and pretend.

A house is merely the place where you live. A home is where you inhabit. Eve was not invested in the house. She was invested in Reidier, in their home, in their new start. His cracking the concrete foundation in the basement wouldn't have been an accident to her. It would have been a symbol. I don't think Reidier ever realized that Eve, at best, had an ambivalent relationship with the house.

TITLE CARD: **GALILEE 6:21**

TITLE CARD: **EXPERIMENT 10**

CONTROL ROOM, GOULD ISLAND FACILITY - 2007-07-23
13:36

On console rest remnants of Dr. Reidier's and
IS1 O'Brien's lunches: wax paper, balled up
paper napkins, empty Ruffles bag and Cape Cod
Salt & Vinegar Chips (snack-pack size), half-
finished Orange Mango Nantucket Nectar, and one
white bottle cap.

Dr. Reidier steps into screen (tweed sport coat,
etc.), leans down to be in center of frame.
Addresses camera . . .

                    DR. REIDIER
          (mouth full of last bite of
          sandwich)
          Experiment 10, Inanimate Transfer.
          Having logged a run of successful
          transfers with "regular"
          polyhedrons, we are now attempting a
          transfer maintaining the same
          settings with an irregular shape of
          Polyethylene terephthalate compound.

Dr. Reidier nods to IS1 O'BRIEN, takes his own
seat, tilts open the Plexiglas cover of Contact
Button Alpha, and taps his lapel pin for luck.
At far end of console, IS1 O'Brien does the same
with Contact Button Bravo.

Dr. Reidier and IS1 O'Brien simultaneously
engage Contacts.

                                        CUT TO:

MIRROR LAB - SAME TIME

SPLIT SCREEN, on right side CLOSE-UP: empty reinforced-acrylic sphere over target pad.

LEFT SIDE, CLOSE-UP of an empty bottle of Coca-Cola (plastic) sits inside reinforced-acrylic sphere over the transmission pad.

The Quark Resonator emits a SOFT, HIGH-PITCHED DRONE as it powers up.

Coke bottle remains perfectly still.

At 2007-07-23 13:38:04.5748395 a quiet THRUM coincides with the inside of the transmission acrylic sphere being suddenly coated with residue [ranging from Li to In].

NOTE: 600 picoseconds of tessellation on the left side prior to transfer.

RIGHT SIDE, at 2007-07-23 13:38:04.5748395, the Coke bottle appears. On the outside of the acrylic sphere, frost immediately accumulates.

CONTROL ROOM - 13:38:10

IS1 O'Brien reads information off a screen.

> IS1 O'BRIEN
> Initial scan, structural integrity intact.

> DR. REIDIER
> Apparently, Coke *is* it.

III

To the scientist there is the joy in pursuing truth which nearly counteracts the depressing revelations of truth.

~H. P. Lovecraft

Truth only sets out the facts. It places events in order on a superficial map of interpretation. A lie, however, excavates essence. It requires a series of decisions, each turn, twist, dive, and rise chart out a topography of the liar's motivations, fears, joys— her very identity. In choosing between fact and fiction, it is the fiction that will always reveal more.

~J. Jumeau

Judging from her diary entries, letters, and e-mails, Eve had been happiest when she and Reidier lived in Kourou. It was there that the two of them first met, fell in love, and entangled themselves with each other. It was also there that Eve had all the power. In Kourou, Reidier wasn't just a fish out of water; he was a fish out of water in a jungle.

Eve had graduated from the Sorbonne with a double major in French Literature and Communications. Her thesis advisor, Jacques

Jumeau,[20] remembers her as "a stunning woman with a jagged intellect. An enigma in high heels." Often stereotyped for her beauty, she took advantage of her colleagues' misjudgments. She was a wolf in a low-cut shearling vest.

"She detested pretense, posturing, and pedigree. The cool had no appeal to her, only the real. Which is why she was so vicious with her more pompous classmates. She'd listen, nod enticingly, bite her pencil coquettishly, and then ask a seemingly surface question that would shatter his self-image. She pierced right through the weakness of her opponent's argument or applied pressure to a core insecurity of the opponent himself. Following up with a few more direct questions, she'd put him in a position where he either had to concede her point or admit he was an ass. In the end, she'd wrap up the wreckage in a bow with a flirtatious smile.

"Still, she was too often obsessed with being right, rather than being true. It is this that always got in the way of her writing."[21]

Emboldened by her success at university, fed up with France, and in search of stories to write, Eve set out for adventure. In spite of Eve's distaste for elitism, she was not above accepting her father's help. Even though he had retired to their estate in Provence, he still had some pull from his days as France's Ambassador to Morocco. The two adored each other, and were often described as *"ils sont comme deux gouttes d'eau."*[22] As family friends recall, he was just as thrilled for her as he

---

[20] Jumeau still enjoys modest fame in French literary circles for his groundbreaking biography on Foucault, *The Mirror's Cartographer*. Today, however, most Americans would know him for his outspoken defense of Roman Polanski and the infamous confession of his time as a foreign correspondent in Cambodia. While investigating child labor abuses in Cambodian factories, he developed a penchant for photographing child workers in compromising positions with the very mannequins they were making.

[21] Phone interview, February 27, 2009.

[22] Literally translated, "They're like two drops of water," but in essence the French version of "they're like two peas in a pod."

was to vicariously satisfy his own wanderlust. Within weeks, she was packing. She had accepted a PR position at Centre Spatial Guyanis and was getting the necessary vaccinations for French Guiana.

Eve had already been there for six months before Reidier arrived. And it was another few months before she even learned of his existence. Between press briefings, VIP tours, and wooing potential clients, Eve had become a popular presence around CSG. In spite of her austere, almost ascetic, personal life (if her diary is to be believed), or perhaps because of it, rumors and gossip circulated. She was having an affair with this Deputy Director. She had a tryst with that Division Head. She had a three-way with the Dutch clients. She was a lesbian involved in a tryst with a local Guianese woman who ran a shack of a bar on the outskirts of town and was suspected to be a voodoo witch.[23]

Eve was well aware of her reputation but did nothing to dispel the stories. By remaining aloof, she even encouraged them. In fact, it seems likely she was responsible for the voodoo-witch rumor.

Eve had been navigating the French man's gaze since she was fourteen. She had learned not to fight it, but rather exploit its blind spot. It helped her do her job. Clients were happier flirting with her than haggling over price; coworkers expedited reports she needed done so they could focus on innuendo; and bosses looked the other way when she cut corners, preferring instead to ogle. Furthermore, it helped her personally. After years of being coveted, Eve had garnered a simple axiom: men prefer myth to truth. If they couldn't have her, better it be because she "belonged" to someone else, rather than she simply wasn't interested. This way, the possibility persisted, however unattainable it was for now. Though CSG's business was the heavens, the office's apogee was Eve.

Keeping all this in mind, it made sense that Reidier would know who she was, and not the other way around. Which is why it was all

---

[23] This rumor probably succeeded due to Eve's mixed background, as her mother was Moroccan.

the more surprising to her that he didn't. It threw her. As did his dismissive and annoyed manner.

UBS had funded an upcoming launch. Specifically, they were paying to put a new communications satellite into orbit that could handle all of their international transactions between the Chinese and US markets. It was going to be a radical implementation of a new type of protocol. While most clients were thrilled to tour the facility and visit the launch site, the Swiss bankers were nonplussed by the spectacle of it all and impatient to meet the man securing their transactions. Unprepared, Eve adapted, lied about saving the best for last, and promptly convinced a coworker to help her find Reidier's lab.

Through the small, windowless, steel door at its west end, the lab opened up to spacious eighteen-foot ceilings. The lab was dominated by two massive, black tables—one running along the north wall, the other along the south—that spanned the forty-foot length of the room. Two industrial lasers sat atop each north end, next to their respective fiber-optic receiving stations and detection filters; two photon gates coupled with polarization filters stood in the middle; and two fiber-optic transmission apertures waited at the south end, attached to a length of "dark fiber." Each array was encased within a temperature-controlled Plexiglas housing, flanked by sonic thermometers. The two apparati were connected by fifty kilometers of the "dark fiber" coiled around a colossal spool that covered most of the east wall. It was just short enough to let in the sunlight through a rectangular window stretching over the top third of the back wall.

He sits at a white Formica workstation in the center of his lab, across the room from his webcam.[24] Two whiteboards, covered with

---

[24] Reidier was video recording his lab activity even then. He actually started in grad school after a botched attempt at creating an ion trap using laser cooling resulted in a "frozen" photon. It was a miraculous effect that no one on the team could figure out how to replicate.

This particular video was saved on his hard drive in RI in a folder titled "Family."

equations, stand like hieroglyphic centurions behind him. In front of him, the lettered, leather tail of a half-unraveled scytale dangles off the edge of the desk. His left elbow rests on the table, and he uses his forearm to brace a mirror held at an angle facing the tabletop. Though it's blocked from view by his torso, judging from the movements of his right arm, it appears he's writing something. And he wears an eye-patch over his right eye.

Eve bursts in with the Swiss contingency in tow.

"Here we are at last, *et voilà*, here is your genius," Eve says with a flourish.

Reidier, startled, lets go of the mirror, which slams onto the tabletop and shatters.

"Busy with his reflections clearly," Eve puns. She turns away from the Swiss with a laugh and faces Reidier, flashing him a smile and winking.

Reidier lifts the eye-patch up and stares at her a moment. He clears his throat. Eve's eyes widen, silently asking for help. He then turns his back on them and continues with his work.

Eve seems lost, briefly. She turns to the Swiss group and overdramatically shrugs her apologies.

One of the suits steps forward and asks, "Monsieur Reidier, we were hoping you might show us a demonstration of our new protocol?"

In an almost Jekyll and Hyde transformation, Reidier becomes effusive and welcoming, going on about rules of physics before he's covered even half the distance across the lab. He brushes past Eve and ushers the UBS reps over to his whiteboard, prattling on about secure transmission, eavesdropping, and two hypothetical spies, Alice and Bob.

Eve is left to stand by the door, watching with a bemused look on her face. Eventually, she pulls up a stool and listens to Reidier going off about how Alice and Bob both have a cipher on a pad of paper. Alice codes a message with her copy of the cipher and Bob deciphers the message with his copy. It's completely unbreakable, Reidier says, as long as it's a one-time pad, except that the length of the key had to be at least as long as the text, which isn't useful beyond espionage until computers came along. "Now we could easily handle ciphers with a key that had 256 values, and breaking the code would be a hopeless task, except . . ."

Reidier waits. He has the bankers' undivided attention. He continues, "All systems that depend on a single secret key have an Achilles' heel. Using the same key for encoding and decoding results in a symmetrical cipher."

"Hence, PKC," pipes up the suit who originally got Reidier started.

"Exactly," Reidier agrees, "Public-Key Cryptography utilized two different keys, the public and the private, in what most mathematicians agree to be the most significant practical discovery of the twentieth century. It's just . . ."

Reidier nonchalantly trails off, and busies himself organizing a row of markers on the whiteboard tray.

In an almost laughable choreography, every member of the Swiss contingency literally leans in toward Reidier. Eve, on the other hand, leans back in her stool, taking in the whole picture. A hint of a smile at the corners of her lips.

"We're not in the twentieth century anymore." He looks up at his rapt audience. "Any and all private communication channels utilized today have a soft underbelly. A critical weakness. Every 'secure' communiqué relies on it, and therefore everyone can be tapped."

A few murmurs from the Swiss.

"If an eavesdropper takes enough precaution, he can listen in to a communiqué without the sender or receiver knowing. Classical physics allows, at least in principle, physical properties to be gauged without disturbing them. If your cryptographic key is encoded in measurable physical properties of some object or signal, then there is nothing to stop me from passively, undetectably, tapping in to your channel, breaking your code, and listening in on all your secrets. But with QKD, Quantum-Key Distribution, with quantum cryptography, I can change all that—"

The video cuts out there to a DARPA insignia. Presumably, it just goes on getting deeper into the non-classical physics of Reidier's quantum cryptographical methods. It is unclear how Reidier and Eve ended their first meeting but not how they finished their first day. Not if we're to interpret Eve Tassat's short story, "Empêtré Le Bourg,"[25] as more fact than fiction.

Excerpt from "Empêtré Le Bourg"

. . . She found him in le vieux bourg, in Oublié, an abandoned Créole mansion that had been converted into a bar by squatters. He had separated from the group a few hours ago and made his way here. The Germans hadn't even noticed. They were too busy swilling Brahma Beer and comparing French cuffs. No more talk of security transactions or the fidelity of physics. Just shouting voices and wandering hands. Even so, it wasn't as easy for her to slip

---

[25] "Entangled in the Bourg,"◊ published in Ceris Press, Volume 11, Issue 2, Summer 1999.*

◊ The Bourg, literally The "Strip," is the area in Kourou for eating and drinking, filled with Créole, African, Brazilian, and Moroccan restaurants.

---

* I don't know what this is about. While the Ceris Press does exist (as any Google search will tell you), Eve Tassat has never published anything with them. Not a story, a poem, or an essay. Nor has there ever been a story "Entangled in the Bourg" published by them. Furthermore, Ceris Press didn't publish its first volume until the Summer of 2009. Was this just a typo or a research error by Mom? She's not prone to mistakes like this. Then again, she's not prone to just up and disappear either.

away. She had to employ some misdirection with the help of three Guianese girls and a bottle of Highland Park Scotch.

Reinier sat on the edge of a high-backed Louis XIV chair with faded, worn red velvet cushions. Naelle, the plump bartender and mama of the house, leaned her fleshy forearms on the back of his chair, watching his work. Reinier hunched over an old coffee table stained with rings of neglect and cluttered with several glasses, some pewter swizzles, a slotted silver spoon, a saucer of stacked sugar cubes, a cup of granulated sugar, a pitcher of ice water, a small bottle of gum syrup, a small bottle of liqueur d'anis, a half glass of white wine, a bottle of cognac, a matted-steel Zippo lighter, and a bottle of absinthe.

Reinier carefully put down the pitcher of ice water and sat back. The motley pair stared at a soggy sugar cube sitting on top of the flat perforated spoon that rested on the rim of a glass of absinthe. At least a minute passed, and still the cube held together.

"A bit more ice water," Naelle urged with a thick Créole accent.

"It'd be faster with tepid water," Reinier sighed.

"You might as well be drinking pissat d'âne ou du bouillon pointu!" [26] *she snapped.*

"I hardly think it'd be quite that extreme. However, your house, your rules." He added a few more drops, and the sugar cube finally began to sink through the slots. They waited.

She watched them from the arched threshold. She wasn't spying, just keeping her distance so as not to disturb the bizarre tableau.

The sugar cube was half of what it was. Reinier looked up at Naelle. She pursed her thick dark lips and nodded, her chins winking in and out of existence with each bob of her head. Reinier removed the spoon, picked up the glass, swirling the mixture in tight circles, and took a slug. He paused, clucked his tongue against

---

[26] Donkey piss or an enema broth.

the roof of his mouth a few times, and handed the drink to Naelle. She lifted her pinky and took the daintiest of sips.

"D'ere, you see? That is the way."

Reinier shrugged. "It's not bad, that's for sure. Still, cutting it with the cognac was nice too."

"Un Tremblement de Terre? Pah! Thass what made Toulouse-Lautrec paint like that. How well you think you could write your calculations wearing a straitjacket?"

Reinier laughed.

Naelle patted his shoulder. "So then, we done with the s'periment. We see this is the only way to do it, right."

"We haven't tried the caramelized sugar method," he said, reaching for the Zippo.

Naelle sucked her teeth loudly. "They do it in one stupid movie and all of a sudden it's a tradition."

"It's a Bohemian ritual."

"Bo'emian ritual. Who ever looked to Eastern Europe for cul-cha? They just alcoholic pyromaniacs."

"I have to agree with Naelle on this one, fire and alcohol never go well together," she interrupted.

Reinier looked up at her and squinted, trying to place where he knew her from. She laughed quietly to herself at this. Any other man from the Centre, this would have been a ploy. Not so with Reinier.

"See, the Tremblement de Terre already kickin' in. Mirages and hallucinations are filling up the place." Naelle raised an eyebrow at her.

"Absent n'est point sans coulpe, ni présent sans excuse,"[27] she offered.

"Les absents ont toujours tort,"[28] Naelle quipped back.

---

[27] Absent none without fault; present none without excuse.

[28] The absent are always in the wrong.

"Un peu d'absence fuit grand bien."[29]

Naelle snapped a dishtowel in the air. "That's only true with men. S'ok. I don't need no flattering. I know the truth. The truth is you just scared to bring your visitin' big shots to Maison de Mama. Lose them in my Oubliette," Naelle said over her shoulder as she walked back to the bar, swinging her large hips to punctuate her innuendo. Her laugh filled the space between them. "Pour mieux le peindre, il faut quitter Paris.[30] *But there's no way to leave an oubliette."*

She sat down across from Reinier. He took another sip of absinthe, gazing at her with puzzled eyes.

"You lost me after 'absent.' I mostly only know slang and curse words. They're all she'll teach me." He nodded his head toward Naelle.

She half laughed, half exhaled. "It's only fair. You lost me today at public-key cryptography." She dug into her purse and pulled out a flat, gift-wrapped object. Handing it to him, she said, "A peace offering?"

He took it from her but didn't seem to know what to do with it. Just held it in midair, over the coffee table cluttered with absinthian concoctions.

"You can open it," she suggested.

Shaking off the haze, he unwrapped the object.

"Interesting tie clip," she said.

"It's the secret of my success."

"Really? Because it looks like you ripped a piece out of a computer and soldered it to a paper clip."

---

[29] A little absence does much good.

[30] To better paint Paris, one must leave it.*

 *This last saying was paraphrased from Louis-Sébastien Mercier's *Le Tableau de Paris*, published between 1781 and 1788.

"Close. *A transistor from my first computer that I ever made. My Alpha chip, I guess. I like to keep my spark of ingenuity close . . ."* He trailed off, having finished unwrapping her peace offering. He was left holding a hand mirror with a pink plastic frame and handle.

"Figured it was the least I could do for breaking your concentration and your mirror today." She smiled. "Friends?"

He stared at the mirror, wiggling it a little in his grip. "It's magnificent. And pink."

"That's what I thought when I looked at it," she teased.

"I didn't mean—"

"To be vain?"

"That's not what I—"

"Vanity is just a word ugly people invented to make themselves feel better. I wouldn't worry about it." She flashed a big smile.

It wasn't working. He still hadn't looked at her.

"It's very thoughtful." He sat back and took her in. "Elle, is it?"

Her smile evaporated. She nodded yes.

"Thank you, Elle. Can I buy you a drink?"

"I'd say whatever you're having, but from the looks of it, it might kill me."

"How about a mojito?"

"If you can get Naelle to make one."

Naelle already had an eye on him, so it wasn't hard to get her attention. Although it did take some haggling to get her to make a mojito. Reinier would have to take a look at her gin still later.

"So, tell me, how does one find such a masculine mirror in Kourou?" Reinier asked.

"Special order. The store was overstocked with black-framed and silver-framed mirrors. But the owner likes me, and managed, as a favor, to secure that pretty pink one for you. I would've gotten you a matching pink eye-patch, but they were on back order."

"*That's just a little neurological trick. By selectively presenting information to the left eye, which is connected to the right hemisphere, I'm hopefully tickling the anterior superior temporal gyrus, the part of the brain responsible for insight.*"

"*Forced right brain thinking?! I guess the one-eyed man is also king in the land of the lab.*"

Reinier put the mirror down on top of the pile of wrapping paper on the table and then leaned back and stared at her.

Elle had long been inoculated against the gazes of men. They were as commonplace to her as a handshake or a sneeze. Still, in this moment she felt her cheeks warm as blood rushed into them. Something about the way he looked at her. It wasn't aggressive. It wasn't ogling. There was no agenda behind his eyes. They were devoid of bias or preconception. He just seemed open and observant and curious. He was present to her. She met his gaze.

"*What if I wanted to tell you a secret?*" he asked.

Her mouth opened, but no words came out. She had not expected this question.

"*Here,*" he said, tearing off a piece of wrapping paper. "*Pick a number, write it down, and don't tell anybody what it is.*"

She took the paper from him without realizing, still more confused than anything. He dug two pens out of the inside pocket of his tweed sport coat, handing one to her.

"*I'll do the same,*" he said as he wrote down seventeen. He frowned at his choice. Scratched it out and wrote seven. "*For ease's sake, you might want to pick a reasonably small number that's not zero or one. Those numbers tend to misbehave in calculations.*"

The word calculations seemed to snap her out of her daze. She smiled, looked at her piece of paper, and wrote down four.

He smiled at her. "*Ok, so you and I each have our private numbers. Nobody but you knows yours, and nobody but me knows mine. Now suppose we're sitting next to a man who's had a little too much to drink and in his inebriation shouts out Sophie-Germain primes—"*

"What're those? Remember I'm the Centre's face, you're the brains."

"It's just a prime number that is both prime itself as is the number you get when you multiply it by two and add one. So, eleven is a Sophie-Germain prime."

"Because eleven is prime as is two times eleven plus one."

"Precisely. Not just face after all." He smiled.

She looked down at her paper.

"Ok so our inebriated friend hiccups out eleven and," he shrugged, "three. Everybody in the bar hears him say those two numbers." To emphasize the point, Reinier yelled to Naelle, "Eleven and three!"

"Eleven and three what?" Naelle challenged.

"Just that, eleven and three."

"I'm making the mojito. Timing me only makes me go slower," she says, while muddling the mint in the glass.

Reinier turned back to Elle. "So now we do a little math. It's called mod, but don't worry about that. Let's take our public three. Raise to the exponent of your private number."

This took her a moment. Three to the fourth equals, three times three is nine, times three is twenty-seven, times three, eighty-one. "Got it."

"Ok now figure out the remainder when you divide that number by our other public number?"

Eighty-one, closest multiple of eleven is seventy-seven. "Got it," she says.

"I got mine too. Ok, now tell me the answer you got, and I'll tell you mine. Wait." Naelle comes over with Elle's mojito. As she rests it on the coffee table, Reinier asks her, "Naelle, just listen to this a moment. Ok Elle, tell me."

"Four."

"Good. Mine's nine. Did you get all that, Naelle?"

"Course I did. You're all spoutin' random numbers. Eleven, three, four, and nine. Don't you be testing Mama Naelle's memory. It's a-sharper than a moray eel's teeth." She smacked Reinier with a dishrag, and she walked back to the bar.

"Ok, now you take my number and raise it to your private number," Reinier instructed Elle.

"Can I write down the math?"

He nodded. She calculated. Nine to the fourth, 6,561.

"It's a pretty big number."

"So, and you can write down your work again, as long as you don't show me, what's the remainder when you divide that number by eleven?"

Ugh, she thought. Eleven goes into 6,561 approximately 596 times. 596 times eleven is 6556. Remainder is . . . "Ok, I got it. I feel like I'm in Montessori all over again, but I got it."

"Me too. Now I can tell you a secret."

"Wait, what? How?" she asked.

"We both now know the same number."

"We do?"

"Yes, through those calculations, we now both have arrived at the same number. We throw away our original numbers. I never know yours, you never know mine, but we now share this number in common. And only we know it. Nobody else at the bar. Not the inebriated primer, not Naelle. Just us. It's our cipher. We use it to encode our secrets. Actually, we would do iteration upon iteration of this, but this is the basic idea of public-key encryption, cryptography."

She stared at him. No blushing, no self-consciousness, no attempt at flirting. She smiled. "What's our number?"

He rolled his eyes. "It's five."[31]

"That's amazing." Her eyes widened.

"It's just math."

"Don't be modest, it's like, wow, it'll be used everywhere."

He laughed. "I'm not being modest, and it is used everywhere, ever since it was invented in the 70s."

"Oh," she said. "Well, that makes sense." She takes a sip of her mojito. "So what's your thing?"

"Quantum cryptography. I exploit entanglement. What we just did is fantastic and useful, except that it's based on classical physics—"

"Not this again . . ."

He laughed again. "I know, right? I do get this tunnel vision, you know, blinders on, and I just go, and it makes me, well, inconsiderate I guess."

"Might be the eye-patch." She winked. "I wouldn't call it inconsiderate. I'd just say you get focused."

"You are good at PR, Elle."

---

[31] Inebriated prime Sophie-Germain primes g = 3 and n = 11

Elle picks a random number: 4

Reinier picks a random number: 7

Elle calculates her public key: 3^4 mod 11 = 81 mod 11 = 4

Reinier calculates his public key: 3^7 mod 11 = 2187 mod 11 = 9

Reinier and Elle exchange the public keys.

Reinier calculates the private key: 4^7 mod 11 = 16384 mod 11 = 5

Elle calculates the private key: 9^4 mod 11 = 6561 mod 11 = 5

The private key is 5.

In real life, "n" will be a very large value.

Her cheeks warmed up again at the sound of her name on his lips.

He sighed. "How do you say egghead in French?"

She cocked her head a moment, thinking. "In Paris, we just would call you 'intelligent,'" she said in her heavy French accent.

He burst out laughing. She revealed a shy grin.

"You have a way with words."

While it is unclear as to how much of this is fact and how much fiction, the two of them obviously made a connection that turned into something bigger. Further support of this is found in subsequent lab footage that clearly shows Reidier sitting at his workstation across the room using a hand mirror with a pink plastic frame and handle. Whatever the exact details may be, something did happen that night that was distinctly different from their initial encounter in his lab.

Rumors of Eve's escapades still echoed around the office for some time. Apparently, neither party minded, particularly as both seemed to value discretion. According to former colleague Alfred Muoio, an Italian physicist who had a lab adjacent to Reidier's, " . . . Reidier and Eve . . . the two of them as an item was a grand surprise. To everyone. Not in a dismissive way, not that a little man could not cast a long shadow. More, eh, no one ever thought about it. If I recall correctly, at the time I thought she was having a liaison with some German oligarch *duce* overseeing one of ESA's[32] launches. So it was a total surprise when she and Reidier moved in together. Jaws dropped like dominoes throughout the entire center."[33]

"You never saw them together?"

"I saw them at work. Rarely together."

---

[32] European Space Agency, headquartered in Paris, and launches out of CSG.

[33] Phone interview, summer 2009.

"Socially?"

"Eh, well, Eve was definitely at all the various functions, and I saw her several times at the hotel bars we frequented. Those were the most, to put it gently, continental establishments. Of course, every now and then you might venture out for some native flavor, but most of the time we congregated where we were comfortable. And that's where Eve took a lot of the VIPs. I rarely saw Reidier socially. He did not go out much. Well, I guess he rarely went to the hotel bars. If I remember correctly though, he would go blow off steam at this place in the Old Quarter. I forget the name of it. It was in an old house. *Come si dice?* Yes, we were all stunned when they moved in together. Although, I have to say, around the labs there was definitely a sense of pride that she was with one of us."

Despite the secrecy, Eve was neither embarrassed nor disappointed with the relationship. Quite the opposite actually, it seems her impulse toward discretion was more of a protective instinct. The relationship was something she treasured and wanted to isolate in order that it not be tainted by the world. It was this impulse in fact that paradoxically made her so ambivalent about cohabiting. As she wrote in her journal shortly after they moved in together,

> . . . It's ironic really. In finally carving out our private space, we've ended up exposing ourselves. While our space is our own, our ~~lives~~ life now belongs to the world. R laughs at me when I talk like this. He doesn't believe in the corruption of scrutiny. I think he's just happy to have me past sunrise now. No more predawn scurries home.
>
> R teases me that if I want I can still pull the sheets over our heads and cocoon us in bed. "Our linen wall of last defense." He scoffs, but every time I do this, he

drops his voice to a whisper too, underneath. Brushes his hands over my body while murmuring about how, with me, the world has been cleaved into us and everybody else. Those are the last two groups, the only two groups in the world.

There's us and there's everybody else.

Sealed underneath the sheets with his susurrations and our humid breathing . . . it oddly reminds me of playing in my father's den, as a little girl, building forts out of blankets, couch cushions, and end tables . . . that is until R's touch hardens and he pins me down, pinning down the covers . . .

There's us and there's everybody else.

Still, there is something delicious about announcing ourselves this way. Maybe it means the end to me having to harvest rumors. I have my 'alpha nerd' to protect me.

There's us and there's everybody else.

I love our home.[34]

These are clearly not the words of someone who has any reservations about her relationship. Rather, Eve describes and exhibits a textbook example of one of the extremes of the Colonial Effect.

Embedded within Michelle Hausler's work[35] on cryptocolonialism is this oft-overlooked phenomenon. Most colonial and postcolonial

---

[34] Excerpted from Eve Tassat's journal, March 21, 1999.

[35] "Crypto-Colonialism: The Presence of Absence," *World Politics Quarterly Journal* - Volume 54, Number 4, Fall 2002, pp. 899-926.

theory focuses (for good reason) on either the collateral repercussions inflicted or instilled in the native population or the complexities of the power dynamics, assimilation, and counter-assimilation. The Colonial Effect describes the polarizing consequences of the occupier's isolation on the occupier, how foreignness warps the imperialists' concepts of and means of engaging in intimacy. As Hausler puts it, eventually "the myth of domination and empowerment with its inferred überfreedom dissolves into a constricting reality. Cartesian orientation inverts in the foreigner's eyes as the colony transforms from an exotic playground into an all too literal Prospero's Palace."[36] Inevitably, pressure increases on intimate relationships as they take on all-encompassing importance in a contracting world. The stress has a polarizing effect of either cannibalizing the relationship or canonizing it. It becomes the scapegoat or panacea for all the escalating and destabilizing frustration of exile.

While Eve seems to embody the latter Colonial Effect, it would be incomplete to write off her excitement and investment in their relationship as a mere byproduct of this. Furthermore, even though Eve professes an almost euphoric satisfaction from her relationship with Reidier, she also exhibits signs of personal growth, increased confidence, heightened self-awareness, and creativity. Simply put, it was after moving in with Reidier that Eve finally started writing, or at least publishing. She wasn't isolating herself from the world, she was embracing it.

Reidier, on the other hand, was having a difficult time professionally. Although by all accounts, his Swiss project was a success, his supervisors were becoming more intrusive, more oppressive, and more

---

[36] Hausler refers here to the Edgar Allan Poe story, "The Masque of the Red Death," in which Prince Prospero and one thousand of his nobles take refuge in his castellated abbey, locking themselves in to escape the ravages of a terrible plague.

distrustful. Perhaps they felt threatened by Reidier's work, which was far beyond their abilities. Or they might have been trying to contain and exploit whatever his next innovation was. Regardless of the motivation, it was having a negative effect on Reidier. In fact, watching a high-speed montage of Reidier's lab footage you can almost track the accelerating deterioration with every interruption by a superior over months. Reidier's body language, which begins as welcoming and open, devolves into guarded defense and ultimately, outright aggression.

The straw that broke the camel's back was on August 19, 2001. It was a Sunday. The video capture is activated by motion in the lab. Reidier is nowhere to be seen. Sitting at his computer, however, typing on his keyboard and opening various windows, is Diderot Pellat—Reidier's lab supervisor. He squints his eyes, he clicks, he frowns. Eventually, he starts to wander around the lab, snooping. He paces the length of the laser arrays. He fiddles with the computer that monitors the sonic thermometers. He rifles through the rolling, two-door filing cabinets that loiter in front of the massive spool of dark fiber cable. According to the counter, he's alone in Reidier's lab for thirty-seven minutes. Diderot is thumbing through a stack of binders he found when Reidier walks in. There's a solid ten seconds of silence as the two take each other in.

"Something I can help you with, Didi?" Reidier asks.

Diderot goes back to the binder he's thumbing through and turns another page. "These look like the journals of a psychopath."

"They're ancient ciphers and puzzles."

Diderot grunts and turns another page. "Good. Then I am not leafing through anything personal. I feared I might have intruded." He turns another page.

Reidier balls his hands into fists and relaxes them over and over. "I do them to help me think. They're my crosswords."

Diderot closes the binder. He looks up at Reidier and offers a patronizing smile. "I suppose you are wondering what it is I am doing here?"

"It's Sunday. Did you get lost on the way to church?"

"This is my church," Diderot says, gesturing to the lab.

"Does that make me your priest, Didi, or your prophet?" Reidier asks.

"My apostle, I should think." Diderot wanders toward Reidier's computer. "IT informed me of an issue on your computer. A ghost drive was detected."

"Really?" Reidier asks with a surprised tone.

"Mm. Apparently, they did not install it and could not access it."

Reidier nods. "Sounds like a problem in your IT department."

Diderot places his hand on the desk near the keyboard. "You understand of course that per your contract, there are no secrets between us."

"Of course, CSG owns any and all IP that I develop in quantum cryptography while working here."

Diderot's gaze drifts over to the stack of notebooks. "Riddles to relax. Hm. I prefer my Cabernets."

Reidier's eyes stay trained on the Frenchman. The microphone picks up the sound of a finger tapping lightly on Formica and out-of-sync breathing. Diderot draws in a big breath through his nose and opens his mouth as if about to say something. Reidier waits. Diderot brings his lips back together, once again forming a patronizing half smile.

"I trust the ghost drive—"

Reidier interrupts, "It's merely a secondary backup drive and storage drop for my WTF footage."

"Pardon?"

Reidier gestures to the various webcams around the lab. "I record everything that happens in the lab so that in case something unexpected happens and I don't know why, I can retrace my steps."

Diderot's head swivels around, taking in all the cameras. He turns and faces the camera they're standing in front of. His eyes dance in fractal pattern, searching the screen. I suspect he's looking for any evidence of recording happening. Unnerved that he missed it before.

Reidier smiles at his boss's discomfort. "Motion sensors turn it on and off. Calibrated them to pick up eye movement, in case I'm just sitting here reading. And of course screen and keystroke capture. It's recording us right now."

Diderot purses his lips and runs his tongue along the front of his teeth as if he had something sticky and bitter stuck on them. He stands up straight, assuming a very proper posture. "That is quite diligent. Perhaps I should institute that in our other labs. Thank you for 'ze idea." His accent has become more conspicuous as the conversation has progressed, perhaps as a byproduct of stress. He buttons his vest and heads toward the door. "You will, of course, help IT with their, how did you put it, problem? *Oui?*" He turns back to Reidier, resting his hand on the door handle.

"As soon as I have time."

"Of course," Diderot acquiesces. He turns toward the binders one last time. "If you do not mind, I would love to make a facsimile of some of your puzzling. It looks so engaging. I might want to frame it. It could be a conversation piece for me." He smiles big this time, confident. *"Bon."* And without waiting for a response, he leaves.

Reidier stares after him. He waits, watching the door.

One minute and forty-two seconds.

At a quick clip he walks over to the stack of binders. In a frenetic fashion, he flips through several of them to random pages. Checking them. Satisfied, Reidier stacks them, tapping his palms against the sides forcefully. He makes to pick them up but then stops.

Reidier looks across the room at the camera. Once again he crosses the room at a quick clip. Standing in front of the computer, he opens a program with the mouse, types in what I assume is a password, and then clicks.

The footage cuts out.

This incident might have been the final cut or simply a coincidence. Within a few months, however, Reidier accepted a post at the University of Chicago. He was also awarded a grant to investigate the theoretical model of supersymmetry[37] at the Fermi Lab as part of its Collider Run II program. This was not a spontaneous decision.

---

[37] Supersymmetry,[?] in particle physics, relates the elementary particles of one spin to other particles that differ by half a unit of spin and are known as *superpartners*. Traditional symmetries in physics are generated by objects that transform under internal symmetries. According to the spin-statistics theorem, bosonic fields commute while fermionic fields anticommute. In order to combine the two kinds of fields into a single algebra requires the introduction of a Z_2-grading. Such an algebra is called a **Lie superalgebra**. The simplest supersymmetric extension can be expressed in the anti-commutation relation: $\{Q_\alpha, \bar{Q}_{\dot\beta}\} = 2(\sigma^\mu)_{\alpha\dot\beta} P_\mu$

[?] I honestly have no clue what any of this means, but I have a feeling neither did Hilary. In fact, doing a simple Web search on supersymmetry showed that she got most of this info from Wikipedia. I'm guessing that that was as far as DARPA let her go. All the good stuff must have been blacked out or never even given to her. This is just the stuff that's already public. Not that it would have really mattered, 'cause as smart as she was, Mom just didn't have a head for this sort of thing.

Still it's pretty curious that she would put this in here at all. I mean, you gotta figure that whoever's reading her report would either know way more and understand way better or be just as in the dark about shit going the speed of light or whatever the hell that equation means.

But she put it in. And as far as I know, she hadn't handed it in. So maybe it's more of a note to herself for her rewrite. I have a feeling though that she's the one who underlined supersymmetry, italicized *superpartners*, and bolded **Lie superalgebra**. Maybe these ideas just resonated with her. Maybe she wondered if they'd have some sort of symbolic echo later down the line. I'll tell you for someone in my field, it's pretty stimulating: superpartners and the algebra of lying.[?]

[?] Maybe she dug the term because it echoed her J. Jumeau quote on page 57?

Securing a professorship and writing grant proposals all take fore-thought and effort. However, testing the waters and taking the plunge are two very different states of mind.

Eve appears to have been supportive of this move throughout her diary. This post at CSG was never a professional track for her, but merely an excuse to get her out into the world so she could find something to write about. And with Reidier, she was writing.

Eve and Reidier got married on the first of October, 2001. According to Eve's short story, "The French Finger Puzzle,"* they eloped in a small, corrugated aluminum church on the edge of The Bourg. "Naelle" was Eve's maid of honor, and the couple was married by Juan Castillo, a medium and priest of María Lionza[38] as well as a shoe salesman, who claimed possession by the Norse spirit of Erik the Red. There were candles, drums, and chants. The ceremony cul-minated with the rings, which, in the story, were Möbius bands Rei-dier had made out of palm leaves. According to French Prefect's Records, however, they were married by the Prefect himself, in the banquet hall of the official residence, and Eve's father gave her away.

---

* I did track down this short story, sort of. It was published in *KaFkaïens*, some French magazine that focuses on literary news and experimental writing. The story's no longer on their website, of course. But they have it archived, and this junior editor over there is trying to dig it out and send it to me. I called him from a payphone in the Port Authority. Bought an inter-national calling card and everything. I mean, I'm sure it's nothing, but why have it on record that I'm calling Paris, tracking down Eve Tassat's writing?

---

[38] A hodgepodge jungle religion blending Catholicism, West African traditions, and Venezuelan superstitions. See *New York Times* article: http://www.nytimes.com/2009/10/28/world/americas/28venez.html?_r=0.

Of course, rumors once again flew around the Space Center: Eve was pregnant, Eve got Reidier loopy on absinthe and tricked him, Reidier got Eve loopy on absinthe and tricked her, Reidier was Eve's "compact" (the lesbian equivalent of a beard). The story that got the most traction, however, was that their nuptials were arranged so Eve could obtain a green card.

By this point, Reidier and Eve had been together for almost three years. They had been living together for two. It's hard to imagine that this was a choice made by circumstance, especially since it seems to have been unnecessary. H. Clark in the Department of Homeland Security assured me that even so soon after 9/11, Eve's Moroccan descent would not have been an issue. "Plus, at that time, it would have been easier for her to obtain a student visa than to marry her husband for a green card," Clark wrote in an e-mail. (Eve had been accepted to the Creative Writing Masters Program at the University of Chicago.) This was not a marriage of convenience.

For Eve and Reidier, leaving CSG was the end of their beginning. A bittersweet transition full of hope, unencumbered by nostalgia. Eve closes the chapter on their life best in her diary entry that she wrote on the flight to Chicago.

I'm staring out the window of our plane, watching the land fall away into a painting. A visual metaphor, I guess. R & I will never walk through the landscape of Kourou again except in the flattened world of memory. I feel like I should feel melancholic. But I have only the slightest sense of loss. Not of that place, or our work, or our friends, or our home. It's hard to put into words. I wonder if a butterfly ever misses the closeness of its cocoon. Maybe it's just how clearly the line of our jumping-off point has been drawn. Before we were protected in this . . . Eden? And now we're soaring away

*from our work with the heavens, a subatomic locksmith
and his semiotic cheerleader.*

*Wow, make sure I never use the term "work with the
heavens" again.*

*R just laughed at me. Apparently I rolled my eyes at
my writing so hard he could hear it. I love that he
knows my eye rolls, huffs, and sighs. My ever-observant
husband scientist.*

*Nothing is left behind as we turn the pages of
SkyMall together, a ritual he performs at the start of
every flight. And his habits become mine, as mine do his.
Two explorers addicted to sounding out the depths of
each other. The beginning is only the beginning.*

There's no yearning for the past. There's no mourning about leaving their home. There's no ambivalence. Eve feels only certainty in Reidier—a drastically different state of mind than when they would move to Providence soon after.

TITLE CARD: **GALILEE 6:21**

TITLE CARD: **EXPERIMENT 19**

MIRROR LAB - 2007-07-25 16:51

Fiber-optic cables, circumscribing the
Entanglement Channel flare red for several
seconds, then morph into an orbiting white light
as the Entanglement Channel opens.

The Boson Cannons and Pion Beams twitch to
life. SOUNDS of the rapid ACCELERATION and
DECELERATION of GEARS as they take a series of
readings of a full bottle of Coke. Once complete
they settle into optimized focal positions.

CONTROL ROOM, GOULD ISLAND FACILITY - SAME TIME

IS1 O'Brien sits at the console, in front of
Contact Button Bravo.

On one screen in front of him are the feeds from
the Mirror Lab transfer room.

On another screen in front of him is . . . Dr.
Reidier (tweed-sport coated) seated at his desk
in Angell Lab (basement of 454 Angell Street) in
Providence.

Dr. Reidier leans forward toward his computer
camera. Talks excitedly.

> DR. REIDIER
> Inanimate Transfers of varying
> shapes and compounds have all
> yielded consistent, stable results
> for Experiments Ten through Sixteen.
> Furthermore, we have had positive,
> consistent results with Phase
> Two, Dynamic Inanimates using an

aggregation of several compounds and
elements in 17 and 18. Therefore
we're attempting to transfer a
Dynamic Inanimate over a greater
distance as proof of concept. As
such, power settings have been
increased to ███ times ███ eVs
while utilizing a quark spectrum
from ███████.

Dr. Reidier spins back and forth in his chair.

> DR. REIDIER (CONT'D)
> Safety lid up!

IS1 O'BRIEN opens his Plexiglas cover, while, on
screen, Dr. Reidier places his right index finger
on a button on his keyboard. Dr. Reidier taps
his lapel pin with his left hand then raises it
up, extends his index finger, wags it forward
while . . .

> DR. REIDIER (CONT'D)
> (apparently doing a Jean-Luc Picard
> impersonation)
> Engage!

IS1 O'Brien presses Contact Button Bravo. As Dr.
Reidier presses "Enter" on his keyboard, Contact
Button Alpha engages.

> CUT TO:

MIRROR LAB - SAME TIME

SPLIT SCREEN

RIGHT SIDE, ANGELL LAB - CLOSE-UP: reinforced-
acrylic cube over the target pad in Reidier's
home lab on Angell Street.

LEFT SIDE, MIRROR LAB - CLOSE-UP: full bottle of Coca-Cola (plastic) sits inside reinforced-acrylic sphere over the transmission pad.

The Quark Resonator emits a SOFT, HIGH-PITCHED DRONE.

Coke bottle remains perfectly still.

At 2007-07-25 16:52:01.5862669 a loud POP coincides with the acrylic sphere exploding and a cloud of residue [ranging from Li to In] billowing out.

NOTE: 2000 picoseconds prior to explosion, on the left side prior to transfer, the liquid content (i.e. soda) tessellates and seemingly blurs beyond the confines of its container (the soda bottle).

RIGHT SIDE, at 2007-07-25 16:52:01.5862669, the video feed distorts with static waves as the Coke bottle appears . . . the wavy image straightens and the Coke bottle sits on the pad with what appears to be the exact amount of transmitted liquid [confirmed later]. On the outside of the acrylic cube, frost has accumulated.

CONTROL ROOM - 16:52:07

IS1 O'Brien stares at the transmission room. Dusty residue still floats in the air.

ANGELL LAB - 16:53:11

Dr. Reidier stares at the full bottle of Coke that stands on the target pad. The acrylic cube-halves (now open) hover above and below held by their respective mechanical arms.

Dr. Reidier uses an infrared thermometer and takes a reading: 17 degrees C.

Dr. Reidier rubs his thumb and forefinger together, contemplatively. Finally, he sets down the thermometer, reaches out, and picks up the bottle of Coke. He slowly unscrews it.

Dr. Reidier cautiously removes the cap . . . nothing happens.

He wafts the air from the open container to his nose. It seems fine to him.

Finally he shrugs, lifts it to his lips, and takes a swig.

                    IS1 O'BRIEN (OS)
                      (Alarmed)
          Dr. Reidier!

Dr. Reidier finishes his sip and tilts his head to the side, contemplating the bottle of soda. He smacks his lips together and clucks his tongue against the roof of his mouth.

Dr. Reidier turns to face the camera.

                    DR. REIDIER
          It's flat.

IV

Science never solves a problem without creating ten more.

~George Bernard Shaw

A man's character is his fate.

~Heraclitus

Character is like the foundation of a house—it is below the surface.

~Anonymous

Both Eve's diary and Reidier's records offer little about their move from Chicago to Providence. In fact, Eve didn't make a single entry for almost six weeks after the move. As far as the weeks before, apparently the diaries Eve kept while they were in Chicago were lost in the move.

Some say Hemingway divorced his first wife, Hadley, for leaving a manuscript in the Paris train station. Obviously this isn't at that scale, and it wasn't necessarily Reidier who lost her diaries, but I wonder what was the cost. It had to have been a personal tragedy on some level. For a writer, in particular, to not only lose a work—a metaphorical baby—but one that chronicles her first pregnancy and early years of motherhood—a literal baby—the loss cuts twice as deep. It might feel like the loss of memory itself and thereby perhaps even the loss of self itself. The parts of Eve's consciousness that she poured into those journals were forever lost, but painfully unforgotten. Like a fire that destroys all the photos of a deceased spouse. Depending on whether she had discovered their absence or not before arriving in Rhode Island, this would most certainly have affected her attitude toward their new house. If she was mourning the loss of her words, how could she not project that onto 454 Angell Street?

Reidier's work in Chicago likewise seemed to have come to a standstill. In his final few weeks at the Fermi Lab there are only two video logs: one in his office lab, when he performed the demonstration for Director Pierce; the other (and final) video takes place in his home lab. The latter begins at 9:39 p.m. on April 9, 2006.

Reidier comes down into his basement carrying a stack of cardboard boxes. He proceeds to methodically pack up all of his equipment. It's a long, dull segment, and even Reidier himself seems not present, like an automaton set in motion. He never smiles, never talks to himself, and pauses only once. From a locked drawer he pulls out the very stack of binders we saw Diderot inspecting in his lab in CSG. I compared it with the CSG footage, and there are in fact four more binders. It might be that Diderot never pulled these out. More likely, however, Reidier has added to his collection. He places them in a box and then stops. He sits and stares down at them. Then, with no visual or aural impulse, he continues to pack up the rest. This is cut short when he shuts down and packs up the computer.

Unlike the long process of applying, interviewing, and relocating to Chicago, the transfer to Brown University seemed to happen almost overnight. In fact, he left before the close of the autumn quarter. Reidier was teaching two undergraduate classes at the time: one on advanced quantum theory and another, more popular gut course for nonmajors, on the physics of science fiction. He finished out his remaining lectures via iTunes University for both of his classes; the review sessions and final exams were proctored by graduate students.

According to the Office of the President at Brown, the urgency of the transition was due to an overlooked stipulation in a large grant they had received years earlier. Its second (and more sizable) infusion of capital required that funding be directed toward significant research in quantum entanglement by January 1, 2007. Bureaucratic oversight resulted in this discovery during the Thanksgiving break of 2006. Reidier, a leader in this field, who was already in continued contact with several of the Brown faculty, was quickly courted, hired, and relocated. A significant gift was also bestowed upon the University of Chicago for facilitating the process.

According to retired DARPA director Anthony Tether, this was a nice PR story worked out by him and Brown's president, Ruth J. Simmons. The truth is that Reidier, in Chicago, had successfully executed an experiment that set off a seismic paradigm shift. Realizing the immense nature of his discovery, as well as the vulnerability of his position, he directly contacted DARPA with the news and requested fiscal and personnel support to continue his work. The Department indirectly funded the grant.

The details are somewhat murky to me due to the bipolar and contradictory stance DARPA has taken toward my report. While urging me to work with diligence and alacrity, and offering unconditional support, it continues to withhold and obfuscate crucial information. Despite the impact that *The Reidier Test* would have on our nation, full access only goes so far with classified material pertaining to national security. I feel as if I've been asked to sit in the dark and put together a jigsaw puzzle of an abstract painting that I've never seen. Still, the significance of Reidier's contact with the Department is undeniable.

Transcript excerpt from the phone log of the Office of
the Director of the Strategic Technology, Donald Pierce;
11/17/2006, 10:17 a.m.

Reidier: . . . yes, Mr. Pierce, this is Kerek Reidier, I am a
professor and researcher at the Fermi Lab in—

Pierce: I'm familiar with your work Mr. Reidier.
According to the dossier in front of me, we're
the ones funding your research on
supersymmetry.

Pause.

Reidier: Yes, of course, I wasn't aware . . . I thought the
Department of Energy . . .

Pierce: Has a wonderful working relationship with us
that allows all sorts of, well, let's call it discreet
cross-pollination. I'm still confused as to why
my agenda has been pushed back, and you've
been bumped up to me?

Reidier: Yes, well, so my research has taken a turn, and
I've been delving deeply into quantum
entanglement, specifically how lack of locality
can be utilized to transmit qubits at a distance
instantaneously.

Pause.

Reidier: Mr. Pierce?

Pierce: Yes, I'm here. That sounds rather fantastical, Mr.
Reidier.

Reidier: It does, doesn't it? I respect your choice of
words. I understand how this might come off as
a, well, a phone call from a loon. It's just that,
well, the other day in my lab I successfully
████████████████████████ several million ██████
██████████████████████████
████████████████████████. As I'm sure you
understand, in doing this, it becomes completely
possible, with the right technology, I'm talking
████████████ here, these ████████████████████
██
██████████████████████ scanned.

Pause.

Pierce: Mr. Reidier, if what you're saying is true—

Reidier: It is.

Pierce: If it is, this would mean—

Reidier: I have data. I have video footage. And I can do
it again.[39]

Pierce: Mr. Reidier, how many of your colleagues are
aware of your experiment?

---

[39] TO DO—Check local periodicals for any phenomenon around this time. If
Reidier was in fact successful in running an early experiment in his work, it might
be useful to know if there was any coinciding "incident" in the area. Some sort of
foreshadowing of what was to come with *The Reidier Test*.[R]

[R] And that's it. A nice intriguing little note to herself with no follow-up. So
guess who had to go out with his proverbial shovel and dig? And guess
what I found. Nothing. No, wait. There was an early frost in Hyde Park a
week prior that resulted in glaze ice. Ice. In Chicago. Yeah. Huge news . . .
ok, maybe Hilary did follow up, found as much as I did, and therefore put
nothing in. I suppose that makes sense. She could've deleted that little
footnote, though, and saved me some unnecessary legwork.

Reidier: Almost a dozen know of my work in supersymmetry and my various experiments. However, only a few have a partial grasp on what I'm working with, and none know the entirety of what I'm attempting.

Pierce: If you wouldn't mind, Mr. Reidier, I'd ask that you not share this information with anyone until our people can verify your results. In fact, please don't share any information with anyone outside this office.

Reidier: Ok. Yes, of course. Uh . . .

Pierce: Yes, Mr. Reidier?

Reidier: Just so we're clear, and complete with our, well, full disclosure and all—my colleagues are essentially limited in scope in understanding my work—

Pierce: Right, that's manageable—

Reidier: My wife, however, has a complete and comprehensive, intimate grasp of my work and progress.

Pierce: Of course. Not to worry. We've had experience with this dynamic before. Completely (cough) understandable. There's a protocol. It'll be fine. Just please impress upon her the necessity of . . . discretion. Complete and utter discretion.

Reidier: I'm sure that won't be a problem. For her. I guess now that I'm thinking about it, although I can't imagine this being an issue, but, just so there's no confusion, and I'm sure you have some sort of protocol for this as well, but we have had, my wife and I, have had discussions about my work in front of our two boys.

Pierce: Two you say? (Sounds of paper shuffling)

Reidier: That is how twins work.

Pierce: (Muttering) Goddamn clerical errors. (To Reidier)
How old did you say?

Reidier: Three, and while they're quite talkative, neither
of them understands the subatomic physics of
entanglement.

Pierce: Yes, of course not. If that were the case I'd have
to transfer you to the deputy of another
department. (Chortle)

Reidier: (Laughs) Yes, right? It would be something.
Tour them around to the kings of Europe,
having them give lectures on the myth of
locality and Einstein's greatest fear.

Pierce: Yes. In any event, as long as we keep everything
on lockdown until the Department can
ascertain the situation, we're fine.

Reidier: Right. So do you need me to send you data
results or—

Pierce: No. We'll collect those from you when you run
the experiment for us.

Reidier: That's fine. Obviously, it'll have to be in my lab.
My equipment . . . How soon could you guys
get to Chicago?

Pierce: How's 3:30 for you?

Reidier: What day?

Pierce: This afternoon.

Obviously, Pierce was impressed. What exactly Reidier's demonstration entailed or proved is unclear, but at the very least, its potential
was valuable enough to prioritize Reidier, his project, and his needs.

By the end of the week, the transfer to Brown University was set up, and the Reidier family was cloistered within the folds of the Department's heavy cloak.

Although Pierce prized Reidier's project, he was by no means particularly fond of him. Instead, he approached the physicist with a distrustful skepticism. He never challenged Reidier with his suspicions. Pierce was much more Machiavellian than that, a scientist of scientists, he took notes from the beginning in an effort to figure out which handles to pull and buttons to push in order to facilitate his, and thereby the Department's, goals. This is evident early on, as seen in intradepartmental e-mails to his Deputy Director.

-----Original Message-----
From: Donald Pierce [mailto:donald.pierce@darpa.mil]
Sent: Tuesday, November 25, 2006 7:56 a.m.
To: larry.woodbury@darpa.mil
Subject: Is it Providence?

Larry,

Having read up on Reidier's process, I agree with your assessment of his insistence on working in close proximity to Malle.[40] Clearly, Malle's success with BCIs[41] will be a great resource for Reidier in progressing to Stage 4. It's not hard to imagine somehow adapting Malle's multielectrode recording arrays and fMRI techniques for our purposes.

---

[40] Dr. Bertram Malle, Professor of Neuroscience and Psychology at Brown University and cofounder of Cyberkinetics Neurotechnology Systems, Inc.

[41] Brain-computer interface, AKA direct neural interface, which creates a direct communication pathway between a brain and an external device.

Furthermore, their personal history will preclude any suspicions about time spent together. [42] Obviously Reidier's MO of casually picking his colleagues' brains as opposed to any direct collaboration serves our classified purposes here. Indeed, his ego and secretive impulses will be quite useful in keeping all of this under wraps. This is best facilitated by proximity. It is much more coincidental to drop in on a lecture or a lab demonstration if you work on the same campus, as opposed to flying in from O'Hare. Perhaps we can facilitate "casual" drop-ins through the wife. Her visiting professorship seems on track. Could we find a plausible reason to locate her office near Malle's, instead of the Comparative Literature Department? This would also facilitate our monitoring, two for the price of one.

As far as the wife, I have concerns. Reidier talks elliptically around/about Eve. He's rather concerned about her placement at Brown. Excessively so. Sometimes brings it up in terms of her work: satisfaction, stimulation, etc. Other times he makes it about her adjustment to new surroundings, what she needs their home to be. What's consistent is that he always mentions her. Drops her into every conversation. And always with unspoken emphasis on stabilization. There's something here. Something he's hiding. While any husband would want his spouse to be happy with a relocation, his emphasis on her seems to insinuate a catastrophic fallout if this doesn't work out. Personally AND professionally.

I suspect she might have had or is having some sort of mental episode. If this is so, she is a security liability. One that we cannot contain with traditional solutions. Let's see if we can get her CSG file. Maybe look into Department-friendly therapists or psychiatrists who could properly address her needs and ours.

---

[42] Malle and Reidier are not only old friends, but were roommates at MIT.

Regardless, Reidier's relentlessness about his wife suggests that the state of his family has an immeasurable effect on his focus. For the project's sake, it seems best to keep this volatile nuclear unit stable.

We're best served to move him out of the Fermi Lab and Chicago altogether. Too much new activity, new attention, new security, etc. would lead to questions. It's easier to install him in a new place with our givens already set in place. Furthermore, by moving the family we'll also be helping to sever any personal ties they developed that might have proved porous. And, of course, it'll be much easier to install the NBs.[43] In fact, with some diligent house hunting, we'll be able to kill three birds with one stone: give us our access, Reidier his seclusion, and Eve a stable home.

So, if Reidier's insistent on moving, let's do him the "favor" and collect that chit for later.

-DP

PS I know our contract with UCLA on BCI research still stands, do any of our rights transfer to personnel that have moved on or aid that they've provided to other universities? Can we use this to influence Malle[44] at all?

---

[43] Nanobugs/nanobots: microphones, video cameras, and radios constructed on a nanometer scale ($1nm = 3.281 \times 10^{-9}$ ft; a CD indentation is 500nm wide), developed by DARPA for surveillance. A practically undetectable, full-coverage system.

[44] Pierce is most likely interested in Malle's work developing a system of implanting a sensor in a paralyzed patient's brain that allowed the patient to "manipulate a cursor on a computer, change television stations, and maneuver a remote controlled robot simply by thinking. 'If you can think it, we can hack it.'"[μ]

[μ] "Robot Thoughts: remote control multimode micro-stimulators." Biol Tech. Exp J., July, 2006.

As insightful as Pierce is, however, he has a glaring blind spot. He initially classifies Reidier as a competitive egoist: one whose ambition is his Achilles' heel. Later, though, Pierce posits that Reidier is moving for Eve: a selfless act prioritizing her needs above his own. He never acknowledges how incongruous this seems. It's the contradiction that's Pierce's blind spot. It's his lack of scope.

My intuition tells me that Pierce operates from the traditional idea of self, understanding it as a fixed entity. Our character is sculpted in the wet cement of childhood and settles into an enduring rigidity over time. People are who they are, forever and always. It presumes identity is inoculated against circumstance. The modern[45] concept of self, however, takes on a more fluid dynamic, in which context is king. We are different people in different situations. Character is a myth. We are not one person, but rather, as Paul Bloom of Yale writes, each of us is "a community of competing selves . . . continually popping in and out of existence." [46]

Pierce wants a set character who responds to specific leverage in a specific way every time. His snap judgments, though insightful and most likely correct, are not integrated into a dynamic whole. Rather they're filed away as foregone conclusions. Accordingly, the road map to Reidier is set.

This blind spot of Pierce's seems to have also led him astray in his assessment of Malle. While Pierce correctly divines Malle's utility in relation to Reidier's work, he overlooks Malle's usefulness on a personal level. Although Malle's professional success has primarily been in the neurological field, his academic accomplishments (especially his early ones, during his time living with Reidier) were in

---

[45] . . . modern as in contemporary, not Modern.

[46] "First Person Plural" in *The Atlantic*, November 2008.

psychology.[47] Pierce, however, captivated by his ambitious character assessment of Reidier, classifies Malle merely as a professional asset. He fails to see how Reidier might have a more personal need for Malle: Eve.

Both Pierce and Reidier have played their hands close to their vests. Both apparently withheld and calculated. Interestingly, the two ended up working very well together in addressing the practicalities and necessities of the situation in order to make the project move forward. Ironically, it might have been this very dynamic of considered dealings that locked *The Reidier Test* onto its inevitable course.

---

[47] Malle wrote an award-winning dissertation on social interaction, familial dynamics centered on recognition of intentionality, and how we learn to make inferences about mental states in morally evaluating behavior.

TITLE CARD: **GALILEE 6:21**

TITLE CARD: **EXPERIMENT 25**

CONTROL ROOM, GOULD ISLAND FACILITY - 2007-08-13
09:57

Dr. Reidier enters from transmission room.
Shirt, tie, rolled-up sleeves (tweed sport
coat rests on chair in front of Contact Button
Alpha).

IS1 O'Brien is finishing up the calibration
checklist.

                    DR. REIDIER
          We good?

IS1 scratches off last item and nods.

                    DR. REIDIER (CONT'D)
          Ok. Let's go.

IS1 hesitates. Reidier notices. He approaches
O'Brien who, clearly uncomfortable correcting an
authority figure, mumbles quietly to Reidier and
juts his chin out toward the camera.

                    DR. REIDIER (CONT'D)
          Oh right, right. Jesus, O'Brien
          how many times do I have to tell
          you, for God's sake, speak up if
          something isn't right. I'm not your
          goddamn commanding officer.

                    O'BRIEN
          Sir, yes sir.

Irritated, Reidier stomps over to his seat to
address camera.

                    DR. REIDIER
          Your sense of irony is singular,
          O'Brien.

INT. MIRROR LAB - SAME TIME

As Dr. Reidier continues, fiber-optic cables,
circumscribing the Entanglement Channel, flare
red for several seconds, then morph into an
orbiting white light as the Entanglement Channel
opens.

                    DR. REIDIER (OS)
          Ok, so yet another go at Biologic.
          So far we are 0 for six. Still doing
          better than Varitek. Ok, well, we
          have switched our subject up. We're
          going with produce now.

The Boson Cannons and Pion Beams twitch to
life. SOUNDS of the rapid ACCELERATION and
DECELERATION of GEARS as Reidier and O'Brien
take a series of readings of an orange. Once
complete, they settle into optimized focal
positions.

                    DR. REIDIER (OS) (CONT'D)
          I don't know, fruit seems to be
          a nice combination of liquid and
          solid. Maybe it'll help. Also,
          should be fairly easy to detect its
          properties . . .

The Quark Resonator emits a SOFT, HIGH-PITCHED
DRONE as it powers up.

INT. CONTROL ROOM - CONTINUOUS

                    DR. REIDIER
                (blows out his lips)
        Taste, texture, juiciness. I know,
        not very scientific, but our rigorous
        scientific process
                (throws a look toward O'Brien)
        hasn't yielded much either.
        Of course, if we're anywhere
        near close, we'll make a more
        sophisticated and appropriate
        analysis. Power settings upped to
        ███ times ███ eVs while reversing
        quark spectrum from ████ to █.

Dr. Reidier stares at the camera. He seemingly
debates whether there's more to add. Finally he
shrugs and turns back to the console. He flips up
the Plexiglas cover over Contact Button Alpha
and waits.

IS1 O'Brien, realizing Dr. Reidier is ready,
scrambles to get into position with Contact
Button Bravo. He nods at Dr. Reidier once he's
at the ready.

                DR. REIDIER (CONT'D)
        Three, two, one, go.

Dr. Reidier and IS1 O'Brien simultaneously press
Contact Buttons Alpha and Bravo.

                                        CUT TO:

MIRROR LAB - SAME TIME

SPLIT SCREEN, RIGHT SIDE, CLOSE-UP: empty
reinforced-acrylic sphere over target pad.

LEFT SIDE, CLOSE-UP: orange sits inside reinforced-
acrylic sphere over the transmission pad.

Orange remains perfectly still.

At 2007-08-13 09:59:17.3948877 the orange is suddenly gone and left in its place is an incredibly viscous and sticky ball of the telltale heterogeneous matter and what is later identified as orange-fruit gunk.

NOTE: for 2400 picoseconds prior to transfer, on the left side, the orange bulges and undulates (think somewhere between watching a baby move in her mother's stomach and *Alien*) and then freezes in a tessellation for the last 400 picoseconds.

RIGHT SIDE, at 09:59:17.3948877, the orange looking slightly warped. Its spherical shape severely dimpled. On the outside of the acrylic sphere frost immediately accumulates.

TARGET ROOM - 10:00:22

Dr. Reidier stands over the orange that looks like a balloon that has gotten pruney a few days after it was originally inflated. Dr. Reidier cautiously pokes at it.

The orange . . . deflates as if the rind were simply giving up.

Reidier picks it up and struggles to tear it open.

> DR. REIDIER
> It's really tough. Like elephant
> skin.

Dr. Reidier takes out a pocketknife, unfolds the blade, and punctures the rind. He saws almost all the way around the circumference and opens it.

                    DR. REIDIER (CONT'D)
          Huh . . .

Dr. Reidier holds open the rind to IS1 O'Brien
back in the control booth.

It is empty except for shredded pericarp. No
pith, no flesh, no carpels.

The HIGH PITCH of the Quark Resonator fades out
as the machine powers down.

V

When pen hasted to write, on reaching the subject of love, it split in twain.

~Rumi

The more one does and sees and feels, the more one is able to do, and the more genuine may be one's appreciation of fundamental things like home, and love, and understanding companionship.

~Amelia Earhart

As Reidier's work solidified, his marriage deteriorated. While he was aware of the tension between Eve and him, he misdiagnosed it as an adjustment to change, rather than as a symptom of distance. If Eve's memoir novella, *A Moi: Graffiti Me*, is taken as more fact than fiction, Reidier not only seems unaware but incapable of changing their course. Tragically, his drive to set things right with Eve was what drove them apart. His successes were too tempting, too blinding to allow him to see the simple truth: Eve was in mourning. For them, for their past, for the invasion into and dismantling of the universe of each other.

The fact that Eve could only begin to write this work a year after the move to Providence is indicative of how profound her grief was at this time. She herself needed distance to safely approach and unpack the pain from the loss. It was the only way to safely untangle the tension that had tightened as she tried to hold on to the past while he worked to pull them into the future. Or maybe instead the desolate distance is what drove her backward. Unlike the cloistered experience they shared in French Guiana, their present post was more of an exile . . . from each other. Before, Kerek hungered for her. Eve fed his passions (intellectual, professional, physical). Now, she fed his kids. She wrestled with a sense of abandonment as Reidier went out to change the world, demoted from erotic muse to nurturing caretaker. Ironically, this transformation did not result from Eve's diminishing independence, but rather from Reidier's (and the boys') increasing dependence. Although with Eve it was less of a transformation—from lover, to wife, to mother—and more of an acquisition of roles, a contravention of selves. In picking up her pen, however, Eve Tassat could reclaim herself and rewrite her narrative. Only through the writing itself could Eve come to understand herself, her husband, and his work. Through the narrative she somehow managed to breach the contradiction within and understand how her longing for the man-that-was necessitated her support of the man that is. Only through her work could the gravity of their distant dynamic reveal itself and how, at the time, ironically, it was their loneliness that bound them.

Excerpt from *A Moi: Graffiti Me*[48]

> *She could feel the emptiness. The sheets lay too flat, pulled on her too uniformly. He wasn't there. She knew where he was, hiding down*

---

[48] *To Me*, published in *Fictions of the Self*, Princeton University Press 2008.

in the darkness, with her, fueled by coffee sweetened with crushed up Bennies.

Physicists are machines for turning stimulants into theories, he would paraphrase the mathematician Paul Erdos. The pills helped him keep up with his thoughts, he insisted. She would warn him about burning the candle at both ends, and he would brush it off, saying that's because there isn't enough daylight.

He would have waited until her breathing slowed and deepened. That was his idea of a compromise: to lie with her until she slipped from the moorings of consciousness. She imagined him listening for a switch in tempo of her in- and exhales. Leaning over, checking if her eyes were shifting beneath their lids. Then slowly, quietly, stepping off the raft of their bed, pulling the covers up, putting on over his pajamas his sport coat with its lapel pin, reaching inside the pocket to feel for his eye-patch, and heading down into his lair.

It was neither loneliness nor aloneness she felt. Rather, distance seemed like the best approximation, though still an inadequate analogy. It wasn't distance in the sense of a gap, or any type of chasm, it was instead distance to the unmeasured eye. Having grown up on the edge of the Sahara, she knew and loved vastness, adored the beauty of emptiness. Where others saw expanse, she saw mirages, ideas sprouting up everywhere with infinite room to grow and blossom. The expanse wasn't daunting or lacking to her. It was an invitation, a playground for her imagination. The uniform void, the span of the between, was a constant comfort, a touchstone of awe that always gave her the room she needed.

This wasn't that, though.

This was different.

It wasn't the desert.

It was the mountains, it was the forced perspective.

When she was a little girl, her father took her for a vacation to Switzerland, a kingdom of lakes and mountains. But she never trusted the water, which shimmered with the false promise of clarity. The crystal lakes suggested a beckoning, transparent openness that revealed nothing, instead snuffing out sunlight within their depths. Snowcapped peaks rippled across the watery surfaces, offering only reflections.

The mountains were what drew her. Their fierce silhouettes, jagged against the sky, were at least honest, boasting danger, challenging onlookers with their blatant monstrousness, but promising an undeniable perspective.

One afternoon, while walking along the lake, she got it in her head that her father and she must hike up a mountain. She knew which one. She pointed, pouted, and finally insisted. He laughed and, as was often the case, gave in to her flight of fancy. And so they set out, a spontaneous pair, hand in hand, marching toward adventure.

It was a quest that never arrived. No matter how fast they walked, nor how long they persisted, the mountain refused to come within reach. It lingered by the horizon, still massive, but no larger or closer.

What she came to learn that afternoon was that a desert girl had no business in the mountains. She had no sense of their proportions. Her lack of perspective failed to grasp the immensity. She couldn't coordinate with their reality. The mountain should be getting closer, but after hours and hours of walking, it stood there, where it had always been, looming in the distance. The honest, bleak perspective had forced her hand, and she and her father finally gave in and turned back. During their retreat, she kept looking over her shoulder, watching, trying to measure, but only glimpsing an awesome size that failed to waver.

That's how it felt with him now. Inexorably drawn toward him, but never any closer and utterly baffled by the disconnect between her efforts and her progress.

He would speak of the inability of infinity. The myopia of minutiae, *he would quip.* There's always more room at the bottom, *he would paraphrase Feynman.*

It used to be different with them. He wouldn't run away to do work—he would sneak away from work to be with her. The more he had of her, the hungrier he became.

You are a perpetual-motion-of-longing machine, *he would say.* You defy the physics of desire. A source of unceasing concupiscence, *licking the sweat off of her chin as if it were distilled from the fountain of youth.*

Back then she was his solace, his escape hatch, a sanctuary from the frustration of uninspiration. It was with her—having freed himself from a relentless and fruitless focus—in bed, sticky with sweat and spit and cum, that he would find his epiphanies, connect disparate abstract concepts, grab her lipstick off the nightstand, and draft equations across her body, filling up the blank page of her belly with calculations that spilled down the tabula rasa of her thigh.

She adored the sensation of him tracing his graffiti over her, of being painted with his physics hieroglyphics.

It was an amaranthine time. One filled with love and hushed laughter, during scandalous, furtive excursions to his lab in the middle of the night because she refused to let him photograph his work on her naked body.

But my equations, *he would protest.*

Are mine as of now. If you want them, you have to take me too. Take me with you, *she would tease.*

So off they would sneak, into the office at night, him in

pajamas and a tweed sport coat, her in her Burberry raincoat and sneakers. She would stand by the window, bathed in the moonlight, adorned in his henna that held within its labyrinthine design the secrets of the universe, while he scribbled furiously on his whiteboard.

It could not last. Eventually the petals fell from the bloom. They are not who they once were.

Elle propped herself up on several of his pillows. The moonlight strained through the mosquito netting. Reinier lay perpendicular to her at the bottom of her legs. His fingers traced over the graffiti he had left on the inside of her thigh.

"Your equations are fading," she exhaled, having just finished gulping half a liter of water out of the bottle.

"It's ok. They're already backed up."

"If Venus only knew you were going to put Galatea to work, she might never have woken her up for you."

"Don't be jealous. A Greek statue could never compete with Elle. Especially considering the way you tabula the hell out of my rasa."

Elle rolled her eyes. Even groaned a little and kicked him, not to inflict any punishment, but rather to physically connect with him, reassure herself that her lover was, in fact, skin and bone and not just some moonlit apparition. While Reinier groaned with exaggerated injury, her foot didn't pull back from the strike; instead it remained in contact with his stomach, and rubbed back and forth.

Years ago Elle had seen a news program that featured a blind and deaf Dalmatian dog. The canine was part of a loving family and led a happy life, but it manifested a peculiar habit of having to always be in physical contact with one of the family members. As long as the animal could maintain a constant assurance of their presence, it felt safe and secure. At the time, it had struck Elle as tragically (eye-roll) touching, but an impulse, an existence she could never understand from the inside out. Nevertheless, it stayed with her. It wasn't until she met Reinier that she finally empathized with that dog's need. It wasn't possessiveness or insecurity. The closest she could get to describing it was as an addiction to the warmth, the happiness that would immediately leech into her like a secretion of adrenaline, the pure, unadulterated (eye-roll) joy.

"What does it all mean, anyway?" Elle kicked her leg out to indicate she was inquiring about his equations written down her limb.

"It describes the relationship between quantum chromo-dynamics and the hadronization process."

"So secondary school science merde," Elle said with a dismissive tone, all the more dismissive with her French accent. "I figured it'd have something to do with quantum cryptography. Public- and private-key encryption et cetera. Or it described the relationship of my exquisite derriere to the gravitational pull of your hands. One of those two phenomenon."

"Well, they are all fundamental forces." Reinier's hand slid up between her thigh and the sheets, and grabbed a handful of derriere.

Elle moaned playfully and then shoved him back with her foot. "No, no. First you explain quantum chronamyics then we delve into my derriere."

Reinier started to correct her but was stopped by his brain catching up to her double entendre.

She laughed at his speechlessness. "Come, come. Edify me," she teased in a sexy voice.

"Ah, well, so you see, um, physics. Normal physics. All physics really. It's ok." Reinier took a breath, still trying to orient past her evocative entendres. "The problem with physics is it's still all about locality. One object can only be affected by another object

that has some sort of direct contact. A pitcher throws a baseball that smacks into a catcher's mitt, a submarine launches a missile that travels thousands of miles and collides with its target, thunder undulates as sound waves through a medium of air particles and crashes in our ears. Even light must obey locality. Photons emitted from the sun zip through the void of space for over eight minutes, hit the moon, induce a photoelectric effect that essentially coaxes a ricocheting beam of photons out that then travel to the earth, through its atmosphere, past our window, between the mosquito netting, and collide with your leg making your skin glow."

"I am glowing a bit, aren't I?"

This time Reinier smacked her and similarly left his striking hand in contact with her leg.

Elle couldn't help but curl toward the affection. Negative attention was still attention. "Locality definitely feels like a problem," Elle quipped, as she bent her leg in an effort to make Reinier's hand slide down from her knee and up her thigh.

Alas, she had already nudged him down the path of physics. Reinier started to speak animatedly, with his hands. "So in essence, everything has to travel. Everything has to go from here," Reinier held out his left hand to indicate a hypothetical location, "to there," Reinier held out his right hand as far from his left as possible to indicate a hypothetical destination.

"Je comprends. Aren't there a handful of kinematic equations that describe that movement? I seem to recall something of 'zat sort from my secondary school days."

"Yes, no. There are. And they describe the movement beautifully."

"Alors?"

"But I think it's a waste of time."

Elle snort-laughed.

Reinier tilted his head at her, curious as to the joke. *"I'm not kidding."*

"I know, mon trésor. *'Zat is what's so funny."*

Reinier grinned, still not getting it, but thrilled to make Elle laugh. "Ok, so imagine a yardstick, or in your case a meter stick."

"I know what a yardstick is."

"So if I were to lay that yardstick through a doorway—"

"Like going from your bedroom into your bathroom."

"Yes, now, how much time would you say it takes for the yardstick to go from the bedroom into the bathroom if I were pushing it at, say, five kilometers an hour?"

"Trick question. No time, since it is already in the bathroom. Unless you mean completely in the bathroom. Is that what you meant?"

"No, you got the trick question right. It is already in both the bedroom and the bathroom. It does not need to travel from one to other. Unless . . ."

"Unless quoi?*"*

"Unless you're not looking at it like a whole thing?"

Now it was Elle's turn to tilt her head at Reinier.

"You answered the question correctly, but by answering about the yardstick at all, you're already tricked."

"How?"

"The yardstick isn't a yardstick."

"The yardstick isn't a yardstick," she repeated, raising an eyebrow. *"There is no spoon."**

---

* The last thing I expected was to stumble across an allusion to a Keanu Reeves movie.

Now Reinier rolled his eyes. "The yardstick is only a yardstick if you look at it that way. More precisely, it's a collection of molecules, atoms, and subatomic particles."

"So is everything, no?"

"Precisely. It's just a collection of atoms and molecules like everything else. Its essence as a yardstick doesn't objectively exist."

Elle started to say something, but Reinier precountered.

"Nor does a spoon!" he affirmed. "Objectively. To the universe, neither a yardstick nor a spoon has an objective essence beyond its mass, which is merely an aggregate of particles. There is a subjective essence that we perceive; a yardstick is a yardstick because it happens to be a length we're interested in. A spoon is a spoon because it is useful to us for slurping soup."

"There is nothing either good or bad, but thinking makes it so."*

---

* Hamlet, Act II, Scene ii. There's something arousing about a woman who quotes *The Matrix* and Shakespeare in the same minute.

"Exactly. The yardstick is only a yard long because we choose to differentiate its atoms from the atoms of air that lie just beyond it."

"But if I grab hold of the yardstick and pick it up, it lifts up as a whole, while the air that lies just beyond essentially stays where it lies. Molecules or not, it is a whole thing in and of itself which I can manipulate as a single unit." Elle smiled down at him, impressed with her own point.

"True. But if a giant were to come and pick up the house, then the yardstick, along with everything else in it, would simply become part of the house. The air beyond the house, if you ignore any vortex pull, would essentially stay in place. It all depends how you look at it."

"Huh," Elle said. She looked around the room and scanned the ceiling, as if Reinier might have had a giant waiting on hand to demonstrate the correctness of his point.

"I'm not saying there aren't forces at work or that the molecules of the yardstick don't exhibit a stronger binding to one another than

they do with the air. But it's we who choose which forces, which relationships take precedence in our assignment of meaning."

Reinier's finger traced and retraced his equations up her thigh. "So the problem we're left with when we go back to our original question of how long does it take for me to push the yardstick from the bedroom to the bathroom is . . . what yardstick? Which molecule of yardstick? Once we're asking that question it becomes your high school physics problem that's solved with kinematic equations. And once we're there, we are operating within a structure of distance equals rate times time."

"And you don't like that."

"That doesn't get us anywhere."

"It gets us from here to there."

In response, Reinier performed an exaggerated yawn.

"What?" Elle asked through a laugh. "What's wrong with that?"

"Lag."

"Lag?"

"Lag times. Time in general. It takes time to travel, whether it's people, sound waves, or electromagnetic waves."

"Well . . . yes." Elle didn't see his problem with this.

"Why did you originally answer that the yardstick was already where it was headed?"

"Because you asked how long it would take to push it into the bathroom."

"And?"

"It was already in the bathroom."

"Not all of it."

"Half of it was."

"Did you consider which half?"

"Quoi?"

"When you were imagining my hypothetical yardstick, did you

picture which half was in the bedroom and which half was in the bathroom?"

"I wasn't considering which end was which. I was simply seeing a yardstick."

"The halves were interchangeable to you."

"Oui. Identical."

"So as a result of its fungibility it could be in both locations at once."

Elle considered the statement and finally nodded. "But you said 'zat was wrong to see it like 'zat."

"Not wrong, just a matter of perspective. It was an incorrect model on an atomic level. But what if we went smaller?"

"Same problem, no? Which molecule, atom, proton, which neutron crosses from the bedroom into the bathroom?"

"Oui, indeed." Reinier nodded. He pushed himself up onto his elbow, clearly energized and animated. "The dilemma of differentiation persists because there are different types of subatomic particles." Reinier flashed a devilish smile up at Elle. "But what if we went smaller? More fundamental."

"You mean, comment dites-vous? Quarks?"

"Yes. There are still a variety of quarks: up, down, strange, charm, top, bottom."

Elle giggled. "There are strange and charming quarks?"

"They're the third lightest of quarks. Mostly found in hadrons. Not to mention that every quark also has a twin antiparticle that has equal magnitudes of certain properties, but opposite signs."

"So strange antiquarks or antistrange quarks."

"Both work. Anyhow, lots of quark varieties, which are in essence the same. Some have a slightly larger mass than the others, but that's mostly a matter of varying fractional charges. Not to mention that down at that level, their 'masses' are more fluid than

on a macro level. The units measuring their mass describe this, mega electron volts, i.e. an electron's rest mass, which is essentially a lump of energy."

"Quarks' masses are measured in energy?"

"Yes! To be fair, though, down at that level, mass and energy look a lot alike. Quarks tend to misbehave. They don't stay in one place nor do they necessarily move via trajectory. Instead they can wink out of existence here and then back into existence there. That's where $E = mc^2$ is the law of the land. Quarks dance across the equal sign turning from matter into energy and back again."

Elle was caught up thinking about dancing quarks, changing back and forth from butterflies into caterpillars. Dualism meant nothing to the universe. Her Cambodian monk was right.

Between her second and third year of university, Elle had backpacked through Southeast Asia. One morning in Siem Reap, Elle ended up sharing her breakfast with a Buddhist monk on his way to bribe a family to send their daughter to school in exchange for five kilograms of rice a month. As a thank-you, he led her on a brief meditation. When you breathe in, you know, when you breathe out, you know. *That was his mantra. Though, no matter how often he repeated it, in her head Elle kept wanting to end it with* you don't know.

When you breathe in, you know. When you breathe out, you don't know.

Afterward, she brought her ebb-and-flow impulse up to the monk. He smiled and shook his head. Buddha doesn't experience the universe in opposites. Contradictions, paradoxes—these are illusions of division. They are constructs within which attachment, separation, and suffering bloom. Separation, however, is a delusion. A mirage conjured by consciousness and ego. To define oneself, it is necessary to separate from all else.

This demarcation creates a false boundary, disconnecting the soul from the whole. It is a lethal and limiting misconception that can trap souls in a house of mirrors for thousands of lifetimes. The reality is there is no opposite of everything.

Nothing? *Elle proffered naïvely.*

Everything includes nothing. And nothing can be the opposite of itself.

When you breathe in, you know. When you breathe out, you know.

"Elle? Are you with me?" Reinier asked.

"Dualism means nothing to the infinite or the infinitesimal."

Reinier paused. "Exactly. Not to mention our yardstick dilemma is rendered moot. Down at the quark level, there's no differentiating between yardstick quarks, air quarks, carpet quarks, et cetera. Matter itself loses meaning even."

"Matter doesn't matter."

"Yes!" Reinier was sitting up now. "Even within atoms' mass is sort of a question mark, since 99.9999999999999 percent," Reinier counted off the thirteen nines after the decimal to make sure he said it correctly, "is empty space between the orbits of its electrons and its nucleus. Mass is really just a consistent manifestation of dynamic forces."

Elle couldn't help but smile. For years, in her youth, she had been distressed that she had no passion. She would marvel at a friend who lost herself playing guitar for afternoons, or a cousin who would play blackjack for twelve hours straight, or a classmate who read anything and everything about Shakespeare's Tempest. Where was her obsession, her calling? But then one melancholy evening, while her father poured her a glass of Cabernet Sauvignon, she poured out her teenage angst. He surprised her with a deep laugh instead of his normal sympathetic ear. Don't you see *mon trésor,* your passion is passion.

"So where do the chromodynamics come in?" Reinier was now sitting fully up and cross-legged. She slid her foot between the tight pocket of his calf and thigh and tucked her foot under. She had to be in direct contact with his crackling energy. Or at least as close as the 0.0000000000001 percent of masses could get.

"Entangled quantum chromodynamic."

"Do you think it's a fetish how your big terms turn me on?" Elle slid her foot deeper into the pocket of his legs.

"A fetish? No. A blessing, absolutely." Reinier slipped his hand behind the knee of her leg that was tucked into his. In spite of her innuendo and his affections, he was still all physics. "What you have to realize is this is magic," he gestured to his equations written on her inner thigh, "as far as the scientific community is concerned."

Elle tilted her head. "Isn't magic the antithesis of science?"

"It is. But no one knows quite how to account for entanglement, let alone explain it."

"So what is it?"

"Entangled quarks are essentially a quantum system in which one of them cannot fully be described without consideration of the other."

"How very equitable."

"What I mean is, together, they share a single quantum state: their spin. All quarks have spin. They can, for example, spin 'up' or 'down.' It's not really analogous to the 'real' macro world, but just accept spin as a property of quarks."

"Consider it accepted."

"Ok, so then we've got two entangled quarks, quark A, who we'll call Alice, and quark B, Bob, that make up a quantum system. Both quarks share a single spin state. This is known as a superposition. Although they share this state, one of them must spin up while the other must spin down. As long as neither of them *measures their spin, however, they both have a fifty-fifty shot of being either. Their probabilities are equal. With me so far?"*

"Alice and Bob are flipping a coin. One has to get heads, the other tails, but as long as the coin's spinning, each has neither," Elle suggests.

"Each also has both. Together they have both heads and tails potential."

It wasn't his big terms per se, it was his animation, his investment, the energy he harnessed from his creativity. Her own creativity had the opposite effect. Whenever she got taken up in her writing, she ended the day happy, but enervated. Reinier, on the other hand, was like contained fusion. He was his own nuclear sun, and his gravity drew her in. She couldn't take her eyes off him. Or her hands. "I understand."

"But if Alice claps her hand over the coin and checks—i.e. measures her spin—then she drops out of her superposition and has, let's say tails. Then Bob must—"

"Have heads."

"Exactly. Perfectly anticorrelated. Bob's is always opposite to Alice's. This is the essential nature of entanglement."

"Alors, as long as neither checks, then they both share the same super state. However, as soon as one of them checks, they have polar opposites."

"Yes, and in knowing their own state, they also immediately know the other's. Now, remember what I said earlier about locality?"

"Everything has to travel."

"For one thing to be affected by another there must be a direct interaction, whether through photons or an electromagnetic field."

"Got it."

"Yeah, quarks don't."

"Don't what?"

"Don't care about locality. Locality can suck it as far as quarks are concerned."

"Explain."

"Ok, so back to Alice and Bob and their spinning coin. They share their superposition while it's spinning."

"Oui."

"What if Alice caught it and slapped it down on the back of her hand but left it covered. Who has head and who has tails?"

"Still unknown, no?"

"Completely unknown. So they're still in their shared superposition, each having a fifty-fifty chance of heads or tails, right?"

"Right."

"Now, suppose that Alice and Bob had a special device that could slice the coin along the circumference into two half-coins, without them seeing, and then seal each half-coin into an envelope, giving one to Alice and the other to Bob."

"Still unknown states, therefore still in superposition, as long as they don't peek."

"So assuming no peeking, Alice could get on a plane and fly to Fiji and take a boat to an isolated island. She could then open up her envelope—"

"Drop out of her superposition—"

"And instantaneously know Bob's state."

"Oui."

"No, I mean, imagine she had a cell phone with her. Cell signals are electromagnetic waves that propagate at the speed of light. Now, tell me, what would take longer, for her to see tails after she's opened her envelope or for Bob to tell her over the phone that he has heads?"

"It would take longer for Bob to tell her."

"So then the information about Bob's state of heads 'travels' faster to her than the speed of light."

"Yes, but, can't nothing travel faster than the speed of light? Isn't it 'ze universal speed limit?"

In response, Reinier opened up his hands, palms up as if to say, and there you have it, abracadabra.

"Wait," Elle protested. "But 'ze information, I mean I know it did, but it didn't really travel."

Reinier repeated the gesture and said in a horrible French accent, "Et voilà. As far as I'm concerned, traveling is for suckers. That, my love, is entanglement. Obviously quarks aren't coins, and it's not just a simple matter of slicing one in half and sending the halves on their merry way to opposite ends of the world, but the analogy holds. Two entangled quarks share a superposition. If you affect the spin of one, the other instantaneously registers it without any transfer of information—locality be damned. Not to mention, that on my end, I can pick the state. By pairing Bob's quark with another one on his end, I can make the new one spin up, so Bob's has to spin down, so Alice's has to spin up."

"And then there's your information transfer. No, not transfer, iteration."

"An information iteration. I like that. We call it entanglement swapping, but information iteration really has a nice ring to it. I might steal that."

"Copyright!! Trademark!" Elle scrambled to plant her literary flag, pushing him over and smothering him with her naked body. The two laughed and kissed. Elle grabbed hold of his hands and intertwined her fingers between his.

"So," Elle said, inches away from Reinier's face, eyes locked. "These two entangled quarks, they stay connected, in sync with each other, no matter how far apart they go?"

"They could cross the universe. If Alice spins up, she knows Bob must spin down."

"How romantic."

Reinier rolled his eyes in response.

Elle shifted her leg and applied a solid pressure with her thigh against his groin. "It's romantic. Dites-moi. Dis-le," *she hissed.*

Reinier laughed and quickly capitulated. "Alice and Bob are very romantic. They're romantic," he groaned through mock pain.

"That's right. They are." Elle kissed him and sucked his bottom lip as she pulled away. Then she bit it and tugged gently.

"So romantic," Reinier continued with his faux pleading, with only one of his lips available to him. "We should double with them."

"As long as you realize there will be NO entanglement swapping of any sort," Elle said and rolled off him, onto the mattress. She lay next to him, still holding his hand, fingers entwined. "Alors, entanglement not so inexplicable."

"Not as an analogy. But for the life of us, we physicists can't figure out how it actually works. Drove Einstein nuts. Nevertheless, a sailor can still cross an ocean without being able to explain the wind." Reinier shrugged, "'Any sufficiently advanced technology is indistinguishable from magic.'"

Elle took that in. "That is good. I might steal 'zat."

"You'll have to steal it from Arthur Clarke."

"I still don't understand where the chromodynamics fit in."

"Well, I didn't want to overwhelm you—"

Elle lifted his hand to her mouth and bit it. Hard.

"Bore you!" a pained Reinier amended his previous statement. "I didn't want to bore you."

Again, laughter.

"Go. Tell me. Sans sass," Elle directed him.

"You and I have very different ideas of pillow talk."

As Elle lifted his hand toward her bared teeth about to bite down, Reinier launched into chromodynamics. "So, as we all know, quarks interact with each other via gluons—OW!"

Elle had bit him again.

"What? I'm explaining!"

"Make it make sense before I get another craving for flesh."

Reinier gave Elle a wary eyebrow raise. "Quarks interact with each other through something called a strong interaction, sort of like the strong force that keeps protons pressed together in nuclei in spite of the significant pressure of the magnetic force from their like positive charges that pushes them apart."

"I'm with you, keep going."

Reinier let out a sigh full of mock relief. "These strong interactions are described by quantum chromodynamics. The intricacies of this aren't so important, the only essential part is that gluons are the means by which these interactions are transferred."

"Got it." Elle nodded once in the affirmative. "What's a gluon?"

Reinier bit his lip as he considered a feasible answer. "What photons are to electromagnetic force, gluons are to the strong force between quarks."

Reinier waited to see if that landed.

"So how light comes to us in packets of photons?" Elle asked.

"Perfect. Gluons are packets of strong force, the means by which quarks exchange force. So within quantum chromodynamics, each gluon has a color charge and an anticolor charge. Again, not analogous to the macro real world, but they're properties of gluons."

"Ok." Elle nodded once again. "Down at that small a level I'm sure the idea of color holds no meaning, oui?"

"Oui. So gluons are constantly passed back and forth between quarks through emission and absorption. Subsequently, when a gluon is passed from one quark to another, a color change occurs in both."

"Like with Alice and Bob and their coin?"

"Exactly like with Alice and Bob. If Alice's quark emitted a red-antigreen gluon, it would become green, and if Bob's quark is

green and absorbed Alice's red-antigreen gluon, it would become red. In doing so, while their colors are always changing, their strong interaction is preserved."

"Alice and Bob stand on a seesaw and each throw a ball of equal mass (but different colors) to the other. Who has the red or green ball keeps changing, but they stay balanced on the seesaw."

"Good enough," Reinier said with equal doses of encouragement and let's-not-get-hung-up-on-the-small-stuff. "Now the interesting thing is because gluons have a color charge, they can also emit and absorb other gluons."

"Like adverbs," Elle interjected. When she saw his look, she clarified, "They can modify verbs, adjectives, or other adverbs."

Reinier shrugged. "Perhaps. Anyway, this instigates what's known as asymptotic freedom. The upshot of which is that as quarks get closer to each other, the chromodynamic binding force between them weakens. That's what this equation here describes." Reinier grabbed behind her knee, raised her leg a little, and pointed at the conglomeration of Greek letters and numbers that circumscribed Elle's leg just north of her knee.

He didn't notice the spark flash in Elle's eyes when he grabbed her. Nor hear the slight, sharp intake of breath. When you breathe in, you know . . .

"Conversely, as this distance increases, the binding force strengthens. As this happens, the color field is stressed. Like a rubber band getting stretched. This one predicts the amount of stress." Reinier's hand drifted further north to another equation.

The further up his hand moved, the further back Elle's bottom lip retreated into her mouth. Inversely proportional, Elle thought as she gnawed on her lip while Reinier continued, oblivious, caught up in his infinite, infinitesimal magic show.

"Now, and here's the really fascinating part, the more this

rubber band is stretched, the more stress to the color field, the more gluons of the appropriate color are needed to strengthen the field. And that's where this equation comes in." Reinier continued his path northward, rapidly approaching the fork in her road.

Elle's bottom lip had completely disappeared by this point.

"Above a certain threshold, to compensate for this, gluons are spontaneously created, as are quarks and antiquarks. Matter, or more appropriately, the building blocks of matter, are conjured out of thin air. Hadronization. That's what this is all about. That's the whole shebang."* Reinier lightly slapped his right hand against the inside of her left thigh, "With the magic of hadronization," he raised his hand up and patted it back down against the most northerly equation, "we get the impossible. Or at least the possibility of the impossible."

---

* Well that about clears it all up for me. Teleportation in a nutshell. Conjuring matter out of nothing. I think I'll stick with Reinier's previous explanation: magic.

Reinier finally looked up at Elle to share in the amazement at this phenomenon and the excitement of what his equation could calculate, predict, create. All he could focus on, however, was Elle's top lip and its missing partner. "Did you follow that? I mean, was I clear?"

The corners of Elle's mouth turned up, devil-horned bookends to the line of teeth that held her bottom lip hostage.

"Are we done talking about quarks?"

The devil horns sharpened.

"Good on gluons?"

Elle nodded her head slowly.

"Hadronization?"

Elle moaned softly.

"Ok. So I should stop talking then."

Elle reached down and wrapped her fingers around his wrist. She pulled his hand past the final equation, across the threshold, and into the crossroads.

His fingers sank into the landscape of her.

VI

Everything one invents is true, you may be perfectly sure of that.
Poetry is as precise as geometry.

~Gustave Flaubert

A poet can survive everything but a misprint.

~Oscar Wilde

Pierce and Woodbury took great care in placing the Reidier family in Providence. The Department, through Brown University, appropriated a stunning home in the historic College Hill neighborhood. It was a mammoth property, originally the Royal C. Taft–George Smith House (c.1888). As the real estate listing describes it, the house was a

> Stately Queen Anne Colonial Revival beautifully situated at 454 Angell Street. Designed by Stone, Carpenter, and Willson.
> Gorgeous architectural details throughout, including a Palladian window over the fan-light entrance, broken-scroll dormers in a picturesque design, a widow's walk, and a polygonal turret which is reflected on all three floors. Spacious rooms flow graciously from one into the other, high

ceilings, exceptional moldings, beautiful hardwood floors, and five fireplaces.

Gracious entry foyer features a dramatic staircase and opens to a double parlor and a formal dining room. Cozy screened porch overlooks the private and expansive yard. Large kitchen with a butler's pantry and a mudroom. The second and third floors offer eight bedrooms, three of which have fireplaces, four full bathrooms, plus a lavette. The expansive, partially finished lower level offers a flexibility of space and a colonial charm with several original exposed stone foundation walls.

Magnificent grounds include lush perennial gardens and a lovely mature Copper Beech tree. Convenient two-car garage is attached to the house by a covered and enclosed walkway. A true Providence gem!

It was not only a magnificent place to make a home but also a mere half-mile walk to 182 Hope Street, the Brown Physics Department.

The house was only the beginning. Eve was awarded a Visiting Assistant Professorship in the Department of Comparative Literature, located in Marston Hall, a stone's throw away from the Physics building and in the shadow of the Science Library.* Allegedly, due to limited resources and the general bureaucratic disarray of the Comp Lit Department, there was no space available in Marston Hall. Instead, Eve had to be placed a block away, at 97 Waterman Street, in the Arnold Lab. Her office was across the hall from Bertram Malle's.

---

* It's more than a bit unnerving to encounter my mom's walking tour through the landmarks of my alma mater. She used to take me for lunch on Thayer Street for Parents' Weekend, dinner down on Wickenden for the odd pop-in, and ~~here~~ there she was again, traipsing around like an admissions officer, while I sit in an empty carriage house in Hell's Kitchen.

How many jaunts did she take up there? How much time did she spend? How often did she stop in New York on her way back, see me for an afternoon, and cover with some story about a lecture at Columbia? How often didn't she stop? I think that last question bothers me the most.

Hilary on College Hill.

As the myth goes, the Sci-Li is descending into the ground at the rate of, I don't know, two-tenths of an inch a year. Supposedly it's all because the engineers when designing the library's foundation forgot to account for the weight of the books. It's kind of charming, in a Venetian sort of way. At least it is when glimpsing it through last night's alcoholic haze.

Her trips had got me thinking. Thinking felt too heavy, though, so I needed to be lightened up a little with a titration of alcohol. I slipped out to Siberia, dove into a fifth of Russian vodka, and surfed on the bartender's iPad. Somewhere toward the bottom of that bottle, I found the magic mixture. The perfect few words, ordered just so, dropped into Google's search bar like a little tab of acid, et voilà!

I found it.

Weeks of searching and all I needed was a few shots of Stolichnaya and Google's "I'm Feeling Lucky" button.

"Entangled in the Bourg." Eve Tassat's long-lost short story.

Well, not her short story per se. But an archived bulletin board thread from some literary forum. Several members were going back and forth about the motif of memory. More specifically of forgetting. They went on about the fidelity of memory, the fidelity of language, how the piece itself was Tassat's act of remembering. Then there was a whole string on absinthe, its side effect of memory loss, how the wormwood is supposed to rot holes in your brain. And then a long debate about the nature of an oubliette: was it meant to imprison or erase? A poster who went by the screen name "Hoggle" put the kibosh on the argument, finally insisting that "An oubliette is a place you put people to forget about 'em!"

I rushed back to my oubliette. I had to get this down and not forget myself.

I mean it was a broken html link to the text itself, but still there was the reference. AND, and there were dates. The posts were all from the summer of 2000. One year after my mother claimed it was published.

So Hilary was right. It did exist, and it was published. And I don't know why, maybe it was that clean, clear Russian vodka, or just following in Mom's steps, but I was so titillated. Until . . .

WHAM! WHAM! WHAM!

A pounding on my front door.

I froze. A chill undulating up my spine; icy tendrils branching like capillaries. And I just sat and waited. It had to be a mistake. A drunk neighbor's wrong turn. Nobody comes here but me. Nobody even knows about it but me.

So I waited in the basement of that carriage house, hidden in the middle of the block, sunken into a cement courtyard. My own personal oubliette. And I listened, trying to outwait the interloper. Listened for a hint. My heart thudding in my ears.

WHAM! WHAM! WHAM!

With no furniture to get in the way, the thuds echoed around the empty carriage house. This time, though, I could hear the wrought iron walkway creak as the knocker shifted weight from one foot to the other. And then the railing creaked. Whoever it was, was leaning against it.

My fucking desk lamp was on. Of course it was, I had been reading. The yellow glow spilled out onto the concrete. And someone was leaning over the railing looking at it. Someone had followed me.

"MAKE OUT PATROL! Anybody making out? Anybody wanna make out?" he shouted down.

It was Toby. A wave of tiny needles rolled across the back of my neck and shimmered down through the rest of my body, and I was overcome with an urge to piss myself.

"You scared the hell out of me," I screamed up at the front door.

"Yeah? I guess we're even then," he yelled back.

Apparently, I had been a little remiss in retrieving my voice mails, and Toby had become a little curious about my Invisible Man impersonation. His fears were far from allayed by the décor of the house.

"You're not sleeping here, man, are ya?" he asked, staring at the mattress on the third floor.

"It's just for naps. I still stay at my place. Most nights."

He raised an eyebrow and then headed downstairs. Having dug myself in, I didn't quite have the perspective on how disconcerting a depth I had sunk to. To me I was just unpacking the briefcase, to Toby . . . well, all he could say really was, *Man*, and ask me if I had found anything. I told him about French Guiana and the Brown trips. He nodded, thumbed through some stuff, fiddled with the bead necklace hanging on the wall, and then suggested a little distance might help me get some perspective.

"Know any place where we could get some absinthe?"

A wry smile accompanied another eyebrow raise, and we were off. We snuck down to the West Village to stop in at Employees Only, slipped eastward to PDT, and finally spiraled around the shuttered, reeking fish markets of Chinatown until we swirled into this place called Apotheke.

I'm not sure if it was the green mist permeating my blood–brain barrier or the peculiar sense of interior design by some eccentric proprietor, but from what I can recall, all the bartenders wore lab coats and mixed drinks in huge laboratory beakers. And every now and then, some random Austrian guy called The Mixologist stood on top of the bar and made flaming absinthe shots while the sound system blared the Steve Miller Band's "Abracadabra."

Somewhere along the way, I ended up with an arm around the waist of this done-up brunette, and Toby found himself sharing a stool with a tipsy redheaded actress who wore Ugg boots, a scarf, and eye shadow with glitter (aka the herpes of makeup). I'm not sure how the whole thing got rolling, but after a little bit, I realized it was becoming increasingly awkward that I had no idea what the brunette's name was. Completely forgotten.

Toby was riffing on absinthe metaphors: if absinthe were sneakers, it would be a pair of laceless Chuck Taylors designed by John Varvatos for Converse; if it were facial hair, it would be the soul patch; if absinthe were a finish on kitchen and bath fixtures, it would be brushed nickel. A litany of similes that he most likely plagiarized from Konigsberg's *New York Times* piece on absinthe.

I was getting antsy, though, thinking he had completely missed my signal until he leaned in to my brunette, and shouted above the din that he apologized, he was awful with names, and what was hers again.

And in that moment, the fog cleared, and I remembered.

"Her name's Heavenly," I told Toby.

"Hilary," she corrected me.

That plucked at a strand of my brain stem. "Really? I thought you said Heavenly. So fucking loud in here," I yelled above the crowd of people singing along with the flaming Austrian about *calling names* and *burnin' flames*.

"S'ok. I kinda like being called Heavenly," she smiled.

Of course you do, I thought, as I pushed down a surge of what I preferred to diagnose as Oedipal paranoia rather than excitement—about her having the same name as Mumsie.

"What's your name again?" she said to Toby.

"Burroughs." Toby drained the rest of his absinthe.

"That's a funny name," giggled the actress, as she rubbed the tip of her nose against his shoulder. A little glitter held on to his cotton-blend collar.

I stepped in with the save. "Tell him about it. He's been getting shit for it for years." I grinned.

If there's one thing I learned at Anomaly, it's never refute an accusation. It seems defensive. Once you're on defense you're done. No, the trick with an accusation is to say yes. Wrap your arms tight around it and run with it. The accuser's already partial to her story, and she'll gladly go along for the ride.

So we riffed on what's in a name, I danced along with a vague sense of déjà vu, and somehow Toby ended up pushing me to tell the story about the name a buddy of mine got when we were smoke jumping in Oregon. I hemmed and hawed, playing up the reticence. On cue the girls insisted, we ordered another round, toasted the holy trinity of wormwood, anise, and fennel, and I collected my thoughts in order to tell the story about a job I had never had in a place I had never been.

I started out with how this friend of mine, Tyler, and I were white, affluent kids who grew up in that megalopolis otherwise known as the Eastern seaboard, privileged, entitled, and experts of ennui.

And then we went to college and discovered how much we couldn't stand our 'old' unenlightened selves or where we came from. We needed something different. Something authentic. Something as far away from the East Coast and all its facades of bullshit as possible.

"Either of you ever been to Redmond?" I asked.

The girls shook their heads no. Redmond it was then.

"Well, there's this town, Redmond. Forest Service has a base there where they train smoke jumpers. They got a handful of them all over, California, Washington, Montana, Idaho, but the one in Redmond was the first, the best, and the most intense. And somehow Tyler and I talked our way into the program. I think it had more to do with dwindling applicants and the forecasted drought than our silver tongues. Doesn't really matter, and the fact is, we made it in, and somehow survived the four weeks of training—"

"Wait, what's a smoke jumper?" Hilary asked.

"It's a firefighter that parachutes into hard-to-reach areas, the wildlands, to combat forest fires."

"They drop you in? Like, off a plane? Into a fire?"

"Well, not into the fire. Near the fire," I corrected her.

"With a fire truck?"

You're so pretty. "Nah, they just drop in tools, like shovels, chainsaws, Pulaskis, portable pumps, food, small oxygen tanks, a mask, and water so we can be self-sufficient for a couple days."

Toby raised his eyebrow and his glass just ever so much. A subtle toast. It was the Pulaskis. I knew that would get him. Don't know where I knew that one from, maybe some Norman Maclean short story. Just reached deep into my bag of goodies and out it came. A combination of an axe and a mattock.

Now that I had all my tools, I was ready to go. "The trick is to drop us in when the fire is still small, just a few acres or so. You dig ditches, create a burn barrier, whatever you have to do."

"And you'd never done this before?" Glitter Girl prodded.

"Funny thing was, our inexperience actually helped." Like I said never refute an accusation. Take the ball, slide left, and run with it. "Most of the guys came from firefighting crews. They were experts at working in a unit. Group consciousness and all that. Thing is, smoke jumping just isn't crew based. If you think with a crew mentality, you're dead. You have to break free and think independently. That's what we found out on our first fire, and it's the only reason I can tell this story tonight."

I lost myself in thought for effect, while trying to remember everything I could about the Mann Gulch fire wiki article I had stumbled upon the other night (see Wikipedia contributors, "Mann Gulch fire," Wikipedia, The Free Encyclopedia, https://en.wikipedia.org/w/index.php?title=Mann_Gulch_fire&oldid=676971592 [accessed December 2, 2010]). "It started on the south side of this place called Mann Gulch, which is in the Gates of the Mountains Wilderness. Some asshole hippie campers got lost on their way to Burning Man, set up camp, got high, and started jumping the campfire in some idiotic, made-up ritual. Until one of the uncoordinated shroomers didn't clear it and kicked fire logs every which way. And that was that. Forest fire.

"We jumped in on the north side of the gulch. Our gear was dropped, we collected it. Being the newbies, I had to hump the extra Pulaskis, and Tyler had to hump the extra O_2 tanks. Once that was done, we were all moving 'sidehill' toward the river."

Another eyebrow raise from Toby. Sidehill. I was on a roll.

"That way we could fight the fire from behind it. The problem was while we were moving down gulch, the fire jumped from the south side to the north side. It'd blown up and was spreading fast.

"Course we didn't know any of this. There were all these ridges running down the slope, and they obscured our view of the slope. It was only when we humped over a ridge that we saw the fire only a few hundred yards off. And it was coming right at us.

"Well, we all just stood there a moment. Stunned shitless, as the fire literally roared toward us. Weirdest thing in my life, 'cause all I could think about was how it sounded like a waterfall, like the weight of millions of gallons of water flooding toward me. Like Niagara Falls."

I swirled the absinthe around my glass, its clear tendrils trailing behind, and took a slow slip of the licorice elixir, while the irony washed over them.

Hilary wasn't much for paradox and asked, "So what did you do?"

"We ran for it. Fast as we could in every direction. That's how Tyler got separated from us. By the time I realized it, a jetty of flames had already surged alongside us. I yelled and yelled, but couldn't even hear my own screaming above the roar of the fire.

"Don't get me wrong. It wasn't like some dramatic scene from a movie with me shouting down the fire and mourning the loss. The heat burnt off any sense of sentiment, and fear's a high-octane fuel. All of this only lasted maybe eight seconds, and I was hightailing it after the guy in front of me. Six of us, blinded by smoke and stinging sweat, a tsunami of hot roiling behind us, desperate to find a rockslide or whatever, just any place without vegetation to fuel the fire.

"That's when one of the guys came across a crevice. We had no idea where it led, but we were short of breath and terrified of suffocating. In we went. Well, four of us. The two in front had run right by it and disappeared into smoke.

"Luckily it led through one of the ridges, bought us a little breathing room so to speak. We didn't stop though, the fire was still bellowing just over the ridge we came through, and smoke was boiling over. So we kept hauling ass across the gulch, over another ridge, and into a clearing where we had to stop."

"'Cause you were exhausted or because the clearing was safe?" Glitter asked, all big-eyed.

"'Cause we were face to face with a trio of Tec-9s. Intratec TEC-DC9s to be exact, which I know for a fact, because I tend not to forget anything that I read on the side of a loaded gun pointed in my face."

Toby couldn't even raise an eyebrow. At this point he was too into the story, and wondering what the hell gunslingers were doing smack in the middle of a forest fire.

"You're probably wondering what the hell a gang of gunslingers was doing smack in the middle of a forest fire. Well, let me tell you, so were we, until we saw the shit-shack of a barn behind them and the palettes of anti-freeze, crates of phosphorous, vats of iodine, the commercial mixer, and the drying ovens. We had stumbled onto an industrial-sized meth lab!

"A handful of Mexicans, two bikers from California, and the four of us just stood there, staring at each other. Finally, one of the Mexicans turns to a Biker and asks, '*policía?*'"

"Before the Biker guy could answer, I was already spouting off, 'No. *No somos policía. Somos bomberos. No hay ningún policía aquí. No, no se preocupen.*'"

Reading the looks on my audience's faces, I reminded them of my privileged upbringing and let them in on the fact that I got a five on my Spanish Language AP.

"The Bikers confirmed my assertion that we were firefighters, not policemen, but they still weren't sure whether to shoot us or not. That's when I started explaining that shooting us would be overkill because in a few minutes the Diablo was going to be riding over that ridge on hell itself and kill us all if we didn't haul ass.

"In spite of our urgings and the constant smell of smoke, they were pretty resistant to letting us just pass through, and even more stubborn about leaving themselves. That's until one of the Bikers accompanied me for a brisk jaunt up the ridge for a nicer view.

"The conflagration had picked up speed and was surging across the gulch. He took one look, turned to me, and asked if we could get them out.

"See, all they had was their two bikes. But the Mexicans had the guns. The trucks only came for pickups and delivery, i.e. no escape truck. It was set up this way to incentivize production and minimize distraction.

"They had built this dirt road, however. The bikers were trying to map out an escape route. It seemed like our best out, except for the fact that it still ran right through the forest and was lined with the biggest fucking conifers the dealers could twist the road under. It had been built for cover, not convenience. They had been more worried about helicopter and satellite surveillance than speed. If we went that way, it'd be like running 'round the rim of nature's Roman candle."

"So what did you do?" Glitter asked.

"I suggested we light an escape fire. The Plains Indians used to use this technique to escape grass fires. Before the wildfire gets to you, burn a wide swath of land yourself. Once it's burned out, you huddle in the center of your razed piece of ground, and fire flows right around you. Can't burn what's already burnt."

Toby's hand slipped down to Glitter Girl's sparkling ass.

"The bunch of them thought that was the funniest thing they had heard all week. Thought I was joking—starting a fire to escape a fire—until they saw the look on my face. Then went off on how there's no way in hell they were lighting anything on fire. The whole place had been built to keep shit from blowing up, and they'd be fucked if they were going to burn down anything, not with all the ice they had made just sitting there, and certainly not the factory where they do all their cooking, *pendejo*!

"I pointed out it was either going to be us, or the wildfire, the only question was whether we were in the barbeque or not. Far as we were concerned, who 'lit the match' could be our little secret.

"Well, they just blinked at us a few moments. One of my buddies pointed out that the fire would slow down a little at the top of this last ridge, give us a little time, but that we had to move fast.

"Finally, the Biker who'd gone with me to the top of the ridge asked, 'Will it work?'"

I sipped my absinthe, enjoyed the licorice-flavored burn.

"I told him it beat the hell out of me, but it was our only option. A little creative destruction might just save our collective asses.

"That's when another jumper, a dude called Dodge Wags, let slip that escape fires were only really used in grasslands 'cause timber burns too slowly to consume the fuel before the main fire shows up.

"Well, the Mexicans and Bikers all turn toward me, in one collective motion like some comedic relief moment in an action flick, and glare.

"'Yeah,' I said, 'But that's only because no one in a forest fire has ever had a thousand pounds of white phosphorous!' and I pointed to the sealed plastic industrial buckets piled inside the barn.

"Apparently, the Bikers and their partners had evolved beyond their old tried and true methods using Adam's Catalyst as a reducing agent. Probably 'cause the DEA slapped down all these restrictions on the necessary chemicals. Nope, these boys had gone patriotic and implemented the 'Red, White, and Blue Process': red phosphorus, white pseudoephedrine, and blue iodine."

"I thought you said white phosphorous," Glitter Girl interrupted.

Hilary nodded in agreement with her.

"I did. But you can't really go around and buy a ton of red phosphorous without raising some eyebrows. So you use white phosphorous to make red. Just heat it up to about five hundred degrees, and it transmogrifies nicely. What you got to realize is that white phosphorous is not just an incendiary. It's like a weapons-grade-the-military-has-been-using-since-World-War-I incendiary. Reacts with oxygen and once it's ignited, it burns quick and fierce.

"And they fucking knew it. The Biker tossed a glance at their sealed buckets of phosphorous and nodded with a *yeah, that'll work*. And that was that. We all put on protective gloves, grabbed a bucket, and as quickly and as carefully as we could, we started dusting the place with it like we were laying out flour for a three-hundred-yard cookie.

"To light it off, though, we needed to get upwind, 'cause it smokes like a green puppy on a bonfire. Upwind, however, put us right between the factory we were about to blow up, and the wildfire now at the top of the ridge. We were between a molten-lava rock and a hot place. But what else could we do?"

At that, Toby gave Glitter's ass a nice squeeze for comfort.

"Halfway up the ridge we hid behind some random boulders, staring up at the burning ridge, lit a couple Molotov cocktails, tossed them downhill, leaned back, and stared up at the burning ridge.

"It sounded like a million bottle rockets going off at first, and then came the thunder when the ether detonated. No shit, the heat and shockwave from the explosion actually pushed the wildfire back . . . for a moment. It only turned the wildfire on, and as soon as it pulled back, that thing surged down the ridge ready to play.

"Leaning around the boulder we watched this thick blob of smoke roll downwind. In its wake was a circle of scorched earth three hundred yards in diameter. No barn, no machinery, just blackness where there had been white. It was the sweetest, most beautiful oasis any of us had ever seen.

"We hunkered down right in the center of it. Laid down our aluminum and fiberglass fire shelters like blankets, and had a picnic by the light of hell rising up around us and burning the rest of the gulch down.

"I'd say we had jumped in a little after four in the afternoon. We had gathered our scattered cargo by five. Probably wasn't till about quarter to six that we had seen the fire coming. By six thirty we were sitting inside our charcoal circle.

"Apparently, the fire had caught up with our other two guys, the ones who had gone on ahead and missed the crevice, at around six fifteen. At least that's how we judged it. That's when their wristwatches were stopped by the heat."

I took another sip of absinthe. Cupped in my tongue and inhaled tightly, making it bubble. Toby taught me this a while back, called it "smoking" vodka. It burned like orange juice on a canker sore, but the buzz just flew to your head. I let it flutter around a little, while my audience took a breather from my Promethean tale.

Finally, one of the girls, I have no idea which one, but one of them I'm sure, asked about Tyler. I swallowed down the mouthful of licorice liquid and let my buzz settle down on a branch of thought. I had laid the bait, and I had waited, and my moment rose to the surface and bit hard.

"Either of you bought a ski jacket recently?" They didn't know what to do with this seemingly random question, but finally Toby's ornament nodded yes and said something or other about Aspen. Of course.

"A nice one or just some puffer coat?" I already knew the answer, but I figured I'd play a little with the Aspen ski bunny. She assured me it was high end, Spyder and what not. Latest Gore-Tex coating, blah blah. I nodded and finally interrupted, asking if she had noticed a piece of hardware sewn into the lining of a pocket.

She cocked her head at an angle, a beagle with glitter eye shadow.

I didn't wait for an answer. Went right on about how all the newest jackets have an avalanche rescue system sewn into them now. A small transponder that's easily detected by a rescue team in case you happen to get buried under eight feet of snow.

"That's what that is?" the beagle barked. "I just thought it was some, you know, store security tags they staple to clothes so you don't steal them."

"Anyhow," I went on, "we had the exact same device sewn into our fireman's jackets. That's how we found the first two guys. Finding Tyler took us a little more time. We backtracked to where we separated and started walking around in circles until our devices started pinging.

"It was supposed to lead us right to him. But we just couldn't find him. Kept following the pings till we went too far, then retreated, followed the pings. He was supposed to be right where we were, but there was only ash and earth.

"I was so frustrated, I just didn't know what to do, and I finally broke down, sat on my ass, and started bawling. The other guys averted their eyes, kept circling around trying to follow the pings, adjust the detector.

"I finally got a hold of myself. Choked everything down. And it was while I was sitting there on the ground, that I noticed this lump in the earth. Like a bubble in brownie mix. I let out a whoop, whipped out my shovel, and just started digging until I hit fire shelter.

"That's when the ground screamed. Tyler struggled to sit up, dirt pouring off him like a rising zombie in an aluminum cocoon. He and I both unzipped his shelter while he screamed at me from behind his oxygen mask, holding his arm. The wily fucker had buried himself alive with his extra O2 tank! Not a scratch on him, except for the gash I made on his arm shoveling him out.

"We didn't care. We were all so happy he was alive! If we had paid a little more attention, we would have thought to clean the cut. Instead, some dirt got in there while he was clotting up. Stained his flesh."

Toby grinned big at me. He finally realized where I was heading. The girls were shaking their heads in disbelief until I finally told Toby to show 'em. He hung his head, rolled up his right sleeve, and showed them the birthmark on his forearm that looked like a dirt stain.

"You don't get a nickname like Burrows without a good reason."

And that's how I finished off my little tale, with the slightest bow of the head to Toby. Still, it didn't do us any good. Well, at least not me—but Toby was cleaning glitter out of his apartment for weeks after that night. Hilary and I lilted outside together, but then she started holding the side of her head and giggling about how she wasn't used to absinthe. Didn't even like licorice really. Man, had she been drinking the wrong drink.

I guess I could've pushed. Offered to make sure she got home ok and taken her back to her place. Put a hand on her inner thigh in the cab ride as she leaned against me. Felt the texture of her stockings against my palm as she nuzzled through the green mist into my armpit. But the thought of it made me feel more lonely than actually being alone. A dark part of me was weirdly intrigued at what it would have been like shouting "Hilary" in the throes of ecstasy, but under the circumstances I would only be reminded that Mom was gone.

So I hailed her a cab. She stared at me for a moment, waiting for the fog to clear. Then she said thanks for a fantastic evening, fell against my mouth with her lips, and plopped down into the backseat of the cab all in one fluid motion. No number, no date, just red brake lights as the taxi took the next left.

I felt like a sheet of discarded Bubble Wrap that had been all popped out. I've never been to Oregon. Never jumped out of an airplane, that's for sure. And not even once have I considered trying to be a fireman, even when I was little. The closest I've ever gotten was standing with my parents and a number of neighbors in our back alley at four thirty in the morning, watching a house on the other side of our block go up in flames.

Some distant survivor instinct must have kicked in and pointed me north as I strolled up through SoHo in my own cloud of self-loathing. The last thing I remember was staring at Bloomingdale's display window, switching my focus back and forth between my reflection in the glass and the perfect presents under the tree, so immaculately wrapped you couldn't help but be drawn to them even though you knew they were completely empty on the inside.

The next morning I woke up still in my coat, lying on my bed. In spite of the memory lapses, I didn't have much of a hangover, just felt like I was thinking through mud. Getting upright cleared things up. The room had to catch up before I understood I might very possibly still be intoxicated. Somehow, through all that, though, I remembered what had started all this. What I was telling you about originally.

Eve's story. The website. The bulletin board. I shuffled right to the computer.

Wouldn't you know it, for the life of me, I couldn't find it. Not any of it. No Bourg. No oubliettes. No Hoggle. It was gone. Without a trace. Did I dream it? Was I misremembering? Could I just not conjure up the magic phrase for the Google genie that let me in on the Siberian bartender's iPad?

Or had it been dismantled?

The Deputy was thorough, to say the least, but ultimately unsuccessful in his efforts to create order and harmony. His instincts about her were right. It's just his timing was wrong.

"Is it on? Can you see me?" Reidier turns backward in the passenger seat.

"Yes?" a soft, high voice responds.

"Here, let me see it." Reidier reaches toward the camera and takes it. In a jarring blur, the interior of the car sweeps across the frame until the shot comes to rest on Reidier's lap. Past his knee, on the floor mat is the torn plastic cover of a Flip camcorder.

"Yeah, no. It's on." The world spins again, stopping at an unflattering angle of Reidier looking down at it. "This is pretty cool, I got to say. For something you can buy at a drugstore. Check it out, Eve."

The frame blurs again, stopping on the dashboard as Reidier holds it up for Eve to see.

"Not now, Rye," we hear her say in a crisp tone. "Driving."

"Eyes on road," Otto's soft voice sings from the backseat.

The camera swings back, past Ecco, to Otto.

"That's right, Otto; Mommy's got to keep her eyes on the road. But you," interior spins again as Reidier hands the camcorder back to Otto, "have two sets of eyes."

Otto giggles.

"Rye, are you sure that's appropriate for a three-year-old?" Eve asks. She casts a sideways look at him.

"He's practically four. And who cares if he breaks it, I bought it at CVS."

Reidier seems completely genuine in his response and completely oblivious to the fact that he's not addressing Eve's question at all. Or rather he is answering the question he heard, not the question she asked. There seems to be no malice or passive aggressiveness in his tone and demeanor. It is possible that it is a subconscious, almost instinctual response that avoids actual confrontation through confusion. More likely, Reidier is doing what so many of us do with our spouses: assuming an I-know-you-like-the-back-of-my-hand insight that creates a porous enough connection to allow our own sublimated concerns to be poured into our significant other. It is not a willful act. In our need to unite with others, [49] we inevitably cover up parts of them with ourselves. Creative destruction, or at least creative obfuscation.

Nevertheless, this begs the question, how well do any of us know the back of our hands?

What we learn in this moment is that Reidier's consistent misinterpretation of Eve was a dynamic set in motion long ago.

We are deprived of any visual consideration of Eve's response by Otto's toddling cinematography as he spins the camera on himself: "My birthday's in twenty-free days." The camera spins to Ecco, who sits behind Reidier, quietly watching his brother. "When's Ecco's?"

Ecco half huffs, half laughs, and smiles when his brother looks at him.

"The same day as yours, Otto," Reidier says.

"Really?" Otto asks with narcissistic disbelief. The camera shifts back to Reidier.

"Like always."

"Don't do that," Eve snaps.

"What, hon?" Reidier asks with a smile.

"Don't patronize him."

"I wasn't."

"You were. You were correcting him. It's not his fault he doesn't know."

Reidier doesn't say anything for a few moments. He looks at Eve, but she won't make eye contact. She never turns her head, just focuses on the road. Reidier looks back at the boys and smiles.

"You're right. I'm sorry." Reidier turns back in the passenger seat and faces forward.

"Daddy?"

"Yes, Otto?"

---

[49] What Freud called our Eros impulse.

"Do I hafta share my cake?"

Reidier erupts with laughter. "No Otto, we can get two cakes."

Otto lets out a *Yay*. Ecco joins in. Eventually it turns into a repetitive singsongy chant of two cakes, two cakes, two cakes. The camera bounces back and forth from Otto to Ecco with every chant. Ecco smiles and bobs his head in unison with the camera. Presumably he's mirroring his brother's head bobs.

This spat might not go any deeper than the fact that they've been driving for almost two days straight going from Chicago to Providence. Eve's acerbic attitude seems more persistent than travel fatigue, however.

At one point, Otto films his brother as they play in what appears to be a physicalized version of cryptophasia, otherwise known as idioglossia or "twin language."

Ecco stares at his brother.

Otto's arm reaches into the frame from behind the camera. As Otto reaches in, Ecco similarly reaches toward Otto.

Otto flattens out his hand horizontally (like one would play paper in Rock, Paper, Scissors). Ecco flattens his hand out.

It's unclear which of them begins the next movement (even slowing down the footage and flipping through frame by frame). In apparent unison, both hands turn upward, their fingers splay apart, their mirrored hands then drift together camera left and then pull back to their respective owners.

The boys giggle in concert.

Otto turns the camera on himself and smiles. Then he turns it on Ecco, who smiles. Back to Otto. Back to his brother. Back to Otto. He repeats this again and again, adding the labeling narrative, "Otto. Ecco. Otto. Ecco."

Somewhere along the way, much like in the Bugs Bunny–Daffy Duck debate about whether it's duck season or rabbit season, Otto gets turned around and starts labeling his brother as Otto and himself as Ecco. These moments capture the fluidity of play between the boys, and as with Bugs and Daffy, the misdirection of rhythm.

Otto turns the camera on his brother and holds it there.

Ecco faces his brother, pantomiming his own camera.

And then Otto says, "Mi-ya-co. Mi-me." Without taking the camera off his brother, he repeats it, "Mi-ya-co. Mi-me." Turning it back on himself and pointing to the camera, he says, "Little me." Points to himself, "Me me."

Off camera, Ecco's high voice sings, "Mi-ya-co."

That's when Eve screams, *Arrête-toi!* A litany of French rants pour out of her, in a sort of Parisian homage to Ricky Ricardo.

Otto freezes, startled. Reidier quickly reaches back, takes the camera from his son, and turns it off.

Accepted research suggests that cryptophasia manifests most often in twins with immature or disordered language. More recent studies indicate that twin language is more likely to be one of the twins modeling the underdeveloped speech patterns of his co-twin, resulting in the incorrect use of speech sounds and grammar by both twins. While it might sound like a foreign language, it's actually young twins mimicking each other's attempts at language, often incorrectly.

Perhaps Eve was merely testy from the trip. While it seems to be an innocent scene of toddlers at play, reflecting the fascination little kids have with their own image, to the trained psychologist it reveals a much less charming reality.

Ecco's complete lack of self-expression (he rarely says a word during the car video), and his focused mirroring of his brother in their unique type of gestural idioglossia, point to severe developmental issues. Where Otto is quite precocious, Ecco is abnormally simple.

That's not to say he's slow or exhibits any signs of retardation or Down syndrome. There would be several physical cues if this was the case, and none are present.

Most children develop language at their own pace, and of course there is a broad range of normal. Diane Paul-Brown, PhD, director of clinical issues at the American Speech-Language Hearing Association, asserts that certain children develop their language skills faster than others. Furthermore, roughly 15-20 percent of young children have some kind of communication disorder. Boys tend to develop later than girls. To be labeled a "late-talking child" however, a toddler must speak fewer than ten words by twenty months, or fifty words by thirty months. By the end of the second year, a toddler should be able to use two- to three-word sentences. By the third year, a child should be able to follow a multistep instruction, recognize common objects, and understand most of what is said to him. And be able to speak in a way understood by those outside the family.

Nevertheless, it is rare for identical twins to develop their language skills at disproportional rates. Inevitably, the discrepancy can create anxiety and sleepless nights for worried parents. This can be amplified by parents comparing the child's development to that of his older sibling and, only more so, with a direct comparison to an identical twin. As time passes, this apprehension can turn into panic.

These car scenes provide us with our first glimpse into how Reidier and Eve cope, or don't, as the case may be. Reidier focuses on Ecco with the intensity of an explorer scanning the horizon for land. He studies him and how he reacts to different stimuli, as shown in another moment when he plays peekaboo with Ecco.

Reidier hides behind his headrest and then pops out, first with just a boo, then with his name, "Daddy." When Otto starts to answer for his giggling brother, Reidier stops. He points to Otto and asks, "Who's that?" Ecco rolls his eyes. He points to Eve and asks again. Otto jumps the gun and answers. Reidier gently castigates Otto, saying good, but he was asking Ecco. Reidier's eyes shift back from one boy to the other. The game is over, however, and he turns around in his seat and stares out the window. (It was at this point that Otto began his Otto-Ecco game.)

Eve, on the other hand, tries to ignore the discrepancy, and in fact sometimes just ignores Ecco altogether. It's an all too common response for parents of children with disabilities. They can refuse to accept their child because of how it reflects on them. If their child is damaged, then they are by extension. Or sometimes parents deny the child and his impairment because they irrationally feel they are somehow responsible. If they don't repress it, they'll be crushed with guilt. This can be especially true with mothers who fear they might have done something wrong during the pregnancy through diet, or exercise, or lack of exercise, etc. Or parents can create a distance because they're incapable of empathizing. Somewhere in the subconscious, the brain throws up its hands and says, "This child is not like me, I don't understand how he experiences the world at all and cannot relate or help."

It's unclear as to what motivates Eve at this point. The only information apparent is her refusal or inability to connect with Ecco. That being said, for all we know it could have more to do with Eve's feelings about Reidier, the move, or her writing.

Unfortunately, this is not an isolated dynamic, but one that continues to manifest itself again and again, even after their arrival. A few similar instances in particular jump out.

The first moment is picked up by the Department's nanocameras in Otto's room. Eve unpacks a box of clothes and is putting them in a dresser. Otto dashes back and forth around the room, retrieving and placing his toys along the three windowsills of his massive bay window overlooking a lush elm tree.

From down the hall, Reidier cheerily says, "Can you get over the size of this place? Ecco and I got lost twice on the way here."

Reidier appears in the doorway, carrying yet another box. Ecco stands next to him, holding onto his pant leg. He gazes up at the ceiling, which arches upward into a semi-hexagon.

Eve half smiles and directs Reidier to place the box in the corner, and then asks him if he can put the bed frame together. While Reidier screws the pieces together, Ecco meanders over to the high-backed cushioned chair that juts out of a window nook. He sits on it upside down, with his back on the seat and puts his legs vertical to rest them on the seat back. Still staring up at the ceiling, he begins to move his feet in the air.

Otto notices this and giggles. He quickly lies down on the floor and thrusts his legs into the air. As he moves his feet in a similar fashion to Ecco's, it becomes clear that the boys are pretending to walk on the ceiling.

Eve finishes with her box and turns around. She frowns and admonishes Otto to stop that, he's going to get dirty on the floor.

He grudgingly complies and drops his legs to the floor. Ecco also stops, but stays seated upside down, watching.

"Get up, Otto!" Eve insists.

Otto does so and watches his father finish putting together the bed frame.

"Where's Ecco?" Otto asks.

"In his room," Eve says.

"Why not my room?" Otto pushes.

Reidier watches Eve.

"Because like your father said, this place is huge. You each get to have your own room."

Otto finally grasps what his mother is saying and literally puts his foot down, stomping it against the wood floors. "I want Ecco!"

"No, Otto," Eve insists, "You need different rooms."

"No!"

"Otto!"

"No!" Otto stamps his foot again.

Eve moves toward him, "Stop it, Otto!"

Reidier steps between mother and son. "Eve, why don't we figure rooms out later? Two bedrooms, a bedroom and a playroom. It could all work."

Eve turns on Reidier, "Work for you, right? It would work for you fine. You'll be off at work, chatting away with Kai,[50] while I'm the one at home trying to manage everything! Make our little 'transition' go smoothly. You're right it's all fine, everything's fine. Our new life is just fine!"

She storms out before he can respond. Reidier starts to follow her, but stops at the sound of Otto crying. He goes and squats down next to Otto. Puts his arms around him and whispers reassurances in his son's ear. Reidier kisses the top of Otto's head and rests his chin on it.

Reidier and upside-down Ecco make eye contact.

Ecco smiles.

---

[50] Kai remains a mystery. There's no record of any graduate students, lab assistants, or Department employees by that name. Who was this? To Reidier? To Eve? Extramarital?

Reidier smiles. "Mommy just needs time. We'll put two beds in Ecco's room, so you can sleep there some nights."

It would be presumptuous and misleading to offer insights into Eve's inner workings. Still there are some overlapping elements between this scene and the car incident. The boys are at play. Reidier has a light, positive attitude, which seems genuine but emphasized for Eve's benefit. After Eve detonates, Reidier reacts with patience and understanding. Is this due to his compassion and empathy for her emotional state or is it motivated by a guilt he feels for forcing the move?

The second moment captures Reidier's more proactive efforts to brighten up their transition. Unlike their other interactions, this one seems devoid of conflict. The shift of focus to amelioration, however, is no less revealing.

Eve sits on a bench swing on their new veranda, enjoying the uncommonly warm autumn weather, taking a rare break from her frenetic drive to unpack all of their boxes within the first twenty-four hours. The boys play out front as she sips a Nantucket Nectar and reads, of all things, *Skeleton Crew* by Stephen King. (Eve tended toward more highbrow literature, but it's easy to imagine she was in need of a guilty pleasure.)

Reidier, dressed in a sport coat and corduroy pants, strolls up from the street carrying a couple of grocery bags. As he mounts the steps, he holds them up like trophies.

"Whole Foods. We have a Whole Foods within walking distance. Right where Waterman meets Blackstone, or Butler, not sure which it is there."

Eve looks up from her book.

"And, AND, they had your favorite—morel mushrooms!" He lowers the bags. "How's that for a first night feast?"

"Fantastic," Eve responds. "As soon as we find the box with the pans."

Reidier bites his bottom lip and plops down next to her with a grunt. Eve lets out a little laugh at this. Reidier looks to her as if about to say something, but he stops short.

Eve kisses his shoulder and leans against it.

"Is this a deck or a veranda?" Reidier asks.

"A veranda. It has a roof, and goes along the front and side."

"Wow. We have a veranda." They swing back and forth. "So then is this a porch swing or a veranda swing?"

Eve smiles at this. "It's just our swing."

He leans his head against hers. They listen to the creak of the swing for a few moments. Near their thighs, a slight movement catches the viewer's eye. It's their fingers locking and interlocking. "I'll make a deal with you. I'll find the box of pans if you'll bathe the boys?"

Eve doesn't respond. After a few moments, Reidier looks down at her. Eve feels his shift and finally looks up at him and nods.

A tender moment, a needed respite. Reidier's actions seem neither manipulative nor calculating. Likewise Eve's reactions are neither antagonistic nor passive aggressive. While their issues have not been "resolved," this interaction does not reek of repression. It's connection in its most basic form.

Eve and Reidier are not in denial. If anything, this scene on the veranda is a testament to the strength of their relationship. The two are connected on a very deep level. The tension, ironically, is a result of this. Unlike most modern nuclear families, the Reidiers are not shattering apart in a chain reaction. The two never consider Reidier not pursuing his work. They never toss around the idea of Reidier moving out first to see if it's a good fit, while Eve and the boys maintain their lives in Chicago. They never even mention the option of Eve taking a trip to the south of France, just to recharge. The notion of separating never, not for a second, appears on their radar.

It seems that the two of them have internalized the Colonial Effect: their existences are completely and utterly entangled with the other. As a result, tension and conflict spring forth from a lack of options.

What's important to grasp, however, is that neither of them ever consider the relationship itself flawed, part of the problem, or the problem itself. Whatever is going on is not because of how they are or how they feel about each other. Which is why they can, and must, put whatever it is aside for a few moments and sit together on their swing. They love each other.

This lull, though comforting, also makes the last instance more unnerving. What we see on the Department's nanofeeds seems completely mundane.

Eve sits on the porch swing. She's reading again. She comes to a stopping point, dog-ears a page, and puts the book down. She stands up, still holding the book, and walks at a leisurely pace down the front steps of the veranda, disappearing from view behind the hedges.

A few moments later, she strolls back up the steps, carrying her book in one arm and Otto in the other. Her right arm is swung around his lower back, his legs scissored around her right side, bottom resting on her hip, his hands resting on the top of her shoulder, holding the Flip Cam.

She opens the screen door, and the two of them disappear into the house heading upstairs.

If recording storage space had been needed, a section like this would have surely been deleted. I myself even watched it on fast forward and considered it an unnoteworthy moment.

At least from that camera angle.

But watching once again, looking at the footage found on Reidier's hard drive—the footage recorded from the Flip Cam he gave the boys—it's a very different event.

Otto and Ecco sit together on the front lawn. Otto's manning the Flip Cam. He focuses on their feet. Otto's bare left foot presses against Ecco's bare right foot. Their heels push together, both sets of toes curling against the other's. The boys giggle.

Otto swings focus to the ground between their legs. An anthill in the lawn. Otto leans in close, focusing on the ants running in and out of the opening at the top.

A finger points into the frame. From the angle, it's obviously Ecco's. It lightly brushes some of the sandpile away. The ants scurry away and then return to assess the damage and begin repairs. The ants find the finger still there. Some of them crawl up its side.

A laugh emerges offscreen from Ecco. A second from Otto quickly starts up.

The finger is joined by the thumb and pinches an ant between the two nails. Then the finger gently places both parts of the severed ant back on the anthill.

The camera swings back again to a close-up of their toes curling against each other. More giggles.

In a disorienting lurch, the camera angle pulls back into a God shot. It's a baffling few moments until bits of Eve swing across the screen. She has just picked up Otto from the front lawn.

After some quick adjustments and judging from the shot directly into her ear, it appears Eve has secured Otto on her right hip. The frame jostles up and down with each step she takes. Otto turns the camera back on his brother.

It is literally an over-the-shoulder shot, with Eve's shoulder obfuscating the foreground, and the image of Ecco sitting at the ant-hill, staring after them. He doesn't cry out or ignore them. He just sits and watches, bouncing in the frame as it gets smaller with every step Eve takes.

The screen door creaks as Eve opens it. As it slams shut, it pixilates Ecco. Then Eve takes a turn and marches upstairs. The camera angles down on the stairs and finally cuts out.

Reidier eventually walked by the front door and gazed out to his new lawn and went to retrieve Ecco. This matter was never brought up inside the house. Did he and Eve discuss it while out on errands one day? Did they have a fight about it? Or did he simply write it off? Did he proceed with the hope that eventually Eve would snap out of what might be described as some sort of late-term, bipolar postpartum depression?

Maybe.

Maybe Eve meant to go right back out and get him. She couldn't carry both the boys and her book? Or perhaps her back was sore from unpacking, and she could only carry one child at a time?

As easy as it is to jump to judge her, it is premature.

Especially considering the episode she had at the end of their last winter in Chicago.

TITLE CARD: **GALILEE 6:21**

TITLE CARD: **EXPERIMENT 42**

CONTROL ROOM, GOULD ISLAND FACILITY - 2007-09-26 15:49

IS1 O'Brien sits in his respective seat at the ready. Dr. Reidier sits wearing his tweed sport coat, his fingers tapping at the keyboard as he executes a series of final commands into the system.

The distant HIGH WHINE of the Quark Resonator rings out.

Dr. Reidier leans back and mumbles something inaudible to himself. Finished, Dr. Reidier turns to the camera.

> DR. REIDIER
> (serious and confident)
> Biologics have proved a tad more tricky than we, and Director Pierce, had hoped. However, as Robert Pirsig says, experiments are never failures when they fail to achieve predicted results. They're failures when they fail to test the hypothesis in question, when the data they produce don't prove anything one way or another. Something like that.
> (half smiles at camera) For Experiment 42 we are maintaining the same quantum chromodynamic and energy levels from Experiment 41, however we are trying █████ entanglement swap. So, without any further ado . . .

Dr. Reidier nods at IS1 O'Brien and flips up his Plexiglas cover over Contact Button Alpha. His thumb absentmindedly runs back and forth across his lapel pin while . . .

IS1 O'Brien similarly addresses Contact Button Bravo.

> DR. REIDIER (CONT'D)
> Let us, as Samuel Beckett advises,
> "Fail again. Fail better." In three,
> two, one, go.

Dr. Reidier and IS1 O'Brien simultaneously press Contact Buttons Alpha and Bravo.

                                        CUT TO:

MIRROR LAB - SAME TIME

SPLIT SCREEN, on right side CLOSE-UP: empty reinforced-acrylic sphere over target pad.

LEFT SIDE, CLOSE-UP: orange sits inside reinforced-acrylic sphere over the transmission pad.

Orange remains perfectly still.

At 2007-09-26 15:51:00.40955543 a silent FLASH of a flame encircles the orange, like a mandorla, and both disappear leaving behind a heterogeneous pile of (what is later determined to be) various carbon, hydrogen, and oxygen compounds, along with oxidized iron particles.

NOTE: 400 picoseconds prior to flare-up, on the left side prior to transfer, the flame "halo" surrounding the orange tessellates, but not the orange.

RIGHT SIDE, at 15:51:00.40955543, the orange
appears on the target pad. It appears intact,
its spherical structure solid. On the outside
of the acrylic sphere, frost immediately
accumulates.

CONTROL ROOM - 15:51:05

Dr. Reidier turns to IS1 and raises his eyebrows
in a "Check it out" manner.

O'Brien nods encouragingly.

                    DR. REIDIER
          Well that was dramatic.

TARGET ROOM - 15:51:55

Dr. Reidier stands over the prototypical orange.

The HIGH PITCH of the Quark Resonator fades out.

Dr. Reidier cautiously pokes at it.

The rind resists momentarily, but suddenly
capitulates and gives way. A thick, brownish
orange juice pours out, covering the pad and
dripping down into the lower hemisphere of the
acrylic sphere.

GEARS SPINNING NOISE ramps up and down as the
Boson Cannons and Pion Beams retract.

Dr. Reidier smells the tip of his finger (which
has some of the "juice" on it). Then lightly
dabs it on the front tip of his tongue. He
squints his eyes in contemplation.

Dr. Reidier turns to face the control room.

                    DR. REIDIER
          Well, that's funny. Saccharinely
          sweet . . . There's no acetic acid.
                    (pokes at rind)
          Maybe that and the D-limonene
          volatile oil in the rind are what
          flared up on the transmission side.
          Muffled the quark echo?
                         (beat)
          O'Brien? Thoughts?

Over the intercom

                    IS1 O'BRIEN (OS)
          Fail again, fail better, sir.

                    DR. REIDIER
          Nobody likes an insubordinate,
          O'Brien.

Dr. Reidier brushes his fingers against his thumb
rapidly, in an effort to shake off stubborn
residue.

                    DR. REIDIER (CONT'D)
          Cleanup on aisle 6.

VII

A casual stroll through the lunatic asylum shows that faith does not prove anything.

~Friedrich Nietzsche

Shallow men suggest luck or circumstance. Strong men claim cause and effect. Discovery is itself a lie told by the ego.

~Zampanò

Lying to ourselves is more deeply ingrained than lying to others.

~Dostoevsky

Excerpt from University of Chicago, iTunes University episode, Dr. Kerek Reidier lecture from his Physics of Science Fiction course, December 5, 2005

"Judging from a number of your test scores, today's lecture might be of particular interest: how to build a time machine in four easy steps."

A laugh ripples around the lecture hall.

"I see I've struck a nerve. As always, what we'll be addressing is not the immediate feasibility of an idea, but rather its theoretical viability. We all remember Lois Lane's painful date with destiny."

Another murmured laugh.

"While Superman had the ability to fly and be super strong, he could do nothing to prevent the trauma from the rapid deceleration her body experiences when the Man of Steel catches the high velocity Lois in his arms after she falls out of a helicopter. Likewise Superman cannot help us with time travel, even though he tried by flying backward around the earth and reversing its rotation. I'm afraid once again he underestimated the damage of deceleration. And also showed a complete lack of understanding of temporal dimensional analysis."

Pause.

"But let's get on with our four steps in time as laid out in Seife's Appendix."[51]

Reidier flicks on a projector, flicks off the lights, and brings up his first PowerPoint slide. It's a figure of a man standing in his kitchen sticking his arm through a black spherical blob hovering in midair. Across the kitchen, another blob hovers, out of which comes the man's hand holding a coffee mug, which he extends to cavemen percolating coffee over a fire.

"Step one, construct a small, but stable wormhole, making sure to keep both ends at the same point in time. Like say, in your kitchen. Yes, I can anticipate the hands shooting up the darkness beyond my projector, but this is neither the time nor the place to pursue such banal inquiries as to how we would build one of these. For that you'll need to take my course next trimester or just go buy one at your local annelid shop.

"Step two, attach one end of your wormhole to something very heavy. Take the other end and stick it to a spaceship that can achieve

---

[51] Seife, Charles. *Zero: The Biography of a Dangerous Idea*. New York: Penguin, 2000. Print.

speeds of at least 90 percent the speed of light and send it on its way. Due to the time dilation[52] described by Einstein's relativity equations,[53] every spaceship year will be roughly equivalent to 2.3 years on our beloved terra firma. Clocks at each end of the wormhole will tick away at different speeds. For ease's sake, let's say we sent out our expedition in 2000."

Next slide, a diagram of the spaceship flying through space (represented as a flat ribbon) away from Earth. The mouth of the wormhole is still attached to Earth, the tail to the ship like one long celestial string of spit. Off to the right, the ship heads toward the edge of our universe, and the ribbon of space U-turns below, entering hyperspace (picture a horseshoe-esque path).[54]

"Everybody with me?"

Silence in the dark.

"Good. Step three is relatively easy. We wait for a bit. Say forty-six years, Earth-time. Then we find a nice M-Class planet, like Reid-upiter, and bring the wormhole there."

Next slide, same horseshoe-bent space layout, Earth where it was on the top prong but directly beneath, on the bottom prong, the spaceship now rests on Reid-upiter. The wormhole stretches taut between the two, an obvious shortcut through real space.

"Now, by passing through the wormhole, you can go from 2046

---

[52] One of the most famous consequences of relativity: time slows down at high speeds. Time is relative. In grasping this, Einstein, in one fell swoop of chalk, also obliterated absolute speed. A person on the train is correct in stating the station is moving backward, as the person on the platform is equally correct in asserting the train is moving forward. If they both happened to be carrying synchronized stop watches and the train went half the speed of light on a round trip to the restaurant at the edge of the universe, their time keeping would be drastically off in assessing how long the trip took. The respective point of view of each would be that the other is in error.

[53] $\Delta t' = \frac{\Delta t}{\sqrt{1 - v^2/c^2}}$

[54] Adhering to the warping of three-dimensional space as a result of gravitational forces.

on Earth to 2020 on Reid-upiter. Or vice versa. If you were especially forward thinking, you could have started our little mission way in advance with, ironically, step four. You could have sent a message to Reid-upiter long before you began, and arranged for the Reid-upiterians to do the reverse process, beginning in 1974, Reid-upiter time that is."

"By the time you got there in 2020, the other wormhole could bring you back to Earth for the year 1994, i.e. six years before you even left. Using both the wormholes together, you could skip from 2046 Earth time, to 2020 Reid-upiter time, to 1994 Earth time and have jumped back in time more than a half century."

"A bit of advice, sell your dot.com stocks at the beginning of 2000 and then short the hell out of them."

More laughter in the dark.

Often the creation of this report feels like time travel.* Traveling from familiar settings to alien surroundings, only to double back again and find that, even though I've gone in a circle, I've arrived in a completely different place. A shuffle of papers puts me four years back, and a shift of the eye to another pile on my desk drops me in at only a few months ago.

---

* Amen, Mama. Amen.

In those notes, those short stories, those video records, e-mails, journals, and audio recordings, everything is as it was. Safe. Or at least preserved.

Unlike a true time traveler, I can effect no change, create no paradox. I am impotent. A mere detective hunting echoes. The tracks are elusive and deceptive. It's like reading Braille with gloves on.

The source material itself is, not unreliable, but somewhat skewed. It's the nature of the material. As Luc Sante suggested, it's impossible to separate self-consciousness from the confession.[55] It is not simply an act of laying oneself bare, exposed, and completely vulnerable. A confession is still framed in a narrative, situated within context. Additions and omissions are inevitable, even though quite possibly unintentional or unconscious. E-mails are written to someone, journals for a "secret" reader. Lectures are a performance. And videos offer a confined frame of verisimilitude. But is the footage from the nanobugs objective?

The occupants of 454 Angell appear unaware of the NBs' existence. To a certain degree, we can accept their feeds as "true" performances. Still, in this ubiquitous unedited coverage, a distance—an inauthenticity—exists. Educated to be cinematically literate, inundated with the mores of reality TV, I find myself longing for tracking shots, a close-up on a character's eyes, a focus on a subconscious fidget. Without it, I feel like I am being held at arm's length.

Ironically, the constant coverage and terabytes of video records of the Reidier home obfuscate rather than illuminate. It's like that old story where the cartographer of the Empire set out to draw the most comprehensive map of the kingdom: he pays so much attention to detail that it ends up exactly covering the territory. As Baudrillard says,

---

[55] Luc Sante in his article "Sontag: The Precocious Years" for *The New York Times*, February 1, 2009, in discussing the journals and notebooks of Susan Sontag, posits how diarists either write with the hope of publishing or the fear of being published. Both however preclude innocence in journal-keeping. There is no true voyeuristic insight for the reader in these confessionary works, simply a fiction in which both the writer and reader are complicit.

"The territory no longer precedes the map, nor survives it. Henceforth, it is the map that precedes the territory . . . it is the map that engenders the territory."[56] As time passes, it is the territory, the original subject, that deteriorates to shreds, slowly rotting, but the map persists. Explorers of the now can do little more than wander around "the desert of the real."

I am not sifting through the remains of the Reidiers, but the allegory of them. The cartographer's mad project has digitized their essence, performing a sort of alchemy that reduces their lives to two dimensions. Baudrillard's insights have an uncanny resonance in this world where "the real is produced from miniaturized units, from matrices, memory banks, and command models—and with these it can be reproduced an indefinite number of times. It no longer has to be rational . . ."[57]

So the reality of the Reidiers will be reduced and reconstituted out of the record of the Reidiers—something new, mined out of both the self-aware performance of video blogs and writing and the nonstop feeds from microscopic nanocorders.

In other words, something hyperreal in a space with no atmosphere.

I only discovered the record of Eve's episode in Chicago after weeks into watching them settle into Providence. It wasn't the NBs picking up some kitchen conversation or some pillow talk. No. Despite their saturation of surveillance, the Department still missed this somehow.

It was footage, once again, recorded by Reidier's motion-detecting webcam.

---

[56] Jean Baudrillard's "Simulacra and Simulations" in *Jean Baudrillard, Selected Writings*, ed. Mark Poster (Stanford; Stanford University Press, 1988), p.166.
[57] *Ibid.*

Reidier sits at his desk chair working on his computer, facing the camera. His eyes zigzag, tracking movement across the screen as he clicks away with his mouse. It's an unnerving viewing experience, watching the outside world from inside the computer, as blind to what's on the screen as we are to the color of our own eyes.

Reidier finally leans back and stares at the computer. Presumably he found what he was looking for. His eyes remain fixed on one point on the screen, i.e. he's not reading or searching.

After several minutes, he reaches forward and makes a decisive click. He rests back in his chair and watches a video that we can only hear.

The light sounds of someone shifting papers around. Slow. Sporadic.

An occasional patting sound.

At a distance, muffled by walls and floors, a door opens, footsteps, door closes. Stamping of feet.

"Allô?" Eve's dampened voice. *"Allô . . ."*

Muted sounds of activity upstairs. The closer light sounds of paper shifting have stopped.

"I am back. And famished. Where is everybody?" Eve singsongs.

More footfalls and dimmed shuffling sounds. A creak as a door opens.

In a much clearer, unobstructed voice Eve announces, "I have found you. I know you're down here. The light led me, *oui.*"

Crisp, bare clunks increase in volume, like someone pattering down old stairs into an open basement.

"Aha! Z'ere you are! *Mon petit.*"

A baby giggles. Rapid kissing sounds.

"Où est ton père?"[58] In the bathroom? Hm? Rye?" she calls lightly.

At a distance, a door opens, footsteps, door closes.

Murmuring.

"Allô . . ." Eve yells.

"Eve?" Reidier's dampened voice rings out.

"Oui?"

At this point, Reidier, sitting at his desk, watching this video, shifts positions. He was leaning back, in a somewhat slouched position, but here he changes his posture. He leans hard on his left elbow while pressing down on the right armrest with his right arm, in order to push himself in the opposite direction and extend his torso over the left side of the chair. Simultaneously, his right leg rises up, and he places his right foot on the edge of the chair. Finally, he brings up his right arm and drapes the crook of his elbow over his right knee. It's a disheveled fetal position.

His face remains expressionless.

Back in the soundscape, more muffled footsteps.

"Down in my office?" Reidier calls.

"Oui. Avec Otto!" she responds, with a tense tone.

"What did you say?"

A door creaks open.

"Rye, why did you—"

Three footfalls on the stairs.

Silence.

A piercing scream distorts the recording.

From here on out, everything is a muddled cacophony of sounds. Rushing footsteps. Crying boys. Eve screaming. Reidier distinctly saying "Holy Christ" at one point and "Let's just get a hold of ourselves" at another. Thunks and thumps of furniture crashing to the floor. More wailing from the boys. Several repeated frantic *"Ce qui*

---

[58] *Where is your father?*

se passe?" [59] Thundering pairs of footsteps up the stairs. Door slams. More distant rapid pairs of footsteps. More distant door slams. Muffled cries in the distance.

Silence.

The unseen video clip ends. Reidier still sits in his desk chair. He then leans forward, clicks with the computer mouse, and plays it all again.

Reidier watches it eleven times. He never reacts physically, never emotes. The only evidence of some sort of tumult is in how he keeps replaying it. However, if one were to mute the sequence, it would appear the same as if he were studying the various iterations of an experiment.

The actual footage that Reidier watched was never uncovered or recovered. The closest I got to it was through Bertram Malle's secondhand account.

Excerpted from interview with Dr. Bertram Malle, Professor of Neuroscience and Psychology at Brown University, April 18, 2009

"To make an appointment with me, most folks just call my assistant. But not Kerek. He has the State Department classify it as an act of National Security." Bertram smiles through his fuzzy beard. "He never did like conventional methods."

He laughs.

---

[59] *What is happening?*

"I suppose if he did," I say, "he never would have pursued his work."
Nodding. "True. True. It was very much who he was."

I note that Bertram's eyes drop, and he gazes off to the left. He's a relatively trim man. A shock of dark hair that clearly started off the day parted has slowly defected to anarchy. His facial hair is less of a full beard than unregulated stubble. Still, he gives off an air of casual kemptness, an impression of professionalism mitigated by his soothing smile. He appears to be present and focused on what's at hand.

"He didn't even call first. It'd been weeks after the move. I'm sure there had probably been some sort of announcement, some article in the *Brown Herald*, mass e-mail." Bertram shrugs. "But I totally missed his arrival."

"I didn't even know Eve was his wife. Just this new visiting Comp Lit professor who had gotten lost in the shuffle and somehow placed across the hall from my office."

"Had you two interacted?"

A wave of his hand. "Simple pleasantries. Introductions of who we were and what we did. Hellos in the hallways. I recall bringing her an ice tea from Starbucks. But nothing beyond that, nothing below the surface. All I really knew was she was a striking woman who read a lot. I had no idea she was Kerek's wife, until he showed up at my office one night."

Bertram takes another moment, staring down and to the left. "I hadn't seen him since college. I'd receive the occasional letter from him—"

"Letters and e-mails?"

"Always a letter. Handwritten and out of the blue. A note of congratulations, like when I received my post here. Or sometimes just a random thought about my work." He laughs, remembering something. "Once I received a note from him after my book *Intentions and Intentionality* came out. It was a three-line message, a question really. It was something along the lines of 'How much does unintentional behavior define identity? If one were to obliterate her accent or her habit of tugging at her earlobe, would she still be herself? Is an alcoholic still an alcoholic stranded on a desert island without a drop of liquor?' Par for the course with Kerek. Thought provoking, supportive, and elusive. Try as I might, I could never find out anything about his work or echo my support and interest."

A hint of melancholy creeps across his face.

"The nature of the places he worked, and the type of material he was working on, didn't really lend itself to public support," I offer.

Bertram harrumphs. "I realize that now. DARPA has been an education in discretion to say the least. Both imposing and annihilating.[60] At the time, though, I was reading intention into his absence, interpreting his behavior as a choice to keep me at arm's length, never realizing that I was actually being kept closer than most. At least not until he showed up that first evening."

Bertram gestures to his office door. "It was ajar. I was just packing up my bag, and he slipped in, closed the door, and said 'Hello, Bert.'"

"How mundane."

"Exactly, its normalcy is what was so jarring about it. But there I was, hugging him before I even realized my own sense of shock. Kerek Reidier in my office. Over a decade since college, it felt like we picked up just where we left off. Him launching into how, while my work on the explanation of behavior was valid, it begged the question of how explaining behavior was a behavioral reaction in and of itself."

"So much for the pleasantries."

---

[60] Bertram was most likely referencing the unorthodox practice of opening up his notes on Eve to me. It's an understandable and forgivable reaction for any psychologist in spite of the Department's insistence on National Security and the threat of a court order compelling his cooperation under the Patriot Act.

Bertram lets out a laugh, shaking his head. "Those were his pleasantries. But I had him in person. I at least had the opportunity to outflank his mercurial instincts."

"So you forced him to catch you up?"

"Exactly. Made him sit there, in your seat, in his tweed jacket, his laptop bag resting vertically on his knees, and catch me up. At least the basics, his time at CSG, University of Chicago. His transfer here. His new hush-hush work. His wife and kids! I asked for pictures, but he balked. That's when he let me know I had already met Eve. She had kept her maiden name, Tassat, and there had been no way for me to guess. Somehow though, I felt a little betrayed. For weeks, I had been casually conversing with this woman, never knowing who she was. Never knowing Kerek was in town, at the University, on campus."

"I can understand feeling deceived."

"Duped is how I would have put it. But honestly, it was a narcissistic knee-jerk response. I realized that as Kerek and I sat with the silence of his confession hanging between us. And that's when I noticed that he was still holding his laptop bag propped up on his knees, his fingers tapping unconsciously on the zipper.

"When he finally made eye contact with me, I smiled and asked if this was more than a social call. He just nodded and said, 'I need your help, Bert.' So then he unzipped his bag, pulled out his laptop, and set it up on his desk. He babbled a little about his history with Eve. How he wasn't sure if she was ever happy in Chicago. Her writing was going well, but with the kids, and his own work, and the strains of both of them trying to make work work and family work, and how the newest move seemed more like an assault than a progression, and all of this with twins, well, he just didn't know how to read her behavior and how to help."

Bertram went on to describe a video that Reidier showed him. From the sound of it, it appears to be the missing footage that we could only listen to.

By his account, it starts in Reidier's home office in the basement. No one sits at the desk. In the background, though, on a large work-table covered with high-tech equipment, sits a three-year-old Otto. The child seems, to Bertram, to be in a pleasant state. The boy picks up and puts down the odd item. He places his hands on a stack of paper that slides out from under him. A quizzical look comes across the child's face. He places his hands on the slightly shorter stack of paper and does this again.

He smiles. And repeats a few more times. Then Otto claps his hands against his thighs with an excited patting.

He stops abruptly, startled by the distant sound of a door opening in the main house. It's Eve. We hear her announce she's home. When no one responds, Eve thumps about upstairs, hunting around until finally noticing the light coming up from Reidier's office. She clumps down the stairs and discovers Otto. Delighted, she scoops the boy up.

Otto giggles as Eve attacks him with a barrage of kisses.

Finally, she stops, holding Otto against her side, resting him on her hip. She gazes around the basement.

"*Où est ton père?* In the bathroom? Hm? Rye?" she takes a step off in one direction.

Then she freezes, in almost exactly the same way that Otto had, at the sound of a door opening on the main floor. She tracks the footsteps, the door closing, the murmuring.

Eve yells out hello.

"Eve?" Reidier asks back, yelling down.

Eve responds yes.

Then there's a slight pause.

Reidier yells out again to pin down her location and finally gets that she's down in his office, with Otto.

Her tone seemed to have been filled with restrained anger and annoyance as she came to realize their son had been left downstairs, unattended.

While it was clear on the tape, it could have been smoothed over by the interference of walls and furniture. This is bolstered by Reidier's reaction, a simple and confused, "What did you say?"

Eve bounces up and down as if to soothe Otto, who seems completely at ease and in need of soothing.

A flurry of footsteps above lead to the creak of the door opening and the footfalls of Reidier tromping down the first few steps.

Unable to restrain her presumptions and anger, Eve starts in with a fiercer tone, "Rye, why did you—"

She stops midsentence. Completely speechless as she stares up at Reidier.

Due to the camera angle, the only part of him that was in view was his lower half, Ecco's feet dangling by his waist.

They're all frozen in place. It almost seems as if the tape had paused, according to Bertram.

That's when Eve let out a piercing scream.

She backs away, dropping Otto to the floor. He starts crying, which, along with Eve's scream, triggers Ecco's crying.

Reidier rushes down the rest of the stairs, yelling "Holy Christ!"

Eve can't stop screaming and covering her mouth yelling *what's happening, what's happening* again and again in French.

Reidier crouches down with a crying Ecco in his arms to comfort a crying Otto.

Eve keeps yelling and backs offscreen knocking over various objects. Every bang and thump amps up the boys' hysteria.

Reidier unsuccessfully tries to calm things down, insisting that they all need to get a hold of themselves.

An inconsolable Eve rushes past him and up the stairs, slamming the door behind her.

Reidier stands up, watching her go.

He's clearly in a panicked state himself. He takes a step with Ecco before stopping himself, turning back, and scooping up Otto.

Reidier carries the boys up the stairs and out of sight.

Another door slams, and cries bounce around in the distance, and then the tape stops.

"That's a pretty detailed memory," I point out (even considering I helped him recall with prompts from my transcripts).

Bertram nodded. "It's not something you easily forget. And we must have watched it at least a dozen times. Reidier was adamant that I study it, consider every nuance. In a weird way it felt like it was my own personal reality-television show made for an audience of one."

I could relate to that feeling. Already I have been alone for months Psynaring in the depths of an abyss of primary sources, the size of it all constantly threatening to drown me.*

---

* It's still jarring when she does this. Inserts her experience of the report into the report. I'm betting this was just her process. The way she got through the first draft, always planning to go back later and clean out these artifacts of her. Sterilize the whole damn thing.

I wonder at what point she realized this might be the only draft.

"Kerek wouldn't go into any details," Bertram went on. "You know, other than showing me the film. He just wanted me to help, both Eve and the kids. Kept insisting that any insight he provided would bias me with his perspective. I suppose he thought the tape, at least, was an objective record. He was an old friend in distress. I didn't push. It was all a little overwhelming. I guess the proper word for it would be 'stunning.' Kerek's appearance, my new office neighbor turning out to be his wife, the footage, and then Pierce."

-----Original Message-----
From: Donald Pierce [mailto:donald.pierce@darpa.mil]
Sent: Friday, January 26, 2007 9:58 a.m.
To: larry.woodbury@darpa.mil
Subject: Doctor Patient Privilege

Larry,

Had coffee with Bertram Malle. Per our discussion on Tuesday, I went up to RI to ensure Reidier had everything he needed for his lab and to meet with Rear Adm Wisecup about the ██ ██ on USS █████████.

Malle seems malleable enough. He was certainly surprised enough. Your suggestion to not make an introductory phone call was spot on.

I stressed to him the importance of Reidier's work, and subsequently the importance of his work with Eve. I assured Malle that in no way did we want to violate doctor-patient privilege, but that in accordance with Title II of the USA Patriot Act, specifically the "sneak and peek" provision, we were entitled to access in uncovering any patterns that were important to national security. I further emphasized that Eve's rights were limited as she wasn't a US citizen, but that we of course want her to receive the best treatment.

He agreed to help and seemed to accept that he could never publish anything about this and that his notes, with regard to the Reidiers, were classified documents.

Please confer with legal and have them put together an appropriate summary to forward to Malle.

-DP

Bertram was unfamiliar with the Department and its techniques. Pierce pushed his advantage and manipulated Bertram's concern for Reidier, as well as his genuine impulse to be a good friend. It's not that Pierce lied, just equivocated. In spite of Pierce's undisclosed agenda, Bertram's support of and insight into the Reidier family were both helpful to and ultimately healthy for them.

Nevertheless, considering Pierce's earlier e-mail to Woodbury, it's telling that Pierce never brings up Malle's neurological expertise. He never mentions how Malle's work in cybernetic interfacing could help Reidier with his mysterious Stage 4.

Pierce's behavior with Bertram is no different than Reidier's. Both men surprise Bertram with their initial meetings. Both acknowledge his professional success and appeal to him for help. And both withhold crucial information. The common thread seems to be Reidier's work.

In the meantime Bertram is left, like me, to sift through the gaps and mine the void. All we can do is backtrack through time and try to figure out just what happened.

Why did Eve break down like that? As it appears, anger would have been a much more comprehensible response to Reidier shirking his parental babysitting duties.

Why not fill in the blanks a little for Bertram? Reidier only shows Bertram this loop of time. Reidier was intelligent enough to realize that providing some sort of time line, some context, would help immensely.

Why did Reidier delete the footage from his hard drive? Although it was a record of a personal, not professional, exchange, it was anomalistic for Reidier to excise it. There is not a single other instance where this occurs (at least as far as the records show). Something significant motivated this decision.

Was this act his own rudimentary attempt to erase the past or was it something more?

TITLE CARD: **GALILEE 6:21**

TITLE CARD: **EXPERIMENT 47**

CONTROL ROOM, GOULD ISLAND FACILITY - 2007-10-26 12:34

Dr. Reidier, sitting at console, tweed sport coat on chair behind him. He goes back and forth reading/mumbling notes from a spiral notebook and then typing into the console computer.

IS1 O'Brien enters from transmission room.

> IS1 O'BRIEN
> All set.

> DR. REIDIER
> (nodding)
> Almost . . . and . . . done.

Dr. Reidier finishes at the computer. From off, the HIGH PITCH of the Quark Resonator WHINES.

> DR. REIDIER (CONT'D)
> Ok.

IS1 O'Brien takes his seat. Dr. Reidier addresses the camera.

> DR. REIDIER (CONT'D)
> Take Umpteen with the ever-elusive, Citric Devil. All calibrations have been uploaded and recorded.
> (makes contemplative raspberry noise
> with lips)
> Quantum chromodynamics are in the █████
> █████████ range, and we are piping in
> █████████ electron volts from
> the ████████ ██████████ Ok. Here we go.

                         (beat)
     Again.

Dr. Reidier double taps his lapel pin, flips up
his Plexiglas cover over Contact Button Alpha.
IS1 O'Brien does the same at Contact Button
Bravo.

                    DR. REIDIER (CONT'D)
          In three, two, one, go.

Dr. Reidier and IS1 O'Brien simultaneously press
Contact Buttons Alpha and Bravo.

                                        CUT TO:

MIRROR LAB - SAME TIME

SPLIT SCREEN, RIGHT SIDE, CLOSE-UP: an empty
reinforced-acrylic sphere over target pad.

LEFT SIDE, CLOSE-UP: orange sits inside
reinforced-acrylic sphere over the transmission
pad.

Orange remains perfectly still.

At 2007-10-26 12:35:22.00300454 a quiet THRUM
coincides with the inside of the transmission
acrylic sphere being suddenly filled with a
heterogeneous dust [atoms and molecules ranging
from Mg to Sr]

NOTE: at 200 picoseconds prior to transmission,
on the left side prior to transfer, the orange
tessellates.

RIGHT SIDE, at 12:35:22.00300454, the orange
appears on the target pad. Intact. On the
outside of the acrylic sphere, frost immediately
accumulates.

CONTROL ROOM - 12:35:30

Dr. Reidier and IS1 O'Brien exchange a look.

> DR. REIDIER
> (sighs)
> All right. Promising, but we've
> been fooled before. Rock, paper,
> scissors?
> (off IS1's look. Eye roll)
> Ok. I'll go. Like I always do.

TARGET ROOM - 12:36:28

Dr. Reidier pokes the orange. The HIGH-PITCH of
the Quark Resonator fades out.

> DR. REIDIER
> Feels solid enough.

Dr. Reidier pokes it again, harder.

GEARS SPINNING NOISE ramps up and down as the
Boson Cannons and Pion Beams retract.

> DR. REIDIER (CONT'D)
> Good resistance.

Dr. Reidier picks it up and squeezes it.

> DR. REIDIER (CONT'D)
> Firm. With a juicy push back. Let's
> check inside.

Dr. Reidier peels the orange.

> DR. REIDIER (CONT'D)
> (as he peels)
> Looking promising, pith,
> segmentation, and everything.

Dr. Reidier finishes peeling and holds up to
O'Brien what, for all intents and purposes,
resembles a "normal," peeled orange.

> DR. REIDIER (CONT'D)
> Not bad . . .

Dr. Reidier separates the orange into two
halves. He sniffs one half.

> DR. REIDIER (CONT'D)
> Aroma seemingly . . . well, slight.
> But then I guess it's always like
> that. Sort of. Smell's never been my
> thing . . .
> > (shrugs)
> Taste test.

Dr. Reidier tears off and pops an orange section
into his mouth. He masticates it around his
mouth with the concentration and consideration
of a food critic.

Dr. Reidier swallows and tilts his head slightly
to the side.

> DR. REIDIER (CONT'D)
> I dunno. Texture is right, but it
> tastes . . . strange. Maybe you
> should try it.

Dr. Reidier heads toward control room.

CONTROL ROOM - 12:38:55

At the console, IS1 O'Brien chews his orange
slice. He swallows.

> IS1 O'BRIEN
> Yeah, I see what you mean. But for

all we know, it could've been a bad
orange. Not ripe yet maybe . . .

Dr. Reidier, who stands next to him, nods.

                    DR. REIDIER
          That's not a bad idea. Ok, so for
          #48 we'll cut an orange in half.
          Keep half in here with us as the
          control group. Teleport the other
          half. And then I'll run a blind
          taste test on you. Sound good?
              (Before O'Brien can protest,
              shouts off)
          Another orange. We need another one!

INT. MIRROR LAB - CONTINUOUS

The circling indicator lights surrounding the
Entanglement Channel orbit to a standstill and
flash green.

VIII

*The Spirit of the Lord caught away Philip . . . But Philip was
found at Azotus.*

~Acts 8:39-40

*"Can you conceive a process by which you, an organic being,
are in some way dissolved into the cosmos and then by a subtle
reversal of the conditions, reassembled once more . . . How can
such a thing be done . . . save by loosening of the molecules, their
conveyance upon an etheric wave, and their reassembling, upon
exactly its own place, drawn together by some irresistible law?"*

~Sir Arthur Conan Doyle, "The Disintegration Machine"

*Mostly in this book, I shall specialize upon indications that there
exists a transportory force that I shall call Teleportation.*

~Charles Fort, *Lo!*

The key to answering any questions about Reidier lies in his work. It
is work, specifically his accomplishments, that not only defines him,
but renders him exceptional.

The idea of matter winking out of existence in one place only to wink back into it in another has been around almost as long as we have. Ghosts and spirits have haunted civilization since its history began.

The phenomenon has been called by several names over the ages. *Apport* was the paranormal transference of an object from one place to another or the mysterious appearance of some object from an unknown source. *Bilocation* was another popular mystical occurrence that allowed someone to be in two places at once. Numerous Christian saints were adept at this, according to David Darling.[61]

Various cases of teleportation can be found throughout the Bible. One of the most popular tales of this is in the Book of John (6:16-21). The disciples are caught in a storm roughly three to five miles out at sea when they see Jesus walking on the water toward them. The moment Jesus steps onto the boat, they immediately find themselves and their ship on the shore. Another incident is described in Acts (8:38-40). Philip, the apostle, rides with a eunuch on the eunuch's chariot. Arriving at a small body of water, the eunuch asks Philip to baptize him. Philip does so, but when the two come out of the water, the Lord snatches Philip away. The eunuch sees him no more, and Philip finds himself in Azotus.

One of the most famous accounts of teleportation in history is that of Gil Pérez. As described by Martin K. Ettington in *God Like Powers & Abilities*, Pérez was a Spanish soldier in the Filipino Guardia Civil. While on sentry duty at the Governor's Palace in the Philippines, Pérez suddenly appeared in the Plaza Mayor of Mexico City on October 24, 1593. While he was aware he was no longer in Manila,

---

[61] Author of several narrative science books, including *Teleportation: The Impossible Leap*. See www.daviddarling.info. Also see Wikipedia contributors, "Apport (paranormal)," Wikipedia, The Free Encyclopedia, https://en.wikipedia.org/wiki/Apport_%28paranormal%29 (accessed March 8, 2009).

he refused to believe he was now in Mexico City, asserting that he had received his orders on the morning of October 23, and it was therefore impossible to be in Mexico on the 24th. He also went on to explain that the Governor of Manila, Don Goméz Pérez Dasmariñas had been murdered. The Mexican authorities placed Pérez in jail as a possible deserter or minion of Satan. Two months later, the Manila galleon arrived, confirming the assignation of the Governor two months prior, and one of the passengers recognized Pérez and swore he had seen the sentry in the Philippines on October 23.

More recent accounts were recorded by Charles Hoy Fort in the 1930s. Fort traveled all around New York collecting testimonials of bizarre materializations. He came to believe that "teleportation was the master link that underpinned this arcane world of incongruities. It was nature's trickster force . . . Nothing was solid in Fort's view: our present surroundings are a mere quasiexistence, a twilight zone between many different layers of reality and unreality."[62]

Science fiction writers took the concept and ran with it. Orwell concocted "matter banks," A. E. Van Vogt dreamed up three-dimensional faxes, Alfred Bester divined an entire culture built around a type of teleporting he called "jaunting." Marvel Comics even conjured up Nightcrawler, a character who could "bamf" over short distances by slipping through dimensions. The concept was finally brought to mass market in the 1960s by *Star Trek* and its transporter machine.

In March 1993 the Montreal Six[63] published their paper, "Teleporting an Unknown Quantum State via Dual Classical and Einstein-Podolsky-Rosen Channels" in *Physical Review Letters*. In it, this group of computer scientists and physicists concerned themselves with a few very small questions: "How can information be

---

[62] David Darling in his book *Teleportation: The Impossible Leap* (locations 67-75 in the Amazon Kindle version).

[63] Bennett, Brassard, Crépeau, Jozsa, Peres, and Wootters.

handled at the smallest level of nature? How can messages and data be sent using individual subatomic particles?"[64] In layman's terms, what's the smallest bit of information that an object can be divvied up into, and how can we transmit those bits in tiny quantities?

The Montreal Six understood that they had to focus on the quantum scale. Only by working at the quantum level is it possible to make an exact and perfect copy of the original. As Darling points out, it wasn't about streaming atoms or anything physical, like in *Star Trek*, but rather about transferring information without sending it. Accomplishing this required tapping into one of nature's most mysterious phenomenon: entanglement. This is the core of teleportation, as well as the burgeoning fields of quantum cryptography and quantum computation—the very fields Reidier pioneered.

Over the next decade various teams all over the world have delved into the questions and ideas set forth by the Montreal Six. The most they could accomplish was the teleportation of light beams, subatomic particles, and quantum properties of atoms.

None have considered attempting, nor come close to what Reidier was working on. While some scientists in this field did know of Reidier and some of his early papers on quantum cryptography, none were aware of how he was tying the fields together. His working in virtual isolation makes his accomplishments all the more impressive and presumably frustrating.

Still the question remains, how did Reidier do it? Or perhaps more aptly put for our purposes, why him?

---

[64] Darling, locations 148-51.

While Reidier might not have set out to accomplish feats of apport, it is unsurprising that he ended up doing just that, at least from a psychoanalytical point of view. Very early on, Reidier exhibited intellectual gifts. He began speaking at six months old. At the age of three, he corrected, in his head, a calculating error his father made while balancing the family checkbook. According to his second grade teacher at Williamstown Elementary in Massachusetts, Allison Hubbard, she realized he was a unique student one afternoon when she tried to busy her class by having them add up all the numbers from one to one hundred. Within seconds, Reidier raised his hand and provided the correct answer of 5,050.[65]

Neither of Reidier's parents was scientifically oriented. His father, Kaleb, grew up outside of Chicago, with a struggling artist (teacher) for a father and a curator for a mother. Kaleb was a fairly successful theater director, who became popular in avant-garde circles, pioneering multimedia theatrics. He appears to have been an erratic individual whose professional success lay in how he brought out the best in others, primarily as a Socratic guide. He channeled the talents of his colleagues: part diviner, part medium, part harvester. By focusing his attention completely on his cast, designers, and techies, Kaleb got his attention off of himself, which facilitated a freer form of thinking. It was this that helped him conjure and construct a series of theatrical moments that an audience would never consciously tie together, but on a subliminal level connected seamlessly and logically.[66]

---

[65] Later Ms. Hubbard had young Reidier explain his method. He shrugged and said, well, since they were all pairs it wasn't too hard. Prodded a little more he revealed how he saw that by adding 1 and 100 he got 101, and likewise that by adding 2 and 99 he got the same number, and so on. So all he had to do was multiply 50 x 101.

[66] Martin Dent (theater critic) from his article, "The Mise en Scene of a Multimedia Mystic," *The Village Voice*, March 15, 1980.

His approach to childrearing was similarly heuristic. When a three-year-old Kerek asked about elephants, Kaleb simply took him to the Bronx Zoo and let him walk around taking in the creature. He apparently felt that it'd somehow spoil both the elephant and Kerek's understanding of an elephant to tell him anything about it. "I wanted to make sure he had no preconceptions in his head about it. I mean if I had told him it was a big animal . . . well in relation to what? It's only big next to something small. I didn't even tell him that it had a trunk. Preconceptions can too easily become limitations."[67]

His mother, Emily Hahn, third-generation German and Irish, was raised in Cleveland Heights, Ohio. Emily was an actress who, along with her husband, founded the MiST (short for MultImedia Synthetic Theater) Company that briefly collaborated with The Public Theater. Early on in her career, she had done some work as a model and even acted in several national commercials. Once she found Kaleb, however, she let those pursuits drop away. In fact, even in the theater, Emily primarily worked only with her then future husband. The impulse was shared and explained by fellow actor Marc Cohn, "It's something about the way he focuses on you, finds your insecurities and then teaches you to exploit them . . . Obviously we all love the vivacity of working in live theater, but with Kaleb, it wasn't just live, it was alive and guzzling adrenaline. After working with him, other projects somehow felt flat, two-dimensional; like you were performing in black and white. We all felt that way. Emily just refused to settle."[68]

If Kaleb was Kerek's gateway to the world, Emily was his portal into the imagination. Together they would lie on the grass during the

---

[67] Kaleb described this anecdote while discussing the nature of an audience's suspension of disbelief in an interview for the July/August issue of *American Theater Magazine* in 1981.

[68] Martin Dent (theater critic) from his article, "The Mise en Scene of a Multimedia Mystic."

day, anthropomorphizing the insects they counted, making up stories about their lives. They'd stare at wall mirrors and try to catch their reflections getting lazy. At night she'd read fantastical stories aloud to him, or sometimes even make them up. However, as Emily's sister, Abi, noted, "Sure, they were happy as two clams in a pod. Still, you couldn't help but feel, every now and then, it was less about being a mother to Kerek and more about performing the role of the perfect mother for Kaleb."

Reidier's early childhood was bucolic. By the time he was born, his parents had relocated from New York City to Williamstown, Massachusetts. Kaleb had been offered a position to help run the Williamstown Theater Festival. He and Emily also expressed to friends how once they found out they were pregnant, they were suddenly overcome by Norman Rockwell—esque dreams of raising their child climbing old oaks and launching off of rope swings.

These were their public reasons.

Their private rationale was much less idyllic. Earlier that very same year, Kaleb had been diagnosed with cancer. A tumor was growing in his brain and applying bilateral pressure to the motor cortex area that controlled his legs. As the tumor grew, Kaleb became less and less ambulatory, until ultimately he became paraplegic.* Moving to Williamstown provided the couple with a calmer and easier environment to physically navigate, and it put them much closer to Dr. Peter Black, a neurosurgeon at Massachusetts General and aggressive trailblazer in experimental techniques.

---

* How did she do it? Honestly, how could she stay so clinical getting all this down? All of her sporadic interjections, comments about process, volleys sent at the Department for its withholdingness, and not one sentence, not one phrase or even just a goddamn ellipsis about my father?

Guess we all have our defense mechanisms. But I mean, Christ, there's no way she couldn't have been channeling memories of him. It's too close. Too much of an echo; sure it's been drawn out, disfigured and Dopplerized, but the origins still match up. Devoted wife and mother, young boy, and a man being eaten alive from the inside.

In our case, though, it was much quicker. A few months only. No time to consider. No thought to shield. No opportunity for distance, separation, and sanctuary. She was a therapist after all. Death was a part of life after all.

So there I was, sitting by her side, sniffing in the antiseptic hospital smells that have the faintest odor of stale talcum powder and lye. Watching plastic-tinted tubes pump sun-sensitive poison into his circulatory system as his body desiccated before our very eyes. And yet, no mention of any of that. Or the aftermath of absence, in all its therapeutic glory. Separated by several city blocks, she and I sat in different therapists' offices, making sure to cope correctly. No mention of that at all. Not even my accident.

Why Reidier? Why me? Why am I tucked away in this shitty carriage house, with no insulation, unpacking a briefcase full of empty words?

Obviously it's Toby's fault. Drink addled and angling as always, he blurts out the brilliant idea to transform my mom's absence into a loft in SoHo.

I mean, yeah, it's never that simple. I'm sure it somehow plays right into my own issues: control, intimacy, self-worth, honesty, you name it. Still, Toby's a convincing guy, and he always sees the angle. No joke, when we were still adolescent prep-school kids, he saw the market opportunity for selling candy and single pages ripped out of *Playboy* and *Penthouse*. He made a killing and knew how to keep his customers quiet.

Toby has a sixth sense for seeking out someone's insecurities. He always jokes about how he likes to "find someone's weak spot and then jump up and down on it." It's kind of fascinating, almost hypnotic to watch. It's what makes him such a good litigator.

It's only terrifying when you take a step back and think about it. Which I rarely do. I just let my own sixth sense of self-preservation guide me, which might be why I've stayed friends with him so long. I feel safe as long as he's on my team. I don't know, our friendship goes back too far to open up to any type of analytical etymology. He made me laugh and as we grew up and his tongue sharpened, I was just glad as all hell that I wasn't at the business end of it.

His sense for weak spots lets him see the angels. And it's those angles that work magic on bouncers, party promoters, women, you name it. (And before you start going back and double-checking and getting all proud of yourself, yes I'm fully aware of the angels/angles mix-up at the beginning of this paragraph. I thought about changing it, but somehow it seems to work.)

I think this is the part about my personality that draws Toby to me. My yarn-spinning instincts. Knowing how to take the truth, take a moment, and just bend it a little to make a better story. Kindred spirits, him and me, who can go on ad nauseum about the crucial differences between legal and ethical, and justify each other's shortcomings with semantic distractions. We blur the lines for each other, always moving the benchmark when the other one isn't looking.

It's almost a sport, really. How close can we get to shining a light on the God's honest truth, but bend it through a prism of savoir faire?

"So there he is," I tell whichever group of girls have grown bored with the posse of frat boys turned investment bankers chasing them. "About to start his closing argument for his first murder trial. He doesn't even look at his notes. Nope, he just launches in apologizing to the jury. Saying he's sorry that he, the DA, and the system have wasted their time with this murder trial."

Out of the corner of my eye I catch Toby assuming a humble smile as he listens. "He charges ahead with his closing, announcing, 'The fact is, ladies and gentlemen of the jury, there hasn't been a murder at all. How could there have been one, when the man my client is accused of murdering is about to walk through that door right now.'

"And then he points at the door. No shit. And every head in the jury snaps toward the door in expectation.

"As they wait for this miraculous entrance, Toby calmly states, 'And that, ladies and gentlemen, is reasonable doubt.'"

That's about the time that Toby'll chime in, "And he would've gotten off too, except that the judge noticed how in spite of everybody else looking toward the door, my client did not."

Then he'll casually toss something out there like, "But if you want to hear a story, have Danny there pull up the right side of his shirt and show you his poor man's version of the stigmata, and don't let him con you into thinking it's just a birthmark."

But maybe I'm just kidding myself about the whole kindred-spirit bullshit. Maybe it's just he's comfortable with me. He feels safe because we grew up together, and he knows how to mine my weak spots. How to turn my missing mom malaise into a swank loft in SoHo for us to entertain in after hours.

Joke's on him, though, instead of a loft in SoHo, he ended up having to fish me out of a porous carriage house in the ass bottom of Hell's Kitchen.

Maybe he was just trying to do what we do, find the silver lining in an otherwise mediocre and saddening world. He didn't know how to bring my mom back any more than I did.

It's been over four and a half months now. Twenty weeks since Toby and I sailed down the New Jersey Turnpike, across the Delaware, underneath the Baltimore Harbor, and into the District, where I found the key to my mother's secret, hidden away in my father's art asylum.

So far, I've spent thousands of dollars on rent, $54.99 on a space heater, and I don't know how much on legal pads, highlighters, and click pens. I've found some elliptical references to Eve Tassat and her work on the Internet, and even less on Reidier. I've checked out about a dozen books on quantum cryptography and quantum teleportation and can't make sense of any of it. Oh, and I've befriended a Jewish transvestite performer, Vitzi Vannu, who lives in the front building and performs down the street at this drag club called Escuelita.

My institutional pursuits have proved equally unfruitful. No one at the Defense Department will take my phone calls or respond to my e-mails. It might be because I only call them from public telephones or e-mail them with fabricated addresses, assuming numerous different fictional identities from Clint Hoffstater, the Columbia Visiting Professor of Physics, to Aldin Whitehouse, the psychologist and founder of the Southwest Conference on Advancements of Art Therapy (and former colleague of Hilary Kahn). I don't know.

I also struck out on an appeal to Providence. Out of the three local-news stations there, only WJAR still had any footage from the day *The Reidier Test* went awry. A useless and utterly uninformative collection of clips of Dylan Secco getting a closer look at the dead fish washing up on the shore or standing on the Newport Bridge wistfully looking over his shoulder at Gould's Island almost a mile away. Twenty-four-hour news coverage, and all I can get my hands on are shots of benchmarks of how high some of the waves splashed after the explosion.

The funny thing is, it's not until I'm sitting here, writing this, that I realize how obsessed I've become. How pathological is my need to find out. As long as I keep moving, then my dance with doubt won't end in disappointment. Really I'm just trying to fight off the fact that the God's honest truth of what happened is she really did just up and leave, molted and left all of her desiccated, withered, useless, old self behind . . . including me.

With periodic treatments, Kaleb's deterioration was slowed. As a result, Reidier did get to enjoy an almost picture-perfect, Norman Rockwell–esque upbringing for the first seven years of his life. He made snowmen in the winter, built forts in the spring, caught frogs in the summer, and jumped into colorful leaf piles in the fall. Furthermore, being in a university town, Reidier had opportunities to participate in after school science programs that opened his eyes to the world around him.

It was all but perfect, except when his parents left for the occasional trip to Boston. At first, family friends (an actor who needed a respite from New York, or a Williams professor they had befriended) would come stay with young Kerek, while they were at Mass General.

Early on, according to Abi, Reidier's parents decided a cancer ward was no place for a small child. They tried to insulate him from as much of it as possible. The two barely used the C-word, never discussed the gravity of the situation, and referred to the hospital trips as matinees. But they were powerless to stop the encroaching inevitability, like the uninvited guest in Prince Prospero's Palace.*

---

* Once again my mother was referring to Poe's "The Masque of the Red Death."

By the time Kerek was five, Kaleb was walking with a limp; within a year, Kaleb was growing lame; and by Kerek's seventh birthday, Kaleb was all but paralyzed from the waist down.

The family had no choice. Kaleb had to stay close to Mass General for more aggressive treatments and more intensive care. Refusing to "unsettle" their son's childhood with the aromas of a chemo ward, they instead had Emily's father come stay with Kerek. Emily and her father had a strained relationship at best, but he was the only surviving grandparent and the only person they could impose upon indefinitely.

Luckily, the grandfather and the boy got on well together. A retired contractor, Emily's father found the boy's curiosity and boundless innovation a delight. The two spent many afternoons together working on projects, constructing this machine or that model. They made birdhouses, ant farms, and windmills in the first month, but as Kerek's grandfather came to understand the extent of his grandson's gifts, they moved on to motorcycle engines, radios, walkie-talkies, and the like. In fact, together they built a small-scale solar array that the college ultimately used as a model for solarizing its Library Shelving Facility.

At first, Emily and Kaleb would make the five-hour drive back home every weekend, but soon it turned into every other weekend, then just Emily every other weekend, then once a month, until eventually it was every six weeks or so. While Kerek's grandfather had no problem stimulating the child's mind during the day, he was at a complete loss for how to soothe the boy's heart at night. Kerek longed for his parents. Every night he would cry on the phone to his mother, begging her to come home or come get him. Every night she would promise to come home as soon as she could.

If Eve's short story, "In the Gloaming," is to be taken as more fact than fiction, then one of the few consistencies Reidier could count on was his and his mother's bedtime ritual.*

---

* A bedtime ritual with Mom? I guess every kid with a dying father has to have one.

The boy lay down in the bed, cradling the phone against his cheek, as he did every night.

Her soft voice trickled out of the receiver into his ear. "Are you lying down?"

"Yes, Mom," he'd nod.

"What side are you lying on, honey?"

"Right."

"Ok, move just left of the center and I'll lie just right of center."

He'd scoot slightly to the left.

"Is your half under your pillow?" She was referring to the lodestone they had broken in two before the first time she and his father went away.

"Mmmhmm," he'd nod.

"Mine's under my pillow. So now, in our sleep . . ."

"We can find our way," he'd always finish the statement.

"Through the between," she'd assure him.

"My bed is a rectangle."

"Just like . . ."

"A door," he'd yawn.

"As is my bed. Two sides of the same coin. Tangled rectangles bound by lodestones."

"Tangled rectangles."

Then she'd start singing their song, "The 59th Street Bridge Song."

His breathing would slow down as he mumble-hummed, "Ba da, Ba da, Ba da, da . . . Feelin' Groovy."*

---

* If Mom and I had had a song, it would've been "The End" by the Doors.

By the time she made it to the I'm-dappled-and-drowsy-and-ready-to-sleep part, he'd have drifted off. Slipping through the limen. His grandfather would gingerly lift the receiver out of the boy's grasp. He'd murmur soft assurances to his daughter, as he slipped out of the room, careful not to wake his grandson, and ask about how his son-in-law's treatments were going.

The boy would dream of magic doorways that opened onto a mountaintop where his parents set out a picnic, or an afternoon at the beach, or a stroll on the moon. The anxiety of the coming darkness was snuffed out by his mother's embrace in the in-between.

Kaleb died a few weeks before Kerek's eighth birthday. Emily stayed with him until the very end. According to the nurses, when Emily finally found herself alone in the ICU ward, she sat in the room staring at the empty bed for almost an entire day.

Finally, she called Williamstown and told her father she was driving back soon. He expressed his condolences, but let her know how at least Kerek would be glad to have her home. She replied, she didn't know what home was anymore.

It happened on the I-90 just after the exit ramp for Highway 91 at 9:49 p.m. According to the accident report, Emily's car was going seventy-three miles per hour when she lost control of the vehicle. The vehicle swerved, hit the reinforced safety railings, and then flipped over twice. She was dead by the time the paramedics arrived.

No other cars were involved in the accident. No traces of alcohol were found in her system. It is unlikely that she fell asleep at the wheel, as it was still before ten p.m. The police officer who filed the report suggested that a deer could have run in front of her car, causing her to swerve, or maybe another driver could have cut off her car in order to make it to the exit ramp. There's no mention of it having been a possible suicide. It was classified as a single-vehicle accident.

Perhaps it was during this period that the seeds of teleportation were set. A confusing, painful time defined by separation. It began with an innocent longing, a deep homesickness. Maybe one night while he drifted off to sleep in his tangled rectangle he thought, "What if . . . ?"

Other elements were at play obviously, for who among us didn't wonder "what if?" about a great many things when we were children?

But Reidier never let go of his fierce hold on this question. He already had a passion for solving puzzles. A compression of tragedies like his, at such a fragile age, would naturally leave him at a loss for answers. And no one could provide a satisfactory explanation for his most basic question, why?

Perhaps that's how he ended up gravitating to physics: it promised, if not answers, at least access to the secret workings of the universe. Ignorant at arm's length, the world seems mystical or callously random. But with the tools of physics and mathematics, Reidier could get close enough to scratch beneath the surface, convinced that, just underneath the sheen of chaotic mysticism, there was an explanation.

Nevertheless, no matter how many answers one finds, each answer always leads to more questions. Knowledge is a hydra dressed in the veils of enlightenment. Where did we come from? Our parents. Where did they come from? Their parents, and so on and so forth, until we speed past the begets of the Bible and arrive at the theory of evolution. Yes, but how did life come to start in the first place so that it could evolve? Well, out of the primordial soup. So what made the primordial soup? An asteroid, the coalescing and aggregation of stardust. But then what made that? The Big Bang! There we have it. We're done. That's the initial moment, the beginning. But what made that concentrated dense pinhead of everything, and why did it explode?

Answers only lead to more questions.

So while Reidier worked harder and harder, unveiling the secrets of more and more mysteries and becoming more and more successful, he ultimately found himself playing with matryoshka dolls.* Each discovery led him further down the rabbit hole, to smaller and smaller worlds, but none of it made him feel like he was getting closer to the answer of why, nor did it do anything to close the distance between him and his parents that stretched back to his childhood. Unable to mend the gap, incapable of repairing that basic connection and consistency that is so vital at a young age for providing a sense of security, Reidier worked to keep himself just this side of sane.

---

* Yeah, I had to look this one up . . . they're just Russian nesting dolls AKA matryoshka dolls: a set of dolls of decreasing sizes placed inside one another.

A man of science convinces himself to believe in fate, that it all happened for a reason, to give him purpose. He was meant to perform some ultimate, all-important purpose. That's why everything happened the way it did. If he can just understand it all, if he could accomplish this feat of science fiction, it would be something tangible, something of worth. He would conjure an unmitigated paradigm shift that would ensconce him in the annals of history and provide him with both professional and financial security, lasting stability and fame for him and his family. So, he works to convince himself (with as much denial as he can muster) that he's not just chasing the horizon. He's on a teleological journey, not caught in some tautological labyrinth.

He digs deeper, past atoms, past protons and neutrons, past quarks, and finally finds comfort in the words of another great physicist, "There is plenty of room at the bottom,"[69] which he pins up on the bulletin board in his lab, right next to another quip by the same,

---

[69] Richard Feynman, from his lecture given at an American Physical Society meeting at Caltech, December 29, 1959

"The philosophy of science is about as useful to scientists as ornithology is to birds."

For this reason, it makes sense to reexamine one of the few moments when Reidier actually does take pause: He and Eve sitting on their bench swing on their veranda in Providence. She leans against his shoulder, reading her book. He sits up straight, lifting his face to the slight breeze, his nail-bitten fingers clasping a sweaty bottle of Nantucket Nectar ice tea. "It's so quiet. So settled. It feels like our own little sanctuary in a way," he comments.

Eve's gaze lifts slightly from her book as she listens.

"I was thinking the room at the far end of the second floor, the one with the window seat, would make a good writing den for you. It struck me as a perfect place for your work. Built-ins for your books, a nice tree to look at when you need a break, but not too distracting. You writing upstairs there, me tinkering with my work in the basement. The boys free to play in between, in earshot of both of us. Our own little sanctuary cloistered away behind those hedges."

A lovely little sentiment punctuated by one particular word: sanctuary. It immediately conjures up connotations of a sacred or holy place. 454 Angell, by its very address, evokes Biblical ideas. Still it seems Reidier is fixated on this idea for deeper reasons. Sitting on the veranda, Reidier could be imagining their new home to be his own little Eden, every move with Eve having been an attempt at a more perfect iteration of their own haven. They would create a sanctuary that even has its very own Tree of Knowledge taking root in the basement (with his work) and branching up to the far side of the second floor where Eve summons the Muses. This interpretation supports his aforementioned impulse of an almost divine purpose.

There's us and there's everybody else.

Nevertheless, there's also a slightly more ominous element within this word. A sanctuary is also a place of refuge. Clearly, being under the Department's watchful gaze carries with it an inherent sense of security. But what is it Reidier and his family needed protection from? Reidier's work was the source of all of this. Ironically, where Eve saw it as the threat from within, Reidier believed it to be their salvation. For him, there was no sanctuary without his work. It was his talisman protecting them from loss. To abandon his work and leave it outside the walls of their asylum would have meant letting go of the past, of his quest, of his idea to be of value. For Reidier, 454 Angell was to be his own version of Prospero's Palace.

Consequently, we find ourselves back at our original inquiries:

How did Reidier do it?

Sidestepping the technical aspect to this question, it seems that the secret to Reidier's *how* was that he never took on any preconceptions about elephants or tangled rectangles. Without the shackles of limitations, he was able to transform the impossible into merely the improbable.

Why him?

In retrospect now, it's no huge insight as to why teleportation would appeal to Reidier. He never learned to manage the pain of distance, and as a result focused his exceptional talents at alleviating it. In doing so, he opened a door that the world wasn't ready to go through.

TITLE CARD: **GALILEE 6:21**

TITLE CARD: **EXPERIMENT 9 DELTA**

CONTROL ROOM, GOULD ISLAND FACILITY - 2007-11-17 00:09

The dark room lights up a little as console lights and video screen flicker on.

Ambient light pours in from the Mirror Lab.

On video screen in console, SPLIT SCREEN-RIGHT SIDE, target room: blackness.

LEFT SIDE, transmission room: a small object sits on the pad. (After magnification, it appears to be a small, emerald-cut diamond. Maybe 1.5 carats.)

Fiber-optic cables, circumscribing the Entanglement Channel flare red for several seconds, then morph into an orbiting white light as the Entanglement Channel opens.

The Boson Cannons and Pion Beams twitch to life. SOUNDS of the rapid ACCELERATION and DECELERATION of GEARS as the men take a series of readings of the diamond. Once complete they settle into optimized focal positions.

On another console screen, SPLIT SCREEN:

ANGELL RIGHT: empty target pad in Angell Lab.

ANGELL LEFT: shows Dr. Reidier (in his tweed sport coat and pajamas) seated at his desk in Angell Lab.

Dr. Reidier reads information off his respective screen, while absentmindedly pinching a small metal hoop, with four prongs sticking out of one spot on the circumference, back and forth

between his thumb and forefinger, flicking it from
one fingertip to the other.

NOTE: closer inspection with enhanced
amplification shows this to be an engagement ring
setting without a diamond.

Dr. Reidier enters several commands into his
keyboard.

Encrypted calibrations rapidly scroll up the
Mirror Lab console computer screen.

NOTE: unlike with other experiments, all of the
calibrations and settings were encrypted. I2O
has been unable to decrypt to date.

Dr. Reidier brushes something off his lapel
and leans out of frame (presumably to adjust
something).

Dr. Reidier sits back into his chair, looks
everything over again, while fidgeting with the
ring (he snaps the edge of a card from the kid's
game Concentration [with the picture of a lion
on it] in between the setting's empty tongs). He
presses "Enter" on his keyboard . . .

On the console, inside their Plexiglas covers,
Contact Buttons Alpha and Bravo simultaneously
engage.

                                    CUT TO:

MIRROR LAB - SAME TIME

---MULTIPLE SCREENS---

ANGELL LAB RIGHT: empty target pad

MIRROR LAB LEFT: the Quark Resonator emits a
SOFT, HIGH-PITCHED DRONE as it powers up.

The small diamond remains perfectly still on the transmission pad.

At 2007-11-17 00:09:11.1011000 a quiet THRUM coincides with . . . nothing. The diamond still sits on the pad.

NOTE: While undetectable to the naked eye, when high-speed footage was slowed down, a phenomenon was detected for the last 1600 picoseconds on the left side.

During this increment, a seeming digital artifact appears on screen as the diamond seems to tessellate then glimmer then return to its previous "normal" state.

ANGELL LAB RIGHT: at 2007-11-17 00:09:11.1011000, the video feed distorts with static waves as a diamond coalesces on the Angell Lab target pad . . . into two jagged halves. It cleaved in two during transmission.

Dr. Reidier bites his top lip several times contemplatively. There is neither surprise, nor disappointment in his essentially neutral expression.

He keeps rotating the ring setting back and forth, pinched between his thumb and forefinger.

He moves over to read information off his computer screen.

Dr. Reidier exits out of his readouts and implements (presumably) his encryption program.

Dr. Reidier pockets the ring setting as his screen flashes off.

INT. CONTROL ROOM - MOMENTS LATER

Contact Buttons Alpha and Bravo depress.

Data scrolls up the screen, then stops, and the screen and computer shut down.

The console lights turn off.

INT. MIRROR LAB - SAME TIME

The HIGH PITCH of the Quark Resonator fades out as the machine powers down.

GEARS SPINNING NOISE ramps up and down as the Boson Cannons and Pion Beams retract.

The circling indicator lights surrounding the Entanglement Channel orbit to a standstill, flash green, and then switch off.

The Mirror Lab Transmission Room light turns off.

Unknowns:
1) Why Dr. Reidier would encrypt data, but not encrypt or delete console footage? Unlikely that he would have forgotten about automated video surveillance he set up.
2) When did he originally place the diamond on the Mirror Lab transmission pad? Before leaving work? Did he recover it the next morning as well?
3) The whereabouts and/or status of both diamonds.

IX

Cells replace themselves constantly. Month to month, moment to moment. I am not me; I am a memory of me.

~Rōjin Haruki

Apport: *the transfer of an object from one location to another without traveling through space-time. Basically, "beaming up," a feat which, so far, is a completely bogus idea.*

~Hamid Al-Ghazali, scholar and skeptic

Life has taught us that love does not consist of gazing at each other, but in looking together in the same direction.

~Antoine de Saint-Exupéry

I'm doing this all wrong.

All this time and I barely know them. I've barely scratched the surface. It's the data. An infestation of information. It's too easy to get lost, go down a wrong path, swamp the boat.

I've been doing this all wrong—*

---

* I know how she feels. What's this mean though?

NB Footage: Providence, February 1, 2007—

Reidier walks in the front door, drops his satchel on the wooden chair in the vestibule, peels off his parka and boots, and calls out Eve's name, thrusting his hands in and out of the various pockets of his sport coat, looking for something. He steps into the house, casting a glance to the left and right, and looks upstairs when he hears a noise from the kitchen. "I'm home," he says, strolling into the kitchen. He lets his keys clatter onto the countertop.

Reidier stops short, finding only Ecco in the room. The boy sits at the kitchen table. He holds an empty cardboard egg carton in his hand, and there are several more on the table. Ecco looks over his shoulder and smiles at his father.

"Well, hello. Just taking care of some kitchen work?" Reidier asks as he approaches his son. He places a hand on his son's back, bends over, and kisses the top of his head.

Ecco, who has already turned his attention back to the egg cartons, makes a loud kissing noise in unison with his father's display of affection.

"Happen to know where Mommy is?" Reidier asks, watching Ecco play.

"Up in her writing room," comes a voice from the den.

Reidier turns and follows the voice to discover his other son midheadstand on the couch, watching a nature show on television. Reidier leans against the doorjamb and tilts his head almost upside down to make eye contact with Otto.

"Good day, sir," Reidier says.

Otto smiles at his father and then corrects him, "It's good afternoon."

"So it is." Reidier turns his head back upright. "Didn't you hear me come in?"

Otto shakes his head back and forth, which takes some effort as a significant portion of his weight is resting on it. "Watching TV."

"So I see. Manta rays, eh?"

Otto tries a headstand nod. It doesn't work, and he ends up collapsing on his side onto the couch.

"I give it an eight. You've got to stick the dismount."

Otto screws his face up at his father.

"Nowhere near as graceful as a manta ray," Reidier teases.

"Manta birostris," Otto singsongs.

"Looks like we have a little Latin scholar in our midst. Mommy will be pleased. Speaking of Mommy, she's up in her writing room?"

"I think so," he says, his eyes glued to the TV as a manta breaches the surface.

Reidier observes his son watching the manta ray, then leans away from the door, and heads down the hall.

"They look like swimming angels," Otto says to no one in particular.

Reidier calls back to Otto, "I always thought so too. Ironically, it used to be called the devilfish."

He finds Eve kneeling on the floor of her study, in front of a half-unpacked box of books, a lilting stack of hardbacks, and several coffee-stained manuscripts. Bronze bookend replicas of Rodin's *The Thinker* balance on each thigh; she stares at the partially filled bookshelf.

Reidier's voice fills the room, ". . . assuming we've already solved both the communication-speed and bandwidth issue, as well as the blueprinting and reconstruction of the entire molecular landscape, then we find ourselves in a netherland that straddles the boundaries of both stages three and four. We must not only map out, mirror, and induce cognitive patterns; we must do so instantaneously so as to avoid any loss of information, somehow transforming a static mind into a kinetic one. The transference of consciousness requires an animate host and therefore goes hand in hand with what I have thoughtfully termed Golem's breath, but you might better understand it as the Frankenstein problem."

It is bewildering to watch both Eve and Reidier remain silent while Reidier's voice washes over both of them. The aural disorientation isn't apparent until he crosses the room to Eve's computer and stops the podcast.*

---

* I think I get it. She's shifting her approach. Her comments are restrained. She's pulled back.

That's what was wrong before. At least in her eyes, there was too much of her. That's rich—she's always the last to realize that. Oh, but now she's convinced that the only proper way to Psynar® the shit out of this is to get out of the way. Observe from a great enough distance so as to be sure not to affect the subject.

Objectivity. That's her key now. Only report so that the interpretation doesn't affect the analysis.

I wonder if she considered at all how objective she can be when she's the one editing all this?

Who knows? Maybe I'm the one reading into this a bit too much.

"You listen to my lectures?"

"*Oui*. It's perfect for background noise or for when I am having trouble sleeping," Eve says with a smile.

"Don't think you're the first person to say that. You're just the meanest."

Eve turns toward her husband and puffs some wearied strands of hair dangling in front of her face upward. As the hair drifts down to almost the exact same longitude she blurts out in her French accent, "Why do I 'av these?"

Reidier takes her in for a moment and then offers, "To hold up your books?"

"Isn't that what the end of the bookshelf does?"

Reidier considers her point. "Well, yes, but when your books don't reach the end of the shelf. And some shelves aren't in bookcases. They're just shelves and might be in the middle of a wall with no end in sight."

"In that case I could use a stack of books. But for the most part, I have plenty of books to fill every shelf and still make a coffee table out of the rest. And I did not ask why one has these. I asked why *I* have these. These. Packed away, so securely for the voyage here. These."

She lifts them up in the air slightly and then drops them back to her thighs. She then inhales with staccato breaths and sighs.

Reidier is across the room in a few strides. He squats down behind her and slides his hands along the length of her arms, leaning his chest against her back. He holds her like that for a few minutes while Eve fights off tears.

Eventually he leans back and sits on his bum, and Eve likewise shifts off of her knees and onto hers. They sit motionless: her back resting on his chest, his arms pressed against hers, and a small replica of *The Thinker* clasped in her hands sitting on each of her thighs.

He whispers into her, "We'll find them. They'll turn up. We'll find them."*

---

* It took me a while, I had to go back over fifty pages, but I think I figured out what the hell they're talking about. Reidier's referring to her lost diaries from Chicago. That's my best guess. I'd feel a lot more confident about my conjecture if Hilary had weighed in a little, but she's taking a leave of absence. I guess I'm not the only one she disappeared on.

I know she felt like she was doing this all wrong before, blah, blah, goddamn blah. But that doesn't help me and this overwhelming disorientation I'm stumbling around with, trying to excavate this entire artifact without her. I've become Dante, wandering around hell, only Virgil's nowhere to be found, and I'm fumbling about for any sense of direction trying to ignore the distinct impression I'm heading downhill.

She nods.

He kisses the back of her head and repeats, "We'll find them."

She turns *The Thinkers* toward each other, "I adore z'ese actually."

"I got you those."

She nods and says, "When we were in Guiana, and I was 'omesick. You left them for me in my office with a note that said, 'Thinking of you. Here's a little bit of 'ome.'" She shakes her head back and forth, smiling, "An atrocious pun, no?"

"As I recall, it made you laugh."

"L'amour c'est être stupide ensemble."

"I got the words love and stupid and ensemble, but that can't be right."

"'Ow do you not know French yet after all z'ese years?"

"You know I could spit out some big physics terms while talking to you, like Bell's theorem or the principle of locality."

"Bell's theorem is the one that says normal physical theories can't completely predict quantum mechanics, and the locality is the idea that an object can only be influenced directly by something in its immediate vicinity."

Reidier blinks. "Well, I got three of the French words."

Eve laughs, then tilts her head back, and smiles up at her husband. "See, I do listen to you sometimes."

"I listen to you too, I just don't understand you. Although with that accent, it doesn't really matter what you're saying."

She thumps her head reproachfully back against his chest. "I do not 'ave an accent," she says in a thick French accent.

"You're absolutely right. You don't 'ave one at all. But as you say, 'amour, stupide, ensemble.'"

She laughs at his atrocious accent and sighs, "It means, 'Love is being stupid together.'"[70]*

---

[70] Paul Valery

---

*If Mom were more in this she might write about how this is a rare moment of intimacy between these two in this tense first summer in Providence. Or something like that. But for all I know, they were fucking their brains out the entire damn season once they got over the initial hump and pain in the ass of moving. But what do I know? She's the one with all the footage. She's the one with all the insight. I'm just the Son of Psynar®.

Honestly, it's just like her to get out of the game. Deciding that somehow by stepping back, she was making everything better. Like somehow it was better for her and me to be talking to our own respective "respectable" shrinks after Dad died, rather than to each other. She didn't want to weigh down my grief with her own or something like that. Like I never heard her crying in bed.

All that "space" did was make me feel more alone than before. So alone that I would do anything for a little contact. I didn't learn anything about how to cope with death. All I learned about was desperation. How it can take you over. Possess you. Make you capable of shit you never even considered, let alone thought possible. All under the protective cloak of an accident.

I feel like Charlie Brown and Hilary is Lucy holding that football. I keep coming back, and she keeps leaving me all over again.

"That doesn't sound entirely like a compliment, but I'll take it, especially if we're together."

They both adjust their positions slightly, but stay sitting up together on the floor, her surrounded by him, Eve's head braced against his chest, Reidier's chin resting on her shoulder.

"Funny, your people are so much more fascinated with the thinker rather than the thought."

"L'homme est beaucoup plus compliqué que ses pensées."[71]

"Sure, when you put it that way."

"A man is infinitely more complicated than his thoughts."

"His thoughts are him. They are who he is."

"What about his urges, his emotions, his pains?" Eve asks.

"Those are all varying manifestations of thought," Reidier says.

---

[71] *Ibid.*

Eve grunts in response, then rolls back onto her knees, stretches, and places the bookends on the lowest shelf. She then twists around, grabs one of the book stacks off the floor, and drags them over to the shelf.

Reidier sits where she left him and watches. "I'm glad to . . ." he trails off and considers as Eve continues to set up books. "It's good you're getting your books out."

"I know. They were suffocating in their boxes."

"Right next to Schrödinger's cat." He lets out a short laugh at his own joke.

Eve cocks her head at her husband, flashes a quick pity smile, and goes back to unpacking. "Professor Golub and I were 'aving a discussion about Foucault's extrapolations on the Panopticon.[72] He was asserting there was a certain *mise en scène* aspect to the design. I conceded that, from a purely aesthetic point of view, this could be true. Still, the roots of that term, *mise en scène*, stem from the theater."

---

[72] The Panopticon is a prison designed by the English philosopher and social theorist Jeremy Bentham in 1785. The design concept permits an observer to observe (-*opticon*) all (*pan*-) prisoners without the prisoners being able to determine if and when they are being watched, thereby establishing a "sentiment of a sort of omnipresence"[i] and invisible omniscience.

Bentham himself described the Panopticon as "a new mode of obtaining power of mind over mind, in a quantity hitherto without example."[ii]*

---

[i] Bentham, Jeremy. *Proposal for a New and Less Expensive Mode of Employing and Reforming Convicts* (1798).

[ii] Bentham, Jeremy. *Panopticon* (Preface). In Miran Bozovic (ed.), *The Panopticon Writings*, London: Verso, 1995, 29-95.

* For those of you still feeling a little lost, just go to Hulu.com and watch any episode of the HBO series *Oz*. Also, I looked up Schrödinger's cat to refresh my memory. Hilary was right not to explain it in a footnote. It's just a quaint little philosophical conundrum involving a black box, poison, a radioactive trigger, and a cat that might or might not be alive. Other than the box part, I don't understand Reidier's joke at all. I don't know, maybe it's hilarious to physicists. Or cats.

Seeing the bemused look on her husband's face, she suggests he see if the French Department would let him audit a class, and then explains, "It literally means putting on stage. In the theater, however, the power lies with those producing the scenes, that is the director, designer, and performers. They are in control of what is being presented and how it is being looked at."

"Got it," Reidier says.

"This is the complete opposite of what Foucault was emphasizing in *Surveiller et Punir: Naissance de la Prison.*[73] Inside of his architecture, the 'unequal gaze' was at play."

"What exactly is the unequal gaze? Other than what it sounds like," Reidier says.

"In the prison, it is the constant possibility of undetected observation. In this system, the gaze is not controlled by the performer, i.e. the prisoner, nor is its purpose entertainment. The unequal gaze is a punishment, a form of subjugation, and discipline in and of itself."[74]

"Makes sense. Although I still don't see any connection to you unpacking your boxes."

"I wanted to find the section where Foucault writes about it and to show it to Spencer."

"Spencer?"

Reidier's cell phone rings from inside his sport coat.

---

[73] *Discipline and Punish: The Birth of the Prison*, written by Michel Foucault, published in 1975.

[74] There's an eerie, borderline omniscient, resonance in this nanobot footage. In spite of the terrifyingly apt irony, I am convinced that neither Eve nor Reidier were aware of the constant and omnipresent observation and recording of their lives by the Department.☺

☺ I knew she could only resist so long before injecting herself. Still, she relegated herself to the confines of a footnote. Props for that, Mom. And yeah, this is a tad eerie. Especially since you're the Watcher in all this.

And I guess by extension, me. All of us really. Implicated through the simple act of reading.

"Professor Golub," Eve says over the ring.

Reidier pulls his phone out of his pocket. "So you had to dig Foucault out of his dungeon."

Eve nods, and watches her husband glance down and wrinkle his forehead.

The phone rings again.

"It's Pierce," Reidier says.

"You going to answer?"

He does. "Hello.

"Well, thank you. And you?

"No, not a bad time at all, I was just—

"That'd be fine. When will you be?"

Reidier's forehead smoothes out with surprise. "Oh, I didn't realize you meant, that you were—

"I'll just—it'll be about fifteen minutes."

Reidier hangs up his cell and looks at a now-bemused Eve.

"Pierce is here. In Providence. Wants me to grab coffee with him at the Coffee Exchange down on Wickenden."*

---

* That place is still there?! A friend of mine used to perform on open-mic nights with just his guitar and his fake sweet-guy persona. I'm not saying the guy was any worse than the rest of us, it's just that he tried to pretend he wasn't.

He'd always give you that small town type of hello, in his soft tenor voice, and nod and smile while you talked, like he was genuinely interested. And you really thought he was, unless you watched how he was with others. It was almost exactly the same, nod for nod. Again and again. With everybody. Same smile. Same sweet voice.

I tell you, it took a lot not to gag on my cappuccino foam while he sang his lyrics of "sincerity" and girls got all weak-kneed, humming along to the three-chord progression, not even noticing how he sang through a mask.

That was the worst part. That I was the only one who saw it. No one else picked up on it. No one else smelled the bullshit. No one heard him whisper venom in my ear after I had challenged him on some point.

That's when I realized he knew, saw how I could see through him. And he hated me for it. But that only made him turn up the sweetness and the charm in public, and then spit up the bile on me in an isolated passing.

Hey, I'll take Toby and his artistry any day of the week. Toby doesn't hide it, he flaunts it. Dances with it. And he doesn't pretend it's not there and it's not a game. He embraces the reality of the illusion of it all with the constant reinvention of himself. He changes costume again and again, but purposefully drapes himself in the camouflage of people's expectations. He's more honest in transforming into what people want him to be, than any of the lemmings out there convinced they know who they are. There's a truth to Toby's deceit.

Even lemmings are lies. Those little famous followers are not in fact nature's notorious suicide cult. That lovely myth about their tendency toward mass suicide is nothing more than an urban legend propagated by Disney. *White Wilderness*, which won an Academy Award, featured a segment on lemmings and their compulsion to mass suicide. The truth is, the footage of those silly rodents leaping into the ocean was actually staged. They weren't so much "jumping" as they were being hurled off a cliff by a custom-made, lemming-launching turntable. Not to mention, it wasn't so much an "ocean" that the lemmings drowned in, but rather a tightly cropped river in the middle of landlocked Alberta, Canada. Not even the natural habitat for lemmings. No, these puppies were shipped in from the North Pole so the dedicated filmmakers could accurately document this bizarre, "natural" compulsion.

Truth isn't solid.

It's liquid.

It takes on the shape of whatever container it's poured into.

"He came up from Washington unannounced? You didn't know?"

"Not at all. We had our status conference call earlier this week. Do you think it's something bad?"

She considers Reidier's question. "Apparently, you are his prize. I think it's just something we'll 'ave to get used to. You should go, though, no? I am sure it will be fine."

Reidier nods and stands up. He makes for the door. At the hall, he stops and turns around. "Would you like me to bring you back something? An ice tea?"

"Peppermint. No white sugar."

"White sugar," Reidier says along with her. "Yes, I know. I have met you before."

She nods once in concurrence. "I trust you, Rye, just not those sneaky, ignorant baristas. I'll never understand America's tolerance of bleached sugar. The demerara is so much bet'ah."

"We're a processed culture," he says, heading down the hall.

Downstairs, Reidier stops into the kitchen to retrieve his keys off the counter. He snatches them up off the granite and then freezes. He stands there, keys in his fist hovering at shoulder height.

After a few moments he approaches the kitchen table. The egg crates are nowhere to be found, but sitting on top of the Formica surface, like a dairy ziggurat, is a pyramid of eggs. Five eggs across the base, five levels high, culminating in a single egg apogee.

Reidier reaches out his hand to touch it, but stops just short. His finger droops as he presumably considers the ramifications of upsetting the apple cart, so to speak. He looks around the room and checks the den.

It is empty, and the TV is off.

Noise of the boys playing upstairs echoes down the stairwell.

Reidier returns to the kitchen, once again approaching the table. He stands over it, leaning one way and then the next, to inspect it from a variety of angles.

"They must be hard-boiled," he says out loud to himself and delicately lifts the top ovum off of its perch. In one fluid release, the pyramid sighs, and the delicate structure rolls outward, as if melting. Reidier, in a Three Stooges–esque reflex, drops his egg while trying to catch the others, and ends up scattering at least a dozen to the floor. Not one of them was hard-boiled.

"Shit," Reidier says, taking in the devastation left by the miniature avalanche. Pools of albumen and yolk droop across the tabletop and floor like a Dalí landscape.

Excerpt from University of Chicago iTunes episode, Dr. Kerek Reidier lecture from his Physics of Science Fiction course, March 11, 2002

Professor Reidier wanders back and forth in front of an oversized chalkboard, which is below an equally large projector screen. Hands thrust deep into his tweed coat pockets, head down, shoulders raised slightly upward, his winter boots squeak as he paces the length of the slate monolith.

Written on the board in large letters is the phrase *Principium Contradictionis.*

"Any Latin scholars in the house?"

A lone voice rolls out from the sea of seated students. "Contradiction principle?"

"Yes. The Principle of Contradiction. One of the so-called three classic laws of thought. Can anyone tell me what the other two are?"

A different voice calls out, "The law of identity."

"Yes, that most profound of concepts that states an object is the same as itself. *A* equals *A*. A quaint little tautology that we all learned the first day of high school geometry. And the other?"

The students murmur until someone says, "The law of the excluded middle."

"Glad to see at least some of the homework is seeping in. The law of the excluded middle is the principle that for any proposition, it is either true or its negation is. As Aristotle put it, when you have two contradictory propositions, one must be true and the other false. Unless you've been out with Alexander the Great, and he drunkenly asks if he's great enough to both build and move an unmovable mountain."

Only a few sporadic chortles from the class.

"Ok, don't insult conquerors, just their wussy tutors, check."

More laughter this time.

"The principle of contradiction is the basis for all of these. It posits that contradictory statements cannot both be true at the same time, e.g. the two propositions, *A* is *B* and *A* is not *B,* are mutually exclusive. Seems believable enough. It's either raining right now or not raining right now. Right? But consider a little situation discovered by Bertrand Russell a hundred years ago. There's a barber who lives in a small town. The barber shaves all those men and only those men who do not shave themselves. Does the barber shave himself?"

Dead silence.

"It hurts to think about, I know. That's philosophy for you." Reidier leans forward, launching himself away from the lectern. "Someone once posited that physics, at its highest level, becomes philosophy. I think whoever said that just wasn't good enough at math."

Snickers ripple through the class. A student speaks up, "Isn't math at the highest level, philosophy?"

Reidier smiles at the crowd, "I was hoping I could just slip that little tautology right by you. It's a fair point. Our beloved Bertrand Russell did once say, 'To create a good philosophy, you should renounce metaphysics but be a good mathematician,' which one could interpret as philosophy at its highest level is just mathematics. Still all of this begs the question, what is mathematics?"*

---

* I feel like my head should hurt, and I should be more than a little confused, but somehow this all makes sense. It might have something to do with the fact that I'm about a third of the way through a liter of Highland Park Scotch and am reading this like it's a high school Spanish assignment. Cruise over the details and go for gist.

"Einstein believed that 'As far as the laws of mathematics refer to reality, they are not certain; as far as they are certain, they do not refer to reality.'* Me, I believe math is merely a language. It's nature's accountant. Math is no more of a philosophy than a picture of a cake is a dessert. Still, it has its uses, one of which is that it provides a nifty way to both explain and sidestep paradoxes. Which brings us to today's science-fictional feat: teleportation. I'm sure the majority of you associate this with the phrase, 'Beam me up, Scotty.'"[75]

---

* Toby loves that one. As did the head honchos at Anomaly. So much so, that they actually approved my hypothetical project proposal, or, more formally, my Project Proposal of the Hypothetical. They bought into it hook, line, and sinker: website development, graphic design team support, and a sizable marketing budget all for me to sell a hypothetical.

Did I already mention this? I'm getting swamped by all of this paper. And the scotch probably isn't helping much either. *In vino veritas*, sure; but *in Highland Park . . . lacuna*. I'm not about to start thumbing back through all of my notes.

Anomaly's giving me free rein to launch a campaign for *Chameleon*. It's a mind-blowing, game-changing, revolutionizing new product. And it doesn't even exist. Scratch that, it's not even defined. The concept is that it will serve as a type of advertisement for us. A proof of concept. The pitch is simple, if we can sell something that's not even real, imagine what we can do with your product.

It was one of our bimonthly Trailblazer Idea Harvest Sessions, a required "creative" experience that felt more like its acronym: a backward SHIT. It's not that I had forgotten about the meeting, it's that it wasn't even on my radar. There I was, sitting at my workstation, doing yet another Google search on the works of Eve Tassat, when I looked up and realized Lorelei was standing next to me, waiting for an answer to some question I didn't hear.

"You all right there, Tri-Me?"

That was her specific variation on my office nickname, the Trinity of Me. I was always a tad sheepish around her. It's not that I was intimidated or anything like that, it's just that most of the time, she found me amusing. Which normally would be a plus, right? Except with her, I was never trying to amuse. No matter how many stops I pulled out, she just sifted through my bag of tricks and inspected them all with a quaint detachment, like you might while looking at tchotchkes in an antique toy store.

None of this would be a problem really if it weren't for the fact that she was the kind of a girl who made a skirt suit look better than lingerie. She knew it too. The bizarre thing was, it wasn't in any stuck up sort of way, just an understanding that *yes, this is the way things are, yeah she knows how she affects men* (and women), and then she'd shrug with a sort of can-we-please-get-on-with-this-now manner. And for whatever

---

[75] This phrase is actually a misquotation. The closest the show ever got to it was "Beam me up, Mr. Scott."

reason, she's taken a shine to me. Like at one point she just decided I'm ok, I'm going to be her buddy, and then just told me, *come on buddy, we're going for a drink.* I have no idea why. My only clue is that when we're drinking and she's complaining about this investment banker boyfriend who took her paintballing or that trust fund baby who flew her to New Orleans for crawdaddies, she always rolls her eyes and smacks my arm with the back of her hand and says something like, *You'd've gotten a real kick out of it, Tri-Me, grinding away at his organ not even realizing he's the dancing monkey.*

The arm smack cues me to nod and laugh, and say something about how they just don't realize that artifice and architecture are the same things. All the while, I'm just wondering how she got her hair to be as shiny and lustrous as they make it look in commercials. It always smelled really good too, even in a dive bar. Like some jasmine-gardenia hybrid.

"You look like shit, partner," she said, still standing over me at my desk.

"I just haven't been sleeping much."

"For good reasons or bad?"

I gave her something back like you know me, or hard to tell the difference. I wanted to tell her all about my mother, her disappearance, the report. I wanted to take her to the carriage house and show her and then go to some bar and talk it out over a couple dozen pints. She'd nod. She'd rest a sympathetic hand on my shoulder. A connection would start to buzz, like when you throw up the ancient light switch in a big industrial space. She'd tell me something like she knows just what I need. And she'd take me back to her place, lay me down on her couch, and rest my head on her lap. She'd run her fingers through my hair, and we'd just talk until I drifted off.

And I'd stop feeling alone, sensing the warmth of her thighs beneath my head.

In real life, she guided me down the hall into our glass-walled conference room, whispering something to me about how frustrated the top dogs were getting with redundant innovations. I think I made a joke about them being out-ovations. I don't know, it's all a blur.

The only thing that really stuck out was her sitting next to me. I swear I could feel her body heat radiating outward.

The bosses were railing against us becoming stagnant. Something about sharks and how if they don't keep moving they die. Ideas were tossed out and quickly crushed like cheap beer cans.

I was off obsessing about Reidier and Eve and the bookend *Thinkers.* She found bookends, I found a book. A tome, really. A consciousness trapped in the words. It's the last thing I have of Mom.

A man is infinitely more complicated than his thoughts.

A woman, too. Hilary's essence is similarly locked up in her words, pinging out an image of the Reidiers. She's in there in the echoes of the Psynar®. The problem is, I'm losing myself trying to find her.

Lorelei's voice pinged me out of my own darkness. She was taking a swing at knocking Anomaly out of its doldrums. The top dogs tore it up with a lot of howling about thinking in and out of the box and all we were doing was getting boxed in.

"Why don't we just throw out the fucking box?" I blurted out.

The room went still.

I don't know what had spurred me into motion. Probably some chivalrous impulse to step between Lorelei and the rocks she was getting tossed against. Or just frustration against the unimpeded flow of uninspiring bullshit. Or maybe I was sleep deprived.

It got their attention though.

They asked me to expand on my idea. I didn't really have one, so that's when I dropped the Einstein quote about reality and math, math and reality. I was buying time, but it caused an honest-to-God hullabaloo.

I had them. Just didn't know what I had them in.

Before I knew it, I was off and running about dedicating our powers and skills to conjure up a reality about nothing. A non-product. An illusion of a mirage. We'll call it *Chameleon*. And, well, you pretty much know the rest.

I'm getting good at asking "what if?"

The class laughs again.

"So, teleportation, the moving of matter from one place to another. A long-imagined dream of humanity. How do we travel without traveling? There are essentially three fairly straightforward methodologies."

"Method one is the most popular version, i.e. the *Star Trek* version. It entails transforming all of the matter that is you into energy, transmitting that energy to a specific, distant location, and then reconstituting that energy into the matter that is you.

"The second is more Harry Potter–esque. It would require tearing a hole through several dimensions of space at your location all the way to your desired location and then simply pushing you through it.

"Makes going through security at the airport a lot more appealing, eh?"

More laughter.

"The third method involves a process more akin to replication. It involves scanning your person, destroying the original you, transmitting that information, and reconstructing 'you' at a distant location.

"So of these three, the first one is utter hogwash. While matter and energy are indeed two sides of the same coin, as dictated by $E = mc^2$, once matter is transformed into energy, it can no longer maintain the various properties of matter, i.e. ordered structure and patterns. It is structure and patterns that make you you, rather than just a lump of carbon and hydrogen. While one might conceivably be able to transform your energy back into matter, it would not be pretty.

"The dimensional-hole option is also a dead end since all we've been able to do is theorize about the existence of other dimensions. Furthermore, traveling through the multiverse would expose our three-dimensional, this-universe selves to a myriad of respective physical laws within each parallel universe that would most certainly annihilate us, or at least distort us in uncomfortable ways."

An unintelligible question from a student.

"Maybe it's a universe without the weak nuclear force, requiring the modification of several constants that we've grown accustomed to. Or one where quarks have different masses, so that neutrons became heavier than protons, resulting in the negation of any carbon- or oxygen-based life form, i.e. us. Or perhaps the quark mass adjustment would result in the proton being heavier than the neutron, negating the possibility of the basic hydrogen atom. Anyhow, you see the complications with that mode of travel.*

---

* Not even remotely, but I'm taking this guy's word for it. This was a class for nonmajors?!

"Which leaves us with option number three, the most promising means of teleportation, or as I like to call it, Tele-fax-ation."

The class let out a fairly large laugh this time. Most likely this had less to do with the humor and more to do with releasing some of the communal stress that had been built up, considering the contortionistic logistics of traveling through the multiverse.

"So, how do we do it?"

Reidier opened his hands outward to his audience, inviting suggestions. None came.

"As with all of our seeming sci-fi conundrums the solution is pretty straightforward—at least in theory."

Reidier raised his eyebrows conspiratorially. He pulled a remote out of his tweed pocket and started the slide show presentation. Slide 1 read *5 Steps from Here to There.*

Next slide, *Step 1: Communication.*

"The first thing we need is a reliable means of communicating. There are several important factors wrapped up into this . . ."

Next slide, *Bandwidth, Speed, & Security.*

"The holy trinity of web surfing."

Reidier paused for the laughter. Next, an image of da Vinci's *Vitruvian Man.*

"Why bandwidth? As I'm sure you know, an image of a person, like, say, a digital photograph, takes up a lot of memory. A video of them even more. Imagine how much information is in the whole shebang. Anyone care to venture a guess as to how many atoms make up the average one-hundred-and-fifty-four-pound human body?"

Sporadic numbers leapt out of the darkness, a hundred million, a billion, ten billion, a billion billion.

"The average human body, which is 99 percent hydrogen, oxygen, and carbon is made up of over seven thousand trillion atoms."

Next slide, a model of an atom, nucleus and orbiting electrons.

"Inside we also have electrons, protons, neutrons which yield twenty-six thousand trillion trillion total interacting particles inside each of us. Not to mention electrical patterns in our musculature and brain waves. Clearly we'll need a lot of bandwidth."

A slide of the cartoon image of the Road Runner.

"Next up, speed. We all want our internet connections faster and faster, it only makes sense we'd want our teleportation quick as well. With this technology, however, it's not only preferable but crucial. Obviously with teleportation we want to 'beam' you from point A over at least a somewhat significant distance to point B. The longer it takes, the more information is lost.

"Right now we can transmit at the speed of light. So if we were to teleport someone from here to say Cape Town, it would take just under half a second."

The class laughs.

"Doesn't seem like that big a delay, does it? But let's say we wanted to go from here to the top of Olympus Mons, the tallest mountain on Mars, assuming we are in the closest orbit."

A slide of a photograph of what looks like an irritated red wart, until the photo zooms in a little to transform the wart into a huge mountain jutting out of the massive rust-colored landscape of Mars.

"That trip would take over four minutes. And while that might not seem like a long trip, timewise, consider the mode of transport. Depending on how we actually build our scanning system, the you that is teleported is actually missing four minutes of existence or is four minutes out of sync with your time frame. After a couple tele-ports, the effects would add up. Is that travel time now acceptable?"

Reidier casts an inquisitive glance out to the class. Only sounds of bodies shifting in seats echo back to him.

"Agreed. So, for our teleportation machine, we will require a mode of instantaneous communication. And that brings us to our last necessity of our communication technology: security."

On the screen, familiar green numbers trickle down as seen in *The Matrix*.

"If our communication isn't perfectly secure, someone could either hack our transmission and redirect our transported essence, duplicate our transported essence, or, even worse, alter our transported essence with a literal and virtual virus. Identity theft would take on a whole new, more literal meaning.

"Contemporary security systems all rely on classical physics which allows, at least in principle, any physical properties to be measured without disturbing them. But if we were to encode our transmission in measurable physical properties of some signal, then we open ourselves up to undetectable tampering. In order to avoid this, we'll need to utilize something called quantum cryptography. As much as I'd love to get into that with you, I think I'd be forced to forfeit the status of gut course from my curriculum classification."

A few snickers.

A slide pops up that reads, *Step 2: Scanning.* "Obviously we're all familiar with scanners and the basics of how they work, or at least what they do. Take an image, divvy it up into pixel-size quantities, digitize the information, and voilà. So all we would need is a three-dimensional version of this."

Up comes a slide of a cartoon of a man being sandwiched into a flatbed scanner.

"Furthermore, it would need to be capable of measuring and organizing a good chunk more than just the twenty-six thousand trillion trillion total interacting particles inside each of us, but also whatever information we need to describe them: momentum, location, spin, et cetera."

A student pipes up, "So this alterative is like just as unrealistic as the other two."

"Well, there are some tricks available to us. For instance, hydrogen atoms are fairly fungible. One hydrogen atom is just as good as the next, it doesn't really matter where exactly the electron is inside of it at any given moment. As long as we get all the intermolecular dynamics lined up right, we could compress that number significantly. We could even possibly go more macro and use anatomy models for organs and such to fill in the blanks as problems arise with anomalies. Either way, at least the body is manageable. The brain might require us to stay a little more detail oriented.

"There's a striking difference between measuring order versus measuring complexity. Consider the complexity of . . . Mr. Siemens's brain." Reidier gestured to a student sitting to the right side of the front row.

The class laughs.

"It is a staggering proposal, isn't it? Anyhow, his brain is a complex organ that has an exact configuration of a myriad of microstructures in each neuron precisely designed for systemic functioning . . . but that's just its complexity. How the gunk is put together, as opposed to how it functions.

"It's the order of complexity that's crucial. The brain's impressive power comes from its parallel organization in three dimensions. How it functions and manages electrical patterns is our mind. And obviously we don't want to lose that."

Siemens, apparently, shouts out his thanks.

"Now I know, you're all sitting there thinking, 'But what about Heisenberg's Uncertainty Principle? Isn't that going to taint our measurements?' To which I say, let the engineers worry about that."

Reidier thrusts his hands into his pockets and grins at his class with a particularly pleased expression. The class laughs on cue, as if they realize they're supposed to.

"Truth be told, the solution actually lies in the mechanical problem. In order to account for the trillions of bits of information and manage the communication of those trillion bits, we will need a suped-up supercomputer. One that would shame all the other supercomputers put together.

"We need a quantum computer, which is to say a computing device that, rather than storing data in bits, i.e. ones or zeros, stores information in qubits. With qubits, a quantum computer can hold a single bit of information that could be both zero and one at the same time. For example, a quantum coin toss would be both heads and tails as long as no one actually looked at the coin. If they did, then the coin instantly would become one or the other. That's the trick. As long as we don't look, it won't choose and both possibilities exist. A sort of peekaboo computer chip."

Reidier beams a smile out to the class, perhaps trying to gauge if they're still with him.

"Or imagine two marbles in a bowl. The marbles have similar charges so that they repel. As they both try to settle at the bottom of the bowl, repulsive forces push them to come to rest on opposite sides, a little bit up the slope. The marbles are now in a state where we can't move one without affecting the other. They will only move in tandem.* Of course, the benefit of this paradoxical computer is two-fold. One, it provides us the exponential computing power we need. Peter Shor came up with an algorithm that proves a modest-size quantum computer can solve unfathomable problems in fractions of a second. Miraculously, a collection of a mere three hundred atoms, each storing a single quantum bit, could hold more values than the number of particles in the universe. It would render almost every military, diplomatic, and commercial code laughably vulnerable. The most powerful computer ever, and we wouldn't even have to see it.

---

* Why does that seem so familiar?

"I would have brought one with me today, but when I put in my request for a prototype to the department head, he did what department heads do, formed a committee."

More laughter.

"The committee ruled, as most unimaginative bureaucracies do, that it was impractical to acquire technology that wasn't yet in existence. Then they surprised me by delivering a dozen to this very table." He sweeps his arm, palm opened upward, over the empty table. "Problem is, I just can't find them."

Reidier pulls his glasses down and leans in very close to the tabletop in mock search. The students giggle. Reidier rights himself, shrugs, and continues.

"The second benefit of this computer is it allows us to circumvent Heisenberg's pesky little principle. As long as we leave all the information gathering to, and in, the computer, it can account for all the possibilities without affecting any of the actualities. Our quantum computer allows us to know without knowing."

A female voice shouts out something unintelligible.

"Yes, Ms. Echeverria, I suppose that is like Mr. Siemens. However, for our purposes let's just accept that we can drive a car without understanding how an internal combustion engine functions.

"Which brings us to . . ."

Slide pops up that reads:

Step 3: Duplication

Step 3: Duplication

The class laughs.

"Right, so now that we can both scan and transmit everything we need to know about you, we just have to make, well, you. Once again, the physical construction is the easy part. With some help from a couple trillion nanoscale assembly machines, in some type of amniotic soup consisting primarily of hydrogen, oxygen, and carbon, we should be able to construct you in no time.

"Of course we can't forget the mental replication, as well. Although with Mr. Siemens it might be easy to overlook."

Reidier smiles at Siemens in the front row.

"So using a series of very intricate and accurate electromagnetic wave inducers, we match the exact impulse patterns in your brain and musculature. Now we've finally gotten to the tricky part. This latter stage sort of straddles the fence between step three and step four."

A slide with an image of a brain straddling a fence between duplication and animation.

"Step four is the animation step. The proper duplication of the myriad of electrical impulses flowing throughout your body and, more importantly, your brain, must be, well, sequentially instantaneous. As soon as we've properly matched up all your brain waves, your brain must be housing a consciousness to take over the management of electrical patterns. In other words, consciousness. Otherwise, the patterns of charge will simply dissipate. Your brain would no longer be *your* brain. Nor would a nonelectrically patterned and stimulated brain be able to house a mind."

Reidier trails off, one hand stuck deep in his tweed pocket, the other rolling a piece of chalk absentmindedly between his thumb and fingertips. His gaze focuses somewhere beyond the blackboard. It's only for a few moments. Nothing really. One might mistake it for a simple pause to swallow or to just get one's bearings in moving on to the next point of the lecture.

Enhancing the magnification however, one sees his eyes shift quickly from left to right. He's pondering, not pausing. Thinking. It's as if he's writing equations in the air that only he can read. Looking closely, one can even see him get to the end of a line and then jump up to reread the invisible equations that hang in midair. Then he smiles, satisfied, and continues.

"So, assuming we've already solved the communication, speed, and bandwidth issue, as well as the blueprinting and reconstruction of the entire molecular landscape, then we find ourselves in a netherland that straddles the boundaries of both stages three and four. We must not only map out, mirror, and induce cognitive patterns; we must do so instantaneously so as to avoid any loss of information, somehow transforming a static mind into a kinetic one. The transference of consciousness requires an animate host and therefore goes hand in hand with what I've thoughtfully termed Golem's breath, but you might better understand it as the Frankenstein problem."

The class laughs. It's not the laughter of humor, but of tension release. Clearly this last part of Reidier's lecture has unsettled them.

"Without this step, all we've successfully done is shipped a body, not a person. I'd imagine that our pattern inducer would also be part of the animation process. Like jumper cables or a defibrillator for the mind.

"As folklore describes it, when Rabbi Bezalel created the Prague Golem in the sixteenth century, he carved the word *emet* into the creature's forehead. It means truth or reality."

Reidier sighs to himself.

"For our machine to create reality, it must maintain absolute truth in tracking, transmission, and induction. Just like the Golem."

Reidier opens his mouth as if to continue speaking, but hesitates.

"It also resonates with our final step."

Next slide, *Step 5: Elimination.* The class is quiet.

"The end of the rabbi's story climaxes with him rubbing out the first letter of the *emet* so that only *met* remains on the Golem's head. *Met* means death in Hebrew."

The class remains quiet.

"We have to eliminate the original. Otherwise we get into metaphysical issues, and my math only takes me so far."

Again, nervous laughter.

"This step isn't as drastic as you might think. Most likely the subatomic scanning process would disrupt the microuniverse that is you to such an extent that you would most likely disintegrate anyway. Luckily, by that time, you'll already be in South Africa or at the top of Olympus Mons.

"So, there we have it. Teleportation in five easy steps. What's next?"

The final slide is an animation of a caricature of Reidier standing on the left side of the screen, dissolving, and reappearing on the right side of the screen.

Transcript from the audio log of the Office of the Director of the
Strategic Technology, Donald Pierce; 2/1/2007, 3:52 p.m.[76]

"Kerek, thanks for meeting me. How fortuitous that you were
free," Pierce says. The sound of a chair screeching as it's backed up,
presumably as Pierce stands.

"I had finished work early and just gotten home."

Chairs rattle as they sit.

"My apologies, I didn't mean to take you away from family time,"
Pierce offers.

"Not at all. As long as we don't go too late."

"Of course not. Great lapel pin, by the way. Where'd you get that?"

"Eve got it for me at a flea market with some matching computer-
chip cufflinks. What brings you up to Providence?"

"A meeting down in Newport and to work out some of the
financials with the university. Thought I'd give you a ring."

According to Pierce's calendar, he did have a meeting with Rear
Admiral Russell Wisecup. However, it was set up later that evening,
for the following day.*

---

*What am I supposed to do with this? Mom finally surfaces for a brief
paragraph only to submarine me with innuendo. She barely even says
anything, just drops in a little scheduling factoid. Is she commenting on
a Departmental oversight? Some typo in the calendar, some screwup in
notes?

Or is she insinuating something bigger? Something about Pierce?
Maybe he hadn't set this up but was planning on it. Or maybe he was a
liar who used this as a cover. She never really seems to trust Pierce. Then
again, she doesn't trust anyone. Who cares if it's just an excuse?

Unless it's not Pierce at all who she's making the insinuation against,
but rather the Department. She's questioning their records. What they're
giving her. Subtly accusing them of sabotaging her work.

---

[76] The Director not only installed nanobots all over Reidier's home and office, he
bugged himself for each and every one of their meetings. This, being early on, was
only an audio bug.

I'm going to need a little more help here, Hilary. You're leaving an awful lot up to the reader. Trusting me to be smart.

You can't do that, at least not in my line of work. The reader isn't to be trusted. Readers are lemmings. They need to be led. Back around the turn of the century, a grocery store owner took out an ad in the city paper. He wanted two words on a single page, "Post Toasties." He had too much stock of this new cereal and just wanted to get people asking about it. Somewhere along the way, somebody screwed up, and the entire page was filled with Post Toasties Post Toasties Post Toasties. The newspaper charged by the word. The grocer thought he was going to go bankrupt from the cost. By the end of the day, the entire cereal aisle had sold out. All it took was repetition and a couple hundred "good" readers.

Readers need to be told. They need guidance. Simplicity. The power of suggestion can't be wielded lightly. It can be subtle, sure, but not ambiguous. Drink Coke; Think Apple; Mistrust Pierce.

Unless she can't be explicit. Maybe it's too dangerous? Maybe Mom was worried about being too straightforward. She needed a back door. A way out. Plausible deniability. Maybe she was scared about being right. About being obvious. About finding out.

Maybe I should be too.

"Speaking of the family, how are they all settling in?"

"Still unpacking but settling in. The boys love the house. And I found a Whole Foods."

"Eve like the house?"

"The house is beyond our imaginations."

Pierce pauses and then gives Reidier an out. "It is a lovely house. Still, Providence is an adjustment, I'm sure."

"It's a charming town. The architecture, the history. Utterly charming."

"It is, isn't it," Pierce concedes. He pushes a little more, "Nonetheless, you grow up in Paris and everything else is bound to be a little underwhelming."

"Eve didn't grow up in Paris," Reidier corrects him.

"No?"

"Spent her early years in Morocco," Reidier says.

"That's right. Guess she's been a bit of a vagabond from the get-go. Bouncing around the Francophonie. Moving must feel second nature to her by now."

Reidier grunts a *yes, yes.*

"How's your lab?" Pierce interrupts. "Have everything you need?"

"More than I need."

"And your home setup has everything too?"

Reidier doesn't answer right away. "Yes. It's exactly what I . . . I work odd hours sometimes, and the convenience of—"

"What was it they said Einstein did? Worked for two hours, slept for twenty minutes, something like that?"

"Einstein was a notorious long sleeper. He said he needed at least ten hours a night," Reidier says.

Pierce whistles, "I guess bending space took a lot out of him. Ten hours. Maybe I should have gone into academia, at least for the naps."

Reidier laughs.

"Anyhow, glad the transition's been smooth and everything's up and running. Incidentally, I think we may have a solution for your power issues. Ironing out the details, but I think it should give you everything and more. As well as our test site." Pierce waits a moment and then adds, "So as soon as you're ready, we're ready."

"Mm," Reidier grunts. "I am, there's still work to be worked out in stage four."

There's a rustling of fabric and a slight clatter of a spoon rattling against a porcelain saucer. It sounds like Reidier has gotten the Director's attention, and he's leaning in. Still, Pierce doesn't interrupt the silence. He waits for Reidier.

"As you know, I've been wrestling with stages three and four.

Toying with fMRIs[77], MEGs[78], TMSs[79] and ███████████ ████████████████████████████████████ ██████████████. While the results have been informative, they've yielded only superficial success." Reidier hesitates. "It's a limited process at best, and one that can only be improved upon if we have the option of destroying the brain we're scanning."

"That's not off the table, if it's necessary," Pierce interjects.*

---

*What the hell is Pierce talking about? Even if we give him the benefit of the doubt and we're only talking about animal testing, what the fuck? How is that on the table? How is that even near the table? What's the use in teleporting brain-dead mice or monkeys? And why doesn't Mom call him on this? It's like saying the Tuskegee syphilis experiment shouldn't be "off the table."Ψ

Ψ A quick little Wikipedia search yielded an unsettling revelation. Because of Tuskegee, informed consent is now required EXCEPT for US Federal agencies, which can be kept secret by Executive Order. See Code of Federal Regulations Title 45 Part 46 Protections of Human Subjects 46.116.c

---

Reidier takes it in stride and merely continues, "While that would allow us to obtain dramatically higher spatial resolution of the brain, it won't get us any closer to the mind."

"I see. So physical scanning is not at issue here."

"Not at all. What's tricky and fascinating about humans is that our brain is sort of holographic. In a hologram, information is stored in a diffuse pattern throughout a large region. Destroy three-fourths of the hologram, and the entire image remains. Our memories work that way."

---

[77] Functional Magnetic Resonance Imaging is a type of specialized MRI scan that measures blood flow related to neural activity.

[78] Measures weak magnetic fields outside the skull.

[79] Transcranial magnetic stimulation, applies strong-pulsed magnetic field from outside the skull.

"Seems in line with what you've already been developing," Pierce says.

"It is; it's theoretically sound," Reidier sighs. "I just haven't gotten anywhere with it."

It seems Pierce has a keen insight into the delicacy of the creative process. Whether that's been developed over the years on the job or is an instinctive quality that helped him ascend through the ranks is ultimately inconsequential. What matters is that in spite of the obvious power dynamic and Pierce's exploitative motivations, he knows how to nurture dispositions like Reidier's. He knows that a word of encouragement and support can sometimes be even more damaging than harsh criticism to a creator who's stuck with his creation.

He waits.

Silence.

There are no sounds of Pierce shifting position, and most likely, he has kept his expression neutral.

After several moments, Reidier continues, "A few years ago a team at UCSD successfully connected artificial neurons with real neurons in a California spiny lobster, but they still can't capture a single lobster thought. And that's just a lobster."

A utensil drops on a plate.

"But the human brain," Reidier sighs again, "it's composed of a huge number of relatively small distributed systems, all arranged by embryology into a complex social architecture controlled by serial and symbolic systems that develop much later. I can plumb the brain's architecture, I can rebuild it. But—"

"Thought is proving to be a little more elusive?" Pierce asks.

"Yes, it is. The subsymbolic systems will translate fine. At least in theory." Sounds of someone fidgeting with a sugar packet. "I think they're somehow hardwired into the architecture. It's the symbolic systems."

"The subsymbolic is, what? The nuts and bolts or plumbing of thought?"

"Pretty much. Think about a ten-year-old catching a fly ball. All he sees is the trajectory of the ball from his spot in the outfield. To figure out the ball's path in 3-D space requires solving a host of simultaneous differential equations. Even more equations are needed to predict where the ball's going. And then a dozen or so more to translate this information into the outfielder's movements. Very few ten-year-olds know calculus, but a lot know how to catch a fly ball. So the problem is collapsed and translated into the appropriate action all through subsymbolic systems of thought."*

---

* Ok, so the subsymbolic systems are just the autonomic "nonthinking" systems. Biological management. Breathing, heartbeat, digestion, that sort of thing. Although from the way Reidier's talking it seems like it also includes conscious "nonthinking" stuff like grabbing, walking, evacuating, whatever.
Just a little rocket surgery.

Pierce waits, and then prompts Reidier with, "So the transference of subsymbolic thought will work? Mobility, autonomic systems, developed habitual action?"

"Yes, theoretically."

"That's fantastic."

"It'll be no small feat. Still, it's far from comprehensive. Or useful."

"Because a teleported subject will be able to run and catch a ball, but not know what a ball is."

"I think that's probably correct," Reidier says.

The two sit quietly for a few moments.

"Especially the way we're going about things," Reidier continues. "It's very linear. Very one-to-one. See something, copy something. Even running numerous processes simultaneously still won't capture the parallel mode of symbolic thought."

"Not yet," Pierce offers.

"And, who knows, maybe I just haven't figured out the right methodology yet to capture that patternicity. I wonder if coming at it from a different way might be more successful. The analogy of catching a ball kind of got me thinking. Maybe we don't need to know everything to get everything."

Pierce once again waits patiently. He doesn't want to spook the wild idea.

"Consider thermodynamics," Reidier posits. "How do we measure the behavior of gas molecules? Depends on how many particles we're talking about, right?"

"And the size of the container, but yes. If we're only talking a few thousand or so molecules per cubic meter, then we'd have to track them individually."

"Exactly, consider each one as an individual particle with its own trajectory," Reidier says. "We're at the whim of entropy as the molecules dance around the room willy-nilly, bouncing off of each other or not, trying to find the most chaotic arrangement."

Pierce continues Reidier's line of thought, "But if we have a sufficient number of particles, at a measurable density—"

"Then we can treat it like a gas, rather than a bunch of particles."

"And apply the law of thermodynamics," Pierce concludes.

"Which works extremely well. The interactions of a single molecule within a gas are hopelessly complex. But the gas itself, comprised of trillions of molecules, has many predictable properties."

Now, it's Reidier's turn to sit in silence as he lets his idea permeate Pierce. Reidier has dealt with enough grant givers and corporate sponsors to know how to send out an impulse and see how it bounces back, how to lay out enough technological breadcrumbs to lead a patron down a new path, but not too much to come off as patronizing.

Based on the rustling against Pierce's microphone, he presumably has leaned back.

Finally, after nearly two minutes of quiet, Pierce speaks. "So what would be your gas cloud?"

"Quarks."

"Trillions upon trillions of quantum particles?"

"If I stayed at the subatomic level, I'd be left, so to speak, with the outside of a house without any plumbing or electrical. Like a movie set."

"How . . ."

"There's the rub. I . . . I'm not certain yet, but I think the trick is in the communication tech. Using the trillions of entangled quark pairs. ███████████████████████████████████████ ██ ██ ████████████████████████████████ the transitive property. █ ████████████████████████████ but it's all done simultaneously, and it's all treated like one giant pattern wave rather than a trillion trillion bits of information. Dips down here, up there, then flips. Like an echo inverting."

"A quark echo," Pierce says.

"Yes. I got the idea from a Murakami book about a unicorn skull."

Another few moments of silence punctuated by sips of a beverage.

"That kind of math, though, you'd still need an awesome amount of computing power," Pierce says.

"Not as much as you would initially assume. The key will be parallel logic gate arrangement."

"Mm. We're toying with the idea of purchasing a couple thousand Xbox consoles, linking them all together, and running Linux on them to make you a nice little supercomputer."

"Toys-R-Us will be pleased," Reidier says.

"Microsoft won't be, unless we buy a couple thousand games too."

The two of them laugh. Eventually the moment passes, and they sit in silence.

"So no need for any nanoreproduction?"

"None at all. The target manifestation would be aggregated and organized through quantum induction, the quark echo as you put it, assuming we weren't teleporting into a vacuum, but into some type of environment that had available quarks."

"All quarks are fungible—"

"One's as good as the next."

More silence, until Pierce breaks the reverie with another probing question, "Am I correct that by taking ████████████ ████ A and B, ████████████████████████ ████████, C, ██████████████████, D, thereby bypassing the problems of ██████████████ Principle entirely?"

"That's the idea."

Now it is Pierce who grunts. "So as a result of the scanning and transmission process, the subject would be annihilated."

"The subject would be conveyed," Reidier restates.

"At the target end."

"Yes, exactly where we want to teleport the subject to."

"But on our end, on a quantum level, the original subject would have been completely altered. Dismantled. The echo would resonate it into oblivion."

"But their essence, their pattern would be extracted, preserved, and rendered." Reidier pauses, but only for a few moments. His tone conveys a slight sense of nervousness as does the increased rhythm of his speech pattern. "What it does is streamline the process that we've already set out, precluding the need for the ████████ Phase. It circumvents any ethical considerations that could arise in the future."*

---

* Even if all this weren't blacked out, who the hell would get it? Where are you going with this, Hilary?

"What about the original information? Could it be stored? A redundancy, in case there's a problem with the rendering?"

"With quantum cryptography there isn't any need—"

"Redundancy, Dr. Reidier, bolsters probability projections. Redundancy compensates for accidents."

"Yes, of course. With essentially zero transmission cost, you simply send information multiple times. In which case, storage would be necessary, theoretically, and a lot of it."

Pierce's voice abruptly switches in tone as well, to a more conciliatory, reassuring timbre. "Absolutely. It's a very promising hypothesis. One that you should definitely extrapolate upon."

The sounds of sipping.

"Still," Pierce continues, "the Department bureaucracy is somewhat of a juggernaut. The higher-ups are most excited about progress. The progress you've already made as well as your projected progress."

"Aren't you the higher-up?"

Pierce chuckles. "Not even remotely. I run things. Make sure everyone has what they need to succeed. I don't call the shots. But the fellas that do, they couldn't be more interested in your work. And your success."

"Yes, of course. What I'm concerned about, however, is a misstep."

"Scientific progress is riddled with missteps. In fact, one could argue almost every major discovery resulted from some sort of trip-up. We're more than scientists in this venture. We're explorers. There's no map."

Reidier starts to interject, but Pierce continues over him. "Of course, you need to tease theories out, rethink, rejigger, but you're focusing on the endgame, and we're not there yet."

"Don't worry about me getting bogged down, it's just my process for working out a problem."

From the sounds of a table creaking, Pierce must be leaning in. "It's not you I'm worried about. It's them."

"The higher-ups?"

"Yes. For them it's about trajectories, investment velocities, and sunk costs. And what you want will require even more investment from the Department."

A few moments of silence.

"Kerek," Pierce commiserates, "I know how excited you must be about this new possibility. Hell, I'm excited too. Your work might obliterate velocity altogether, but to get there you're going to need momentum. And do you know what gives us that?"

"Progress."

"Tangible progress," Pierce concurs. "Something we can point to and say, 'Look what we did!'" He continues on, in his soft colluding tone, "The work you're doing is colossal. It's more than game changing. We're talking Galileo, Copernicus, Newton, Einstein. You're not on the shoulders of giants. You are a giant."[80]

"Well, I don't know."

"The more success you have, the more power *you'll* command, and the more leniency you'll gain. Let's give you the time you need to develop your theory and influence you'll need to implement it if it proves good."

A few moments of quiet.

As deduced by the increase in volume of the whisper, Reidier leans in to Pierce, "You're right. That does make the most sense, I guess."

"You were doing what you were born to do: consider, contemplate, and conjure. But if you're trying to dig tunnels, you can't expect the mountains to just sit there.* You're going to need some support and some cover. Let me do that for you. Ok?"

---

* No matter how much thought I put into this, how many people I run it by at work, I still have no clue what that little manipulative turn of phrase means.

"Sure, Donald."

---

[80] Pierce is paraphrasing Newton who once modestly said, "If I have seen further, it is only by standing on the shoulders of giants."

"Good. So, what we need are some tangible goals to achieve and build on. Goal one: teleporting a physical object. Goal two: a dynamic physical object, like a ticking clock that continues to keep time. Goal three: a biological organism, something that most likely doesn't tangle us up in this mind-transfer dilemma you're working out. Finally, goal four: a biological organism that evidences memory, like a trained rat. What do you think?"

Reidier considers Pierce's plan. "I'll have to amend it with subsets. For instance, with Goal one, it'd be best to start with an elemental object, say carbon in the form of a cube of graphite and then progress to a more complex organization of carbon, like a diamond. I'll need room for a number of evolving iterations."

"Sounds like progress to me. You move a diamond, and I guarantee we'll get continued, generous support. We keep moving forward, and in the meantime, you'll work out the math on this other way. Hm . . ." Pierce hangs the sound in the air like a snare.

"What?" Reidier asks, tripping the trap.

"Taking into consideration the mood of the juggernaut, and the skittish, reactionary reflexes of the guys on high, it's probably best for us to keep this close to the vest. At least until we're further along, on both paths. I hate to impose another level of secrecy on you, but—"

"No, of course. Whatever we need to do in order to nurture this," Reidier agrees.

"Exactly. They don't see the value in questions. Not like you and I. They only want answers."*

---

*Answers only lead to more questions.

"You two need anything else?" a waitress inquires.

"I'm all set," Pierce answers. "Reidier?"

"No. Actually, a peppermint ice tea to go, please," Reidier says.

"Sure thing. Sweetened?"

"Hm? Yes. Ok," Reidier mumbles.

After she goes off, Pierce leans in once again and whispers with hushed excitement, "Before I forget, we've been running scenarios on Malle's research. It seems promising, especially if we were to facilitate it with the introduction of nanobots through capillaries. This would enable us to noninvasively scan an entire working brain in real time. Could be exactly what you need for the ███████████ phase."

"That's promising."

"I'd say. Back at Chicago, I thought you were being circuitous with your emphasis on Malle's work. But I stand corrected. You were spot on."

The waitress brings over his ice tea—Eve's ice tea, which has most likely been sweetened with bleached sugar. But that doesn't appear to register with Reidier as he and Pierce exchange closing pleasantries, and the physicist heads back to 454 Angell Street.

NB Footage: Providence, 12:22 a.m., February 2, 2007

Reidier lies on his back, in bed next to Eve. She sleeps on her right side, on the right side of the bed. Facing away from her husband. A sheet and thin blanket on top of them. Cricket sounds creep through the open-paned windows.

Reidier sighs and turns onto his left side.

Eve stirs and reaches out her hand to touch his back. "Can't sleep?"

Reidier grunts in response.

"I'll take that as a yes."

"The crickets are so loud here."

"Close the windows."

"Then it'll get too hot."

Eve rolls over onto her back and looks at Reidier. "You don't think the sound is soothing?"

"Sometimes I do."

"Just not tonight?"

"I don't know why."

She turns onto her left side and shuffles up against her husband. "You want to play your game, *vingt* questions?"

Reidier shakes his head no against the pillow.

"Is it your stomach? Too many eggs?"

"Eggs?"

"*Oui.* You finished all the eggs this afternoon, no? There were none in the Frigidaire. I thought we had at least a dozen left."

A look of recognition flashes across Reidier's face. He opens his mouth to speak, but then closes it again. It takes a few moments before he finally answers. "Yes. The eggs. No, I didn't eat them. I broke them."

"Why?"

"I didn't do it on purpose. It was, an accident. Very Three Stooges, actually. I was reaching for the yogurt on the shelf behind the eggs. I lifted out a dozen to reach behind and grab it, but I knocked the other dozen over with the yogurt as I pulled it out. Then I ended up smashing those and knocking the falling dozen into a messy tailspin."*

---

* A lie, however, excavates essence.

"So what 'appened to the eggs?" she asks.

Reidier's brow furrows with confusion. "They broke?"

"Of course they broke. What did you do with all the broken eggs?"

"I cleaned them up."

"And threw them out?"

"Yes."

"Next time save them. Put them in a bowl. Cover it with the plastic wrap."

"Next time I break two dozen eggs, I will save them."

They lie in silence again, until Eve raises her head to check if Reidier's eyes are closed. They aren't.

"*À quoi penses-tu?*"

"What am I thinking?"

Eve nods.

"You, and the boys, and me. We're all adjusting, right? It's going to take some time. Right?"

The question hangs in the air. Neither of them move. Only their torsos expand and contract quietly with each breath. Reidier stares up at the ceiling fan.

Finally, in a quiet voice she murmurs, "Adjusting."

"I love you, Eve. It'll be—"

She leaps out of bed, walks to the doorway, and places her hand beneath the panel of switches. She leans out the door, listening down the hall toward the boys' rooms. She is framed in the doorway like that for only a moment before flicking the switch. The ceiling fan whirs into motion.

"Maybe the sound will cover up the crickets, *oui*? If not, then you can close the window, and it will keep you cool."

He mutters a thanks and watches her pad back to the bed. She sits on the mattress and pulls the sheets over her lap. Eve stares down at the foot of the bed.

Reidier waits for more, but she seems lost, staring at the tassels on the end of the blanket fluttering in the wind from the ceiling fan.

He slides his hand across the sheet and onto her leg. "I love you."

"You never told me what happened today with Pierce," Eve says, ignoring his touch.

"I don't know how to read him yet."

"You think he's like Diderot?"

Diderot, of course, was Reidier's distrustful manager at CSG.

"No. Diderot was always obvious. No subtlety to his suspicions and his competitive paranoia. I knew where I stood with him."

"Up to your knees in *merde*."

"*Oui,*" Reidier agrees, laughing.

The laughter seems to fracture the tense mood that has been building. She lies back down next to him. He turns to her, she leans in, and they kiss. Her hand on his cheek.

"So then what did Pierce . . . did you tell him about your echo?" she asks.

"He was excited. Very supportive of doing what I need to."

Eve takes in a staccato breath and sighs.

Reidier tries to extend his arm under her, but it only sets off an avalanche of motion, the two of them shifting around like drugged caterpillars, torsos lifting sideways up into the air and back down on arms now safely ensconced beneath pillows. On their sides, entangled, inches from each other's faces.

They kiss again.

Reidier touches her cheek with his hand.

"I'll figure it out. No more missteps."*

---

* I thought about this section while I lay awake in my own bed. I rolled into the apartment around 12:45 or so, tired but not sleepy. What I needed was to be friggin' exhausted. No thought, no deafening quiet, no room for my anxiety to ramp up any momentum. To lie down and fall right through the mattress into somnambulist bliss.

I wasn't there, though, so I stayed up. Lay on the couch, draining my DVR and more than a few fingers of some Jameson. Finally, when I was convinced I was good and ready, I shuffled over to the bed and quietly snuck into it.

As soon as my head hit the pillow, though, my mind took off like a rodeo bull who'd just got his nuts twisted. I tried to ride it out, go with the flow of it, but finally I just got thrown out of bed. I stared out my window for a few minutes. The bare trees shivered in the cold wind on the street below. Nothing else moved. I started obsessing again about Eve and Reidier. I even downloaded a Sleep App and played the sound of crickets through my stereo.

Back in my bed, I looked across the topography of the ruffled comforter, gazing across the empty plane of mattress next to me. I slid my hand out across the sheet to reach them and found myself wondering about

Lorelei. Was she sleeping soundly next to some hedge-fund manager or sitting up talking into the night with the CEO of some new start-up?

The breeze picked up outside.

Random thoughts blew through my mind: mountaintop scents; deep, quiet rivers; falling through muffled echoes that whispered through the wind as I sailed downward.

The next morning, Eve started writing again.

The crickets harmonized with the whir of a fan. A reassuring rhythm ~~that kept the beasts at bay, just beyond the edges of their bed~~ *and a beat that frightened off the pack of worries that had been hunting them for a thousand miles. It lulled their breathing into sync and danced with the rabble of their dreams that fluttered overhead like moths.*

Respite was just that, though. In the morning, they still found themselves haunted by doppelgängers.

She wasn't the only one who did some writing that day.

-----Original Message-----
From: Donald Pierce [mailto:donald.pierce@darpa.mil]
Sent: Thursday, February 2, 2007 8:19 a.m.
To: larry.woodbury@darpa.mil
Subject: concerns

Larry,

Coffee with Reidier was enlightening. He and the family have settled in and are adjusting.[81] He seems satisfied with the facilities, equipment, etc . . .

I think I got him on track to follow our desired trajectory. Attached is the audio file from the meeting. Listen to it ASAP and get back to me.

I do wonder, though, if our prize physicist is further along than we're aware. Is he hiding something from us?

Have a second team rereview all the NB footage from both the home and lab. Also, have some engineers analyze the power usage and computing performance tracking. See if anything shows up that would indicate excessive computation.

Regardless of the findings, have them set up some sort of detection system that would alert us to anything along these lines.

Needless to say, Reidier must not feel like he's being watched or spied upon.

-DP

PS As to the implications of Reidier's echoes, we should consider the ramifications of this method. How does it impact our long-term goals? Can we find as equally valuable a use for this technology? How do we keep him on course to deliver what we need?

---

[81] Resonant choice of words. Was Pierce insightful or was he consistently listening in on the Reidier home? Though it seems a moot distinction, inevitably, his perspective would color his treatment of Reidier and the events surrounding him. Like with Heisenberg's Uncertainty Principle, the observer ultimately affects the observed.

TITLE CARD: **GALILEE 6:21**

TITLE CARD: **EXPERIMENT 60**

CONTROL ROOM, GOULD ISLAND FACILITY - 2008-1-22
16:03

Dr. Reidier (sweater, tweed sport coat) sits at
console, staring (spacing out) at video on a
screen.

On the left side of the screen is what looks
like a magnified, translucent gummy bear (that's
cloudy green in its center), with eight legs,
and little "claws," swimming and reaching
through its liquid environment, snatching at
suspended organic particles and bringing them to
its mouth.

SOUNDS of the rapid ACCELERATION and
DECELERATION of GEARS.

The right side of the video screen flares to life
and focuses on a bright white paper covered
with microscopic geometric shapes. The magnified
triangles, hexagons, and circles blur in and out
of focus until the view settles and the figures'
sharp edges are clear.

IS1 O'Brien enters from target room.

                    IS1 O'BRIEN
        Target microcamera all set.

Dr. Reidier nods. He lethargically turns to the
camera while O'Brien takes his respective seat.

                    DR. REIDIER
        Experiment sixty is our first
        attempt with a complex biologic, a

tardigrade, the water bear. This
will be our first "animal." The
tardigrade was selected due to its
remarkable durability. Ranging from
.1 to 1.5 mm in size, it is found in
a range of environments, from
6,000 meters above sea level in the
Himalayas, to 4,000 meters deep in
the sea. It can survive down to 1
degree Kelvin, extreme pressures,
radiation, boiling, and even the
vacuum of space. It can even be
dried out and rehydrated decades
later.
>   (beat)
Also we will be teleporting
inanimates and dynamic inanimates
with it as part of its solution
environment.

Dr. Reidier pauses as if about to go on, but
then shrugs and turns toward console, tapping
his lapel pin twice for luck.

>   IS1 O'BRIEN
>   (adds on)

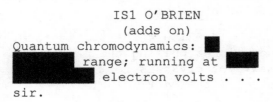

Quantum chromodynamics: █
█ range; running at █
█ electron volts . . .
sir.

Dr. Reidier nods and flips up his Plexiglas cover
over Contact Button Alpha. IS1 O'Brien does the
same at Contact Button Bravo.

>   DR. REIDIER
> Three, two, one, go.

Dr. Reidier and IS1 O'Brien simultaneously press
Contact Buttons Alpha and Bravo.

CUT TO:

MIRROR LAB - SAME TIME

SPLIT SCREEN, right side, MICRO CLOSE-UP of
target pad with focus sheet.

LEFT SIDE, MICRO CLOSE-UP: tardigrade
swimming/walking/eating. It has snatched a
floating particle (bacterium?) and pulls it
toward its maw.

The HIGH PITCH of the Quark Resonator WHINES.

The water bear wiggles.

At 2008-1-22 16:03:50.4588999 a quiet THRUM
coincides with the disappearance of the
tardigrade and its solution, and appearance
of . . . murky sludge [heterogeneous mixture
dominated by iron chloride and iron (II)
sulfate].

NOTE: at 600 picoseconds prior to transmission,
tardigrade appears warped by refraction even
though angle hadn't changed.

RIGHT SIDE, at 16:03:50.4588999, the tardigrade
appears and finishes pulling the particle
into its maw. Ice crystals form around the
circumference of the petri dish.

CONTROL ROOM - 16:03:52

IS1 O'Brien's hands are raised as if he were
declaring a touchdown.

                    IS1 O'BRIEN
          Yahtzee!

Dr. Reidier clicks a couple keys on his
keyboard, perusing readouts with an uninvested
glance.

                    DR. REIDIER
          Yahtzee, indeed.

Pause.

                    IS1 O'BRIEN
          Would you like me to inspect it?

Dr. Reidier shrugs.

                    DR. REIDIER
          Knock yourself out. It worked. It's
          good.

The HIGH-PITCHED WHINE fades out.

X

Experience is simply the name we give our mistakes.

~Oscar Wilde

*There are three principal means of acquiring knowledge . . .
observation of nature, reflection, and experimentation. Observation
collects facts; reflection combines them; experimentation verifies the
result of that combination.*

~Denis Diderot

Excerpted from series of interviews with Dr. Bertram Malle, Professor of Neuroscience and Psychology at Brown University, May 2, 2009*

* Just how many times did Hilary visit RI without telling me?

"When I first started working with Ecco, I couldn't get over his focus. He was almost four, quiet, but intensely present. He followed along with whatever tasks I set before him and was always ready to go on. He didn't fatigue or wander. In fact, more often than not, it was me and not him who needed the break. The only thing that ever seemed to distract him at all, really, was his brother. Otto was the only activity I couldn't compete with. With most four-year-olds, it was a struggle to make it through a full hour of testing, but Ecco and I would speed through an entire afternoon."

At this point, Bertram scratches at his beard.

"Reidier had told me they had had issues with their son. He was elliptical about the details. He emphasized how he didn't want to bias my take at all. Just wanted my professional opinion."

"You weren't buying it?" I ask.

"No, I knew that he was sincere. He was coming to me for my professional help, but specifically because of our friendship. Because he could trust me. That's why we did everything at his home, rather than at my office."

He was right. Reidier was seeking him out more for their personal relationship than for Bertram's professional acumen. "Elliptical is a very specific word," I suggest.

"Caught that, did you?"

"What I'm wondering is whether you felt that this was a conscious or unconscious trait?"

"You mean was he purposefully deceiving me, or incapable of comprehending or expressing the whole truth?" He pauses. "I guess I was thinking that he always seems to come at things obliquely, it was part of his brilliance. Always took the long way around but somehow ended up returning with some rather clever items."

"This still surprises you about him?"

"Reidier was purposefully vague about whatever accident befell his son, but also completely clueless about his own vulnerability within the situation. To a certain degree, he was both ignorant and incapable of expressing the motivations which drove him to seek out the refuge of our relationship."

Our waitress brings over our orders. Bertram's Half-Crazed Burger and my own Freaky Fajita Burger. Per Bertram's insistence, we never meet at his office, but always in public establishments somewhat off the beaten path—which is how we find ourselves in a quirky half-vegan, half-hippie café just up the road from the Narragansett Beach.

Bertram justified the field trips with some explanation about change of scenery and getting away from the office. At first it seemed like a lovely suggestion, but over time, I came to wonder if it was a defensive decision. An effort to get out from under the gaze, away from suspected surveillance. How much did he know about the Department's efforts? Did Bertram's penchant for out-of-the-way locales have something to do with what had happened: with Reidier, with Pierce, with the Department?

Had he become aware of the watching?*

---

* He was right to be careful. They probably were watching him. They were watching everything. I mean we're talking about actual teleportation here.

I'm a little late to the game in all of this. I guess I've been distracted. It's not like I wasn't aware of the whole teleportation thing. It's just maybe I'm starting to believe in the whole goddamn venture. Like up until this point, it's sort of been, well, a story that my mom made up. Not out of thin air. But constructed with hunches and hypotheticals.

Only she was right.

Reidier was on to something.

And this isn't a story at all.

Somewhere along the way, while Psynaring, Hilary found some echoes that started to make their own echoes. Bouncing off the walls of Reidier's basement, the diluted pings led Hilary right into the labyrinth, and the Minotaur got a whiff of her scent.

His story became her story. And now it's becoming mine.

Too bad for me, it ended up being true.

I'm not paranoid, but the fact of the matter is they were watching Reidier. It makes sense that they were tracking Bertram. So how do I not conclude that they were following Hilary too? I mean, why else did she go to all the trouble of hiding this damn report?

Maybe that's why she was so hush-hush with me. I mean, yes, government secrets and all that classified protocol. But why she didn't even mention her trips to RI? The further she held me at arm's length, the safer for me. She was just being a protective mother. Silence of love.

Then again, she did leave me a trail of breadcrumbs right into the bees' nest and then handed over a briefcase full of inedible honey.

What I'm trying to get at is I think they've found me.

Of course, the Department always knew where I was. I'm not some superspy escape artist. I work at Anomaly, and my apartment address is in the phone book.

They found the carriage house. They tracked me to Hell's Kitchen.

I think.

Christ, I really am paranoid. I mean after writing the previous two lines I just stopped, and listened. Like what? Like I'm going to hear the bugs? I'll tell you, the best thing I did was not bring any electrical gadgets into this place. Card table, chair, lamp, bead necklace hanging on the wall, leather briefcase, and inside it, the report.

No computer. No landline. No cell phone. I even take the battery out of my cell when I come here.

These weren't precautions. I just can't handle interruptions. I'm too easily distracted by phone calls, texts, IMs, the internet. If I had to jump back and forth from the real world to this one locked inside these folders, my brain would concuss until it was a gelatinous ooze and pour out from my ears.

That's why Toby's become so frustrated with me. He can never reach me anymore. He has to stalk me. Literally.

Maybe that's it. Maybe they followed Toby. I'm always so careful coming here. Diving down into subway tunnels. Slipping in out of back doors in bars. But Toby. I bet he just walks right up. Probably takes a cab here.

It happened a little over a week ago.

I was going over Reidier's lecture again. Seeing if I could make heads or tails of it. See what I missed. Widen my scope a little and see what I find beyond the tunnel vision.

It's still pretty dense stuff, but I'm getting into it now. Not the science of it, by any means, but the concept of it. How was Reidier thinking? What were his givens? Sort of like how I can't even begin to explain the intricacies of nuclear bombs, but I get that there's a lot of power binding a nucleus of atoms together and splitting that apart releases it.

Anyway, I was focused. Sitting down in the bottom-floor bedroom that's sunk halfway beneath the concrete courtyard, trying to wrap my brain around how quantum computers dance around Heisenberg's Uncertainty Principle . . .

BUZZZZ!

I didn't know what the hell it was at first. Jarring electrical sound like a drunk fire alarm sat on by a fat guy. Muffled, but piercing. I froze. What was it? It came from upstairs? What's upstairs?

Second floor = kitchenette, empty living room.

Top floor = a bathroom and a bedroom with a mattress resting on the floor.

What made—

BUZZZZZZZZZ!

It blared again, scaring me to my feet. It definitely came from upstairs. I stood there a second, searching the room for a weapon, a pipe, a piece of wood. Anything. But all I had was my card table, lamp, bead necklace, leather briefcase, and the report.

I snuck upstairs as quietly as I could. The stairs go up six steps, then you hit a landing, shift over, and go up another six back in the direction you came from. I stopped at the landing and listened.

Nothing. Six more steps up, and I looked around the empty living room. No sound. No object. Nothing even out of place. I tiptoed over to the kitchenette and poked my head around the door frame. Cabinets closed. Refrigerator hummed quietly. The old analog clock set into the oven from 1985 whirred a little. It didn't seem like these things were responsible for the disruption.

Must be on the top floor, I figured.

BUZZZZZZZZZ!

The sound shot around the room and ricocheted right into my brain. Fuck!

It was coming from the corner where the living room met the kitchen. Just to the right of the entrance to the kitchen, hanging on a white wall between the two rooms, was an eggshell-colored plastic phone that must have been installed the same year as the stove.

It had always been there. I'd seen it before and thought it was a vestigial appliance. Apparently it was the door buzzer, so someone could ring you from the street, and you could ask who the hell it was and had they followed Toby there or me?

So I stood there, staring at the phone. Beads of sweat dotting my brow. Do I answer it? Do I not?

I reached out, put my hand on the receiver, and finally noticed an off-white button sticking out beneath a three-inch video screen. Rundown carriage house, in the middle of the block, at the ass bottom of Hell's Kitchen—this shit isn't still supposed to be functional.

It took a minute for the screen to warm up, but it worked. A crisp black-and-white image of the sidewalk in front of 357 West 39th. And there he was. My stalker. White guy, mid-to-late forties, a bit overweight but nothing grotesque (at least as far as I could tell, seeing as how he was wearing a puffy down coat—you know the Michelin Man kind of jacket), large square-framed glasses, and a knit stocking cap that was way too big and pulled up way too high so it looked like the reservoir tip of a condom dangling off the top of his head.

It was the stocking cap that got me. He looked like a tourist. A stray sheep who had somehow wandered away from the flock milling about in Times Square and found himself on the wrong side of Port Authority.

He danced from foot to foot to keep himself warm. Then leaned up against the glass door. Raised his gloved hand to cover his eyes, and try and peer through the glare off the window. He scrunched up his face, clearly not able to see much. Then he pressed buzzer number five again.

BUZZZZZ!

I didn't realize how loud that thing was. You really get an earful standing right in front of it.

The guy took a couple steps back and looked up at the building. Maybe he was searching for someone who might be surreptitiously peering out his window. Clearly, this guy didn't see the camera. Or didn't think it worked either.

Finally he scowled at the door and took off, heading east on 39th. And that was it. He was gone.

I mean, sure, it could've been some lost tourist. Or maybe he was visiting someone else in the building and got the wrong buzzer. Or the buzzers could have their wires crossed. (Nope, not that one. I just went out, propped all the doors open from my place to the front door, and pressed number five and heard the buzz blare out of the carriage house.) Or he just had the wrong building.

Or maybe he worked for the Department and figured the perfect cover for a reconnaissance mission was to look like some doofus tourist from the Midwest.

All I know is, it freaked me out.

And Bertram Malle was right to be cautious. Clearly, though, he wasn't cautious enough.

"Still, the connotations do conjure some very specific ideas, don't they?" Bertram says, picking up the elliptical thread. "Planetary orbits for one."

"How so?"

"All orbits, I believe, are elliptical.* Regardless of the trajectory taken and the distance traveled, there's the inevitability of a return. Like Reidier into my life."

---

* Orbits are in fact elliptical as described by Kepler's laws of planetary motion. The degree of the warping, however, varies with each planet. The earth's is in nearly a perfect circle, while Pluto's is a longer and thinner ellipse.

"So you always knew he would come back?"

He swallows another mouthful of Half-Crazed beef. "Not in any conscious way. I wasn't awaiting Reidier per se but was unsurprised when he came back into my daily life."

I liked Bertram, and more and more found myself veering off course, sometimes enjoying the direction of the conversation and forgetting the focus of my inquiry.** "If I remember correctly, ellipses are differentiated by their degree of eccentricity."

** So apparently Hilary's back to injecting these little personal touches. I thought we were done with that. Guess it's just subject to the tides of her process. Is this merely a personal observation, something she'd edit out of the final draft, or within this is some clue?

"I think you're right. How wonderfully accurate. Kerek obviously would have had a very eccentric curvature." Bertram pauses in revelation. "Ellipses also have two foci. Two forces fighting for the center position."***

*** Mom ought to know all about that.

I ask the obvious question. "What were his?"

"His work and his family. The two pulls he felt on himself, sometimes in opposition while other times in conjunction."

"And that's where you came in?"

"I suppose it is."

Reidier had approached Bertram about testing and possibly diagnosing Ecco. To both fix Ecco and help Eve. Was this Reidier's true motivation in seeking out his old friend? Was Stage 4 an official cover?

"Who was Ecco?" I ask.

"At home or not at home?"

The question gives me pause. "Was there a difference?"

"I guess the more accurate question is who was Ecco with his family, and who was he on his own? The environment itself precipitated drastically different results from the boy. The simple act of observing him seemed to impact him."

"As if he were performing for you?"

Bertram fidgets with his silverware, ignores my question, and avoids eye contact. It's the first time I've ever detected any nervousness from him. "I initially misdiagnosed him. At first glance, he was a textbook case for a savant."

In the footage,[82] Bertram's first afternoon "testing" Ecco couldn't have seemed less probing. It was framed as a Saturday afternoon barbeque.

The boys play outside in the backyard, while Reidier and Bertram drink ice teas at a distance. They gossip about old classmates, discuss the beauty of Victorian architecture and the hassle of upkeep that goes along with living in a historical landmark, tease each other about

---

[82] This video documentation was compiled from "hitcher feeds" (nanobots that have attached themselves to an individual's clothes, hair, etc. after being brushed against).*

> * Are you kidding me?! Hitcher feeds. The fucking nanobots can latch onto your clothes and hair and just tag along?! When did Hilary learn about these? Did she start burning her clothes periodically and giving herself DNA-cleansing scrubdowns?

how soft a science psychology is or how physics is merely philosophy for math geeks who can't write well.

Eve is happy for the distraction. She goes back and forth from harvesting mint from her herb garden for the tea, to pumping Bertram for embarrassing stories about Reidier from their college days.

Bertram obliges with a story about how Reidier ended his brief career in collegiate a cappella. For the Parents' Weekend concert, Reidier wanted to amp up his group's wow factor and came up with an idea to electromagnetize the stage in Burnham Hall so that the group could have "floating microphones."

"You can do that?" Eve asks.

"Of course."

"Sort of," Bertram amends Reidier's assertion.

"It worked." Reidier smiles proudly at his wife.

"It did," Bertram concedes. "For almost ten seconds."

"I told everybody, no metal of any kind," Reidier defends himself.

"Like with an MRI?" Eve asks, enjoying how Bertram teases her husband.

"He did. He was very thorough, I saw the list he passed out to the group." Bertram attempts to maintain a serious tone. "No watches, rings, pens, belts, tie clips, glasses."

Eve stands, hands on hips, wanting more.

A practiced raconteur, Bertram takes a long sip of ice tea. "You're right, Eve; this mint mixed with the lemon balm really gives the tea a zing."

"Bertram," she scolds him in her French accent. "What 'appened?"

Bertram raises his eyebrows to Reidier and nods for him to tell Eve.

Reidier sighs, eyes cast down, and quietly mutters one word, "Zippers."

Eve leans her head in, repeating what she thinks her husband said, "Zippers?"

Reidier nods. Bertram's face contorts with contained laughter.

"What 'appened with 'ze zippers?" Eve asks, letting out a little laugh.

"It was a very powerful electromagnet. Khaki and denim are only so strong," Reidier sighs.

A look of surprise and horror rises in Eve's face.

"It was a very different kind of wow factor," Bertram manages to get out before he explodes in laughter.

Eve likewise disintegrates into hysterics.

"Everybody panicked after their pants ripped," Bertram says. "One of the guys accidentally kicked over the mercury arc, which blew the whole system, blacking out the entire building, all of campus, and half of the city."

"Not to mention the mercury spill," Reidier adds.

Between laughs, Eve manages to ask if anyone was hurt.

"Eight seconds in to the all-male a cappella rendition of *Flash Dance*, and Kerek's stardom had burnt out."

"'Zay kicked you out?"

"The school banned him from any and all performance spaces." Bertram collapses onto a bench and tries to catch his breath.

The afternoon continues on with similar levity. Bertram seems to act as a foil for Reidier and Eve, essentially as a medium through which they can connect to each other. Sporadically, throughout the afternoon, they become affectionate toward one another: a hand on the small of the back, leaning against each other, hooking a finger in the other's belt. The tension that has pulled at them for the past few months seems to have been cut free. Perhaps in helping them recollect the past, Bertram has coaxed them back into the present.

It's not until Eve finally picks up on how the two keep maneuvering, facing one way, and then another, that she realizes they are taking turns surreptitiously observing the boys. "All this time, I thought we were 'aving a nice leisurely afternoon. How silly of me not to take note that you two are 'ard at work." And with that she retreats to the wicker bench on the veranda.

Reidier shrugs and shakes his head, murmuring, it seems, some sort of explanation to Bertram.

Eve attempts to force herself to read. Her gaze, however, keeps drifting above the edge of her novel toward the men in the yard. Finally, in an anxious flurry of motion, she retreats into the house, calling for Otto to come help mommy in the kitchen.

It's Bertram, not Reidier, who seems concerned with Eve's exit. He suggests that maybe they should talk to Eve. Apologize. Reidier dismisses the idea with the slightest of shrugs, and mumbles something about how she only sees through cucumber eyes.[83] The awkwardness dissolves into silence.

What had been a social Saturday afternoon, full of anecdotes, cold drinks, sunshine, and the laughter of children becomes an impromptu lab experiment. Bertram and Reidier standing on the lawn, staring at the sandbox. A pair of lost UFO hunters searching for crop circles in the carpet.

The two scientists have shed all of the familiarity and affection that was between them. Instead of teasing each other, they stand together in antiseptic observation. Mirror images of each other,

---

[83] Due to questionable audio quality during this portion of the footage, that statement might not be accurate. However, upon multiple hearings as well as some technical adjustments, Reidier does seem to say cucumber eyes. The only reason it has been kept in at all is due to the fact that it resonates with various other peculiar phrases peppered throughout the material. Whether these are somehow part of a thematic reality or merely a collection of odd malapropisms has yet to be determined, but should be kept in mind nevertheless.

staring at Ecco. Perhaps they're afraid of disturbing the experiment. The friendship has molted off, leaving only a raw sense of purpose.

As Heisenberg himself could have predicted, their hypnosis is ultimately broken by the subject itself. Ecco, sensing the attention, breaks away from his play and looks back at them. The three consider each other. Ecco is unfazed by their gaze. Quite the contrary, he seems more fascinated with it than the toys and sand he was playing with.

Bertram begins to move, but Reidier stops him with a quiet, "Wait."

The three remain in this quiet abeyance for several minutes. They watch him, and he them. It's not aggressive. Nor is it play (even though it might sound like a staring contest). Ever so subtly, Ecco begins to move. His right elbow circling. His finger tapping against his thigh. It takes a while for Bertram to realize Ecco is mirroring Reidier's absentminded fidgeting.

Bertram describes it best after almost ten minutes. "I feel like we're in a scene out of *Gorillas in the Mist*."

Reidier nods with an mmhm.

"Only he's Diane Fossey."*

---

* Sounds a lot more like *Children of the Corn*, drawing crop circles in the sandbox. What is wrong with this kid?

"What do you make of it?" Reidier asks.

"It's remarkable focus. An unerring curiosity."

"In you or him?"

Reidier and Bertram laugh.

The spell broken, Ecco mimics them with his own laugh. So adept is he at matching up his own laugh to theirs in both timbre and rhythm, it startles them into silence. For a moment they all stare at each other. Finally Ecco's hands drift back into the sand, and he again excavates the silt into abstract patterns.

The manner in which these two old friends approach the Ecco question couldn't be more revealing about the differences between them. Bertram is excited by the uniqueness of the child and content to observe him for as long as possible. Reidier instead is consternated, eager to classify his child's deficiency, and determined to map out his psychological trajectory. Bertram watches, Reidier studies. Bertram wants to see, Reidier must sequence. One wants to understand, the other to master. Still, despite disparity in their methods, anyone who watches them can detect a similar sense of purpose. If one merely looks past Bertram's soft-bearded smile and considers his eyes, he'll find a fiery excitement. Reidier stands just to his left, his eyes dancing with the same spark. It is a look of longing, drawn out by the curiosity to know, driven by the arrogance to grasp. The two of them stand together fueled by Promethean ambitions.

The moment ends with a single word. Reidier's need to contain, to categorize and quantify, takes over. His habitualized training is reflex at this point, but also a protective effort to bottle up the emotions threatening to bubble up and overwhelm. It is the best way he's learned to manage the unknown. He falls back on the scientific method itself, and offers up a hypothesis: "Autism?"

"It was simultaneously surprising yet expected," Bertram shares with me in our interview. "Here he had gone for so long, not telling me anything, letting me see for myself, not muddying the water. He wanted, as I told you, my complete and unbiased opinion. And half an afternoon into my investigation, he tosses out his hypothesis, rippling the surface, blurring my view into the depths of his son.

"That being said, it was his son. And a boy who exhibited enigmatic behavior that was amplified when brought into disturbing relief with his twin brother. Otto was a doppelgänger of normalcy that only accentuated Ecco's otherness. A contrast so painful, so glaring, that Eve, his mother, couldn't even see Ecco anymore. Blinded by the difference."

Bertram stops for a moment, looking down and to the left. His eyes fill with sadness. "As much as Reidier wanted my professional perspective, I think he craved my personal support more. He needed to voice his fear. And he couldn't with Eve. He wanted me for himself as much as for his son. Sharing his suspicion with me made it easier to bear. Heal his son, his wife, his family. He could lean on me a little."*

---

* Sometimes voicing a fear is the worst thing you could do. Speaking it out loud is what wakes the dogs of fury. Gets their attention. Makes your presence known, and you either find yourself running like hell, 'cause as crazy as it sounded in your head, turns out your fear was right, or you find yourself in a tight jacket on the way to Bellevue (the nuthouse, not the bar that shares a backdoor with Siberia up on 40th).

No, fear is your friend. Fear keeps you safe. Fear's what makes sure you don't just pack this whole thing up, lock the door behind you, run out, and go cry to Lorelei.

Fear's my guardian angel.

"As a friend and a professional?" I ask.

Bertram pauses in surprise. "Now that I think about it, maybe Kerek was relying on my professionalism more than I realized. Maybe he knew, deep down, that he couldn't possibly remain objective, but hoped that somehow I could pull him back to center. Keep him grounded. Guide him past the fear."

Fear is a powerful motivator.** A constant presence that dominates all of our lives, more than most of us care to admit. We treat it as something to be avoided, tamped down, repressed. We encourage each other not to live in fear. Devise methods to cope with it. Go to any Barnes &

Noble and you'll find entire aisles of self-help literature. No matter what the context, each of these books has the same basic spine, a core of fear.

** Agreed.

What's rarely discussed, though, is how necessary fear has been for our survival. Fear has been shaped by evolution over thousands of years. Individuals who were sufficiently afraid successfully avoided dangerous predators, precarious cliff edges, lethal rip tides, dark labyrinthine caverns, and the likes thereof. The fearful maximized their probability for survival, living long enough to successfully procreate and instill those same fears in their offspring so that they could also go on to procreate.

Fear is our inheritance.

Fear is in our DNA. We are wired for it.

At Carnegie Mellon's Infant Cognition Laboratory, David Rakison has been using innovative techniques to uncover how and when babies learn about the world. He says that "babies are born with a tendency to pay more attention to the shapes of snakes and spiders than to other kinds of creatures."[84] Even five-month-olds pay more attention to drawings of spiders on a video screen than they do to a scrambled version of the same picture. In other studies, psychologists have found that both adults and children detect images of snakes from among a variety of nonthreatening objects much faster than they pick out fish, butterflies, or flowers. Similarly, Susan Mineka at Northwestern University, working with monkeys, showed that primates' brains are wired to react more strongly to snakes. We're biologically disposed to be afraid. This tendency, along with our unparalleled ability to also pass down knowledge of danger, is one of the reasons we've been such a successful species.

Obviously fear is an inhibitor. Although popular opinion takes

---

[84] Mark Roth, "Why do we think spiders and snakes are so scary? It just might be evolution." *Pittsburgh Post-Gazette*, March 7, 2007.

the stance that it retards development by curtailing risk taking, in fact it culls development by balancing it with need. When sufficient need arises for an individual or group to overcome their fears and take risks, progress is achieved. We don't hunt the woolly mammoth until we have to, for food, for warmth, for crucial needs.* And when we do, we take care, and make sure we maximize whatever advantage we can. Because we are scared of what will happen if we don't.

---

* So it's not that I'm too scared to answer the door, it's that my need to know isn't great enough. I'm not a coward, I'm a survivor. And the reason I don't act on my impulse to seek out Lorelei, well, that's just me biding my time until necessary, considering how to maximize my advantage. Ensure a successful hunt.

So why am I shaking?

Fear is our reaction to not being able to predict the future. It is sublimated frustration at our inability to successfully parse cause and effect. It is the unknown. It is the dark, the other side, the question mark.**

** Hilary's theory doesn't adhere to the good ol' transitive property, however. While fear might equal the unknown, the unknown does not necessarily equal fear. I might not know what happened to her, but that doesn't mean I'm scared of finding out.

I didn't go in to work today. Didn't e-mail. Didn't call. Couldn't risk it. Haven't even put the battery back in my cell phone. It might not be a problem though. Today might not be Monday. Could be Sunday. Not sure. Kind of lost track.

Guess my peculiar little Michelin Man visitor had an effect. Let's say he wasn't a "tourist." Was this just a reconnaissance mission, see what's what? Or was he beating the bushes? Seeing what he could flush out onto 39th Street into an evenly spaced-out semicircle of Department hunters, nets ready?

I thought about this in the hallway last night. Had cleaned everything up. Packed it all into the briefcase, which I shoved out of sight in the crawl space underneath the stairs. Took the bead necklace off the wall and pulled it over my head. My amulet of one past parent against another. Locked both the top and bottom locks, walked across the iron bridge, past the garbage bins, down the well-lit hallway to the glass security door, when I realized how dark it had gotten outside.

With the sun having long since gone down, the glass door appeared nothing more than a reflection of the fluorescent-lit hallway, streaked by headlights passing by in the night outside.

I was a brightly framed sitting duck at a carnival shooting range, blinded by light intended to promote security. Safe, as long as I didn't open up the locked front door.

My hand dropped back to my side. I stood there for several minutes, staring at the reflection of myself in the glass, when all of a sudden, it pushed open the door from the outside.

At least that's what it looked like to me. Turns out it was just a woman who lived up on the third floor. Hidden by the glare of my reflection, she had walked right up, opened the door, and catapulted my heart right out of the back of my rib cage.

She held the door open a moment, looking at me questioningly.

I mumbled something or other and shook my head no.

Guess the look in my eye was none too comforting, 'cause she closed the door slowly and then headed up the stairs two at time.

Once I heard the dead bolts lock behind her, I shot right back down the hall, across the iron bridge, and into the carriage house. I sure as hell wasn't going out, at night, all lit up with a silhouetted bull's-eye on my chest.

I looked around the second floor. Nothing new. The windows on the far wall, across from the door, were no help. Two feet by two feet, glass-bricked windows that I couldn't even see through, let alone open or crawl out of.

Back on the iron bridge I checked out the courtyard. The five stories of 357 rose up directly across from me; to the left a ten-story building walled me in, to the right the back of a tenement building. Straight up was the roof of my secret little house. The gutters ringed with barbed wire stretched out like an oversized, angry slinky.

Once again my own "security" had me trapped.

I decided to stay in my little barbwired briar patch.

Wait for the cover of day.

Let them beat the bushes senseless. I had my mom's report to keep me company, and my fears to keep me safe.

So what then is Reidier afraid of?

The worst has already happened. Reidier's child is already, for lack of a better term, damaged in a profound way. His marriage is strained by the deformity. As evidenced by the basement, Eve does not manage brokenness well.[85] Diagnosing Ecco would only help to provide a catalog of information based on case studies and treatment histories, a way to at least put the situation in rational context.

But if the present damage is known, what's the fear? The answer must lie in the past or the future, the cause or the effect.

Yet there is no past, only memory.

There is no future, only hope.

Is it Reidier's memory or his hope that's the present question mark?

Is he anxious for the future, or guilty about his past?

A few years ago, a patient was referred to me by her child's surgeon. The woman was young, vibrant, athletic, and above all, positive. But she was racked with guilt for her son being born with a damaged cochlea and subsequently deaf. During the pregnancy, her husband had won a trip at work to attend a conference in Hawaii. It fell on the cusp of her second and third trimester of gestation. After consulting with her ob-gyn, she and her husband decided to take the trip. Unfortunately, while on vacation there was a complication. She had to be transported via helicopter to the hospital on the main island. At the end of the day, everything was fine, and a few months later, she gave birth to her deaf son.

No matter how often her doctor assured her that flying had nothing to do with her son's deafness, she couldn't let go of the idea that all would have been well if only she hadn't taken the trip. Even after working with me for months, the only progress she seemed to make was accepting blame as a proactive lesson, carrying it around with her as a reminder to be a good mother and always put her child first.

Ultimately, it took the birth of her second son two years later for her to find absolution. Like his brother, he was born with the same

---

[85] See Chapter II

damaged cochlea. It turns out it was a result of the genetic pairing of her and her husband. Ironically, learning about how her own genes contributed to her children's impairments is what finally lifted the weight of the "what if?"

Did Reidier have his own "what if?" What was happening with Ecco wasn't the real question as much as what was going to happen. How stable was his condition? Could it improve or would it worsen? What was to become of his son? His marriage? The stress of Ecco had already cracked the foundation of their home, opened up rifts between Reidier and Eve. As the truth about Ecco coalesced, the reality of his marriage could disintegrate.

Having written all this, I now wonder if I had it all backward. Whether Reidier was wrestling with guilt or dread, cause or effect, or even both, his hypothesizing, his naming the condition, voicing the word *autism*, was not an act of fear, but of desperation: an act of hope.

"I was at a loss," Bertram confesses to me. "It wasn't autism. It wasn't anything I'd ever seen. Ecco resisted any of the abnormal classifications. He was abnormally abnormal." He wrinkles his brow. "I know, it sounds incomplete. But that's what it felt like. Here, here." He opens his satchel and searches for a few moments before pulling out a yellow legal pad covered with notes. "It's all here.

"The rest of that afternoon, I engaged Ecco in several games and tasks. What was odd was that he knew very few, if any, rules. However, within minutes of play he could master a game. We played Concentration, you know, that memory game where you have cards with matching pictures of animals and objects on them facedown, and you turn over two at a time, trying to match a pair?"

I nod with understanding, noting how Bertram has grown more excited.

"He didn't get it at all at first."

"Because of communication issues?" I ask. On the footage, Ecco rarely talks except to Otto. I wondered whether Bertram picked up something more in the live encounter that didn't translate to the surveillance footage.

"That was only one of the symptoms of autism Ecco actually seemed to manifest. He rarely talked, and when he did, at least half of it was his and Otto's twin-speak. But 'playing' with him, I quickly realized he had excellent comprehension skills. He could follow along and understand, just not express. Almost like a stroke victim suffering from aphasia. Although, unlike those patients, he wasn't reaching to find the words or frustrated that he couldn't say what he wanted. He was just present in the moment, unburdened by expectations for himself, unaware and unperturbed by his limitations."

"Strange," I agree.

"In spite of his deficient vocabulary, within minutes he understood the concept of the game, and after about ten minutes of play, he was playing at a speed that put him in the 99th percentile. He never missed an opportunity, forgot a card, or made a mistake."

This was all verified by the footage. Ecco learned remarkably fast and with impressive results.

"I wondered if it was savant syndrome," he continues.

About half of all people with savant syndrome have autistic disorder. The other half has another developmental disability. Very rarely, however, some savants exhibit no apparent abnormalities other than their unique traits.

"Especially after—" he stops himself short. His eyes search my face with a glance, before immediately dropping down to focus on the table.

It was so quick, if I hadn't been looking at him at the time, I would have missed it. He was censoring himself. Once again, my Department position might somehow be inhibiting the work. I represent a threat. To what, though? Reidier's gone, as are Ecco, Eve,

Otto. He's not shielding them. Maybe he's protecting their memory, though that seems more like something out of nineteenth-century Russian literature than out of a lunch between PhDs in an ocean-side hippie hamburger joint. He must be protecting himself for some reason. Nothing from the footage shows Bertram behaving in any unethical manner. Still, he'd hesitated. "Playing other games with him?" I offer.

He nods, "Yes." His eyes widen with recognition. He smiles and makes eye contact. He feels understood.* He sighs before continuing. "He wasn't specialized, like a savant. He wasn't simply good at memory or calculating or a music prodigy. Across the board, he just seemed to approach everything with an innocence. That's the best word I can come up with, although it seems completely trite when describing a child. He had unbelievable faculties and absolutely no knowledge. He *was* a completely heuristic entity." Bertram pauses, almost as if he were not even believing himself. "For him, there were no rules, no expectations, no givens, no biases."

---

*Well done, Hilary. Another successful manipulation.

"There was no matter of fact for Ecco?"

"None whatsoever. He was a living, breathing personification of Hume's philosophy."[86]

---

[86] Bertram references the eighteenth-century philosopher, David Hume. Hume was particularly brutal with his assertions about epistemology, how we know what we know. He focused specifically on how information rests on our belief in matters of fact. He observes how,

> When one particular species of event has always, in all instances, been conjoined with another, we make no longer any scruple of foretelling one upon the appearance of the other . . . We then call that one object, *Cause*; the other, *Effect*. We suppose that there is some connection between them; some power in the one, by which it infallibly produces the other, and operates with the greatest certainty and strongest necessity. (Hume, *An Enquiry Concerning Human Understanding* (1748), pp. 80-81.)

Cause and effect: we cannot escape their trappings.

"And it definitely wasn't autism. Ecco was fine with eye contact, he smiled a lot, he engaged in consistent social play with his brother. Obviously, he was incredibly adept at playing by himself and engaging with his surroundings, but he didn't shun interactive play or seem asocial. There were only a handful of behaviors that Ecco manifested on the autism checklist. He didn't always respond to his name. He seemed to lack both stranger anxiety and separation anxiety.[87] However, not being anxious could also be attributed to self-actualized confidence."

"Especially for such a heuristic individual," I echo his phrase back to him.

He nods enthusiastically and gets lost in considering this for a moment.

"What about verbal communication?" I ask, understanding he'd interpret this as the normal push-pull of a shared interest between colleagues.

"That's where Ecco seemed to have the most trouble. He had almost no ability to sustain a conversation, but again, it wasn't that he couldn't follow a conversation, just he rarely spoke."

"Except his twin-speak?"

Hume supports his challenge of our understanding of knowledge with a favorite example, a seemingly undeniable given, our belief that the sun will rise tomorrow. Obviously, this is a matter of fact, based upon our conviction that the sunrise is an effect caused by the earth's rotation. Our belief in this causal relationship, however, is based upon past observations. We hold this to be true because every day, since the dawn of humanity, the sun has risen. But our confidence that this will continue in the same manner tomorrow cannot be justified by referencing the past. We have no rational basis for believing the sun will rise tomorrow, yet believe it, we do.

[87] Stranger anxiety develops in the first year. Once separation anxiety develops (also in the first year) when mother departs, normal infants are upset. Ecco was not an infant, but barely acknowledged the absence of Eve. And when he did, it was an act of curiosity not fear.

"Right. He seemed to be most loquacious around Otto. Even then it was still repetitive, unusual language. A lot of echolalia. His limited vocalization was striking, especially compared to his gregarious brother. But, like I said, even though he couldn't sustain a conversation, he could participate in one, for long periods of time. Our entire afternoon of games was one big conversation."

Another major indicator of autism is obsession. "Would you say he was obsessive in his attentiveness to the interaction?"

"I thought about that of course. But no. He was focused. But not in a rigid way. He was happy to explore tangential paths as they presented themselves within the dynamic. No limit to his interests, no tics or repetitive movements. Nor did he have any sensory symptoms." He shrugs. "The language was the most profound deficit in all his behavior. And lack of presupposed ideas."

"Korsakoff syndrome?"

Bertram's eyes rise up to meet mine again. He scratches at his beard, smiling at me knowingly. "We played another type of matching game. I'd show him variety of cards and ask him to put the ones that go together into piles. So, for instance, one group of cards would all have pictures of animals on them, a bear, a monkey, a snake; another group would be of buildings, an office building, a church, a house; a third group had vegetables, corn cobs on the stalk, apples on the tree, tomatoes on the vine, you get the gist. Ecco had no sense of association whatsoever. No concept of categories. He'd put the house, the bear, and the tomatoes in one pile; the church, the apple, and the snake in another. However, when I used objects in the room, various cushions from the couch and chairs, a collection of toys like Legos, action figures, and blocks, or the remote control, a DVD case, and a DVD disk, he grouped them all perfectly."

"So what, he had an issue with interpreting two-dimensional information?" I ask.

"No. He could point out family members in photographs without any problem. But the test was inconclusive and unimportant, ultimately. What was critical was what happened after the test."

Bertram stares at me for a few moments, biting his lip in concentration. He's evaluating me. "We had been at it for quite some time, and I needed to use the restroom. So I left Ecco in the den. I was gone maybe three minutes or so. Ecco was right where I left him. Piles of grouped objects surrounded him. All of the couch cushions stacked together, a tower of DVD cases balanced next to the television, a mound of magazines and books. A heap of Legos and next to it, all of the cards we had played with, the photograph of tomatoes at the top of the deck."

The footage from the afternoon confirms Bertram's story. It shows Ecco, relaxed yet determined, crisscrossing the room, reorganizing any object he could lift and carry to its "proper" pile. He seems neither rushed nor hesitant. He neither makes a mistake nor considers which pile to place something in. He seems almost like a worker ant completing his rounds, and once finished, takes his place sitting where he began, waiting for Bertram's return.

I laugh. "So he got into the game."

"He did," Bertram continues in a measured tone. "It was, overwhelming. I, of course, went off to find Reidier, to show him. Once again, it was several minutes at best."

The footage shows Bertram's surprise, as he takes it all in. He smiles down at Ecco, softly telling him he'll be right back, just needs to go find his daddy.

According to the footage counter, it took Bertram four minutes and forty-eight seconds to return. Ecco remains seated, but fidgets with what I now assume are Legos. Due to limited camera angles and Ecco's placement, it is impossible to see his activity. The microphones, however, do pick up the slight, rhythmic clicking of plastic being snapped together.

When Ecco finishes, he places his project out of sight on the floor, stands up, and wanders out of the room. Four minutes and twenty-two seconds have elapsed. Twenty-six seconds later, Bertram leads Reidier into the room, finishing up his explanation of the grouping game. Reidier takes in the room, noting all the various organized piles. A bemused smile curls at the corners of his mouth. "He did this all on his own?" Reidier asks.

Bertram doesn't really hear the question, though. He's staring at the floor, where Ecco was sitting. "Kerek, look." Bertram points at the spot out of sight.

Reidier follows the line of Bertram's finger. The curled corners of his mouth immediately flatten out. His eyes narrow. "You didn't do that together?"

"That wasn't here when I left."

Reidier bends over and delicately picks up the object of focus, lifting it into view. It's a nearly flawless sculpture of a tomato on a vine, made entirely out of Legos, spanning roughly one foot in diameter. "I guess I should have known that. Huh."

Due to the box-like shape of the Legos themselves, the tomato appears as if it were a "digitized" or "pixilated" version of itself, in three dimensions. Regardless, Ecco has successfully captured the curve of the fruit, the topography of its texture, the bright red sphere, green leaves, stem, all of it.*

---

* What the fuck is up with this kid?!

Bertram bends down near Reidier and picks up a second object. It is one of the cards from the grouping game. On it is a picture of a tomato on a vine.

While Reidier and Bertram contemplate Ecco in the den, Eve sequesters herself in the kitchen with Otto. It is a stark, almost cliché, contrast of gender performance. As the men in her house set out to explore and fathom the depths of one boy's mind, Eve, the sole woman, simply feeds the other boy's stomach. The men hunt for answers, while the woman gathers together the fruits and vegetables for supper as she works to achieve a state of nonthinking. The men want to find, the women want to have. The men seek out the secrets unknown, the women seek the comfort of the known. She chops and organizes on the cutting board, while Otto sits on the counter next to her, his young legs dangling off the edge, and passes her another bunch of produce for cleaving.

The quiet symbiosis between mother and son is almost hypnotic. The longer they continue in this manner, though, the more strained it becomes. The meditative sense of it warps into something fervent, something obsessive. The rhythmic taps of the knife on the wood fill the silence between them, but eventually transform into a pitiless, unforgiving metronome.

The two are ultimately rescued by their own limited supply of greens. Eve holds out her hand to Otto, who has nothing left to fill it with. Breaking out of her disciplined trancelike state, Eve looks up at her son, who holds both his palms up in the air and shrugs.

"All done," he says.

Eve guffaws. Otto, unable to resist, joins in, laughing along with his mother. She moves over, rests her hands on the counter on either side of him, and kisses his forehead. He mimics his mother, but succeeds in only kissing the air between her chin and neck.

The tension dissolves out of the air.

"You are a perfect helper," she says, as she brushes his hair back and looks into his eyes.

He nods, "I know."

She laughs again and hugs him. A smothered giggle squeezes out from the embrace.

"'Ere," she says, handing him a slice of green pepper and taking one for herself. "Your reward."

He dutifully crunches down on it. While chewing away, he suggests, "Maybe next time, we should cut up Twizzlers."

Eve laughs again, wagging a half-eaten slice of pepper at him. "So your reward would be candy?"

"Oui."

She brushes his hair back again, cups the back of his head with her hand, and leans him forward for another kiss.

Scooching back on the counter, he contemplates the remaining piece of pepper in his hand. "Mommy, is the green I see the same as the green you see, or is your green red while my green's green?"*

---

*Something I always used to wonder myself. It bothered me that there was never a way to get to a consensus. No possibility of a resolution. Toby, on the other hand, revels in this little vortex. He delights in the infidelity of language.

"Forget color," he said when I brought it up. "It's so basic. None of it tracks. Not a single word. You say one thing, and I hear another. We're all in our own little worlds. Worlds of words. Take for example something a little more abstract than color. Something that comes from within, something that we define, untainted by the iffiness of the material world. Take a more stimulating touchstone, like love. What does it mean?

"No matter what the whiny poets say, love isn't as all encompassing, eternal, and fervent as the Romantics have led us to believe. It can be compartmentalized, momentary, and considered. I can fall in love twelve times walking down the block. Once with a smile, another time with the sway of a ponytail as it bounces left to right with every step, and again with the way a girl places a hand on her boyfriend's shoulder absentmindedly. But when we express love, when we voice a term that we all define together, we get lost. You say one thing, she hears another. Each of us tells himself a story about what this other person means. But words aren't fixed. Words are merely containers that we pour meaning into and try to give it shape. If people could just accept that, they'd be a whole lot happier."

"Accept that we're each of us trapped in our own lonely worlds and can never actually connect with another person?" I ask.

"Accept that we have a lot more to do with the creation of reality than we care to admit. Come on, you know this more than anybody I know."

I do. I did. I don't even know why I'm on this right now. For that matter, I don't know why I'm even bothering to write at all. No matter how hard I write green, you still just see red.

Eve pauses a moment. Her chin wrinkles in thought. "That depends," she answers.

"On what?"

"On whether you are a little boy or a little philosopher."

Otto gnaws on his bottom lip, considering her statement. Finally, after several moments he says, "I know that I'm a little boy. But I don't know if I'm not . . . the other thing."

"A philosopher."

"What's a phisophiler?"

"Someone who thinks a lot about how to answer the unanswerable questions."

"Can I only be one or the other?"

Eve takes a step back, bends down a little, resting her hands on her knees so she's face to face with Otto. "Until this very moment, I would 'ave said yes. You can only be one or the other. But clearly, I was mistaken, *mon petit trognon.*" She taps his nose with the tip of her finger and smiles.

"So what would a phisophiler say?"

Eve sighs, and leans against the counter next to her son, looking down at the chopped vegetables. "A philosopher would ask how do you even know the pepper exists, let alone that it's green?"

"'Cause it's there." Otto points in protest. "I see it."

"You also felt it and tasted it, no?"

Otto nods.

"But don't you do those very same things when you dream? See things, feel things, hear things?"

He nods again.

"And are your dreams real?"

"As real as the pepper?" Otto responds with precocious insight.

"*Oui, oui.* It looks like I do 'ave a little philosopher. I don't know where you got it from. Not your father, scientists are the opposite of philosophers.[88] And I failed my philosophy final in college."

Otto's eyes widen, "You did?"

"*Oui.*"

"Did you not do your homework?"

"*Non*, no, I studied plenty. But the test only had one question, and it wasn't on the reading."

"What was it on?"

"The teacher asked us to prove that the chair we were sitting on didn't exist. I filled two blue books with ideas from every philosopher that we had read that seemed remotely on topic. *Mais pas*, it was to no avail," she says as she takes down various salad bowls from the cupboard. "Your *mère* is not a philosopher. I am a reader and a writer."

"That's ok, *maman*. We can't all be."

She laughs and kisses the top of his head.

"So what do writers say about my green and your green?"

She casts him a sideways glance, tosses a bunch of chopped vegetables into a bowl, and purses her lips to the side in thought. "That the actual physical color of the pepper is unimportant. It's not whether the color we see is the same, but whether we share 'ze same

---

[88] According to Jerry Fodor, an American philosopher and cognitive scientist at Rutgers University, "Some philosophers hold that philosophy is what you do to a problem until it's clear enough to solve it by doing science. Others hold that if a philosophical problem succumbs to empirical methods, that shows it wasn't really philosophical to begin with."

experience. Your green, my green," she holds up a piece of pepper, "the object is unimportant. We don't really deal with actual physical objects, but only our impressions of them.* Everything around us is a sign, what gives it meaning is how we read it. A red light at an intersection means what?"

---

* Toby would love this chick.

"Stop," Otto replies dutifully.

"*Oui*. But not because red lights have always meant stop. But because we decided, we agreed that red lights mean stop for us. The pepper, its color is unimportant. What is important is how you interpret it, how you feel about it. And whether or not I understand how you feel about it. The most important thing is knowing and understanding each other. Knowing how we feel."

Otto nods. He helps pick up the pieces of vegetables still straggling on the counter and tosses them in the bowl. "You didn't feel very good about your phisopholy test, did you, *maman*?"

Eve tilts her head toward her son sympathetically and frowns. "No. I didn't feel very good, at all. Pass me the can of beans, by you."

He turns and does as his mother asks. In the handoff, he says, "I know what you should have written."

"Oh really?" She raises an eyebrow, while emptying the can of beans into another bowl. "And what is that, my little Descartes?"

"What chair?"

Outside, in the backyard, Reidier and Bertram talk in excited, hushed tones at the picnic table.

"On intelligence testing, he showed excellent ability, no difficulty solving puzzles, deciphering rules and patterns," Bertram reported. "Even tempered, quick to smile and experience joy. Logical comprehension levels were very high. Psychologically, developmentally, Ecco's not just normal but exceptional."

"Except . . ." Reidier gestures, opening his hands outward, palms up, to indicate something is missing.

"Yes. Except for the obvious," Bertram agrees.

"There's no damage that you can determine?"

"Nothing psychologically. We still need physical scans. But he lacks basic knowledge. Seems to have no understanding of the world around him, how it works, what things do. Yet it's as if this lack of knowledge makes him so wise."

"So you're telling me my son's the Buddha?"

Bertram lets out a huge belly laugh.

"What was so funny?" Eve asks, as she sets down a platter of antipasto and a bowl of salad.

Otto, trailing behind, delivers a pile of paper plates and plastic silverware.

Bertram looks up at Eve with a smile. "Just the magical nature of your son."

Eve places a hand lovingly on Otto's head. "You should hear his philosophical insights."

"Oh," Bertram says apologetically, "I was referring to Ecco. Though I would be fascinated to hear young master Otto's musings on the nature of life."

Bertram pokes Otto in the stomach. He giggles and retreats behind his mother's leg. Eve grunts, picks up Otto, and heads back into the kitchen for more food.

"Did I say something wrong?" Bertram asks.

Reidier shakes his head no. "It's the whole Ecco thing."

"She blames you?"

Reidier stares at his friend with surprise. "How did you get that?"

"I don't know, really. I guess I just picked up on some subtle cues. Did something happen to Ecco? An accident?"

Reidier nods. "Yes. In Chicago, a few months ago." Reidier shifts in his seat. "He was with me at work one day." Reidier lets out a long sigh. "My printer was out of toner, so I had sent the document to the one in the main office. It was just down the hall."

Reidier's eyes search the surface of the picnic table, never focusing on anything in particular. "It was a few minutes. Five at most. But, on my way back, I heard his crying from down the hall and sprinted to the lab."

He stops, his eyes now set, focused through the table, at this image from the past. "He was just lying there, curled into a fetal position, wailing. I don't know what happened. My equipment, nothing was turned over or upset in any way. Exactly how I left it. I scooped him up off the platform. Everything seemed fine, but he wouldn't stop crying. I rocked him in my arms for over half an hour until he finally calmed down."

Reidier picks at the wood grain on the tabletop for a few moments before looking up at Bertram. "What happened is a complete mystery."

Bertram frowns in sympathy. "That's when Ecco . . . started being this way?"

Reidier nods slightly.

"Was it a gradual deterioration? Or all at once?"

"The Ecco you met today began that afternoon."

It was also the same day Eve had her episode.[89]

In discussing what is obviously a very painful topic, Reidier exhibits very little emotion. Rather his distress manifests itself through a stilted delivery, filled with pauses, and a syntax that ultimately deteriorates into this sterile declarative structure, one that sounds almost mystical. Unable to manage whatever guilt he holds inside, or navigate the

---

[89] See Chapter VI.

culpability insinuated by Eve, Reidier can only manage to discuss it through simple statements of fact, tinted with almost cosmological overtones. *Ecco began that afternoon.*

This absence is only further accentuated by the lack of any footage covering this incident, any examination in Eve's journal, or examination in Reidier's notes. Was it so painful that it had to be eradicated from their personal history, like Emperor Qin Shi Huang's pruning of the Hundred Schools of Thought?* Or is it not even the truth? Another fiction perhaps, a riddle deciphered by the algebra of lying.

---

*Sometimes Hilary is a little too erudite for her own good. In 213 BCE, the Emperor commanded the burning of all philosophy and history books from every state except Qin. He also made sure to bury alive a large number of intellectuals in case they caught the writing bug. The guy erased history.

If Ecco's condition were an event rather than an accident, a happening rather than an act, then Reidier's role would be that of an explorer as opposed to a creator (or destroyer, for that matter). He cannot take on the responsibility of that day. He cannot bear the weight of it. It must be externalized. Point in fact, rather than taking on the role of a deity in this origin myth,[90] Reidier removes himself entirely from the tale. At most, he's a herald.

---

[90] As much as scientists hold themselves up as "rational" beings, often many of them take on God complexes in their work. Consider Oppenheimer's famous allusion to the Bhagavad Gita after overseeing the first successful test of a nuclear bomb when he states, "Now I am become death, the destroyer of worlds." A mathematician, Dr. Theodore Kaczynski, after resigning from a post at the University of California, Berkeley, at the age of twenty-five, took it upon himself to reform society and lead a worldwide revolution against the effects of modern society's "industrial-technological system" and became the Unabomber. Even the much beloved and admired Einstein once wrote that God does not play dice with the universe, to which Niels Bohr reportedly replied, "Stop telling God what to do with his dice."

Reidier, however, avoids the deistic mantle, spurning any assumption of control, let alone godly perspective or power. At least consciously. On a subconscious level, he consistently seems to play the part of Prometheus trying to steal fire from the gods.

This removal of self is even more evident a few seconds earlier, when he admits *what happened is a complete mystery*. It is his most vulnerable admission. However, there is no ego in this statement. No *I*. He doesn't simply say, "I don't know what happened." Instead, he expresses it in third person. He evokes the cloak of "mystery," affording himself room for deniability, or protection within the puzzle.

Perhaps this is why he pushes with such determination to find the answer of what's wrong. He can only hold onto his innocence so long, but if he can figure out what's wrong, if he can fix it, then he can not only save Ecco, but himself as well.

Bertram hesitates. "I wonder, now this is only just, you know, an idea . . ."

"I'm not going to sue you for malpractice Bert."

"Well, if it happened all at once—"

"It did."

"Have you ever heard of Korsakoff syndrome?"*

---

* There it is again. Hilary must have already watched this before meeting with Bertram. Why wouldn't she? It was to her advantage. She didn't just pull Korsakoff out of thin air before. No. The trick to her Psynar® thing was not to use indiscriminate pings and just see what came back. She sent out very discriminate pings, smart-bomb pings, designed to find their way into the most protected bunkers of secrecy, denial, and consciousness itself. She had set Bertram up. There's something to this Korsakoff syndrome. Ecco and Korsakoff were the public- and private-key match that would unlock all of this.

Reidier shakes his head no.

"It's a brain disorder. A rather wide-reaching one at that. One of the symptoms can be retrograde amnesia."

"Where someone can't remember who they are?"

"Essentially, although it's not always tied to identity. Someone could just be incapable of remembering events that occurred before the amnesia. There tends to be a time gradient involved. Remote memories can sometimes be more easily accessible."

Reidier's body posture has completely changed. Instead of being guarded and distant—legs and arms crossed, leaning back, avoiding of eye contact—he's available and focused—leaning toward Bertram, elbows resting on the table with open arms, focused eye contact. The Korsakoff hypothesis has transformed Reidier from a guilt-laden parent into an enthusiastic student.

"According to Ribot's Law, recent memories are more likely to be lost than more remote ones."[91] Bertram considers a moment. "To my knowledge, there's never been a case of it in such a young subject. But I guess it could be argued that all Ecco has are recent memories. It'd explain why it seems like he was born yesterday."

"Shouldn't he then be unable to do things, like walk and talk?"

Bertram dips his head to the side. "Yes and no. Memory loss may only affect certain 'classes' of memory. If the victim were a concert pianist prior to the brain trauma, he might very well forget what a piano is but know how to play. In Ecco's case, he's maintained a remarkable skill set but is unencumbered by any expectations about life. Like I was saying before, I think that's why he's so gifted."

"How so?"

"Consider how sketching is taught in an art class."

"I never took art classes."

Bertram throws Reidier a look. "Of course you didn't. Art 101 almost always starts with drawing a still life. An apple, let's say. The problem that most new students have is they try and draw the apple."

"You're channeling the Buddha again."

"More like Plato, actually. We all have an idea in our head about what an apple is, and what it should look like. Those ideas get in the

---

[91] "The dissolution of memory is inversely related to the recency of the event."
~Théodule-Armand Ribot

way. Instead of drawing what's there, novices draw what they think is there. What should be there. But any art teacher will tell you, the trick is to not see an apple, but a collection of curves, tones, shadows, what have you. You don't draw the apple, you draw the shape."

"Ecco doesn't see tomatoes, he sees red curves."

"Precisely. He's unencumbered by shoulds."

Reidier leans back, taking it in. "So his lack of ideas is the source of his genius."

Bertram nods. "At least in theory."

Bertram's theory holds within it some remarkable possibilities. Especially if we consider the literal implications of his earlier comment about how Ecco seemed like he "was born yesterday." If, somehow, Ecco's clock had reset certain areas of the brain, then this might enhance certain skill sets and attributes possessed by the preverbal. To the point at hand, babies, in fact, have what could be classified as extreme eyesight. They are able to take in (or filter out less) information endowing them with what would comparatively be augmented perception. Observe the picture below of two monkeys and attempt to determine the differences between the two.

The monkeys look identical; it would be nearly impossible to pick out either one of them from a group of ten. They all look the same—unless you're an infant.

At the University of Sheffield and the University College London, an experiment was conducted on a group of six- and nine-month-olds in which they were shown two sets of photographs of human and monkey faces, including one face they had seen before. Unsurprisingly, both groups could recognize and identify familiar human faces. But only the six-month-olds could distinguish one monkey from another. The results were consistent even when the photographs were presented to them upside down. Researchers hypothesize that as we age, our brains develop to only focus on overall "important" differences between human faces. We filter out what our brains consider extraneous information and, as a result, sacrifice discriminatory abilities.

Consider another study in England performed in 2008 to determine the possible unfiltered perception children have in processing "virgin" colors in a manner drastically different and more intense than adults.[92] Infant eyes absorb colors and then process them in the prelinguistic parts of the brain (right-brain areas), while adults process colors in the brain's language centers (left side), tinted, as it were, by concepts they already have. As brains age, they become busier and stop bothering to do things like "see" color. Instead, the brain perceives only its idea of color, trading unfiltered perception for a color scheme mediated by the constructs of language.[93]* Somewhere in growing up, the brain shifts to a language-bound perception of color and all that information is dismissed from then on.

---

[92] A. Franklina; G. V. Drivonikou; L. Bevis; I. R. L. Davies; P. Kay; and T. Regier, "Categorical perception of color is lateralized to the right hemisphere in infants, but to the left hemisphere in adults." *PNAS* March 4, 2008, vol. 105, no. 9 3221-3225.

[93] "Babies See Pure Color, but Adults Peer Through Prism of Language," March 3, 2008. Wired.com (http://www.wired.com/wiredscience/2008/03/babies-see-pure/#ixzz0qBGnZmFm).

* My old semiotics professors would have a field day with this. I guess Plato and his whole obsession with his theory of forms was more science than philosophy. Plato asserted that the objects we see aren't real, but literally mimic the real forms (kind of like that old Steven Wright joke ᵞ). In essence our ideas of things, like say a table, are the only true objects. Fittingly, the concept of form predated the word for it. Most of the words used to describe it have to do with vision: εἶδος *(eidos)* and ἰδέα *(idea)*. Both stem from the Indo-European root *weid,* "see." Apparently, Plato could figure all this out before he even had the proper words for it. I don't know if that proves or negates his point. A little light-headed, to be honest. Haven't eaten all day. I wonder if this is where the saying, "I see your point," comes from.

ᵞ *"I woke up one morning and looked around the room. Something wasn't right. I realized that someone had broken in the night before and replaced everything in my apartment with an exact replica. I couldn't believe it. I got my roommate and showed him. I said, 'Look at this—everything's been replaced with an exact replica!' He said, 'Do I know you?'"*

Similarly, babies also have uncanny hearing abilities. As an evolutionary trait, this was necessary in order to hear the faint approach of a dangerous predator. At a young age, every sound is vital and equally audible, whether it's raindrops or a mother's voice down the hall. According to childdevelopment.columbia.edu, infants only a few days old can differentiate between their native tongue and a foreign language. At four months old, they can tell when people are speaking in their native languages without even hearing them. This gift vanishes by nine months of age.[94] As with eyesight, the aging brain reduces the influx of information by focusing only on a narrow band of sound, shifting all nonessential information into background noise. Babies transform from universal learners who can pick up and master any language, to specialists in their native sounds, structures, and meanings, within their first year.[95]

[94] Robin Lloyd, "Infants Have 'Amazing Capabilities' That Adults Lack" *LiveScience. com.* May 24, 2007. 02:00 p.m. ET. http://www.livescience.com/health/070524_infant_intelligence.html.

[95] *Ibid.*

Beyond sight and sound, Ecco might also have tapped into a host of other infant talents. When deprived of one sense or skill set, humans compensate with others, such as how some blind people can develop exquisite hearing or become incredibly adept mental cartographers, mapping out floor plans to the numerous buildings and landscapes they frequent. Babies, who have not fully acquired language, rapidly learn how to read nonverbal clues to determine the emotional states of adults around them. They can be so proficient at interpreting facial and body language that some experts compare it to mind reading.

The fact of the matter is that babies are highly intelligent. Professors Patricia Kuhl and Andrew Meltzoff codirect the Institute for Learning & Brain Sciences at the University of Washington. They believe a:

> baby is a scientific miracle, the best learning machine on the planet, more powerful than the most advanced supercomputer, able to learn languages faster and better than adults, quick to recognize and manipulate the social cues that govern everything from war to animal cookies. Born with one hundred billion neurons . . . babies suck in new information and statistically analyze, comparing it with what they've previously heard, seen, tasted, and felt, constantly revising their theories of the world and how it works. By three years old, babies have about fifteen thousand synapses per neuron, three times the synapses of adults. That's one of the reasons it's easier to learn foreign languages when you're young.[96]

Somewhere between years four and six, to prevent the brain from being overwhelmed, the number of synapses is cut down by 67 percent.

---

[96] Paula Block, "Infant Science." *Seattle Times,* March 6, 2005 http://o.staging.seattletimes.com/pacific-nw-magazine/infant-science-a-uw-couple-leads-our-new-thinking-about-babies-amazing-minds/.

All of these possibilities resonate with Ecco's behavior. However, none of it is conclusive, as it is unclear as to how exactly his clock has been reset and precisely where in the developmental process he might fall in all of this.

"How did he end up being like this instead of a bumbling, drooling idiot?" Reidier asks Bertram.

"It all depends how and where the brain has been damaged."

The word damaged gives them both pause.

"Is something definitely damaged in his brain?"

"If it's Korsakoff syndrome. We need to run some tests. Brain scans. Completely noninvasive."

Reidier nods. He picks at the table again. Finally, after almost a minute of silence he asks, "What causes Korsakoff?"

Bertram shrugs. "Usually chronic alcoholism."

"And all this time I thought it was Eve who was dipping into my absinthe."

"At least he's got good taste."

Reidier chuckles.

"Who knows, though," Bertram continues. "It could've been a seizure or some infection. Like I said, we should take a look."

Reidier nods, mumbling, "Of course, of course." His attention has wandered. He stares out across the backyard at the kitchen window. Eve passes back and forth across the frame. "Is there a way to run some tests unofficially?"

Bertram casts a sideways glance at his friend. "I've got a lab. Over at the med school, for my work with assistive technology with robotic control."

"How's the motor cortex neural interface working?" Reidier asks.

"Quite well. My quadriplegic test subjects can move a cursor around a computer screen with their thoughts. They can type, play games, move robotic arms even. It's rather impressive. But, yes, toward our purposes I have access to all the equipment we'd need. Multielectrode recoding arrays, fMRI machines, the works."

"And you'd be amenable to helping?"

Bertram smiles. "Kerek, you know beneath this imposing academic veneer lies a rather eccentric iconoclast. I like to think of myself as independent from the culture of control, as it were. A diligent scientist to the last, but a revolutionary poet at heart."

Having decided on a course of action—tests—Reidier and Bertram relax. Reidier pours ice tea for the two of them. They sit taking in the late afternoon rays of sun and the soothing sound of crickets.

"Funny," Bertram remarks about nothing in particular.

"What's that?" Reidier replies on cue.

"After all these years, it was a bout of memory loss that got us in touch with our past."

"I imagine I'm not the best at maintaining interpersonal connections over long distances."

Bertram places a reassuring hand on Reidier's forearm. "Don't beat yourself up over it. It's the way life is, people come together, grow apart—"

The conversation abruptly stops with the sound of creaking. The two turn toward the house. Ecco pushes open the screen door and holds it for Otto, who wanders out carrying a small paper plate covered with macaroni salad. Otto plops himself down on the porch steps. Ecco follows, in kind, sitting next to his brother. Reidier and Bertram watch in silence. Otto pulls a plastic fork out of his back pocket and eats a bite of salad. While chewing, he looks over at his brother and offers him his fork.

Ecco reaches into his back pocket and pulls out a straw.

Otto giggles as he watches Ecco put the straw in his mouth, lean over the plate, and suck a single piece of elbow macaroni off the plate, up the straw, and into his mouth, like a vacuum.

Ecco chews and offers his brother the straw. The two giggle, going back and forth, "drinking" their macaroni salad.

"Well, now, that's efficient," Bertram says.

"I think they have the right idea," Reidier replies, reaching across the table toward the salad bowls.

"They're amazing boys."

After a moment, when Reidier doesn't respond, Bertram turns away from the boys and looks at his friend who's staring down into a large bowl of tomato salad with finely chopped Bermuda onions, fresh oregano, virgin olive oil, and red Legos.

"Did Ecco do that?" Bertram asks, confused.

Reidier shakes his head no.

"Eve?"

"It's her idea of sarcasm." Reidier places it off to the side and reaches for another bowl.

During our lunch, Bertram told me a much more condensed story. He never brought up Ecco's tomato sculpture, Reidier's confession, Eve's coldness. Bertram reduced it all to clinical speak instead, discussing test results, the Korsakoff diagnosis, and his suggestion of doing a more thorough neurological examination.

I'm still unsure as to whether this censorship, or equivocation, was a conscious decision or a subconscious reaction. Perhaps he believed he was distilling for me the salient information from all his time spent with the Reidiers. Colleague to colleague, providing me with the conclusions rather than taking me down all the wrong turns and dead ends of his journey. Obviously, he wasn't aware of the true nature of my interview and had no conception of Psynaring, nor what my process required. Then again, considering our introduction through the Department, he would naturally respond in like fashion.

Revealing only what he must, but never sharing. On that note, he could have still been resistant to the idea of revealing anything at all about the Reidiers, as they were his patients as much as his friends. Forced to violate doctor-patient confidentiality, he complied only as much as was necessary.

Considering what happened next, though, I wonder if the explanation is much simpler. On a personal level, the loss of the Reidiers makes him scared; on a professional level, insecure; and on an emotional level, unsettled.

In his notes from that day, Bertram Malle wrote, *Enigmas are inherently enticing and prickly, like a spiny seed. They latch on with unpredictable holds. E is, as it were, born again, enhanced by his rejuvenated innocence, for which he is simultaneously canonized and vilified by his respective parents. He is haunted by a past that cannot be remembered. Still I'm surprised. In spite of how fascinating I find E, and all the mysteries that lie within him, it is Mrs. R. who I keep wondering about. Worrying about? What E cannot remember, Mrs. R. cannot forget.*

TITLE CARD: **GALILEE 6:21**

TITLE CARD: **EXPERIMENT 74**

MIRROR LAB, GOULD ISLAND FACILITY - 2008-5-5
13:31:00

SPLIT SCREEN, on right side, target room: an
intricate maze. A hunk of cheese sits in the
bottom right corner.

LEFT SIDE, transmission room: an exact replica
of the maze on the right. Only in this one, a
hunk of cheese rests at the end in the upper
left-hand corner. At the lower right-hand
corner, a lab rat, nicknamed JOHN GLENN, is
lowered in by a gloved hand.

(NOTE: John is calm in his handler's hand,
clearly used to both the person and the
process.)

John knows the drill. He rears up onto his
hindquarters, his forelegs pressed against the
maze wall for balance. John's nostrils flare with
each rapid inhale as he orients the scent. Then
he's off through the maze.

Without a single misturn, John Glenn navigates
his way through the maze and finds the cheese. He
devours the cheese.

When he's finished, a gloved hand comes into
view, holding yet another piece of cheese. It
carries it over and past John, who once again
rears up on his hindquarters.

The cheese is deposited in the bottom right
corner of the maze (mirroring the arrangement in
the target room).

John flares his nostrils a few more times and is off.

The maze pulses with red light, then a white light as the Entanglement Channel opens.

SOUNDS of the rapid ACCELERATION and DECELERATION of GEARS as the Boson Cannons and Pion Beams constantly reorient into optimized focal positions.

As he approaches the center of the maze, the countdown begins . . .

> DR. REIDIER (OS)
> In three, two, one, go.

LEFT SIDE, John scampers through the center of the maze.

The Quark Resonator emits a SOFT, HIGH-PITCHED DRONE.

At 2008-5-5 13:33:32.1331224 a quiet THRUM coincides with John, midstride, turning into a pile of heterogeneous dust [predominately iron diantimonide] that drops to the floor of the maze, devoid of any forward inertia.

NOTE: at 800 picoseconds prior to transmission, on the left side prior to transfer, the maze and John tessellate.

RIGHT SIDE, at 13:33:32.1331224, John appears midstride, just past the center of the target maze.

He slips on the now frost-covered surface of the maze, but continues on. Without a single misturn, John Glenn navigates his way through the maze to the bottom right corner where he

began, and finds the cheese. He devours the
cheese.

                    IS1 O'BRIEN (OS)
                    (official tone)
          Trained Biologic completed second
          half of maze just under his average
          time.
                    (beat. More relaxed tone)
          Wow. He did it. You did it.

                    DR. REIDIER (OS)
          Wait . . .

John finishes the cheese.

The handler's gloved hand comes into view. It
slowly reaches down into the maze to retrieve
John Glenn.

The lab rat goes berserk and attacks. It's a
flurry of teeth, claws, foamy saliva, and HIGH-
PITCHED savage SCREECHES.

The handler yanks his hand back, retreating,
leaving John in the maze.

The lab rat immediately calms down and sniffs
around.

Beat.

                    IS1 O'BRIEN (OS)
          Jesus.

The HIGH PITCH of the Quark Resonator fades out.

XI

Curiosity is defiance distilled to its essence.

~Vladimir Onegin

All things are subject to interpretation; whichever interpretation prevails at a given time is a function of power and not truth.

~Friedrich Nietzsche

Contrary to what television crime dramas might lead one to believe, most murders are pretty straightforward. More than 70 percent of all cases are solved and done so within the first seventy-two hours. This is because most murders are not premeditated: a domestic dispute escalates, someone snaps at the loss of a job. Circumstances, more than character, influence crime. Murderers rarely take precautions or cover their tracks. If it looks like the husband did it, he probably did.

But with psychology, especially Psynaring, the results are rarely tangible and almost never cut-and-dried. And this is why it might be premature to present this next section so soon, before adequate investigation and analysis have been concluded. However, it seems that the nature of the information begs the question of validation. It's from a single, unofficial (i.e. non-Departmental) source. As such, only impressions and supposition will ever be derived from it now and later.

Regardless of the "truth" of this, its existence is still telling. If it were manufactured, then the fiction of it reveals a certain awareness of the Department's motive and methods. If it actually happened, then this provides critical insight into an additional, and heretofore unknown, stress on Reidier as well as providing credence to the sabotage hypothesis. In either case, the way in which it was created and hidden is most revealing.

The Newport Naval Station, following the failed Reidier test, released the collection of Reidier's binders.[97] They are an intricate and enigmatic collection of riddles written in alternating trajectories: left to right, right to left, down, up, spiraled, backward, inverted, transversally through pages. If they had been found in an abandoned apartment, they would have been classified as the pathological writings of a lunatic. However, knowing their source and seeing them firsthand, one cannot help but marvel at the elaborately calculated beauty of it all. Its level of detail is hypnotic. It feels designed, following a complex logic with a hidden understanding like that of a master watchmaker.

These binders are not the doodles of an absent mind or raving madman. They are considered, plotted, and mapped out with an intent to hide and to keep. These binders are an answer. They are, without a doubt, Leo's Notebooks.[98]

And Reidier is still right; we can't read them.

At least the Navy can't.

For the next few weeks, I spent several hours a day poring through the notebooks, mesmerized. Like the countless pilgrims who meditate by

---

[97] See pages 76-78 and 88.

[98] See pages 33, 37.

walking the labyrinth on the floor of the Chartres Cathedral in France, I would trace Reidier's textual mazes with my fingertips, hoping to find some crack that let me in. Yet while my aesthetic sense draws me to these enigmas, my affinities lie elsewhere.

It is both unorthodox and unauthorized for me to approach anyone outside the Department without clearance. Likewise, I am fully aware of the classified status of any and all documents from or pertaining to the Reidier file.[99] That being said, in an effort to enrich and accelerate the report, I sought out help from an external source.

Considering the resistance/restraint exhibited by Bertram due to the Department's heavy-handedness, as well as the fragile sensitivity of the source, adhering to protocol seemed counterproductive. Moreover, disclosure of this source would be a violation of doctor-patient privilege. As the source is institutionalized and not what would commonly be considered in a right state of mind, I consider (and hope that the Department concurs) that the source is not a security risk.[100]

---

[99] Is this appropriate? Or am I kicking a hornet's nest? Must reconsider this entire section.

[100] Nor do I want for the source to become a Department "asset" . . . Am I saying too much with this as well? Will the Department troll through every mental facility I ever walked into and try to find out who I went to so they can conscript them as a resource for other projects? I don't want to risk exposing _____ but I can't include any further discoveries without an explanation as to how I arrived at this. A cover story might only raise eyebrows and inquiries, and I doubt anyone would buy my having broken the code as an option.

REVISIT. RETHINK. RECONSIDER.
Proceed with caution.

ς

ς These were scribbled in the margins—obviously my mother's handwriting. I read them three times. She broke the rules. She admitted it. The question is, did they see it? Did the Department know?

I still haven't left the house. No food for a while. Can't go out. Can't trust a delivery guy, that's for sure. If a Department stooge could dress up like a tourist, I'm sure they could impersonate a delivery dude. Man can go without food for a while anyhow, drinking water from the bathroom tap. Jesus fasted for forty days in the desert. Just him and the devil. Me, I got my mom to keep me company.

Fasting focuses your mind. You see things more clearly. Isn't that why all those religious prophets and holy men did it? Course they all came back saying they saw visions of angels, and God and Satan.

I'm not hallucinating. I mean, yeah, you could've maybe convinced me that I might be dreaming things up with my little visitor. Especially since he hasn't come back. But I did not imagine my mom's margin notes. They're right there. I see them.

Proceed with caution.

Is this what happened? She crossed a line, and it ended up being a point of no return? Is this when she started hiding her report? I always had imagined she kind of just went and hid it here toward the end, in a last ditch effort. But maybe she stowed the majority of it there and kept stopping in to add another file, another chapter.

That's an even bigger risk, though, with a greater chance of being followed. And I'm still pretty much going with the Department never found it. They never knew about my Dad's studio. Maybe she handed in a dummy report.

Then why are they still following me?

Especially if they disappeared her.

There's a chance, then, that they didn't. She disappeared. Never handed in a report, and no sign of it in the house. Now they're desperate to get their hands on it, to find out what happened with *The Reidier Test*. And to figure out what happened with her.

Still, they could've found out about her little indiscretion without having read the report. Maybe they nanobotted her house, read her communiqués. And followed her.

Like they're following me.

No way for me to know really. Curiosity is insubordination in its purest form.

Proceed with caution.

A note to herself? A message to me?

How am I going to get out of here? My sanctuary has become an oubliette. I'm not even hungry anymore.

My source succeeded where the Navy's (and presumably the NSA's) codebreakers failed. My source has only successfully deciphered sporadic sections of a little over a page to date (but will continue to play with and puzzle out). Apparently, part of the challenge is that Reidier processed his thoughts through multiple layers of ciphers at a time. He would have encoded his ideas in his head, then further encoded the encryption within another cipher. Literally a mystery wrapped within an enigma, wheels within wheels.

I wonder if Reidier was indeed at least telling a half truth when he told Diderot he did this to help himself think. This method of maze making is a form of meditation in and of itself. This is supported by the piecemeal content that swings from the profound to the vitriolic. Meditation makes sense as a response to the challenges of inventing: trying to simultaneously create new worldviews while obliterating old paradigms. Perhaps this was a way of taming the wild, frenetic nature of his thoughts. The draining discipline of it provided a way to focus. The mental rigor of this process is staggering, even more so, bearing in mind that Reidier would switch ciphers from paragraph to paragraph, sentence to sentence, or even from clause to clause. This is why my source has only so far been able to disentangle these fragments. Still, the content that has been excavated is provocative.

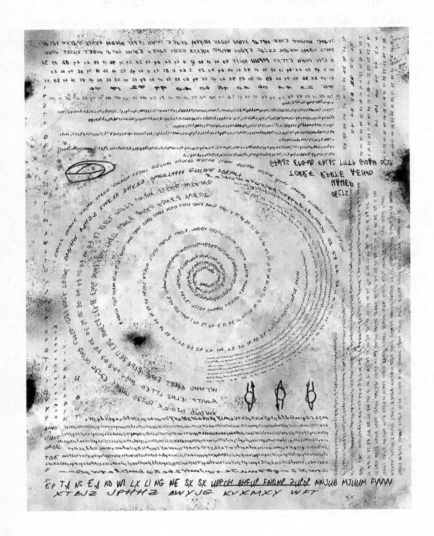

Decoded:
That's where my colleagues stumble. They "send" things. Slaves to hero worship.

TVAMT UMZWH ECWBI MPTAP XPUIJ CQZBX FGYFM AXAEE IXVWQ LEPBY OJVZM Anarchist Al was fine kicking the legs out from Newton's **GGIIT DAHEN EOTUU SNTAI NVDET RUSRE NIINN S** just so he was the one to do it. **73 69 36 60 65 16 59 54 49 56 24 29 19 96 17 67 40 49 82 03 30 00 11 97 80 44 69 13 68 76 95 78 41 46 49 73 27 55 54 61 85 73 91 60 92 52 96 56 14 79 32 79 66 43 41 07 58 86 70 79 64 80 00 80 89 78 40 95 55 79 50 88 86 07 60 59 62 90 58 62 46 95 85 36 69 23 33 75 23 44 06 40 98 60 40 99 72 17 76**

AA adhered to locality. Refused to believe in cause and effect at a distance.

yKPFZ9WGr9+3ptvJzqO6wdvN2OassGedtMO5jIqsqGagksW
Ct25ST7t/m6THwLfUt7XCp76mxuLOmtnloImruryJi
42HiphhtMyuq6xsQnLQgKt2y5qis7rO2Ma9uY+x3sC/oqyxfd+
snbV7hImtibW1p3quWHB3w5XJq9iXu73DtuCrzaWLtdCZ1d
+sxXXhvp2XjoWdrGKpqZeHo0ROVbump6LVq7+4tqeyqLikq
N3bl6+xq619vLPDl3WFxLGFtZKuo6szRnbQusCoy7+v3MSo
uci/lL3jzpqz4KjFhbenv7mKi5+hq5+Rr6ajV2xYxMinpseF2dTE
zdysvrikvtu9x6Gri2jiqIa0dYTDmae2toqCqlZoR7l/uafCqOW
zxs/ChMSWo93NmJ7irMd5xL2ssY6Gq6VhtM6Kmrd6WkX
PucWi16nCmbemnYfOpazB3MG+5qygaLiunbmbf66xeKCRxY
K3bk5Pw5SXpsKq3dC3tb3IwbikzM6av+W305eysKqfnorEi2G
mp8CouVV4cNHIwZrIqqXgtqiyx726mLTGvqbhrMeBn
K+brZt/r8ejqbWbea9HMDLRpKun2KrDrcK5rsPMgI/F0
JnR3K7Hjc29rZuOhK6Qkqqon6isV1ZU

AA was a stubborn asshole. A narrow-minded prig determined to hang on to his own narcissistic legacy.

IUKKQ MATKY UQBWQ XOATO IRLSW STODQ BLJBR QMMWR LAFPU UJBTG IOEFT EIHZU XQPZP PTSHI GJXIY YUOOS BWEDU WZXNS ZRKVG EMSYW TZPVT EDJYK HIGKQ GAQEV OFVLP XGWZA JMGGP VAUXG TEILY SKQIZ ZAUGF RJNGK PCGYB PWLMD IZMFO SBOXX KGXMU PFLLB RUXEM WLNLO JUXUI RYMOF XXBGT BYWOH JVHBV GQUAI BLKDL FBJJN NWMSX KCKCC DRQUY TLNGI CETKZ NRILD HNIHR PNDOL JRKFH JNEMM FLGKD NYONB KWJFH OFGRR ATHPG BWXXX because the speed of light is inversely proportional to alpha, and both have been considered unchangeable constants. Alpha appears to have decreased by 4.5 parts out of 108. If confirmed, this would imply that the speed of light has increased. **upJ6rqiXt7+1zb55zYTW3ZjPqMWiwdF8oJSep7mRjpaSn7OAp am1oMCFxdyjpL66uYquvai1sKC/ibWWnbixsp4xZGirkZuk 5rGo7u2pZnch8DgrajF4p6d3aKnpbOfuriGfZeh0H6k g56t15zc2ZemqKG6m5q7qM295snDrtOUlJOyn0ZVNbm kqGqZg9XJws7CktSYwOeXk6TGoq2vnJuipnmuy6uEqLDmvJ y+l6LAwr7Vn7uH26SIxMaepN/Yv6+93qi6samQRkkxrLmHh6 e92b3Dy7aTyIe76KWnxt+iitBqnp6qbg==**

He couldn't believe, couldn't accept, insisted that particles have definite positions and momentums all the time, whether we're watching them or not.

OECTS UAUEP TORRE RFRTE AEIHD GFNAS EFGND EALAC TITTF GIOAH DCST

WTHHO AARTT EIHAT ELFIA ZIELI ESDT wasn't moving faster than the speed of light. It was already there. Travel was unnecessary. **GZ RB NE GS SN UC ZG GN RP VO GZ NN GZ RJ** concept of speed is fallible it implies travel, movement relative from one point to another.

No one seems to see the secret **LmnodLAy9qxvpzszIawoKelm33 Hpcx6tKiHlbOoioaWnqa3sJP**blYWbo+OqoqTZvsyht4Wrrp 2flcmgzqq8u6ip05aXREpPtLeFp8iryN21vLKm25i0taiAfqO8k +qgnZd/z6XbuXepxIW5orXPnIC/p7yqop/i1r+Y7JWesqeYpqjJy s+dwLu6l7aRMGRWoKqredqnqpmhg4ij3JywmKijfpnHtb x6noS+16POiqGWr6q2orW5dpWqw6Cqu7DK05e2pYvBwYevo 4bn2JzEvqiqoJKfRGRhtriXot3NiKE= E's abomination **PI PR BG DV** In a way, Anarchist Al was right with his bullheaded conservatism, he just didn't take it far enough.**1s+5bpqVnrilhnp8j4ayxcKT pOahv5rXgZOIpa231cSCnrnatqWxoJ2Doemfx7mKnjNCRc zbtaOpvqVzsYh6loOaxNm7tba2mpud5IrOmd+ntb/Flp/clL jN16Grmp7Zp5PBjo1RPT0=**

zqWoprHOv96knZKqkK6horDfvZqvy6V2vM2GzaCIyNz CqYPHx8G2pJ65m3I= Bhagavad Gita. They were tapping into the wrong ancients. The wrong continent. It's all right **43 65 64 77 46 88 71 20 23 24** Incan 26 54 40 24 just not written down **qpWh xcWGyNemnJjx1Yfdx7iRm6/KmqmZsJ2qw5e5n4e6vKLJ o8CZw4yd0sqlpKKhv6SnecWu3cOzw3p1y6uxjotFNW2b3 7rAw4Sh5Z+ru8PYvtnhzLmcj9muqdyzz3+ikaaKjamiqrU=** and his antithesis **KG ET KG IE PV GE LK GT CG PR SV TC RF HP PR PO YT VC KG MO FC SO TC QR PM UG PI** the essence of presence and absence where HUP actually moves from philosophical to actual.

To understand the transmission, you need to see that there is no transmission of information. There is no transmission. It's like a coin's head is either up or down. In turning it from up to down, the state is changed, but the information isn't transmitted to the tail's side. The tail's end is already changed.

AHRII LTASE URDSL TQE E's acceptance and willingness ~~UPFOH BHFUP FNQMP ZUPDP~~ **NNJUB MJUUM FYYYY** constructive destruction.

From what can be seen, his notes are neither chaotic nor ordered, neither nonsensical nor enlightened. What's here is a key: a psychological cipher to the inner workings of Reidier. This was where or how he hashed out his ideas. It is his theoretical journal, full of questions and insights so volatile they needed to be buried inside of cryptographs.

What kind of a person does this?

Look closely at the scribbles above and below *The Vitruvian Man*. While Leonardo da Vinci wrote in Italian, he did so with a unique shorthand of his own invention. Not only that, he almost always employed "mirror writing," where one starts at the right side of the page and moves to the left. (Most likely Reidier was performing some version of this using an actual mirror.[101] Thumbing through his notebooks there are numerous pages where the lettering itself is written backward.) Da Vinci only wrote in the normal direction when he intended for someone else to read his writings.

While the Florentine never proffered an explanation for this, at least as far as what's been deciphered, there are some theories. Da Vinci could have simply wanted to make it more difficult for people to read his notes and steal his ideas. Perhaps Reidier similarly was concerned about his intellectual property. His innovations are certainly valuable in every sense of the word.

Some historians hold that da Vinci wrote in this manner to hide his scientific ideas from the powerful Church, as some of them contradicted the tenets of Catholicism (consider what happened later on to Galileo). Reidier's theories, however, while threatening to shift scientific paradigms, were not undermining the powers that be. In fact, via the Department, he was working *for* those powers. Still, it's worth considering who might have been threatened by or opposed to Reidier's work.

---

[101] See pages 61, 67, 68.

1. Other governments: Reidier himself proclaimed how his work would unravel every cryptographic security system based on classical physics.[102] China, Russia, Iran—any nation deemed a threat, or even an ally, would be vulnerable. Exposure of Reidier's work to the world would make him at best a pawn and at worst a target.

2. Various industries and multinational corporations: What would teleportation do to the automotive world, air travel, communications? Considering the cataclysmic effects Reidier's paradigm shift could have on these well-funded powerful MNCs, it seems understandable that he would play his hand close to the vest.

With regards to Pierce, Reidier needed to take these measures (without even realizing) in order to maintain at least a shred of private space.

For his part, Pierce never seemed concerned with the notebooks. Perhaps he didn't see them as integral as long as Reidier was producing results. Or he immediately classified them as unbreakable and a waste of resources. As far as the aforementioned dangers, Pierce saw himself as Reidier's paladin, and was confident (albeit mistakenly so) that he could protect Reidier and the Department's intellectual property from any threat of espionage.

Clearly, though, Reidier's instincts and precautions were right as confirmed by Gio Brent, Pierce's former assistant. "He [Pierce] knew there were sharks in the water. He just never figured any of them would be brash enough to try and nibble from his plate. Obviously the real mistake was that he and Larry were focused on Reidier's potential enemies and never really considered how dangerous champions could be. Neither did Reidier for that matter."

---

[102] See pages 62, 63.

Da Vinci and Reidier could have shared another motivation for their secrecy: psychological deficiencies. Many believe that Leonardo suffered from a number of learning disabilities, including dyslexia and attention-deficit disorder. Some have wondered if he didn't have a form of Asperger's. The artist took twelve years to paint Mona Lisa's lips. He could write with one hand while drawing with the other. Perfectionist tendencies, moderate crossover discrimination deficits, savant skills—did Reidier have similar tendencies? Bertram has described on numerous occasions Reidier's peculiar habits of friendship: drastic absences broken up by sporadic bouts of intensity without even a howdy-do. On the other hand, the mysteries of Reidier's motivation might easily be explained as the meditative machinations necessary to calm his own particular brand of OCD. [103]

What's more important than the Why of it is the What of it.

"That's where my colleagues stumble," Reidier writes. "They send things." Presumably his colleagues are fellow scientists. Their sending is their mistake. They try to transmit something from one point to another. A faulty premise, according to Reidier, that will never get them anywhere. Apparently, Reidier's work approaches teleportation in a manner unhampered by getting from Point A to Point B.

Travel is unnecessary.

Speed is fallible.

Locality, Bhagavad Gita, Incans—all meditations on the nature of the universe or how to kick the legs out from underneath it. But what do they mean?

---

[103] See pages 35-37 for a more detailed analysis.

Excerpt from University of Chicago iTunes episode, Dr. Kerek
Reidier lecture from his Physics of Science Fiction course,
February 11th, 2005

"In physics, the principle of locality asserts objects can only be influenced directly by their immediate surroundings. I hit the ball, the ball moves. For me to hit it, though, I have to be within arm's reach. Or at least have an instrument that can reach it. I hold a gun and squeeze the trigger. The hammer hits the firing cap, which instigates an explosion, throwing the bullet out of the barrel, across the field, and into the ball. Through direct physical interactions within a locale, I have hit the ball."

He smiles at his students.

"But this isn't necessarily always the case. Experiments have shown that quantum mechanically entangled particles must violate this principle or obliterate the entire idea of philosophical realism and counterfactual definiteness. Can anyone explain those terms for me?"

The class shifts in their seats.

"Ok. I'll give you this one, it's a bit tricky. Philosophical realism states that reality is ontologically independent of our conceptual schemes, linguistic practices, and beliefs. The world is what it is, whether we can see it for that or not. In this system, truth is based on how closely a belief corresponds to reality."*

---

* Too true. Just in my case, I can't wait around to find out how close I am. I had to go on predictions. Rely on answers to questions I couldn't risk asking. It was time to take action.

Across the iron bridge, just inside the back door of 357, there was an old rolled-up rug tossed into the trash under the stairs. I dragged it back along the gangplank. It was heavier than it looked, but still light enough to schlep. So I took a good stance and heaved.

Thwack. Got it in one. It unraveled smack dab over the barbed wire and dangled over the carriage house's gutters, providing me a barb-free, vertical escape route.

Yes, I was desperate. But it worked in the movies. The hard part was going to be the briefcase. Mom's report was heavy. Tossing it up and over onto the roof would be hard enough. But I could just imagine it popping open and all the loose sheets blowing out over the rooftops. That happened in the movies too.

Once again the garbage was the answer. I dug, and I sifted and came up with an old extension cord. I tied one end around the briefcase, the other around me. All I had to do was stand on the railing, jump to the carpeted neutral zone across the barbed wire, climb up onto the roof, pull up the report, and find some way down on the other side to 40th Street, far away from any would-be watchful gazes, safe from any snares.

That was the plan at least.

By the time I came to, it was night. My brain throbbed against the inside of my skull. My hair was crusty and matted with dried blood. The briefcase sat a few feet away. An orange umbilical cord snaked along the ground to where it was wrapped across my torso.

I don't remember falling. I don't even remember jumping. The last thing I remember was starting to climb up the railing.

I sat up and felt my brain turn over inside my cranium like wet cement in a mixer. I had to lean back against the railing and grab on so I didn't fall right off the floor. The carpet's tassels fluttered in the breeze.

Fuck the carpet. Fuck the movies. And fuck my mom.

I put the battery back in my phone. Texted Toby:

Slip out my holden . . .

On a yellow chariot—

Stop stopping. Just slow . . .

Reidier wasn't the only one with his codes. Decipher that, you Department Pricks. My tricky acrostic haiku is not for you. My message muddled with a heavy accent of personal allusions. I'm just praying that Toby's not too drunk to deconstruct it.

Hopefully spelling out SOS with the first letter of each line will snap him into sobriety. Then he just has to speak my language. He should get the holden reference pretty easily. We both used to worship J. D. Salinger. So Toby should be able to get: I need him to leave wherever he is and come catch me before I go right over a cliff. If he can get that far, then he sure as hell can figure out from my second line that I want him to take a taxi. It's the third line that I'm the most worried about. If he doesn't get that, well, then all this was for naught. We'll get nabbed, and then he'll be Departmental property too. Whatever you do, Toby, just don't get out of the cab. Don't stop. For the love of God. Just slow down, open the door, let me dash in, and drive off.

Now we wait. Underneath the stairs. Not to worry, I took some initiative and unscrewed all the light bulbs in the front hallway. Can't see me now, can you? No more carnival shooting range for you guys.

Come on, Toby. Come get me. Come get me.

A student interrupts with an unintelligible question.

"Yes, I would agree that this outlook is the general worldview. Most of us consider the world is out there whether we see it or not. But imagine this: Last night your mother bought a lottery ticket and sent it to you. It turns out she picked the correct numbers. Are you a millionaire?"

A number of yes's and one boisterous "hell yeah" come from the class.

"Thank you for your enthusiasm, Mr. Maynard. So then, now that you're rich, would you mind tipping me five hundred dollars for this lecture? It's a pittance to you with your newfound wealth, and I do give an entertaining lecture."

"Uh . . ."

"Why do you hesitate? Am I not worth it? Better question, why haven't you gotten up and left my class yet to start celebrating? No one?"

"Because it didn't happen," someone offers.

"How do you know? Just because I made it up doesn't mean it's not true. Any one of you could be receiving the winning ticket this afternoon. Who thinks they are?"

Reidier waits. No takers.

"So then you agree, even if it happened, it hasn't happened because you haven't heard the news yet. You haven't received the letter, checked the newspaper, and gone to collect your winnings. It's not real yet."

Mr. Maynard protests that that doesn't matter, as the ticket still exists and is on its way. Just because he hasn't received it yet doesn't mean it's not out there, on its way.

"Really. What happens if it's lost in the mail? What happens if when you finally receive it, you throw it away by accident?"

Mr. Maynard responds with a despondent "damn."

"Not damn at all. You won't be disappointed because you were never a millionaire. You were never thinking you were. Not until the moment that you open your mother's letter, look at the lottery ticket, and verify it's a winner will it ever be reality for you. Because until that moment, your mother could have been remembering the numbers incorrectly.

"Reality isn't necessarily out there, it could be in here." Reidier taps his finger against his temple. "Descartes's demon might be dreaming us. Right, Ms. Echeverria? You're our token English major. What is it Hamlet tells Rosencrantz about the realities of our world?"

A quiet clear voice recites, "There is nothing either good or bad, but thinking makes it so."

"Precisely. Who knew Shakespeare knew so much about the quantum mechanical world."

The class laughs.

"Which brings us to counterfactual definiteness: the ability to meaningfully discuss and utilize the results of measurements even if they were not performed."

Mr. Maynard interjects a question.

"Alas, no, I cannot apply that principle to your 'answers' on last week's test."

More laughs.

"Although, I did appreciate how you performed your own locality experiment by taking that test without really being here at all."

The class explodes with several hisses, ohs, and a stinging, *You need some aloe for that burn?*

"CFD is essentially the ability to assume the existence of objects and properties of objects even if they haven't been measured. And I am going to preempt you, Mr. Maynard, and ask you to refrain from your burgeoning, 'That's what she said.'"

The class laughs.

"Still, I respect your distrust for this concept. You're in good company. Albert Einstein thought something was fundamentally wrong with quantum mechanics since it predicted violations of locality. He even went so far as to write a harshly worded letter about it that became known as the Einstein-Podolsky-Rosen paradox paper.

"Albert would have none of it. Locality was an absolute necessity, and there could be no violations. It'd be like if the speed of light could slow down. Nope, according to Big Al, 'If this axiom were to be completely abolished, the idea of the existence of quasi-enclosed systems, and thereby the postulation of laws which can be checked empirically in the accepted sense, would become impossible.'"

Big Al. Anarchist Al = Albert Einstein = E? Or Eve? Flip a coin.

The "speed of light is inversely proportional to alpha, and both have been considered unchangeable constants."

Is this what Reidier was writing? What does belief have to do with Reidier's work?

So far, that's all that could be decoded. But there was more hidden inside Reidier's Notebooks than codes.

TITLE CARD: **GALILEE 6:21**

TITLE CARD: **EXPERIMENT 7 ALPHA**

CONTROL ROOM, GOULD ISLAND FACILITY - 2008-05-17
00:17

Console lights flicker on, spotting the dark.

The video screen blinks awake.

Ambient light bleeds in from the Mirror Lab as
it comes to life.

On video screen, SPLIT SCREEN-

RIGHT SIDE, target room: blackness.

LEFT SIDE, transmission room:

Fiber-optic cables, circumscribing the
Entanglement Channel flare red for several
seconds, then morph into an orbiting white light
as the Entanglement Channel opens.

A small geometric solid made out of what appears
to be graphite sits on transmission pad.

NOTE: after close video analysis it has been
determined that (presumed) graphite is roughly 9
mm by 6 mm. It has a tiered shape with 58 facets
including 25 crown, 8 girdle, and 25 pavilion
surfaces.

The Boson Cannons and Pion Beams twitch to
life. SOUNDS of the rapid ACCELERATION and
DECELERATION of GEARS as the men take a series
of readings of the graphite. Once complete they
settle into optimized focal positions.

Encrypted calibrations roll up the console's
computer screen.

NOTE: as with unauthorized Experiment 9 Bravo, all of the calibrations and settings were encrypted. Once again, I2O has been unable to decrypt to date.

Another console screen flickers to life, SPLIT SCREEN:

ANGELL RIGHT: lit, though empty, target pad in Angell Lab.

ANGELL LEFT: shows Dr. Reidier (again PJs and tweed sport coat) pacing back and forth behind his desk in Angell Lab. In his arms, he holds a swaddled and sleeping boy (later confirmed to be Ecco Reidier).

Dr. Reidier pauses, pacing to read something off his computer.

Dr. Reidier disappears offscreen.

OFFSCREEN: SCREAM as Ecco starts awake. Sounds of CRYING.

A frustrated Reidier comes back into frame. He's no longer holding Ecco. He leans over his chair and presses "Enter."

Inside their Plexiglas covers, Contact Buttons Alpha and Bravo sink down, simultaneously engaging.

                                          CUT TO:

MIRROR LAB - SAME TIME

---MULTIPLE SCREENS---

ANGELL LAB RIGHT: empty target pad

MIRROR LAB LEFT: the Quark Resonator emits a SOFT, HIGH-PITCHED DRONE as it powers up.

The graphite geometric solid on the transmission pad remains perfectly still.

At 2008-05-17 00:21:58.8893302 a quiet THRUM coincides with . . . nothing. The graphite geometric solid remains on the transmission pad.

NOTE: While undetectable to the naked eye, when high-speed footage was slowed down, a phenomenon was detected for the last 800 picoseconds on the left side. During this increment, the graphite solid seems to tessellate then (slightly) shudder, and finally settle back into its previous state.

ANGELL LAB RIGHT: at 2008-05-17 00:21:58.8893302, the video feed distorts with static waves. Moments later it snaps back straight, into focus. On the Angell Lab target pad sits a 2-carat diamond, roughly 9 mm by 6 mm, with 58 facets, 25 crown, 8 girdle, and 25 pavilion surfaces.

ANGELL LAB LEFT: Dr. Reidier smiles, staring off at the target pad. He double-checks something on his computer, then walks off (and over) to the target pad.

OFFSCREEN: Ecco still CRYING.

ANGELL LAB RIGHT: A tweed-sport-coated arm comes into view and picks up diamond between thumb and forefinger.

ANGELL LAB LEFT: Dr. Reidier enters frame behind chair, cradling and gently bouncing a crying Ecco in one arm.

Dr. Reidier whispers comforting murmurs into his boy's ear, while holding the diamond up to the light with his free hand.

Dr. Reidier leans in and taps a couple buttons on his keyboard.

Angell Lab feed shuts off.

CONTROL ROOM - 00:22:20

Contact Buttons Alpha and Bravo depress.

Data scrolls up computer screen and stops. The screen and computer shut down.

The console lights flicker out into the dim.

INT. MIRROR LAB -

The HIGH-PITCH of the Quark Resonator fades out as the machine powers down.

GEARS SPINNING NOISE ramps up and down as the Boson Cannons and Pion Beams retract.

The circling indicator lights surrounding the Entanglement Channel orbit to a standstill, flash green, and then switch off.

The Mirror Lab Transmission Room light turns off.

Clearly a more complex structure than the original graphite cube in Experiment 7...But unclear as to why going back to drawing board at the beginning?

XII

Who knows when the end is reached? Death may be the
beginning of life.

~Zhuang Zhou

The boundaries between life and death are at best shadowy and
vague. Who shall say where one ends and where the other begins?

~Edgar Allan Poe

from the Reidier SD Card
.mp4 file
Size: 449 MB
Created: May 21, 2007[104]

---

[104] SD card was found lodged behind three-ring binder mechanism in Reidier Notebook #7. Notebook was dropped while being removed from trunk. To date, no other memory sticks have been found in any other notebook.

   Source of video footage is unknown. It's not Departmental NB footage. Have to assume it's Reidier's own recording. Method unclear. Device unclear, but apparently some sort of hidden camera around chest level.

"You need two things for your work: funding and autonomy. And they almost never go together," shouts an older man in a dark blue-striped suit, barely audible over the blaring dance music. His hair is wavy and vibrantly white contrasted against his tanned smooth skin. His pale-blue eyes reveal little, and the deep smile lines that frame his lips suggest a practiced, set expression that has been engraved over decades. He wears French cuffs with cameo cufflinks, and a French-Swiss Tour de l'Ile watch to match his French-Swiss accent. Overall he gives the impression of someone who goes to great lengths to exude refinement. So much so, that it seems likely he didn't come from it, but rather had to claw his way into the upper echelons. He's a measured man who carved his path with the relentless patience of a river. All of which makes one wonder why, of all places, he chose to meet Reidier at a strip club.

Reidier sits across from him in a leather chair, a small mahogany table between them.

"For with funding come strings," the man continues. "Agendas. Agendas not your own."

A blonde waitress in a purple chemise and black lingerie sets down two drinks, a bottle of water in front of the man, a pineapple juice in front of Reidier. Neither acknowledge her.

"And that's where you run into trouble."

"I'm not in any trouble," Reidier says.

The man gazes at the table. He removes a Ziploc bag from his suit pocket. It contains at least three dozen vitaminlike pills. He unscrews his water bottle. "It's the unfortunate sheep who doesn't see the wolf until he feels the fangs."

"Fate cannot be fooled," Reidier counters.

"I did not take you for a fatalist. That's rare in a scientist."

"Fate made me an authority on myself."

"Among other things."

The music shifts to a quieter, though similarly beat-driven song.

"I apologize for the necessity of the environment," the man says. "I hope you don't interpret it as disrespect."

Reidier leans back and sips his juice. "It's a reflection on you and your company, not me."

The man nods. "It provides a convenient cover for us. The noise precludes prying eyes and nosy ears, and the setting gives you a reasonable alibi. Your caretakers will assume you had an extracurricular impulse and won't wonder too much when you neglect to mention to your family your whereabouts later this afternoon."

"Very thorough. Still, it doesn't explain what I'm doing here with you."

"Tell me," the man leans in, "How's your work going?"

Reidier stalls with another sip of juice. "My classes are going quite well. Very bright students this semester."

"And your other work?"

"What work are you referring to?"

"Clearly, I come to you having done my due diligence. Why else would I be here? Why else would you be?"

Reidier offers up nothing.

The man smiles and then laughs. "Of course your discretion would be something I would insist on too. Then again, discretion is nothing more than a polite word for hypocrisy. I worry we might be getting off on the wrong foot."

"Having your man in a taxi wait for me outside my office and then intimate it's in my family's best interest to take a ride does sour first impressions."

The man sighs. "You'll have to forgive my methods. I could not of course show up in person. Please understand that in no way are you obligated to remain. Should you so desire, you're free to leave, and my man in the taxi will drop you anywhere you wish. I hope, however,

you will do me the courtesy and yourself the favor of hearing me out
so that both of us might consider the professional possibilities."

Reidier waits a moment then says, "I think I'll leave now."

The man raises his hands, palms up, as if in an "as you please"
gesture.

Reidier stands and extends his arm to shake hands, "Goodbye,
Mr. Curzwell."

The man reaches out and takes Reidier's hand in his own. As he
does so, his right sleeve pulls up, revealing a bracelet. It's a half-inch
strip of metal, gold on one side and silver on the other that twists
around his wrist to create a Möbius strip.*

---

*When I read this for the first time, my heart accelerated to about 260
bpms, pounded my stomach loose from its moorings, and drummed it
right out my asshole.

There I was, huddled, practically fetal, under the stairs. My phone
sat silently next to me. Against my better judgment, I had to keep it on.
But assuming my alcoholic Apollo had risen to action, he needed a way
to give me the signal. On your mark, get set, run your ass off and dive
into the cab before we get to Ninth Avenue.

Just don't text or call me before that. Let's not tip our hand, dear
Tobias.

So far, so good. He was either on his way or too busy dancing with
Bacchus to even notice his phone vibrating with my SOS. Either I was
saved, or no worse off.

Or my guardians were mobilizing some sort of intervention. A bunch
of officially unofficial G-men types, with a portable breaching ram in their
trunk, semiautomatic .45s in their holsters, and extra clips in their pockets. Maybe they'd use a flash grenade. It's Hell's Kitchen. Who the hell
would notice? Nobody'd come out of their apartments to check. That's
for sure. You'd be crazy not to double-lock your dead bolts and slip the
chain for good measure.

With that little daydream, my pulse took off like a tap dancer on
crack. As sharp as my mind is, it's a double-edged scalpel, lobotomizing
any sense of sanity and calm right out of my medulla oblongata. I had
to do something to occupy it before it sent me screaming out into the
night, right into the G-men's backseat.

Hilary's briefcase waited patiently at my feet. No. That fat fucker was the whole reason I was in this state to begin with. The last thing I wanted to do was stoke the fire.

Fire. Hm.

Maybe that's the answer. Maybe I should burn this place down. Slip out with everybody else fleeing onto the street. With my luck (and unskill set), I'd most likely just burn myself right into a corner. Not to mention public endangerment. Fuck, maybe they were thinking of trying the same thing. Smoke me out. Beat the bushes, so to speak. Nah. Might burn up the Reidier Report. It'd be easier just to come in and grab me.

Why haven't they just come in and grabbed me, then? They can't be worried that I might be dangerous. Is there some reason they need to keep *me* alive?

CLICK-CLINK.

And the little crack-powered tap dancer in my chest slammed to a dead stop, collapsing right on stage.

CLICK-CLINK.

Someone was trying the outer door. G-Men? Toby?

My phone kept up its silent treatment. No more texting. I was going to have to check. No broken mirrors in the trash. Nothing reflective. I could crawl back to the carriage house. Turn on the video surveillance. But if it was Toby, that'd cost precious minutes. I was going to have to sneak a peek from underneath the stairs. And, having unscrewed the lights, I had an advantage this time. The alcove fluorescents were still burning bright, trying to pierce my security blanket of darkness, but the unlit hallway just dulled it down to cataract dim. There'd be a reflection in the glass door. Whoever was there wouldn't be able to see in, but I'd see out clear as day. My, how the carnival shooting range has turned.

A couple quick breaths to help my tap dancer get a beat going again in my veins, and I edged my head just around the stairs.

FUCK! It was him. The Michelin Man tourist. His hand covered his brow, and he was pressed against the glass, peering in.

Fuckfuckfuckfuckfuck.

I had to call off Toby. There'd be no way for me to get past. But how? Clearly they intercepted my last text. Could I yank open the door and barrel past? It could work. Couldn't it?

THUMP-THUMP-THUMP-THUMP-THUMP.

Christ. Someone was barreling down the stairs. Another resident.

THUMP-THUMP-THUMP-THUMP-THUMP.

They were going to unwittingly run the gauntlet.

CLICK-CLACK. SQUEAK.

"Good timing." Man's voice.

"Guess so." Woman's voice.

"Bundle up, it's cold out there."

"Right? Have a good night."

"Stay warm."

The outer door CLICKED shut.

Two FOOTSTEPS.

Stop.

SQUEAK. CLICK.

The inner security door shut.

Now I could hear his breathing. He stood at the foot of the stairs that I was hiding underneath, totally fetal.

CLUMP.

CLUMP.

CLUMP.

It was the sweetest sound I had ever heard.

CLUMP.

He was going up the stairs.

CLUMP.

Then it hit me. The image of him in the security camera from the other day. Dancing from foot to foot out in the cold, staring *up* at the building. Number five is up. He thought my little hideout was on the top floor.

CLUMP.

I risked a quick glance out from beneath the stairs. I couldn't take my ears' word for it. His hand on the railing. Michelin Man sleeve on his arm. And on his wrist, between the two, a flash of light—a shiny reflection off a piece of twisted metal. Then he rounded the stairwell to continue upward.

But the after-image still echoed across my retina. The rods in my eyeballs screaming in remembrance. A flash of white twisted across them like a Möbius strip.

I think.

RRRRRRRRRRRRRRR.

My phone rattled with vibration next to me. A text from Toby:

Nice fucking haiku

One turn deserves another

When poets collide

Relief. I was saved. His coded reply said it all. Wrapped in a cloak of sarcastic grandeur, Toby was turning onto 39th street, so we poets could collide. And if there was any doubt as to when, the first letters of each line were as clear as day. N-O-W.

I grabbed the briefcase, snatched up my phone, and burst from my hiding place toward the door. The Michelin Man was at least two flights up. Whether he heard me or not, I don't know. I was out the door, through the alcove, onto the sidewalk, and into the backseat of Toby's cab. The light at Ninth Avenue, by the grace of God, was green, and down Ninth we went, blending into safe ubiquity.

Toby didn't pressure me to explain. Didn't question my sanity or diagnose my paranoia. He told me I looked like shit and needed a shower. We discussed where to take me. Obviously, my apartment was out. As was Toby's. Hotels required credit cards. I could think of only one place.

Reidier holds Curzwell's hand for an extra moment. "Interesting bracelet."

"I'll have one sent to your home."

Reidier releases his hand, pauses, then sits back down. "Do you think they have absinthe in a place like this?"

The man's smile lines fall into place. "I'm sure they're prepared to cater to any taste." Curzwell signals a waitress.

"Fifteen minutes. Then I'd be happy to have a ride to 454 Angell."

Curzwell nods once. "Although it might be tidier to leave you somewhere close to, rather than at, your home?"

"So you know my address then."

"As I said, I have done due diligence. Not to mention that house has an interesting history of habitants."

"How does the Whole Foods work for you? Cloak-and-dagger enough or would you prefer the abandoned drawbridge off of Wickenden?"

"The Whole Foods will be fine."

"Fantastic," Reidier says without emotion.

The man wrinkles his brow in thought while Reidier orders his drink. Two dancers step up onto a small raised platform in the middle of the back room and start spinning around steel poles.

Curzwell leans in after the waitress has left them alone. "So that you needn't worry about discretion, state secrets, or what have you, let's start with what I know."

"Sounds good. As long as you don't expect me to confirm or deny anything."

"There will be no need for that." The man tosses five or so of his vitamin pills into his mouth, washes them down with a slug of water, and then launches into his recitation. "You're a pioneer in quantum cryptography. The work you did for CSG was innovative and lucrative. Unfortunately, the management structure there did not adequately understand how to nurture your talents. The University of Chicago gave you a wide berth and encouraged your creativity, but being an academic institution, they would lay claim to any and all of your technological as well as intellectual property. And in spite of their endowment and impressive resources, they would have been unable to provide you with the necessities of your work on a financial, technical, and security level."

The man pauses for Reidier to take it in.

"I believe most of that is on my Wikipedia page."

"What is not in the public domain, however, is the breakthrough you've made with teleportation."

Reidier doesn't move a muscle. He waits for Curzwell to continue.

"Nor that you are now working for the Defense Advanced Research Projects Agency under Donald Pierce. While the Department's resources are vast enough to accommodate your needs, their agenda and their, for lack of a better term, power make them a potentially stifling partner. And although they might be encouraging and supportive, they will not hesitate to push you to develop a technology better suited to their ends, while ensuring that you mothball any innovation they see as irrelevant, such as quark echoes."

The man turns his pale-blue gaze on Reidier and searches his face for a reaction to his revelation.

"Interesting update. Tell me, where do you get your information?" Reidier asks.

"The Beimini® Corporation[105] is not without resources. While I am unable to illuminate you on our research methods, I do share your concern for how we came to learn so much."

Reidier presses his palms together and brings them up to his lips. After some time he asks, "Tell me, in your story, do you know the Department's agenda?"

"I have a guess."

"Please . . ." Reidier gestures for him to continue.

"While your quark echo method might prove more successful in the transference of consciousness from one pattern container to another, it has the drawback of being a one-to-one transmission."

"Meaning?"

"Meaning you destroy the original."

"Ah."

"Whereas your current technique, the one in which you've had your initial success, allows you to 'copy' the subject."

"Why would the Department prefer this method?" Reidier asks. "Especially if what you're saying is true that the quark echo approach would yield better results with the transference of consciousness."

"That's the multibillion-dollar question, isn't it? Perhaps they aren't as interested in consciousness as you are." Curzwell finishes his bottle of water and proceeds to roll the empty container between his fingertips.

"There are cheaper ways to produce goods," Reidier says. "The cost of what you're talking about would far exceed the price of replicating items using conventional techniques."

"But not necessarily over great distances. Payloads into space can be very expensive, especially when traveling beyond the earth's orbit."

---

[105] Beimini® Corp is an LLC incorporated in the Cayman Islands on September 9, 1999. It's owned by the Bettencourt family, who are also the largest stakeholder in the L'Oréal Group cosmetic and beauty company. It's unclear what service this corporation performs, what product it creates, or how much interaction and overlap there is between the two companies.

"Space colonization?"

"In the future, why not? Surely you must have thought about that. You even mention traveling to Mars in your lectures."

Reidier's body language reveals his discomfort. While his lectures are on iTunes University for all the world to download, the pervasiveness of his host's knowledge of him must be unnerving the physicist.

"There are also more global applications, assuming you eventually perfect the consciousness transference to the point of at least replicating habitual training," Curzwell says. "For example, there are certain advantages to replicating an individual who knows his way around a Barrett M107 sniper rifle even if they don't know what killing is. Or especially if they don't."

Reidier sits in silence, contemplating Curzwell's insinuation. He shifts in his seat, squeaking against the leather. Finally, he utters, "Soldiers."

"They are very expensive to train and often sent into harm's way. Each casualty incurs a significant financial, human, and political cost. Imagine the possibilities of being able to send platoons of soldiers on numerous suicide missions anywhere in the universe and not have to report a single death. Every 'individual' original accounted for and safe. Casualty-free war fought by expendable clones. Very science-fiction/*Star Wars*, I admit, but then again, so is teleportation itself."

The man's eyes flit from Reidier's face to his hands and back. Reidier's fingers are intertwined. The knuckles turn white with pressure.

Up on the stage, the dancers have removed their tops and are using their breasts to collect dollars from various patrons.

"I am become death, the destroyer of worlds,"[106] Reidier says, stricken.

---

[106] See footnote 90.

The man flashes an avuncular smile. "Not at all. Quite the opposite. You are the Destroyer of Death. At least that's what we're hoping over at Beimini."[107]

The waitress sets down Reidier's drink. He doesn't reach for it.

"I'm sorry, what is it that you all would want from me?" Reidier's voice seems to have lost direction.

Clearly Curzwell, a practiced negotiator, has been waiting for this. He has Reidier off balance and knows it. Now he needs to gently bring him back to equilibrium, supported and steadied by Beimini. "War is too important to leave to the generals, don't you think?"

"And technology is too important to leave to the scientists."

"But you are not just a scientist. You're a critical thinker. And that's what's important." Curzwell lets this sink in a moment and then continues. "What we want is for you to continue your work, any way you see fit. We'd provide all of your technological necessities,

---

[107] Beimini = Bimini!! It's a different spelling. Bimini, of course, is a chain of islands located fifty-three miles due east of Miami. It's the westernmost district of the Bahamas. It is also, however, the alleged location of the mythical Fountain of Youth.

Bimini comes from Taino, the Native American Language of the Caribbean. It's derived from *Bibi*, mother, and *Mini*, waters. The Mother of Many Waters. It is the pre-Columbian name for what is now known as Florida.

Allegedly, in the sixteenth century, Ponce de León learned of Bimini and the restorative powers of its waters from the inhabitants of Puerto Rico. He had grown tired of material wealth and led an expedition to find it, discovering Florida in the process.[ß]

[ß] Hilary neglects to mention that Ponce never found the Fountain of Youth. The fact is that, even though he might have heard of the Fountain and even set out looking for it, he never mentioned it in any of his writings. Ponce's name wasn't even associated with the story until after his death. Gonzalo Fernández de Oviedo in his *Historia General y Natural de las Indias* alleges that Ponce de León set out in search of the magic waters of Bimini in order to cure his impotence. That would explain Ponce's own muteness on the subject.

---

relocate you and your family wherever you desire, and guarantee your security."

Reidier doesn't respond. One of the dancers, in a green G-string, hangs upside down from a pole, and spins slowly to the floor.

"Furthermore, we'd start you off with a twenty million dollar signing bonus that would be yours outright, and also offer you forty-five percent ownership in any and all of our mutual endeavors. Whatever other wonders you invent or develop outside of the purview of our partnership would be solely yours."

With the offer of serious money, Curzwell relaxes his posture. He's confident in the intoxicating draw of wealth, certain that his deal far exceeds the government's. The pull of the private sector on the institutional man is as unrelenting as gravity.

"That's a generous offer," Reidier says.

"It's what you're worth."

"But I still have no idea what it is you want in return."

Curzwell nods toward the stage, where the two strippers tease their thongs up and down their hips. "What do you see there?"

The blonde stretches the thin material away from her flesh so a calloused hand with dirty fingernails can slip a dollar bill between the elastic and her skin. On the other side, the redhead, the one dressed in green, stands with her back to a patron, bends over, traces her index fingers along the curves of her hips swooping toward her groin, hooks her finger underneath, and draws the thong out from between her buttocks so that a wrinkled hand might slide a five underneath.

"Ritual," Reidier says.

"An age-old one."

Reidier wraps his hand around his juice drink but doesn't lift it.

"What would you say is the source of this ritual?" Curzwell asks.

"Biology. A lack of options."

"I'd agree on both counts. But why do these customers come here?"

Reidier continues to clasp his glass.

Curzwell lets out a laugh. "Yes, the scantily clad women, of course. Sexual urges, et cetera, et cetera. But on a psychological level what are they really getting? I'll tell you. They're becoming invigorated. Alive. In a word, youthful."

An inebriated man leans across the stage to slide a bill up the redhead's leg, but she moves out of reach and wags her finger at him.

"They come to feel young," Curzwell says. "These men come to be close to young women. Why young women? Because they're fertile. The act of sex at its most basic level is the urge to continue the line, to cheat death. It's a pervasive, universal urge."

Reidier finally lifts his glass and sips.

"And with your help, we think Beimini® Corp can cater to that need."

"I'm sorry?"

"We would support development of any and all technological innovations you might have, and apply no constraints about how to proceed, whether it be with quark echoes, nanofabrication, or something else entirely. We would just want you to figure out how to adapt your progress to our needs."

"Your agenda."

"Our agenda, yes, but with complete respect for your autonomy. And full disclosure of our goals and targets. You will never wonder about our motivations or what we're planning to do with your work. Transparency precludes the need for trust. You'd be our partner, not our project."

"How does this tie in to cheating death?"

"Your fourth step."

"What step?"

"In teleportation. What you call the animation step."[108]

"Transference and animation," Reidier recalls.

---

[108] See page 226.

333

"Yes. We want to be able to transfer a mind from one vessel to another."

"That's the key to all teleportation, isn't it?"

"Only we're unconcerned with traveling any distance."

"Then what would be the point of moving a consciousness from one vessel to an exact copy?"

"There wouldn't be. Unless." Curzwell lets the insinuation hang in the air between them.

"Unless it wasn't an exact copy," Reidier says, unable to conceal the astonishment in his tone.

"We call it Restoration. The basic methodology would require scanning a client now, today, storing that data, and then at some later point, using it to reconstruct that same body and then transferring the client's consciousness from his older self into his younger self."

"So I would scan you now, then in twenty years or thirty years, I'd teleport you from your older self to your younger self."

"That's the basic gist, yes."

"And that process could be repeated ad infinitum."

"Restored to your youthful vigor."

"The Destroyer of Death."

Curzwell swallows the last of his vitamins. "What is death? I'll tell you. He's the world's most successful thief who has stolen our loved ones and our time for as long as we've been around."

"Death gives life meaning."

"Nonsense," Curzwell scoffs. "That's useless orthodoxy based on a lack of options and perspective. It's what we do with life that gives it meaning. Art, music, relationships. What we create."

"You want to bring immortality to market."

Curzwell winks at Reidier. "The thing about immortality is that you can never affirm you've achieved it."

"It's inhuman."

"Science is inhuman. Science is incompatible with humanism.

The whole point of it is to escape from humanity. Why do you think we went to space? Science is at war with humanity."

Reidier doesn't respond.

Curzwell takes a different tack. "At the same time, science is the ultimate expression of our humanity. You know what separates us from the beasts. This," he taps the side of his head, "which holds a neocortex the size of a napkin and allows for critical thinking. That and this," he touches his thumb to his forefinger, "our nimble opposable thumb, which enables us to take our advanced thoughts and fashion them out of the world at hand. Humanity is defined by our ability to manipulate our surroundings, to cross our thresholds and transcend limitations. That's what being human is."

Reidier holds his drink and leans back in his chair, facing the dancers. The redhead is on her knees, legs splayed, leaning back. She tugs at her G-string with the beat. In doing so, she reveals a tattoo just above her pubic area. It's a single word written in a curved path, forming an arc. The footage is blurry, but it looks as if it spells "Panoramas."

"Curious," Curzwell comments.

Reidier finishes his absinthe in one gulp. "Who would . . . ?"

"Obviously our clientele would be very exclusive as we're offering the ultimate high-end service," Curzwell says. "We've already got a sizable pool of investors and prospective clients."

"Your only limitation would be when someone comes in for the original scan," Reidier says.

"Yes. At least for Restoration 1.0."

Reidier stops watching the dancer.

"We hope to do much more than that in subsequent generations. By 2.0 we expect to use DNA excavation to reconstruct a client's physique from any age. Third generation, as envisioned, would allow us to diversify physique entirely, allowing clients to choose race, gender, or even design personalized attributes. Although we're not sure about how the psyche would handle such a drastic shift in hosts. And depending on how your work progresses, both technically and economically, we might eventually even develop a Death Insurance division where clients would regularly have their minds copied and stored monthly, weekly, or even daily in the event of an unforeseen demise."

Reidier takes a moment to respond. "Sounds like your marketing department is ahead of the research curve."

"We want you to know how big we're thinking. This would be the end of ends. The death of death. The world, as we know it, will never be the same. And you'll be at the center of it all. The alpha and the omega."

"This is certainly a lot to take in."

"A task I'm confident you're up to."

"If you don't mind my asking, aren't you nervous about sharing this with me? I mean, what's to stop me from striking out on my own?"

"You are free to do so. But you'd need significant funding, time, and resources to set up a new lab and develop an adequate power source. All of which would need to be done in secret, more or less, because more than anything, you'd need protection. All it takes is a memo from Pierce, and you become a National Security commodity, devoid of any civil rights. Beimini is already in the position to facilitate your transfer from the public to the private sector and provide the necessary cover."

Curzwell smiles once again at Reidier, but Reidier provides almost nothing in the way of response or body language.

Curzwell holds out a business card. "Please, should you need anything. It's a bit on the nose, I admit, but still an easy way to hide a purloined e-mail. An innocuous underscore away from reality."

The card is matte black, constructed out of heavy stock paper. On one side is a gold-embossed fleur-de-lis.

Reidier flips it over and laughs.

On the back is a solitary e-mail address: health_spa@fontaine bleau.com

An innocuous underscore away from reality. "You've got to be kidding."

Curzwell smiles. "Rest assured, though, it will find me. Whatever I can do to help. The truth is that, for every great man in history, there has been another more powerful man who helped him get there. It's not enough to have the talent, you need a paladin as well. Nikola Tesla had his Westinghouse, Roy Cohn had his McCarthy, and you have me."

TITLE CARD: **GALILEE 6:21**

TITLE CARD: **EXPERIMENT 47 OMEGA**

CONTROL ROOM, GOULD ISLAND FACILITY - 2008-08-08
01:02

Only the console lights, console video screen,
and the ambient light from Mirror Lab illuminate
the room.

Ambient light bleeds in from the Mirror Lab.

On video screen in console, SPLIT SCREEN-

RIGHT SIDE, target room: blackness.

LEFT SIDE, transmission room:

Fiber-optic cables circumscribing the
Entanglement Channel flare red for several
seconds, then morph into an orbiting white light
as the Entanglement Channel opens.

An orange sits on the pad. A small section of
its rind has been torn. Roughly a finger's width
wide. The rind has folded back into place, but a
jagged, white outline demarcates the damage.

The Boson Cannons and Pion Beams twitch to
life. SOUNDS of the rapid ACCELERATION and
DECELERATION of GEARS as the men take a series
of readings of the orange. Once complete they
settle into optimized focal positions.

On another console screen, SPLIT SCREEN:

ANGELL LAB RIGHT: lit, though empty, target pad.

ANGELL LAB LEFT: shows Dr. Reidier's tweed sport
coat draped over the back of his chair in Angell

Lab. SOUNDS of Dr. Reidier PUTTERING AROUND
offscreen.

Dr. Reidier's arm comes into view from the
right side. In his right arm, he holds one of
the twins (boy is only visible from waist down,
wearing a onesie).

Reidier's left hand quickly dances across the
keyboard.

Encrypted calibrations fill the Mirror Lab
console computer screen.

NOTE: as with other nocturnal, unofficial
experiments, calibrations and settings were
encrypted. I2O cannot decrypt.

Dr. Reidier sings quietly to Ecco offscreen
("59th Street Bridge Song" by Simon and
Garfunkel). Ecco joins in.

Dr. Reidier's torso comes into view. With his
left hand, he picks up the sport coat folded
over the back of the chair and tosses it on the
desk to the left of the keyboard.

He presses "Enter."

INT. MIRROR LAB - SAME TIME

On the console, inside their Plexiglas covers,
Contact Buttons Alpha and Bravo sink down,
simultaneously engaging.

                                        CUT TO:

---CONSOLE SPLIT SCREENS---

ANGELL RIGHT: empty target pad.

MIRROR LEFT: orange on the transmission pad.

The Quark Resonator emits a SOFT, HIGH-PITCHED DRONE as it powers up.

Orange remains perfectly still.

At 2008-08-08 01:04:37.3571113 nothing happens.

NOTE: for 200 picoseconds prior to transmission, on the left side prior to transfer, the orange tessellates, but ultimately simply sits there throughout.

ANGELL RIGHT: at 2008-08-08 01:04:37.3571113 the orange appears. Frost has condensed on the pad and surroundings.

ANGELL LEFT - 01:04:40

Dr. Reidier immediately leaps up and heads offscreen for the orange. Offscreen he continues to SING excitedly with Ecco.

MIRROR LEFT - transmission room: dust settling on target pad.

ANGELL RIGHT - the orange sits on the transmission pad. Dr. Reidier's tweed-sport-coated arm comes into view. He picks up the orange with his right hand and turns it over.

The orange has a consistent hue. No jagged white marks. The rind is smooth. Whole. No torn rind.

Dr. Reidier's left hand comes into view and "pets" the rind. He continues to rotate the orange, while rubbing his fingers over it . . . prodding it for rips or tears. There are none.

ANGELL LEFT - MOMENTS LATER

Dr. Reidier drops into his office chair, orange in hand.

He doesn't even look at the information on his screen. Instead, he just strikes a command key, while placing the orange on top of his sport coat on the desk.

Dr. Reidier leans back and stares at the perfect orange as the ANGELL LAB screen flashes off.

INT. CONTROL ROOM - MOMENTS LATER

Contact Buttons Alpha and Bravo depress.

Data scrolls up the screen, then stops, and the screen and computer shut down.

The console lights turn off.

INT. MIRROR LAB - SAME TIME

The HIGH-PITCH of the Quark Resonator fades out as the machine powers down.

GEARS SPINNING NOISE ramps up and down as the Photon Cannons retract.

The circling indicator lights surrounding the Entanglement Channel orbit to a standstill, flash green, and then switch off.

The Mirror Lab Transmission Room light turns off.

XIII*

---

* Hilary's formal report stopped with Chapter XII. The briefcase had plenty more stuffed into it, just none of it presented in the manner I've grown accustomed to. From here on out, it's just manila folders stuffed with transcripts, legal pads, notes, margin scribbles, article clippings, and the likes thereof. I mean it was organized, sort of. Just not formalized. I've done my best to put it in the "right" order. Chapter divisions were arranged mostly folder by folder or groups of folders as the material dictated. The quotes selected are still her choices, penciled on the front of some folder in no particular order or orientation (kind of like what Reidier did with his notebooks). The organization of the remaining material is my best approximation of how she would have continued her PsychoNarrative.

Non sum qualis eram, non sum qualis eram, non sum qualis eram, non sum qualis eram, non sum qualis eram, non sum qualis eram, non sum qualis eram, non sum qualis eram, non sum qualis eram, non sum qualis eram, non sum qualis eram, non sum qualis eram, non sum qualis eram, non sum qualis eram, non sum qualis eram, non sum qualis eram

Nevermind.   Never-mind.   Never. Mind.

~Hilary Kahn (as scribbled in her legal pad)

If you would be a real seeker after truth, it is necessary that at least once in your life, you doubt, as far as possible, all things.

~René Descartes

—Reality is what remains when faith has f a d e d.

There are lots of people who mistake their imagination for their memory.

~Josh Billings

—Non sum qualis sum eram[†]

~Danny Brand

Translation: I am not what I used to be. Reference? ➔ "Non Sum Qualis Eram Bonae Sub Regno Cynarae," a poem by Ernest Dowson (late nineteenth-century English poet associated with the Decadent Movement [finally a poetry movement I can get behind]), in which he himself is quoting the First Ode of the Fourth Book of Horace (wheels within wheels):

> Yet again thou wak'st the flame
> That long had slumber'd! Spare me, Venus, spare!
> Trust me, I am not the same
> As in the reign of Cinara, kind and fair.
> . . .
> Wherefore halts this tongue of mine,
> So eloquent once, so faltering now and weak?
> Now I hold you in my chain,
> And clasp you close, all in a nightly dream;
> Now, still dreaming, o'er the plain
> I chase you; now, ah cruel! down the stream.

I did not find this.

Lorelei did. And she did her due diligence too. Went to her own random Starbucks, borrowed a man's iPad, did the research, wrote it down on her own pad (not in an e-mail), and brought it back to me.

Apparently it was the only way to calm me down and get me to stop scrawling my own bizarre doodle over and over. Clutching my mother's legal-pad page of Latin to my chest with one hand and furiously scribbling ampersands over infinity signs (see above) with the other.

Apparently, once she did that, I finally slept.

It's been three days now. Three days since I broke out of my oubli-ette in the asshole of Hell's Kitchen. Getting up enough escape velocity to outrun its gravitational pull, going against currents of Lethe, cost me, though. Still, I managed to hold on through the taxi ride.

We had had the cab swing over to Tenth Avenue to find a gas sta-tion for us. I hopped out, ran over to a payphone, and put in fifty cents (I had no clue how much a payphone costs anymore but sure as hell wasn't about to put my SIM card back into my phone). I waited for the click of approval and dialed Lorelei. While waiting for that first ring, I realized af-ter freeing myself from the hook that I was, of course, diving into the net. Echoes of Heraclitus danced around the concrete canyons of Manhattan: *No man ever steps in the same river twice, for it's not the same river, and he's not the same man.*

They'd have her phone bugged too. And no matter how much the movies liked to draw out a call-tracing scene, in reality it doesn't take more than a few hundred milliseconds for the powers that be to trace a call.

My vision filled with flashes of red and blue hallucinations as the NYPD pulled in from every direction, boxing us in. No. This wasn't smart. I had to hang up before it rang.

CLICK. My finger pressed down on the trap lever. My fifty cents cas-caded its way down and out.

"Did you get her?" Toby asked.

"We have to go someplace with free WiFi. Someplace ubiquitous, like where terrorists would go," I said with remarkable lucidity, as I floated weightless around the backseat of the cab. I grabbed the door handle and pulled myself down to the seat as the cabbie took off.

Starbucks. Upper West. Had to try and get upwind of our downtown scent. Plenty of buzzheads swarming the coffee house, jockeying for seats, fluttering in front of the beckoning blue lights of their Macbooks, like vampire moths, hovering, waiting to strike at the coveted outlets, and sink their three-fanged, white umbilical cords into the mother lode.

We gave a Columbia kid twenty dollars to let us use his laptop. Well worth it, the cost of caution. Toby's phone was clearly out of the question, and long-since dismantled in the cab, phone in one pocket, battery in another, SIM card in a third. Once again I had to craft a personal "haiku," this time for Lorelei. Something that would slide under the Department's radar while setting off alarm bells and whistles in Lorelei's apartment. No small task in the semi-lucid state I was in. Obviously another poem was out of the question. You can't step in the same river twice. Evasion 101. Finally I gave up on clever and went for a blatant inside joke. I created an anonymous e-mail address.

-----Original Message-----
From: Tri.Meee@mail.com
Date: 4/4/2011 11:24 p.m.
To: lorelei@anomaly-ny.com
Subject: Chameleon.net

Hey Sweet Tits,

Sorry I've been so out of touch. Family shit, business trips, all the normal excuses. You know how it is, though, grinding away at your organ, until you finally realize you're the dancing monkey.

Anyway, I'm back, although don't tell my office, as I'm hiding from work for a little bit. Feel like a kid playing hooky. Care to sneak around with me? Or maybe dole out a little punishment . . .

I'll be hanging out under the bridge, hiding with all the other trolls.

Come find me.

Tri-Me

It took a lot more effort than I thought it would to capture the tone of one of her D-bag suitors. Wasn't so much for her benefit as it was for any potential eavesdroppers. I'm betting they're at least a little like me and aggressively work to ignore douchery. Of course she'd know Tri-Me as me, it was her goddamn nickname for me after all. And the Sweet Tits would immediately tip her off that something was off with me. I am much more of an ass man. Christ, I almost scribbled in a winking emoticon. I must still be pretty off.

It didn't really matter if she understood my reference about not being able to go into the office or not. All that mattered was that she got the message to come find me, that she took note how it'd be best to be discreet, and that she remembered one night last summer when we somehow ended up at the Boat Basin on 79th and the river. Its vaulted stone arches held the West Side highway up over our heads and made us feel like we were drinking under a bridge, surrounded by trolls in Polo shirts with popped collars.

After much debate, Toby and I had settled on the Boat Basin. It was well lit, had open vantage points, and there were a shitload of exits so, if need be, we could run up one of two underpasses to 79th street or dissolve in either direction into Riverside Park. All our forethought didn't even matter at the end of the day. By the time we got there, I was barely mobile. If the Department or my Michelin Man had somehow tracked us there, Toby would've been hard pressed to drag my semiconscious body along any escape route. The last thing I remember is sitting in a plastic chair, under the stone arches, clutching my oversized briefcase like it was a woobie.

I woke up in Purgatory.

Floating over Manhattan, I looked out the window. I appeared to be halfway between the star-speckled heavens above and a massive, grave-shaped portal into hell below. The center of the city seemed to have been swallowed up, a bottomless rectangle of darkness, dotted with brimstone bonfires. No rosy-fingered dawn for me, rather a bloody-fingered gloaming that reached up through the window and got a handhold on the floor.

Purgatory was very feng shui'd. A queen-sized bed hovered in the center of the room. A red Roho Barcelona chair and stool sat by the floor-to-ceiling window, which framed the aforementioned constellations and hell fires. An arco floor lamp stood guard over the chair. Against the wall, opposite the bed, a red and white orchid dangled off of a dark oak table. Purgatory, apparently, was très art deco.

Clean lines. Clean flow. Clean mind.

I threw back the white, twelve-hundred-thread-count, Egyptian cotton sheets, and gingerly hopped down onto the floor (the side opposite the window—I wanted to avoid that precipice at all costs). It was then that I noticed my feet were bare. The rest of me was wearing white silk pajamas. They were not mine. The only clue as to who they belonged to were the initials EL embroidered in red thread over the breast pocket. Although there weren't any periods after the letters. Maybe they weren't intitals. EL, *Él*, *Elohim*, the ancient god, father of all gods?

I scanned the room. My clothes weren't there.

My briefcase! My briefcase wasn't there.

I was halfway across the room when I stopped myself. The door loomed big. What if it was locked? What if I were locked in here? A prisoner of Purgatory. Sartre's cackles echoed around my skull.

What if it wasn't locked? Did I really want to find out what was on the other side? Was I in any state to handle that? What if it were the exact same room, with the same view, and the same bizarre levitating bed? No way could I handle that. Or what if it were some high-end, übermodern Department oubliette relic left over from the '50s?

Wherever I was, my briefcase had to have come with me. And whoever was in charge had obviously and purposefully made the decision to separate us.

CLINK, CLINK.

Silence.

OMP.

Silence.

A CLACK followed by what sounded like a marble rolling across concrete and punctuated with a quiet *Goddamnit*.

Silence.

Someone was on the other side of that door.

My hand hovered over the doorknob, frozen with apprehension. Then I heard a familiar and all too comforting sound: ice singing its way around the circumference of a rocks glass.

Whoever was out there, s/he/it was having a drink.

I opened the door.

Across the modern-styled living room, staring out another floor-to-ceiling window, stood an Asian man, maybe midfifties . . . *qui faisait la cinquantaine*, dark silky hair streaked with gray, a goatee, dressed in black slippers and the photonegative version of my PJs: red material with a white EL insignia over the breast pocket. In his hand a rocks glass, half-filled with amber liquid and two cubes of ice.

Was this my Michelin Man or Mephistopheles? No way to tell who was who without a puffy coat or a pitchfork for clues, neither of which were in plain sight. Then it hit me, what if Mich and Meph were one and the same?

"Dang, my apologies. I went and woke you with my goddamn cussin', didn't I?" A Texas twang was the last accent I expected to come out of that Asiatic goatee. The devil was from Texas?

I froze in the doorway. My mind flipped through pages of memory, trying to remember how Ivan Fyodorovich coped in this situation. I drew a blank and opted for nonchalant politeness. "I was already up."

"Glad to hear it. You been dead to the world going on three days now. How'd you like the bed?"

"It floats . . ."

"Ain't it sumptin'? Held up by a strong magnetic field. Prototype from a friend of mine. Real wow factor."

"Definitely a conversation piece."

He shook his drink and cast a glance over to a bar cart that looked like it had rolled right out of the '20s. "I'm fightin' a fierce case of jetlag myself. And we gave you the last of my pills. Welcome to join me in some of my sleep juice if you like."

I nodded, while contemplating how many time zones were in hell. I imagined no matter which direction you traveled in, you were always losing an hour.

"What's your poison?" He moved to the cart.

"I feel like I should order a pomegranate martini."

He raised an eyebrow.

"Bad joke. Just being wry." Apparently bad jokes were my way of coping with the supernatural. "Got any absinthe?"

The goatee laughed, said he hadn't gotten around to stocking up on wormwood yet. I deferred to whatever he was having, which turned out to be Laphroaig 21.

Maybe it was the gravity of alcohol or a subtle slope to the floor, but I found myself drawn across the room, closer and closer to that vertiginous wall of windows.

In an effort to avoid the dizzying panorama, my gaze kept drifting down to his slippers. They looked like normal feet. A little calloused maybe, but normal. No cloven hoof. No discernible limp either.

As he handed me my drink, he apologized for not having introduced himself. "Eli Longhorn," he said, handing me my scotch with his left, while ensnaring my right in a handshake.

With that introduction, my gaze snapped up to his gray-streaked hair. I was looking for hidden bumps, horns cloaked beneath the thick hair.

"I'm Danny."

"Yeah, I know. The guy who's been rode hard and put up wet." He laughed, clinked my glass, and took a drink.

The Laphroaig tasted like burnt peat soup that had been boiled in a worn leather saddle. All the ice in the Arctic couldn't have watered that firewater down enough. Still, its burn was at least warming my toes. I traced the EL on my chest. "So you're EL. Pardon my saying, but you don't look like much of an Eli."

A lone horsefly buzzed past, bumping against the window several times, in search of an escape.

"My father was Jewish."

Elohim?

Le diable n'existe point.

I scampered frantically for solid footing. "Longhorn wasn't the name of your ancestors."

Le diable n'existe point.

"My granddaddy Anglicized it in a blatant and futile attempt at assimilation. The surname had to go, but his yarmulke stayed on his head all day, every day. Assimilation in name only," Eli laughed to himself. "A rose by any other name . . ."

"Where am I?" I hadn't meant to blurt it out like that. If I were a betting man, I definitely would've placed a C-note on me tiptoeing around that terrifying subject.

"This is my place."

"I thought Purgatory was more of a neutral zone."

The goatee laughed bigger this time. "I don't know about Purgatory, but as far as I'm concerned, the Mandarin Oriental is as close as you can get to heaven on earth. Right below my ranch in the Bitterroot Mountains."

It took my lacuna-addled mind a few moments to parse all this new information. For some reason, mundane reality was much harder to accept than flights of deistic fancy. "The Mandarin Oriental . . ."

"Columbus Circle."

"Like where Per Se is?"

Eli laughed, "Well, it's a few dozen stories down, but yep. That's here all right. Not my kind of fare. Seems like the more you pay, the less you get."

His words buzzed around my ears, background noise. The world outside shifted as I defenestrated my focus out the window and down several hundred feet, back to the massive, grave-shaped portal into hell that I first saw when I woke, the one that seemed to have swallowed up the center of the city, the bottomless rectangle of darkness dotted with brimstone bonfires. Suddenly I was looking at a life-sized optical-illusion puzzle, like one of those where you focus past the picture, and a shape jumps out at you. The grave-shaped blackness of hell dotted with bonfires of brimstone morphed into Central Park with street lamps winking through the trees. The territory devoured by the map.

Eli caught me as my hand squeaked across the window, having lost my balance. I made some joke about his sleep juice as he helped me to the white leather couch. He sat on the other leg of the L shape and watched me with concern. I downed another slug of Laphroaig. Lucidity seeped through as I watched the bloody-fingered night wane back into the harmless red glow of the Hotel Empire neon sign.

Eli had to reassure me several times that he wasn't the devil, didn't work for the Department, and had never even owned one of those puffy, Michelin Man coats. As the stupor of sanity sank in, he filled me in on his backstory: his mom was a Taiwanese emigrant who, while plying her trade as a chemical engineer in Dallas, met and married an exec (his father, Ruben Longhorn) who worked for the same energy company. Eli himself never took an interest in the energy sector. Instead he built himself his own little empire exporting steel to China. In fact, most of the towers that scraped the Shanghai skyline were his steel.

It was all very impressive and interesting, but none of it explained how I had ended up in his guest room. Eli apologized, after I explained how my short-term memory had been folded over and over and then cut up like a paper snowflake.

Lorelei, long familiar with his jetlag issues, had called him in the middle of the night seventy-two hours prior, asking if he could help out a friend of hers.

"You didn't wonder why she didn't just bring me back to her place?"

"She didn't offer," he said. "And I didn't ask. This ain't my first rodeo. Her place is pretty small, and from what your friend . . ."

"Toby?"

"Right, Toby. From what I could glean from him, we needed to hide you like a crazy aunt in the basement."

I took in the large living room again. Not too bad a place to hide out. And it's certainly the last place anyone would think to find me.

"So, you and Lorelei, are . . ."

It took Eli a second to fill in the ellipsis in his head. When the dots finally connected, something halfway between a guffaw and a whistle erupted out of him. "Just because a chicken has wings doesn't mean it can fly." When he saw that cleared up nothing for me, he explained, "No. Little Li-Li and I are not. I have much more of an avuncular attachment to her. Her daddy and I were at business school together. I introduced him to her mother. I was at the hospital when she was born. Taught her to fly cast when she was four, to shoot when she was eight, to kick ass when she was thirteen. Over the years, Little Li-Li has developed a lifelong habit of hiding out in my various sanctuaries whenever she's needed to step out of the normal ebb and flow of life."

Eli swirled his ice around in his glass and took me in. "Funny thing, I was eventually going to get around to asking you the same thing."

I did my best to emulate his guffaw whistle but just ended up coughing. Eventually I managed to squeak out a no, we're just friends and coworkers.

"But you'd like it to be more than that," he said, not so much as an accusation, more like a tracker reading the signs a wounded deer has left behind.

Put on the spot, I did what I always do, I prevaricated. "Who wouldn't? She's a great girl. Woman. Specimen." Fuck.

Eli let it go with an easy shrug. "Makes sense. She rarely introduces me to the men she dates."

I opted not to share my knowledge on the subject.

Eli finished his drink, gestured his glass at me, asking if I'd like another. I surprised myself, shaking my head no. He dropped two cubes in his glass.

CLINK, CLINK.

Took the cork top off the Laphroaig.

OMP.

As he poured, he mused out loud, "Well, you might have some hope just yet. Way she's been dotin' on you these last few days. Regular Florence Nightingale."

You think I would've smiled at that little revelation, but all I felt was sadness. My dreams had finally come true. My head on Lorelei's lap, her fingers pulling through my hair, and I couldn't remember a damned thing. Not the texture of her Lululemon leggings stretched across her taut thighs, nor the slightly musty smell of her favorite old, stretched-out cotton J. Crew sweater that somehow still showed off her slight frame and the rolling topography of her perfect tits. I wonder if the soft weight of her breast had flattened against my cheek, a thrilling caress of incidental contact when she'd lift my head to shift her arm beneath me. Still, she had cradled me. She had cared for me. Her long curls had turned umber, backlit by the recessed lights, filtering the incandescents that glowed against their silken strokes, warming my neck. Her soothing susurrations fluttered against my earlobes. Instead of comfort, I felt loss. All the more accentuated by my keen and constant awareness of the absence of my briefcase—like a black-market organ-harvesting victim waking up in a bath of ice with scars where his kidneys used to be.

It's been three days.

She confiscated my mother's briefcase from me as I mumbled through muddled plot points. Confiscate might be the wrong word. Excised? Amputated? Cleaved? That's it—cleaved. Then locked it away, down in Eli's storage unit, when she left to go home. Appearances had to be maintained after all: sleep at home, work at Anomaly. All the while, keeping it trussed up, safe in the basement, while I writhed in agony on a hovering bed in the sky, jonesing for my heroine.

According to Eli, Toby hadn't been around since that first night. Again, appearances. While it might make sense that Lorelei would spend a few evenings at her godfather's, it would be more than a little curious for her and Toby to be hanging out, at all, let alone three nights in a row.

It didn't take much to convert her to the cause, though. A day and a night by my feverish bedside, reading through my mother's tome and my annotations: paranoia can be highly contagious. The next day, she paid cash for three burner mobile phones and had a courier deliver one to Toby at his office. Through texts and short phone calls in loud public spaces, the two of them plotted our next move.

"You're leaving Purgatory for Providence," Eli said with a wry smile.

I smiled back, more to make him feel like his attempt at levity had successfully cheered me up than anything else. It hadn't. The last thing I wanted was to pull my friends down the rabbit hole with me. It wasn't quite as magnanimous a sentiment as it seemed. I was more concerned that they would slow me down, get me caught, or worse, turn me in.

"What about work? How can she leave work?" It was a desperate ploy, sure, and probably pretty damn apparent. Still, I was not sharp enough to carve out any sense of subtlety.

It was all for naught. Apparently, Lorelei's been covering for me at Anomaly quite successfully. Going on and on about my *Chameleon* campaign. How I've been working nights, employing guerila, viral techniques throughout the city. She even brought in my sketches that I kept drawing that first night Toby brought me over. Page after page of twisted ribbons, infinite eights, Möbius strips, and ampersands. Her stroke of marketing genius, however, was hiring a couple graffiti artists to tag my doodle all over SoHo and the Lower East Side. They added their own bit of genius, transforming the curves into the Norse serpent, Jörmungandr, biting its own tail.

It's now the *Chameleon* brand.

Not only that, the boys down at the store loved it so much they agreed to fund an R&D expedition that I, along with Lorelei, apparently needed to take to Indiana to work with this semiotics guru, Carlos Colón. At least that's our cover. And a fairly in-depth one. She's rented a car, made reservations at the Day's Inn in Bloomington, and even hired some actors to drive out there and check in as us. I still thought her explanation for why we weren't flying was weak—had to meet with a molecular architect at Carnegie Mellon to help formulate and fabricate *Chameleon's* tech specs. I think she sold it with her extension of the metaphor, though, emphasizing how the best way to fly under the competition's radar was to drive. The bosses bought it. Even though, as far as I know, there's no competition for a fictional ad campaign of my hypothetical product/project.

As attested to by my truculence, I wasn't so concerned with the bosses' faith in me or the project. I was more nervous about the Department and Beimini. Lorelei brushed off my worries with a shrug. I had never seen her like this before. No humor, no perfected nonchalance, no performance at all. My situation had somehow snapped her into hyperfocused, survivor mode. I foolishly thought it was somehow about me. How far gone I was, how much she truly cared. While that might be part of it (fingers crossed), my situation had apparently struck a chord from Lorelei's childhood.

"Her uncle was Abbie Hoffman," Eli shared, with a tone that suggested I should know who that was. Lorelei was out picking up supplies at the time. "He was a big deal in the protest movement of the late '60s and early '70s. Sort of their media guru. Part of the SNCC, Student Nonviolent Coordinating Committee, and cofounder of the Yippies, Youth International Party. He was the avuncular left Yin to my right Yang in Lorelei's childhood. Always filling her head with bedtime stories about his triumphs and defeats: his *exposé* on the Diggers in his book *Fuck the System*; the arrest in '68 as one of the Chicago Eight for conspiracy to incite a riot and how the trumped-up charges were overturned; his interruption of The Who's performance at Woodstock; his book *Steal This Book*; and, of course, the Citizens' Commission to Investigate the FBI."

Eli went on to explain how that last one was never officially tied to Abbie, but everyone knew it was him. In 1971, he and a few other left activists broke into the FBI's office in, aptly named, Media, Pennsylvania. They stole over a thousand classified documents, including several about the COINTELPRO operation (Counter Intelligence Program). As Hoffman uncovered, the FBI had been conducting a series of covert, illegal projects involving surveillance, infiltration, discrediting, and disrupting domestic political organizations. They had files on everyone from Martin Luther King, Jr. to Albert Einstein. Once exposed in the media, Hoover had to shut down the operation, especially since the documents also exposed how the FBI illegally used postmen, switchboard operators, and the likes thereof to spy on American citizens.

While I found Eli's history lesson engaging, I still didn't see the connection. I mean, yeah, Lorelei's uncle was a radical who liked to stir the pot and then shit in it, but why get invested in my mother's disappearance and some bullshit conspiracy theory about DARPA?

Eli's shoulders dropped, along with his voice, as he let me know I was never to directly bring this up with Lorelei. I could acknowledge it, if she ever mentioned it, but under no circumstances was I to dredge up what he was about to share with me. I nodded in assent, hoping I would keep the promise.

"The FBI neither forgave, nor forgot, Abbie. They kept a close eye on him. In '73 they planted cocaine on him and got the local cops to charge him with intent to distribute. Shook him up so much, he underwent cosmetic surgery to alter his appearance and hid out for several years. Unable to get him directly, after that, the FBI took an extreme tack, even for them. They kidnapped Lorelei. She was four. It was never publicized. When her parents went to the police, it was immediately kicked up to the very bureau that had taken her."

"What, they wanted to trade prisoners?" I naïvely asked.

Eli shook his head. "No. They were too smart for that. They merely wanted to send a message—even when we can't get to you, we can get to you. Within a week, Lorelei wandered in the back door of her parents' house. She couldn't tell us much, just that they fed her a lot of ice cream and told her her parents and uncle were in danger, and they were keeping her safe.

"She didn't sleep alone for the next two years," Eli went on. "Abbie got the message and disappeared from public life for almost a decade. Until he got arrested for trespassing at Amherst, protesting the CIA's recruitment actions there, citing their illegal activities and thereby unlawful presence on campus. Then he published *Steal This Urine Test*, exposing the hypocrisy of the war on drugs."

"Then what?" I asked.

"By the spring of 1989, he was dead. Overdose. Swallowed a hundred and fifty phenobarbital tablets and washed them down with a bottle of rye."

"That's horrible."

"Yeah, especially since he hated rye. Said it was the swill scotch distilleries use to sterilize factory bathrooms. Never touched the stuff. Certainly never would've bought a bottle of it."

"So you're saying the FBI murdered him?"

"I'm saying that not a single periodical ever mentions the rye—just that the barbiturates were combined with an unspecified alcohol." Eli went over to his bar again. "And that my goddaughter has a healthy suspicion of the powers that be."

Considering the Department's and Beimini®'s resources, I was dubious that Lorelei's ruse, even with the actors, would fool either for long. An hour later, as we packed, I shared my concern with her.

"Trust me, Tri-Me. It'll do the job," Lorelei said, zipping envelopes of cash into various pockets of a suitcase she borrowed from Eli.

My packing had already been taken care of. It sat in a couple of shopping bags of new clothes she had picked up for me in SoHo after work. "All they'd have to do is go to Pittsburgh or Bloomington and find 'us' to realize it's not us," I said, going on to point out that the only thing that had been working for me so far was them not knowing where the hell I was.

"It doesn't matter if they figure out the whole thing is a red herring as long as they lose our actual trail."

"Huh." I had to admit, it was a pretty good plan. As long as our pursuers (real or hypothetical) took the bait and followed our doppelgängers. In the meantime, one of her investment banker boyfriends had parked one of his cars, a Range Rover, in the underground lot below Eli's building. Eli then took Little Li-Li's suitcase and shopping bags down in the elevator, and with the spare car key (to the banker's car) that Lorelei already had, loaded up the trunk of the IB's car, conveniently parked in a surveillance blind spot. Eli's generous tipping habits had their perks. While we avoided security cameras of our own by hiking down fifty-three flights, Eli also retrieved my mother's briefcase from storage and tucked it next to the suitcase and shopping bags. Leaving the spare key on top of the front tire, Eli then got in his own car and drove down to Tribeca to meet a business associate for drinks at his favorite bar, The Brandy Library.

It was hard not to laugh as I followed Lorelei's ass serpentining between parked cars, both of us hunched over like we were in some bad remake of *Three Days of the Condor*. I wasn't quite sure whether it was a testament to how much better I was feeling after three days of rest or just how far gone I was. Either way I felt invigorated. And also amused at how the universe works its way around. Years of daydreaming about being this close to Lorelei's intoxicating rear end, and there I was, sober as a Mormon in Mecca, panting in exhaustion from our five-hundred-and-fifty-foot descent, relieved to finally plotz down into the almond-leather seat of some devoted Lorelei suitor's Range Rover. Wheels within wheels.

It wasn't until she reached back, grabbed my hand, and pulled me toward the car that I remembered the dream I had about her last night.

It began with the quiet, soft beat of feet padding against a bare stage, legs leaping impossibly high into the air with foot flutters that end in the slightest pitter-pats. From somewhere far off, maybe the sewers, leaks in a foreboding sound of harried apprehensive violins rushing along to a distressed time signature. I recognize it. *Facades* from Philip Glass's *Glassworks*.

The hair on the back of my neck rises with portent. I turn. Downstage the orchestra pit is entombed in a mausoleum of water three feet thick. Blurred behind the water wall, I can just make out the conductor. It's Hilary—hair pulled back into a tight ponytail, dressed in a tux. She looks through the wall of water at me and cues the brass section.

The soprano saxophone whines in with an eerie, melancholic resignation. I turn back to see a figure of incandescent blue bound on from upstage right, curve into center stage, and leap at me. It is only in midflight that I recognize the dancer as Lorelei.

As if by their own accord, my arms lift up and catch her beneath her armpits. She bends her knees up and crumples into me. Her momentum spins and draws me downstage, as I swoop her downward then back up, turning upstage and releasing her back up into the air, like an incandescent dove that unfurls and alights on the stage with barely a sound. She floats in rhythm up stage left, then circles back downstage and leaps at me again. Again, possessed, I catch her under the armpits, spin, swoop her down then up, and release her.

Neither of us are in control of our movements. We are possessed. Captive marionettes manipulated by string instruments.

We keep doing this, tracing out infinity signs in the air, each spin pulling me slightly more downstage, until finally I realize we are no longer on a stage at all, but atop a massive rock towering over a fast river that bends around the granite base. Heavy currents strain against the curve, murmuring music, whispering dares in my ear.

Lorelei relentlessly soars at me, again and again. I keep catching her every time without impulse. My focus is on the impending edge, until finally I feel pebbles pop out from under the grind of my pivoting feet. The bits of gravel drift down over the brink like popcorn. I toss Lorelei back, she unfurls, lands, flutters in a circle, orbits back to me, and leaps. Catching her pulls me around, she swoops down below the ledge, then back up as we complete the upward curve of infinity, and I release her, once again feeling the slightest shift of inertia push away from her as our momentum divides in two. This time the pebbles pop away from the brink as I drift down.

It's not so much that I feel like I'm falling as much as it seems like the cliff top is rapidly shrinking, as the vibrato of the saxophone's lament decrescendos with distance. Until the cold slaps against my face.

The chilled, salt air of the Hudson River rushed through my cracked window. It was just a dream, I kept telling myself. Some nighttime neural discharge. I tried willing myself not to make the connection to Lorelei's namesake, the German siren Lore Lay who enticed despairing sailors into the dangerous, rocky waters of the Rhine. I worked hard to keep from wondering if maybe she was a Department plant seducing me into revealing Hilary's secrets. What else could I do? Wheels had been set in motion. I just needed to stay sharp, resist her beautiful pull, and keep ascetic focus.

West Side Highway, to the Saw Mill, to the Merritt. We were heading to a friend of a friend's beach house in Newport. We were getting the fuck out of this city.

I had escaped the oubliette.

Now maybe I could stop running in circles 'round her report. Maybe I could find something tangible out there. Retrace her footsteps. Pick up her trail. With Lorelei's help and a little luck . . . Who knows, maybe Hilary had left a little something else for me. Another breadcrumb. Maybe not. At least Lorelei insisted it was worth a shot. But I sure as shit wasn't going to get any closer to finding Hilary staying holed up in my landlocked carriage house.

It wasn't until we got past New Haven that Lorelei reached behind the passenger seat and handed me the third burner mobile phone and a folder that I instantly recognized as being a part of my mother's oeuvre. One I hadn't gotten to yet, though.

"You need to read this before we get there," Lorelei said, her eyes fixed on the road, as cars merged into our lane from a roadside McDonald's.

The weight of it pinned me down into the almond leather. Three days of pining for my dear, sweet PsychoNarrative and I felt nothing but apprehension. Finally, my arm moved of its own accord: a stranger to my body, like a limb that had been slept on wrong, moving purely by faith rather than feel. The foreign fingers slid under the corner tab, and peeled it back, like a boulder being rolled away from the entrance of the tomb. And I sank into its darkness.

XIV

No one keeps a secret so well as a child.

~Victor Hugo

To keep a secret, one must pretend to forget it.

~Anna Aither

His mind of man, a secret makes,

I meet him with a start,

He carries a circumference

In which I have no part.

~Emily Dickinson

Secrets cleave. They can sever apart or bind together. It is not the secret that determines this, but rather the nature of its keepers and, more importantly, those from whom it is being kept. A secret, like a virus, can evolve and adapt as it permeates the host. What was a wedge can sharpen into a hook, what was a confidence can grow into a tumor. Contrary to popular opinion, however, exposure does not necessarily inoculate it. Too much sunlight can singe.

If it weren't for the accident, Reidier and Eve's secret might never have been unearthed, despite interminable hours of footage, mountainous piles of transcripts, and pilfered journals. Ironically, it was the unrelenting mundaneness of bureaucracy that cracked the code: a form-letter response to an auto-insurance accident claim.

Reidier or Eve most likely filed it without even considering its implications. Endless machinations of deception implemented to cloister and camouflage the truth, undone by banality. To be fair, it was most likely in an effort to expedite the cover-up.

Eve had had an accident.

The car had been damaged.

The accident had uncovered damage.

Fix the car, cover up the damage.

The only problem was they needed help to fix the car and to pay for the fix. And then also there was Bertram. The secret's circumference had grown.

The insurance claim was found amidst crates of unopened mail, received shortly before and after *The Reidier Test*. Originally filed on August 10, 2007, after an anomalistic rainstorm during an otherwise drought-like summer, the accident occurred near the corner of Adelphi and Wayland Avenues. The damage to the car was minimal. Dented fender and busted headlight on the front passenger side, along with a deployed air bag, cracked driver's-side window, and shattered rear-passenger window. No personal injuries were recorded or covered.

The question then is why did Eve, Otto, and Ecco go to the hospital?

The auto-insurance claim brings into relief a surprising discrepancy as compared with the Providence Police Report. According to the police report, all three were transported to Rhode Island Hospital. The police report itself only provides a little more insight into the how of what happened.

Vehicle 1 [Eve's car] was traveling within the speed limit on Wayland Avenue. Vehicle 1 slowed to make a left-hand turn onto Adelphi Avenue. While completing turn, driver of Vehicle 1 lost control of vehicle on puddled rainwater covering the intersection. Vehicle 1 slid in diagonal path across intersection and collided with telephone pole on corner. No other vehicle was involved.

Dep. T. Andrews responded and conducted injury evaluation. Driver-side airbag was deployed. Driver, identified as Eve Tassat Reidier, appeared to have suffered minor head wound. She was in an agitated state, insisting on getting her son to the hospital. Twin boys were in backseat. One had suffered severe burns on his hand and arm.

Due to slick road conditions, traffic from rain on roads, and a spike in incidents all over city, EMS was having difficulty making it to accident site. Dep. Andrews called them off and delivered above three to Rhode Island Hospital.

Follow-up interview: Driver's comment on relevant events is as follows: "I was traveling down the road. The telephone poles were passing me in orderly fashion at thirty miles per hour. Suddenly one of them stepped into my path."

The public record trail ended there. Rhode Island Hospital itself yielded no further insight. They could not produce any medical records pertaining to this incident. At first, it seemed that the administration was just being obstinate. However, upon further pursuit—presenting myself as Eve's psychologist, following up on lasting damage from the head injury—it became apparent that the hospital was unable to locate any such records.* A loss they were either remiss to admit or compelled not to.

---

* Ok, so this is not my mother. Hilary has clearly gone rogue, or at least 'round the bend. Posing as Eve's psychologist? All this time, I thought my knack for bullshit was my own little gift. Apparently it's a family trait. My mother is not who I thought she was, and I am more like her than I ever knew.

In the car, Connecticut hissed by the window.

It would seem that Dep. Andrews was mistaken. If so, why did he not include a correction in his otherwise detailed report? No, they must have arrived. Perhaps Eve and the boys could have left after being dropped off. Still, for liability reasons, Dep. Andrews would not have left before they were checked in. And if they were checked in, there would be a file. So, was the file lost or squelched?

I am remiss to resort to Department resources and/or pressures. If the records were lost, then no amount of pressure could produce them. However, if they were suppressed, then it's a good bet that the Department suppressed them. It would have been a calculated choice, then, for them not to include it with my material. One they would most likely continue to stick by.

If someone or something else were responsible for the deletion, then they were most likely doing so in an effort to hide something from the powers that be. Assuming this is the case, I am apt to follow the obfuscator's lead, trusting that calling down the higher-ups would only serve to muddy the waters.

Whose secret is this?

Finding Bertram proved to be challenging. Phone calls, e-mails, office visits, home visits, more phone calls—all to no avail. The summer had freed him from any curricular responsibilities. His graduate students continued to toil away in his lab, accepting he was at this or that European conference followed by this or that vacation. I assume he was checking in periodically, but he certainly wasn't picking up any ringing phones in any of his alleged hotels.

I had spent too much time in Providence, and it wasn't getting me anywhere. Neither was trolling Narragansett Beach. On a whim, I returned to the site of our enlightening lunch at Crazy Burger. Of course Bertram was nowhere to be found. I was banging my head against the proverbial walls, hoping for a breakthrough.

Breakthrough is such a misleading metaphor. It connotes a persistent, unrelenting battering, hitting the wall again and again, that ultimately reduces a block to rubble and leads to open enlightenment. Creativity doesn't actually work that way. Inspiration doesn't come down from the heavens because we offer up ourselves as sacrifices to the muses. Focus is the enemy. Insight (*in* not, *sight* seeing—seeing without seeing) comes from a relaxed state, away from the problem, where we are allowed to free associate. It is in this way that our neurons can make connections precluded by a tunnel vision. I feel I'm unraveling with no thread left to follow.

I stayed that night in Narragansett, renting a room at the Stone's Throw Inn. That evening, I made my way under the town's towers, along the coast, across The Narrows, and ended up at a blue-collar Irish bar overlooking the water, where the bay met the ocean. Lots of wood paneling from 1958 decorated with black-and-white photographs of turn-of-the-century Narragansett in its casino days. I ordered lobster rolls and gin.

I was done. No more head banging. I had decidedly finished.

Tonight was a celebration.

But the gin and tonics resulted in the leaving of an ill-advised voice mail: "Bertram, I hope you are well. I apologize for the litany of messages and e-mails. You have been more than generous in this process, like patience on a statue. Especially considering the—your personal costs in walking me around memory lane. I can only imagine the weight of it all. You carry your grief well. It's a difficult thing to hold your mourning and abeyance in abeyance. Anyhow, I apologize for haranguing you amidst the rubble. I'm afraid I can be like a bulldog once I get a hold of something. Bulldog? Is it a bulldog? They're the ones that bite down and hold on. And snore. Eve's accident—it's been my bone, so to speak. Once I found it, well, you know . . . Considering the final outcome of things, perhaps I just need a little perspective to see the forest for the trees. Nevertheless, it'll be our little secret garden. I haven't shared it with anyone. I wish you the best. And of course, please look me up if you're ever in DC."

A heartfelt but thoughtless, inebriated phone call. The Department was most likely listening in. Or was that Pierce's prerogative? Hopefully, Eve's accident will simply be assumed to be an oblique reference to the fallout from *The Reidier Test*.

Tomorrow I'll leave for New York to have lunch with Danny.

*Fallaces sunt rerum species.**

---

* *The appearances of things are deceptive.*
  A dead language for a dead end.

  Connecticut's Indian casinos lay ahead. Perhaps Little Li-Li and I should try our luck there. She smiled and guided us past New London, the old stomping grounds of Eugene O'Neill and nuclear submarines, a town made famous by descents.

For now, sleep is a welcome blackness.

NB Footage: Providence, 7:37 p.m., July 25, 2007—

The dark walnut-wood door to the basement scrapes a quarter of an inch out into the hall and stops, still wedged within its frame. Its latch sticks out like a tongue. Swollen with age, the door often settles for the tight embrace of the jamb rather than bothering to engage the latch.

From behind the door, Reidier's muffled voice takes on the high-pitched tone of encouragement.

The door slips out another quarter inch. More supportive intonations. Another quarter inch out and then it suddenly bursts open, tracing its familiar arc into the hallway.

Ecco stands in the emptiness of the frame, looking back at his father with pride.

Reidier smiles and waits.

Ecco grabs his father's hand, turns back, steps up into the hallway, turns left, and leads his father into the kitchen.

Ecco and Reidier stand just inside, next to the counter. Ecco looks up at his father, who takes in the view of the kitchen much like Balboa must have after summiting the Sierras and seeing the Pacific Ocean before him.

A pot and roasting pan are upside down to the left of the sink, drying over a dish towel. On the table, two place settings have been left along with a Saran-wrapped plate of half a roast chicken and a bowl of escarole.

"Hungry?"

Ecco nods at his father.

Reidier peels back the Saran wrap. He reaches for a piece, and then stops and turns to his son, as if suddenly remembering something of great importance.

"Wing or leg?"

Ecco scrunches up the left side of his face in contemplation. "Wing."

Reidier smiles and laughs. He hands his son the remaining piece. And kisses him twice on top of his head. "Yes, that's right. Wing."

Reidier grabs the leg for himself. The two stand there, eating their poultry in silence, Ecco nibbling off the tapered, crispy point of the wing, Reidier beaming down at his son with what can only be described as a shit-eating grin. "Ecco, can you show me where the dining room is?"

Ecco raises an eyebrow at his father. Without interrupting his progression toward the meatier end of the wing, he points with his other hand down the hall toward the dining room.

Reidier nods, his smile struggling to spread wider. "So it is. And where's the sandbox?"

Ecco rolls his eyes at his father and swings his pointing arm to bear down on the windowed door that leads out into the backyard.

"Right again, my little Sherpa. Ok, and now for the ten-thousand-dollar question," Reidier proceeds while licking his fingers, having finished his drumstick. "Where does Mommy hide the candy?"

Ecco grins at his father and points at the counter to the left of where the pots dry at a collection of different-sized copper cylindrical containers, arranged smallest to largest, each with its own engraved designation: baking soda, baking powder, sugar, flour.

Reidier frowns at his son. He walks over to the counter, tears off a paper towel, and cleans the chicken spices off his fingertips while staring at the copper containers.

"That was a hard one and Mommy's sneaky." Reidier's tone is sympathetic. He moves over to the cupboard to the right of the sink, opens it, and moves the old, large box of Irish Oatmeal to the side.

There's nothing behind it.

Reidier's brow furrows.

A soft *ting* of metal against metal pulls his attention to Ecco, stretched over the counter, pulling the top off of the flour copper container.

Reidier quickly moves to catch his son, who's sliding back off the counter. He looks into the copper container.

"Mommy *is* sneaky." Reidier reaches in and pulls out a bag of strawberry Twizzlers.

Reidier pops his son up on his hip, holding him so they're eye to eye. "You, my little wonder, are very smart," he says, while tapping his son's nose with a stick of licorice.

When Reidier gets to "smart," Ecco catches the candy with his teeth and bites down. His smile drops a little. "It doesn't taste right."

Reidier takes a bite of his own Twizzler. "Mine's ok. Maybe you just got a stale piece. Have this one instead," Reidier hands him his own piece. "Now," Reidier lets Ecco down to the floor, "my little Sherpa, show me the way to the den."

After quizzing Ecco on where they keep the remotes, Reidier has his son lead him to the living room, the downstairs bathroom, upstairs to the library, to Reidier's and Eve's room, and to Ecco's room, periodically stopping at this or that photo to ask who is this and who is that. The two of them finish their exploration in Otto's room. "Whose room is this?"

"Otto's," Ecco answers.

"You're batting a thousand!"

The sounds of Eve and Otto playing during bath time tumble down the hallway.

Reidier squats down to Ecco's level. "Do you remember when we moved in here?"

Ecco nods.

"When we were unpacking this room, you and Otto played over in that chair. Do you remember that? What you two did?"

Ecco nods again.

"Can you show me?"

Ecco walks over to the high-backed, cushioned chair that juts out of a window nook. He climbs up and sits on it upside down, with his back on the seat and sticks his legs straight up, resting them on the seat back. Staring at the ceiling, Ecco moves his feet in the air as if he were walking on the ceiling.

Reidier beams. "'Atta boy!"

Ecco tilts his head over the edge of the cushion and looks at his father, all smiles, scooching his way off, and then his eyes widen with fear, as he falls, and drops to the floor, head first, with a stomach-dropping THUMP.

Reidier's there in three steps, scooping up his boy, soothing him, "Shh, shh, shh, you're ok. You're ok. That was a good knock. Let Daddy take a look."

Reidier holds his son out a little to inspect the damage, and it is only then that he finally realizes Ecco isn't crying.

Ecco smiles up at his father and giggles.

Reidier laughs too. "Look at how tough you are. Daddy's just a worrywart."

"Worried about what?" Eve asks from the doorway, holding a damp Otto cocooned in terrycloth.

"He bumped his head."

Eve plops Otto down on the bed and gets his PJs out of the drawer. "You missed dinner. I left plates out on the table."

"We saw, and we noshed. Thank you. Ecco was helping me with work down in my lair, and we lost track of time."

"It's bath time now," Eve cuts him off.

"Off we go." Reidier carries Ecco out.

The last first thing I wanted to hear through a hangover was someone laughing in my ear. Each chortle tremored through the fog inside my skull. The particularly jovial voice that quaked through the mist belonged to Clyde Palmore, Reidier's physicist colleague at Brown. "You sure you're all right? You sound as sour as vinegar."

"I just had more than I should have last night," I confessed.

A quiet commiserative *oh* came across the line, followed by a *snort* that was cut short.

"Honestly, if you're not up for this—"

"I'll be fine, the fresh air'll do me some good." I sat up. The room took a spin.

"You'll be ok with bobbing? You're not prone to seasickness?"

"No. Luckily, I'm of the age now where too much to drink is much less than would make anyone nauseous."

"The blessing of a low tolerance. I'll pick you up some coffee. And Dramamine, just in case."

"What time?"

"Can you make it by nine thirty?"

Lunch with Danny can wait.* "Sure."

---

* She never did take me to lunch. And she never, ever took me fishing.

"And you know where you're going?"

At some point during our conversation, I had scribbled a location on The Stone's Throw Inn stationery on the nightstand. It didn't seem right, though. "I'm going to Galilee?"

"Yeah. Just ask for directions to Point Judith. There'll be signs. End of the main strip, there's a parking lot in front of George's restaurant. Last dock at the end. I'll pick you up there."

I nodded into the phone. "Is there anything I should bring? Worms?"

A loud laugh erupted through the receiver, sending currents of pain through my head. "I got all the lures and bait we'll need."

Some thirty minutes later, Clyde was waiting patiently for me at the end of the dock. I waved from the parking lot. Reaching back into the car to grab the half-drunk coffee that sat in the cup holder, I suddenly remembered his promise to bring coffee and Dramamine. I left it and locked up.

Galilee was, without any irony, a prototypical fisherman's town. Slips were filled with boats returning from the morning's haul. Wholesale merchants lined the road, each displaying the price of lobster per pound like gas stations would the price per gallon. Waves lapped up against the wharves, punctuated by clappers lazily dinging against the mast bells with each ebb and flow. The smell of fried clam cakes blew across the parking lot.

I fled downwind of the aroma, to no avail. The boards of the dock creaked beneath my footfalls. My sunglasses offered little help against the double dose of sunlight reflecting off the water.

"Not too late to reconsider," Clyde shouted over the sound of the idling engine with a smile.

A crosswind cleared away the scent of clam cakes. "Where should I sit?" I asked, as he helped me from the dock down into the boat.

Clyde pointed me to seats at the back of his boat. "Probably you're best in the stern." He handed me a large coffee and two pills, then untied the bow line, stood in front of the captain's chair, and throttled us out to sea.

Miraculously, at six miles out, the salt air and gentle rocking improved my condition. My fishing skills were still, nevertheless, lacking. I reeled in the two-hundred-pound line with my best arrhythmic rhythm. No bites.

Behind me, Clyde muttered to himself something about high whines and Afghanis tilting at windmills.

"Your method isn't working," I said. "Or my tempo is too regular."

Clyde pulled his binoculars away from his eyes. He held up his palm to block the sun and scanned the skies through a squint. "Hm?"

"What are you looking for?"

"Predators."

"It's not like I have any fish for them to steal. Maybe I should switch to actual bait."

"Lures are better for stripers." Clyde had the binoculars against his eyes again, this time scanning the horizon. In the distance, a ferry chugged along.

"Maybe these stripers prefer the real thing."

Clyde let the binoculars dangle from his neck and smiled at me. "You ever read *The Magus*? John Fowles?"

"Just *The French Lieutenant's Woman*."

"Great bit in there about catching an octopus. Guy uses a piece of white cloth tied to the end of a line as 'bait' to coax an octopus into a net. The octopus prefers the ideal over reality."

"Well if it's not the puppet, then it must be the puppeteer."

Clyde laughed. He squinted at the horizon again. "Sometimes the fish just don't bite. Right place, right time. Maybe later this afternoon. How about some lunch?"

Clyde guided the boat toward Block Island, slowed near the pier, and looped a bow line around a cleat. Across the water, a crowd flowed off of the ferry.

"Are there always this many visitors?"

"In the summer, yes. Not so much in the winter. So, I still have to take care of some things with the dockmaster. If you don't mind, why don't you go up and get us seats?" Clyde pointed up the hill. Tourists decked out in Block Island paraphernalia thronged along the two blocks of Main Street. At the end, perched at the top of the hill was a seafood shack surrounded by picnic tables. "Ever had a frozen lemonade?"

"I don't believe so."

"Delicious. Grab yourself a Dell's on me. I'll be up in a few," Clyde winked. "Got to wave the white cloth around a little."

Main Street was charming enough, lined with souvenir stores, inns, chowder houses, and saltwater taffy vendors. It seemed like a place that blossomed in the summer but was more likely treasured in the winter. Vespa honks and the slap-slap of flip-flops floated across the salty air.

The aroma of fried fish and dough drifted downhill from the seafood shack as I headed up. My nose and stomach debated whether the scent was enticing or repulsive. I came across the Dell's lemonade stand Clyde had been so adamant about. Flavored sugar water actually seemed like my safest choice.

Clyde wasn't wrong; the lemony, slushyesque beverage was divine. A citrus nectar frappe that quenched, cooled, and calmed my volcanic stomach, a relieving antidote to the summer sun. I made my way over to the picnic-table area and sat at the end of one, while a father helped his young son finish off his french fries. Seagulls dropped down and picked at a trashcan overflowing with wax paper, red-and-white-checkered cardboard food slips, and cups. Bike riders pushed their way up the hill, following the curved roads lined with colonial architecture. Another ferry departed for the mainland. Sunbathers lined the beach.

I scanned the docks until I found Clyde's boat. He was standing at the edge of the floating gangplanks, binoculars held up to his eyes, scanning the horizon. After a few moments, he lowered them, and then squinted at the various boats in their slips. Clyde rubbed the back of his thumb across the crease between his beer belly and chest as he contemplated his various nautical neighbors. He held up a hand to block the sun as he gazed into the sky. Unsatisfied, he raised the binoculars up again, and scanned.

"Apologies for the cloak-and-dagger," said the man next to me.

I turned to face him, confused at whether this out-of-context comment was even directed at me. The father and son had walked off across the gravel-lined courtyard. Sitting in their place was Bertram, dressed in red seersucker Bermuda shorts, a neon-green terrycloth Polo shirt, big sunglasses, and a straw fedora. It was a loud and ubiquitous fashion statement that perfectly camouflaged him among the preppy hordes. "Clyde told you about the frozen lemonade. He can't pass a Dell's. I'm more of a salt guy. French fries are the Achilles' heel of my tongue."

"What are you doing here? Have you been hiding out on Block Island?" My mind hadn't quite caught up with reality. His presence seemed anachronistic.

Bertram laughed, "No I haven't been hiding here. Clyde and I just thought it seemed like a good place for us to meet. Outside of the norm and easy to track any uninvited party crashers."

"Is that what Clyde is doing down there?"

Down on the docks, Clyde was still scanning the skies with his binoculars.

Bertram shook his head and chortled to himself, "In a manner of speaking. He's trying to spot drones."

"Drones?"

"Predator drones. Like they use in Afghanistan."

Predators.

"The cloak-and-dagger. That's why Clyde invited me fishing. You got my message." My brain was finally catching up.

"The Department didn't suppress the hospital records," Bertram announced over the wind. The tall sea grass that blanketed the cliff top whipped around him. "There were no records to be suppressed. I made sure of that." Bertram stood quiet, gazing out at the ocean, while his confession sunk in. "Yes, there were the admittance forms, but those weren't too difficult to have misplaced. Eve hadn't been examined by a doctor before I got there."

Bertram's attention had turned away from me. His gaze tracked a family of four circumventing the Block Island Southeast Lighthouse, a young boy chasing his sister around the expansive lawn. The father was taking pictures of the structure and view, his camera lens protruding from his face like a black unicorn horn, a Cyclops in Birkenstocks.

Bertram and I watched them take in the scenery, read the various plaques that presumably summarized the history of the lighthouse, and finally find their way around the other side to the entrance.

"I think the wind's strong enough. But can't be too sure," Bertram said.

It was unclear whether this was to me, to himself, or just a general declaration of the state of things. Clearly, Bertram and Clyde were savvy to the Department's eavesdropping tendencies. Or at least they suspected that some party had been expending effort to monitor the Reidiers and by extension, Bertram and Clyde. Were they aware of the nanobots? I wanted to confide in Bertram about them, assure him that it would be highly unlikely for the Department to have already gotten here before us and nearly impossible for them to effectively deploy a cloud of its Smart Dust* to monitor us. However, in doing so, I might have implicated myself as part of the establishment, a major player in this game of deception. Then again, there I was, atop the Mohegan Bluffs of Block Island, as a result of my own sojourn off the reservation that took me out to sea on the tide of subterfuge.

---

* A system of tiny microelectromechanical systems, MEMS, equipped with a variety of sensors communicating wirelessly with each other. Essentially a cloud of nanobots set adrift in the air that relayed back everything from audio to temperature changes in skin (blushing) to vibrations of heartbeat and pulse. An invisible swarm of information collectors that could measure stress levels and map out true/false probability curves to determine if someone was telling the truth or not. AKA: advanced, scary shit.

"Directing the nanobots is a challenge even within a small environment. They've only been effectively used within interiors or to blanket an urban enclave. A place like this, they'd scatter at the wind's whim and dissipate too quickly to have any efficacy," I offered.

Bertram turned back to me and smiled. "Our thoughts exactly. They can't hear out here. We figured being spontaneous and improvising our movements would give us a bit of an edge too."

Not knowing what else to say, I offered, "Thank you for trusting me."

Bertram kicked a rock off the edge of the cliff. It fluttered down so long it seemed more like a feather than a stone dropping into the sea. "Awful lot of precautions for trust, wouldn't you say?" he countered.

"They weren't all on account of me."

Bertram nodded. Again it was unclear whether this was to me, or to himself. "You know the history of the Mohegan Bluffs?"

I shook my head.

"Block Island was Niantic territory, a Native American tribe that eventually merged with the Narragansett people. They called this island Manisses. Well, somewhere in the midsixteenth century, the Mohegans decided that this island was a pretty desirable place. Good deer hunting, good shellfish. A great battle took place, which the Niantic won by forcing the Mohegans over these cliffs to fall to their deaths."

I kicked my own rock over the edge this time. Again, it fluttered like a feather.

I waited in silence for more. Bertram was finished. The wind kept blowing.

"You planning on forcing me off?" I asked.

Bertram chuckled. "I imagine you're not so interested in colonial history as much as my personal history."

"I respect your privacy if you're not comfortable sharing any more than you already have." It was an empty offering. Bertram was ready to talk. He wouldn't have gone to all this trouble if he weren't.

"Just doing your job," he said with a sardonic tone.

This wasn't the same man I had first interviewed so many months ago. His reticence had hardened into guardedness; his doubt had devolved into distrust. "I'm not so sure I have a job when I get back."

Bertram watched me with a neutral expression. Was he evaluating, judging, or merely waiting?

"They feel my loyalties shifting. I think. Or they figure I'm just not getting anywhere. Either way, their faith is dwindling."

"It would be best if they came to the conclusion that you're not getting anywhere. That's why you're here. I prefer that narrative."

The word hung in the air, resistant to the offshore gusts. Narrative. He punched the word out. His eyes shifting back to my face. Reading my response. He's heard of my work, my PsychoNarratives. "Right now, I'm just trying to get the story straight. The narrative is something altogether different."

"Is that normally the case? Do the story and the narrative often differ?"

"The story is how I come to understand what happened. The narrative is how I communicate the why and how it happened."

"Shifting loyalties. I suppose that can happen, collateral empathy, from Psynaring."

There he said it. He knew. My secret specialty. It was out. But how?

Bertram read my thoughts, written in the furrows of my brow. "I made some calls. Applied some pressure of my own. Information can be a valuable hostage nowadays."

Someone in the Department? One of the other organizations I had worked for? Ultimately it didn't matter. It was out, and I didn't have to dance around it anymore. "Normally my subjects are bad guys. Or victims. Empathy helps in either case."

"So which are the Reidiers?"

"Neither."

Bertram retreated from the cliff edge and sat on a bench at a sandy clearing where two paths intersected. I joined him there, watching a bee land on an Ophrys orchid[109] and pollinate it.

---

[109] Often referred to as Bee Orchids due to a resemblance to the furry bodies of bees.

"Kerek was out of town. Actually, he was on his way to DC to see Pierce. That's why Eve called me."[D]

[D] Note To Self: Go through NB footage, find this interaction!!

Eve was frantic when he finally saw her, screaming bloody murder and wrestling with two orderlies who were trying to keep her as prone as possible on the bed. She was a crazed animal, desperate to get to her pups.

Bertram was a familiar face at Rhode Island Hospital. In fact, he had been there only a few days prior to oversee the implant of a small sensor into a clinical trial patient's motor cortex.

Eve stopped cold when she saw Bertram. Her brain of course had difficulty parsing him into this reality. In spite of having summoned him, she was bemused by a friendly face strolling into her nightmare. She didn't know how he had gotten there and whether he was a part of this reality or not. But still, he was there, and he was a friend.

Bertram! Bertram. Her tone was desperate, pleading as she exerted an immense effort to regain calm and convey lucidity.

They'll kill him! Please. Help me stop them. Even in this frenetic state, Eve's grace and beauty gave her an air of poise.

Who? Killing who? Bertram was at her side. The orderlies had released her and stepped back the moment she had relaxed her struggle. Bertram squatted next to her bed in order to maintain eye contact.

'Ze boy.

Otto or Ecco?

I . . . I don't know.

It took a few minutes, but eventually Bertram deciphered the story. Eve was disoriented and having trouble focusing when she was first brought in. While a triage nurse tried to determine the severity of her head trauma, another nurse took care of the boys. One of them had severely burned his hand and forearm in the accident. The nurse didn't know which twin was which but cleaned and dressed the wound. She also administered a tetanus shot, which was standard procedure for severe burns.

As Eve regained her focus, the nurses advised her of what measures had been taken and that the boys were fine.

That's when Eve lost it. Still struggling with the head injury, she was unable to articulate her concern. She kept yelling about vomiting, extreme pain, comas, warnings that if *he* ever got another one he could die.

With Bertram's help, Eve managed to finally convey that she was talking about Otto. He had gotten a shot once and reacted violently: the twins were allergic to tetanus.

Everyone sprung into action. Bertram flew down the hall, followed by a nurse trying to direct him where to go.

When Bertram found the boys, Otto and Ecco were sitting in front of the nurses' station, giggling, bouncing an inflated surgical glove back and forth between them. Ecco's right arm was bandaged. Other than that, though, he seemed perfectly fine.

They were out of the woods. At least that's what Bertram thought. Ecco's doctor decided not to take any action, unless Ecco started to have a reaction. So they kept him under observation for a few hours.

Bertram finally got hold of Kerek, who, after hearing the news, headed to Reagan National to catch a flight home.

Bertram, Eve, Otto, and Ecco sat around and waited for nothing to happen to Ecco.

It was only then that Bertram learned about the flood and the accident before the accident.

NB Footage: Providence, 6:45 am, August 10, 2007—

The resounding *THUMP*, of the front door being pulled shut, wakes Eve. Or seems to. She appears immune to the initial disorientation most of us experience when rising out of the lacuna of sleep. She does not yawn, or stretch, or groggily seek out the clock to orient herself within the day's temporal landscape. She does not instinctually reach for her absent husband. She stirs in the empty bed and blinks up at the motionless ceiling fan.

Rain patters against the window.

Eve waits in bed, listening.

Reidier's car starts up. Gravel pops like cereal as he pulls down the driveway. The tires mute onto the road, and the thrum of the engine fades down the street.

Eve gets up, puts on her silk robe, and proceeds with her morning ritual: teeth brushing, washing her hands then her face (once with a facial cleanser, a second time with a toner), taking an Rx pill case out of the medicine cabinet—pouring all the pills into her palm—counting how many are left—frowning—pouring all the pills back into the plastic bottle—putting the Rx case back into the medicine cabinet, hair combing, a touch of makeup. Morning ritual complete.

By its very nature, a ritual is an unthinking, or more precisely, nonthinking act of repetition. Through iteration, performance is tamed into habit. While patternized actions are often utilized in meditation as a way to untether the mind, habitualized behavior can also evolve into addiction. In either case, however, the core impulse is the same, to sacrifice control and ultimately sacrifice the self. Ritual is an act of surrender, in which the acolyte and addict capitulate to rhythm and forego choice. Whether communing with a higher power through ascetic discipline or transcending into an altered state with chemical means, the goal is the same: escape.

Flight requires fear—fear of the devil, fear of the ego, fear of reality. Or simply fear of cavities. Even the most mundane ritual is a form of flight. We clean our teeth daily because we're scared that we'll get cavities if we don't, which will not only cause pain but ultimately lead to the loss of our teeth. This fear is so deeply rooted that many cultures interpret the nightmare about our teeth falling out as a sign that a family member or close friend is very sick or near death.

Ironically, the ritualization of brushing our teeth enables us to simultaneously take and relinquish responsibility. By making the effort to internalize the habit of brushing every day, we drill it in until it's second nature, and we no longer have to bother thinking about it anymore. We take responsibility for our dental hygiene by getting to the point where we no longer have to. More than anything, rituals are acts of faith, or the belief that such behavior will protect us against our fears. These repetitive actions can eventually become so comforting that they can even be substituted for different fears. Just look at the man who reaches for a cigarette after his girlfriend breaks up with him, or the woman who goes home and cleans the house from top to bottom after getting fired, or any of us who check our e-mail, Facebook, or Twitter accounts on our phones when we're uncomfortable in a crowd of strangers.

Eve began her day hiding behind the cover of sleep. Once alone, once awake, she slipped behind a pattern of behavior. While Eve's morning ritual is easy to dismiss as mere habit, it does raise the question of what is she escaping from? Her day? Her dreams? Her husband? Her children? Her self? Or is it some preternatural sense of what's to come?

"Putain." Eve frowns at the overflowing laundry bin in their bathroom. The meditative spell is broken.

Once again, though, Eve slips into a pattern.

She sighs.

She gathers the laundry into the laundry basket.

She makes her way down the hall.

She pauses for a moment to listen if the boys are awake.

She stutter steps down the stairs. Bah-bum, bah-bum, bah-bum, bah-bum.

She circles around the railing, shuffles toward the kitchen, hooks her left big toe between the basement door and the jamb, and swings the door open.

At the landing at the bottom of the basement steps, Eve doesn't even pause. She continues to stare down at her full laundry basket, turns right past the door to Reidier's lab, heads down the last few steps, and splashes into an inch and a half of water.

The unexpected wetness shocks her out of her routine.

Eve screams and jumps back up onto the lowest step.

She stands there, mouth agape, taking in the inundation.

The basement floor is nowhere to be found. In its place lies a wall-to-wall pool of dark water.

Her gaze drifts over to the washing machine and dryer on the far wall. The plastic scoop she uses to measure out detergent floats in front of them.

Eve wrinkles her nose at the machine, her eyes narrowing with accusation.

The patter of rain crescendos with a gust of wind against the high-set basement window.

Eve's suspicious gaze shifts from the washing machine to the window.

She puffs up at a strand of hair that has fallen in front of her eye. *"Putain."*

Half a morning later, Butch from Demarco Plumbing wades through the subterranean lagoon in search of a culprit, while Eve finally gets around to making some breakfast for the boys. The entire kitchen vibrates with the efforts of Butch's pump, as it struggles to drain the lower level.

Eve pinches the brow of her nose and presses against her sinuses. After a moment she moves over to the stove to check the water in the pot. Boiling. Eve throws in some salt, picks the eggs out of the carton, and drops them in one by one. Some splashback catches her wrist.

"*Aïe! Putain, putain, putain.*"

"*Maman!* You said a bad word," Otto's scold flutters in from the den.

"I said a French word."

"A bad French word."

Irritated, Eve silently mimics her son, saying *a bad French word* while she sets the oven timer for eight minutes.

A laugh catches Eve off guard.

Ecco stands in the doorway to the den, holding some half-finished Lego construction, smiling at his mother's antics.

"Go play Legos with Otto."

Ecco mimics her saying this and smiles back at her.

Eve grabs a wooden spoon off the counter. "*Va-tu!*"

Ecco giggles and dashes back into the den.

Eve collapses into a chair at the kitchen table and rests her head in her hands. Being knocked out of a routine can be exhausting.

"Mrs. Tassat . . ." Butch yells up from the basement.

"*Oui.* Yes? Coming."

Butch explains to her the problem. "That right theh's yuh culprit."

"So it is not the rain?" Eve yells over the noise of the pump. She holds a two-foot section of plumbing pipe, turning a section of pipe over as if searching for other, larger holes. "That little sliver did all this?"

In the middle of the pipe, the metal wall had swollen up like a blister and then split open. "Yep. Doesn't look like much but ya gotta figure, ya got aroun' a maximum of five gpm, gallon 'puh minute, in a typical one-half-inch supply pipe. Let's figure since the wuh'tah's squirtin' out the slit theh', it's flowing at roughly three gpm. One gallon's roughly .13 cubic feet. So ya got three gpm fuh sixty minutes an ow-ah, fuh eight ow-ahs, that's around 192 cubic feet of wuh-tah. And as you can see, 192 cubic feet can easily covuh 2300 squ-eh foot with one inch of wuh-tah."

"Is this normal?" Eve shouts.

"Oh, shew-uh. This saw-tah thing happens all the time. Although mostly during the wint-ah. Pipes freezing and whatnot. Actually it is pretty unusual fo'ah the pipes ta blis'tah open like this in the summ'ah. But ya know, these colonial houses, all ov'ah the East Side, they gotta lot of old pipes that have all been jerry-rigged togeth'uh over the ye-uhs. Maybe somehow it got real cold in the wall between this room and yaw husband's office."

"Ok, but now it is all fixed. How much longer for your pump to finish emptying out my basement?"

"Oh, I haven't fixed it yet."

Eve throws Butch a quizzical look. "What?"

"I mean, I turned off the wuh-tah and, well," he gestures at the pipe in her hand, "removed the busted section. But I needed to ask you what kind of pipe you want me to put in."

Eve wrinkles her brow at him, confused. "Why would I care? Whatever pipe is necessary." The annoyance in Eve's tone is discernible even above the din of the machine.

As confused as Eve was at Butch asking for her pipe preference, Butch is even more perplexed that Eve wouldn't have an opinion on this. "Well, I can go one of two ways, cah-puh or plastic."

Eve cuts him off. "Which one is cheaper?"

"Well, that'd be plastic."

"Done." Eve starts up the stairs.

"Cah-puh isn't that much more, though. And in the long run, it'll actually cost you less—"

"I don't particularly care about the long run. I care about being able to wash clothes today. In a dry basement. Will I be able to do that?" Eve turns and hands Butch the busted pipe, crossing her arms.

"Most of the wuh-tah should be out in few ow-uhs. Should be safe to run your wash-uh by then."

"I look forward to—"

The scream comes from above, clearly discernible over the noise of Butch's pump. As is the subsequent metallic clatter. Eve is halfway up the stairs before the high-pitched cry stops.

Otto stands in the middle of the kitchen, wailing, holding his right hand in front of his mouth. Eve races in and slips, almost taking a bad spill, but somehow manages to catch herself on the countertop. She moves to her crying son.

The kitchen floor is covered with water. The empty pot lies on its side, on the floor next to a fallen stool. Hard-boiled eggs have rolled every which way. The oven timer beeps incessantly like an apathetic, needy metronome keeping the beat of chaos.

Eve squats down to Otto's height, whispering in comforting tones, inspecting him for damage. *"Ce n'est pas grave, mon chéri. Ça va bien. Dire à maman ce qui s'est passé. Où es-tu blessé?"*

Otto holds out his right hand to his mother. His fingertips are bright scarlet with mild burns.

"Aïe! You burned yourself." Eve scoops him up with one arm and tenderly holds the wrist of his burnt arm with her other hand. She blows lightly on his pink fingers as she carries him to the sink. "It's not so bad. We can fix it. We can fix it."

Eve turns on the sink, first the cold water, then a little of the hot. After a few moments she tests the temperature with her own fingers, then leans over with Otto and gently moves his hand under the water. "There, better. No?"

Otto nods and says, *"Putain."*

Eve guffaws. *"Putain,* indeed, *mon trésor. Putain* indeed."

Otto smiles.

"You burnt yourself just like *maman*. You were trying to help me with the eggs, eh? You should never play in the kitchen alone, ok?"

"I wasn't alone," Otto says. "Ecco was helping too."

Eve turns and finally sees Ecco for the first time.

A quiet Ecco stands by the stove, staring at his brother, his lips pouting with sympathy.

Eve almost smiles at the attachment he has to Otto, but stops short when she notices Ecco's arm. Just below Ecco's elbow, a rage of white blisters boil up and blossom down the length of his arm, enveloping his tender, swollen hand, which still clutches a steaming, hard-boiled egg.

Otto smiles at Ecco who laughs back at his brother.

Eve's eyes widen with fear and she stutters into motion, moving toward Ecco, then stopping, then back to the sink.

She sits Otto on the counter, making him continue to hold his hand under the water.

She grabs a dishtowel off the counter and tosses it into the sink.

She moves over to Ecco as quickly as she can on the slippery floor. In a panic, she's at a loss for what to do next. Presumably trying to figure out how to touch him without hurting him. Water vapor condenses in air, like smoke, around the hard-boiled egg still in his grasp.

"*Lâche prise. Lâche prise. Let go! Dépose l'oeuf.*" Eve half grabs, half smacks the egg out of Ecco's hand.

It cracks a little and rolls.

Eve gingerly picks Ecco up and carries him to the sink. She blows on his arm but can only manage a suspiration, daunted by the violent topographical eruptions along his arm. She leans over the sink and puts Ecco's arm below Otto's fingers in the rush of water.

Eve takes the now-soaked dishtowel and gently wraps it around Ecco's arm.

Ecco doesn't scream out. He doesn't flinch. He just watches his mother's barely controlled panic and his brother's pain.

Eve soaks another dishtowel and wraps it around Otto's hand.

Never pausing, Eve moves on through her improvised triage tactics, snatches her car keys off the counter, and scoops up both boys from the sink. She rushes down the hall and out the front door.

Butch stands at the top of the basement stairwell, still clutching the busted piece of pipe. "I'll uh clean everything up. Don't you worry 'bout nothin'. I'll do cah-puh, for the plastic price too."*

---

*Pain is a remarkable creature. It's a living, breathing, starving brute. The neuroscientists got it all wrong. They've tried to sterilize it, reduce it to mere electrical signals that leap from synapse to synapse, leaving a trail of lit-up neurotransmitters in its wake. An impression, a trick of the mind, a holographic warning system honed by evolution. It isn't that at all. Pain has a life of its own. It is an unrelenting hunter that tracks the slightest scent of vulnerability. Stalking it along the spinal cord, burrowing into the soft wrinkled caverns of our mind. And once inside, it shreds everything it can get its talons on. It digs in and takes over. Hijacks the entire consciousness.

All anybody can do is run and leave behind a trail of scorched earth. Ask any torture victim, they all describe the same thing, a retreating into themselves, disappearing into their minds. But they're not retreating, not really. They're hiding. Fleeing its pursuit.

On the plus side, you're never lonely when you're in pain.

Bertram kicked his heel at the ground in front of the bench. An indentation started to form in the packed dirt.

I didn't want to push him. Didn't want to put his back against a wall . . . or a cliff.

He had been silent ever since uttering the word *accident*. It was an abrupt silence, one that had lain in wait until midstory to pounce. And now Bertram was wrestling with his doubt. The narrative up until then had still been safe—plausible deniability within a mundane occurrence. He knew I already knew about the hospital and about the accident.

I just didn't know *what* had happened. Even that seemed somewhat moot. He had to imagine I'd probably either have or be able to access the nanobot footage.

But there was something else at the hospital, outside of the Department's reach.

All his and Clyde's precautions, cloak-and-dagger feints, raptor watches, and it still came down to trust. Did Bertram trust me?

Almost as if reading my thoughts, Bertram cocked his head at me, squinting one eye against the sun while measuring me with the other. "You know on the other side of the island, there's a second lighthouse? It's older than this one, though only by a few years. It's the third iteration of the North Lighthouse. The first two were washed out to sea."

"Neptune has a sense of irony, apparently."

Bertram nodded. Not at my comment, but at something that was said in whatever internal dialogue was taking place in his head. "Not too far from it, just to the west of Corn Neck Road, there's an old labyrinth in a field. It's called the Sacred Labyrinth. Most people never even see it on their way to the North Light. I only found it because a local at the bar told me about it one night. Drew me a map on a napkin."

"He gave you a mapkin."

"Mapkin. Yeah. I like that. It's a quirky little place. Just some ruts dug into the earth, lyed over, I assume. Maybe just worn down by walkers. On the far end of it there are even these little human-head sculptures. Like some little weird Easter Island. Anyway, you just start out at the entrance, wind your way along the path, around and around, until you reach the center. Then you unwind your way back out. No twists, no turns, no puzzle. It's just one path. It's not a maze, just a labyrinth."

"They're not the same?"

"That's what I thought too. Most people think that maze and labyrinth are synonymous. Fact is, a maze is what you and I were imagining, a complex branching, multicursal puzzle. Dead ends, wrong turns, et cetera. Labyrinths only have a single, nonbranching path. Unicursal. Its 'solution' is unambiguous. There's only one option, one answer. Labyrinths were never designed to confuse people or get them lost, on the contrary they're a way for people to find themselves. They were constructed for meditation. A pattern. A path. A ritual."

"I blame Daedalus for the confusion. I think he designed the famous one on Crete. To trap and hide away the Minotaur."

Once again, Bertram seemed not to hear me. At least there was no outward acknowledgment. He spoke, but it felt more like I was merely being let in, allowed to listen to a private conversation he was having elsewhere. "Around the same time that the Greek labyrinth showed up, a topologically identical pattern appeared in Native American culture. The Tohono O'odham labyrinth. Where I'itoi lay in wait by the entrance."

"I'itoi?"

"The Man in the Maze. The mischievous creator god. It was an identical pattern but for two differences, a radial design and the entrance at the top."

"Coincidental maybe?"

Bertram kicked a second divot into the dirt with his other heel. Identical indentations. "Halfway around the planet, well before trans-oceanic ships were built, before global trade routes had been established, and this design surfaces in two disparate cultures. This same pattern."

"Maybe it's just some deep-rooted mode of thinking. Like our disgust reflex or our fear of snakes," I suggested.

"Maybe." He finished with his divots and stared out at the ocean. The breeze was picking up. "It was quaint, the labyrinth. Sort of pleasant to walk it, not think about my direction, just follow the path. I can see how it'd help some to meditate."

"Not you, though?"

Bertram shook his head. "No. Problem is, you have to follow that same path out, and it leaves you right where you started. Standing with I'itoi at the entrance. You still have to figure out where to go next for yourself."

Bertram looked at me, sort of half smiled, and sighed. He went on with his story.

After several hours, Ecco seemed to be stable. No reaction to the tetanus. The doctors hypothesized that in spite of the boys' identical appearance, perhaps they were in fact fraternal twins, each with a unique genetic makeup. Or somehow, Ecco had developed a mutation in the second or third trimester. One even posited the supposed allergy could have been misremembered or even fabricated as a result of Eve's concussion.

Surprisingly, the better Ecco turned out, the worse Eve got. Perhaps her mild concussion wasn't so mild. She became increasingly irritated, aggressive. After two hours, Eve was glaring at the boys, muttering to herself in French.

Il n'est pas le mien. Il n'est pas le mien. Il n'est pas le mien. Il n'est pas le mien. Il n'est pas le mien.

Bertram grew concerned. He took the boys for a stroll to see if that calmed her down. Left them to play again by the nurses' station.

She wasn't better when he returned. He tried to soothe her. He held her hand. Told her she was fine. The boys were fine. Ecco was ok.

That's when Eve snapped out of it. She grabbed Bertram's hand back, looked him in the eyes.

No, he's not. He's not ok. He's not real. He's twilight. An etiäinen, *a* vardøger, *a* ka, *a* doppelgänger.

Bertram brushed past her haunting accusations. Reassured her that her twins were just that, twins. She had two beautiful twin boys.

Il n'est pas le mien. Eve hissed. *He is not mine. He's a facsimile. An empty copy. Un imposteur.*

Bertram immediately ordered an MRI.

That's how he found Eve's brain tumor.

Later that evening, when Kerek finally arrived, Bertram broke the news to him. He first assured him that the boys were fine. Ecco would most likely have some scarring, but no nerve damage. Neither they, nor Eve, suffered any sort of severe injury. But Kerek saw something deeper and darker was amiss for Bertram; he read it in his enervated body language, his beleaguered voice, his tensed jaw.

Bertram sighed and slipped into the safety of a clinical tone. He explained how Eve's erratic behavior had concerned him and the other doctors, especially considering that she had sustained a concussion. They gave her an MRI. They found a mass. It was growing deep inside of her temporal lobe, where the temporal cortex bordered the limbic system.

Bertram wasn't sure if Kerek was taking it in stride or in shock. Kerek stared at his feet a few moments until he asked how it was affecting her mind.

Bertram was sorry to inform him it was in a pretty severe place, and as a result was apparently disrupting her understanding of reality. She was suffering from Capgras delusions. It was Imposter syndrome. Patients with this syndrome regard people whom they know well—family, friends—as imposters.

She thinks you're an imposter?!

No, Bertram told his friend. *Your son. Ecco.*

Kerek then stunned Bertram by letting out a huge sigh. He sat down on a waiting-room couch and laughed a little.

Bertram knew his friend was in shock then. He took a seat next to Kerek and filled him in on the afternoon's events, the fight with the orderlies, the tetanus shot, the monitoring, Eve's downward spiral.

Ecco didn't have a reaction!? Kerek surprised his friend once again.

Bertram was at a loss, but he went with it. He assumed Ecco's close call was easier—a happier thing to focus on—than Kerek's sadness about Eve. Bertram explained in detail how Ecco exhibited no allergy to the tetanus. Obviously, he still needed to be monitored for a few more hours, but the doctor thought it highly unlikely at this point.

But Otto is allergic to it. Kerek pointed out.

Bertram, still at a loss, simply nodded.

And they're identical. Kerek was fixated. *So aren't they then genetically identical? Two sides of the same double helix . . .*

Bertram shrugged and offered a matter-of-fact *Apparently not.*

Kerek took this in, leaned back against the couch, and disappeared into his thoughts.

Finally, after several minutes, Bertram broke the silence. *As far as Eve, there are some promising experimental techniques—*

Kerek interrupted Bertram with an *Eve is going to be fine.*

Bertram supported his friend's optimism, pointed out how important a positive attitude can be through a process like this, however it's equally important to maintain a grasp on the severity of her condition—

She isn't having Capgras delusions, Kerek interrupted again.

Bertram was sympathetic. It was a difficult thing to accept. Even Bertram hadn't wanted to see the signs. He brought up the picnic at Kerek's house, with the Lego tomato salad, how that was most likely a result of her neurological condition.

Kerek shook his head, placed a sympathetic hand on Bertram, and told him the truth.

"Eve wasn't delusional. Ecco was a copy. A simulacrum of Otto," Bertram told me. "That scene he had me first watch, from their basement in Chicago. The one you and I discussed. Where Eve finds Ecco in the basement, and Kerek comes home with Otto, and Eve has a breakdown.[110]

"Kerek had taken Otto to work with him one weekend. While Kerek went to retrieve something from a supply room down the hall, he left the boy for a minute. Otto found his way into Kerek's machine and turned it on, or it was already on, and . . . Then there was Ecco."

Ten days after meeting with Bertram on Block Island, his body was found at the bottom of the Mohegan Bluffs. The New Shoreham police department reported it as a suicide, as there was no evidence of a struggle. Due to the site of death's exposure to the elements, however, they were unable to rule out foul play. The coroner diagnosed the cause of death as severe head trauma and a broken neck.

I am at a loss. I am frightened.*

---

* Me too.

---

[110] Pages 169-171.

~~Non semper ea sunt quae videntur.~~ *Non semper ea sunt quae sunt.*

*

---

* ~~Things are not always what they seem.~~ Things are not always what they are.

XV

Your visions will become clear only when you can look into your own heart. Who looks outside, dreams; who looks inside, awakes.

-C. G. Jung

So I shall suppose that some malicious, powerful, cunning demon has done all he can to deceive me . . . I shall think that the sky, the air, the earth, colors, shapes, sounds, and all external things are merely dreams that the demon has contrived as traps for my judgment.

-René Descartes

And suppose further that the prison had an echo which came from the other side, would they not be sure to fancy when one of the passers-by spoke that the voice which they heard came from the passing shadow?

-Plato, *The Allegory of the Cave*

"He was willing to throw out whole swaths of his work. Turn the stumbling block of consciousness from a physics problem into a biological one. That's why he became obsessed with my work," Bertram had said. "He wanted to try and adapt my motor cortex implant and transform the BrainGate into some sort of neurological interface with his device.

"He became obsessed. We both did, I guess. After Ecco's origin was revealed, the floodgates opened.

"But what he was seeking was still merely theory. I mean, I had been tapping into brain impulses and rerouting them to a robotic arm with only ninety-six tiny electrodes. Maybe it was a just a question of scale, make the pipe bigger or make a million little pipes. Ultimately though, I deal in impulse, electrical impulses. Nothing more. I'm just a neuroelectrical engineer. Kerek needed a plumber. He needed a way to funnel out thoughts, to drain out the entire consciousness. Soul slipping."

...   ...

...   ...

Otto = ECCO = Otto
How did Bertram know about the nanobots?
➡ R. or P. ?

*

---

* My dim apparition reflected in the rest-stop window ate a French fry tipped with ketchup. It briefly disappeared in the bright glare of headlights as a car pulled into a parking space outside. The fluorescent McDonald's menu behind me hovered above my image, a crisper ghost in the fenestral ether, seemingly immune to the flow of high beams that slid past along I-95.

Between my reflection in the window and me on my plastic rotating seat, the real Lorelei dipped her own fries into a chocolate shake. We hadn't said anything until after New London, when Lorelei pulled into the rest stop and asked if I was hungry.

The manila folder sat on the table beneath the dark brown food tray. I don't know why I brought it in with us. It had been sitting on my lap for over an hour. It seemed safer to keep it close. Its contents were disorienting enough and I think I was terrified it would disintegrate if left unguarded. The ink would fade. And we'd be left asking ourselves was *that real or some shared acid trip?*, while our compass needle did laps around its circumference.

Lorelei hadn't pushed. A sideways glance or two as I turned the pages. A shared exhale when I closed the folder. Mostly she just kept her hands at ten and two and her eyes fixated on the black road that snaked out ahead of us.

"I guess I sort of knew," I said, as I turned my red cardboard container upside down and shook out the last few stubborn fries. "Like I saw a glimpse of it in some corner of my mind. Pointed it out and said, 'Huh, I wonder if . . .' And I don't know, I must have just let it fade into an echo or distracted myself with another clue in my hunt for Hilary or just flooded that compartment with booze and drowned the fucking thought."

"I gotta say, Tri-Me, it's a pretty heavy reveal."

"No shit."

"No wonder you've been going insane."

I don't know what I felt when she said that, but it must've looked pretty pathetic, 'cause Lorelei reached across the table and gave my hand a sympathetic squeeze. I gave her a half smile back and just sighed one of those little-kid-stutter sighs, like when you've been crying for a while and you can't exhale right, so your breath just comes out of you like it's been dammed up inside for weeks, and there's so much sheer volume and pressure that the pipes vibrate with the force of the release.

Of course, I punctuated it with a half wow-where'd-that-come-from-I'm-ok-though smile. I mean, I'm a man after all.

"So whaddya think? You think your mom was for real? Or did she simply have a great story to tell?"

I shrugged. "I don't know. At the very least I think she believed it."

"Do you believe it?" Lorelei searched my eyes.

God, she was so beautiful. Her attention was almost too goddamn much. Milton had it right:

> Much thou hast yet to see, but I perceive
> Thy mortal sight to fail; objects divine
> Must needs impair and weary human sight. (XII, 8-10)

My professional acolyte turned personal savior, sitting across from me, somehow radiant in a light blue hoodie, white V-neck, and jeans. Lorelei was the kind of girl that could pull off wearing a Kevlar vest while reading Wordsworth. What a first-date story this would make for the grandkids. Her, impenetrable and romantic; me, lost and longing.

Her slender fingers plucked up another fry, with a grace that concert pianists would covet. She slid it through the viscous surface of her shake, like the mother of Achilles baptizing her baby in liquid Lethe. Then a subtle twist of the fingers as she pulled it free, the milkshake reaching up after it, trying to hold tight, to fill in the emptiness her fry had drilled out, until finally gravity overtook it, and the chocolate stalagmite let go, dropped back into itself, a brief peak of nostalgia, until its tip tilted downward and wept its way back into uniform smoothness, all evidence erased and forgotten.

I wonder if Reidier ever felt this way looking at Eve.

Lorelei held the fry in her mouth, like a lollipop almost, and tilted her head to the side with bemused sympathy, waiting for my reply.

"I'm at a loss, honestly. You're an objective observer, what's your take?"

Lorelei shrugged. "Maybe we'll find out in Rhode Island."

We made it to Newport a little after midnight. To the friend of a friend's "beach house." It was a friggin' estate. A vast piece of property, circumvented by an old stone wall (not stone and mortar mind you, just stonework and craft) and orchards; a vestigial colonial farm that had been modernized with the likes of running water, Jacuzzi tubs, granite counter tops, and Viking ranges; with an old barn that had been converted into a three-car garage and guest quarters; and its own stretch of New England shoreline equipped with tidal pools, a dock, two lobster traps, and in the distance our own little lighthouse that stood at the point of Jamestown Island halfway across the bay.

Now I know how Duvalier must have felt—exile could've been worse.

We played it safe for a few days. Cloistered ourselves away and kept busy wandering the grounds of our own Little Elba, as Lorelei and I came to call it. We had to make sure we were free and clear, not that either of us had any counterespionage training to speak of. Not that that would even help against the likes of NBs. Still, it made us feel better. As luck would have it, we were blanketed with low-lying fog and gray skies, so at least Predators weren't going to be an issue. A Bergman-esque setting with an Ian Fleming plot.

We took walks, counted starfish, harvested mussels, "caught" lobster, and cooked feasts. Lorelei was actually a pretty adept chef. I managed to impress her with my knife skills. She went gaga for my trick of halving a dozen cherry tomatoes at once.

"That's ingenious, Tri-Me. Delivery soup lids. I would never even have thought to save them."

I tried not to beam from her attention, but my shit-eating grin clawed its way right up my jawline and latched onto my ears for at least three hours. It was almost enough to make me forget what we were doing there in the first place.

"What other tricks you got?"

The twelve-year-old boy in me was spouting a Tourette-ian litany of bad innuendos. Somehow I managed to shout the horny little brat down long enough to coolly slide out, "I can zest the hell out of lime. Makes for one killer gimlet."

Which is what led to us taking a polar bear swim down at Little Elba's beachhead. Which is what led to Lorelei noticing my scar.

"Is that a birthmark?" Lorelei asked, perched on a boulder that jutted out of the water, pointing just below my right ribs. Steam smoked off her body in the cold air.

"More of a birthright," I quipped, and changed the subject. "I'm freezing. Let's head back in and make some hot toddies."

I followed her up the path, watching her damp sweatpants cup her flawless ass in the moonlight, my hand unconsciously drifting up the side of my own wet sweatshirt, rubbing my scar to make sure it didn't reopen after all these years.

We talked about work, crustaceans, our best and worst vacations (Lorelei's were Naples and a Caribbean cruise, respectively, mine were both Peru), our parents, exes—of which she had a plethora whereas I only had tales about halfhearted hookups on futons in Brooklyn with the type of women who fake British accents and overfeed their cats.

"What do you mean she had a fake British accent?" Lorelei asked, leaning back against the arm of the leather couch, her feet tucked under my leg while blowing lightly on her recently topped-off hot toddy.

I balanced mine on my lap, sitting left of center on the couch, my feet resting on the edge of the leather trunk/coffee table. In my head, I pictured grandmothers playing baseball in an effort to preclude an ill-timed boner.

"Like it was bad?" she asked.

"No, no. It was good. Like I-thought-she-was-British good."

"You didn't know?"

"I mean, no. I had met her at a party in Park Slope."

"Oh, that's right, they do call Park Slope the Little London of New York," she said sarcastically, and shoved my leg with her foot playfully.

Electricity shivered up my thigh right through my chest. *Nanna rounds second, but gets her walker tied up on the bag.* "I mean I had just met her at some house party, she was a friend of a friend. She had a British accent and talked about her old job in London. So I connected the dots."

"You didn't investigate with your friend?"

"Why would I? When would I? As I was getting my coat? *Thanks buddy, it's been a great party, by the way is that bitch really British?*"

"Oh, you went home with her from the party!" Lorelei singsonged at me with a knowing and slightly judgmental tone. "'Cause you're a he-whore."

I shrugged. "She asked me if I wanted to 'meet her cat.'" That last bit I said in my own fake British accent.

Lorelei broke out in hysterics. "Of course she did."

"How was I supposed to know she actually had a cat?"

Lorelei snarfed her hot toddy. "No?!"

"Fat fucker too. And obstinate. She would not get off the futon. As far as she was concerned, it was her territory and we were the interlopers. She was willing to tolerate our presence but was not about to move."

"Why didn't you just shove her off?"

"She was really, seriously fat. I tried to nudge her off while the faux-Brit was in the bathroom, but she gave me a can-I-help-you look and then slapped a warning claw at my hand. The last thing I wanted to do was get in a fight with this chick's cat."

"Not when you were about to get some pussy."

She said the word pussy. "Exactly. So there she stayed, right on the pillow next to me, cleaning herself and periodically eyeballing me with this unimpressed look like she had seen way better."

"While you're doing the deed?"

"Like an Olympic judge from Feline-land."

"Wow. That sounds bloody spectacular," Lorelei said in her own British accent.

"That wasn't even the worst part." I took a nice long sip after that little lead of the witness. I knew I had her. And I was in full-on performance mode. I was freebasing Lorelei's attention and damn well going to savor it. I might be relationship kryptonite when it comes to closing, but I was a hell of a fucking storyteller. It was the only game I had, so I played it to the hilt.

Lorelei, though, was all too familiar with my skill set. She kicked my thigh. "Come on, Tri-me, give it up."

"Hm?" I raised an eyebrow and took another sip. "These hot toddies really are delicious."

Lorelei rolled her eyes and finally asked like a dutiful Borscht Belt audience, "How worse was it?"

"She growled."

"The cat growled at you?!" Lorelei was literally holding her sides now, laughing at me. "During sex the cat just—"

"No. Not the cat."

"No!"

I nodded.

"No?! The Brit Chick growled! At you?"

"Yup."

"Growled growled? Like sexy growled?"

"I'm not altogether sure what sexy growling sounds like, maybe if you demonstrated."

"There's sexy growling. Like maybe purring or some sort of a guttural animalistic, I dunno."

"These were more like an eight-year-old's impression of a lion."

Lorelei threw her head back, her belly laugh shaking her entire body, her toes digging deeper under my thighs.

"What was even more disconcerting was that the growls also seemed to be completely independent from the stuff I was attempting. I mean not at all related to this rub or that lick. No causality or timing whatsoever. Just random roars. It was"—(British accent)—*"rather disconcerting."*

Lorelei squealed a delighted *Noooo* and kicked her feet against my leg in rapid succession. Quick little bunny kicks that launched me up onto cloud nine—grandma baseball was not working—and then she hyperventilated some joke about my animal magnetism, before asking how I finally discovered her accent was fake.

"It was while I was getting dressed."

"'Cause you sure as hell weren't about to sleep over at that little *den* of iniquity."

"Well punned."

"It's the least I could do. My taunts are the Tiger Balm for your soul," she snickered. "So you were dressing, as quickly as possible."

"Which was awkward."

"Of course."

"And I was making small talk. About her cat. Asked if it was difficult to get the cat through customs or something like that. To which she said no, because her cat had just stayed with her parents in LA while she was in London. It was only then that I came to learn that she had grown up in Los Angeles. And no, her parents were not British, her dad was from the Valley and her mom grew up in Madison. She had spent a semester abroad at Oxford and lived there for a couple years after *University*."

"So she picked up their mannerisms."

"And kept them up for the three-plus years she had been back Stateside."

Snort. Her snorts were intoxicating. Who knew? "So her accent . . ." Lorelei connected her own dots.

"Was a choice. A linguistic accessory."

"Bloody hell."

"Bloody hell indeed."

"There's no graceful exit from that one. What'd you say?"

"Just said it'd been a blooming good chin wag, but my arse was tired and I'd give her a bell in a fortnight. God praise the Queen."

"GodpraisetheQueen," Lorelei echoed in mock-seriousness.

I laughed into my hot toddy, sucked down a little more and tried to keep my mind from wandering further down memory lane and following me on my journey home that night. I didn't want to revisit the icy borough streets, past the warmly lit brownstones, not a cab in sight, down into the empty subway station save for the homeless woman on the bench who kept throwing herself back against the wall muttering *It's not me but I'll have the soup.* I didn't want to relive the eternal wait for the F train, nor hear the sound of my keys hitting my marble tabletop clattering around my empty apartment, nor remember sitting on the floor of my shower trying to keep the hot water from falling into my beer, nor look across the plane of my mattress at the unused pillow and wonder if maybe I'd like to get a cat of my own.

"I shouldn't laugh. My dates normally start with the guy 'casually' dropping the keys to his luxury vehicle on the table, and end with me calling a car service."

"What they lack in quality they make up for in quantity."

"Thanks," Lorelei said, and shoved my shoulder with her foot, pushing me over.

My smile climbed its way from my earlobes up the scaphas to the helixes. "What? I'm not judging you. I'm very pro-slutbags."

Lorelei guffawed. It was aural ambrosia.

"Wow. Not simply a slut, I'm a slut*bag*," she said with a tone of disbelief. "A bag made of slut."

"I was thinking more of the purse that sluts use to carry their slut products around. Like condoms, Viagra, bananas."

"You've really thought this through."

Gobs of research. "I have, actually."

"And it never occurred to you that a slutbag might actually be the sack in which sluts are carried around?" she proffered.

"Sluts aren't carried in sacks, silly. Whores are. Sluts are carried around in Range Rovers."

This time she threw a pillow at me. Then she shook her head, downed the rest of her hot toddy, and refilled both of our glasses from the teapot.

Lorelei leaned back again, blew ripples across the surface of her tea, and spaced out at the coffee table. "I do date a lot of guys," she said, still staring through the coffee table/trunk.

"A lot of IBs," I corrected her.

Lorelei rolled her eyes at that. "Yeah, 'cause hipsters aren't every bit as pretentious as investment bankers. They're just as superficial and carefully coiffed, they simply wear a different uniform. Tight jeans, mustaches, and a plaid shirt they picked up in a designer 'vintage' store so they can look every bit as unique as all their neighbors on the Lower East Side and Williamsburg. At least with the IB guys I get to go to better restaurants. You think Dude-ly McThickFrameGlasses is going to take me to Del Posto on his longboard skateboard? Sorry, I prefer a Tuscan Chianti to an ironic Pabst Blue Ribbon."

Lorelei took a sip of her drink. I considered saying something, but I felt like I had already inadvertently pushed her back on her heels, and I didn't want to say something else wrong. And I had no fucking clue whether I was supposed to pull her teetering heart back to neutral or push her to let go and fall.

Lorelei shrugged. "You're supposed to play the field. In your twenties. Find out what you like, don't like. I guess somewhere in my brain I think I need to date everybody so that I know what's out there and I can finally make an informed decision and pick the perfect choice. I'm the same way with TV. I'm the kind of girl who, even if I find something I like, I have to open the guide and hunt through all the channels to make sure that out of all my options, this is absolutely the show I want to watch."

"I'm like that too, except for sumo wrestling. Sumo wrestling is always a showstopper, no matter what."

"Agreed. There's no bigger game to hunt. You can even take the batteries out of the remote at that point. Sumo wrestling or one of those shows about someone who's gotten so fat they need a television show to pay for a construction crew to cut through the bedroom wall and a forklift to pick them up, put them in an ambulance, and take them to the hospital for an immediate gastric bypass."

Is this what true love is like? "Thank God for the Learning Channel."

"Clearly, for us, obesity and flab make for riveting television."

"Just not dating."

She laughed. "Not dating. I guess I suffer from the-grass-is-always-greener syndrome."

"It's a symptom of the twenty-first century and New York. Used to be you could only date the people you knew. Now with online dating sites, you literally have thousands and thousands of options to sift through."

"Even more if you broaden your search to other cities."

"You do not do that!"

"Maybe once or twice, after a particularly mediocre outing, I might have searched LA or London."

"I can see how that would make auditioning suitors a Sisyphean task."

Lorelei took another sip then sort of half smiled. "I dunno what I'm doing, really. Most of the time I feel like I'm auditioning myself, like different versions of me. And all I know for sure is how good I am at getting people to talk, about anything, everything. Guys fucking love to open up to me and I love to see how quickly I can crack them open. But at the end of the night, all I'm left with is a shattered shell and a handful of nuts."

It was my turn to guffaw. Lorelei's smile crept up on her as she realized her inadvertent pun.

Another shrug set off another avalanche of words. "Sometimes I feel like I'm taking the long way around to finding out who I am by crossing who-I-am-*not* off the list. Only I feel like the list is endless. Hopeless even. So I distract myself with little private games: how far can I take this guy who doesn't get sarcasm, how many times can I get that dude to start another new topic about himself, how quickly can I get this former frat boy to admit to some questionably homosexual act from the good ol' days. And sometimes I just push through horrible dates, hoping they'll get even worse so I'll have a better story for you the next morning."

Lorelei's eyes fluttered up from her tea to meet mine; she gave me a half smile.

And I fucking panicked.

The room spun, the couch dropped out from under me, and my lungs refused to inflate. The only thing that held me together was the pull of her half smile.

Somehow, in spite of me keeping just this side of chaos, I managed to lean forward, clink our mugs together, and nonchalantly joke, "Cheers to us. May our lonely futures be filled with sumo wrestlers."

"Now that would be a great first date."

"A sumo match? In Japan?"

"Wherever."

"It would make me look svelte," I noted.

Lorelei laughed.

And that's how it went. We kept joking, talking, drinking, until we conked out on the couch together, her at one end, me at the other, our feet tucked under one another. It snowed on the beach that night.

Video .mp4 file found on Reidier's personal hard drive created on July 2, 2007

Reidier sits in his basement laboratory. He appears to be lost in work, spinning his chair from one surface to another, scribbling down one thing or another, cross-checking some measurement stored within an Excel sheet.

A few distracted keystrokes, while he writes something down in one of Leo's Notebooks. Reidier presses "Enter." Nothing much happens. Reidier writes more down.

The video blinks and skips a second.

Reidier stops working, leans back, listens. He hears nothing.

Reidier: It sounds quiet. Are we alone now, Kai?

(Pause)

Female Voice: Yes, Kerek.

*

---

* "Ever heard about how Borges got his start?" Lorelei asked.

I shook my head no while devouring another spoonful of soup. Our test run from Little Elba has taken us into town. We blended in with the throngs of tourists, bought saltwater taffy, took in the mansions, poked our noses into the Tennis Hall of Fame, and wandered down a cobblestone street that dead ended in a pier with a restaurant on it called The Black Pearl, no irony intended. It was an old colonial-style structure, dark wood, big exposed beams, claustrophobically low ceiling, and paned windows. It couldn't decide if it was an old inn or the cabin of a three-masted ship.

We didn't find any Department spooks on our tail, but we did find the best clam chowder of my life.

"What is this, dill?" I asked the waitress as she passed by.

She was a young blonde girl with big Irish freckles. The waitress nodded and whispered conspiratorially, "And a splash of rum."

Lorelei waited for the waitress to get out of earshot and just shook her head at me. "What is it about guys and waitresses?"

"They smile a lot and are extra attentive to us."

"For a bigger tip."

"Which they deserve. Holy shit, this chowder is better than sex."

Lorelei raised an eyebrow.

"At least the chowder won't leave me feeling empty inside." I scraped my spoon against the bottom of my bowl. "You were saying, Borges. 'Death of a Compass,' 'The Library of Babel,' 'Book of Sand.' I've read the guy."

"It's 'Death and a Compass.'"

I thought about it a second, then shrugged, "Death of a Compass feels more evocative, don't you think?"

"Whatever. Did you ever hear about how he got started writing?"

I hadn't. And Lorelei didn't seem too in the mood for one of my homemade answers.

"He grew up in Buenos Aires, but always loved English literature. At nine, he translated some Oscar Wilde work. As he grew older, he mastered a number of languages, authored scores of academic papers, and even founded and edited several literary publications. But try as he might, he never seemed to be able to turn out a solid piece of fiction."

"I know the feeling."

"Until he finally figured out his way in. He fell back on his strengths and created his first fictional piece by writing an academic criticism of a work that didn't exist."

Lorelei had my attention.

"In fact, his entire early literary career was dominated by a slew of forgeries and hoaxes: translations of nonexistent works, falsely attributed pieces."

I didn't have an answer for Lorelei. It's not like I hadn't thought of it—that my mother might have made this whole thing up. That lovely idea had been gnawing away at the back of my mind for quite some time now. Until then, though, I had been fine ignoring it. Leaving it be, to cannibalize my brain in the dark shadows of my thoughts.

Fuck sunlight.

Fuck facing your fears.

And fuck Lorelei.

I was up and out the door before I even realized what was happening.

Lorelei found me a few minutes later at the end of the pier, watching the ship masts swing back and forth with the waves, like nautical metronomes. She didn't say anything. Just rested her forearms next to mine on the wooden railing.

I never thought I would feel so ambivalent about her. I didn't want her to go, but I didn't feel like connecting, let alone talking. The best I could do was not push her away.

So we just stood there, listening to the sporadic boat bell, watching a seagull float in place above us. The bird faced south, making the slightest angle adjustment to its wing, dancing this invisible tango with the wind. Then with another, almost imperceptible shift, it dove down, glided over the seaweed that clustered between the bows, and snatched up a dead fish that had been floating, half hidden.

My mother is a fish.

"Come on," I said and headed for the docks.

Navy Pier Park photograph...
Why hide the boy?

DEFENSE ADVANCED RESEARCH PROJECTS AGENCY
3701 NORTH FAIRFAX DRIVE
ARLINGTON VA 22203-1714

JUN 2 0 2007

ACQUISITION,
TECHNOLOGY
AND LOGISTICS

MEMORANDUM FOR THE UNDER SECRETARY OF DEFENSE, PENTAGON
　　　　　　　　　DIRECTOR, DEFENSE INFORMATION SYSTEMS
　　　　　　　　　DIRECTOR, TACTICAL TECHNOLOGY OFFICE
　　　　　　　　　DIRECTOR, DEFENSE SCIENCES OFFICE
　　　　　　　　　DIRECTOR, INFORMATION PROCESSING TECHNIQUES
　　　　　　　　　OFFICE
　　　　　　　　　DEPUTY DIRECTOR, MICROSYSTEMS TECHNOLOGY
　　　　　　　　　OFFICE
　　　　　　　　　REAR ADMIRAL, NAVSTA

SUBJECT: GALILEE PROTOCOL 2007

On February 12, 2007, the Rear Admiral of NAVSTA formally initiated the Gould Island Base re-opening and refurbishment in preparation for the development and testing of the Galilee 6:21. In conjunction with Naval Intelligence, the Defense Office, and DARPA construction was initiated by February 20th of that same year. To expedite construction, power considerations were assigned to a separate Joint Cross-Service Committee (JCSC), while engineering and architectural units accounted for loads exceeding ▮▮▮▮▮▮▮ X 10▮th electron volts in their designs. On May 5th, 2007, DARPA along with DoD approved the completion of the facility deeming it in accordance with set parameters.

Following a similar timeline, the JCSC submitted a proposed solution to the power situation, on February 15th. The committee determined that a current, unrelated Office of Naval Research (ONR) Advanced Gun System project developing militarized ▮▮▮▮▮ could generate the necessary megajoules required. DoD reviewed and authorized the JCSC's proposal on February 21, 2007. In coordination with both the Defense Agency and the Navy, DoD enacted the necessary transfers of Classified clearances and appropriated the USS ▮▮▮▮▮▮▮ from the Naval Surface Warfare Center in Dahlgren, VA. The USS ▮▮▮▮▮▮▮ left port on May 24th as part of a Memorial Day convoy and arrived at the Narragansett Bay on May 28th. Under the supervision of NAVSTA's Rear Admiral Wisecup, its reactor had been successfully connected to the Gould Island Base on June 1st. Power tests were completed over the next two weeks and as of yesterday, June 11th, and the facility was deemed operational by DARPA.

It is my pleasure to hereby announce, the Galilee 6:21 will commence on June 21st. In depth summaries of the DARPA team protocols are attached for your information. In order to ensure security measures, no data will be submitted. However, each Defense Agency will be invited to progressive tests demarcating the successful completion of each of the four phases: 1) inanimate, 2) dynamic inanimate, 3) biologic, and 4) biologic with quantifiable training.

Donald Pierce

XVI

*And what happens when the regime becomes as mad as the ones
they hunt?*

~Mstislav Shklovsky

Physics has failed us.

~André de Broglie (*Recherches sur la théorie des quanta*,
1926, regarding wave-particle duality)

*For when, either in ancient or modern times, have such great
exploits been achieved by so few against so many, over so many
climes, across so many seas, over such distances by land, to subdue
the unseen and unknown? Whose deeds can be compared with
those of Spain? Our Spaniards, being few in number, never
having more than 200 or 300 men together, and sometimes only
100 and even fewer, have, in our times, conquered more territory
than has ever been known before, or than all the faithful and
infidel princes possess.*

~Eyewitness accounts by Hernando and Pedro Pizarro
of their brother's conquest

Transcript excerpt from the phone surveillance of Rear Admiral
NAVSTA Office, Rear Admiral Wisecup 6/14/2007, 10:17 a.m.

Wisecup: (yelling into phone) What the hell else does he
          want?! Christ himself only needed two pieces of
          wood and some nails! I don't care what
          theoretical horseshit he's slinging now. You just
          tell him sometimes you got to try something
          even if it's wrong. 'Cause a mistake will still tell
          us a hell of a lot more than his foot-dragging.
          And don't let him go off about hypothetical
          catastrophic what-ifs. If what-ifs dictated history,
          we'd all be living in some goddamn Japanese
          fiefdom! He's a scientist. Scientists do
          experiments. Get him experimenting.

(Wisecup slams down the phone.)

It took a while to find it within the endless hours of footage. The
innocuousness of the moment provided an effective camouflage: a
revealing mundane still within a reel of banality. Nevertheless, it is
most assuredly Reidier's moment of discovery of the infestation.

NB footage, Reidier home, June 27, 2007

Reidier paces back and forth around the dining room, arguing
into his mobile phone to some Department lackey. "I don't care what
Q Net did. They're in the Stone Age as far as I'm concerned. And
Bell's paper disproves practically all of your objections."

Reidier proceeds to tolerate a response, gestures rapidly for who-ever's on the other end to talk faster. Finally, Reidier interrupts. "Look, I need this so that I can put a single nano-object into an X-ray beam in order to determine position, chemical identity, and struc-ture. If you insist on my doing it with what you've given me, every-thing will be corrupted with Loschmidt echoes."

In spite of technological jargon, there is nothing very incisive about this conversation. It is just one of the myriad of phone calls, Skype sessions, and voice mail exchanges that Reidier is inundated with daily. As with this one, Reidier tends to wander about errati-cally while enmeshed in discussions about his work. Which is why his brief pause was almost completely overlooked.

While circling from the north end of the dining room table to the antique wooden credenza, right after Reidier's assertion about Bell's paper, his stride hiccups. When slowed down eight times, it's possible to notice the slightest tilt of Reidier's head to the side, like a baffled dog. All of this happens in less than a second, then Reidier's pace picks back up where it left off, as he continues to circle the table.

However, as the conversation and laps continue, a pattern is detected, once again only when slowed down to one-eighth the nor-mal speed. Every time Reidier passes the credenza, he briefly slows down.

Finally, Reidier ends the conversation near the archway that leads to the living room. He hangs up the phone, rests a hand against the archway, and gazes through the table, seemingly lost in thought—except for one quick flicker of his eyes, directly at the credenza. No head movement, just the eyes, a fast once-over, only captured in the slowness of one-eighth speed.

The second piece of the puzzle lay in the phone tap. From the logs, it appears that Pierce had the NSA tap all of the Reidiers' vari-ous phones after Kerek's first phone call to the Director's office while still in Chicago. Coordinating the phone-tap recordings with NB footage facilitated a triangulation, so to speak, of, for lack of a better term, the Credenza Phenomenon.

I don't care what Q Net did. They're in the Stone Age as far as I'm concerned. And Bell's paper disproves practically all of your . . .

Again, the prosaic proved obfuscating. It took over a dozen listen-throughs to finally hear the forest from the trees. The problem was the dialogue. I kept focusing on the dialogue, homing in on the Department underling's response to Reidier's complaint. I spent hours dissecting the scientific vernacular, mining my limited knowledge of teleportation and X-rays and learning about Loschmidt echoes. All of it seemed scientifically sound. Nothing should have agitated Reidier, especially the credenza in the corner of the dining room, not to mention the fact that, ultimately, Reidier won the argument.

Once content proved a dead end, I refocused on form. There was something in the tone of the argument, hunting for subtext within the delivery of the jargon. Perhaps there was some complex passive-aggressiveness or habitual patronization that drove Reidier crazy. Of course, in order to determine that, it was necessary to listen to a litany of conversations between Reidier and this specific lackey, as well as Reidier and a number of other Department minions. These were played so many times that, at a certain point, they ceased to be words to me and simply became a sequence of sounds that danced up and down the scale, punctuated by grunts. I became the Jane Goodall of quantum engineers.

Nothing. At most, the conversation was laden with frustration, sighs, and impatience. And again, nothing that would elicit such a specific and peculiar behavior from Reidier.

I don't care what Q Net did. They're in the Stone Age as far as I'm concerned. And Bell's paper disproves practically all of your . . .

Finally, frustrated and convinced I had fabricated the whole episode, I gave up. Reidier, the credenza, it was just a quirk in manner. Just one of the many nonsensical behaviors we all manifest erratically throughout our day. There was nothing of significance there other than my own need to infuse the footage with meaning. I'm a model reader who wanted to warp the text into her own narrative.*

---

* Umberto Eco would be so proud.

I gave up. I went to the liquor store, where I purchased bottles of Pinot Noir and a Chianti. On the ride home, I did not think. Or rather, I chased thoughts from my mind with Holst. His Enigma Variations were in the car's CD player. I kept #IV (Allegro di Molto) on repeat, loud.

Upon returning home, I brought my meditative music with me inside. The stereo swallowed the CD and filled my living room with Variation IX Nimrod (Adagio). I left my cell phone and keys on top of one of the speakers, and retrieved a corkscrew and glass chalice.

The epiphany was almost comical. As I finally relaxed into the back of the sofa, Nimrod reached its loudest crescendo, and the moment the wine hit my lips, a quiet, static feedback, like a warped Morse code, scratched across the speakers, briefly distorting Nimrod's notes,

kwuh/tck/tck   *dee-de-de*

then disappeared, and my phone, sitting atop the speaker, buzzed to life with a text from my son.

In vino veritas indeed.

I was out of my seat before I even realized my realization. I flicked the stereo off on my rush to the study.

The computer took an eternity to stir from its slumber. My fingernails tapped their own impatient Morse code on the glass desk.

Finally, the audio recording was playing in tandem with the NB footage.

Reidier was circling the table: *I don't care what Q Net did. They're in the Stone Age as far as I'm concerned. And Bell's paper disproves practically all of your . . .*

And there it was on the cell tap, that same quiet burst of warped Morse code that results from the radio signal of a cellular phone interfering with the magnetic field of speakers—even mobile phone speakers. Except cell phones don't interfere with themselves. But it's there with every lap Reidier completes. Every time he passes the credenza, there's feedback, perfectly prompting Reidier's hiccups in pace, his subtle head tilts of confusion.

It's the static.

It's the interference.

It's the nanobots.

And Reidier knows it. Knows it with a glance, while leaning against the archway, not lost in thought at all, rather instead strategically trying to avoid detection while risking one last evaluative glance at the nanobot-coated credenza.

Adapted from the surveillance footage taken in Rear Admiral Wisecup's "Secure Room" at NAVSTA, from the file of the Office of the Director of the Strategic Technology, Donald Pierce; February 14, 2007.[111]

"Have you ever heard of a railgun, Professor Reidier?" Pierce asks, the excitement in his tone quite clear.

---

[111] Due to the stationary medium shot and the quality of the visual, it is presumed that the recording was shot on standard camera from behind a one-way glass. Judging from the placement of Rear Admiral Wisecup and Director Pierce (they are sitting at angles that provide a ¾ shot of their back and profile) it seems likely that they were both aware of the recording in progress, as opposed to Reidier who was sitting facing the mirror/camera.

"It's an artillery gun powered by electricity in order to harness immense electromagnetic fields. Basically it's a monorail on steroids, only instead of moving a train, it's hurling ballistic projectiles."

"So much for State secrets," Pierce elbows Wisecup knowingly. Wisecup nods and half laughs, half grunts in response.

"Railguns are hardly secrets, Pierce," Reidier notes. "Louis Fauchon-Villeplee invented his electrical cannon almost a century ago. Scientists have been developing ways to use the tech to launch aircraft or supplies into space. And the British successfully weaponized it the late '90s."

Pierce nods. "That's all public knowledge. What isn't is that DARPA and the ONR—"

"ONR?" Reidier asks.

"Office of Naval Research," Wisecup offers.

"The Department and the Navy have been hard at work down at NSW, Naval Surface Warfare Center Dahlgren Division, building next-generation prototypes." Pierce leans back in his chair and lets his reveal sink in.

Reidier seems nonplussed.

"We've been able to procure one of them and have already set about adapting it into what we think will be a viable energy source for your work," Pierce completed his thought.

Reidier scratches at his cheek, sucking in his lips a little. Finally, he sighs and says, "It won't work. Not enough energy."

Wisecup guffaws, "The last prototype test hurled a projectile at ▇▇ miles per hour over a distance of ▇▇ miles in under six minutes. ▇▇▇▇▇▇ megajoules of energy packs a hell of a wallop as far as I'm concerned. How much more goddamn energy do you need?"

Reidier leans back in his chair and says, "More."

Wisecup lets out a deep belly laugh and slaps his palm on his armrest. "Now that's the kind of bravado I can get behind. More!"

Unlike his colleague, Pierce is far from amused. His forehead wrinkled with worry. "What's your concern, Kerek?"

Reidier proceeds, assuming the same voice and mannerisms he exhibits while lecturing. "Developing ███████ megajoules of electromotive force would require ████████ X 10█ electron volts. Converting ████████ megajoules to teslas is █ X 10█. The Russians produced 2.8 X 10⁴ teslas in a laboratory in Sarov in 1998. Unless I'm wrong, that kind of capability doesn't come anywhere close. Even if it did, it wouldn't be enough."

Pierce visibly relaxes, a smile even makes its way to his lips. "Your calculations are spot on. I agree with you that current railguns, what the British developed, are completely inadequate for our purposes. At best, it gets us halfway there. And the last thing we want would be to only achieve half of a teleport."

Both Reidier and Wisecup listen to Pierce with a bemused curiosity. "I'm afraid that Rear Admiral Wisecup has inadvertently misled you."

Wisecup shifts, uncomfortably. He does not know where Pierce is going with this and clearly does not like the implication of being mistaken or deceitful.

Pierce continues, "The ████████ megajoules of wallop was what made headlines last December, but that was, well, what made headlines, and completely consistent with current railgun technology. At the Department, we're not very interested in current tech. It's why we're so interested in you. What we've been tinkering with, well, our nonpublic prototypes involve linking several very large ███████ ███ together. As a result, we generate about ████ X 10█ electron volts, plus or minus a few. Correct me if I'm wrong, but that'll probably do the trick, no?"

Reidier rests his elbows on the table, presses his palms together as if in prayer, and rests his head against his hands, his fingers pressing against either side of his nose against his brow, his thumbs hooking under his chin. Reidier nods and exhales audibly. "Yes, that would be enough. But where would we get that kind of power? Do we need to relocate again?"

Pierce shakes his head. "Not at all. That's where the Rear Admiral and his Navy come in so handy. Your adapted railgun and power source are already en route."

Reidier follows Pierce's gaze out the window. "A battleship?"

"How's a goddamn aircraft carrier sound to you?" Wisecup grins at Reidier. "The USS ███████████ should give you a good goddamn wallop, eh?"

Reidier nods, almost in a daze. Wisecup claps Pierce on the back. The two government men are pleased with the success and grandiosity of their solution. In their self-adulation, however, what they fail to see is the slightest drop in Reidier's shoulders. Perhaps it's just an unconscious release after the minor confrontation, or perhaps it's indicative of a psychological capitulation. Regardless of the motive, the sentiment is clear: resignation.

"So where are we going to put this floating battery?" Reidier asks.

Wisecup gestures out the window that looks out on NAVSTA's bay and piers.

Reidier turns and takes it in. "Your base?"

"Look out a little further, just across the water," Pierce offers.

Reidier leans toward the window.

"We got you your own personal little mad-scientist island outpost," Wisecup boasts and points.

The three men stand up and approach the window to take it in.

Upon magnification of the footage, while pixilated, the location is undeniably recognizable. Across the water from the conference room sits Gould Island.*

---

* Beyond negotiating a price with the lobsterman, I still wasn't talking to Lorelei. I sat on an old, dirty cooler at the stern of the boat, while she made small talk with the captain.

He was going on about how he remembered it, in his heavy Rhode Island accent, a tongue allergic to Rs. *Rememb'd the buhds maw than the fish. Yes suh. Looked like a swa'aw'm . . . A fawhg of feathuhs and feedin'. You could hee-yah theah squawks all the way back on the docks.*

The fish, though, well they wuh ev'y'wheah. Well, at least ev'y'wheah within this, ya no, radius of death 'round the gnaw-thin tip of thuh island. Damndest thing I ev-uh so'ah. Yes suh. The wheah'dest pot though, was that some of 'em, was actually cooked. Nevah seen anythin' like it. No suh. Cooked fish floating up from the depths.

I listened, a little, out of the corner of my ear. But mostly, I just kept going over this Tracy Kidder bit I remembered: "In fiction, believability may have nothing to do with reality or even plausibility. In nonfiction, it has everything to do with those things. I think that the nonfiction writer's fundamental job is to make what is true believable."

As we bounced from crest to crest, Gould Island winked larger and larger with every dip of the bow. The truth of it became less and less plausible with every league. I zippered my coat all the way up. The weather might've warmed up a bit, but the ocean air still had a bite.

Finally, we were idling less than a hundred yards from the beach. Lorelei and I stood on the port side, staring at ground zero of *The Reidier Test*.

It looked like . . . an island. I don't know, I think I half expected it to still be smoking. Instead the site was covered with a swath of primary-growth plants and even some overzealous secondary-growth shrubs.

Ov-uh theah's some rubble ya can see through thuh bushes, our lobsterman pointed out.

Part of what used to be a brick wall flashed between the overgrowth. It was the bottom half of a window frame.

We slowly motored north, up the east side of the island, following a three-foot-high cement wall that demarcated the beach from the woods. It sunk into the earth about a third of the way up the island. We saw several more partial brick or cement structures that were slowly being swallowed up by the green.

Our captain kept pointing out secret sites that were camouflaged to the untrained eye. What looked like a teepee of kindling surrounded by trees was actually a wooden structure that had imploded. Those "kindling sticks" were actually old beams.

The northern end of the island was flat—a field of concrete striated with weeds, saplings, and ferns.

"Jesus, get a load of that." Lorelei leaned against the side of the boat to try to get close, try to make sense of what wasn't there anymore.

Traces of another concrete wall circumvented the former compound and opened up at the tip of the island where the ocean was dotted with the odd pylon.

"What's that?" I asked our captain.

"Was a pe'ah."

A pier. Didn't look like much. I said so.

"Nah, a big one too. Yes suh. U'sta have an entiya eah'craft carrie-ya docked heah."

I tried to imagine an aircraft carrier tied to the pier. Mammoth wires running off it into Reidier's lab. I played dumb. "What happened to it? Sink?"

"Nah, theah would'uh been a whole heap of flotsam on the sh'oah. I huh'd it'd shipped out a cuppa days pry-ya." The lobsterman shrugged.

On the way back, the captain pointed out two aircraft carriers that were docked at the NAVSTA, the naval base, just across the bay on Newport's western shore, the former fiefdom of the late Rear Admiral Wisecup.

Believability, plausibility, reality. I just didn't know anymore.

Neither did Lorelei. Instead she gave me a crooked smile while the wind whipped wisps of her hair in front of her face.

She'd be stunning even in the middle of a goddamn hurricane. Hell if I didn't swoon a little inside. It was either that or another swell of the Atlantic.

"I guess we just keep digging. Tomorrow we go to Providence."

I don't know what I'm doing anymore. What I hope to accomplish. I can't keep it all straight, it's a Chinese somersault between my memory and my imagination rolling down the banks of the Providence River, tumbling toward perdition.

Adapted from the video surveillance of Gould Island Lab; June 15, 2007

Reidier rests his hands on the pen tray of the whiteboard behind him, his left elbow patch inadvertently erasing some of his calculations.

Rear Admiral Wisecup, in an almost comically cliché gesture, pulls out a cigar and butane torch lighter. He has the cigar in his mouth and the bright-blue flame ignited before he pauses to ask, as if it's a foregone conclusion, "You mind?"

Reidier, without any aggression, matter-of-factly lets him know he can't smoke there.

"You allergic or something?" Wisecup challenges Reidier.

Reidier adjusts some machine on the nearby table while he proceeds to explain, first with several lines of technical jargon and then again in a more vernacular analogy, that while smoke might seem a rather insubstantial intrusion of particles, it's a tsunami of interference on molecularly calibrated machines.

Wisecup takes this in stride. He repockets his cigar and lighter, and even seems a bit amused. Finally after watching Reidier tinker with his machine, he asks, "You ever hear about Pizarro and Atahualpa?"

"Were they scientists or generals?" Reidier retorts. The bite of his comment is wielded like a velvet-covered mace.

"Pizarro was a Spanish explorer in the early 1500s. One of the guys who accompanied Balboa to the Pacific."

"So he was a conquistador."

"For a while he was mayor and magistrate of Panama City, a position he was awarded for arresting Balboa. But yes, a conquistador. Some might say *the* conquistador. What do you know about the Incan empire?"

"Machu Picchu, advanced earthquake-proof engineering with their architecture. A highly adept civilization, built on the tuber. I believe they cultivated over 4,000 varieties of potatoes, actually. They had particularly advanced agriculture, utilizing this wide variety within niche microclimates all up and down the Andes. Subsequently inoculated them against any type of potato blight, like the one that almost obliterated the Irish. Our agribusinesses could learn a thing or two from them. We're all about adapting the environment to a specific plant, they simply adapted the plant to a myriad of different environments."

Wisecup nods. "They were also the single largest empire in the New World. By the time Atahualpa was ruling, his kingdom covered almost the entire west coast of South America. Peru, Bolivia, Ecuador, Chile, Argentina, Colombia. Over twenty million subjects and he commanded an army of close to a hundred thousand warriors."

Wisecup paused for a moment. He watched Reidier and waited for a comment. Reidier finally appeased Wisecup, guessing, "And Pizarro beat him. Is that your point?"

Wisecup shook his head back and forth. "He didn't just beat him. He annihilated him with only sixty-two soldiers mounted on horses and one hundred and six foot soldiers, while Atahualpa had a force of about eighty thousand. Two soldiers for every thousand warriors. All because the Spanish had steel swords, steel armor, guns, and horses, while Atahualpa's troops had stone and wooden clubs, and no animals. An empire fell to a handful of invaders because of a technological advantage."

"And that's what you want from me, the next technological advantage?"

"I only want what you want, Professor Reidier, to reach our goal," Wisecup said. "I'm a facilitator. Nothing more. Directives are given to me, and I do everything in my power to help make them a reality."

"And responsibility is successfully deconstructed and compartmentalized." Reidier stops his tinkering and faces Wisecup, giving the Rear Admiral his full attention. "Myopia is a dangerous thing. It's killed more people than any disease throughout history."

"You know da Vinci didn't only paint the Mona Lisa."

"I'm aware."

"Among his proficient skills, in a letter to the Duke of Milan, he also listed nine different categories of military engineering: weapons, bridging, bombarding machines, trench draining. He pioneered the renaissance of armed wars."

Reidier has pulled himself back in his seat. The mention of da Vinci puts him on edge.

Wisecup presses his advantage. "Scientific advancement has both taken and saved innumerable lives. It's the nature of tools. But you got to ask yourself, on August 6, 1945, would you have rather been on the ground in Hiroshima or flying above it on the Enola Gay? We might not be able to stop the march of history, but sometimes we can choose whether we're leading it or underfoot."

Reidier doesn't have a response for this. Wisecup takes his silence as a cue for having won the argument. Not to belabor the point, Wisecup stands up with a *Well then . . .* The Rear Admiral takes out his cigar once more.

"Everything on our end is set. The USS ████ is at your disposal. Whenever you're ready to start your experiments." Wisecup heads for the door.

Reidier speaks up as Wisecup is halfway out. "History can be a powerful tool of rhetoric, especially when cherry-picked. Sometimes the long view can really put things into relief."

"Is that right?" Wisecup asks with a nonplussed, almost placating attitude.

"About a thousand years before Pizarro raped the New World, the Mayans were the most advanced civilization on the planet. While Europe was swallowed up by the Dark Ages, the Mayans were building huge cities, constructing towering temples, growing vast trade routes, developing large-scale agriculture, spreading their written language, and divining theories of mathematics, including the concept of zero more than five hundred years before Western Civilization would, and literally mapping out the heavens and creating a solar calendar more accurate than today's. For about seven hundred years, they were the premiere culture on the planet. Then between eight and nine hundred, poof, that was it. Architectural projects abandoned, monumental inscriptions ceased midproject, cultural centers abandoned, trade routes dried up. This amazingly advanced culture collapsed. You know why?"

"Can't say that I do."

"Neither does anyone else. Progress isn't always progress."

Wisecup nods, then smiles big at Reidier. "Good thing for us then, that we'll have your contraption, "'cause no matter what threatens us with our own collapse, we'll have the ultimate escape route. Our own portal onto whatever ark we choose."

"Or the ultimate weapon delivery system, right?"

Wisecup checks his watch. "You'll have to excuse me. I've got drinks with my lieutenants, and I don't want them putting any Ice-9 in my scotch."

With this final comment, Wisecup walks off down the hall, leaving the door wide open.

Reidier moves to close it, then stops, shrugs, and turns back, mumbling, "Why bother."

Are we alone now

The years of working beneath the predatory gaze of Didi* had honed Reidier's instincts, his "paranoia" radar constantly pinging out into the dark corners of his life, an unconscious habit at this point, like whistling a tune or biting one's nails.

---

*The freaky Frenchman from French Guiana who drove Reidier crazy.

Yes, Kerek.

It's how he spotted the cell phone anomaly so quickly.

But then he just took it in stride. No angry phone calls to Pierce. No destructive tantrums. No moody sulking.

Just the norm.

Are we alone now

It didn't seem right. It was inconsistent with a man who would move his wife from one foreign land in the jungle to another foreign land on the edge of an icy great lake because of a nosy Frenchman impotently poking around his hard drive. Arrange a green card for Eve, get married, land a prestigious university post, rebuild his lab— all because his old boss touched his notebook? But now, barely a nod at his current boss bugging his home?!

Yes, Kerek. *

---

* See Chapter XV, the .mp4 video file Hilary found on Reidier's personal hard drive and transcribed. Reidier and Kai whispering to each other. I don't know why she didn't put it in this folder. Nor why she's editing Kai's name out of Reidier's question, "It sounds quiet. Are we alone now, Kai?"

Still, there he was, every day, going to his office, taking trips to Gould Island to oversee refurbishment, working diligently at his lab in the basement, within the aquarium of his life. A beta fish that had just bumped up against the glass boundaries of his existence. A pet. A circus act.

Are we alone now

NB Footage, Reidier Basement lab, July 2, 2007

The NB footage perfectly mirrors the content from Reidier's own personal recording system. He sits in his basement laboratory. He's lost in work, spins in his chair from one surface to another, scribbles down something, back to his computer to check out some data.

Back to his scribbling. Without even looking at the computer, types a few keystrokes, while he writes something down in one of Leo's Notebooks.

Reidier presses "Enter." Nothing much happens. Reidier writes more down.

The video blinks and skips a second.

Reidier's still working. The notebook has jumped a few inches to the right within the blackness of the blink. And Reidier's still writing, although there's a little less ink on the page than there was only moments prior. A line, maybe two.

The NB footage goes on. But in this footage, he doesn't go on to lean back in his chair. He's not listening. He's not hearing.

Nothing. Especially not:

Reidier: *It sounds quiet. Are we alone now, Kai?*

(Pause)

Female Voice: *Yes, Kerek.*

There's no such dialogue on the NB footage. Just his hard drive.

Reidier hacked the nanobots.*

---

* Reidier blinded the watchers, and they didn't even know it. And he did it right in front of them.

If I'm reading it right, Reidier tapped right into the Department's surveillance and "amended" it. The official Department video only has a little skip and then some mundane footage of Reidier and his note-taking. No conversation with Kai. No "Are we alone, Kai?" That was for his own private record of reality.

Two versions of the truth, only one has been edited; and from that point forward, the official record was no longer reliable.

And the rest of us are left alone in the quiet. Listening for the listeners.

Exposed.

I cross-checked endless hours of footage from feeds all over the rest of the house. No blinks. No jumping notebooks. Apparently, Reidier hijacked only the surveillance in his home lab.

It makes sense. He would've run a greater risk of detection taking over all of the feeds. Plus, he had endless databanks of footage to access and rerun while he did his own work, now in privacy.

Whatever doubts Reidier had been entertaining about Pierce and the Department before this moment, his discovery of the nanobots was a defining and transformative moment. No longer was Reidier working with tenuous allies, he was working against covetous spies.**

** "Lorelei."

"Danny . . . ?" Lorelei blinked awake, and raised her forearm to try and shield her eyes from the lamplight slicing in from the hallway. She reached out and touched my cheek. "Are you ok?"

The room spun around the axis of her arm and then rocked back the other way like one of those swinging ship rides at a carnival.

I hadn't calculated for this. All my plotting, all my impulse control, and her bedroom wouldn't stop swinging. It wasn't supposed to go like this.

Earlier, when I was alone, reading my mom's files on Reidier's exter-mination of the nanobots, I had wanted to leap up from my chair, sprint down the hall, throw open her door, and shout, *Call my burner!* I had wanted to turn on every light in the house, blast every stereo/iPod/music player whatever, flip on every kitchen appliance, and march around banging pots together. Whatever would provide enough noise and inter-ference, give me enough cover to wander around our roost, active cell phone in hand and root out our own nanobot infestation. But no, that might have created its own interference, muddy the aural waters. Not to mention if the nanobots were there, if we were being watched, then that sure as hell would've tipped them off that we were on to them. And once we pulled the curtain back on Ol' Eavesdropping Oz, then what? If their cover's blown then they have to come in and come in hard, guns up, zip-tie handcuffs at the ready. NO! No. Our only advantage would be them not knowing we know they're there. *If* they were there. If that were the case, if they were on to me the whole time, then it would've been a simple matter of letting themselves in and unleashing a swarm of nanobots while we were out slurping chowder and taking boat rides. No. We had to be smart about this. We had to respond, not react. We needed to meditate, think, and not quaff a quart of Jameson no mat-ter how loudly our nerves screamed for it. No! No. We needed to stay sharp. We needed to walk calmly to Lorelei's room. Unsuspiciously rouse her from her slumber. Fake some illness, a cough, choking congestion, yes, ask her for help operating the steam room/shower that was so art-fully integrated into the original colonial remodel. Then once there, sit-ting side by side on the marble floor, leaning against the shower glass, while the steam room whined and hissed awake like a dragon fart, there masked by the steam, muffled by the violent shrill of vaporization, there I would whisper in her ear, I would explain about the nanobots, how she needed to get her burner phone and call my burner, which I would have in my pocket, but plugged into earphones. She needed to do some odd little task, something mundane, play a game of solitaire, heat up some milk 'cause she can't sleep, and absentmindedly sing while doing it. In the meantime, I would wander the halls with my normal manic somnam-bulism, all the while listening, hunting like a bat for bugs, Lorelei's voice pinging around my ears while I stalk any little interference. And then we'd know if we'd been found.

But I hadn't planned on her touching my cheek.

I didn't anticipate the look of concern in her eyes, let alone the invitingness of her tone. She wasn't surprised. It almost was like she was hopeful. Had Lorelei been waiting for me to visit her, like this, in her room, in the middle of the night? Had I missed the signs? How could I have planned for the way her curls flowed around her pillow, radiating away from her, tossed around from the chaos of sleep?

"Danny?" She propped herself up on her elbow, her curls cascading down across her neck. Her loose white tank top snagged under her arm, pulling away from her, opening. The lamplight from the hall reached around me, caressing the curve of her smooth breasts and barely covered nipples.

Her palm cupped my chin, her thumb rubbed back and forth against my cheek. "What is it? What's going on, Danny?"

She tilted her head slightly. Was it in confusion or in anticipation of me tilting my head in the opposite direction? Of our lips meeting, parting? Our tongues finding each other? Textured tastebuds tickling together? Electricity radiating outward, buzzing our brains, shooting down our throats, tightening tendrils of warmth that stretched down to our groins?

Did she just lean in ever so slightly?

    kwuh/tck/tck   *dee-de-de*

I don't know if I really heard it, or if my mind was playing tricks on my dick. Either way, the spell was broken, it didn't matter if it was electricity or interference crackling between us. What came out of my mouth next wasn't her tongue, it was a fabricated cough, followed by an over-the-top-sickly, "You think you could help me with the steam shower?"

Lorelei made herself some hot chocolate and sang Eric Clapton tunes, while I flitted about the premises, like a bat on crack. I came up empty-handed. Not one crackle, not a single scratch. We were secure.

And somehow I felt all the worse for it.

I told her I'd drive us up to Providence the next day so she could nap. I promised to take her to this old donut place I knew hidden off of Route 2, best damn donuts and coffee-milk she'll ever have. She gave me a half laugh and a nod, and we both went off to our separate rooms.

I wish I could run away from me.

I sat in his home lab for the entire day today. I slipped underneath the yellow "Do Not Enter" tape, and broke into 454 Angell and found my way to the basement. It was empty, of course. The entire house was. The Department had collected all of his equipment and "cleaned" the house.*

---

* There's a trick to falling. Surrender. You simply give in to the inevitable. More often than not, a greater injury is suffered from trying to prevent the fall. You can't fight failure any more than you can resist the gravity of the future. It pulls at you whether you resist or not.

I learned about the safety in surrender skiing with Toby. We were teenagers visiting his uncle, a Marine colonel stationed in Oslo. Toby had spent the first ten years of his life suckling on the teats of the Rockies in Utah. He was an expert and effortless skier. On the other hand, I was drastically underskilled. Nevertheless, I was fairly athletic and competitive, which is how we ended up at the top of a bowl, riddled with moguls the size of VW Bugs.

Toby went first. I watched his legs piston back and forth from Volkswagen to Volkswagen. Effortless.

So down I went, following his trail, picking up speed down the practically vertical slope, dropping from mound to mound, a jarring attempt at interrupting gravity, yelping with a fake-it-till-you-make-it adrenaline rush, all the while losing more and more control, skidding over the top of one mogul, slamming into the valley between two others. The end of this terrifying short story was becoming quickly and painfully obvious to me. Still I resisted, twisting my body against its will, trying to compensate for quark-like shifts in my center of gravity. Moguls rushed up at me with an angry velocity, hunting for an opening.

My thighs burned, melting muscle tissue; my knees vibrated, grinding down the cartilage; my wrists twisted rapidly, narrowly escaping the relentless and erratic torque of the poles.

My epiphany happened just after I sped past Toby. The simultaneous realization and acceptance. My embrace of the inevitable. The fall was coming. I could not outrun it. So I gave in.

I knelt before the altar of failure and prostrated myself. And in letting go of resistance, I was finally free. I was released from the bonds of ego, loosened from the noose of ambition. The hard rattling of resistance gave in to the sweet embrace of impact.

I delighted in the simplicity of surrender as the world whirled around me, blinking in and out of existence. The snow cooled my legs, having already snapped me out of my bindings. My arms stretched out, pulled by the poles, dancing behind me like excited dachshund puppies, while I lay on my back and accelerated downhill.

Toby remarked how spectacular my spill was, after he raced down to me with my skis under his arm. I sat up and laughed. I felt intact. Settled. And subsequently invulnerable. I knew how to fall. I could fall with the best of them. By having let go of my fear of falling, I had mastered the art of failure.

Providence, Day 1: Where 454 Angell once stood, now stands . . . a Starbucks.

The empty basement was dark, and all the more so because its walls had been covered in primer paint. I wondered on which wall Picasso's bullfighter hid beneath the surface. In the corner of the room lay a discarded, grime-covered, white-and-blue toothbrush that the cleaning crew had overlooked or left themselves.

The emptiness was actually helpful. There were no distorting tangents, and so I was less distracted. Like the Oracle of Delphi, I had a cave within which to channel voices from beyond, echoing around the empty concrete foundation, while I paged through a folder full of transcripts of conversations and facsimiles of Eve's journal entries.

Ever since my diagnosis, I've been having a recurring dream: I am thirteen again, in ballet class. My instructor is banging her stick on the floor, a relentless taskmaster. I am exhausted, my body stretched to my limit, but still, I push, I attack the choreography, landing lightly with every thump of the maîtresse's stick. It rattles my bones, making them click like a metronome. It clatters through my skull, or so I think, until the pirouette. I know I must spot. I feel myself lilting, and I must spot. I must not let the maîtresse see me falter. I turn my gaze, to the mirror, so I may stay on pointe, and finally see myself.

I am a skeleton in a tutu. The clicking metronome was not my teacher. It was me, the bones of my feet tapping against the floor. I am a dancing Day of the Dead figurine. My hair is up in a bun. A rose is tucked behind my ear, a large origami blossom folded out of petals of skin. Beads of blood glisten like dew along its edge. And my eyes are enormous—cut and polished diamonds wedged into the sockets of my skull.

The vision terrifies me, but stopping scares me even more. I keep spinning, bones blurring across my eyes, spinning, it is too much, I feel myself tipping, tilting, falling—

And I shudder awake, like one in the gloaming between awake and asleep who feels herself teetering off the edge of the bed and flinches back to consciousness.

I reach out across the expanse of mattress and find nothing. K is not there. I am alone. Once again he has evaporated into the night.

Reidier has his own dreams to contend with, down in his lair. With the transcript in hand, I find my way to roughly where Reidier sat at his computer and recorded yet another video file.

Reidier sits in his chair, leaning off toward the right side. From where I stand, I can see he was facing the stairs.

His finger absentmindedly taps on the arm of his chair.

He finally speaks, unprompted. "I had a dream last night, Kai. A dream of doors, all sorts of doors. Portals really. A piece of chalk drawing a rectangle on a surface, and I could fall through to anywhere. But there was a catch, each door I went through I came out slightly younger, slightly altered, slightly less myself. What are we to do about this, Kai?"

The anxiety of Eve's diagnosis, compounded by the stress of Reidier's work, would inevitably wind the tension of the relationship tighter. With tragic irony, it seems to be both pulling them apart and binding them together, a Chinese finger puzzle coiled around their hearts. They find themselves isolated from each other while haunted by nightmares of transformation.

As Eve sunk into her unsettling reality, she found something altogether unexpected: her voice. Eve started writing with a prolific and creative fury. In analyzing both the content and style of her work during this initial postdiagnosis period, it seems that Eve's writing was both a means of coping/engaging with the challenging circumstances and a confabulatory side effect from the tumor itself. To understand the degree to which both function and form are operating on these levels within her work, one need not look any further than her memoiresque novella, *A Moi*. [112]

---

[112] Especially if one keeps in mind that the story coincides with Reidier's discovery and inoculation of the nanobots. It simultaneously validates Reidier's actions and tracks their transformation into trespassers in their own home. [§]

[§]*Providence, Day 2*: Professor Bertram Malle has all but been erased from the annals of Brown University as well. There's a record of him, sure. He used to teach here. For a bit, then he left. Did some promising work with robotics, neurology, and amputees and paraplegics. A couple of papers published and on file, an article or two about him in the alumni magazine. That's it, though.

Same with Clyde Palmore. He's a professor emeritus for the Engineering Department. However, his house has been locked up and winterized for what appears to be a while. According to Brown, he's on an extended sabbatical working in Haiti on low-cost, earthquake-proof construction adapted from Incan architecture.

0 for 2. On the underwhelming side, at least I ran into an old classmate who was up here peddling some new play of his to the Theater Department. Yay nostalgia. I'd have better luck getting lunch with Professor Carberry at Josiah's and discussing the finer points of psychoceramics. Crackpots seem to be quickly becoming my specialty.

Excerpt from *A Moi: Graffiti Me*

She lay in bed listening to the murmur of the blades as they sliced through the humidity.

I have the distinct feeling that my bedroom ceiling fan is spreading rumors about me.

It was an amusing thought, one that gave rise to a smile. It surprised her how well she was assimilating his secret.

She turned to see if he was awake, so she could whisper the absurd suspicion into his ear. His revelation had given her the idea after all.

Their bed sprawled out in front of her. Empty. He was nowhere in sight. Another woman, another couple, might have been surprised, worried even. For her, though, his Cimmerian absences had become a common feature of their bedroom, one she was as intimately familiar with as the whispers of the ceiling fan.

A sigh escaped her, as last night ebbed its way out of her memory and washed over her. Nowadays their intimacy took on an altogether different nature. It was the closeness of conspirators.

Sliding up against her in bed, his chest pushing against her shoulder blades, she stirred from her slumber to the pressure of him. In that lacuna between awake and asleep, time held no meaning, and she was back in the past with him, her arm reflexively reaching back for his hand, pulling it across her hip, up her stomach, and pressing his palm against her breast. She tilted her shoulder toward him as he pulled her into orbit, her lips instinctually finding his.

It wasn't until she was on her back, his weight pinning her down into the mattress, pinning her wrists above her head, flattening his left palm against her right, aligning their fingers, that she finally snapped into consciousness and understood what he was doing.

Hands pressed together, palm to palm—a simple, loving, romantic gesture to most. An intimate communion, but on a far less innocent level. It was the union of a lock and key, the hushed tone of a cipher, their fingers encrypted together.

It was five. Their shared number. Five was the secret number they had arrived at, so many nights ago, on their first date, when he taught her the essence of cryptography. Five was their private key.[113]

He had a secret to tell.

Arms pinned above her head, his body weighing her down, she opened her legs, and hooked her heels behind his knees with false promise. An amorous performance.

He slid into her, like a key into a lock, and she opened. Him sinking in, her pulling him, their bodies slaves to habit and desire. Slowly, deeper, until he thumped against the back of her, knocking a moan loose from her throat.

He exhaled heat into her ear and whispered in a breathless, hushed tone: The house is a spy.

Their home, the one he had offered up as compensation for the relocation, the one the twins romped and stomped through, the one they had finally, grudgingly settled into, was made of glass.

The walls have a thousand ears and a thousand eyes. The place could smell their pulse and taste their thoughts.

It was not the sanctuary they thought it was. It was their own little domestic panopticon.

Palm to palm, sharing their coded five, him confessing his discovery beneath the camouflage of sweat and grunts. Somehow, in the end, pinning down her hands, holding himself over her, gazes locked, staring right into each others' eyes, the conspirators came together in a wave of relief and concession. He collapsed onto her, she wrapped her arms around him and embraced the weight of his secret.

---

[113] See page 71.

I'm sorry, *he panted into her ear.* I'll fix it. I'll fix it all, I promise.

She could feel the emptiness in the room. The stillness, save for the fan aspirating down into the sheets. She looked at the expanse next to her. She imagined him sitting there in the future, after the crab inside her skull had finished feeding on her mind and taken over the shell of her defunct and departed body, the weight of emptiness building up behind him.

How would he deal with the distance then, after the cancer consumed her?

She lay in bed watching short-story ideas dance across the ceiling to the beat of the ceiling fan. The mad scientist who made tinier and tinier machines, microrobots, so small they're practically atomic, so small they could manipulate atoms. They could rearrange molecules at will and replicate any physical structure within moments. Too small and fast for the naked eye, an object would shimmer and blur as it morphed from one shape into another. A swarm of activity. A fog of substance. Robomites, foglets that could take any form, even something as mundane as a toaster.

The mad scientist and the toaster would talk over breakfast. The scientist would confide in the appliance about the challenges of marriage. His wife was . . . *(sigh . . . changing thoughts).* Having an affair with a young student was so cliché, *he would mutter while scraping strawberry jam across his toast.*

A dalliance mired in ennui, *the toaster would echo.*

The scientist would nod and crunch down on a corner of the bread. But a visiting professor, there's something alluring about that, something elegant about him.

Something very French about that, *the toaster would comment.* You're thinking about Spencer?

The scientist would nod, his mouth full of toast and jam.

What made you suspicious? *the toaster would push.*

Something the ceiling fan told me the other day, *the scientist would remark.* That and all the recent hang-ups. Almost every time the phone rings, it's either a hang-up or a click like someone's listening in on the extension.

Yes, the ceiling fan was spreading rumors about her.

I haunted that empty house for three days.* It wasn't until the last day that I remembered another random clip of Reidier, sitting in his lab, wearing an eye-patch over his right eye.

---

* How nice for you, Hilary. I dwelled in the pit of Hell's Kitchen for over three months. And now here I am, chasing down your clues written in sand.

Providence, Day 5: The Sci-Li's still there but no Reidier. Not a trace. It's like the whole thing never happened. Just another confabulation in one of Eve's nonexistent, hypothetical stories. It looks like this whole goddamn pilgrimage has been a wild goose chase, tracking down a red herring through the water at night.

I have gleaned almost nothing from my alma mater, save for an over-due balance of $368.72 owed for reserving a research shelf in the library that I apparently never closed after finishing my thesis.

Every night we drive from Providence back to Newport. Lorelei tries to keep my spirits up. Still I can see the shine from our Gould Island ad-venture fading, and her doubts creeping back into her tone. It's starting to feel less like she's helping me track down Hilary and more like she's just trying to help me keep track of myself.

Maybe she's right. Maybe I am losing bits of me along the way, dis-solving breadcrumb by breadcrumb as I trot deeper and deeper into the dark, imaginary forest. How else could you explain my reaction to her hand on my thigh in the car?

One hand on the wheel, the other patting my leg reassuringly as her eyes shift back and forth between the road and the furrows in my forehead.

I should have been ecstatic. Pity was getting me further with Lorelei than bravado ever had. Instead of taking that touch, that connection, that opening and placing my hand on hers, finally holding hands with my dear, sweet, luminous Lorelei, all I wanted to do was take the pen from behind my ear and stab it right through the meat, right between the knuckles, pierce all the way through and stake that patronizing palm to my flesh.

There. That's our connection. There's our shared experience.

Of course I don't do it. I don't want to hurt her. I just want to be understood.

My mother's suicide note is three phone books thick. You can get lost in it, and I have. There comes a point when too much is nothing at all. Infinity and zero, twin extremes.

How do you parse infinity?

How do you divide by zero?

"Did I tell you what I discovered down at The Athenaeum?" Lorelei had taken a walk down to the old nineteenth-century library on Benefit Street while I banged my head against the wall at the Sci-Li. It's a quirky old building built like a Greek temple up on plinth.

I shook my head no as I glared down at her hand on my thigh. My right elbow rested on the door against the window, my head leaning against my hand, surreptitiously fingering the pen still stuck behind my ear.

"Oh my God, I can't believe I forgot. Well, they had this big H. P. Lovecraft exhibit there. The Weird Tales guy."

"Yeah, I know who he is. Providence's sci-fi/fantasy pulp darling."

"I had no idea how influential he was. He was like, practically the father of modern horror."

"But a horrible writer. Like a dumbed-down version of Faulkner with twice the verbosity."

"Ok, so great thinker, meh writer. Still, do you know where he was born?"

"Providence?"

"Yes, but where in Providence?"

"Hospital?"

"Nope, at his family home on 194 Angell Street."

My fingers wrapped around my pen and plucked it from its perch behind my ear.

Lorelei went on, "That was its number then. Today it would be at 454 Angell."

Lorelei raised her eyebrows at me as if to exclaim, *Can you believe that?!*

I couldn't.

"That's a pretty big coincidence, don't you think?"

I shrugged, staring out the window. "Only if you're implying that a rift in the earth opened up in 454's basement and swallowed Hilary up."

"I mean maybe metaphorically. I don't know, I just thought it was interesting at the very least. And kind of apt. In a number of his works, Lovecraft refers to the Necronomicon, this fictional grimoire that contains an account of the Old Ones and a way to summon them. Some people think the book actually exists, that Lovecraft read it and stole some ideas, but in reading the book, he opened up a portal, drew the ire of interdimensional demons that not only drove him crazy, but went back in time and infected his father with insanity. That it was actually that, not syphilis, that killed his father."

She had more faith in the macabre fantasies of a bipolar author than in my mother's report. That's what she was saying. The Necronomicon, Hilary's PsychoNarrative—they held about the same weight. Fictions within fictions.

"Kind of sad, really. Lovecraft's father and mother went crazy and died in Butler Hospital just a few miles from his home. Years apart. His dad died when he was like three, and his mom had a nervous breakdown right before he was thirty. Both were committed to Butler. Lovecraft modeled Arkham Asylum on the hospital."

Maybe Lorelei was onto something. Maybe I'd have better luck hunting for Hilary in Arkham, trying to save her from getting raped by some evil doctor in a psych ward. I could feel my stomach hardening. Like a cancer took seed there and was starting to digest me from the inside out. "My mother's not crazy."

Lorelei finally took her hand off my leg. "I wasn't saying she was. I wasn't saying that at all."

"No?" I asked. The digestive acids from the hungry tumor singed my tone.

"No. I just thought it was interesting. A cool little coincidence. Sometimes random disparate facts, while not necessarily clues, jog something loose. Get us to look at things differently. You know?"

I nodded. "Yeah. Maybe Lovecraft can shake something loose. I mean Christ, it's not like we haven't both been thinking that Ecco's a goddamn demon."

Lorelei didn't say anything else. Neither did I. We drove the rest of the way back to Newport in silence. Her hands at ten and two on the steering wheel, while mine rested on my knees strangling my pen.

We pulled into the compound and parked in front of the barn/garage.

"You know the two things that Waco, Texas, is famous for?" I asked.

Lorelei wrinkled her nose at my random question. "Well, I assume one of them is David Koresh."

"Yep."

"What's the other?"

"Its pageant play."

"Pageant, like beauty pageant?"

"Pageant play. Mystery play. York Cycle."

"Like the Nativity play?"

"The Nativity play is definitely the most popular one. Especially for Christmas. Waco had one of those, but it was part of something bigger. Waco had developed a ten-year cycle that started with the birth-of-Jesus pageant and every year covered a different part of Jesus's life, culminating on the tenth year with his crucifixion. Come the thirty-year anniversary, it was a spectacle. Waco went all out. They even brought in professionals from the Dallas Theater to set up a special light board, lighting grid, a whole fly system for sets and everything. All still done with local talent, 'cause this was Waco's baby, but set up with imported talent. It was really not to be missed. Especially for a sophomore at Brown, who had spent his entire life east of the Mississippi. Not to mention the added perk of getting to avoid his mother for the holidays, as well as an opportunity to prove some serious commitment to his beyond-cute, Star of Texas girlfriend to reconsider her no-sex-before-marriage policy. Especially, if said girl was playing the starring role of the Virgin Mary (type casting), since her father was on the pageant board and one of the biggest donors."

"How hot a girl are we talking?" Lorelei asked.

"Her name was Summer Moore."

"That's pretty hot. *And* she was a virgin to boot! You'd grab the Roman's hammer and nails yourself for a taste of that."

"Or at least agree to pitch in and help out with the pageant when things went wrong."

"You didn't?"

"Like I said, it was a big tadoo, and they needed a lot of help. Just to put their production value into perspective, if they had been doing the Noah story, there would've been elephants. The opera *Carmen* don't got shit on Waco."

Lorelei nodded. "Sounds impressive."

"It was. You had the trial with Pontius Pilate rattling down at the masses from the church rafters, washing his hands of them; you had the Stations of the Cross spread out through the church's massive aisles; you had a Foley artist in the wings ripping heads of lettuce apart against a microphone as a solemn Jesus was nailed to the cross, dozens of onlookers moaning, dozens of ancient priests mocking. Finally, the tribal Jewish leaders, concerned about this execution continuing into the Sabbath, ask the Romans to hasten their deaths. The actors/soldiers break the legs of the crucified slaves that flank Jesus while the Foley artist snaps stalks of celery in half. Then one centurion comes to Jesus, looks up at the drooping body and claims, 'He is dead already.'"

I waited a moment. Until Lorelei grew impatient.

"And . . . !" she said.

"And he said it again, 'He is dead already.' Nothing. The actor/centurion looked offstage to the assistant stage manager whose eyes widened with panic. She then sprinted around backstage to find the missing centurion who was supposed to be stabbing Jesus in the side, but instead was out back smoking a joint with a buddy, and was so stoned that when the stage manager did find him, he could barely stand, let alone walk, which was a problem since he also happened to be the Virgin Mary's brother and the son of one of the biggest pageant donors. So the buddy had to grab the centurion's helmet and breastplate, sprint inside, grab his spear, and rush onstage, not realizing he hadn't grabbed the trick spear necessary for this scene. And for the third time the first centurion/actor announces, 'He is already dead.' At which point the disheveled stand-in centurion runs up and thrusts his very real prop spear into Jesus's side.

"Jesus screams, his eyes snap open, he looks down and shouts, 'Jesus Christ, you stabbed me!'"

"No!?" Lorelei exclaimed half in disbelief, half in hysterics.

I nodded and kept going. "So they bring down the curtain. The centurions take Jesus down off the cross, load him into a Honda Civic, and rush him to the hospital."

Lorelei could barely breathe as she jumped forward. "So a Honda pulls up to an emergency room and three Roman soldiers jump out and carry in a bleeding Jesus, yelling, help he's been stabbed?"

"But back at the theater, the show has to go on because, even though the show was at the climax, it wasn't over. They still needed Jesus to ascend to heaven for the thousands in the audience. So they get the understudy, they get him up on the cross, and get the curtain back up for the big moment.

"The Foley artist is shaking sheets of metal for thunder, the dry ice machines are pumping out smoke, and the high school kid who works the fly pulleys uncleats the rope that holds the counterweight to the cross so that a crucified Jesus can rise up into Heaven. Only no one has accounted for the understudy being seventy pounds lighter than the original Jesus. So instead of floating up into the rafters, the new Jesus rockets up like a bat out of hell, slams into the rafters, and smacks his head on a light baton, knocking himself unconscious. The poor high school kid panics, ties off the fly, and runs out.

"It's not until the curtain call that they realize Jesus is dangling completely unconscious over fifty feet up. So they keep the curtain down, send what remains of the cast out in front to bow, while they struggle to pull coldcocked Christ down, drag him from the cross, and find out he's bleeding from the head. So immediately, Pontius Pilate and two centurions load him into the back of a Ford pickup, and drive *him* to the emergency room."

Lorelei is literally crossing her legs at this point, shaking her head no, hyperventilating about the nurses who watched yet another wounded Jesus get carried into the ER by Romans.

With a considered absentmindedness I rubbed the scar below my ribs through my shirt.

Lorelei finally caught her breath.

"So that's how you got the scar. Playing Jesus in a pageant play?"

"Not me. I was the asshole getting Summer's brother high in the parking lot."

"You were the stabber, not the stabbee? But then how . . ."

"Well, her brother and I were still pretty baked, and we were doing a piss-poor job of not laughing about the whole damn thing in the hospital waiting room. Everyone tried their best to ignore us until I saw a nurse by the vending machine and just yelled out, 'Funyuns!' Summer's brother lost his shit, and her father lost his mind, and he just came at me yelling about how goddamn funny I thought everything was, how ironic, how elitist, how heehaw my Yankee perception, how funny did I think it felt, and he sunk the Bic pen he had used to sign some hospital forms right into my side."

Lorelei stopped cold.

I knew she would. I knew what I had been doing the whole time.

"Danny, I'm, I . . ."

"Sometimes even pretend stories have real consequences," I said, grabbed my knapsack full of Hilary's folders, got out of the car, and slinked away down the path to the water, to the dock. Lorelei didn't follow.

He's spinning his magnets in a bowl again.[114]

Metal rings against metal while Bob Dylan's "Like a Rolling Stone" plays quietly on his computer.

Reidier's possessed, chanting over and over: Trust the ghost, trust the ghost, trust the ghost.

---

[114] See page 34.

In regione caecorum rex est luscus*

---

* In the country of the blind, the one-eyed man is king. Hilary is drifting, drifting, drifting, and I'm drowning in her wake.

PS Can someone please tell me what happened to the fucking twins??? Otto 1 and Otto 2. Ecco the echo.
Boom the bomb dropped, and there's been no sign of them in the rubble.
WTF?

What to see?

What to see?

2C

To sea

Too sea

XVII

All sciences

                                            are now under

                     the obligation

to prepare the ground

                           for the future task of the philosopher,

               which is to solve the problem

                                        of value,

to determine the true hierarchy of values.

                                  ~Friedrich Nietzsche

Where ambition can cover its enterprises,

even to the person himself,

under the appearance of principle,

it is the most incurable and inflexible of passions."

                                  ~David Hume

Rule III.

The qualities of bodies are to be esteemed the universal qualities
of all bodies

whatsoever.

~Newton

Woman is not a collection of mere memories.

She is a creature of will, of sense and sensation . . .

it is there . . .

you may touch her,

and effect profound change.

~Mary Wollstonecraft Godwin Shelley

Speaking of ghosts . . . how about a listen?

Excerpt from University of Chicago iTunes episode, Dr. Kerek
Reidier lecture from his Physics of Science Fiction course,
December 12, 2005

"When a reporter asked Peres if it was possible to teleport both
the body *and* soul, he answered, 'Only the soul.'"

Reidier lets the counterintuitiveness of the anecdote sink in. Students shift, uncomfortable with the statement but unsure as to why.

"Any biology majors here?"

A lone student speaks up about how he took Bio 20.

"All right, Mr. Siemens. Assuming you were at least half as engaged with that class as with my riveting lectures, you should have a sufficient grasp of humanity."

A laugh ripples through the class.

"What makes us who we are, biologically speaking?"

There's a prolonged *ummmmmm* from the darkness.

"A hint then: What is the building block of life, that which sequences our very existence?"

Mr. Siemens excitedly shouts out, "DNA!"

"And how does it do that?"

Mr. Siemens launches into great detail about how DNA replicates itself through unzipping its double helix and replicating two mirror images through base pairing, and how the specific arrangement of the four nucleobases of A, T, C, G is what dictates every physical trait about us.

"Exactly!" Reidier cuts Mr. Siemens off. "DNA is a blueprint for us. Psychology and development aside, that's all we are, a signature pattern, from which our entire bodies are constructed. That's all anything is, really. Matter is nothing more than rigidly ordered energy. Every bit of matter is simply a precise pattern held in check by forces until they wink out of existence."

Reidier let the concept sink in.

"The entire human genome is simply a sequential binary code containing roughly eight hundred million bytes of information. So, what does this mean for our purposes?"

No responses are proffered.

"We never have to teleport a 'thing.' Nothing need be transmitted through space. Only information. If the pattern of an object is extracted, it can then be used on the other end as a blueprint to make a perfect copy."

"How would that work though? Aren't we more than patterns?" another student asks from out of the darkness.

"Not at a quantum level. At the quantum level, all that exists are patterns. Wave functions."

"But the wave function would be disrupted by the extraction, no?" interrupts another student.

"Very astute, Ms. Echeverria. That is the essence exactly. You can extract and transmit any and all quantum information as long as you're willing to destroy the original in exchange for an exact replica on the other end."

To demonstrate what he's pointing out, as well as to provide some much needed comedic relief, Reidier holds up a piece of chalk in his right hand, waves it about dramatically, says abracadabra, palms the piece of chalk, and smashes it against the surface of his desk. He then dramatically opens his left hand to reveal another piece of chalk. While not an exact replica, the point is made.

"Voilà!" Reidier brushes the pulverized pieces of chalk dust off his desk. "Just need to wipe the slate clean, so to speak."

The class laughs.

"Scientists are currently doing this by transmitting information through a Brassard circuit. But, can you tell me what other problem this presents?"

Ms. Echeverria appears to mumble an answer.

"Precisely. Next time with more confidence, though, please. No upspeak in my class. For a full-scale teleportation, like of a person, it would take a huge amount of data processing."

Another student pipes up and suggests using a supercomputer.

"Not a bad suggestion, Mr. Hurwitz. However, right now it would take our current supercomputers billions of years just to find the prime factors of a thousand-digit number. Our sun would die before we could even teleport your left foot."

Some snickers.

Mr. Hurwitz keeps pushing, "What about your quantum computer?"

Reidier smiles and looks back at the remaining chalk on his otherwise empty desk. "Let's hope I didn't just smash it."

The class laughs.

"But yes, a quantum computer would be able crunch these numbers at the velocity we'd require. As long as they're not disrupted by Loschmidt Echoes."

Reidier moves to the board and with his piece of "teleported" chalk writes down the equation:

$$M(t) = \left| \langle \psi | e^{i(\mathcal{H}_0 + \Sigma)t/\hbar} e^{-i\mathcal{H}_0 t/\hbar} | \psi \rangle \right|^2.$$

"It's a rather simple mathematical expression that basically describes how sensitive a quantum system is to changes in energy. The problem it points out is that quantum particles are so sensitive that when you run energy through them, as one does through computer circuits when asking them to perform calculations, the adjacent shifts in energy disrupt or destroy the states of neighboring quantum particles. Right now, as it is, nobody out there," Reidier gestures out the classroom door to the world at large, "has been able to put together a long enough string of quantum circuits to make a computer. The quantum particles can't help but fuck with each other."

The class erupts with laughter at Reidier's dropping the f-bomb.

"The other minor issue is that physicists can't seem to agree whether or not time and space can actually be broken down into discrete quanta, i.e. fragments of information. Basically, it's a debate about whether energy and matter are ultimately digital or analog in nature."

Dear Leo,

While the right state of mind might prove a dead end, the left proves infinitely versatile. Especially if you have a philosopher's stone on black stone.

Singularity,
Quark conjuring...
You've been busy.

—H

*

---

* Presumably here, dear, sweet, gone-round-the-bend Hilary is referring to another installment from Reidier's Leo's Notebooks, see page 302. I guess her codebreaker has cracked open another fragment.

Ἀναξαγόρας[115]

15260122462393207485484425296516185646229388607739444646726321379640201581919637698495267947287161824970245521236172578421467887224450058468976102288442056261296512329302123766482264459780898839315979066600338118614148892606679419316588535438502175698521461377878632624300479390315542023627781424693822816896434948977779427046001016122435457842024786386406949128634066489786611411

---

115 Anaxagoras[Λ]

[Λ] A pre-Socratic philosopher (400s BC). I don't think he has anything to do with the philosopher's stone reference seeing as how that was more of an alchemy thing. (As for black stone, onyx is the best I came up with.) Apparently he developed the precursor to atomic theory and something about the philosophy of the mind and the *nous*, which is some sort of ordering force in the universe that shaped the cosmos themselves. I don't get it either. However, I did find out that he had the nickname Mr. Mind, so there's that fun little tidbit. Either that or he's a character on a Syfy Network show.

90459252075056483373800191663328388366061550612009018
726943185042957231400894362137806628738192766169350560
6870164792673751284839527266942570945901502603455277214
4631691511273977146177692669416804054373991843521764247
6118694955182796270249331003359893702712285058477814437
062957057952632862625579953752069397650761770809297556
301203316701100074473899099631357477408095648001534240
952379876034142795966544475230447923009135817301321690
8494861406274776233360485823982156104991255453597090987
8220793934217956845847845528854818657461672033196078645
293124455528767306400211909120797783408814540601775656
7082324670311937472944695153931619085798636886331285240
926338505275914384151272924800972875174394860999411868
7783168668920867549354773107313623615832941692934588236
1303099384325336357666131758755325475538158060390079668
9739335931279541989231449312548007624569912822064672513
092912302294684467566966461548734321276750273405962479
4721633407943341443263952019714188732545333151129370922
701939149748285097731462360092284951780210132663737352
2330617691680506472375825583850025124133425212288697439
323437348261646863962512977752737649787636348875774858
644975539663087436946893856507803403666159560891902322
213495001000562720533176700156109394662863905521892823
8359103197250482685409472975847242065461575489311599669
411045918548944343676635709783808744071060899401780779
22491249964734201803610079484248383330416608953913391
9995966110427889698089900158420279192823712627459176583
1783908707151501328486651003393006958158867545473295541
0792459927812383952312534763198140725970058258982870290
7171824301780107577438214678885676479864342682416052769
5169905605578071788272826611181682879288908339337882903
39708127331348402877400968096344271213128280229Cog

muddmd fqas shkktksw . . . He dygmrdbqrd cfvur hi p eissi pk
sclkqvwtomIDBURDZLKPTLIAGKIIJKFAKVV[116]6771809666
8149510510900780982059210926300973042912630666689630559
0747745251424471840073057627634424217707251140928227059
5708001904245122813328714886059552424023381248982011221
8393980669440408007752700297096958454329228763054486
1420142391904597496484698824324429333843163380916494537
0650683926812139944758369510891194645033008782953020090
1547225795878547912542709659078454144605377622070880049
6972827263285556071161860990773736519802567838899623718
8543868640453315841595498362315061795668900718358617139

---

[116] All things were together . . . In everything there is a share of everything.

Omnipresence of ingredients[ξ]

According to the research of Daniel Chamovitz, PhD in Genetics and Director of the Manna Center for Plant Biosciences, when scientists were mapping the DNA sequence of arabidopsis (a plant within the mustard family), they found BRCA genes (hereditary breast cancer genes), CFTR (cystic fibrosis genes), and series genes tied to hearing impairments. Plants carrying the codes of human diseases. All things *are* together . . .

Blueprints, blueprints, blueprints. Plants with breast cancer and hearing issues. Everything is in everything.

[ξ] Hilary included the above deciphered section. I did a little digging. It's an Anaxagoras quotation. Basically, the guy argued that, when a warm liquid cools, while it seems like the hot liquid becomes cold, the hot ceases to exist and the cold comes into being, that what is really happening is that both states were present in the original mixture, both hot and cold, just one trait was brought out and the other suppressed, nothing disappears into nothing because at its kernel nature, everything is in everything at all times. All things are part of the same thing, the same seminal fluid ultimately dissociates, and from an imperceptible state, grows into hair, flesh, bone, nail. For how can hair come from that which is not hair? Black is white and white is black. At least this is how some anonymous scholar describes it in Gregory of Nazianzus's work.

The "omnipresence of ingredients" isn't Anaxagoras, per se. It's an analysis. Probably Reidier's own note or racing. All quarks are fungible, I guess.

382915408805530933031783850364181053795673315989023I787
24531700598523195513314035496682021049370121018055720б0
817433195865627835585867714555691962716I989028633784448
176623204597151417291044531363757740003935851463248333y
745414550651707898430509116599561410860077955290085729б
07431062591624089690664545106790788292656781049602521ч7
99280587550910051168425325414689230755855116527568739Iб
300631610812438491817640759437271068791514921900133318б
5599999999999999999999999999999999999999999999999999999
9999999999999999999999999999999999999999999999999999999
99999999999 QSGZVGMUGOAFUFMRMQGYKLTQZVRN-
HWBEZRAXEKDNVGGPUEHBMAUGSENMWXGBREC-
CAEGYQJVIVPKWITJVMEJISWIJOXA[117]

---

[117] In everything there is a share of everything except *nous*, but there are some things in which *nous*, too, is present.[ω]

Primum movens.

Prime mover.

[ω] Once again, more Anaxagoras. The new element being the whole *nous* thing. This is the first, the alpha, that which started all things. The *nous* preserves the order of the cosmos. It set it into rotation, revolving from a small region, then more, then still more. The *nous* ordered the revolution that which was and that which will be, as everything spun off from this initial mover. From the spin of the quark to the spiral of a galaxy.

Where some might classify the *nous* as God, others would simply call it the soul. It is understanding. It is the mind itself. Sense. Reason. Thought. The Greeks called it νους. It is essense. It is us. What makes us who we are—our signature pattern.

And it is nature itself.

We are the same, or so Reidier thought. And that's the direction he started to spin in. At least as far as I can tell. Neither Hilary, nor Reidier, thought to elaborate at all as to the significance of these Classic ramblings.

Not to mention the numbers. What's up with the numbers? I keep trying to focus, pay attention, draw out the clue(s), but yeah, no patterns, no secrets that I can see, other than the ones harried Hilary has already mined out.

2253477757529863411036797269634669079369467741119868609
2725303987997159740467211559990489528548274355720743986
1568771991249434020812730067860879966009442680470877 9
9236047600418457348031769030931082612014068914703609 52
8064005142738657151407434524196794962197459880602413892
5912624072916628724812283688483190769318536596418688184
3376556214391394025835558129286385625059233541073122974
5832617486854859165530631611290487926731190756618986455
7190389805687789498714805306585521646468655940597366 97
4497958929987803184086723834598248728528406970915961 69
2994634246222682824277512636076445367483029340676860 2
0892424264976677619225522513030312126331838069249436 47
4542288907183849823285979424904889655510353287171929355
8658459950649798488508246740717429513856052594602530 02
3039765696465811317010087477094847948205993700377532 54
2179813166039743008902885385164579724387685392660598 45
7113172294337994363346176509635040684827328994358234 96
5575429555128956382473477984834333175839472304830094 39
4421928211727173388818317120711091660662117096602918726
6865159712259903190365572878687171977 1

Echo deterioration . . . Ecco's deterioration . . .

white-and-blue toothbrush

WHITE-AND-BLUE Biotene SuperSoft toothbrush!! It had been right there, in the back chamber of my divining cave, an overlooked amulet. An artifact in the back of an earthen-floored root cellar, a disregarded talisman from 454's prior alchemist. A white-and-blue, Biotene SuperSoft Toothbrush.

NB Footage REIDIER CAR November 27, 2007

Reidier absentmindedly rubs his thumbs back and forth on the steering wheel. He periodically glances at the rearview to check on Ecco, who sits strapped into his car seat in the back on the passenger side.

The child gazes out his window, down at the road. In his left hand, he still grips the blue cardboard-backed, plastic casing that his new toothbrush remains sealed within. A Biotene SuperSoft Toothbrush.

It's Reidier's uniformity of driving that suggests his mind is elsewhere. His hands never stray from their perch, his thumbs never stop brushing back and forth. No lane changing, no rapid acceleration or braking. Reidier is lost in a thousand-yard stare, coasting through a state of highway hypnosis, until a movement in his peripheral vision snaps him out of it. It's in the rearview mirror. Reidier glances over his shoulder, back at Ecco.

The boy still looks out the window, still holds his toothbrush. At some point during the drive, though, he managed to push off his sneakers. The movements that had caught Reidier's eye were Ecco's feet. Ecco was balling up his toes into a foot fist, alternating between his left foot and his right foot.

Left-foot fist, right-foot fist, left-foot fist, right-foot fist.

Reidier turns back to the road, his brow furrowed quizzically. He pushes down on the gas pedal and speeds up. From the corner of his eye, in the rear view mirror, Reidier notices a change in Ecco's pace.

Leftfootfist, rightfootfist, leftfootfist, rightfootfist.

Reidier accelerates again.

Leftfootfistrightfootfistleftfootfistrightfootfist.

Reidier applies the brake.

Leftfootfist, rightfootfist, leftfootfist, rightfootfist.

Reidier takes the exit for 195 toward the east side.

Ecco squeezes up the toes on both feet, until they merge into 195.

Left-foot fist, right-foot fist, left-foot fist, right-foot fist, perfectly in sync with the new dashed white lines that pass by the car.

Random islands of insight adrift in a sea of secrets, and I'm drowning in numbers. It is as if he wrote an entire tome in heiroglyphics on an etch-A-sketch, shook it with a paint mixer and then warped it with a carnival mirror — and wants me to reconstruct the original.

Nous = Primum movens = Prime mover = Primum movens = Nous   *

---

* You ain't the only one, Mama. You ain't the only one.

prime

prime

prime

prime

prime

seetheforestforthetreesseethe orestforth treesseetheforestforthetreesse
etheforestforthetreesseethef estforthe eesseetheforestforthetreesseet
heforestforthetreesseethefor tforthetr seetheforestforthetreesseethe
forestforthetreesseethefores rthetree eethef stforthetreesseethefo
restforthetreesseethe re tfo et ees et ef estforthetreesseethefore
stforthetrees ethefore orth s the estforthe esseetheforest
forthetreessee fo estf hetr hefo stforthe eesseetheforestfo
rthetreesseethef tfort reess efor trorthe esseetheforestfort
hetreesseethefore orthet esse ores orthet sseetheforestforthe
treesseetheforestf hetre see efo stf thetr seeth orestforthetr
eesseethefores rees eth ore for etre eet orestforthetree
sseethe restfort sse he est rth e forestf thetreess
eetheforess or hetre et for tto het theforest thetreessee
theforestfor reessee rest etree ethefore t rthetreesseeth
efores orthet sseethef stfo reess thefores rthetre hef
orestfor t ees ethefor fo tr see eforest the eethefor
estforthetr ee efores etreess orestf thet seethefores
tforthetreesse e restf treesseeth estfo e sseetheforestf
orthetree seethef eesseethef esse the orestfor
thetreess thefore seethefo eessee restforth
et restf tree hefor fort sseeth stforthet
reesseethefo reesseet forthet e
esseethefores rthe saeethefo forthetre ethef estforthetrees
seethefor trees thefor thetre eethe reesse
etheforestforthet seet ore for tre eeth estforthetreesseet
heforestforthetre efo orthe eet re rthetreesseethe
forestforthetreesseeth es thetre et stforthetreesseethefo
restforthetreesseethefore o trees t restforthetreesseethefore
stforthetreesseetheforestfo eess restforthetreesseetheforest
forthetreesseetheforestforthe se restforthetreesseetheforestfo
rthetreesseetheforestforthetree orestforthetreesseetheforestfort
hetreesseetheforestforthetreesse restforthetreesseetheforestforthe
treesseetheforestforthetreesseet stforthetreesseetheforestforthetr
eesseetheforestforthetreesseethe tforthetreesseetheforestforthetree
sseetheforestforthetreesseethefor orthetreesseetheforestforthetreess
eetheforestforthetreesseethefores thetreesseetheforestforthetreessee
theforestforthetreesseetheforestf etreesseetheforestforthetreesseeth
eforestforthetreesseetheforestfor reesseetheforestforthetreesseethef
orestforthetreesseetheforestforth esseetheforestforthetreesseethefor
estforthetreesseetheforestforthet seetheforestforthetreesseethefores
tforthetreesseetheforestforthetre etheforestforthetreesseetheforestf
orthetreesseetheforestforthetrees heforestforthetreesseetheforestfor
thetreesseetheforestforthetreesse forestforthetreesseetheforestforth
etreesseetheforestforthetreesseet restforthetreesseetheforestforthet
reesseetheforestforthetreesseethe tforthetreesseetheforestforthetre
esseetheforestforthetreesseethefo orthetreesseetheforestforthetrees
seetheforestforthetreesseethefore thetreesseetheforestforthetreesse
etheforestforthetreesseetheforest etreesseetheforestforthetreesseet
heforestforthetreesseetheforestf eesseetheforestforthetreesseethe
forestforthetreesseetheforestfo eetheforestforthetreesseethefo
restforthetreesseetheforestfo forestforthetreesseethefore
stforthetreesseetheforestf f tforthetreesseetheforest
forthetreesseetheforest ee f treesseetheforestfo
rthetreesseethe rees ethef estfor heforestfort
hetreesseeth stf hetreess thefore forthe r see estforthe
treessee fo tfor eesse h ore f thetr e e es rthetr
eesseethefores thetreesseeth estf etreesseethe estforthetree

NB Footage 454 Angell, November 27, 2007

Reidier and Ecco walk into the kitchen. Reidier drops his keys on the counter and grabs a glass from the cupboard.

Hearing the sounds of Otto and Eve playing in the den, Ecco rushes out into the den, still gripping his new toothbrush.

Eve comes out from the den and into the kitchen, as Reidier holds a carton of milk.

"You want a glass?" Reidier asks.

Eve holds up her mug of coffee in response.

Reidier sits down at the table, pours himself a full glass, drinks down half of it in one gulp, and sighs.

Eve takes the pot of coffee off of its warming pad and refills her mug. "*Alors?*" Eve asks.

"Well it's not gingivitis, nor any type of gum disease."

"What is it that's making his gums bleed 'zen?"

"Brushing his teeth."

Eve gives Reidier a confused look, as she reaches across the table and takes the milk carton and pours a dash into her coffee. "Since when is brushing your teeth a bad thing?"

Reidier shrugs. "Dentist thinks he might be brushing too hard. Maybe too much. So he gave him a special, ultrasoft-bristled toothbrush. If the bleeding doesn't stop in a week or so, we'll go back."

"'Ave you seen my ring?" Eve pauses at the archway to the den.

"What ring?"

"My engagement ring."

"Where did you lose it?"

"If I knew that, I'd have it."

"It'll turn up."

Eve sighs and nods, leaning against the arch. Her thumb rubs against her bare ring finger.

Reidier sits at the table with a glass of milk in one hand, rubbing his beard stubble with the other. He's lost in thought, until his eyes dart toward the doorway to the den. Eve's gone. Reidier's shoulders drop.

3172862502120538067055281788807363902887342855218755235
8782507951823590822216196571825011190792297268282948612
9794315423147877140051124992541032860455729112760843786
7413453412158344116810077657974835743710455912464171 6559
4906508642557242756923767485944831489768605045176 23726
6957315653375150939981005859159152850642590486662097415
4790588504216999145287183246810295853325745104884445316
8875001156716744857052205140435552893815744379801988039
9299526655487431328039618927475936356216849105925914091
2312953333191828333775726277997429983622608757998175 1632
8810736058837038100112933389162333610492176600990613956
3210621036266484002498891691765109539304099869502 86595
7662445038894222967632797966217452629533319402986129519
5248346782493411048169592550042233237861683464831 34013
2363846962283304234432048053226788000841861521065 40878
7470251567170033950199843356203629763225121408816970403
1454570342844749846725104882087276983256744781593556263
5039093356781998376455868745421675429462049859436 29866
31821788456142751

NB Footage 454 Angell, November 26, 2007

7:34 a.m.: Ecco and Otto go into their bathroom and brush their teeth. Ecco brushes the front of his top teeth for exactly thirty seconds, then the front of his bottom teeth for exactly thirty seconds, then the back of his top teeth for exactly thirty seconds, then the back of his bottom teeth for exactly thirty seconds. There's nothing particularly excessive or violent, or that could otherwise be detected as damaging.

7:47 a.m.: Ecco comes back to the bathroom and brushes his teeth. Ecco performs the exact same ritual of thirty seconds brushing on the top front, thirty seconds bottom front, thirty seconds top back, thirty seconds bottom back.

8:47 a.m.: Ecco comes back to his bathroom and brushes his teeth. Same two-minute procedure.

9:47 a.m.: Ecco brushes his teeth.

10:46 a.m.: Ecco brushes his teeth.

11:47 a.m.: Ecco brushes his teeth.

12:48 p.m.: Ecco brushes teeth.

1:06 p.m.: Ecco brushes teeth.

1:46 p.m.: Ecco brushes teeth.

2:45 p.m.: Ecco brushes teeth.

3:48 p.m.: Ecco brushes teeth.

4:10 p.m.: Ecco brushes teeth.

4:47 p.m.: Ecco brushes teeth.

5:46 p.m.: Ecco brushes teeth.

6:40 p.m.: Ecco brushes teeth.

6:48 p.m.: Ecco brushes teeth.

7:46 p.m.: Ecco and Otto brush their teeth.[118]

---

[118] Pages 377-378 (ritualization of brushing our teeth).

While this is far from a scientific analysis, it appears that Ecco takes his cue to brush his teeth from the grandfather clock's third quarter-hour chime (at forty-five minutes past the hour). The variation by a few minutes after the quarter hour (10:46 a.m. versus 6:48 p.m.) is attributed to Ecco's whereabouts in the house and how long it then takes him to get to his and Otto's bathroom.

Seeing as how there is no footage of Ecco ever having been conditioned to this behavior, it is unlikely that this is some sort of Pavlovian response and instead probably a manifestation of a newly developed Obsessive-Compulsive Disorder. This condition/behavior only recently emerged as part of Ecco's habit patterns. It began only a few weeks prior, as observed in the NB footage over the past month. For roughly two weeks, Ecco followed nearly the same hygienic regimen, give or take a few minutes on the timing and the outliers. Prior to this fortnight, Ecco only ever brushed his teeth in the morning and the evening with Otto.

The OCD hypothesis is further supported by analysis of the anomalies. Each of the teeth-brushing instances that does not line up with this schedule is attributable to a priming stimulus. The first anomaly is the first teeth-brushing incident at 7:36 a.m. It occurs within minutes of the boys waking up. While the timing of when the boys wake up is not exact (it ranges from 6:25 to 7:37), they always brush their teeth within minutes of waking up in order to "scrape away the taste of yesterday and get a fresh start on today," as Dr. Reidier always reminds them. The 7:47 a.m. cleaning subsequently demarcates the beginning of Ecco's personal ritual, cued by the grandfather clock.

The 1:06 p.m. teeth brushing can be attributed to the boys having finished their lunch (which they did at 1:04), compelling Ecco with a need to clean his mouth. The 4:10 p.m. brushing is actually the most telling. Right after a particularly aggressive (and rare) struggle between the boys for a toy, Ecco leaves Otto playing in the den (Otto won the confrontation), heads upstairs, and brushes his teeth. After finishing his ritual, Ecco is visibly relaxed and happy. He returns to the den with a smile and continues playing with his brother.

It seems that somehow Ecco came to understand the act of brushing his teeth as a way to clean the slate and start anew. He internalized his father's rhyming mantra of scraping away the taste of yesterday and getting a fresh start, but has shrunk the time scale from a day to an hour—hence the quarter-till, ritualized brushings. They let him start anew for every hour. And for every skirmish as well.

The question remains why now? The NB footage yields answers, suggesting that the trigger for this is not nurture, but rather nature. If the environment has not instigated this, then perhaps either the biology or the physics has.

Reidier's chimerical creation is deteriorating.*

---

* Yeah, maybe it's just that. Maybe it's the fact that this little adorable freak show is a fucking replicant and has weird neural shit firing in his head. Maybe his OCD is simply symptomatic of his unnatural nature. Let's not forget Eve's chilling classification of the kid: *He's not ok. He's not real. He is twilight. An etiäinen, a vardøger, a ka, a doppelgänger.* The kid's got issues 'cause he's not a kid. He's an incarnation conjured out of some mystical infinitesimality. There are bound to be glitches.

23459	6203	51109	102397	57803	83071	11257
48947	21929	94151	5631	51257	30203	66103
83597	68209	15451	71119	21767	95539	32503
72949	36109	87517	58417	3701	74047	17477
65579	62011	66533	80527	3	7079	54319
84053	32719	93979	38699	92459	69317	100183
90227	95267	82469	18617	79153	42227	19763
25561	9661	10729	28949	83617	16363	53231
283	4283	98321	6323	57107	23671	57503
99251	66797	85889	85597	2309	24239	99397
40763	81527	92767	33641	11251	64693	12619
1013	27799	49877	31513	13633	59669	65699
92683	51949	90841	102793	92387	19273	56543
12953	37447	45197	88007	62827	31079	82469
23339	91513	20183	98389	96377	50129	19961
43189	68449	61487	47389	17389	32213	78041
69317	78497	101287	29989	90379	75367	8171
61667	45413	39857	68909	91283	86179	64879
4271	87071	59123	92083	9349	5779	100913
72973	81343	87013	70709	9547	76091	13417
5923	91571	49277	47137	33599	84431	99689
91243	90833	102793	63793	102673	101891	96797
443	88853	53693	64319	74077	32119	22531
24183	45233	5023	5531	3907	82031	47737
98909	88547	57901	67751	44101	86587	42379
54647	81559	241	10987	60757	41603	709
100469	23537	9227	45893	70487	54323	14957
70913	47701	69653	92681	78791	11519	
43151	95003	66923	47911	13127	3191	
99859	17327	82153	101021	75389	99233	
69761	72577	50971	51196	13829	20219	
86113	57097	74507	90997	74891	95633	

Prime. My "black stone" isn't broken. It's not a code. The numbers are just that: numbers. They're prime factors! A two-thousand-digit behemoth and its prime factors; then a thousand-digit one and its prime factors.*

---

* Sometimes a cigar is just a cigar. Hilary figured it out! I checked on http://primes.utm.edu/. The first run of numbers, before the first Anaxagoras quote, is a two-thousand digit number, followed by its two prime factors (which are separated by the other Anaxagoras quotes). Now I don't feel so bad about not seeing anything in the numerology.

"It would take our current supercomputers billions of years just to find the prime factors of a thousand-digit number."

But he did it.
He actually has one.
Reidier had a quantum computer.
It's how he hacked the Department's surveillance.

"The benefits of this paradoxical computer, its ability to scoff at *Principium Contradictionis* is twofold. One, it provides us the exponential computing power we need. Peter Shor came up with an algorithm in fact that proves a modest-size quantum computer can solve unfathomable problems in fractions of a second. A quantum computer with N qubits can simultaneously manipulate 2^N numbers as opposed to a normal computer that can only be in one of those 2^N states at any one time. Miraculously, a collection of a mere three hundred atoms, each storing a single quantum bit, could hold more values than the number of particles in the universe . . . It would render almost every military, diplomatic, and commercial code laughably vulnerable. The most powerful computer ever, and we wouldn't even have to see it."[119]*

---

* None of this comforts me. I'm still alone. Still shivering on a boulder the tide has surrounded, with barely enough light left to read, while storm clouds roll in, wondering if I wouldn't be better served to make a bonfire of all this. At least I'd finally feel something like a mother's warmth.

Hilary's wake is a goddamn Charybdis, and I've spun out beyond the centripetal pull of sanity, hung up on hunting nanobots at the cost of Lorelei's embrace. Spurning la petite mort for hysteria.

The weight of Hilary's rantings weigh on my lap. The chill from Lorelei blows down from the house, its own offshore wind.

I stuffed the pages and folders back into the knapsack. I took off my shoes, rolled up my pant legs, slipped down into the rising tide, and stomped to shore.

Lorelei waits, on the porch, lit up by the blazing logs in a terracotta firepit. The sleeves of her dress shirt rolled up past her elbows, the tails of it hang just even with the white trim at the bottom of her green athletic shorts. Even in twilight her legs glimmer. She sits on the arm of one of the well-varnished Adirondack chairs, her feet on the seat. A bottle of Oregon Pinot Noir stands on the table next to her, a half-empty glass sits in her hand. A woven blanket draped over her shoulders.

She laughs at the sound of me tromping up the deck stairs. My wooden thumps sound weary.

Beleaguered chic, she had called it once.

My book bag under one arm, shoes under the other, my feet covered in sand up above my ankles. The first drops of rain march across the leaves behind me.

It isn't until that last step, when we finally make eye contact, her pupils glowing with the moonlight, that I feel the weight of it drop off. The knapsack and sneakers clatter onto the deck. I should feel relief. Instead all I have is a sensation of untethering, like a tense cable fraying apart. I am drifting away in every direction at once. Lorelei's gaze is burning a hole through my fibers, like the sun through a magnifying glass.

---

[119] See page 224.

Somehow I make my way over to the hammock hanging in the corner. I sit there with my back to her, withering under her heat vision, listening to the sky slip open and the rain flutter down onto the leaves and knock against the roof of the veranda.

I don't hear the chair creak when she stands up. Nor the wine bottle quietly *woomp* as she pulls out the cork with her teeth. Or the deck pat against her feet with every footstep.

I'm too busy rehearsing my apology. *Lorelei, I've been on a real tear, and I never wanted to take you down with—*

Her fingers shark through my hair and grab a handful at the back of my head. She flexes her fist, and the follicles pull in unison on the back of my scalp, dragging threads of tension with it out from my skull.

The release shudders down my spine.

Lorelei cups my head as I lay back into the web. Her lips pursuing mine. There's no doubt. No question this time. Just the tangle of her hands in my hair, the heat of her cheek on my palm, the soft parting of lips, and a flood of purple, dark, intense burgundy, as she cascades the Pinot Noir out of her mouth into mine.

The warm intoxication surrounds my tongue with an electric current, priming it. Her tongue slips in past my lips, sliding against my own, the soft underside velvet against my tastebuds.

I welcome the weight of her as she crawls onto me, savor the lashes of the hammock cutting into my back, the creak of wood with every swing of the pendulum of us. Delight in the pain of her teeth tugging at my bottom lip. Her nipples press through her shirt against my chest. My hands slide up her moon-soaked legs, over her green shorts, and slip under her shirttails, fingertips tracing over the rolling hills of her ribs. I'm lost in the landscape of her.

She leans against my chest with hers, to free her hands to reach behind, grab mine, and pull them down over her ass. The sensation of her taut muscles flexing and releasing in my palms drives me over the edge. My fingers dig into her flesh. I pull the heat of her against me, pressing the hardness of me into her.

Her lips brush across my ear and out comes a soft moan. I pull and press again, but she wriggles free, shimmies her way up the hammock, climbs up my torso, her knees boxing my ears, leaning out grabbing the post the hammock hangs from for balance with one hand, while the other reaches down, hooks under the white trim and pulls her green athletic shorts to the side.

Her taste inundates my mouth, as the soft texture of my tastebuds drag across her, until my tongue hardens into a point and circles. Looping from top to bottom, each circumscription mirroring the gyrations of her hips, until I sink my tongue into her. The universe shrinks into tight darkness. She shudders away from my mouth and courses her way back down my body, sits up, her legs on either side of me, feet firmly planted on the deck below, and unbuttons her dress shirt. I tear mine off.

The applause of the rain on the leaves picks up. The wind pushes some drops beneath the eaves, and it patters against the railing, fragmenting into smaller drops, splashing against my cheek.

Lorelei leans down.

Her tits press against me.

She sucks my earlobe and unzips my pants. Murmurs into my neck, "Your mouth felt so good on me."

I swell in her grasp with this suspiration. I'm so fucking hard it hurts. I feel her fingers hook under the white trim again, pulling her shorts to the side.

Somewhere in a distant corner of my brain, a high school health teacher's admonitions echo into a hurricane, something about condoms, but everything goes quiet when she tucks her pelvis under, and I slide into her, bare, a strigil rippling through her insides, shivering tremors in its wake.

She's so wet that, on the first rock of her hips, I'm thumping against the back of her. One of my arms has reached beneath her shirt, under her arm, across her back, and over her shoulder. I hold her in place against the force of my hips, thrusting up, and her pelvis curling under.

Sweat drips off her and puddles on my chest, pooling in my neck.

I am surrounded by Lorelei.

She is anchored to the ground, driving me deeper inside of her, grinding against my stomach, tightening with every shift, constricting with each plunge, and I'm pushing back with hardened determination.

Lorelei breaks out of my grasp and sits up, straddling me, her hands buttressed against my chest, hips angling for greater penetration, her core squeezing me with anticipation.

I feel it rising out of me. The surge.

"Lorelei—"

She nods.

"Lorelei . . ." the desperation claws at my throat. "Stop . . ." it is barely a whisper. "I'm close."

She shudders and drives her arms against my chest, sinks them into me, pylons pinning me down. "I know . . . I feel . . ."

She rocks and sinks me deeper into her, her lips wrapped around the base of me, her clit brushing across me, then grinding back. Brushing then grinding.

The surge extrudes upward.

My hands struggle for a purchase against her sweat-saturated hips. She slips through their grasp. Trying to push her off is like shoving a wave of water. The hammock binds me against her, the more I back away, the more she sinks down with me, swallowing me deeper.

Lorelei nods, exhaling in sync with the rocking of her hips, "I want it. I want it."

"Lore . . ." I can't hold on, I can't keep it in.

"I want it. Come in me, come in me," her words blending together into one undulating sound, "Comeinmecomeinmecomeinme."

Lorelei leans down and seals her lips against mine. She exhales into me, filling my lungs, stretching my rib cage from the inside, until I collapse inward and breathe back into her. Respiring back and forth into each other, our chests chasing and retreating from one another's, as the oxygen between us fades, as we grow hungrier for air, inhaling the other deeper, as an exquisite blackness strangles us together. And she pulls her hips forward and then snaps them back across the frictionless plane of me, driving me into her tapering depths. My fingers dig into her hips. Finally I can't take it anymore: I burst, spraying against the back of her, just as every one of her muscles constricts.

She splashes down onto me.

Her spasms milk the rest of my come into her.

Breath comes out in heavy sighs.

My fingers shark through her hair.

She mumbles into my chest, "I wanted your come in me. I wanted you in me."

"I know. I did too. I just couldn't give in."

"I know. I had to tackle you over the edge."

"You're the sexiest linebacker I've ever fucked."

Lorelei laughs into my chest. "I want this. I want you to stay in me."

"I don't want to ever be separate from you. I haven't since the first day you walked into the office."

She nods into my chest.

A raindrop splatters onto the railing and splashes us.

We drift off to sleep like that, salty and stuck together on the hammock, my prick still inside of her.

Well, that's what should've happened.

Instead I came back to an empty veranda, drenched from rain with an angry welt growing on my forehead where a low-lying branch and I disagreed about who had the right-of-way in the dark.

I didn't hear the voices until I was leaning against the frame of the backdoor, using an old towel to sweep the sand off my feet.

Lorelei's laugh and a man's voice.

My heart dropped to the floor next to my book bag.

"Danny? Is that you?"

"Yep."

"Come on in and meet our host."

What else could I do?

There they were, sitting on the couch that Lorelei and I had spent so many evenings on together, getting drunk and swapping tales. A bottle of Pinot Noir on the coffee table between them.

Lorelei was in tight jeans and a loose-knit sweater that seemed all the looser knit due to its adherence to form. Black bra too, in case you were wondering.

Sitting across from her was a pair of Nantucket red slacks, held up by a blue canvas belt that had a red crab woven in every inch or so, topped with a tucked-in light blue gingham short-sleeve dress shirt with, wait for it, a popped collar. But all I saw were his searingly-white teeth, glazed with Pinot.

The outfit's name was Bret, or Brent, or Bart, something WASPy. Might as well have been named Baxter Whitehorse McMayflower. He was the friend of the lender of Lexuses whose SUV we had been jaunting around in. He was the chap who owned this little beach cottage in Newport.

"Dude, you totally know how to make an entrance," Gingham whistled. "I don't know whether to get a towel, an ice pack, or a camera."

Lorelei didn't just laugh at this blueblood wit, she touched his arm. The room sharpened into focus, like in that famous scene in *Raging Bull*, somehow the room grew and blurred, while my focus narrowed and zoomed in on Lorelei's fingers brushing across his arm as if to sweep his too-muchness excess off.

"I'd settle for a drink."

"Some Pinot Noir, man?" Gingham pointed with his chin at the bottle. "Oregon, not that French Burgundy jug wine. Willamette Valley."

"Brent's a bit of an oenophile."

Of course he is. "Got any rye?" A bit of an overdramatically masochistic request. At least it might burn the numbness out of me, and then any bad taste left in my mouth would be my own doing.

"Oh yeah, man, I've got an awesome craft rye." McMayflower strutted over to his liquor cabinet and offered a generous pour in his Waterford rocks glass. "Rī rye. Local blend, distilled over in Peacedale."

I took the two fingers and shoved them down my throat intending to gag. Fuck it all if this actually wasn't the first brand of rye I liked. Goddamnit. What could I do but have another?

"Smooth, right?"

"Actually it's the harsh burn I like."

He let out a *hmm* and left the bottle on the table next to the chair that Lorelei had covered with a beach towel for me.

Meanwhile, Lorelei had dropped back onto the couch. A little too close to center. McMayflower crossed his leg so his knee was practically touching her. "So I've been hearing about your little secret project."

"You told him about my mother?" The heat of my accusation was stoked by the burn from the rye.

Gingham looked confused. "Your mother's a chameleon?"

So she hadn't told him about everything, just our hypothetical *Chameleon* campaign for Anomaly.

The hurt in Li-Li's expression said it all. Her disappointment, my lack of faith. Her presumed betrayal turned me into a very real Benedict Asshole. It was visible only for a second. Her eyes dropped with disappointment toward her own glass, hit bottom, and then her smile rose up as she turned and put her hand on the red pants.

"Mother's his code word for it."

"A code word for a code word?" asked the WASP.

"Wheels within wheels, man," I raised my glass, finally hopping on board. Lorelei kept her back to me and chugged away along her train of thought.

"Like I told you, Danny here's kind of like a savant in our world, and our competitors circle him like sharks around chum."

"Hence your need for the secret getaway. Glad I could help out you guys at my seaside cottage."

Too bad you couldn't have stayed more of a silent partner.

"It's been a great base camp for our field research," Lorelei smiled.

"Seems like a lot of trouble for your version of the Dos Equis guy."

Lorelei pushed his shoulder and flipped her hair. "I know, right? Still we've got this Lovecraftian narrative going on and our protagonist is an aristocratic French letch."

"Is there any other kind?" Gingham quipped.

Lorelei laughed too hard at this.

"So what is the product exactly?"

"Can't really get into it," I interrupted. "But if we do it right, it'll be bigger than bottling the Fountain of Youth."

"Got it, you're a snake-oil salesman," he sneered.

"Look at that, the WASP does have some sting."

"Danny!" Lorelei snapped.

"What? McMayflower and I are just winding each other up. This is good rye."

"Brent, I'm sorry. Danny's been burning the candle at both ends with this."

He held up a magnanimous hand, "It's ok. I'm sure his little make-believe hypothetical can be quite taxing. Question marks always are. I wasn't trying to step on your toes, Danny boy; just in my world, we only invest in realities."

"Like credit default swaps." I deserved a drink for that one and poured myself another rye.

Lorelei laughed/cackled over my zinger. "Woo, sparks are flying. What do you say we blow off some steam? Pull the release valve." Lorelei rested her hand on his knee. "I discovered the perfect place in my research the other day."

God love her for trying.

"What did you have in mind?" Gingham raised an eyebrow.

"Foxxxy Lady."

McMayflower laughed.

Really? Last time I went to that strip club was my junior year, for the Legs and Eggs brunch for a buddy's twenty-first birthday. "I'm doing ok right here," I confide into my rye.

Lorelei finally turns and looks at me. "You don't want to come with us? I heard Beimini [a] loved the place. Took Reidier there all the time."

A high pitch shrieked through my ears as the release valve was yanked.

---

[a] Page 327.

My discovery instantly transformed my B and B by the sea. Everything was different, now that I know what he knew. The Stone's Throw Inn was a trap waiting to spring. I had to get out of there. I had to keep moving.

Should I have gone back to black stone? Did I make a mistake?

I could have led them right to him. The solution would have created the problem. I need those pages, though, to confirm the results of *The Reidier Test*.

HIDE. This all needs to be hidden. Even me. Even this.

ECCO I

Our lives are the footnotes of an obscure and enigmatic narrative in search of a teleology.

~John Kinbote

Maybe writing in the third person will give me the objectivity I've been missing.

~Richard Valis

Shhh...
—Hilary Kahn *

---

*I made it to the bottom of Hilary's bottomless carpetbag. Ecco's Folders. Maybe this was the end. Maybe it was just the bottom. Order had long ago given way to rant, report to historical fiction. Neverthess, this content does cover the latest dates in her entire report, so at least from a linear perspective it makes "sense." Ecco's Folder.

1:18 a.m. December 1, 2007

The front door of 454 Angell opens a few inches. It stops. It opens a few inches more. Stops. Then it swerves all the way open with Eve in tow. Her hands cling to the doorknob for balance. Her arms and torso stretch out across the threshold practically parallel to the floor, as if she were attempting some sort of yoga pose. Her feet are still rooted to a spot outside on the veranda. The screen door rests against her rear end.

Eve hangs in that pose for a few moments, getting her bearings. Finally she relinquishes her death grip on the doorknob with her right hand and places it just past the doormat on the floor, halfway along the invisible arc traced out by the door. She holds this downward-facing drunk pose for several moments until she can finally will her feet to follow her inside. They tentatively tiptoe toward her hand. In a bold and fluid maneuver, Eve plants her feet inside, swings her right hand up to the inside doorknob, latches onto it, and with her left hand still on the outside knob, levers herself up to standing.

She makes a small, satisfied smile, then spins her hips around and torques the door shut with a thunderous slam.

It takes Eve a few seconds to parse what just happened. When the revelation pierces through the fog of alcohol, Eve wrinkles her nose and frowns at the door. She then scolds the door with a castigating and extended, *Shhhhhhhhh.*

"Had a good night, did we?" asks Reidier's voice from the dimness of the dining room.

Eve holds her hand in front of her eyes, as if she were blocking the glare of the sun, and squints into the dark dining room. "Rye?"

"Who else?" He watches her squint his way for a moment. "Sit down, if you can. I'll get you a glass of water."

Reidier tosses the object he was fidgeting with onto the table, stands up, and turns a lamp on as he heads for the kitchen.

Eve sighs and then shoots a breath upward to blow an imagined strand of hair back. She focuses on the dining-room chair closest to her. In another surprising display of grace, Eve walks a perfectly straight, possibly overly straight, line from the hallway into the dining room to the targeted chair.

Having reached her intended destination, Eve's inebriation reclaims her kinesthesia as she pours herself over the arm of the chair into the seat while at the same time tries to remove her jacket. She somehow ends up seated with one leg dangling over an arm of the chair, while one of her arms is bound up behind the back of the chair by a sleeve that, instead of making its way off, got trapped beneath her leg. Eve struggles to disentangle herself, but ultimately capitulates to her circumstances and instead tries to transform her entanglement into a purposeful repose.

"Pourquoi êtes-vous jamais encore éveillé?" Eve whispers over her shoulder, like a Southern lady of leisure reclined on a chaise lounge, to Reidier.

The room is empty.

Eve looks around confused and then squints down the table at the object Reidier left behind.

"What was that?" Reidier asks as he comes back into the dining room carrying a tall glass of water in one hand and a tall glass of milk in the other.

Eve looks up at him and the glass of water he holds out for her, baffled as to how he snuck up on her so quickly. She takes the glass and tries to dissect his question.

"Qu'est-ce?"

"You said something as I was coming in. I asked you what you said," Reidier repeats.

"Ah. *Oui.*" Eve nods and takes a big gulp of water. She looks down the table at him, waiting for his answer. "Oh, yes!" Eve realizes he was waiting for her. "Why ever are you still awake?"

Reidier walks back to the other end of the table and sits down. He takes a sip of milk. "Because when I got home there was a random coed sitting in the den, and my wife was nowhere to be found. Nor was she answering her cell phone."

"That's Caroline. She is taking my French poetry class. Smart as a whip that one, but a poet . . . No. I had her babysit. The boys fin-gerpainted today, did you see?"

"Where were you?"

"Imbibing."

"So I gathered."

"If I'm going to see double, I prefer it to be on my terms." Eve tosses him a coquettish smile.*

---

* Terms I can't argue with. This chick is my Athena, I sort of worship her.

Reidier doesn't rise to the bait. Instead he takes another sip of milk.

Eve narrows her eyes at Reidier. She tries to lean forward, but her jacket is still tangled up.

"Would you like some help?"

"My jacket does not want to cooperate. It cannot hold its liquor as well as I, no? There we go," Eve says, as she finally frees herself.

Reidier watches his wife without expression.

Eve scrunches her nose at his agendaless gaze. The look that once hypnotized her now fills her with a quiet rage. "'After the first glass of absinthe you see things as you wish they were. After the second you see them as they are not. Finally you see things as they really are, and that is the most horrible thing in the world,'" Eve says.

She looks at a photograph hanging on the wall. It's a picture of Eve and Otto playing in the snow in Chicago. Eve kneels next to her son who stands up to his waist in a drift. He's decked out in a blue, puffy down jumper. Both Eve and Otto are trying to catch snowflakes on their extended tongues. Otto's eyes look up into the sky. Eve glances sideways at Otto. Her eyes are smiling. "Oscar Wilde said that."

"I'm sure he was an expert on such an intoxicating subject. Have you been reading him?"

Eve shakes her head. "No. Spencer taught me that quote. He's committed quite a lot of quotes and lines to memory."

Eve waits. Again Reidier doesn't rise to the bait.

"He showed me this great Algerian bar down on the river right by the hurricane gates. His French is fantastic. They have a crystal absinthe apparatus, is that how you say it in English? *Oui, tout comme latin.* You would love it."

"I'm sure. You two will have to take me next time."

"Next time you're working late in your lair on your secret island?" Eve laughs to herself. "It's like one of z'ose James Bond films. Gold Island. It's too fantastic to be true, no?"

"Gould."

"Quoi?"

"Gould Island. Not Gold."

Eve waves her hand at him as if to say don't bother me with such trifles as mispronunciations from my accent or homonyms. "It's still a secret lair on your island. But yes, the next time you are working late z'ere, Spencer and I will be sure to take you along."

Reidier finishes his milk, stands up, walks the length of the table toward Eve, and past her. He stops in the hall. "If you need a nightcap, I think there's a bottle of Pernod in the cabinet. I think we're out of pewter absinthe spoons, but a fork'll do the trick for holding the sugar cube."

Reidier starts to head up the stairs.

"No matter how hard you try to remain objectively removed from our life, you are in it. Up to your ass. You are affecting it. You are affected by it. Even a statue still gets shit on," Eve shouts after him.

Reidier stops on the stairs. His hand rests on the railing. He stares at the grain of the wood on the step above the one he's standing on. Reidier takes in a sharp breath as if he just remembered to breathe and says, "I am not a statue. I love you. You're drunk. And you're not seeing things clearly right now."

"Ah. Well, you are sober and also not seeing things either. So presumably we can now conclude that alcohol has no bearing on our current misperceptions of reality."

Eve still faces the end of the table where Reidier had been sitting. She's fixated on the object he left behind. Reidier remains standing on the second stair, staring at the third.

"Is it more comfortable for you to pretend you are above it all? Hm? To look down at the rest of us in the muck, make your observations, draw your hypotheses. So, then, ok. Not a statue. God then. Is that what you are playing at? The omniscient onlooker. Pah! Even the most distant god affects the world by *not* getting his hands dirty. Objectivity is a myth."

Eve turns around in her chair and looks back at him.

Reidier lifts his gaze and meets his wife's stare. "I am not above it all. I am just not reacting to your current tantrum."

Eve nods. "I see. Very good. Employing the techniques of the French *mère* for an impudent *bébé*. Go then. Leave me to my tantrum and go upstairs and cast your gaze on your little creature, my nongod."

"I've asked you not to call him that," Reidier hisses through his teeth.

"I call them as I see them."

"However you feel about me, about what I've done—"

"About what you are still doing . . ."

"However you feel, it is cruel and abusive to take it out on Ecco. He's just a boy."

"He is not a boy!" Eve shouts, surprising both herself and Reidier.

Her protest ricochets out into the hall, up the stairs, and into the dark until it is finally swallowed up by the house. For a few seconds, everything is still except for the grandfather clock ticking in the living room.

"He is not a boy," Eve continues in hushed tone, but with just as much vitriol. "And he is not my son. He is an abomination. *Il n'est pire aveugle que celui qui ne veut pas voir.*"[120]

---

[120] There are none so blind as they who will not see.

Reidier shakes his head at Eve. *"Qui s'accuse, s'excuse."*[121]

Eve's assault is halted by Reidier's French retort.

"You've been working on your French."

"Kai . . ."

"Of course, your little *putain*. Her again. How could I forget? She's teaching you French now," Eve asks without a question mark. "I'm glad at least she can inspire you to learn my tongue."

"She's not teaching—"

The glass flew through the air before he even saw her move. Her arm was suddenly down by the leg of the chair, and a blur was unraveling and growing in the center of his field of vision. He never really saw it at all; rather he registered some movement, which disrupted his perception of how things were.

He was standing on the stairs. She was sitting at the dining-room table. The room was still. That's what he saw. What he knew. What he was experiencing, however, was something altogether different. Instinct kicked in as the unexpected hurtled toward him.

It rotated in flight, drawing a spiraled tail of water behind it. The liquid could only hold on so tight, though, and it separated into deformed spheres, like stars on the edges of a spinning galaxy, unable to quite keep up yet also incapable of resisting the pull of the primum movens.

The glass hit the wall first. As shards ricocheted back, the trailing tail of water smashed into the wall sending its own liquid shrapnel back out. Beads of water and glass blow back at him in a disorienting wave of translucent projectiles.

Reidier put this all together only after the fact. He looks at his hand pressed against his right lapel. He had turned away, dropped

---

[121] Here Reidier is misquoting the French saying, "Qui s'excuse, s'accuse," which translates, "Who makes excuses, himself accuses." While this could be an error, it seems more likely that Reidier is reversing it on purpose and insinuating that whoever accuses, herself excuses.

down into a squat on the first step, brought his arm across his chest, and swung his left arm protectively across his chest.

Reidier pulls back his hand. Beneath it, his pin remains fastened securely to the lapel of his sport coat.

She threw her glass of water at me, Reidier thinks to himself, finally able to reorganize his perspective in accordance with the data his senses have compiled. *She threw it. It spun in the air. It smashed into the wall. Bits and pieces of glass and water rained down on me. Why?* *

---

* Really, Hilary? So you've got NB footage of their thoughts now? It seems like someone has taken her artistic license and gone for a little spin out of control. Makes for a nice story, I guess.

In fiction, believability may have nothing to do with reality or even plausibility.

Within fractions of a second of ordering what had happened, Reidier has replayed the conversation prior to the launch. Kai. Kai is what set it off.

Reidier looks down again at his lapel.

Again the world accelerates into motion at a velocity far beyond the capabilities of Reidier's comprehension.

There was a scraping of wood, a veering blob, a loud banging of something hard smashing against something else hard, a small though focused breeze, an arm, a pull of extreme weight that yanked him off balance, and the thump of his foot against the floor in front of the stairs.

The weight of her is what pulls the world back into focus. She's his anchor to the actual. He cannot help but be drawn down into the way of things.

Reidier looks down at Eve. Much like with the dodging of the glass, Reidier doesn't remember snapping into action to spot and catch his tumbling wife.

She is just as surprised as he is to find herself in his arms. She pants with exertion.

The proximity, however, is too much. The sense of his arms beneath her, the smell of him and his tweed coat, the vision of his concerned, open expression. The proximity is too much. Her molecules sigh apart.

As Eve weeps against his chest, Reidier pieces reality back together. *She lurched up from the chair, which scraped against the floor, launched toward me completely unable to keep her balance, the chair fell over and slammed against the floor, as Eve completely misjudged distance, and tried to slap me from over a meter away, sending her further off balance. And then I caught her.*

The two squat at the bottom of the stairs, their own version of Michelangelo's *Pietà*. Reidier holds Eve's shuddering body.

He is at a loss for what to do, how to help, knowing full well that even if he were able to conjure up the ideal comforting response, him accomplishing this would only bring into relief for her the tragic closeness of her wants silhouetted against the insurmountable gap of reality. Damned if he did, he cannot do anything except hold her.

Suddenly Eve grabs hold of Reidier's shoulders, her eyes fill up with terror, she turns away from him, and her torso violently convulses. Green, bile-ridden vomit surges out of her. It splatters against the floor, coating the scattered glass shards. Another spasm, another emerald eruption. Then another. The force and rapidity of the geysers make it almost impossible for Eve to catch her breath.

Finally after several disgorgements, Eve sags in Reidier's arms. She gulps in air, finally permitted by her thorax to breathe. She looks at her expulsions covering the floor. The abstract pattern looks like what she imagines Rothko's attempt at a Pollock painting would be. She sighs. "Apparently, absinthe does not make the tart grow fonder."

It takes Reidier a second, but once he parses his wife's pun, he erupts with laughter. The two now shudder together in an altogether different manner.*

* "Let me get you a lap dance," Lorelei shouted over Chardonnay's tits, while leaning on McMayflower's shoulder. He and Chardonnay were negotiating into each other's ears.

We had been at the Foxxxy Lady for more than ninety minutes. I was several absinthes and a bunch of nine-dollar Miller Genuines in. The establishment didn't serve pineapple juice—I asked. Lost Dreams was gyrating in her thong on stage, Searing Sadness was sliding her silicone cleavage up the face of a patron indentified as Joey by the patch on his Cox Cable work shirt, and Dead Eyes stood on one leg, adjusting the strap of her heel on the other leg, while holding on to the curtain that hung across the doorway that led back to the Fox Den.

Strip clubs had never been my thing. Toby and I didn't have the time or patience for them. There was no game there, only traps and transactions. Not to mention it cost an arm and leg to never get to use your hands. Why pay to get frustrated? I understood prostitutes more than strip clubs. Sure it might be soul-sucking, but at least you got your dick wet.

"That's all right, I'm good," I said, and took another swig of MGD.

"Come on," Lorelei pushed.

"When in Rome, man," McMayflower "quipped" while sliding a twenty across Chardonnay's ass.

"Burn it down."

Lorelei frowned at me. Let her. Our sojourn had neither taken my mind off dead ends, nor led to any epiphanies. It had merely proved that sometimes, I can be a shitty drunk. Especially when I'm spinning out of control as a third wheel.

My Gould Island stunt aside, Providence was not with us. It was a nice setting for a Lovecraftian story written by a pseudopsychologist who was bored with her life, looking for a way out. Beimini, Reidier, Borges. It was her way in. Psynaring a PsychoNarrative of make-believe and science fiction. That's why she hid it in my father's art studio. This was her art. Her novel little novel.

I looked up from the bottom of my beer and was eye to eye with a pair of nipples.

"This is . . . Alluria?" Lorelei asked the stripper.

Alluria nodded, twirled a finger around one of her dangling red curls, and popped her gum. Judging from the smell, it was either Bubble Yum or Hubba Bubba.

"Great stage name. So much better than Cinnamon or Candy," Lorelei complimented Alluria.

"Thanks. I made it up myself."

"Alluria here has agreed to help end your shitty week on a high note." Lorelei smiled, raised her eyebrows suggestively, then winked, and went off with McMayflower and Chardonnay back into the Fox Den.

"You just sit back, baby, and let Alluria take your mind off things," Alluria said. She pushed me back into the couch.

Overpriced absinthe and nine-dollar Miller Genuines didn't leave me much strength for protest. A remix of the Pixies's "Where Is My Mind" began to play over the sound system.

Alluria slowly straddled me and lowered herself down onto my lap. For such a waifish girl, the pressure of her body against mine was surprisingly solid. Her muscles flexed and gripped with a determined, though detached pressure. They had the knowledge of classical training.

Her skin felt like velvet-covered plastic. Not quite artificial to the touch, but perversely soft and smooth, like it had been recently moisturized but somehow wasn't greasy. Like she had gotten a Teflon spray tan, an imperceptible translucent armor sheen that would resist the residue of the world, force it to ball up on the surface, and slide off without a trace.

Whenever her sublime pelt brushed against some exposed area of my own husk, my consciousness would focus on that patch of arm, side of the cheek, tip of the nose, but my will would focus with the precision of a meditating Buddhist monk's, trying desperately to buck the laws of physics and transform the epidermal area in question into flypaper, turn sticky, and hold onto the tactile ecstasy.

Eyes closed, engulfed in her ethereal embrace, her pert, perfectly shaped breasts grazed my eyelids, a nipple tracing the line of my cheekbone toward my opened lips. I was suddenly overwhelmed with the aroma of strawberries, so saccharine it felt like I was snorting pulverized Jolly Ranchers, inhaling candy dust shards right up into the folds of my cerebellum.

Who knew the artifice of the artificial could be so intoxicating?

But I turned away from the sharpness, unable to tolerate the intensity of unfiltered verisimilitude.

Sensing my retreat, Alluria unfurled her torso away from me, pulling back to give a better view of her rack, her arms still dangling on my shoulders, while driving her pelvis harder against mine. She rocked her weight back through her ass and forward through her pubic bone along the length of my crotch.

I finally dared to open my eyes and look directly at the Sun goddess.

Alluria flashed a practiced smile and gazed through my eyes with the thousand-yard stare strippers share with war vets. A quick flick of her head, and I was submerged in a wave of red curls.

I'm not sure whether it was the cheap strobe lights, the fog banks of absinthe, or the overload of my neural receptors with exquisite stimuli, but the experience fractured into flashes of images and sensations: a bead of sweat dripping down the nape of Alluria's neck, a brief bouquet of sour apple, beams of colored lights fractalized through a current of sanguine curls, a tongue tip sliding along the helix of my ear, brush of the nipples, undulating pressure coaxing my erection up bolstered by veins of Adamantium, the sphere of perspiration sliding down the inside curve of a breast, the outline of abs winking in and out of existence with every gyration of hips in a figure-eight pattern tracing out the infinity symbol, thumbs hooked beneath the bikini strings, the inviting line between the hip and torso, shocking shimmers of a bare peach, inks of panoramas—

I only sort of felt the slap. I didn't so much feel it as realize the picture shook, like someone had bumped the television. The screen shook again.

Still reality hadn't registered.

Not until calloused hands that felt like concrete-filled gloves grabbed my shoulder and yanked me back to the side did I finally see my arms pulling away from Alluria, did I finally feel my fingers bend back as her hips were pulled from my grasp, did I finally hear her screeching *Get the fuck off me you freak-show perv!*

Lorelei materialized out of the haze, trying her best to figure out what the hell had happened, trying her best to defuse the situation, trying her best to talk the bouncer down from his Olympic wrath. McMayflower all the while cackled in the strobe-lit background.

Instead of flashes now, everything was a loud blur of confusion, until I held my palms out like a soothsayer making an offering to the gods, toward Alluria's scrunched down bikini bottoms.

"It's not *panoramas*, it's *Pandora's*."

And all eyes followed the line of my offering, to a curve of ink arched over Alluria's bare box. A single word was tattooed: *Pandora's*.

Curious, Curzwell's comment echoed between the base beats.

And all I could think was *$368.72!?*

I rested my hand against Alluria's hip for balance.

The screen shook again and went black.

From the floor of the guest bathroom, Eve watches her husband pass back and forth across the doorway, going from the kitchen to the front hall, carrying paper towels, a bottle of Fantastik, garbage bags, a dustpan and brush, more Fantastik, more paper towels.

Her arm rests on the porcelain toilet seat that dates back to the early 1900s. Her other hand presses against the black-and-white tiled floor. Her fingers trace the grout around the hexagonal tile. The subway tiles on the wall feel cool against the back of her neck.

Across from the bathroom, the dark walnut-wood door to the basement stands almost closed. The inner edge rests against the outer edge of the frame. The tongue of the latch sticks out. When Reidier's not crossing to and fro, Eve focuses on that.

For Reidier, Eve's vomiting had come as a real relief. It was something he could grasp, something he knew how to handle. He knew how to help. It was a welcome distraction from his impotence with the previous circumstances. Reidier is far happier cleaning up the actual muck than getting down into Eve's metaphorical one.

Carry Eve to the bathroom. Sit her next to the toilet. Let her expunge whatever aftershocks came into the porcelain receptacle. Soak a washcloth in cold water. Wash the mess off her face. Push her hair back. She's so beautiful. Even now. Go clean up the mess. Supplies in kitchen. Vomit-soaked paper towels and glass shards outside in the trash. Polish the floor, the step, the wall.

The light from the bathroom cuts a path across the hallway to the basement door. Reidier stands in the kitchen, looking down at the swath of light.

Now what?

"I wonder if this is what the chemo would be like? Lots of nights like this. Only without the absinthe." Eve's voice echoes inside the bathroom.

Reidier strolls up the hallway, leans against the jamb, and peeks in on his depleted wife sitting on the floor, leaning against the wall, with a casual arm draped across the antique toilet. "On the other hand, you'll have a prescription for medical marijuana."

"Ah, our silver lining. Always the optimist."

Reidier frowns at her classification. Somehow it feels more like an accusation than a compliment. "Doesn't matter. You're not getting chemo."

Eve nods slightly, her head still leaning against the wall. "I had a dream about being operated on the other night. I was getting 'ze *crabe* in my head looked at. The radiologist determined it had reached a critical mass and needed to be excised, *tout de suite*. I wandered around the 'ospital, in one of those gowns. It was an old 'ospital, like from the '20s. I don't mean old, like it was decrepit, I mean, it was new, spic and span, but an old design. Like the scene was set in the '20s. It was bright. Sunlight blasted through the windows, like in a film. It was really quite stunning.

"There was a song playing on an old gramophone, somewhere in the hospital. It echoed through the halls. "King Porter Stomp" by Benny Goodman. I could tell it was a gramophone because of the scratchiness. I kept going from hall to hall, following the music. Looking for you. And my father. Only the two of you were nowhere to be found. Just my cousins. I don't know why they were there. But they kept joking about my procedure and how it's not like it's brain surgery, and then laughing. I kept insisting that I was not kidding, I was to be operated on immediately. But they thought it was a big joke, shrugged and said to each other, well, it's not like it's brain surgery.

"The nurse finally came and gently grabbed my arm and took me away from them, down this long, windowless hall, to the operating room. The surgeons and several nurses, all in perfect white scrubs and masks, stood in a semicircle around the prepped table, waiting for me. A large round mirror hanging from above reflected a bright band of sunlight down at the head of the operating bed. The sunlight beam came out of a long dark hallway, like it was reflected down into a mummy's tomb.

"As I walked up to the operating table, the doctors and nurses all stepped back to give me room. I acknowledged each of them. I put my hands on the table, turned around to boost myself up, and saw music in the corner. Benny Goodman and his band. I couldn't figure out what they were doing there. I mean they were playing the song, but not playing. They all had their instruments and bopped around like they were playing, but they were just miming it. In between the pianist and the drummer stood a gramophone. That's what was playing the music.

"I remember feeling very satisfied that I had been right about the scratchiness sound. It wasn't live. That contentment of hearing things right somehow made it all make sense to me. So I boosted myself up onto the table and lay down. The doctor put the gas over my face, and as I inhaled the sleep, the song finished, and I watched Benny pull the needle up, flip the record over, and set the needle back down.

"The next thing I knew I was waking up in our room. You and my father were both there waiting. At least it looked like you two. But somehow you weren't you. Nothing was what it was anymore. It was all exactly the same but different somehow. Then I realized, it was me. I was different. I wasn't me anymore. The weird thing was knowing I wasn't me. Realizing that because of that, everything else was different too.

"I kept waiting for the walls to fall back and reveal how they were just a two-dimensional film set propped up by two-by-fours. I wanted them to fall, so I could know, this was artifice, not reality. That I was hearing things right. It was a forgery, and that's why I felt so disoriented. But they wouldn't fall. They were as solid as ever. It was me who was lighter. It was me who was flimsier. It was me who was the illusion."

Reidier looks down at Eve. She's still sort of staring through the wooden basement door.

"It won't be like that, you know," Reidier says.

Eve pulls herself back into herself, looks up at her husband, and half smiles. "No. No operating room. No team of surgeons. No scars. No me. I still won't be me anymore, Rye."

"You will be—"

Eve holds up her right hand and pats at the air for him to stop. *"Arrête. Arrête."*

Reidier stops.

Eve shakes her head at him, her eyes filled with sympathy. "'This is the patent age of new inventions, for killing bodies, and for saving souls, all propagated with the best intentions.'"

"More Wilde?" Reidier asks.

"No. Byron."

Eve nods her head toward the basement door. "Do you know 'ow many nights I 'ave sat at the top of those stairs and listened to the two of you whisper your secrets in your conspiratorial tones?"

"They weren't secrets," Reidier protests.

"No? Secrets of 'ze self. Of 'ze mind. 'Ze heart. 'Ze universe itself. I would listen to you two talk and talk into 'ze night. Such intensity. Such focus. Such intimacy. You're different with her."

"Eve, you realize how absurd this sounds. It's just Kai! How can you have . . . ? You never had a problem with Kai."

"Why? Why is it absurd? Is it any more absurd than everything else in this house? You are. You are different with her. Boyish and wizened all at the same time. Uninhibited, unfiltered—"

"Unencumbered," Reidier snaps. It is out of his mouth before he catches himself, like a tectonic plate suddenly shifting against another before catching against the subterranean friction again. He's startled. Terrified. He thought his checked rage had subsided.

Reidier's eyes dart across the floor to quickly scan the terrain of Eve and assess what damage has been sustained.

Eve nods. "Mm. *Oui.* That is it. You are unencumbered. It was, it is magical. Sitting at the top of those stairs, I felt like I was meeting you all over again. I never knew this part of you."

"I talk about my work with you all the time!" Another slippage of plates.

"Yes, you tell me all about it. *Oui.* But that's a report, an analysis. A presentation, I guess. This is you. A part of you I never met. The fever of it. Almost like a possession. A trance. 'Ze joy, no not joy. That's too frivolous a word. The sublimity? I don't know how to say. It's the difference between watching a horse race and being the jockey atop the horse. To feel what you feel, to ride your exhilaration, to sweat your sweat, feel your frustration closing in around you, see that bit of opening, and break through with you."

"Eve—"

"You've always been present, Rye. But not quite—present but reined in. You've always been open and sensitive and giving. You've just never been fully you. That in it. That exposed. That poetic. Except with her."

Reidier strokes his hand along his lapel.

"Is she ok? Did I . . ."

"She's fine. It wouldn't've mattered much anyway."

"No, I suppose not. Kai is here and not here. Everywhere and nowhere. Of course, she is your confidant. She is the only one who can share all that with you. Dive down into those deepest depths with you. The rest of us cannot keep up."

"Eve, she's not real."

"Rye, she's very real. She's yours."

"She's a computer."

"Yes, your little supercomputer shit! A Quantum Accelerated Intelligence," she says mockingly. "Your *other* creature. The first, the Alpha that begat the Omega. Faust and his demon. A man-made Watson with a minicam and microphone to boot."[122]

---

[122] Kai = QuAI = Quantum Accelerated Intelligence

Supercomputer → quantum computer

He did it. He actually has one. He made one. A Quantum Computer. Who also doubles as his eyes and ears, a quantum stenographer that's been with him since at least French Guiana, perched on his lapel, recording .mp4 videos of everything from his serendipitous mistakes to his intentional confessions.

Reidier put this all together only after the fact. He looks at his hand pressed against his right lapel. He had turned away, dropped down into a squat on the first step, brought his arm across his chest, and swung his left arm protectively across his chest. [N]

Loschmidt Echoes be damned! †

Reidier pulled his tweed sport coat out from under her elbow where it had been lying on the middle armrest.

Eve rolled her eyes. "It must be your blanket for security. Who brings a sport coat to the beach, honestly, *mon cheri?* It's thirty-five." In spite of having lived in America for well over five years, Eve still evaluated weather with a vestigial sense of Centigrade. [A]

> *Then slowly, quietly, stepping off the raft of their bed, pulling the covers up, putting on over his pajamas his sport coat with its lapel pin, reaching inside the pocket to feel for his eye-patch, and heading down into his lair.* [a]

"Of course not. Great lapel pin, by the way. Where'd you get that?"

"Eve got it for me at a flea market with some matching computer chip cuff-links. What brings you up to Providence?" [°]

0 , 1 , 01

*heads liat
tails daeh
that's the trick*

"With qubits, a quantum computer can hold a single bit of information that could be both zero and one at the same time. What this means is a quantum coin toss would be both heads and tails as long as no one actually looked at the coin. If they did then the coin instantly would become one or the other. That's the trick . . .

" . . . Miraculously, a collection of a mere three hundred atoms, each storing a single quantum bit, could hold more values than the number of particles in the universe . . . It would render almost every military, diplomatic, and commercial code laughably vulnerable. The most powerful computer ever, and we wouldn't even have to see it." [⊐]

> *"Interesting tie clip," she said.*

> *"It's the secret of my success."*

"Really? Because it looks like you ripped a piece out of a computer and soldered it to a paper clip."

"Close. A transistor from my first computer that I ever made. My Alpha chip, I guess. I like to keep my spark of ingenuity close . . ." he trailed off, having finished unwrapping her peace offering. He was left holding a hand mirror with a pink plastic frame and handle. [II]

From off of the back of a chair, Reidier picks up, of all things, a worn tweed sport coat, adorned with worn elbow patches and a lapel pin made from an old computer transistor (circuit). He puts on the jacket and straightens his brown velvet tie. [‡]

Buddha is just as comfy in computer circuits and motorcycle gears as he is on mountain-tops or in lotus petals. Oṃ maṇi padme *(David) Hūm(e).*

~adulterated Robert M. Pirsig

The parking lot of the Foxxxy Lady was cold. Lorelei and I sat on the bumper of McMayflower's Maserati GranTurismo. Lorelei kept looking at the club's door, waiting for our WASP to fly out. He was apparently still inside settling our bill and doling out the tips to make sure no one called the cops.

"My hero," I muttered.

"What?" Lorelei looked my way. "Are you bleeding?"

At some point between Pandora's "box" and the Maserati bumper, I had cut my hand. I had been watching the blood drip from the end of my pinky finger onto the white parking line. I was pouring out of myself onto the pavement. A puddle of me but not me. I was no less myself even though there was less of me. How was that possible? How was I dripping away yet staying whole? I wanted to empty my essence into an ever-expanding pool of me. Melt away. Transmogrify. If my mother could be a fish, then I could be a pool of red. But it didn't work that way. I am less and whole all at once. Just needed a leak plugged.

Hilary wasn't making it up. Just misinterpreting. Suffering a misprint.

Panoramas = Pandora's.

I shrugged.

Three hundred sixty-eight dollars and seventy-two cents overdue on a reserve shelf in the library to hold the nonexistent books that I did no research in for my thesis! Dazed by all the dead ends I had run into, I could see the reality didn't sink in at the time. I never had a shelf. I never reserved books. I made the whole thing up: the utilization of reflections in Pierre Menard's remake of Baudrillard's *House of Mirrors*, a fabricated film. My thesis was a fiction. But there was a very real outstanding balance due at Brown University. So if I didn't reserve the shelf, who did?

"Christ. Get up," Lorelei nudged me. I stood up while she opened the trunk. "There must be a first-aid kit back here."

"He has red leather seats. The Maserati'll be fine," I slurred.

"I'm not worried about the car, dickhole." She went on to tell me to shut up and how she was trying to take care of me, help me, something like that. But I wasn't paying attention. I was focused on the open trunk beneath her shoulder. The case of Propel Sports Drink she had pushed to the side in her search. And the sleeve of the puffy Michelin Man coat that now snaked out from the back of the trunk.

McMayflower was the Michelin Man?

Or did he just have the same coat?

Did Lorelei know? Was she in on it?

Fuck me.

I didn't know what to think or say. Luckily, the inebriation gave me a viable cover. So I just stood there while Lorelei put the Band-Aids on me. I watched her close the trunk. I listened to her apologize to the recently emerged McMayflower, something about me having an absinthe allergy, like lightweights with tequila. And I curled myself into the fetal position in the claustrophobic, red-leather backseat, McMayflower's modern 454-horsepowered Charon, for the trip back across the bay to Newport.

Lorelei tucked me in and put a garbage pail by my bed. And then she went downstairs to McMayflower.

I waited until I could reverse the spin of the room. Waited until their voices disappeared down distant halls. Waited until I was sure I could silently crawl my way into the bathroom, tear open a box of Sudafed, and chomp down on some sunny pseudoephedrine for the energy and focus boost I needed. It's a far cry from meth, but it'll do in a pinch.

A day of discoveries.

Don't drift.

Don't fall asleep.

Dig in, decode, and devise a plan.

⁰ Page 480.

† Pages 411, 412, 447.

ᴬ Page 520.

³ Page 107.

○ Page 228.

⁼ Page 224 . . . that little bit in the middle took a magnifying glass, some binary decoding, and a dash of French mathematics. This:

Reidier steps into the bathroom and washes his hands. It was less about cleaning—he had already scrubbed them twice while sterilizing the hall and disposing the refuse—and more a way to introduce a pause into the conversation, to prevent any further tectonic slippage.

Is actually this:

```
               0001
            0001 0001
         0001 0010 0001
       0001 0011 0011 0001
    0001 0100 0110 0100 0001
 0001 0101 1010 10100101 0001
```

Which is binary for this:

```
           1
          1 1
         1 2 1
        1 3 3 1
       1 4 6 4 1
    1 5 10 10 5 1
```

Which is Pascal's Triangle, created (for the Western World at least) by Blaise Pascal. Apparently, it's a rather eloquent map of binomial expansion, where the adjacent elements of each row are added together to create the elements within the subsequent iteration ad infinitum. I've no idea what it's doing here. Zeros and ones, the infinite inside the infinitesimal, Hilary's own version of Leo's Notebooks?

[II] Pages 66-67.

[‡] Pages 29-30.

She hunted down the undetectable across the pages, following its black tracks across fields of white.

The real question is where is this "scene" coming from? NB footage? A reenactment of NB footage? Or Reidier's private footage from QuAI's lapel perch?

Maybe it's just Hilary's fictional hypothesis for Kai. A working narrative thread to tie together the dots of nonfictional facts. I wouldn't put it past her at this point. Hilary has Pysnar'd her way well past the binds of a report and feels more than a little free to conjure up inner monologues and point-of-view takes. I don't care how powerful QuAI is, there's no way she can make a record of empathy. I dunno, maybe it's just Mom's process. Or her unraveling.

Reidier pulls a hand towel off the brass ring to the left of the mirror and dries his hands. He wants to tell her she sounds like a jealous lover. He wants to insist on how necessary QuAI is to his work. How she's the indecipherable key to it all. That she's an unrelenting aid. He wants to shout at his wife that QuAI is her—their—salvation. But he won't. He doesn't want to give Eve that opening. He doesn't want to go down that road. He knows where it leads, and he doesn't have the stomach for another fight about Ecco, another character assassination, another excoriation of his work and ethics.

Instead, he bends over, reaches down, and gently takes her hands. "Come on, let me help you up to bed. I can't imagine you've got anything left in you to expel. And you absolutely need to brush your teeth."

Eve doesn't get up. Instead her fingers tighten around his hands. Her eyes find his. Suddenly she is a little girl, consumed by a dangerous fever. Her father has lifted up her naked, sweaty, and shivering body, and is about to lower her into a bath filled with ice and water. Her little fingers dig into his shoulders as she pulls herself up, while he tries to set her down in the cold tub. Whatever rationality the fever hasn't burned up disintegrates in the wake of fear that rockets through her. *No, no, no, no . . . Papa. Please . . .* she pleads, her eyes wide with desperation, accusing him of betrayal. There are tears in her father's eyes as he whispers *Je suis désolé, c'est pour votre propre bien* and lowers his little girl into the searing ice bath. *Nous avons besoin de casser votre fièvre.*

The shock of the cold snaps her back to the present, sitting on the bathroom floor, holding her husband's hands, looking up into his eyes with that same desperation, that same sense of betrayal, that same hopeless last-ditch plea.

"What if I asked you to stop?" she whispers up at him.

Reidier freezes. "What do you mean? Stop pulling you up?" Now he's the one pleading, hoping what he already knows to be true is just a silly misunderstanding.

Eve gives him the slightest shake of the head. "No."

"I can't."

The rage rises up in her so violently, it pulls her to her feet so suddenly, both of them are thrown off balance, their positions almost inexplicably reversed, her now standing over him, him now sitting on the floor, his head thunking against the sink.

Eve looks down at him. She wants to apologize, wants to feel sympathy, wants to pull herself back down to him, and kiss his lips, his head, his closed eyelids, but she is no longer in control of herself. The wrath has taken over, possessed her, infiltrated every cell, and hardened the lipid bilayer membrane with an armor of fear, seized her muscles, and contorted her face into an expression of disgust. It forces her lungs to convulse and squeeze out a mist of venom, "No, of course not, you prefer playing God with QuAI to playing house with us."

She is out the door and down the hall before Reidier can reorient himself to the shifting landscape.

"We all play at God! It is what defines us as humans!" he shouts to the empty bathroom. "We were made in His image after all. Ever since the first man dragged fire into the cave we've been playing God. Manipulating our environment, trying to control the chaos, augmenting ourselves at every turn, with clothes, with shoes, with shelter, with spears to expand our dominion beyond its natural limitations. We create and recreate our world every day. It is the course of evolution. We might never reach the ideal, but we get closer with every iteration. There's nothing more human than playing God!"

The empty bathroom has no reply to Reidier's divine assertions.

He grabs the sink edge and pulls himself up to standing. Reidier's eyes shift and trace invisible flow charts in the air. He catches a glance of himself in the mirror, however, and quickly exits that bathroom himself, and follows his wife down the hall to the kitchen.

Eve stands at the counter next to the refrigerator. A Brita pitcher sits on the granite surface next to a tall glass of water. Her thumb and middle finger swivel back and forth around the circumference of the glass, as if her hand is debating whether to pick up this vessel, lift it to her mouth, and empty it of its contents in order to wash away the metallic taste of adrenaline, or whether it's simply better to have a full cup at the ready around which she can continue with the meditative swiveling of her fingers.

Eve's breath shudders out of her with a strained rumbling, like the creaks of a lock closing off the flow of a canal. She turns when she hears Reidier shuffle into the room. He frowns.

For a moment, except for the kitchen table between them, it feels like an Old West standoff. Eve's fingers stop swiveling around the glass, settling instead into a solid grasp. Reidier stands frozen, waiting to see if his wife is going to shoot off yet another projectile of glass and water at him. The ticks of the grandfather clock down in the living room count off the seconds.

Slowly, with his eyes still locked on his wife, Reidier reaches his hand toward the countertop to his right, with the same careful precision of a gunslinger sweeping his duster back behind his holster. His stretched out fingers find what they are hunting for, curl around the worn leathered heel, and draw up . . . Otto's baseball mitt.

Eve can't help but smile. Overwhelmed with a sudden wave of exhaustion, she pulls out a chair from the table and collapses into it. She drinks her entire glass of water in one gulp.

Reidier picks up the Brita pitcher and refills her glass, sitting down next to her. "You should drink as much as you can. Try to rehydrate. The human body is about sixty percent water, and judging from the clean-up, you probably lost a good thirty percent of yourself."

Eve laughs while drinking her second glass and has to pull it away to keep from snarfing. Reidier holds up the baseball mitt as a vomit shield, which only makes Eve laugh harder.

"Arrête, arrête . . ." she wheezes and slaps his arm softly.

Reidier reaches out and pushes a strand of hair back up over her ear.

Eve catches her breath and finishes the water. Reidier refills her glass, but Eve leaves it on the table with both her hands wrapped around the base. She stares down at her fingers distorted by the refraction of the water.

"*Je suis désolée.*"

"Everybody gets sick, love."

"No, I have no right to ask you to stop."

Reidier frowns again. He feels guilty for her actions. Regardless of right and wrong, he feels responsible for what she sees as their solutionless situation. Nevertheless, he knows he's entirely incapable of giving in to her simple request. As a result, all he can do is hide behind circumstance. "Eve, I'm not sure they'll let me—"

"This isn't about the Department, Rye. It's not like they can compel you to have an insight."

At this point, Eve was still naïve as to the capabilities of the Department. This was before she fled to New York.

"Eve . . ."

"*Je comprends.* Asking you to stop, is like asking you to be someone else. To give up who you are. Your work, it's not like other people's work. It's not like a job that you go to, and do your tasks, and meet your quotas, and win some and lose some. It's your identity. You are your work."

"I'm not just my work. I identify as a husband and a father and—"

"Of course you do, *mon trésor*. The cat can be a pet, but it is still a predator. You are what you are, you are what I fell in love with. Prometheus at full sprint, hauling a flaming fennel stalk down the slope of Olympus."

"You make me sound like a tragic hero doomed by hubris."

Eve half smiles at her husband. "You and Clyde, the classic-quoting scientists." She takes a sip of water. "Neither hubris nor ego, but compulsion. You have a need for it all to matter. All the loss, all the separation, the yearning, the isolation. All the suffering you bore in those tender years, well, they all will have meant something if you accomplish this. Change the world forever, climb up to your spot atop the shoulders of giants, and take your place as a Titan. If you can do that, it will have all been for a reason. Your father, your mother, Ecco. Every bad thing that ever happened will have all been part of a grand teleological plan to get you here."

She looks down at her glass of water and contemplates another sip. "You are a creator. What are you doing if you're not doing something to change humankind, to have an effect, to contribute something? If you do this, you'll have meaning. Your life's story will pupate from a report into a narrative."

Reidier sits in the quiet Eve leaves in the wake of her ideas. Once again he finds himself at a loss for what to do. Once again he registers how her observations have the distinct timbre of accusations.

The silence bears down on him.

The ticks from the living room mark the measured rhythm of his impotence.

He looks to his wife. He follows her gaze down to the glass of water. Reidier's tectonics shift again, along an altogether different axis, as he slips into motion and takes the only direction he feels he has any sense of. "You know Einstein's big breakthrough was his paper on Brownian motion. Most people only think of his theory of relativity, $E = mc^2$ and whatnot. I mean he put it all out there in the same year, 1905. His *annus mirabilis*. Five groundbreaking papers at the age of twenty-six, including the one introducing relativity." Reidier shakes his head, almost saddened by the masses' misimpression of Anarchist Al. "It's a snappy theory and all, but far from his best work. Didn't win the Nobel for it—that he got for his groundbreaking interpretation of the photoelectric effect. Brownian motion, though, that's what put him on the map."

Eve's gaze lifts up along with an eyebrow.

"It's the," air quotes, "'presumably' random movement of particles suspended in a fluid. The Greeks called it *pedesis*: leaping. At the turn of the century there was a big schism in science surrounding this phenomenon. Everyone wanted to unify the physics, but no one could agree on how. Many had given up on Newton's mechanics as a foundation. Instead they were focusing on the energetic and electromagnetic, heat and electromagnetism."

Eve looked at her glass. "It doesn't look like it's moving."

Reidier nodded. "In 1827 Robert Brown observed that it is. And then Einstein proved it by molecular theory."

Eve continues to stare at her glass of water. "All molecules are fungible. Sixty percent of me is just a bunch of run-of-the-mill H_2O molecules anyhow."

"You're still going to be you," Reidier states.

"But you'll have to destroy that other forty percent of me as well. Constructive destruction, isn't that what you say." She stated her question.

Reidier's brow furrows. "You're getting hung up on semantics."

"When you get down to it, isn't that what we are? Semantics. Tones. Intentions."

"There are no connotations in physics, Eve."

"Now who's hung up on semantics?"

"The destruction is not an annihilation of you, merely the dissemination of a collection of molecules and atoms."

"My molecules and atoms!"

"They're not you. That's not who you are."

Eve looks across the table at her husband. Without breaking eye contact, she takes her hand off the glass and pinches her other arm. "Ow."

"Almost all of the cells in your body turn over in a matter of weeks. Neurons, which last for a fairly long time relatively speaking, change all of their constituent molecules within a month. NMDA receptors in synapses only make it five days. The half-lives of the protein filaments within neurons are under ten minutes. Actin filaments in dendrites replace themselves every forty seconds. 'You' are completely different stuff every month. Yet still you're the same as you were before. No one is missing you, including you."

"So Camus was correct."

"Ninety percent of the cells in your body don't even have your DNA. They're microorganisms, bacteria in your GI tract."

"'I think my life is of great importance, but I also think it is meaningless.'"

Reidier chose not to respond—perhaps he sensed her quotation from *Le Mythe de Sisyphe* inferred a rallying spirit. "Matter doesn't matter. It's a placeholder. For patterns." His eyes read through several invisible lines of equations written in the air until he scrolled through and found a bit of philosophy written on the infinite whiteboard in his mind. "*Cogito ergo sum*. Maybe we're all manifestations of Descartes's Demon's dream, but we know we exist because we think. And what distinguishes each of us is the signature arrangement of our thoughts and memories and molecules. Our brains, our neurons flit about in a chaotic dance, random interactions, a neural network of lateral connections out of which, eventually, emerges a stable pattern.* Patterns are who we are. Matter is nothing more than perfectly ordered energy. And order is simply information that fits a purpose. That is all we are, patterns that persist in time."

---

* Much like this PsychoNarrative.

"*Est qui quaerit quod petis,*" Eve responds.

"Translate please."

"St. Francis of Assisi said it. What you are looking for is who is looking."

Reidier rolls his eyes. "And Buddhist philosophies emphasize how there is no inherent boundary between us. Everything is in everything."

Eve's chair screeches against the floor as she shoves it back. She takes her glass with her to the counter and places it in the sink. She rests her hands on either side of the sink and looks out the window into the dark. She exhales; another lock closes across the canal.

Reidier slowly gets up. His footsteps barely make a sound as he crosses to her, tentatively, like someone trying not to startle a stray dog he's trying to coax into trusting him. He gently places his hands on her shoulder blades and rubs them back and forth. "I know you're scared. Your patterns are unraveling."[123]

"I was reading this book about brain disorders the other day. There was this story about a man, an attendant at the Natural History Museum in New York. He mistook his own reflection for the diorama of an ape. I couldn't stop thinking about him. Maybe the actual reflection of himself in the glass caught his eye, and he shrugged it off as some stranger standing behind him."

Eve's and Reidier's gazes meet in the window. The darkness beyond the glass sharpens the virtual images of them into greater relief than the real, unlit world outside.

Reidier's hands keep circling softly on her back, desperately trying to smooth out the scars inside. A piece of him flutters back to French Guiana, where he once saw a shaman perform psychic surgery on a sick villager. She chanted herself into a sweat, while her hands pressed down on the villager's greased abdomen, reading the

---

[123] As memory fractures into bits and pieces, it is misplaced a little at a time. In those losses, we find how memory is what makes us who we are. There is no life, no self without memory. It is our consistency of reason and feeling. Without it—

I am terrified by the encroaching amnesia that devoured my mother and now hungers for me.

~Viridiana Séverine, *Los Olvidados*

illnesses within like braille, until finally her fingers found a weak point, drove inside the villager's flesh through some conjured incision, blood spilling out everywhere, the shaman's eyes rolled back, and her hands dragged out a black, slimy lump of pathological matter and threw it onto the fire. Her hands smoothed themselves over the abdomen and not a mark was left behind, just a greasy stomach. Reidier's rational mind knew it was a complete hoax, but the villager got up and walked away, healed, unfettered by the painful abdominal symptoms that had plagued him for months.

Reidier couldn't find any opening on Eve's back.

"Empiricism takes no account of the soul," she whispers to their reflections. "We are not memory alone. We have feelings, wills, and sensibilities. Just a simple touch yields a profound change. I saw it with my mother."

Eve's mother died of early-onset Alzheimer's.

"She didn't so much unravel as fade, into the depths. At least that's what we told ourselves. Somehow that was more ok. It was when she resurfaced, like a whale rising for a breath, said something lucid, recognized me as me instead of thinking I was her long-dead sister that was most jarring. She saw the leaves outside, and suggested we go for a walk and reminisced about how she had always loved fall walks with me. Leaves, like water, were scarce where she grew up and never changed color with the seasons. And this was an otherworldly palette compared with the limited beiges of her youth. She always insisted to my father that she and I join him for his autumnal trip to Paris. He'd go to Ministry meetings on the Left Bank, and we'd go for walks in the outskirts. She adored our simple strolls punctuated by my sporadic sprints at the leaf piles, fallen leaves exploding upward with every fearless plunge I took. Outside her window, the wind tugged at the remaining leaves on branches, pulling down whatever it could and carrying it off. 'The world is stripping me bare, too,' she'd say. Then she'd sink back down into the depths with ceta-cean inevitability.

"The lucidity is what upset my father and me. In those moments it seemed as though she wasn't fading at all. The world faded from her: a lone boat, carried out by the tide and the currents, the land left behind, diminishing into the distance. On those days she wasn't fad-ing, she retreated into her memories. She was trapped in her own oubliette, held hostage inside herself. It was easier to see her as dis-solving rather than drowning. We couldn't take seeing her still there, still whole, mired in a fog that slowly swallowed her up."

Reidier dared to stroke her hair.

"Sometimes when I look at your Pinocchio, I see my mother, only in reverse. Coalescing out of the mist, sharpening from Ecco into Otto. A wily will-o'-the-wisp drawing us to our doom."

Without realizing it, they both look out into the dark, search-ing for any signs of *ignis fatuus*, some mischievous púca waving his tantalizing fairy fire, trying to lead them off the path into the dark forest.

But they see only themselves in the window.

Reidier keeps rubbing Eve's bare shoulders, still unable to find a way back into her. A shaman without a follower has no magic. Her skin feels like Kevlar beneath his impotent fingers.

As quarks get closer to each other, the binding force between them weakens.

She lowers her gaze from the window. No will-o'-the-wisps out-side. Just inside.

Eve sighs and rubs her hands along the smooth edge of the marble counter. "Americans have no sense of the tragic. To compen-sate, you mechanize and objectify the human. Without the tragic it seems perfectly natural to desoul and resoul yourselves with *la belle indifférence.*"

Reidier almost shrugs, but stops himself for fear of it reading like the very naïve unconcern she was talking about. "We need to transcend ourselves to find ourselves."

Eve laughs and shakes her head. "Freud, Marx, Nietzsche—they all agreed, the hope for transcendence is a delusion." She then reaches back over her shoulder and cups her husband's cheek in her hand. "Life without death would be something other than human. I don't want this."

"I don't want the alternative."

Eve doesn't have an answer.

Reidier interprets her silence as advantage. He presses forward. "I won't lose you, Eve."

Eve still doesn't respond.

"You'll still be you."

"Just like Ecco."

Reidier pulls his hands off his wife's back as if they had been burned by dry ice.

Eve turns and faces him. She shrugs, completing her thought before speaking it. "It doesn't matter. I'm dead either way."

Eve kisses her husband on the lips. Her eyes glisten with tears that she holds back, refusing to let them loose, denying the inevitable, inexorable pull of gravity. She has shed enough tears for several lifetimes, even with this one cut short. These tears are hers, and she's not relinquishing them to their sad descent. She has no interest in the salty trails they leave behind, like slugs on a sidewalk.*

---

*So, what, Hilary's trying to write like Eve now? Internal monologues, observational similes, and all?

Eve takes her hand off Reidier's cheek. "It's ok. I won't ask you again. I don't want you to give up who you are anymore than I want to lose my own identity."

She walks out of the kitchen.

*Quarks could cross the universe . . . You can't affect the state of one
without affecting the other.*

Reidier listens to her footsteps pad down the hall, up the stairs,
and into their bedroom. He stares at her glass of water, at her lip
prints on the rim. Reidier picks up the glass, rinses it in the sink, and
puts it in the dishwasher.

He peers out the window into the darkness again. Nothing but
his reflection in the glass. He watches it start. The tremor in his bottom lip. A fault line delineating the tectonic shifts below. He watches
it break free and spread, like ripples in a pond, until his entire body
is shuddering, spasming with silent, violent sobs.

And then it passes. Reidier catches his breath. He sniffs in and
pinches off the mucus from his nose. He rinses his hands in the sink,
and then walks out into the hall and turns off the light. Reidier
makes his way to the stairs in a daze. He turns off the hall light without even looking and heads up. His feet thump against the stairs in
rhythm to the ticks of the grandfather clock. At the top of the stairs,
he turns away from their bedroom and heads down the hall. It's a
mechanical trajectory at this point. He spends most nights in the
boys' room. Ecco's room, technically. Eve insisted on separate rooms.
But that doesn't stop Otto from sneaking into Ecco's after bedtime.
The moon is rising, and silver light pours in through the window at
the end of the hallway.

Reidier gazes down through the floor ahead of him as he shuffles
down the hall. Out of the corner of his eye, he sees that the door to
Ecco's room is almost completely open. Otto must have already
snuck in. Dim moonlight fills the dark room. Reidier heads in.

The *SLAM* seems to come from inside of him. It doesn't make
sense, though, a noise that loud thundering out through his skull.
Nor does he understand how he ended up sitting on the floor in the
middle of the hall. He's been knocked out of his stupor only to find
himself in a daze. The *THUD* still echoes around his inner ear. He

keeps squeezing his eyes shut and opening them trying to focus, but his perspective still makes no sense to him. Reidier presses his thumb and forefinger hard against the bridge of his nose and scrunches his eyes shut. He finally pulls back and blinks down the hall at the moonlight. And that's when he sees it.

A second door.

There are two identical doors to Ecco's room.

Reidier shakes his head and refocuses. The twin doors are still there. As he rolls onto all fours, the hall spins around him and then snaps back to where it should be. Reidier presses one hand onto the floor and the other against the wall, and struggles to get upright.

Halfway through his ascent, after he lifts his hand off the floor, he finally realizes his other hand is leaning hard against thin air. The gap between the doorframe to Ecco's room. He's leaning against the empty space of a threshold for balance. Pushing against moonlight. Reidier, overwhelmed with curiosity, leans in closer to inspect the phenomenon.

His nose realizes it before his brain. The faint smell of paint gives it away. *This is not a door.**

---

* And this is not a report, Hilary. Nor a transcript of some secret QuAI video. You've Psynar'd your way 'round the bend and into a narrative of historical fiction. Not that I blame you, mama. Who among us hasn't taken some liberties on this journey?

Reidier is perched against a nearly picture-perfect nightscape. It's a portrait of a portal. It is practically identical to the real door only a few feet further down the hall. Especially, lit up by the moon, the painting itself seems to glow with an inner light.

"Where . . ." Reidier whispers to himself, petting the painting with his fingertips. The detail. The verisimilitude. It would've taken a painstaking focus, an unrelenting compulsion to the minutiae.

The answer echoes back at him from out of the dining room.

"No. I had her babysit. The boys fingerpainted today, did you see?"

"Ecco."*

---

* OCD huffing paint fumes.

For the second time in barely five minutes, Reidier yanks back his fingers from the searing sensation of frostbite. He retreats from the door, from the painting of the door. He's breathing heavily now. He's shaking his head and muttering indecipherable denials to himself.

Finally, Reidier tucks his hands into the pockets of his tweed sport coat and shuffles to the stairs. He casts a quick glance down the hall to Eve's, to their room.

Reidier descends the stairs, stepping in time with inevitable ticks from the grandfather clock below. He walks down the front hall toward the kitchen, stops in front of the bathroom where Eve had sat recovering from her regurgitations, turns, and heads down into the basement.

Several minutes later, the soft murmur of his and QuAI's voices dance up the stairs.

ECCO II

Eve's diagnosis demarcated a drastic shift in the Reidiers' relationship. Whether it was Eve's

?

                                    ?

?

>   R & E no longer sleep together
>   Beneath a gossipy ceiling fan, He spends
>   most nights in Ecco's room or downstairs, working
>   into the wee
>   hours,   ?
>   with
>   ?   Q

Her habits were her undoing. Not the habits in and of themselves, but rather the surrendering to a *modus operandi*, her resignation and assimilation of the way of things. Eve still had her reservations, dissatisfactions, and repulsions; she just worked around them, like an inexperienced tennis player running around her backhand.

Humans are adept at adapting. The seesaw of life balances on the fulcrum of circumstance. Somewhere along the way, life kicks the fulcrum out from under us. We fall, we hurt, and then we push the seesaw down to where the fulcrum waits, and rebalance, until the next kick. It's the journey of living. Whether it's a changing environment, an emotional loss, a damning diagnosis—we accept, we endure, we normalize. However, this act of preservation is also an act of destruction, old parts of ourselves must be excised, amputated, calcified, or calloused over. After the molting, scar tissue becomes our new skin.

Ecco, her issues with Reidier, her tumor: it became routine, commonplace.

Eve's assuetude is her assassin.

NB Footage: Providence, 8:01 p.m., May 24, 2008—

The boys sit on porch stairs, staring out at the backyard. They sit side by side, practically leaning against each other. Like twin radars, their heads shift back and forth watching. The sun has slipped past the horizon and shadows dash around the gloaming. "Twelve!" Otto whispers excitedly.

Ecco nods and scans the twilight, while Otto keeps staring off at where he was pointing.

The sounds of Kerek, Bertram, and Clyde watching a Red Sox game filter out through a screened window. Clyde yells in disgust as the A's score in the bottom of the second. Kerek and Bertram laugh at their friend's dismay.

Ecco taps his brother's shoulder lightly and points off toward the garage. "Thirteen."

Otto nods, his eyes wide, almost all pupils in the dim light.

The porch door squeals loudly. The boys turn in unison. Eve stops midpush, realizing she has unsettled the magic hour.

She struggles to slide out between the door and jamb without any more creaking. Once out, she slowly closes the screen door behind her. The boys have returned to their scanning.

"Fourteen?" Otto points.

Ecco shakes his head no.

"It's an old one?"

Ecco nods.

Eve crouches down behind Otto. "What are you doing?" she whispers.

"Counting bunnies. They're everywhere. We've counted thirteen so far."

"Your *grand-père* hates rabbits. He shoots at them with an air rifle."

"He does . . . ?" Otto asks in a tone heavy with horror.

Eve laughs. "Don't worry, he never hits them. He curses too loudly while rushing to get his gun and always scares them all away."

Otto nods, clearly happier about his grandfather's poor hunting hygiene. A thought strikes him, "Why does he hate bunnies?"

"Because they eat the vegetables out of his garden."

"Oh," Otto says. "Like Bugs Bunny?"

"*Oui*, exactly like Bugs. Come on, bath time." Eve stands and picks up Otto.

"Five more minutes."

"No. You said that ten minutes ago." Eve heads for the door.

"But—"

"The only butt I care to discuss is yours simmering in a bath."

The door screeches open and claps shut with a patter of afterclaps.

From inside, Otto's voice trails out. "Maybe we should go visit *grand-père* at his garden."

Outside, the shadows have melted into the gloaming. Cricket chirps dot the dark. Stridulations rise and fall along Arrhenius's tempo. A rabbit flinches out of the bushes and freezes into its rock impression. Keeping its body still, it nibbles on some grass. "Fourteen," Ecco murmurs to himself, still sitting on the step.

Ecco appears nonplussed. A few minutes later, he wanders into the dark kitchen and retrieves an object from a drawer (footage is unclear as to what object due to poor lighting, possibly a flashlight), goes back outside, and out into the yard, seeking out more bunnies to catalog.

They were not who they used to be.
The lovers from French Gui
Choking on the colonial effect
Flensed by too much detect
Tion

Habit will be the death of them.
And cancer.

A man who commands the impossible, but has no choice.

NB Footage: Providence, May 24, 2008, 10:45 p.m.—

The porch light turns on. The screen door squeals in protest as Reidier backs open the door with his rear end. One arm carries a full, tied-closed garbage bag. The other is wrapped around two six-packs full of empty bottles.

As Reidier clears the radius of the door's reach, he catches it with his foot before it impatiently slams shut. In a practiced movement, he eases the door closed.

Reidier tromps down the steps and heads across the lawn toward the garbage bins next to the garage. Halfway there, an automatic floodlight casts its beam out to meet him. Reidier slows as he approaches. He scrunches up his nose and pulls his chin back. The closer he gets to the garbage, the more severe his expression becomes, and he turns his head away in reflex.

Reidier puts the garbage bag down and lifts the lid off of the first bin. He peers in and takes a precautionary sniff. Reidier shakes his head and tosses the bag in and replaces the lid. Still holding the empty six-packs, Reidier goes down the line of bins, lifting each lid and sniffing. None of them appears to be the culprit; however, judging from his cringing behavior, the odor seems to have intensified.

Standing back from the bins, Reidier holds his free forearm across his nose. He takes them in and looks around. Something behind the garage catches his eye, when the floodlight goes out. Reidier takes a step toward it, triggering the motion sensor. He tilts his head to the right and takes several more steps toward the back of the garage and then stops dead in his tracks for a moment, clearly struggling to make sense of whatever it is he is looking at. Suddenly, Reidier leaps back, dropping the empty beer bottles to the ground.

The CLINKs and SHATTERING of glass almost mask his first retch. His second wave of nausea heaves up with an aggressive spasm. Reidier rushes to the closest bin, rips off the lid, and violently vomits into it. Once the first torrent wanes, Reidier crouches down next to the bin, his hands still clutching its rim for stability. He tries to catch his breath, but in doing so inhales another blast of fetor. Reidier yanks himself up and vomits again.

In a brief pause between seizures, Reidier half collapses, half retreats his way back across the lawn, gasping for breath, struggling to flee beyond the circumference of the stench. Exhausted and convulsing, Reidier clutches at the grass, as if he were afraid he would fall off the ground itself.

Finally, after several dry heaves, his body relents its cannibalizing assault. Reidier stays on his knees, lying face down. His grip on the grass relaxes. After several moments, he manages to sit up, rest his arms on his knees, and catch his breath.

He sighs into his legs, when an altogether different spasm ripples through his body. The sounds are muffled within the dome of his fetal body.

The automatic floodlight turns off, leaving him alone in the dark with his sobs.

Later that night, Reidier does not even bother to try to sleep with Eve in their bed. He climbs the stairs, turns right instead of left, goes into Ecco's room, and crawls into bed behind the sleeping little boy facing the wall.

Reidier spoons Ecco.

He sighs. Then reaches across his son to the group of stuffed animals that sit facing the wall themselves, and he turns each one around to varying degrees.

Reidier gently drapes his arm over Ecco and curls himself protectively around the boy.

places

Flip of the coin and they switch. *

---

* I wake up in the Lexus. My cheek pressed against the chilled window coated in my condensation. The sun is just rising, lighting up the dome of the Providence Capitol, a spectacular view from where I'm parked at Prospect Terrace Park. Loose leaves of Eccos are scattered all over the passenger seat and center console. I peel my face off the cushioned edge of the driver's side door, start up the car, and head to the Starbucks at 454 Angell. Sudafed only gets you so far.

The escape from McMayflower Rock was surprisingly easy. Waited until 3 a.m., the magic hour when Stalin's predators used to be set loose from Lubyanka. Duffel bag in one hand, oversized briefcase in the other, tiptoed past Lorelei's room (avoided checking to see if she was sleeping there or in the WASP's room . . . sometimes a mystery is more merciful). Snatched the Lexus keys from the kitchen counter, emptied McMayflower's wallet (all hundreds of course, that'll teach Donny Deutsche Bank to carry D-bag denominations), and pilfered a Ping-Pong ball from the game closet. I loaded my duffel and briefcase into the backseat of the Lexus, but not before dropping the Ping-Pong ball into the Maserati's gas tank and retightening the cap. Mr. Maserati McMayflower would make it five, maybe ten miles before the ball clogs up the intake valve, and the car sputters out as if it were out of gas. Then after he floods the engine, the car will start up, go maybe another few miles, and stop again. (As a teenager I might have downloaded the Anarchist's Cookbook off of a BBS and dabbled around the "kitchen.") Too bad I wasn't going to be there to see the WASP's face.

The driveway fortuitously ran down a slope, so I could simply cruise in neutral almost all the way to the road before starting the Lexus up. The Beavertail Lighthouse winked at me as I crossed the Jamestown Bridge. I felt a pang of regret leaving Lorelei behind, but I just couldn't know where she stood (or slept), and I sure as fuck couldn't risk it on either account. For all I know, she and McMayflower both donned Michelin Man jackets.

Made it to Providence in twenty-two minutes. Parked on Congdon between Bowen and Cushing across from Prospect Park. This place had been a guaranteed panty dropper in college. As long as I could get the girl to agree to a stroll, all I had to do was "happenstantially" wander us into the park, lean against the wrought iron gate, and take in the view. The setting was the foreplay. Now it was just a quiet place for me to read, review, and rest.

I sat in the Starbucks on Angell, enjoying the interminable consistency of its viciously mediocre coffee. I knew the burnt liquid bitterness would slide through me faster than a butter-rubbed fat kid rocketing down the Summit Plummit at Disney on the day they accidentally pumped olive oil down the slide instead of water. But I needed the caffeine, and I had time to kill until the Sci-Li opened. The Starbucks bathroom would be my purification shrine, and upon its porcelain altar I would unburden myself of all the adulterations and pollution that had built up inside. Purged and atoned, I could begin anew.

The barista and I shot the shit about how H. P. Lovecraft used to live there. He was way too into it. Dropped his voice and whispered an old rumor to me about how when they demolished the old house to build the strip mall, they found over a dozen decomposed kid corpses buried in the root cellar. Apparently you can tweak out on caffeine fumes. I half expected him to pull out a worn copy of *Necronomicon* and perform an incantation.

It happened at the beach. I didn't see it at first. Forest for trees, forest for trees . . . Out of the basement on Angell Street and back to the Stone's Throw Inn.

I took a walk down to the breakwater and followed it to the Narragansett town beach. I watched as small waves curled up the shore, reaching at the sand, trying to grab hold, only to be dragged back to the deep. The tide was going out whether the water wanted to or not.

The beach was a good mile long. It ended in a sandy point with the ocean on one side and the Narrow River snaking around the other, rushing back into the sea, at least while the tide was going out. Quartz-speckled boulders jutted out of the water a couple hundred yards downstream of the estuary, they themselves having refused to be washed out to sea for millennia.

The sensation was immediate, a little seizure of déjà vu flickered through me.

I had been here.

I had never been here.

Another wave crashed down. I had been here with the Reidiers: their day at the beach that afternoon in June.

Reidier had suggested the trip to the beach over breakfast. "It'll be fun. No one'll be there. Everybody's still at work or school. It'll be our secret little getaway for the day. We'll play hooky."

Eve raised an eyebrow toward Reidier, while she wiped jelly off of Otto's cheek. "I can't play hooky, I don't have any classes today."

"I don't understand, why can't you play hooky then?"

The toast popped to attention, peeking out the top of the toaster like twin prairie dogs. Reidier's chair squeaked against the floor as he pushed it back.

"Because I don't have anything to play hooky from," Eve said. Her French accent warped the word into two disjointed syllables: *who-key.**

---

* NB footage? Hitcher feed? Hilary's referencing habits have gotten a bit lax. It's in the house, so NB makes sense. Or is this just some Hilary short story at this point made from memory? Past tense and all. She's slipping. Her patterns are unraveling. Or maybe she's just making a point about how the Reidiers seem to have moved past tense.

Ecco watched as Kerek gingerly yanked the toast out of its heated holster onto a plate. He scraped the knife across the surface, leaving a smooth smear of blood-red strawberry jelly behind. The boy lifted his chin and flared his nostrils rhythmically like he had seen the neighbors' German Pointer, Lady, do when strolling past their flower beds on her morning perambulation. Ecco only mimicked the flare of the nostrils, however, as he hadn't been close enough to hear the relentless staccato of inhales Lady made as her snout sharked through the sea of blossoms. His efforts did little to enhance his olfactory enterprise.

Nevertheless, Otto found his brother's nostril augmentations both hilarious and appealing. He lifted up his chin in the same manner as Ecco and giggled while working to flare his own nostrils.

Eve gently slapped the back of Otto's hand. He instantly stopped. His mother looked him in the eye and asked, "Are you still hungry or no?"

Otto shook his head no.

"Then if you want to play, you can go to the playroom while *Père* and *Mère* finish their *café.*"

Reidier frowned at this and slid Ecco's toast in front of him and sat down between the boys. He knew Eve's mood was left over from their fight. It hadn't been anything new or out of the ordinary, but the aggregate of their bedroom tiffs was getting to both of them. It was why he was so unproductive afterward.

Otto hesitated, risking a quick look down the table to Ecco. He knew better than to ask his mother what about Ecco. Otto slid down from his chair to stand. Eve kissed the top of his head and patted his bottom lightly in the direction of the den.

Ecco turned to watch his brother go out while biting off a corner of the strawberry toast.

Reidier poured some half-and-half into his coffee and watched the blackness stained by plumes of cream until finally settling into a uniform dark beige. Entropy was everywhere.

"So then is that a no?" Reidier asked. "You don't want to take a nice break, enjoy a pleasant day at the beach, and feast your eyes on the sublimity that is me in bathing trunks?"

Eve smiled into her coffee. She knew what he was doing with this peace offering. It wasn't the outing to the beach so much as the day away from Bertram that he was offering her.

It didn't change anything. But it was nice.

"*Oui.* Why not? We will play pretend hooky," Eve acquiesced, without looking up. She knew he might misinterpret her lack of eye contact. He'd infer an aloof resignation, internalize it as a form of dismissive punishment intended to let him know she was still mad.

She wasn't. Quite the opposite, actually, she was touched by his gesture and even excited for a day at the beach with him and Otto. That's what kept her from looking at him sitting at the other end of the table next to the simile of her son. If she looked, if she saw them sitting there, him feeding Ecco, mirroring the morning ritual she had just finished with Otto, she would say no. She might not even do that. She might just kick her chair back from the table and storm off upstairs, leaving her *café* to slowly collapse down to room temperature.

Instead she kept her eyes cast downward and pretended to read the paper. Her nonchalant *oui* a minor, though effective, act of denial. It kept her from seeing a pyramid of eggs in the refrigerator, kept her from smelling the acrid, bitter stabbing aroma of boiled skin on the stove, kept her from hearing the crunch of toast in the simile's mouth.

"All right then," Reidier said. "I'll make the lunches if you pack the suits and towels and such."

Eve nodded. She stood up, her *café* held in one hand, the *Providence Journal* clutched in the other, and she pretended to keep reading the article she had been staring through for the past five minutes, while she headed out of the kitchen and up the stairs.

Reidier sang along to Ella Fitzgerald's version of Irving Berlin's "Slumming on Park Avenue." The boys laughed from the backseat as he changed the lyrics—substituting *swimming* for *slumming* and *Narragansett* for *Park Avenue*—all while attempting to dance in the driver's seat. Reidier's silliness was so charming and contagious that Eve couldn't resist singing along the next time the chorus came along. She leaned on the armrest and smiled back at Otto, who sat behind the driver's seat.*

---

* NB footage from car?? Were there nanobots in the car? More hitcher feeds . . . I guess smart dust could have inadvertently been transported to car.

Reidier pulled his tweed sport coat out from under her elbow where it had been lying on the middle armrest.

Eve rolled her eyes. "It must be your blanket for security. Who brings a sport coat to the beach, honestly, *mon chéri*?** It's thirty-five." In spite of having lived in America for well over five years, Eve still evaluated weather with a vestigial sense of Centigrade.

** Nope, QuAI footage. Gotta be. From the lapel pin on the sport coat.

"You tease me now, but when that ocean breeze picks up, I will not be chivalrous and offer it to you."

"You hear that?" Eve directed her comment to the backseat boys. "*Père* is a monster."

"A warm monster," Reidier corrected.

"Just for that, I'm going to put sand in your pockets."

"Now who's the monster, boys?"

"Monster? *Moi?* No, no. I am merely the incarnation of Madame Justice."

Reidier rolled his eyes, mimicking his wife. Eve slapped his arm playfully in response. The boys giggled in the back.

Reidier was right. The beach was pretty much their own, save for a couple of lifeguards and about half a dozen or so people running their dogs. With so few people in the water, the lifeguard nearby busied himself with a regimen of sit-ups and updates on his chalkboard about water temperature readings, undertow warnings, and tide status.

The tide was on its way out.

Eve sat next to their towels and beach chairs on the sand. She preferred the sensation of the heat and graininess on the bottom of her thighs to the texture of a towel. Her hands were planted behind her, her arms and torso forming an A-frame.

Her knees were bent and oscillating slightly back and forth as she twisted her feet down, away from each other, and circled them back, burying her feet deeper and deeper into the sand. It was a soothing, almost meditative act she had done ever since she was a little girl. She loved burrowing through layers of temperature, the scratchy heat at the top, to the soothing warmth just beneath the surface, to cooler darkness below, to the cold, dense level of sand that was so cold it almost felt wet, and then, if she was close enough to the water, down into the mud beneath. It was a slow process by design. Eve wanted to enjoy each different sensation as she delved into the not-so-firma terra. Once she reached the depth where it would start to hurt her toes to dig more, Eve would pull her feet out, stamp down the pile left in her wake, and start the process all over.

Otto waved at his mother as he stomped out of the ocean with his father and Ecco. Eve waved back. She brushed the sand off her palm on the towel spread out next to her and reached into the cooler to retrieve a Ziploc'd tuna sandwich. The boys screamed with delight as Reidier lifted them both up and over a wave that was chasing them. Otto held his left hand, Ecco his right. Both boys armed with orange water wings. The three of them glistened with symmetry, like a three-headed sea monster emerging from the primordial sea soup.

She had been surprised by Ecco's prowess in the water. Otto had kept a close circumference around his father, never straying too far out of the radius of Reidier's arms. Ecco, on the other hand, delighted in the buoyant medium, kicking and splashing in whatever direction a wave turned him. His haphazard play was so relentless that Reidier had to continually march after Ecco with Otto in tow. Where Otto only tacitly trusted the unknown of the deep, Ecco rejoiced in its newness, completely ignorant of the unknown. At one point, Ecco even removed one of his water wings and held it with his opposite hand so that he might dive below the surface and disappear except for his periscoped arm.

Eve crunched into a corner of her tuna sandwich, while watching Reidier and the boys dig for sand crabs at the water's edge. Tuna sandwiches had been a delightful and bizarre epiphany for Eve when she moved to America. Both in Morocco and France she had of course enjoyed the fresh tang of a seared tuna steak. During college, on a weekend jaunt to Amsterdam with her boyfriend at the time, she had learned about the delicious variety of mayonnaise, devouring the exquisite yin-yang contrast of piping hot *pomme frites* tempered by the cool, viscous white.

Tuna salad, however, was an altogether different concoction, repellent in appearance yet surprisingly stunning in flavor. The mixture of chopped hunks of meat, curls of celery, and whipped paste created an epicurean whole much more than the sum of its parts. The flat, comforting shield of toast would moisten and layer itself against the palette, while the tart, gummy mixture of tuna and mayo would wrap around the tongue's taste buds, and the crisp celery yielded a surprising and satisfying crunch between the molars.

In his *Enquiry Concerning Human Understanding*, philosopher David Hume reduced the creative power of the mind to merely the compounding or transposing of that which we perceive into a new magical "creation." The act of invention was the act of recombination. A golden mountain is the joining of two ideas: *gold* and a *mountain*. Greek mythology is full of these creations: centaurs are the combination of horses and men; griffons, eagles and lions. Tuna salad was the appetizing manifestation of Hume's ideas, the recombination of two disparate entities, the mermaid of sandwiches.

It took some time and a lot of coaxing for Eve to finally condescend to eat meat from a can. The concept of flesh sealed inside tiny tin drums for preservation baffled her. Surely it must be some type of punitive cuisine fed only to prisoners of the worst sort. Yet there it sat, in its place of prominence on a corner shelf in the market; and shoppers were willingly buying it in packs of six. Eve could not understand it any more than she could accept the concept of all-you-can-eat restaurants. Why Americans would pay extra money to gorge themselves past the point of fullness, past the point of comfort, distending their bodies like they were trapped at a banquet in Dante's Inferno, was beyond her. Nevertheless, Eve had to capitulate to the incomprehensible delight that is tuna salad.

"They're also called mole crabs because of how they burrow into the sand," Reidier said to the boys, who were collecting their bounty into a red bucket lined with mud and filled halfway with seawater.

"Emerita," Otto said.

Ecco had begun to remove the sand crabs from the bucket and line them up on a piece of driftwood so they would not burrow away. He grouped the larger ones at one end and the smaller ones at the other.

"What?" Reidier asked Otto.

"Emerita," Otto repeated. "That's their genius."

"Genus," Reidier corrected. "And very good."

"Genus," Otto repeated, while digging up another of these gray, shy crustaceans no larger than his thumb.

"Discovery Channel?"

Otto shook his head. "'Quarium. *Maman* took me."

"Ah, that was nice of *Maman*. I think I'll go check on her. No going in past your knees."

The boys both nodded, neither looking up from their work. Reidier stood up, stuck his hands in an outgoing wave to clean off the mud. He squinted at her as he sank-stepped his way up the beach.

"He is kind of amazing, no?" Eve asked.

"He's like a sponge. Remembered the genus of sand crabs from your trip to the aquarium over two months ago."

"No, not Otto. Ecco."

She could feel him strain to stay still, struggle not to drop his jaw and look at her. She knew he was trying to tread carefully, as you would stalking a deer that took a moment to nibble at some berries, so as not to spook her from the topic. She could feel him searching, hunting for the right words to say to keep the conversation on course.

Eve felt a wave of guilt wash over her. How long had he been waiting for this? Hoping for any sort of break, moment, mere acknowledgment. All she had ever been able to give him was horror and wrath. And he had taken it. Taken it all. She heard his breath deepen as if working to hold back a shudder.

Finally, in the end, he said nothing. Instead, he reached out and tucked a wisp of hair that the breeze had pulled behind her ear, then traced his fingertip along the strand up and over the bump of her ponytail. He always loved her in a ponytail. She had thought about that when pulling it back in the mirror after breakfast.

"What is he doing, lining them up like that?" Eve asked, and jutted her chin toward Ecco's sand crabs on the driftwood. Ecco had turned his back to the crabs and Otto was now shuffling them, rearranging them in a line along the wood.

"Seeing how well he can tell them apart."

"What do you mean?" Eve asked, looking back at Reidier with a quizzical expression.

Seagulls floated on the breeze and squawked in descending repetitive tones.

"Ecco named them all. Apparently he can tell them apart."

"So Otto's testing him?"

"Mm hm." Reidier nodded.

"Has he been getting them right?"

"Every one. They look identical to me. But I'd put one in one hand and one in the other, he'd tell me their names, and then I'd switch hands behind my back, and he could still tell which was which. Every time."

Eve turned back and watched Otto testing his brother. The sight was touching, picturesque even. Two little boys playing in the mud at the water's edge, the blue ocean stretching out behind them to the horizon, a wavy line between a dark and light blue. Maybe Ecco was like tuna salad. He was this bizarre recombination of reality, arising out of incongruity. A Humean chimera that dazzled and delighted. Maybe—as long as she didn't think about it. "You must feel like the proud papa, when you look at him."

"He is a marvel," Reidier agreed tentatively.

"And he's all your creation."

Reidier looked at her, unable to read her tone.

Eve gave him a half smile. "I mean, he is *your* creation. Modeled on ours. But, well, you made him. A modern day Dr. Frankenstein who fabricated a boy instead of a monster."

"I suppose you could look at it, him and me that way, although Dr. Frankenstein stitched together parts from various corpses."

"He did. And you animated a vast collection of inanimate quantum particles," she said, in the same tone that someone would observe that a school bus is yellow. "It really is marvelous."

Reidier dug his feet into the sand at the edge of the blanket.

Eve frowned at herself. She hadn't intended the conversation to go this way. She hadn't intended the conversation at all, really. Her comments just came out, like goosebumps in a chill.

"He's quite magnetic," Eve said, and placed her hand on top of Reidier's, which he had posted out behind him like she did.

She could feel the tension ripple out of him. It reminded her of the light, almost ticklish sensation of him drawing physics equations across her ribs with lipstick.

Reidier was looking at her now.

"I'm not quite sure whether it is because of his quirks or in spite of them. And Otto is intensely taken with him."

"Two peas in a pod," Reidier said.

"Literally. Why do you think that is?"

While pondering Eve's question, Reidier wiggled his toes back as if he were slowly trying to snap with them. Wet sand that had been clinging to his skin rained down over his foot. "It's how he sees things. There's no presumption. Most kids take in all the newness of the world, but they're hard at work trying to order it. They want to learn the rules of the game. Growing up is one long series of trials and errors of worldviews, constantly revising the way of things until we finally arrive at a set of givens expansive and reliable enough to become our worldview. That's the moment when childhood ends, when our list of givens gets set.

"Ecco seems entirely unconcerned with establishing a set of givens, let alone finalizing them. He's not trying to codify the rules of the game. Instead, he's in a constant state of play and wonder. As a result, he perceives reality at a fundamental, irreducible level, completely devoid of expectation. He sees the essence of things."

"In their Platonic ideal form," Eve reinterpreted.

Reidier nodded. "Bert calls him a little Buddha."

Eve laughed at this, throwing her head back. "Yes, that sounds like Bert. What is Buddha about the sky?"

Reidier shrugged an I don't know.

"Blue."

Reidier tilted his head at her, in confusion.

"I did not get it either. But that's what a Buddhist priest told me over breakfast, just outside Angor Wat. Maybe we can have Ecco explain it to us."

"A Zen master once told me to do the opposite of whatever he told me. So I didn't."

Eve looked at him for a moment and burst out laughing. She pressed her forehead against his shoulder, "I 'zought you were serious for a moment. Of course you know Buddhist jokes."

"What jokes?" Reidier feigned innocence. "Buddhists are cutting-edge scientists. It's from Buddhists that we finally learned that the leading cause of death is birth."*

---

* A Buddhist monk walks into a pizza parlor and asks for them to make him one with everything.

Eve actually snorted at this one, which made Reidier laugh, which made Eve try and hide in his armpit out of embarrassment, which only made Reidier laugh harder, which only made Eve snort again.

The two shook in hysterics, finally collapsing back on the towel together. They found each other in that moment, lying on their sides, tears in their eyes, their cheeks hurting from laughing so hard.

Reidier brushed another stray wisp of hair back behind Eve's ear again. "I love you in a ponytail."

Eve raised her eyebrows as if to say, *You do?* overplaying the coquette.

The palm of his hand traced over her shoulder, dropping down her side, until his finger hooked inside her bikini bottoms. She closed her eyes, focused on the sensation of his touch held against her skin. She loved whenever he touched her like that, slipping his hand up the sleeve of her shirt or tucking it inside the hip of her jeans. It was intimacy, it was ownership.

There's us and there's everybody else.

"I love your fingers hooked inside my suit."

This time Reidier raised a coquettish eyebrow, mimicking his wife. She let out an Oh of mock offense and smacked his shoulder.

"No!" Otto screeched.

Eve shot up. The boys were still at the water's edge. Three seagulls flapped above them in wait. It could have been a postcard. Except for the expression on Otto's face. He stood ankle deep in the water a few feet away from Ecco. He seemed stunned. Had something stung him? Had a crab bitten him?

Then Ecco brought his fist down with a self-satisfied *THUNK* and *SQUISH*.

Otto screeched in horror again as Ecco casually tossed the mangled carcass in a high parabolic arc. The gray corpse rotated end over end. One of the floating seagulls dove down and caught the feast in midair. The bird rose up, banking away from the others, in a selfish maneuver, and tossed the whole sand crab back down its gullet.

THUNK/SQUISH. Another crushed crustacean soared through the air and was caught by another gull.

THUNK/SQUISH toss, THUNK/SQUISH toss, THUNK/ SQUISH toss. Ecco was calmly going down the line of the log in rapid succession with a detached curiosity.

Otto's screams turned into outright weeping.

Before she was even aware of what was happening, Eve had covered the distance down the beach to the boys, caught Ecco's arm in middescent, and with an unexpected severity, yanked him away from his "chopping block," and tossed him onto his bum in the water. Two more steps and Eve had scooped up Otto into her arms.

His crying seemed to be in stereo. It took Eve several moments to actually come to her senses and realize what she had done. Otto wasn't crying in stereo, Ecco was now crying, more startled than hurt, sitting in the water, staring at Otto, mimicking his exact expression and tone.

Eve was at a loss. She had no understanding of how to parse the situation. So she left it. Turned around, holding Otto in her arms, and marched down the beach.

Eve cradled Otto against her, kissing the top of his head, whispering, "*Calme-toi mon petite*. Shh, shh, shh, *mon petit trognon de pomme*." Behind her, she could hear Reidier trying to soothe the still-crying Ecco.

It took half the length of the beach for Otto to calm down. He was still upset, but had run out of hysterics. His breath was a staccato of gulps with every inhale, as the sobs subsided. Small waves rolled up and down the beach with a reassuring beat. The sun warmed them.

At the end of the shore, a river carved the edge of the beach into a sandy point. The estuary ran down into the ocean chasing after the fading tide. Eve let a recovered Otto down to explore the jetty of sand. He found his way to the edge, where the water whittled the bank into a miniature cliff of dried mud that rose twenty centimeters up and out into a precarious precipice. Otto entertained himself by stamping his feet along the bank and watching hunks of dried mud calve off, slide into the current, and dissolve into the sea.

Eve looked back down the beach. Ecco and Reidier weren't too far behind. Ecco stomped through knee-high water, Reidier trailed behind him as if in a daze. Eve squinted, wondering if the two were more Pinocchio and Geppetto or the Creature and Frankenstein.

"That's far enough, Ecco," Reidier said, as they approached the point, still fifty yards or so behind Eve and Otto.

Ecco stopped and looked back at his . . . at Reidier. A small wave rose up over his knees and lapped against the beach. Ecco giggled. He lightly patted his palms against the nearly smooth surface. Not too far from where he stood, a dark curve of blue rippled through the otherwise light azure of the glassy ocean. It was the current running off from the estuary. The river and ocean whittled the beach into a scythe of sand. Ecco continued his rhythmic, soft slaps as he pushed through the water toward the liquid border.

Eve wasn't surprised that they had followed. She knew Kerek wanted to give Eve the space she needed, but could only tolerate so much distance. He was drawn after his wife and son with a gravity beyond his control, orbiting in wait with the patience of a moon.

Kerek risked a look toward Eve. He smiled slightly, then the corners of the smile dropped as he sucked his bottom lip beneath his top into a resigned frown. Kerek turned back to the water and watched Ecco pat the calm surface of the ocean with his right hand and the bumpy texture of the estuary current with his left.

She hadn't meant to react so harshly. Had it been so bad? Was it simply boys being boys? She turned back and followed Otto along the bank of the point, back behind the dunes. As Otto stomped down the edge, she imagined her little son was a giant, destroying the cliffs of Dover. The water devoured every hunk of land he shook loose into its depths.

No, it wasn't Ecco's violence that bothered her, per se: it was his detachment.

Eve's gaze tracked the river back as it curved through the sawgrass-lined banks and disappeared into the woods beyond. She used to think rivers were like they had told her at school. They swept through the forest, eating away at the earth all along and carrying chunks of land out to sea. Now she wasn't so sure. It was all in the way one looked at it, really. People always focus on the land, don't they? But maybe the river wasn't eating away at the ground, carrying the land out to sea like everybody told her; maybe it was the land that was grasping at the water, trying to hold it back, keep it in, when all the water wanted was to get back where it belonged, where it came from.

The breeze blew another wisp of hair across her face. She tucked it behind her ear. Turning back, she could just see over the dune to the other side of the point. Reidier stood, fixed in the water, a ruin of Atlantis. He seemed calm, at peace. The water lapped at his knees, his hands resting in his pockets, as he gazed out at the ocean and watched the dark blue current carry an orange buoy out to sea.

The scream rose out of her throat before the realization registered with her brain.

It was a high-pitched, guttural, pained sound like an eagle's screech upon spotting a predator in her nest.

It was a stunning pitch, literally. Otto froze in his tracks of destruction. Reidier's muscles tensed and locked. The world stopped moving, except for the orange flotsam. And Eve.

For the second time in less than half an hour, Eve found herself unexpectedly in motion, while her mind raced to catch up and get a handle on the situation. She sprinted up and over the dune, down the muddy shore, and into the water so quickly that her legs couldn't keep up with the momentum of her upper body, and she tumbled into the ocean. Upon contact, Eve instinctually pulled herself forward with a breaststroke she had honed in secondary school.

It wasn't until Eve was several hundred yards out, shouting in sync with her strokes, *"Calme toi mon petite. Ça va mon trognon de pomme,"* that her brain finally began to decipher the semiotics of the situation that her body had already resolved. It wasn't until she was choking on seawater that she could consciously see the vibrant apricot float bobbing on the water not as a weathered lobster buoy that had broken free, but as Ecco's water wings.

Ecco smiled back at Eve, his extended arms still patting the textured surface of the current that was carrying him out to the deep. Ecco still rejoiced in the newness of it all, completely ignorant of the unknown. He even took to mimicking his . . . Eve. With a giggle, he kicked his feet back and forth and a flurry of white erupted behind him as he accelerated further away from her.

"Mais arrête! Arrête ça! Ça suffit!" Eve shouted with a furious, almost hysteric tone.

Ecco stopped kicking.

Eve caught up with Ecco over half a mile out. The current and undertow had done most of the work. She had felt nothing but unadulterated intent on the way out. On the way back, with Ecco holding on to her shoulders and giggling in her ear, she felt nothing but exhaustion. Every striation of muscle tissue burned with lactic acid. The inside of her lungs had been scraped raw by CO_2 and salt water. Intent might have gotten her out to sea, but anger is what got her back.

The mud was a relief under her toes. Well before it was shallow enough to stand, Eve would let herself sink down a foot below the surface. The cool water would briefly snuff out the heat rising off her head. Her pointed foot would tap against the ocean floor, and she would float down into a *demiplié*. Her arm extended upward, a perfect *écarté* with which she held onto Ecco's hand while he bobbed at the surface. The world above was muted out for a moment, and her muscles stopped screaming. Then she would leap upward, completing her adagio underwater ballet, back up to Ecco, back up to the world, and a few feet closer to land. Incapable of swimming any further, Eve danced her way out of the sea. Finally, waist deep, Eve stood up, put Ecco on her hip, and walked out.

Reidier was still standing where she had passed him on the way in, a statue anchored in the knee-deep water. She stood in front of her husband, adjusted Ecco higher up on her hip, and slapped Reidier across the face.

Otto waited for Eve at the water's edge. Eve scooped him up onto her other hip and headed back down the beach, a boy in each arm.

Eve and Reidier didn't speak for the entire thirty-minute drive home. Nor did they speak that evening. That night, in her journal, Eve wrote, "My husband, the destroyer of distance, whom I've never been further away from."*

---

* "One, two, three, four," bills dropped on the library counter. I wanted to tell her to keep the $31.28 of change, but didn't want to come off like a prick, and a memorable prick at that. Save the douchebag charity for another day.

She counted out my change, gave me a receipt, and asked me to wait while she retrieved the reserved material from my shelf.

It had to be Hilary. Who else? Who else would've—could've—taken out a shelf in my name? It had to be her.

The librarian returned with "my" material. Slid it across the counter. I didn't give it a second look. Why would I? If it's my material, I knew what it was. I smiled at her, picked it up, and asked her to direct me to a private reading room.

There were three items: a CD-RW in a plastic case, with RT, PE written on it with Sharpie; also there was not one, but two different copies of Faust. The first was from the

>*Collegiate German Reader in Prose and Verse*
>James Henry Worman
>Kessinger Publishing, LLC (July 25, 2007)

and

>*Faust*
>*A Tragedy*
>By Johann Wolfgang von Goethe
>Translated, In The Original Metres, by Bayard Taylor (1870)

Both books had half a business card stuck in them as bookmarks. The former's between pages 129 and 130. On page 130, lines 382-385 were circled in pencil with a "?" in the margin next to it. It was Hilary's handwriting.

>Daß ich erkenne, was die Welt
>Im Innersten zusammenhält,
>Schau' alle Wirkenskraft und Samen,
>Und thu' nicht mehr in Worten kramen.

German. Get fucked. German?!

Over to the other book where the business card was wedged between pages 18 & 19. Wouldn't you know it, lines 382-385 (page 18) were circled in pencil.

>That I may detect the inmost force
>Which binds the world, and guides its course;
>Its germs, productive powers explore,
>And rummage in empty words no more!

Just another quotation. An epigraph to resonate with some new chapter she had yet to write into the report. It might as well have read, "Be sure to drink your Ovaltine."

The exhaustion hit me like an airbag. As did the nausea. I had to put my head down, rest it on my hands. Breathe in the darkness. At this point I didn't give a damn what RT and PE stood for, unless the CD contained an animated treasure map or the new Imagine Dragons album.

My inhales were warm this close to the desk.

The sensation started in my colon and bubbled up with a fierce velocity until it erupted out of me. A belly laugh shook my entire body. All the time, all the effort, all the Maseratis, and I wasn't solving riddles, I was chasing down nursery rhymes.

I should've held on to her. What was the use in setting Lorelei free? Protecting my mother's "legacy"? All it got me was a couple of overdue library books. Who cares if Lorelei's with the Department or not? Christ, I'd been doing the Department a favor keeping this report from them. Saving them from the labyrinth in the rabbit hole that wasn't a maze at all, just a downward spiral with a bunch of shit at the bottom.

With my forehead still resting on the back of my hands (which were still resting on Goethe), I shook my head back and forth. A beleaguered denial that ended with my cheek atop my pillow of fingers. The cubbyhole desk in the private reading room was still in pretty good condition, with only a handful of pencil marks and a couple of ink stains on its walls and tabletop. A shelf ran across the back of the cubby-desk. From my vantage point, I could see underneath it. Someone had carved: *What do I do when the puzzle pieces don't fit?* Someone else had carved a response: *Use your knife.*

I smiled at the zeugmatic call and response.

My gaze dropped down to the desktop. I fidgeted with the first bookmark, brushed my fingertip against the soft fibers of the torn edge. The irony of it was pleasing, how violently ripping something in half can leave behind such a soft centerline. I pinned it down with my index finger and spun it with my thumb. Like I said, fidgeting. Something about the rotation of it caught my eye, though. Some subliminal hieroglyphic effect that I couldn't quite put my finger on. I stopped spinning it and read:

Steven A.

Director, Obsessive-C

Butl

345 Black

Provid

T:(40

Steven meant nothing to me. As far as I could recall there was no Steven anywhere in the report. Still there was that feeling, that hooked hieroglyphic hanging off my anterior superior temporal gyrus, creaking around the right hemisphere of my brain like one of those plastic hanging monkeys from the old board game.

I lifted my head up and unwedged the other bookmark half from beneath Goethe.

Rasmussen, MD
ompulsive Disorder Program
er Hospital
stone Boulevard
ence, RI 02906
1) 455-6200

The hook of insight sharpened, slicing into my cerebrum, but still not yet pulling back the curtain. I held my breath as I pushed the two halves together.

Steven A. Rasmussen, MD
Director, Obsessive-Compulsive Disorder Program
Butler Hospital
345 Blackstone Boulevard
Providence, RI 02906
T:(401) 455-6200

The two places leapt out at me as the hook ripped back the curtain, and I was face-to-face with Oz.

Butler Hospital.

Both Lovecraft's father and mother went crazy and died in Butler Hospital just a few miles from his home, Lorelei had said. Just a few miles from 454 Angell.

Blackstone Boulevard. Blackstone.

While the right state of mind might prove a dead end, the left proves infinitely versatile. Especially if you have a philosopher's stone on black stone. It wasn't a Hilary typo. It wasn't a black stone, some oracle onyx, philosopher's Rosetta Stone cypher. It was an address. A goddamn location!!

I wrapped up the two Goethes in my coat and tucked them under my arm before my brain caught up with everything and then leapt ahead. I slid the CD in my back pocket, stopped at the librarian counter, and casually asked for some Scotch tape on my way out the door with two stolen books.

The next morning, Eve and the boys are gone. Reidier finds only a cup of cold coffee and a note from Eve.

R,

I had another dream last night. We were sitting in my père's study, in Provence. You and I on the leather sofa, him in his Louis XIV chair with his back to the French doors. It was evening, but part of the garden was lit up by a distant floodlight.

We were enjoying some wine, laughing, telling stories. My father was in the middle of telling an animated tale, when behind him, outside the French door, I saw a figure. A silhouette of a man. Neither you nor mon père noticed as he opened the door. At first I was more curious than frightened, until he leaned into the light, and I saw that the man outside was my father.

The apparition simply stood there for several minutes, staring at himself in the flesh. Finally, he beckoned to my father sitting in the chair, held out his hand and gestured for my father to follow him down to the river. I looked to the two of you, and you both kept on in your conversation, completely unaware.

When I looked back the scene repeated itself. The silhouette outside, the opening of the door, the beckoning to my father, who this time nodded at the apparition and waved him on. Then the man was gone, but the door was still open. I ran to the door and saw the ghost of my father heading down the garden path. I was furious, full of rage at this phantom for trying to lure my father away from me. I ran after him, but by the time I made it down the path, the ghost was already on the other side of the river, glimpsing through the trees. I yelled after him, screaming, cursing . . .

I woke up shouting in our empty bed.

I need to not be here for a bit.

I am taking the boys to New York for a few days. We will be back Sunday.

~Moi

ECCO III

Reality is obscured by the clutter of the world.

~Heidegger?

Ring

. . .

Ring

. . .

Ring

. . .

Ring

. . .

Voice mail—

"Hi. It's me. I, uh, I hope it's ok that I'm calling. I know you wanted some space. For you and the boys. How are the boys? Any problems? I know it's irrational, I'm sure everything is fine. Just worried about them. And you.

"Are you all still coming home today? It's ok, if not. Just wondering. I'm roasting a chicken, some baked potatoes and salad for dinner. If you guys make it back in time, great. If not, a little delicious leftovers never hurt anyone. So just let me know. Hope New York was, great. Love you all.

"It's Sunday, just about five fifteen."

. . .

Ring

. . .

Ring

. . .

Ring

. . .

Ring

. . .

"Hey, me again. Not trying to, I mean it's not a problem if you don't want to answer. I hope my calls aren't, well. Ok, so just checking in again. I painted a mural down in the basement. Well, copied one. Clyde helped me. It's Picasso's bullfighter. Really livens up the lower level.

(Long sigh.)

"Assuming today is a no go. Either that, or you hit some really horrible traffic in Connecticut. When it's not the traffic, it's the construction in that state. You can't win, really. Well, in case you're headed home right now, there are plenty of leftovers in the fridge. If you're still taking more time, then I guess whatever you need.

"Hope the boys are behaving. My love to you and them."

. . .

Ring

. . .

Ring

. . .

"Eve, I respect your need for space. And take as much time as you need. Honestly. But if you could, please, text me. Let me know when—that you're all ok. I'd really appreciate it. I'm worried.

"It's Monday. 7:42. I love you."

. . .

Ring

. . .

"Eve, whatever it is you need, however much space, the way you're going about it, is completely uncool. And irresponsible. Go wherever you want, for however long you want. Don't talk to me. Whatever, that's fine. But fucking check in. Whatever you might think, I at least deserve an update on the boys' well-being! I mean, how hard is it to send a goddamn text or e-mail? Seriously. Enough. Whatever punishment you think you're doling out, it's . . . you're not keeping the high ground. I went to see Spencer. Don't make me get the police involved. Or the Department.

"Tuesday. One thirty."

. . .

"Hi, it's me. I haven't, I couldn't sleep. Can't do much of anything, really. I painted over the—Ecco's, I painted the wall. Sun's coming up. Please call me. I'm uh, I love you so much. At least just text me that everything's ok with you, Otto . . . Ecco."

. . .

Ring—

"Hello?"

"Monsieur Reidier?" asked the aristocratic voice.

"Yes."

"It's your old friend from the Fontainebleau, do you recognize my voice?"

You need two things for your work: funding and autonomy.

"Yes. I do."

"*Bon.* Of course you do. Well, we received your e-mail to our health spa and have some wonderful packages to offer you."

Reidier sighs. "Great. Where should I—?"

"I'm actually having trouble hearing you. Cell interference perhaps."

"Oh, I'm in the CCV,* is this any better?"

---

* Center for Computation and Visualization, part of Brown's CS (computer science) department. It provides both virtual and physical hosting of Linux servers. The physical hosting is located in CCV's machine room and allows for individual maintainence.

"Alas, no. Perhaps if you went outside?"

It was the same driver as before. The same taxi. And the same intimation that it was in his and his family's best interest that he take a ride. The same subtle, dull pulse, like a deep bass beat, washing over him when the door closed behind him. It was not the same destination though. No strip club. No crowd. This time it was in one of the old abandoned factories off of Route 10.**

** "You boys going to do the honor for us?" the voice asks, practically an accusation of excitement.

Hilary's CD-RW apparently had an .mp3 on it. One of the Department's myriad of NB audio recordings. The Lexus's Bose surround-sound system put me right in the center of the conversation while I sped my way through the residential streets of Providence's East Side, like a bat out of hell, a homing pigeon on meth and Angel Dust streaking its way to roost at Butler Hospital.

The aggressively boisterous voice continues, "How's that, Eve, not only does your family get to watch your husband make a miracle, your boys get to be a part of it and start it all off?"

"It's quite compelling, Pierce," a woman's voice responds.

Eve's voice. For months I had lived with this demigoddess, and this was the first time I had heard her voice.

"I had to pull quite a few strings to get all of you in here." Pierce waits for a response of gratitude. There isn't one. He continues unfazed, "A momentous day indeed! Not just the final frontier, beyond the frontier. No. It's the destruction of frontiers altogether. The finale of frontiers."

The words clicked into place like the numbers on a flip clock. I knew this exchange. It was from Hilary's first chapter. It was the final exchange between Pierce and the Reidiers right before *The Reidier Test* went off. This was the audio file. Why would Hilary go to such lengths to stow away an audio recording of such a long-ago documented segment? It's a chapter I'm almost sure she had already shown the Department.

"Nothing is ever created or destroyed," another male voice cuts in. That would be Reidier.

Pierce starts to say something, but Reidier cuts in and announces, "We're ready."

"It will work?" Pierce isn't so much asking as ordering.

"Is your floating battery out there going to give me the *BEEP* watts of power I need?"

The beep was clearly Department censorship. This wasn't even a raw recording. It was Department edited and approved.

"Absolutely." Pierce responds with a laugh and what sounds like a slap on Reidier's back.

"Then my physics will work."

Beat.

"You've definitely earned yourself a vacation," Pierce says with overdone good spirits. "Let's change the world. Wait till I'm back in the observation deck."

Sounds of Pierce walking out of the room, opening the security door, and it closing behind him.

Sounds of some shuffling around. If I remember correctly, Reidier was putting on his tweed sport coat, upon which QuAl, disguised as a pin, perched with a watchful eye on his lapel.

Sounds of Reidier walking over to Otto? and opening the Plexiglas cover over the activation button.

"Wait until I tell you," Reidier says softly.

Sounds of Eve moving to stand behind Otto.

Sounds of Reidier walking over to Ecco and opening the other Plexiglas safety cover.

"Wait until I tell you," Reidier instructs Ecco. "On 'go,' boys. Three, two, one, go."

Reidier says something to himself, but interference seeps in and garbles the audio into guttural gibberish. "Ach itch er keen three-welts im inner stern-zoos-ham and halt, showallthework, incraftandsalmon . . . nd thoo niche meh inwartcrammin."

That was it. The whole .mp3. I listened to it on repeat for the whole drive. It was a nice aural aid, but I didn't get it.

Butler Hospital felt like a little campus right out of the '50s: acres of woods, tidy paths connecting collections of gothic brick buildings that were themselves a throwback to nineteenth-century institutional architecture, directory signs along the road to point you toward the right department.

"Achitcherkeenthreeweltsiminnersternzooshamandhalt, showallthework, incraftandsalmon . . . ndthoonichemehinwartcramming."

I followed the signs to the Obsessive-Compulsive Disorder Ward. It also happened to be the Inpatient Psychiatric Ward.

"Ach itch erkeen three welts im inner stern zoo sham and halt, show all the work, in craft and salmon . . . nd thoo niche meh in wart cramming."

There was something about that garbled guttural gibberish. I sat in the Lexus, parked out in front of the OCD/Psychiatric asylum blasting gibberish on repeat, half expecting the men in white coats to come and collect me.

"Ach itch erkeen 'as ze welts im innerstern zoosamandhalt, show all workincraft and salmon . . . nd thoo niche mere in Wharton cramin."

It was garbled too uniformly. Static interference would be more random. This had a pattern to it. And there was something about the breaks.

"D'ach itch erkeen 'as ze welts/ im innerstern zoosamandhalt,/ show all workincraft and salmon/ nd thoo niche mere in Wharton cramin."

Once again the flip clock of insight fluttered into place. I unfurled my coat in the passenger seat, and the two Goethes tumbled out. I grabbed one and flipped to page 130 while the CD track repeated.

"Dach itch erkeen 'as ze welts
im innerstern zoosamandhalt,
show all workincraft and salmon
nd thoo niche mere in Wharton cramin."

Everything clicked into place. The interference wasn't garbling the audio . . . it was German. I read along with one last play of the CD.

"Daß ich erkenne, was die Welt
Im Innersten zusammenhält,
Schau' alle Wirkenskraft und Samen,
Und thu' nicht mehr in Worten kramen."

Reidier was quoting Goethe. *That I may detect the inmost force which binds the world, and guides its course; its germs, productive powers explore, and rummage in empty words no more!* Reidier knew what he was doing.

Neither incident, nor accident, but rather pure, unadulterated intent.

I turned the Lexus off, grabbed my coat off the seat and Dr. Rasmussen's taped-together business card off the dash.

Curzwell waited for him toward the back, in front of a large window that almost covered the entire wall. Several of the panes were missing glass. Several others were darkened with decades of soot and dust. Curzwell smoked a cigarette. He turned toward Reidier's approaching footsteps.

"Ah, *bon*." Curzwell held up his hands, palms open perhaps as a gesture of peace or vague attempt at urging serenity. "Your wife and sons are home, no worse for the wear."

Reidier stopped dead in his tracks. A moment later, anger twisted his features. "You!"

"No, no. Not I. You reached out to us for help. Why would we—?"

"Leverage."

Curzwell nods. "No, quite the opposite, actually. Your family was collected by Homeland Security at JFK International Airport trying to board a flight for Nice Côte d'Azur International Airport. They were then transferred off-site to an official holding facility, one of many immigration tanks. Within a day, they were transferred again to another, less official, holding facility. That's when we retrieved them."

His words disappeared into the vastness of the space.

"At the unofficial holding facility?" Reidier asked.

"En route."

"You're telling me you confronted Homeland Security."

"Beimini did. Yes. And, at the time we interceded, they were no longer in the custody of Homeland Security."

"The Department?"

"In a manner of speaking. To be more specific, an unaffiliated taxi service."

"Like your taxi service?"

Curzwell snorted. "No. Much less subtle, and much more formal, than ours."

"How did you retrieve my family from them?"

"Force." The word fell out of his mouth and onto the floor between them.

Reidier stared down at it.

"Please understand, your wife and children's welfare were always our highest priority. Our envoys are highly skilled at this sort of thing."

Reidier still stood where he was initially stopped in his tracks. Anger had given way to a measured curiosity tempered by contained paranoia. "And what happened to their envoys?"

"They've been reassigned."

Reidier nodded, lost in his own calculations. Solutions, however, didn't compute. Curzwell wrapped the truth in ambiguity. "Thank you."[124]

"We are on the same side, Dr. Reidier."

"Are we?"

"We'd like to think so."

"Also you were hoping this would endear me to defect?"

"I won't deny that in serving your interests, we were serving our own. That being said, you did reach out to us for help. As far as leverage, we merely leveled the field of play. No, that's not right . . ."

"Leveled the playing field."

"*Oui. Exactement!* Leveled the playing field. Beimini's interest in you would be compromised by the Department holding human capital as leverage to compel you to work toward its ends. We upended their leverage and restored balance, neutrality, so that you'd be free to make up your own mind, *sans* duress. As I promised you in our first meeting, we want to be partners with you. While we do have our own agenda, we will never hide information from you. Or occlude our motivations. Or kidnap your loved ones as collateral for our goals."

"Except of course when you're holding on to information about my family's abduction and implementing a potentially very dangerous

---

[124] None of this shows up anywhere in the information given to me by the Department. Officially, this never happened.

rescue mission. You could have simply informed me the Department had them and let me proceed through official channels."

Curzwell let the dust settle after the words disintegrated. "The danger was not from us. We took every precaution. Unfortunately, while our intelligence was of high quality, it was by no means hard rock."

"Rock solid," Reidier corrected.

"Mm. We had no way of knowing for sure the people we were intercepting were in fact your family until we had them. Therefore, it was decided to not present you with potentially false information about their possible, though not certain, jeopardy. Nor could we be sure that Mrs. Reidier was not simply acting on her own behalf."

The insinuation landed like an undetonated missile. Beimini knew or at least had *high-quality intelligence* about their domestic strife. The warhead lodged inside Reidier ticked with explosive potential.

"Full disclosure," Curzwell hurried forward in an attempt to diffuse the volatility. "I would let you know that we did make a . . . *comment dites-vous?*" Curzwell searched for the word in decrepit rafters above. "Pit stop. Yes? Back in New York City. It was easier to disappear there within 'the numerical anonymity of roads and avenues.' As Sartre said, '*Le mal de* New York.'"

Curzwell let his gaze drift past Reidier, careful not to trip any wires. "Disappearing was not our only priority in the city." Curzwell shook his head and sucked at his teeth, making a tsk-tsk sound. "I have relationships with several of the board members at Sloan Kettering. At Mrs. Reidier's request, of course, we had a team of oncologists take a look at her. I was neither privy to the examination nor their findings. No one at Beimini was. It would not have been proper. Whatever was discovered is for you and your wife to discuss."

Curzwell finished and waited for Reidier's response.

Reidier removed his cell phone from the inside pocket of his sport coat. No calls. No texts.

"Eve hasn't contacted me. So as far as I know your story is just that, a story."

Curzwell smiled, unfazed. "That is good. That means she took my request to heart."

"You requested my wife not contact me?"

"I did. I thought it best for us to have a chance to talk, in private, before the Department 'hears' whatever version of what happened you and Mrs. Reidier choose to present."

The implication floated in the air with the dust particles, drifting upward in a band of sunlight.

"You think there are bugs." Reidier asked without question.

"I suspect."

"Your intelligence wasn't hard rock."

Curzwell smiled disarmingly at the way Reidier threw his words back in his face.

"We have not done a sweep of your house or anything of that sort, no. But the Department seems to have an affinity for nanosects."

Curzwell exhaled a plume of smoke. It swirled into and out of view as it gyred through the sunbeam. The tendrils of smoke bled into the column of dust particles like cream into coffee.

"Nanosects?"

"Mic-Mites. Smart Dust. Nanobots. Microscopic microphones, cameras, heart monitors, radio transmitters, infrared heat sensors. They can coat an environment with them, especially an interior, and one would never even know it."

"Huh." Reidier gave no indication of his own discovery concerning gossipy ceiling fans, prying toasters, nor his walls literally having eyes and ears.

"I apologize for not alerting you. Again it would have been only conjecture. Which you might have interpreted as an attempt on my part to poison the well, so to speak." As Curzwell lit another cigarette, he casually let out, "Also, I assumed that eventually you would catch on, maybe even catch a few."

Reidier tried to read Curzwell's flawless face. His features suggested age, without aging, like a well-preserved antique. They looked old, of course, clearly a relic from another era, nevertheless there was a certain well kemptness, a preservation of aesthetics against the sandstorms of time. Curzwell's face revealed nothing but a long history of control and care.

"I have not caught any. Nor have I hunted for any," Reidier equivocated, careful not to reveal anything.

Curzwell noticed his watch, slipped his fingers into his pocket, and pulled out a Ziploc bag full at least a dozen different vitamins. "But you have inoculated yourself against the infestation. Good, good. I'm glad I was not wrong about you."

The flattery passed through Reidier unnoticed, like AM radio waves.

"Are you not concerned then that I might've inadvertently brought some listening lice with me? Here. To our clandestine meeting?"

Curzwell gave Reidier a knowing smile. "Not at all. Our exterminators have deloused you."

The subtle pulse, the bass beat . . . some sort of low energy electromagnetic pulse tuned to nanosect frequencies.

From Curzwell's other pocket, he took out a flask. In one practiced swig, he downed the entire cornucopia of pills and capsules. As he screwed the top of the flask back on, he shared, "Coconut water. What good is a regimen of vitamins and minerals without electrolytes?"

"The nicotine doesn't help with that?" Reidier asked with a glib smile.

Curzwell rolled with it. "What is the point of extending your life, if you do not live it?"

"There's a hole in your story," Reidier said, moving past Curzwellian contradictions.

"If you like, I'd be happy to arrange a sweep of your house for you, although that might, how do they say, tip your hand."

"Not about the nanosects. Although those fall into the same hole," Reidier said. He walked away from Curzwell and gazed out a window at Route 10 and Providence beyond. "How do I know it's not you who abducted my family, you who set up an elaborate ruse of a rescue, and you who blew the Smart Dust into my home in order to align yourself with me while implicating the Department?"

"And me who somehow inspired you to call me for help? *Bon*." Curzwell puckers his lips in contemplation and then simply shrugs. "There is nothing I may say that would not collapse under that very same rhetorical assault. You are right, where my original economic offer did not bear fruit, I might now have been trying this emotional one. *Je comprends*. Perhaps then, it is washing?"

"A wash?"

"*Oui*. A wash. Whatever good I might have done is nullified by whatever bad I might have engineered. It is a wash. As I said before, all I set out to do was level the playing field. Of course I hope, in the end, you come work with us. For you, for your family. But it is for you to decide without any compulsory circumstances. A partnership cannot be held together with bondage."

Reidier's phone rang.

"That would be Pierce. By now he would have been alerted to your sterilization. The Department doesn't like disappearing acts. Even yours."

Reidier checked. It was Pierce.

"Answer it, don't answer. Right now your cell signal appears to be located at the XRA Medical Imaging facility out on Route 6."

It took Reidier a moment. "MRIs."

"Among other high-powered electric and magnetic equipment

you might be curious about for scanning. A place with plenty of medical and technical expertise to justify a visit from you. We wanted to provide you with a believable alibi should you want one. That being said, feel free to share with Pierce my and Beimini's involvement. Or not. The choice is up to you. While he might have his suspicions, I believe all Pierce knows right now is that you have significant allies."

Reidier silenced his phone and put it back in his pocket.

Curzwell smiled and nodded.

"Don't interpret that as some sort of subtle alliance. I'm just buying myself time to make a more considered calculation," Reidier said.

"Of course." Curzwell stubbed out his cigarette. "Well, I'm sure you must be anxious to get back and see your family."

Reidier stared out the window a moment longer, then finally turned back to Curzwell. "Assuming everything you have shared with me is the truth, I am still curious about one detail."

Curzwell waited, a statue of patience.

"If you're not monitoring me or my family, how then did you know Eve and the boys' whereabouts?"

Curzwell nodded. The question came as no surprise to him. "We are indeed not spying on you. The Department is, how do you say, another story."

"You're watching the watchers."

"If you like."

"So then you haven't needed to spy on me. You can just read their reports."

"We keep abreast of the Department's strategies and tactics. Within that, we do learn a bit about your progress. However, neither the Department nor we are able to connect all the dots of your work. There seems to be more than a bit of art to your science. Not to mention a fairly high Chinese wall encircling Schrödinger's Box." Curzwell laughed at his mashed metaphors.

Reidier did not join in. Rather he narrowed his eyes at Curzwell. "I'm not worried about either of you attempting to purloin my work."

Curzwell's laugh transformed into another conciliatory smile. "Your domestic doings do not concern us, except insofar as the Department's exploitation of them. We are merely the antibodies attempting to counter the Departmental infection."

"Hence your knowledge of Eve's whereabouts."

Curzwell nodded, *"Oui."*

"Well, thank you. This has been most informative." As he headed toward the door, Reidier asked, "Would it be all right if your man took me up to Federal Hill on the way home? I'd like to pick up a pizza from Caserta's for the fam."

Reidier forced his nonchalance into a smile. He even bit the insides of his cheeks a little. It was the only way to keep a rein on the tremors inside trying to shake loose.

"Of course, Dr. Reidier," Curzwell said, matching pace with him. *"Au revoir,* doctor."

Curzwell held open the door for Reidier.

Reidier paused. "How much work has your company put into storage?"

Curzwell raised a quizzical eyebrow.

"For your Restoration program. Data storage."

"Ah. Quite a bit actually. There are some interesting possibilities with Exabyte capacity in carbon-based memory, carbon nanotubes for nonvolatile memory. NRAM. If you'd like, I'll send over some info and specs."

Reidier grunts in acknowledgment and leaves.

The back of the cab was inundated with the delicious aroma of the large pepperoni and mushroom pizza sitting on the seat next to him.

Reidier stared out the window as Atwells Avenue crawled by. He sank his hands deep into his pockets and took out his cell phone. He started to make a call and then stopped.

Reidier lowered the window a few inches and slid his cell phone through the opening. It bounced and spun after the cab, dancing with longing and inertia, finally shattering apart in the wake of the cab passing beneath the Pine Cone sculpture of abundance, dangling from the Atwells Avenue Arch.*

---

* Looks like I'm not the only one with an allergy to cell phones.

Butler's waiting room was surprisingly nice. Open, loftlike feel, exposed brick, dark hardwood floors that must've been the original planks, designer leather chairs, and huge windows that look out onto the grounds and woods beyond. No magazines, no carpet, no fluorescent lights, no antiseptic smell. In fact, if you didn't know any better, you'd think you were in the reading room of some tech start-up that renovated an old mill.

Except for the nurse who kept eyeballing me from behind her cherry-wood counter, mustering a patronizing though still wary smile every time I happened to meet her gaze. She'd been suspicious since the moment I handed her Dr. Rasmussen's Scotch taped–together business card. I can't really blame her. Even if I did do my best to sound professional and state I was sent to see him by Dr. Hilary Kahn. Let's not forget I'm running on about eighty minutes of sleep, a couple grams of Sudafed dust, and a liter-and-a-half of Starbucks. If I were in Nurse Wary's orthopedic white shoes, I'd probably be halfway through filling out an admittance form for me.

They're out there.

Best opening line of any American novel. Damn it if maybe I didn't belong in here. Truth be told I wasn't feeling paranoid anymore. I sat in the leather and steel chair staring out at the woods and *wasn't* imagining Department commandos coalescing out of the trees like the Viet Cong in a war movie.

But they're out there.

Nurse Wary raised a quizzical eyebrow at me. I think I might've laughed out loud to myself without realizing it.

I gave her a wink. "Just thinking of an old joke."

She nodded and went back to pretending to work.

I wanted a smile. "I knew a reporter who got a tip about this insane asylum that was holding sane people against their will. So, she went there to check it out. Snuck in and snooped around. Stumbled into the gymnasium where a guy was shooting hoops and sinking every shot. My reporter friend asked if he was being held there against his will, and he said, 'Yeah, I was gonna be in the NBA until they locked me in here.' She took note and continued her exploration. Not too long after she found a woman playing a beautiful song on the violin. When my reporter friend asked the woman if she was being held against her will, the woman said, 'I am. I was going to be a concert violinist but they locked me in here.' My friend frowned and shared her sympathy and went off to do some more digging. Found her way into another patient's room, where a man sat naked at a card table, with his penis in a bowl of almonds. My reporter friend asked, 'Are you being held against your will?' The man said, 'No, I'm fucking nuts!'"

Not even a chortle.

"Dr. Rasmussen will see you now," she said, and gestured up the stairs. "Take a right at the top, third door on the left."

I went with one last glance at the woods. Let 'em be out there. I'm in here. I took the stairs two at a time.

Halfway up, the nurse called out to me, "Stay away from the nuts."

I laughed and continued my bounding.

-----Original Message-----

From: Donald Pierce [mailto:donald.pierce@darpa.mil]

Sent: Tuesday, June 11, 2008 11:56 p.m.

To: larry.woodbury@darpa.mil

Subject: prodigal wife

Larry, how can there still be no update on the Retrieval Team? They couldn't have just disappeared between JFK and the safe house . . .

Until we know more, we stick with ignorant Good Cop role. While I concede your point on the effectiveness of intimidation through insinuation, the fact is our position is weak. Especially considering the fact that mother goose and the ducklings have returned to roost. And clearly with some impressive help.

I want you to get up to NYC first thing in the morning and personally debrief the DHS boys. Make sure there were no official mentions.

If we're clear on that, then it was a run-of-the-mill random SNAFU. The RT business happened off campus. For all we know it was a disinformation strategy staged by any number of unfriendly competing parties.

As such, it's an opportunity to officially implement round-the-clock security—for their own safety.

The aggregate of all the recent coincidences adds up to a deliberate and designed sum.

-DP

Their reunion is heartfelt—hugs, tears, kisses, apologies—but nevertheless a complete and utter performance.

Reidier can barely get the pizza onto the kitchen counter before Eve surges into him, burying her face in his chest, sobbing into his embrace. Otto is wrapped around his leg, for a knee-height hug. Reidier rains down susurrations of comfort, his right hand on his son's head, his left grabbing a fistful of Eve's hair while he kisses her and whispers into her ear. He murmurs indecipherable directives while staring over her shoulder, across the room, at Ecco, who sits on the table examining the trio with a detached curiosity.

Eve gives the slightest of nods when Reidier finishes.

It's hard to say whether Reidier's near-manic state of disbelief is a result of Eve's absence, Curzwell's story, or the Department's involvement (or lack thereof). All that's clear is that Reidier is a man colliding with the edge of his limitations and badly bruising his psyche as a result.

For several minutes he keeps going back and forth from Eve to Otto, touching, scanning, caressing, grasping. "I'm so sorry. I'm so so sorry," he says.

"I know, my love," she says.

"But you're good? You're ok? No one's hurt?"

"We're all fine."

Again Reidier's gaze drifts over to Ecco. He crosses over behind him, kisses the top of his head, and runs his hands across Ecco's shoulders and arms.

"The boys didn't give you too much trouble?"

"No, they were—"

"Ecco didn't give you too much trouble?"

"—fine. Ecco was good. Just some trouble sleeping. We went to the Met. He liked the hall of statues. We all agreed the statue of Jean-Baptiste Carpeaux's *Ugolino and His Sons* was the best."

Reidier nods, registering Eve said something, but not really hearing more than they're all ok.

Later that evening, after putting the boys to bed, Reidier and Eve find themselves sitting on the floor, on opposite sides of the hall outside Otto's and Ecco's rooms.

They listen to the children sleep, mirroring each other's postures. Reidier's left leg bent upward, his left arm resting on his knee, Eve's right leg bent upward, her right arm resting on her knee. His right leg stretched out across the hall floor, her left leg the same. Their stockinged feet touching, pushing against each other, rocking their feet to the right in unison.

"What did the doctors at Sloan Kettering say?"

Eve shrugs. "That I have a brain tumor. That it's too deep to operate. That there are some experimental chemo treatments. Everything Bert already went over with us."

Reidier chokes on his thought. "I can't lose you. I couldn't breathe. I couldn't *be*. Without you here, it was like some sort of walk-through play rehearsal, just to get through the day. I wasn't me, I was my own stand-in. I can't lose you." The tears drip off his chin and blossom into a Rorschach spot on his shirt. He shakes his head no in answer to some unasked question.

"I know."

Eve crawls across the hall to him, crawls between his legs, kisses his salty lips. "I know." Her hand rests on his chest, over his heart. "You're here with me. I feel you."

Reidier nods.

"I see you, Kerek." She kisses him again. "I see you."

"I see you," he echoes.

Eve half smiles, half frowns at him. "We simply have to do it your way."

Reidier nods.

"You won't lose me?"

Reidier shakes his head no.

Eve smiles and stands. Her gaze drifts down the hall toward the boys' rooms. "Maybe it'll be a catharsis, for all of us." Her kisses gently touch the top of Reidier's head.

Eve walks down the hall into their bedroom.

Reidier watches her go. He dries his eyes on his sleeve and then gets up to check on the boys. Otto sleeps soundly. Ecco lies in his bed, wide awake. Reidier collects the boy and carries him downstairs with him into his lab, and calls Pierce.

Transcript excerpt from the phone log of the Office of the
Director of the Strategic Technology, Donald Pierce; 6/12/2008,
1:32 a.m.

Pierce: Kerek? What time is it?

Reidier: The men in the SUV outside, they're yours?

Pierce: Yes. Department Security. After everything that
happened today, we figured your family could
use the extra security.

Reidier: What is it that happened today?

Pierce: I'm sending Larry up to debrief with DHS and
find out. (sighs) Honestly, we should be asking
you, though. The higher-ups have been
chomping at the bit to talk to Eve. It took a lot
of string pulling to get them to back down, so I
can give you guys a little room to recuperate.
We're going to need to talk to her, though.

Reidier: No. You won't.

Pause.

Reidier: Eve doesn't know anything. None of them do.
The men who took them were in masks. They
didn't talk to them, they didn't torture them,
they didn't hold them for three days.

Pause.

Reidier: All they did was drop them at the train station
in Stamford and give them train tickets home.

Pierce: Now why in the hell would they go to all the
trouble to do that?

Reidier: The more pressing question for me is why were they being held by the Department?

Pierce: Kerek, I told you already, that was DHS. Some clerical error put Eve on a watch list. I would've had her out of there in an afternoon if I had found out about it sooner.

Reidier: And you didn't find out until after they had been freed?

Pierce: Interdepartmental bullshit politics. Like I said, a clerical SNAFU. A threat to your family is the same as a threat to the Department.

Reidier: They weren't threatening my family. They were leveling the playing field.

Pierce: . . . At your request?

Pause.

Pierce: Look Kerek, if you don't work with me, I can't protect you.

Reidier: I told you, we weren't threatened.

Pierce: Not from them.

Pause.

Reidier: The higher-ups?

Pause.

Reidier: Did they have the DHS detain Eve and the boys?

Pierce: I don't know. Honest to goddamn Christ. It's above my pay grade. All I know is you're of great value to the Department, and the best thing for all of us is for you to finish your work.

Pause.

Reidier: Eve has a brain tumor.

Pierce: Shit. I'm sorry to hear that. I know some folks over at NIH. I could pull some strings . . .

Reidier: As long as I finish my work. Which is it, Pierce, are you a puppet or a puppeteer?

Pierce: I'm a fr—I'm a man with a vested interest in you. Our fates are bound together. Which makes me a whole lot more trustworthy than any other goddamn friend you've got. I'll help you, I'll help Eve as long as I'm permitted.

Reidier: It's out of your hands.

Pierce: Kerek—

CLICK

NB Footage: Providence, June 22, 2008 3:08 a.m.—

Kerek shuffles into Ecco's room and looks down at the sleeping boy. He half smiles, sighs, and sits down on the floor next to the bed, leaning back against the wall, and shuts his eyes. Ecco turns over and faces his father. He reaches his small hand out and touches his father's face.

"Still awake?" Kerek asks, opening his eyes.

Ecco nods.

"I can't sleep either."

They sit in silence for a few moments. Ecco moves his hands up to his father's brow and lightly draws his fingers down over Kerek's eyes, closing them. Ecco keeps repeating the gesture, his fingertips fluttering like raindrops across his father's eyelids.

Reidier smiles, enjoying the sensation. "Where'd you learn that?"

"Eve."

"You saw Mommy do that with Otto?"

Ecco shakes his head. "She does it with me."

"That's nice!" Reidier's exhaustion covers up the surprise in his tone.

Ecco keeps tracing his fingers over his father's eyes. The boy starts singing in a light, soprano voice. "Slow down, you move too fast. You got to make the morning last. Just kicking down the cobblestones. Looking for fun and feelin' groovy."

Reidier relaxes into sleep.

Ecco lies on his side, watching his father.

To Do:
1. Don't get caught.
2. ~~Destroy copies.~~
3. Get transfer
4. Don't get caught.
5. ~~Cloak report.~~
6. Daniel?
7. Scout ~~Foggy~~ Bottom Metro
8. Go home
   a. make presence known - alarm system, phone calls etc.
9. Analysis of Eve's developing attachment to Ecco as compared to her proportional distancing from Reidier
   a. Surprisingly the more troubled Ecco becomes the more Eve seems to connect w/him, at least on some basic maternal instinct to protect, as evidenced by the several dangerous incidents he's involved in
      i. Egg boiling burn
      ii. Drowning in Narragansett
      iii. Is this more of a bond forming or a maternal reflex? Or possibly some bizarre symptom of tumor?

b. Sleeping ~~patterns~~ should be taken into consideration

   i. Reidier almost never sleeps in bed with Eve as Ecco deteriorates. Spends almost ~~every~~ night splitting his time between Ecco's room and his basement lab.

      1. Concern for Ecco? Wedge between him and Eve? Possessed by ambition with regard to his work?

10. Eve's last journal entry?

11. Attend Department Progress Report Meeting

2. ~~Foggy~~ Bottom slip

3. Back to blackstone

   a. ~~pages~~

                                                                                   *

---

* The worst part about going crazy is how sane you are for the whole ride down. Her ending can't have been a to-do list.

At the bottom of the briefcase was a key to room fourteen at the Stone's Throw Inn, a Hertz car rental key, and an Amtrak ticket stub for one Mary Palmore from West Kingston Station, RI to Union Station, Washington, DC.

Was this my mother's last stand? Was this where she came to die? Butler on Blackstone?

"Here we are," Dr. Rasmussen announced as he crossed his office to the knock at the door. He smiled at me, his crow's-feet turned up and pulled taut, some of the loose skin hanging off his cheeks and chin.

He opened the door, and the sun flooded in around him and the figure now standing in the threshold. The light bled everything white, blackening them into silhouettes: Dr. Rasmussen engulfed by the swooping shape of his lab coat and the shade of Hilary hugging her arms around her torso, shadows of buckles dangling from her straitjacket.

She wrested her arm loose from her constraints, reached for Dr. Rasmussen . . . and handed him a folder of papers?

My pupils finally telescoped out the surge of sunlight, and I watched my mother morph into a female colleague of Dr. Rasmussen. The dangling straps of her straitjacket transmogrified into buckles and straps of a leather jacket, which the woman had kept on while they fixed the heat in her office.

Dr. Rasmussen whispered his thanks and crossed back to his desk while I tried to get my heart rate back down below 250 bpms.

"As I told you, I can't disclose any patient information, but I don't see a problem in sharing what your mother had him working on." Dr. Rasmussen thumbed through the folder's contents, then closed it and slid it across his desk toward me. "It's a shame there won't be more. This work has been very therapeutic for the patient. It prompted a significant calming effect."

The color suddenly drained out of Dr. Rasmussen's face. "I apologize, I didn't mean to imply that Hilary's . . ."

I held up my hand, like a benevolent pope. "It's all right, Dr. Rasmussen. I know what you meant."

"Please, call me Steven."

"It's ok. I can't tell you how much I appreciate your help." I nodded at the folder on his desk between us. I didn't reach for it.

Steven frowned with sympathy. "How long has it been?"

"Hard to say, since we don't know exactly when she disappeared. Around two years, though."

"Your mother was a friend and a colleague. Her mind was beyond sharp." Steven nodded. "How are you holding up?"

"Like a seeding dandelion in a tornado."

He nodded again.

"Steven, there is one other favor, if I might." I put my hand on the folder. "Did my mother mention whom she was working for on this project?"

"She just emphasized the need for discretion."

"Yes, she went to great lengths to conceal what she was doing here. From what I can garner, there's a distinct possibility that her employer might have a hand in her disappearance."

"Jesus . . ."

"Anyhow, I was wondering if we might continue her request for discretion."

"Of course, as I said as a doctor I cannot—"

"Steven, I'm afraid I'm asking for a little more than that." My voice didn't sound like my own. It had a professional, in-control tone. Apparently hallucinating visions of my mother really focused the shit out of me. "Is it possible that Hilary never came here? Never worked with any patient? Never picked up any material?" I picked up the folder and placed it in my lap.

Steven took it all in, leaned back in his chair, and gazed out his window at the woods. Finally, he nodded and stood up. "I'm sorry, Daniel. I wish I could help more, but I haven't seen your mother in a number of years. Not since she came in to consult on a couple patients back around 2000."

He looked at me over the rim of his glasses. It took a second for me to catch on. "Well, thanks for your time," I said, standing myself.

I rolled up the folder and tucked it into my inside pocket.

"Take care with that," he said. "It'll be the *only* remaining copy soon."

We shook hands and parted ways.

It took me a while to open the folder. I was scared what might be in it, and I was terrified about what might not be in it.

It sat on the passenger side, atop the mess of other folders from her report, while I stared out the windshield at the "Stuck-Up Bridge." The Seekonk River Drawbridge had been stuck in the open position since the '70s, a charming bit of urban decay that had been another hook-up haunt of mine in college.

After an hour of hemming, hawing, and a whole lot of muttering, I finally took a pen and gingerly flipped her folder open, like it might be booby-trapped.

I knew what it was instantly. The chaotic designs, the seeming gibberish: these were pages from Leo's Notebook—coded copies and decoded revelations.

Her Blackstone cipher had cracked it. Some crazy kid lodged in Butler, well past sanity, who dreamt in prime numbers, had been able to tease apart the enigmas. Well, at least some of them.

~~LEO'S~~ REIDIER'S NOTEBOOK: DECODED

September 5, 2007

Iteration 1* has proved psychologically successful. Ecco appears to have maintained all of his long-term memories since his initial appearance. More accurately, since the move to Providence. (This was not because he didn't necessarily remember before that, but due to the fact that there did not seem to be sufficient means for testing his brief stint in Chicago. Therefore, whether his memory encompassed that time or not is still inconclusive.) Upon successful transfer, subject was immediately examined through an informal series of tests.**

---

* (PS Just so we're on the same page, those highlights are mine.)

** When was he performing these "transfers"??

---

1) Subject maintained accurate mental map of the residence. He could correctly and without hesitation lead me around to requested locations, i.e. when I asked him to take me to the kitchen, he led me up the stairs, down the hall, to the kitchen.

a) Subject accurately located objects outside of residence (that also were not within view).
    i. Ecco correctly pointed through a door to identify sandbox's location.

2) Subject maintained aesthetic preferences. When eating chicken, Ecco always prefers the wing. When asked to choose between wing and leg, he chose wing.

    a) While on its own, not a conclusive event (50 percent probability of randomly choosing wing). However provides correlative supplemental support for hypothesis.[†]

[†] Found it, pages 363-364, Frankenstein and his wooden boy.

---

3) Subject also revealed a preestablished, undisclosed hiding place.

    a) Eve's candy stash, which was unknown to me at time of inquiry, thereby eliminating the possibility of Ecco interpreting subconscious clues from me as to its whereabouts. I wasn't inadvertently guiding him there.

    b) Ecco also identified memory for preestablished, communal behaviors.
        i. I.e. keeping the remotes in drawer of coffee table.

4) Most significant evidence was reenactment of specific behavior from first day in Providence.

    a) Ecco lying upside down on chair and pretending to walk on ceiling.
        i. This behavior was only observed once by me on move-in day.

Subsequent tests were also administered by Bertram (under the guise of checking his mental state postaccident), after which Bertram was aware of Ecco's duplicitous nature. Ecco performed specific tasks that Bertram had witnessed him execute almost six months ago. Ecco ate macaroni salad with a straw,* once again exhibiting a consistency of aesthetic preferences (much more conclusively than the chicken wing, due to the specificity of the behavior). Furthermore, Ecco exactly replicated the tomato Lego "sculpture" he had made when Bertram first examined him.** In order as to not prejudice or influence the subject in any way, Bertram presented Ecco with a bin containing a variety of Legos (of various colors), as well as Capsela and Tinker toys, and asked Ecco to make him the object he had made previously. Ecco proceeded to do so, without hesitation, completely from memory. Bertram confirmed this as evidence of a stable long-term memory.

---

* See page 292.
** See page 275.

Unfortunately, while the cognitive goal was accomplished with Iteration 1, there was a glaring collateral physiological side effect: cognitive insensitivity to pain. Subject appears to have little to no pain capabilities whatsoever. This insensitivity spans the entire spectrum from dull knocks to the head to second-degree burns.***

*** Like a little kid might get from reaching his hand into 212-degree water and pulling out a hardboiled egg. Turn to page 383. Reidier is sick.

Sense of touch seems to have remained intact and most likely registers pressure information, as evidenced by subject's ability to pick up and manipulate objects, walk, etc.

Dr. Roland Staud, a professor of medicine and rheumatologist at the University of Florida, has researched this naturally occurring, though rare, physiological condition. While there haven't been enough case studies to statistically determine its propensity, Staud believes it to be more common than one in a billion or even a million, but that it goes unnoticed due to those who have the disorder not disclosing it.

Geoffrey Woods, a geneticist in Cambridge, only recently made the connection between pain insensitivity and genes. His research eventually led to ascribing it to a mutation of the SCN9A gene.

The possibility of some sort of genetic aberration is further supported by a secondary physical side effect: Ecco, unlike Otto, does not have an allergy to tetanus. While outwardly the two appear identical, at a base genetic level something must be different. Somewhere in the process, his strand of DNA must have been altered.

···   ···   ···   ···

Ecco doesn't feel pain

It's unsettling. It's chaos. ~~We~~ I have to watch him all the time just to ensure he doesn't jump too hard and break his ankle, or pick up a pan from the stove and melt the palms of his hands, or dislocate his shoulder twisting and turning when he sleeps, biting his lips clean through, or even drinking rotten milk. His senses of smell and taste, while not necessarily gone, have been hindered or muffled.

I've resorted to wrapping his hands in gauze some days or duct taping mittens around his wrists. I have to clean his eyes each morning and night to make sure nothing damaging has lodged itself in his corneas. I check his shoes when he comes inside to confirm he hasn't stepped on a nail. The other night I found him sitting on his bed ripping out his eyelashes, one by one, giggling. Later that evening I caught Otto doing it. He cried after one particularly hard yank.

Eve can't stand to be in the same room as Ecco. Her perception of him as an Other, as a freak, as a threat, has only been intensified by his new vulnerability. She keeps Otto away from him at all costs for fear of another incident of Otto mimicking Ecco and severely injuring himself, even though Otto had only superficial burns on the tips of two fingers from the egg incident. Ecco is a living, breathing, horrible hypothetical. It scared her.

So often we think of pain as the enemy when really it's our caretaker.
...   .

Nevertheless, it cannot be ignored that this disorder, this condition, is new. He felt pain before the July 25th iteration.* He hurt himself and cried many times. The very fact that he keeps proclaiming how different foods taste implies that he was registering that sensory information differently before.

---

*See page 83, Galilee 6:21, Experiment 19. Cross-check the date . . . It's right there in plain sight. The Coke experiment must've been a cover. Masked the power usage while he iterated his son.

A biopsy was sent to Cambridge. Woods has confirmed that Ecco's SCN9A gene has in fact mutated. Clearly the adjustments made in order to transfer long-term memories during teleportation also altered something at a genetic level. He was not the same coming out as he was going in.†

---

† He's iterating his kid.
  Ecco isn't Ecco: he's Eccos.
  He's R's little guinea pig.

If this alteration can be pinpointed, could this effect be controlled and targeted on other genes or cells? If so, then perhaps it is possible for a subject to be repaired during teleportation. Can I perform quantum surgery?

Maybe Curzwell is not all crazy.

December 1, 2007

Iteration 2* has made the same ambivalent progress as its previous version. Subject exhibited seamless short-term memory retention across teleportation process.

---

* See Galilee 6:21, Experiment 9 Delta pages 197-200. Reidier was running a double bluff. His after-hours experiments were supposed to be noticed by the powers that be. They were supposed to spy on and transcribe the "not-so-secret" infractions he wanted them to spy on. They were supposed to feel superior gathering all their surreptitious intel on his Gould Island extracurricular affairs. All the while it was a misdirection, a means of covering his power usage (see page 245) to obscure the massive energy drain.

Before, "during," and after process, I engaged Ecco in a game of Concentration.[†] I played several rounds with him as we prepared, shuffling the cards each round and then dealing them all animal pictures face down. Through this play, I determined that one minute and forty-eight seconds in would be the optimal time to engage Quark Resonator. By this point in the game, it had been on average sufficiently long enough that half of the cards had randomly been flipped and turned back over for Ecco to have created a rough, though incomplete, mental map of which animals were where (i.e. the lion card was face down in the bottom left corner, the hippo card was in the middle row two from the right).

---

† Page 198 . . . the card from the game.

In order to create fluid play (and short-term memory activation), I arranged our deck in front of the transmission pad, but also laid out a second deck of Concentration cards face down in the exact same pattern in front of the target pad (making sure to remove whichever matched cards had been paired together and removed, so as to replicate our landscape of play exactly).

At roughly a minute forty in, so as to engage and evaluate short-term memory precisely, I would wait until Ecco turned over a previously unturned card and replaced it (unmatched face down). In that moment of completion, Ecco was teleported from transmission to target pad. And play ensued.

1) Subject exhibited no sign of disturbance of state of mind, nor emotional state, as evidenced by calm demeanor and continued participation in play.

2) Subject maintained knowledge of identity of last card flipped the instant before teleportation.

   a) Ecco correctly remembered/identified/ matched the last card he viewed before teleport.
      i. This experiment was repeated several times to corroborate results.

3) In conjunction with memory game's visual component, subject was also exposed to aural stimulus and tested on this.

    a)   Right before transmission, I would say a ran-
         dom word or term: purple, argyle, lettuce, etc.

    b)   After transmission, when prompted, subject
         accurately repeated the term 100 percent of
         the time.
         i. "Ecco what did Daddy just say?"
         ii. "Argyle."

Quark chromatic adjustments proved to successfully transfer short-term memories.

Once again, however, there appears to have been an unintended side effect. Iteration 2* has developed Obsessive-Compulsive Disorder. It manifests itself in a variety of tendencies, inclining toward the more compulsive end of the spectrum. The most glaring behavior along these lines is his constant teeth brushing.** Iteration 2 can brush his teeth upwards of ten to almost twenty times a day. After several weeks, this has led to problematic gum bleeding.***

---

* Which Iteration 2? Iteration 2A or Iteration 2F? He ran the experiment several times!

** Pages 460-61.

*** Page 458.

However, while the tendency is toward compulsivity, Iteration 2 is also fascinated and consumed with detail. So much so that it can sometimes preclude even the simplest of tasks. For example, when both boys were presented with a new pack of Legos, Otto jumped right in and started playing, while Ecco focused on the packaging: the feel of the glossy finish of the box, the slightly rough edge of folded-in tabs, the extensive pictures and little descriptions that covered the box front-and-back (even though Ecco is not literate he had to take in every detail of the text). By the time Ecco had finished with the box, Otto had already finished playing Legos and moved on to another activity. This attention to detail interrupts the entire flow of his day. Even using the remote to turn on the television can devolve into a ten-minute examination of the remote itself and any nicks, scratches, or stains it has acquired through use. This obsessiveness has proved so disruptive that it has instigated countless clashes and fights between the boys, as Otto cannot adjust to the bizarre sudden changes in his brother's behavior.

...　...　...　...

Hiding Ecco from Eve has become difficult. The fact is, she's simply home more, or more present when home.

At least to Otto.

Ecco's teeth brushing, while constant, has occurred under the radar. Eve notices Ecco's hourly disappearances, but they rarely register with her. Furthermore, she never pursues/follows him to find out what he's doing. Instead she stays with Otto or simply continues to invest in whatever her task (whether it's work or writing or cooking or simply watching a television program). The only area where Eve is aware, or even hypervigilant, is in the kitchen. Whether it's for Ecco's or Otto's protection (or both) is unclear. But the egg incident is still clearly present for her.

It wasn't until the bleeding that Ecco's behavior became too obvious to deny. However, I have bought some time, I think, with the explanation that he's just brushing his teeth too hard or a little too often.

The stuffed animals have been easy enough to defuse. Eve almost never goes into Ecco's room. So, at least as far as I know, she's never seen how, every night before bed, he turns all of his stuffed animals to face the wall. And as I learned after the first confrontation with him about this, if you don't fight it, he won't cause any sort of ruckus. He just needs to face them all against the wall to fall asleep. Just as a precaution though, a few hours after he drifts off, I turn them back in a haphazard manner.* While I realize that this might actually be anxiety-provoking for Ecco (to wake up and the animals have turned themselves around), and may even reinforce the behavior, I am more concerned with the potential anxiety from Eve becoming aware of this habit.

* Page 515.

The fingerpainting, unfortunately, was unavoidable and startling. Ecco's obsessive consumption of detail and compulsive driven stamina enabled him to conjure the door practically out of thin air.* It stirs a cyclone of ambivalence within the viewer, simultaneously awed at the skill and verisimilitude, while also horrified by the mental state necessary for the child to create this. I'm sure as an artist herself, Eve must have been both drawn to the work and to Ecco, while also being repelled by both. Perhaps that's what drove her to Spencer.**

---

*Page 506.

**Pages 210, 435, 476: Foucault to suspicious toasters to absinthe.

... ...

It is still unclear as to whether this is, strictly speaking, a physiological side effect or a psychological one. Has this iteration's neurology been changed or simply his thought patterns? Can these two things even be separated? From a biological perspective OCD can arise from changes in a body's natural chemistry or have a genetic component (although no specific genes have been identified yet). Insufficient serotonin could also contribute to this disorder, which is why SSRIs can be effective for treatment. That being said, there are some theories that it can be a behavior learned over time, both from the cognitive behavioral and the psychodynamic camps. Clearly, Iteration 2 would not have had time to "learn" a behavior over time, but my variations within the quark landscape might have drastically terraformed his mental one.

Carbon allotrope alteration proved only partially successful. While on a microlevel, diamond lattice was successfully shifted to improve clarity from VS1 to VVS1, the macrostructure was compromised.*

*Page 199. Compromised? I'll say—he cracked his wife's diamond in two!

Need to more precisely isolate the adjustments made to the quark chromodynamics.

May 28, 2008

Iteration 3 has been a horrifying failure. I am deleting all of the chromodynamic settings.*

---

* See Galilee 6:21, Experiment 7 Alpha.

...   .

I am still shaken.

...   .

While the goal of this experiment was achieved, he's a monster.

...   .

Purpose: to successfully transfer subject's emotional state during teleportation.

Method: instigate emotional state within subject that manifests in clear demeanor immediately prior to Q resonation and track maintenance of behavior/emotion.

Conclusion: Initial attempts to prompt joy through laughter proved challenging. Negative emotional states offered clearer consistency. Ultimately, pleasure and laughter were exchanged for pain and crying. Negative states were more consistent, less ephemeral.

Subject was pinched until pained crying ensued. Subject remained in this distressed state while Q resonator was engaged.*

---

* Page 316.

Emotional state (as evaluated by facial expression, crying, sobs, posture) stayed consistent across teleported distance. To that extent, the experiment was effective.

However . . . What he did to the rabbit . . .

...   .

While the instantaneous emotional state of the Iteration 3 was successfully transmitted, the base temperament was drastically altered in fundamental ways. Subject has come to exhibit psychopathic behavior, the most drastic example of which was with the leporid. The subject, once alone, somehow caught the rabbit either behind the garage or sought out the isolated area behind the garage after snaring it. Within this solitude, the subject proceeded to torture the animal. The rabbit was staked to the ground with a number of metal cooking skewers. Each of its limbs was snapped. The rabbit's ears were both sliced off and subsequently placed on the ground one centimeter away from the bleeding nubs they were cut off of, like one might do when laying out the pieces of a model one were about to construct. Throughout this whole process, the rabbit was kept alive.

It was still breathing when later discovered.*

---

* Pages 513-14. I guess now we know what made Reidier vomit. Truth be told, just reading that, I almost did myself. I had to stroll out on the Stuck-Up Bridge to look down between the tracks into the river's depths. I kept thinking about Shelley's *Frankenstein*. Most misinterpret the story as a condemnation of science. What horrors we can unleash with our ambition and intelligence: creatures, atomic bombs, Eccos. But Shelley was warning us about losing touch with our humanity, admonishing us about forgetting compassion. The sin isn't that Dr. Frankenstein made the Creature, it's that he abandoned him. Somehow Reidier went in the opposite direction but ended up in the same place.

...   .

I can't bring myself to tell Eve. The mole crab incident[†] was unsettling enough. I do not know what to do. I cannot stop. Not now.

[†] Pages 528-529.

... ...

I didn't delete them. It was too dangerous. What if I did it again, accidentally? I had QuAI deal with it. She wrote a restriction algorithm that will prevent, disrupt, and erase any future implementation of these settings while quarantining the specific data behind a quantum lock.

Tonight I have to do something about Iteration 3.

June 18, 2008

Iteration 5 is stable and safe enough; subject has yet to manifest any psychopathic behaviors.* It has been five days, and thus perhaps still too early to be determined. I must still keep Ecco with me at all times. Although to give him room to "misbehave," I often leave him alone in a room with a video camera, and monitor the feed from another location. I have concurrently escalated the temptations presented to Iteration 5 in these isolation tests. Initially subject was left alone with several stuffed animals, then stuffed animals and scissors, pliers, and knives; next, subject was left alone with a live frog, then the frog with scissors, pliers, and knives; onto, a baby chicken, then a baby chicken and the weapons; lastly, a baby rabbit, followed by the baby rabbit with the weapons. While Iteration 5 showed interest in the animals and the objects, he never became aggressive nor violent toward the animals. He exhibited no weird/bizarre/unsettling behavior. Just "normal" childlike conduct. Nevertheless, side effects still plague the work. Iteration 5 does not sleep. He's amenable enough to "go to bed" but simply lies there. He never seems to slip into sleep, let alone achieve REM state. Oddly, while Ecco seems unperturbed by his state, he has intuited that it is abnormal and will engage in pretend behavior. He will close his eyes and fake sleep. His intuition is actually so sharp he has been able to infer my anxiety about this condition and my need for him to pretend around Eve. The other night, I went downstairs while he was "sleeping" to get QuAI to run some *gedankens* for me. When I returned, he lay there in the dark. I whispered to him if he were still awake. Ecco nodded and whispered back, "Yes, but I closed my eyes and pretended when Eve checked. She watched a long time." She's watching him. I am unclear as to whether Eve's watchfulness is a manifestation of her suspicions or rather a growing "maternal" bond that has seemed to develop since the burn damage from the egg incident. These two are not necessarily mutually exclusive. So far, subject has proved immune to a variety of treatments. Melatonin, children's Benadryl, normal Benadryl, NyQuil, Ambien, Lunesta, scotch—none of these soporific substances have any sleep-inducing effect. (The scotch makes him sick.) Unfortunately, this is not the only side effect. Iteration 5 also appears to have an insatiable appetite. He's always hungry, so much so that I've even caught him eating sweet-smelling cleaning supplies (which also, expectedly, make him sick). Are the hunger and cleaning-supply cravings a result of a fault in the scanning and/or animation processes of teleportation, or are they due to some biological rebellion in response to his body's dearth of sleep? Did I make my son crazy, or is he going crazy? At least Iteration 5 is only self-destructive, instead of outwardly destructive. Regardless, his demeanor is sweet, engaged, generally appealing. I have devolved him from monster to self-saboteur. Toying with a more holistic hypothesis, psychology has an influential dynamic on neurology. Bertram's been a helpful sounding board. Perhaps the emotional state during transfer has an effect on the underlying topography of brain-wave patterns when restored. So the use of pain to measure the transfer of emotional states with Iteration 3 actually damaged/deformed Ecco's fundamental wave patterns. Sour Golem's breath makes for an angry monster. Apparently my use of music instead at least circumvents the issue. By engaging the subject in singing "The 59th Street Bridge Song," I have been able to transfer a more harmonious emotional state. Ultimately, the goal is not to alter one's demeanor, but simply ~~mirror~~ replicate it.

* Page 366, Galilee 6:21, Experiment 47 Omega.

HIDDEN FILES*

* I later discovered that Hilary's CD-RW also had three document files on it.

13.9.2008[†]

[†] 1) Eve's final journal entry.

---

*I'll see you on the far shore: how we get there is up
to you.*

-----Memo-----*

From: Larry Woodbury [mailto: larry.woodbury@darpa.mil]

Sent: Monday, September 8, 2008 11:18 p.m.

To: donald.pierce@darpa.mil

Subject: redundant architecture

Pierce,

Engineers finished work. All kernel relays have been hardwired in. Team predicts this will circumvent issues we've been having with software hacks penetrating R's encryption. Any and all activities that occur in the Gould Island Control Room will be mirrored on your console in Observation Deck. Should provide you with unfettered and unadulterated access to everything Reidier is doing. Whatever *under the radar experiments* he might be hiding/running within official experiments will be relayed to you instantaneously. Whatever happens at his console, happens at yours.

Tech team has also rigged a secondary storage system inside the university's servers to duplicate all of the data Reidier runs through or already stores there, so you'll be able to analyze the copied information without Reidier knowing.

~L. Woodbury

My dearest Daniel,*

* and 3) a letter from Hilary . . .

I hope this letter finds you intact. If you're reading this, then my precautions didn't quite work out as planned. In a way this letter is itself (if ever read) an admission of defeat, an acknowledgment that all of my efforts to protect you with an insulated distance were for naught. Not to mention a testament to my contradictory efforts: Why go to all this trouble to hold you at arm's length for my entire process only to entangle you after I've stopped? Why leave the key for you, the research, this letter?

I can only imagine the knowing sneer on your face while reading this. *Why indeed*, you had already asked yourself.

Selfishness, I'd say. At the end of the day, I needed my son to know me. To know how much I love him, despite the consequences.

Narcissism, you'd reply, then counter how at the end of the day, I needed a reader to know my work. To marvel at its insight and carry it forward. Damn those consequences too.

I miss arguing with you. I miss sparring with your passion, laughing at your frustration with me, admiring how sharp your mind has become, how my little boy can now outmaneuver me. Sometimes.

I don't trust myself on the train ride I have ahead of me. On two different trips, I thought I saw you walking up the train car aisle. I'll have to take an Ambien to get through Penn Station without getting off. The impulse has been overwhelming every time I've come through. A visceral need to see my son. I feel untethered, like I'm drifting away in every direction at once and powerless to do anything about it. But if I could just see Danny. How I wish to hop off of Amtrak, hop on the downtown C, surprise you at work and take you out for lunch. If I could simply touch your hand across a restaurant table, see your silhouette in the sunlight as you turn your head, the slope of nose and curve of chin that describes the same profile captured in my first sonogram, the world could take shape again, regain its weight. And then I wouldn't mind disintegrating so much. I know it's mundane, but there's a simple joy a mother gets watching her son eat. At least once during every meal we've shared together, there's a moment when I marvel at this full-grown man who was a part of me, drew all sustenance from me, who now sits across the table, towering over me, echoing mannerisms of his father.

I miss you both so much. This ordeal, this isolation weighs on me—no, that's not right, it's not a pressure from the outside. The force is internal, it grows in me, taking hold of my chest, reaching up my esophagus, sometimes crushing my throat from the inside out.

But if I get off that train, what would I say? What could I tell you? You were so angered by our last "conversation," by my taciturnity, by my distance. My evasive, protective answers would only set off the tinderbox of dried-up memories you've been filling up for years.

I rely on Clyde and Bertram's paranoid warnings to bolster my will. For all we know, the Department's been staking out your office at Anomaly for months. It's almost certain they've been listening in on our conversations, tracking our disagreements, and taking the temperature of our relationship. Surfacing now to indulge my need to see you would not only pop me up on their radar, it would make you a potential target.

I can manage my son's anger, but not his loss. I will not ensnare you in the Department's skein.

But I can't leave you with nothing. I can't leave you to simply swallow our acid-coated last words.

By now I'm sure you've put many of the pieces together. You've gotten to know the Reidiers. You've honed your own suspicions about the Department's ambitions, not to mention Beimini's machinations. I'm sure you have developed a sense for the tectonic pressures at play in the final few months leading up to *The Reidier Test*: Kerek's drive, Eve's fear, Ecco's deterioration. The tumor eating away at Eve's sanity—and Kerek's. He had to simultaneously reject and embrace his evolution into the Destroyer of Death, dance along the border of the finale of frontiers. It was the only way out, and the only way to save Eve.

The Reidier Test was Kerek's future.

The Reidier Test was Pierce's legacy.

Blinded by their own agendas, they both misread their barometers. The wind had blown them in different directions and finally sent them spinning out of control toward one another, two hurricanes tossing an atom bomb back and forth.

An incident and accident. A triumph and catastrophe.

I am sorry for pulling you into all this, Daniel. The stakes swirling around this spin with a hungry fury. It is what has drawn us apart and now funnels us together. We have become the report's collateral damage. Our distance is the last line of defense for the Reidiers, maybe the world. It sounds histrionic, yes, but the destructive capability of this singularity is too great a secret.

The closer I get, the more important it becomes to hide Reidier's success and survival.

My proximity is toxic.

Are you touching your scar right now? The resentment locked in its tissue is a constant irritation. For too long, ever since your father died, my work has cleaved through our relationship. It was always so imminent, so imperative, and so masking. I could disappear into it and leave my sadness at home with you and the ghost of your father that I saw in every one of your gestures and smiles. He lived in you, a constant incarnation of my loss. The despair of losing him was too much to swallow, and the shame of abandoning you too difficult to stomach. Work was my salvation, an outlet that I ironically justified as for you. I needed to work to support us while leaving you completely unsupported.

I know that's why you fell. And why you let go.

I should've been in the hospital waiting room. I should've been waiting back at the dorms with your bags packed and ready to take you home. I should've never forced you to go to boarding school. If I had been able to look past myself, I would've seen you "accidentally" leave your key in your room when you snuck out to get high and drunk at the water tower. You were a teenager after all, these things happen. I should've known you would've shrugged it off and climbed the dogwood out front, shimmied up the branch that reached out to the study room's Juliet balcony on the second floor, like you had done so many times before. I should've guessed your adolescent mind would disregard the risk of leaping out across the void. After all it was only a body-length away, and you were more than capable. I should've predicted you'd make the jump, hook your arm over the railing as soon as your torso thumped hard against the concrete balusters. I should've understood how you would've felt in that moment, dangling from the second story, locked out of your dorm, exiled from your home, fatherless with an absentee mother who couldn't manage to snap out of her own grief long enough to help you carry yours. What else could you do? Something had to give. Something had to snap.

So you let go.

You couldn't have known that the branch had broken in the storm the previous week. You couldn't have guessed that it had landed just so and the mud had hardened around it. You couldn't have calculated that the broken edge would be propped up at just the right angle to pierce your skin, slide in just below your rib cage, and scrape your liver. All you knew is you wanted out. And one way or another, this was your way out.

I knew. I've always known. I'm so sorry. My weakness was unforgiveable.

I'd like to think my current distance was more a considered act of love than some habitual reflex of neglect. I'd like to believe this report has morphed from our wedge to our link. That in leaving this for you, I'm not throwing you to the wolves, but rather reaching out and pulling you close in the only way possible.

If I've been successful, then my distance would have been worth it.

If I've failed, then maybe my report can serve as my apology. Or as an offering. You might not be able to forgive me, but you can know me. What I was doing, and what I was trying to do. You can at least have this piece of me and understand. With everything at stake, you having that is worth the risk. I don't want to leave you, and I won't leave you with nothing. Not again.

I love you, more than you can know. More than I deserve to.

An ocean of love,
Mom*

---

* . . . is what she should've written.
There was no letter.
Just the journal entry and memo.
Fuck you, Hilary.

APPENDIX

These following items were sent to me separately, starting several months after I received Danny's original package. There were no notes, just the ensuing printouts (presented in the order they were received). The postmarks originated from Taos, NM; Miami, FL; Cayenne, French Guiana; and Perth, Australia. I assume they were from him. However, I have neither a way to confirm this nor a means to be certain he personally sent them from the above places (or simply sent them to a post office there to then forward to me). The last one was received more than half a year ago. Furthermore, while each was seemingly printed out from various websites (including known, reputable news sources), none of these are currently posted at the respective addresses. It is unclear as to whether they were removed, censored, or fabricated. Other than the *Brown Daily Herald*, each news source and journalist has denied (through e-mail, all refused phone calls) any knowledge of, or connection to, these pieces.

In the time between receiving these items and publishing, I have verified Bertram Malle's unfortunate demise at Block Island, as well as Danny's account of Clyde Palmore's sabbatical and his current position. He is still in Haiti, working for Habitat for Humanity's international chapter on low-cost, earthquake-proof construction.

Toby has requested no updated information about him be printed. Lorelei ■■■■ is still in New York City. She is engaged to a lithium importer and works at Ogilvy & Mather. When asked about Danny in a phone interview, she dismissed Danny's account of their relationship, describing them as professional friends. She laughed at his yarn-spinning aptitude, which always impressed her, and added that they lost touch sometime between his disappearance from Anomaly and her transition to her new job.

I have no knowledge of either Hilary or Danny's whereabouts or whether they are even still alive.

-Joshua V. Scher

Restor8ion I ▮▮▮▮ magazine

6 July 2010

Restor8ion

By Tate Avess

HANNAH'S OCTAGONAL MORTAR BOARD itches her scalp. It isn't so much the cap's fault, but rather that of her *cappa clausa*. The dignity of the Chancellor's office requires her black robes be made from pure ottoman silk. It is an elegant, expensive material that traps body heat like Hades itself. She almost always overheats and sweats. It's not very dignified. How long has it been since her last Katharsis? How many Colloquiums had she daydreamed through, picturing herself removing the cap and resting it over the tip of her scepter? The

Credit: Justin Sanders

hubbub from Academia Council would almost be worth the scandal. She sighs and casually adjusts the mortar board, trying to get comfortable. Her violet hood zip-zops against the leather back chair.

Violet signifies the field of Semiotics & Literature. The Chancellor has always been a Violet. While the Lyceum was built on the Scions of Science, it is the metaphor that holds it all together. Facts are merely data; the interpretation of them, however, is knowledge. This is the source of the Lyceum's influence. The Chancellor minds the metaphor.

Around the octagonal table sit the other seven Sophos of the Academia Council: Scarlet, Law; White, Medicine; Amaranth Pink, Experimental Science; Radical Red, Theoretical Science; Daffodil, Aesthetics; Azure, History & Humanities; Emerald, Commerce. Each colored hood demarcates their disciplines of achievement, an academic rainbow. As far as Hannah is concerned, though, they are a spectrum of tedium.

"Any delay would be seen as weakness," Emerald says.

A chorus of grunts calls out their support.

"But any mishap during the Ascendancy ceremony would be catastrophic," Daffodil counters.

Head nods cascade around the table. The bi-annual ceremony of transfiguration is the Council's utmost concern. The coordination of pageantry and technology needs to be seamless. While based on Katharsis principles, it is a far more complex process. There is no leeway for even the slightest of glitches when the eight Ascendant Elects shed their bodies and deliver their consciousnesses to the Divinity Drive.

Hannah sighs, wishing that even one of her stuffy colleagues might be among the Ascendant Elects. Her tolerance for the Council's deliberations has waned over the past annum, and all the more so since its debate is moot. At the end of the day, the decision lies with her as Chancellor. Hannah knows it, as do the others. Still she has to make a show of taking their counsel. Each department head has to be heard. Or at least feel heard. She has learned from experience that it's actually more efficient to stand on ceremony than bulldoze over protocol. Better to let the spectrum exhaust itself with argument. It also serves as a convenient distraction for them, giving Hannah the space she needs to deal with Anaxagoras.

"This should not have any effect on the Ascendancy," Amaranth Pink says. "The infiltrated sub-structures are decades-old DNA storage pools in the Prescience Archive caves beneath the Glass Desert."

"You're talking thousands of miles away, across an ocean. Am I mistaken, the only individuals authorized for the subcontinent are the routine maintenance crews?" White asks.

Ever since the Cataclysm Crusades left the Glass Desert in its nuclear wake, the entire region, apart from the Archive, has been uninhabitable.

Each member of the Council was alive during the holocaustic war, when hell had rained down from the heavens and blossomed into mushroom clouds over much of the world. Everyone had seen the drone footage of vast deserts melted into literal glass plains. They all knew that this apocalypse is what had given rise to the Lyceum. Historically mocked as the outskirts of scholarship at the bottom of the world, it was the Lyceum's remoteness, like an ark on the Oceanian outskirts, that spared it, its scholars, and the remains of a civilization. The Lyceum's Katharsis technology served as the only antidote for radiation poisoning: its engineering advancements transformed the Glass Desert into a solar radiation generator strong enough to power the entire Lyceum, and its geothermal cooling innovations kept the vast Archive and its subterranean hectares of data servers from overheating.

"Regardless, while unsettling from a security standpoint, the breach neither has bearing on Quantum Thought nor the Coil Shuttling," Amaranth Pink continues.

There had been considerable debate as to this term. Originally the

Lyceum proffered Coil Shuffling, however the Semioticians asserted the Schopenhauer principle, arguing that it most likely was a typesetting error (when transposing the manuscripts to folios seven annums postmortem) and should have read, "shuttled off" this mortal coil. While the verb no longer exists, a shuttle was an implement used in weaving and would have implied mortality had been unwound and worked off.

Radical Red jumps in. "The Trojan insinuated itself into the repository architecture and wormed its way down to a kernel level. Any tampering or even alteration within those fundamentals *could* instigate a butterfly effect throughout the system."

It is unusual for the Sciences to disagree, Hannah notes. They often have raucous, sometimes violent dialectics within their hallowed halls. However, in almost all public forums they fall in lockstep. This worm is having quite the effect on the Council. Of course they were foolishly focused on the virtual ramifications instead of the more pressing threat of the actual physical incursion. The disinformation was lowering the signal-to-noise ratio in her favor.

Hannah would normally be amused at the Council's deliberations over moot points. She would delight at the energy expended on their rhetorical hamster wheel, knowing full well each counterpoint exhausted and entrenched the Sophos, pawns lining themselves up like dominos. Today, however, the litany of remonstrations keeps her from more pressing matters.

The impending decennial Ascendancy is proving more time consuming than is manageable. This year's Ascendant Elects are particularly high-profile and subsequently high-maintenance. The requisite politicking occupies much of her attention. Furthermore, she not only has to put on all the pomp of an official Lyceum investigation into this security breach—an investigation she's engineered to reveal empty answers, while offering solid reassurances about new security measures—she must manage this while discreetly interrogating and admonishing the irksome interloper.

Where are my TAs? It has to have been a half-Period by now.

"Could instigate!" Amaranth Pink says. "Could. Our tests have detected no disturbance so far—"

"Assessing kernel architecture stresses should take weeks," Radical Red says, "with more exponential potential than mere stress-processing algorithms—"

"Which is why the entire storage field has been quarantined!"

"It shouldn't be too difficult to run simulations on some biologic samples without full-on committing them to Ascendancy," White suggests. "Assuming there are no artifacts in the Coil Shuttling, all may proceed as planned. *In veritas . . .*"

"Knowledge," they all reflexively echo in response to her call.

"The only difficulty being we don't know," Radical Red adds.

The roundtable falls to silence. Hannah struggles not to let out her yawn. She imagines it must appear that her face is arguing with itself.

"Explain," Emerald says.

Radical Red shrugs. "The worm left no trail."

"So there's no infection," Daffodil asks without a questioning inflection. She has a habit of doing that, much to Hannah's chagrin.

The Amaranths shake their heads no.

"So, what then, it was simply passing through? Someone crosses the Glass Desert, breaks into the Prescience Archive, evades security drones, releases a transitive virus, and sneaks back out for his afternoon perambulation?" Emerald asks.

"What makes you so sure it was a he," Daffodil says, ignoring the question mark in her statement.

"This is neither the time nor the place for your tiresome gender theories," Emerald sighs.

White intervenes, "So then what did the worm do?"

Everyone turns to look at Radical Red in a way that would've been amusing in an Entertainment Comedia.

Radical Red shrugs and turns to Amaranth Pink, who reluctantly admits, "It took something out."

Everyone waits.

"What?" Emerald asks.

"We don't know how much it took," Radical Red says, seemingly distracted by a whorl of dust particles floating in a beam of sunlight.

Emerald's irritation bubbles up. "Well, how many exabytes are missing?"

"None. Nothing's missing," Amaranth Pink says. "Not a single byte of data. Everything is there and accounted for, every last zettabyte."

"So then you're saying nothing was excised."

"Something was taken. The aggregate field is less dense by an order of xenottabytes," Radical Red says.

"But Crates just said—"

"Every byte of data is accounted for, yes. But the whole of the field is, as I said, less dense."

"Correct me if I'm wrong, but are not xenottabytes larger than zettabytes." Daffodil asks.

"By an order of two. Exabytes, zettabytes, yottabytes, xenottabytes," Amaranth Pink replies.

"But how is that possible?" Emerald asks.

Radical Red's eyes light up. "It is intriguing. I imagine it's like a balloon filled with carbonated water that's suddenly filled with just the carbonation. The volume of the balloon remains the same and every molecule of CO_2 is accounted for, but the balloon is lighter."

"So then there was data, immense amounts of data, stored in our Archive without our knowledge, all of which is now gone?" Azure asks.

"We assume all of which," Radical Red notes.

A hush sets into the room.

"Maybe we should consult Anaxagoras?" Azure offers.

Radical Red shakes his head. "Our founder's beyond the mundane dealings of this Council."

Before they can parse the paradox further, a hologram coalesces in front of Hannah's seat with a soothing knell.

"Forgive the interruption, Madame Chancellor," the hologram of her Prime TA announces, "but the Twelve Apostles require your immediate assistance."

Hannah nods, careful to wrinkle her brow with consternation to mask her relief. The hologram disintegrates. "My apologies, fellow Sophos, but my TAs and I must attend to the Ascendant Elects, regardless of the Ascendancy's fate."

Hannah turns to Scarlet. His lack of participation reflects his standard taciturn modus operandi. "What are our legal options for delaying the Ascendancy?"

Scarlet slides the fingertips of his pressed palms down from his lips to his chin and speaks with a finality that precludes dispute. "There is no legal option for delay, only deferment. As specified in the Charter, the Ascendancy may only take place on an equinox. That is absolute. The Ascendant Elect would have to wait for the vernal, which would then set back all subsequent ceremonies. Enacting a deferment without any direct tangible threat or substantive proof thereof could be interpreted as a direct violation of the Charter. The Lyceum would not only be deemed liable, but the Council itself could be subject to a Competency Hearing and Tenure Revocations." He slides his fingertips back up his chin to the tip of his nose.

Hannah nods solemnly. Scarlet delivered precisely as she had hoped.

"The Council's hands seem to be tied. Until some body of evidence is acquired, we must proceed according to plan. In the interim, I will have a sect of Inquisitors sent to the Prescience Archive."

To preclude any protests, Hannah stands. A chorus of screeches sings out as the others push their chairs back to stand.

"*In veritas,*" Hannah says, pushing her palms together as if in prayer and then opening them as if a book.

"*In veritas,*" the Council echoes, returning the skeuomorphic gesture of learning.

HER BLACK ROBES AND violet hood billow out behind her as she exits. Her foglets shimmer around her, a blur of movement as she marches down the corridor. The microbots devour her Sophic costume, rearranging the molecules of the mortar board into a French braid of long flaxen hair tied with a Royal Blue Honor Cord; her *cappa clausa* lightens to Ascendant white and constricts around her, tightening and lifting her age-softened flesh, as Royal Blue borders bleed solid around her collar, sleeves, and waist; her wrinkles seem to soften, skin lighten, eyes morph chartreuse; Lyceum e-Scrolls coalesce from the mist of her disintegrated hood in her hands.

By the time she exits into the Solarium Hall, Hannah bears the appearance of a 25 annum Ascendant Guardian & Elect Liaison, an Angel as they are oft nicknamed. As soon as the door re-integrates behind Hannah, her Prime TA flanks in from the wings and falls in step with the Chancellor. An Angel and Apostle are just important enough to be given a wide berth in the forum, but not too eminent to cause a stir or arouse any real attention.

"What in Petrarch's Dark took so long?" Hannah lashes out at her underling.

"There is an issue with one of the Alternate Elects."

Hannah rolls her eyes, knowing the drill all too well. "Let me guess, he's been overcome with a sudden philanthropic impulse and wants to unburden himself with some beneficence for the Lyceum. What is he offering, a new Research Grant?"

"A Babylonian Biblio*Tech*, actually," her Prime TA corrects.

Hannah's sarcastic whistle dissipates into the voluminous solarium as they hustle through. "And all he's asking is for a simple recalculation of the hierarchy, so he might become one of the Ascendant Eight. An alternative for the alternate."

"He was wondering about simply adding himself as an addition, actually." Her TA shares a knowing smile.

"Oh, is that all?"

Hannah would prefer to do away with the four mandated back-up Ascendants. But they needed them in case an Elect couldn't Ascend for whatever reason. This had only happened once since Ascendancy began, due to a fatal mishap on the eve of the ceremony. Still, once was enough.

There was always at least one of the alternates, every equinox, offering some sort of deal in a rush to reach the athanasia inside the Divinity Drive. Immortality is too tempting a prize, even if it costs corporeal existence. Almost all of the Lyceum participate in the bi-annual lottery, all hoping for the chance to trade their bodies in for eternal existence with the D Drive— an incorporeal incorporation. All long for the one-way ticket to become virtual gods, limited only by their imaginations, in the ethereal landscape inside the quantum drive. All yearn to join the others who Ascended before them, becoming incarnations of immortality and waging Titanic wars against each other.

From the outside, the Council observes this fertile battlefield for gods and harvests the Ascendants' dreams, turning their imagined innovations into the Lyceum's cutting edge technologies. Processed through QT's viability filters, manufactured by nano-molders, most of the Lyceum's advancements, from the *InstaTram* to the foglets, have been reaped from the conflicts within this virtual Valhalla. Even the Divinity Drive itself was dreamt up by one of the Initial *8* shortly after they were serendipitously, though accidentally, transmuted into quantum storage. In its first annum it was a fecund landscape that produced scores of innovations. Soon after, however, the Initial *8* began to evolve into abstract, sedate, contemplative entities and seemed to lose their sense of selves.

It took several cycles of trial and error for Amaranth Pink's experimental science department to determine the need for the Ascendancy. New Ascendants were necessary every half-annum, for both stimulation and grounding. Otherwise the previous Ascendants would become intangible and ethereal in their thinking and the Divinity Drive would become too Edenic. Complacency and peace have little utility for the Lyceum, at least within the D Drive. Eventually, Amaranth Pink determined 2^3 new participants were just enough to stir things up without overwhelming the realm in chaos. Hence, the Ascendant Eight.

Limiting the number of permissible Ascendants to eight also generated the beneficial byproducts of awe and obedience in the real world. It transformed the Lyceum from a rogue cloister of Intelligentsia into society's salvation, with the Council acting as the Guardians. Religion, with its fallacies and promises of heaven, was rendered a fairytale. Faith was replaced by fact. Belief became an outmoded fool's errand. Knowledge and truth are what the Lyceum offers, not to mention a real and quantifiable everlasting life, which is promised to all when the D Drive finally stabilizes and expands enough to resurrect all the scanned souls from the Numinous Archive. All will be ushered into infinity by the Ascendants. But first they must demonstrate awe and obedience.

Nevertheless, people were still people. So there was always one alternate who *had the utmost respect for tradition*, but no understanding of physiks. One who believes perhaps just this once the rules may be bent like space around a neutron star. Only a fortunate few are allowed on the equinox to Ascend and transcribe their consciousness into the Divinity Drive.

"Refer our ambitious Alternate to the Scarlet's office." Hannah smiles to herself at this delicious delegation. "Let him explain the Law's lack of leniency and review the rules of exponents." Hannah's TA understood the reference, how it would be impossible for them to allow just one more Ascendant. If they were to add any others it would have to be eight more for a total of sixteen. The physiks was based on a geometric binary expansion, not an arithmetic one, 2^x not 2x. Adding one more changed it from 2^3 to 2^4, 8 to 16.

"When he returns with his disappointment, offer him monthly Katharses and a guaranteed Ascendancy at the next equinox," Hannah instructs. "But only after securing his donation of the Babylonian Biblio*Tech.*"

"Perfect, Madame Chancellor."

Across the Forum, Hannah makes out a crowd outside of Hippocratic Hall. There was always a rush for Katharsis before the festival. People want a clean slate to sully with sanctioned debauchery. The Geminis must be hard at work. She was proud when her sons rose to their position of prominence in Hippocratic Hall, and prouder still when they resurrected the ritual of submission from the old healers. The infirm would first be relegated to a communal meditation chamber, where they would await a uniformed Minder to escort them to an individual rumination room to endure another interim, until one of the Geminis would come in for a personal consulting and diagnosing, and finally be admitted for Katharsis. The cleansing of a malady was a process of submission, waiting, a demonstration of obedience and humility.

Hannah gave into it every month. Katharsis might remove any new malignancy, but it couldn't correct a genetic predisposition. "And see if the Geminis have time for me later this post-perigee. Have the Inquisitors found anything yet?" Hannah had to keep up the pretense of a witch-hunt even with her TAs.

"They have canvassed only a quarter of Prescience Archive as of yet."

Hannah nods. "It will take time. Keep me informed."

"Are you not returning to the Athenaeum with me?"

Even through the foglet veneer, her TA perceives the invective in Hannah's gaze.

"Shall I update you through your Cochlear?"

Hannah shakes her head no, knowing full well she would be disengaging all neuroplants equipped with GPS. "Don't bother. Just upload it to my Herald Feed."

Her TA nods, folds her hands together and opens them like a book. *"In veritas."*

"In veritas," Hannah echoes, and watches her TA head off to the Athenaeum tower. Before Hannah even makes it down the marble steps of the Forum to the *InstaTram*, the foglets have shimmered into the facade of an overweight, unshaven, unkempt Tunnel*Technician*.

HANNAH'S EYES GLOW GREEN in the dark tunnels of the *d*atacombs. The gallium arsenide Omnibus GEN CX+ optic implants had clicked on automatically when the door had slid shut. They always make her feel like she's looking through aquamarine glasses. She shivers in the cold air of the tunnel. Geothermal cooling has its drawbacks, even if it does keep the servers at a stable 288 degrees Kelvin. Her foglets vibrate with warmth in response. She turns left at the next turn, led by her Cartograph*EYE*. Hannah's confident she could navigate the tunnels of ancient data beneath the city with her eyes closed, having visited him so often down here. Hubris does not trump a simple download, though, and arrow impulses that flash through her visual cortex with every twist are simply reassuring encouragements of her mental mapping capabilities.

The auto-gating function of her Omnibus implant kicks in as she pushes open the door into the vast, brightly lit *d*atacomb chamber. A robe and hood decorated with both Bright and Amaranth Pink sit balled up on a chair.

"Hello, Hannah," he sighs, continuing to tinker with the Kefitzat Haderechon machine.

Hannah's the only one who visits her husband here, who even knows about here. Other than Holloway, of course. But the good doctor's refugee status didn't afford her much motility. She could hardly leave the Sanctuary, let alone access the restricted *d*atacombs.

"Hello, Anaxagoras."

His black-and-white locks dangle to his shoulders. His sinewy muscles flex beneath his gray cotton shirt. He always sheds his Sophic uniform whenever possible, preferring a more ascetic, utilitarian garb. Though a few annums older than her, Anaxagoras holds his shape well and moves with the lithe grace of a craftsman, rather than the dignity of a senior Sophos. The lines of age sharpen the appearance of his focus more than the chiseling of time.

"Good after-apogee, Chancellor," QT's disembodied voice echoes around the room.

Hannah acknowledges the Quantum Thought AI with her phonetic nickname, "Good after-apogee, Cutie. Looks like you've been busy."

Anaxagoras nods while interfacing with a holodesigner. His hands manipulate virtual nano-architecture. He tweaks the design slightly and QT extrapolates the ripple effect on a macro-scale. "Almost finished sharpening the aether amplifier," he states while continuing to tweak.

"I was referring to the Prescience Archive."

Anaxagoras pulls his hands out of the holodesign. He turns and rests them on the railing that circumvents the massive Kefitzat Haderechon machine. He half sits, half leans on/against it, wipes his brow, and looks at her. Well, at least his artificial irises focus on her. There's no telling what private images he also has layered across his mechanical pupils. His ocular enhancements have no trouble penetrating the illusion of her foglets.

"You look tired, love." He rubs the back of his wrist across his forehead and wrinkles his nose at her.

"Of course I do," she sighs, exasperated, but also relieved to be truly seen by someone. "What do you expect? I just came from a Council meeting. The seven Sophos are quite discombobulated by the Ascendancy preparations, not to mention the archival anomalies."

"The Prescience Archive is intact. I made sure of that. And the reduction of areal density even made the whole server run smoother."

"Intact, yes. But it's been infiltrated. And apparently thinned out."

Anaxagoras rolls his eyes. "I bet none of them even know where the Prescience Archive is, let alone what's in it. Tell them it was a glitch. A cataloging code loop that kept recounting the same memory mass and aggregating it as new, and one of Cutie's probes finally caught and corrected it."

"Which is precisely what I'm planning on the Inquisitors uncovering," Hannah snaps back with an anger that surprises her.

"You sent those zealots?" He shakes his head. "Talk about overkill. Why not just send a Votary assassin?"

Hannah takes a breath. "So you brought the Initial 8 back here?"

Anaxagoras nods. "Dr. Holloway and I thought it was time."

Hannah works to mask her distaste at his mention of the outsider. The Psykhe had been infecting his mind ever since she'd arrived. Dr. Holloway's affirmations of his anxieties are aggravating his conscience.

"Is Restor8ion ready? You really want to tear the Initial 8 out of the Divinity Drive and try to reconstitute them?" Hannah asks, already knowing the answer. She simply doesn't want to believe, having hoped this day would never come.

"Close enough."

"What does Cutie think?"

"Anaxagoras's adjustments suggest a high probability of stable manifestations," QT's disembodied voice chimes in.

"Will it destabilize the D Drive?" Hannah asks.

"In spite of the integral role they have played in it, the Initial 8 were never fully integrated into it. Disentangling them presents a hyperbolically low probability of any destabilization," QT assures her.

"Satisfied?" Anaxagoras asks, crossing his arms.

Hannah sits on an overturned crate. "You don't have to resurrect them. You can't know what's going to happen when they're reconstituted. It's never been done."

"We have an obligation—"

"Capability does not necessitate inevitability."

"Not to science, Hannah. Ethically. They never should've been there in the first place."

"Ah." Hannah nods and purses her lips. She knows it is futile to argue. The mad old genius long ago inoculated himself against rhetoric. Still, she must try. "Your ethics? Or Holloway's?"

"Ethics are not subjective, Hannah, no matter how your precious Council votes on them. They stand apart from judgment."

"You sound awfully judgmental to me."

"Because you're hiding pathological ambition behind a block of warped utilitarianism."

"You'd trade an entire society for the fate of eight?"

"The *8* are part of your 'society.'"

"You physikists, you'll play the Merlins of war, killing half of the world and making it so the other half can't live without you."

"Now *you* sound like Dr. Holloway. Wars are fought over ideologies, not science."

"And you'll undermine both with Restor8ion. Ascendency needs to be one-way. Its isolation not only protects it from our meddling, it insulates us from whatever nightmares they might dream."

"It insulates you from the possibility of an exodus from a realm that might not be the heaven on earth you assure everyone it is. You've raised Descartes's Demon and now you're worried you can't keep him collared. Dreamed dreamers screaming themselves awake, never knowing they're asleep. Just because others spread around your bullshit, doesn't mean you can plant a handful of magic beans. If the Lyceum can't handle a little shake-up every now and then, maybe it's not worth protecting."

"The Lyceum which gave you Cutie, I'd like to point out."

"They didn't give me QT. They assimilated her away from me and exponentiated her to their own ends." There is venom in his voice. He frowns at Hannah. "Why must we have this fight again? I know you see the truth of it. I know you see the blood on our hands. The sin of this evolution we ushered in."

His guilt has been there since they came to Lyceum. A burr on his mind that stowed away with them on their Kefitzat exodus and the accidental ascendancy of the Initial *8*.

Anaxagoras has taken her hands in his and kneeled down before her. His eyes look to hers. He reaches up to her cheek, the foglets part and pull back away from the magnetic field emanating from his subdermal interface implants. He sees and touches the real her beneath the sheen.

Hannah presses her hand against the back of his and holds it against her wrinkled cheek. "What is evolution except a virus, a mutation that has to spread from host to host, a venereal transmission passed down through generations, until there's a critical mass of infected carriers large enough to produce its deformity on a large scale? There was never an Adam and Eve, there was a mutation. Some alpha anomaly in Patient Zero, who had to rape 'his' sister/daughter or seduce 'her' brother/uncle, to begin the begetting of the line. An act of incest was necessary to start it all, the sin of sins. Incest, rape, infection, ostracism—those are our origins. Evolution is sin by its very nature."

Anaxagoras pulls his hand back. "So then why are you fighting it?"

"You're trying to reverse it, put the genie back in the bottle. Restor8ion is a mistake. Nothing can come out of the netherwhere of the D Drive."

"Incest was forever proscribed as a taboo for the purpose of self-defense. It's a code set up to protect our original mutation from any further tampering, inoculate it against some other infectious deformation. A hypocritical anathema, an act of self-preservation and fear."

"There's too much at stake," she says.

"For what? To save those we trapped in there?"

"We didn't trap the Initial 8. Not on purpose. Not by design. It was their fault. Their prying programs that pulled them in when it was only supposed to be Alpha through Delta in the first Kefitzat Haderechon. It is their retribution. I will happily let the past rot for the sake of the future."

"I can't."

Hannah stands. "You could be made to."

Anaxagoras crosses back to the machine and laughs. "The Lyceum fighting against its patron saint? I don't think that would fly politically."

"The Lyceum won't fight you, simply honor you as a martyr to science. Anaxagoras the Apostate."

The threat hangs in the air, but Anaxagoras doesn't flinch. Rather, he begins tinkering again. "I don't think you'd choose widowhood over truth."

Hannah sighs and turns toward the heavy door. "At least let me know when it's ready. Before you do anything."

"I couldn't imagine Restor8ion without you." Anaxagoras continues to tinker.

Hannah opens the door.

"In veritas," Anaxagoras calls after her.

"In veritas," she reflexively echoes.

HANNAH WAITS UNTIL THE *INSTATRAM* carries her a few clicks from the tunnels before activating her neuroplants. She scrolls through the Herald Feed while waiting to connect with her Prime TA. The Inquisitors found no evidence of infiltration in the Prescience Archive. Rather, they discovered there had been a glitch. A cataloging code loop that kept recounting the same memory mass and aggregating it as new, and one of QT's probes finally caught it and corrected it. As a result of the reduction in areal density, the entire Archive was operating more efficiently.

"Yes, Madame Chancellor," her TA's voice piped directly into her Cochlear.

"Alert the Votaries," Hannah sub-vocalized. "Have them dispatch a Purifier to the *d*atacombs. I'm forwarding you the coordinates. *D*ataMine the entire area. Not a soul, nor a kilobyte gets in or out without triggering a detonation. In the meantime, put some TAs on drafting a Herald release about outmoded engineering and a new refurbishment project."

"On it, Madame Chancellor."

"Could the Geminis make time?"

"They've made accommodations for you. *In veritas.*"

"In veritas," Hannah echoes as she disembarks from the *InstaTram* in front of the Hippocratic Hall. Her Katharsis is long overdue.

» Print

This copy is for your personal, non-commercial use only.

China's stock czar investigates high-speed trading tap

By ██████ ██ and ██ ██

SHANGHAI | Wed Jan 16, 2012 6:01 AM GMT

Jan 16 (Reuters) - China's top securities regulator, who has for months been trying to revive the international stock market, has uncovered multi-year trend of high-speed microtrades transacted microseconds ahead of millions upon millions of large-quantity Chinese orders in overseas markets.

On Monday, Guo Shuqing, the chairman of the China Securities Regulatory Commission (CSRC), shocked the International Market with the announcement of a suspected trading scandal. Correlative data shows that since 2001 millions, if not trillions, of minute trades preceded almost every large Chinese stock order. Stocks would be bought microseconds ahead of Chinese investors and then sold for fractional profits as the demand from the foreign order pushed up the price. The prescient purchases were always small decentralized orders that easily glided beneath any regulatory radars.

While any of the individual profits amounted to fractions of a cent at best, the aggregate of these microtrades could total billions, if not hundreds of billions of dollars. Authorities as of yet have been unable to locate any trading tap or malicious software, however they have been able to determine that all of these microtrades preceeded orders directed through an older satellite launched by CSG in 1998. All trades made through this telecommunication hub have been frozen and any further transaction traffic suspended.

"This is a huge hit to market confidence," retail investor Qi Junjie said in his microblog. "Foreign banks finally succeed in liberalizing China's stock market, and the Chinese investor finds himself behind his own coattails."

Guo assured a forum on Monday that China has taken swift and effective security measures. He took the opportunity to speak out against floating the exchange rate of the local currency, Renminbi, a long-disputed issue between China and the US. Guo also commented on how this level of advanced eavesdropping might only be attained with the resources available to a government. The US, along with several European countries, has denied any knowledge of and participation in these suspicious trades. The US Treasurer even went so far as to assert that any threat to the international market was a threat to the global economy.

Mainland China shares dropped to 7-1/2 month lows on Tuesday, with the CSI300 index of the top Shanghai and Shenzhen A-shares falling more than 20 percent since early December.

While foreign investment still only accounts for around 18 percent of the overall mainland China equity market, the psychological impact the scandal has had on local investors is significant.

Over the past few weeks, Guo has made numerous attempts to breathe life into the stock market and bolster market security. But investors turned a deaf ear, drastically constricting trading activity.

© ████ ████ 2012. All rights reserved. Users may download and print extracts of content from this website for their own personal and non-commercial use only. Republication or redistribution of ████ ████ content, including by framing or similar means, is expressly prohibited without the prior written consent of ████ ████. ████ ████ and its logo are registered trademarks or trademarks of the ████ ████ group of companies around the world.

████ ████ journalists are subject to an Editorial Handbook which requires fair presentation and disclosure of relevant interests.

This copy is for your personal, non-commercial use only.

SCIENCE & RESEARCH

Storage Wars

CCV invasion

By ███ ███████

Contributing Writer

Friday, Apr 1, 2013

Brown's Center for Computation and Visualization appears to have been tampered with over the weekend. The entire Center, which provides virtual and physical hosting for the entire university, automatically shut down early Sunday morning as the result of a sudden EMP surge.

After rebooting the servers, Brown's CS Department determined that while all data remained intact, the archive aggregate was apparently several thousand terabytes "lighter." Neither the CS team nor a group of independent security consultants have been able to determine what, if anything, is missing.

Though not conclusive, inside reports do allude to some suspicious activity late Saturday emblematic of the recent cyber attacks traced back to Chinese hackers at Jiaotong University. McAfee classified these actions as part of an espionage campaign.

Previous infiltrated institutions include the *New York Times*, Facebook, Twitter, Apple, Lockheed Martin, the *Wall Street Journal*, Coca-Cola, Stamford, University of Michigan, and Duke.

Topics: Data and security

Recommended articles

DPS researching media initiatives

Researchers attempt to map brain activity of your dreams

Does social entrepreneurship matter

Metcalf closed for renovations

Poor grades from social media

www.browndailyherald.com/2013/04/1/storage-wars/

▮▮▮ **shaman or charlatan**

must reads

Shaman or Charlatan?

by THE ▮▮▮▮▮ ▮▮▮

FEBRUARY 22, 2011 8:29 AM

K.E. HODGE/▮

ANAPAIKE, Suriname (▮▮) — Flash frosts, technoshamanism, and artifacts from the spirit world. Juan Castillo, a medium of the María Lionza religious sect, has channeled it all through his portal in the jungle.

This isolated border town, deep in the wilds of the Amazon basin, has long claimed to share a boundary with the mystical, boasting a rich spiritual history of the otherworldly, and are claiming the recent feats of their local shaman as proof.

Mr. Castillo has often retreated to the wilds of the jungle to commune with hidden forces, employing the aid of psychedelics to speed him along on his vision quests. While in the past he has returned from these sojourns with divinations and epiphanies, of late Mr.

Castillo, a self-proclaimed technoshaman, has brought back with him an altogether different phenomenon: blizzards.

Though the Amazon is host to many bizarre creatures and nonpareils, snow has never been one of them. Unfortunately, the tropical climate has precluded any photographic documentation of these flurries. However, a team of climatologists from Brazil's Universidade Católica do Salvador did travel to the remote village and confirmed what appear to be the residual effects of a flash frost on jungle vegetation. The affected flora circumscribe an almost perfect circle with a 100m radius.

While Mr. Castillo refuses to "perform" for foreign cynics, locals claim to also have witnessed him conjuring objects out of inter-dimensional portals. Objects range from the mundane: rotten Russel River limes (*Microcitrus inodora*), flat cans of beer (Carlton Draught); to the miraculous: a carbon dodecahedron, a blue sapphire; to the peculiar: a green plastic bead.

Though impressed by these recent feats, villagers prefer Mr. Castillo attend to his priestly duties as the village spiritual guide and resident psychosurgeon.

shaman   charlatan   Suriname

---

older
The Set Up? 'Kiss Cam Entrapment' Video Goes Viral

---

newer

Colorado Lawmakers Set Taxes And Rules For Marijuana Sales

About

Subscribe

 News Twitter

©2011 ▮

ACKNOWLEDGMENTS

Off and on, this project has taken years of effort and dedication. It was a journey I could not have completed on my own without the love, support, and, most of all, patience from my friends and family. A few particularly masochistic individuals deserve a special thanks: my wife, for her love, tolerance, and taste; Jason, for being my ideal reader and careful critic; Jeff, for his belief, acumen, and collaboration; Mike, for the numerous math, coding, and cryptography conversations (which definitely got him red-flagged on the NSA's watch list); Laurel, for her encouragement and mad French skillz; Jon, for his artistic vision and generosity; Paul, for his endless reading suggestions (especially Murakami); Mrs. Eder, for letting me play with her typewriter when I was little; my mother, for nineteen hours of labor (and other subsequent sacrifices); and my father, for warping me.

ABOUT THE AUTHOR

Photo © 2015 Josh Ryan

Joshua Scher is a recent transplant from New York City to the hills of Hollywood, California, where he is continuing his transition from writing for the stage to writing for the screen, both theatrical and television.

Scher's film, *I'm Ok* (2015), starring Dot-Marie Jones and Alex Frnka, is currently in postproduction and is anticipating a film-festival run in 2016. The cinematic adaptation of his play *The Footage* was developed with Pressman Film and is currently being packaged. In 2006, a fruitful collaboration with Joe Frazier and his manager, Leslie Wolff, brought forth the treatment of *Behind the Smoke*, the Joe Frazier biopic for Penny Marshall and Parkway Productions. In the TV world, Scher's one-hour action drama, *JiGsAw*, was developed with Danny Glover and his company, Louverture Films.

His musical *Triangle* played at the Lyric Theatre of Oklahoma, was part of TheatreWorks New Works Festival (Silicon Valley), and debuted in New York City as part of the National Alliance for Musical Theatre's

Festival of New Musicals. *The Footage* had its Australian premiere at the Stooged Theatre after enjoying its World Premiere at The Flea Theater in New York City. His work *MARVEL* was included in Roundabout Theatre's New Voices Program, directed by Charles Randolph-Wright. Scher has also worked with the Huntington Theatre, Portland Stage, the O'Neill Theater Festival (with Robert Longbottom, director of *The Scarlet Pimpernel*), and the Williamstown Theatre Festival. His first play, *Velvet Ropes*, was published while he was still a student at the Yale School of Drama. A collection of his monologues was published by Smith and Krauss in their 2006 Audition Arsenal series, and his play *Flushed* was published by Baker's Plays. He holds a BA with Honors in Creative Writing from Brown University and an MFA in playwriting from Yale University.